A GLIMPSE INTO THE SCIENCE FICTION WORLD OF "A GENERATION RETURNS" :

"We arrived on time! "Stuart's voice shook with energy. "Thanks to Ferdinand, we were well-equipped with laser and missile guns and proper military uniforms with laser protector panels. That gave us the confidence that we needed to launch an offensive in the face of the androids' guns set for death rays. Sarah and Ruth were ready to pass us other weapons when Diana, Randolph and I broke through the front lines, falling into disorder, enabling Peter, Mathieu, Isabel, John and Jonathan to pass behind. Our strategy was to surround them as they were pushed into."

"Seeing Stuart fueled my determination to win." Diana had a big smile on her face. "We trained and worked together and I knew..." "Me too," Stuart interrupted, "We were a deadly couple!" Our laughter was a spontaneous evocation of admiration. "They came marching in straight lines, android style. That was what I was hoping for

PAMELA SERIES 13
VOLUME 2

A GENERATION RETURNS

By

Patricia Lee Strunk

AB FILM PUBLISHING
NEW YORK USA

ISBN: 978-0-9971715-3-2

Cover Design by Thomas Romano, USA

Published by
AB Film Publishing
290 West 12 Street, Suite A
New York, New York 10014
(212) 741-1441

2017

ACKNOWLEDGEMENTS

After a long period of reflection and a long book, there are many people to whom I owe my heartfelt gratitude.

I feel strongly indebted and thankful to my children, my source of happiness, Trevor and Vinciane, for their unrelenting patience, love and confidence in me, without which I might never have finished Volume 2.

I want to thank my brothers, John and William and their families, along with my nephew, David, and his family, for their high-spirited support and encouragement. And, with tender thoughts of a distant past, I want to thank my sister, Pamela, for her imaginative vision of a better world, and my parents, Robert and Hermana, for leaving me those fond remembrances of their love and belief in me which continue to give me courage and creative inspiration.

I want to thank those who so kindly read my manuscripts and provided me with precious suggestions, corrections, and encouragement. I am particularly grateful to Christine for her well-thought out and insightful comments and suggestion, Cornelius for his in-depth reflections on the nature and substance of my work, and Stephane T. and Robert D., for answering all my many, varied, sometimes bizarre questions, about different species of reptiles. And, finally, I want to give special thanks to Gwenaëlle, Carole, Debbie, and Marie-Christine for their continued praise and reassurance, as well as all my other friends and acquaintances who, in their own way, have helped me with the promotion of Pamela Series 13.

I want to extend my most profound thanks to Dr. Frank Romano, a friend, colleague and author, for giving literary life to my second volume through his critical, demanding and elucidating editing of my rough manuscript. And I want to praise Thomas Romano for the originality of his magnificent illustration.

And, finally I want to extend my most sincere and humble thanks to my publisher, Alan Baxter, of AB Film Productions, for the confidence he has placed in me by giving me this extraordinary opportunity to present Pamela Series 13, Volume 2 "A Generation Returns," to the public.

Dedication (Volume 2)

To My Children

and

In Memory of my Sister and my Parents

Chapter 1: Aftermath

I was standing behind my laboratory table wearing my white lab coat, my long hair pulled back in a ponytail, with loose wavy bangs delicately framing my face to heighten the vibrant green of my eyes. My high-tech equipment was in place, the vials of chemicals were neatly arranged ready for my next experiment and the white wall behind me was covered with formulae, a scene reminiscent of the day that Elisabeth Reinhart ordered her android opposite to self-destruct when Peter entered the room. His presence today disturbed me and I hid the foreboding of it from him, smiling as he approached me, taking me tenderly in his arms. Over all these years, I never tired of him. He was my guiding force, my inner strength, my true love.

"So, what is your decision, Pamela?" He asked in that lively, spirited tone one uses when the answer seems so evident.

But, I was not yet ready to tell him, so instead I looked up at him and stared intensely into his serious, yet compassionate and loving eyes, and watched the last ten years pass before me.

⚜

I was filled with both happiness and despair. Only a handful of people had brought down a massive system of repression. We were back in control of our lives, our history, and . . . our destiny. Our smiles of pleasure were real and genuine. Yes, we won! We could and should be proud of our courage and determination.

The group of 5 was locked up in the small padded room. It was too dangerous to let them prowling the night air without any

1

surveillance. We sent the small group of programmed humans to their cubicles where their boxed dinners awaited them. Their pathetic unawareness of the changed circumstances surprised and saddened me.

We all left for the inner circle to wind down and celebrate our victory. I wanted to know what happened, to have all the details of how they put down the android attack.

Peter was the first to speak. "I took the children to a sheltered area, close to the center. I told them to wait there, that they would be safe and that we would be back soon. I was surprised. They did not show any signs of anxiety or apprehension. To the contrary, they saw this as an opportunity to play tag on unfamiliar turf, at least until I gave them the message that John and I had prepared in case of defeat."

He stopped and looked at us. We all understood how difficult it must have been for him to tell the children that they might never see us again. "I didn't want to dramatize our situation but I had to tell them that if anything happened to us that they should re-member that we loved them and_wanted them to go on living and not be sad. Just saying that brought on tears as they begged me to stay with them. My voice raised high in hopeful triumph, as I em-phatically promised we would win, attenuating my own fear and uncertainty. I left for the cavern to join the rest of the group in the transport center."

"We arrived on time! "Stuart's voice shook with energy. "Thanks to Ferdinand, we were well-equipped with laser and missile guns and proper military uniforms with laser protector panels. That gave us the confidence that we needed to launch an offensive in the face of the androids' guns set for death rays. Sarah and Ruth were ready to pass us other weapons when Diana, Randolph and I broke through the front lines, falling into disorder, enabling Peter, Mathieu, Isabel, John and Jonathan to pass behind. Our strategy was to surround them as they were pushed into."

"Seeing Stuart fueled my determination to win." Diana had a big smile on her face. "We trained and worked together and I knew..." "Me too," Stuart interrupted, "We were a deadly couple!" Our laughter was a spontaneous evocation of admiration. "They came marching in straight lines, android style. That was what I was hoping for." Diana's eyes were blazing. "So Stuart and I broke down the line by striking at their weak point, the extreme sidelines, or the outer limits. I went for the right side and he charged from the left and together we opened up the center for the others to charge in from behind us. This strategy seemed the best because the androids in center position were those who were trained for combat and their training made them more cunning and lethal." I knew nothing about military strategy so I didn't know if it was the best approach, but. . .it worked.

She moved next to Stuart and playfully tapped him around a bit. There was certainly a natural complicity between them because Stuart's face lit up with joy. In fact, he let down his guard with her and showed me that he could be light hearted.

And then she turned to Randolph. "I never knew that one," she said as she pointed to Randolph. "But, I was certainly happy to have him with me. He ran with weapons strung all over him, firing and splattering androids into small pieces. Where did you learn to shoot like that?" She asked.

"Are you kidding, they were like clay pigeons!"

"They were firing back and you dodged their rays like a professional. You looked like you had been doing this all your life." Her mouth stretched in a smile, a patented, toothy devilish look. "You know that, even with our protections, we could have been injured or killed. We were vulnerable, no helmets to protect our heads. That was dangerous because those androids are well-trained sharpshooters."

"I just did my best," he said flashing one of his sexy smiles, accentuating his handsome profile. I guessed that he was looking at Diana in another way.

"Diana is right." Stuart cut off their flirtatiousness. "We actually put chaos in their linear attack. Once the line was broken the androids panicked, scrambling every which way."

He stopped abruptly and stared off into space. "I think that I should explain Diana's and my strategic attack in more detail." He spoke in a low voice. "The android programming for military intervention was very rudimentary. I saw videos of their offensive

3

attacks when I was in the martial arts training program. As you know, my deprogramming as a young child inspired my curiosity in general and gave me a more critical approach to what I saw, read and heard. So even as a child, I was amused rather than impressed by the videos depicting android forces marching forward, as the opposing army retreated in fear." His eyes sparkled. "As I see it, Dr. Murdoc rapidly programmed them to fight and kill, but he did not have time to develop a complex program in military strategy. He was hoping that the monumental size of the android forces, equipped with highly efficient military hardware, would so intimidate the non-intellectuals that they would surrender, extinguishing forever their quest for freedom. I was hoping that the Group of 5 did not have the foresight to improve upon their program, which was fortunately the case. So, the androids did not win, yesterday, just like they lost thousands of years ago, because they had no tactical military skills."

"Just a quick comment, Stuart." John interrupted. "Would you agree that the reason why they did not improve upon the military program was because they never expected us to wage a war?" Stuart nodded. "Is it also possible though that even if they considered the possibility of a future rebellion, their own programming would have prevented them from creating an organized and efficient military force?" All eyes turned on me.

"I have no idea." I spoke boldly. "Reinhart was cruel, but she did not wage wars. She disposed of the non-intellectuals in unorthodox ways, like ushering them aboard spaceships programmed to explode in deep space. Today, we know that she invented those visual receptors to assure complacency and complete cooperation from the non-intellectuals. And, quite frankly, in her final days, she refused to program the androids to kill and argued against it." I paused to get their attention. "I think that the Group of 5 sees themselves as above the degeneracy of human wars, which is why they resorted to programmed humans fighting us humans in a final battle."

There was a long silence, which Stuart broke, resuming his impressions of the battle. "To finish what I was saying, our offensive strategy worked, making it easier for the rest of the group to move in."

"They may have found it easy!" Mathieu broke in. "Stuart and Diana were a killing force. I never saw hands, feet, arms and legs, move so fast. They made extraordinary aerial attacks. Their bodies looked like they were suspended in mid-air and when they finally moved, it was with some sort of centrifugal force that accelerated with each deadly blow they struck and the androids fell, crippled by the effect of the attacks. All this time, Randolph was firing on them, dropping them to the ground, like he was just working out in target practice."

Mathieu swallowed, coughing slightly, like his throat was still burning from the rage of the battle. "When I heard them call out to us to move it, I stood petrified. I knew that I couldn't hit so hard and direct. "John," he looked over at John, "you grabbed me and dragged me on. I thought at that moment, that if you, with no training at all, were going to rush them, then I had no excuse but to move out." He clenched his teeth. "I took blows that I thought were going to kill me. I feel now like I was sent through a grinder. My body is bruised and I ache everywhere." He stopped again. "Only because I have pain do I know that I fought, because whatever I did, I did it in a trance. It was like I was watching someone who looked like me hitting those crazy machines."

"Don't worry, I saw you, the physical Mathieu, hitting and hitting hard. I was right behind you, finishing off whatever you left behind." Isabel said, her eyes wide with wonder and pride.

"Peter, you were not bad at all." Diana was more talkative than usual. "I had the feeling that you shared my pleasure. . .to-wipe them out!" There was mutual respect. "The couple times that I was alongside of you, I wondered if you hadn't had some marital arts training earlier in your life because your moves were too smooth. I know that you didn't get that from training with me. You were so effective and impressive...and under that pressure!"

"I think that I was just motivated by the promise that I made to the children." His face turned bright red.

"Ferdinand, Ralph and I did our best." Jonathan homed in. "I had the strength to crush them once they were on the ground, but not the agility to fight, even though I did find myself in hand-to-hand combat a couple times. I think that I was lucky to have disposed of the ones I encountered." He looked at Ferdinand and Ralph. "Ferdinand and Ralph did what they promised, they rolled around the floor tripping up androids and making it easier for us to pounce on them."

"I can't handle violence." Mathilda cried out, elevating her voice enough to underscore her contempt for violence. "That is why I stayed in the background with Ruth and Sarah. Fortunately, we never had to prove our self-defense skills."

"I can empathize with Mathilda," Benjamin interceded. I noticed that Stanislas was nodding. "But Stanislas and I did not just stand around doing nothing. We actually went back to get the children and bring them into the center once the group moved into the hallway. We did the right thing, because there were android drones circulating the area and the children could have been killed."

"We were very lucky that you did that!" I said unable to hide all the emotions that built up inside of me just thinking about losing my Frederic.

"They were scared when we got to them." Stanislas said. "Instinct told them to hide from the drones. We grabbed them in our arms, I had Frederic and Samuel, and Benjamin carried Rebecca. We ran fast dodging the drone attacks."

"When we finished with the first offensive, we had to rush the others in the corridors. They were protecting themselves by hiding behind corners, using doors as shields, and poking their heads out from adjoining corridors. That was complicated so Randolph's skills were very important." Diana said cutting off Benjamin and continuing to describe the offensive attack. "I know how to fire those weapons and did when I needed to, but I am much more effective in physical combat. I let Randolph and Stuart clear things out for me." She snickered. "I stayed in a comfort zone behind the two of you." They looked at her askance. "Well, it was easier for me and I had to save my energy for more fun things like ripping them apart with my hands." We all let out an eerie laugh.

"That was when the other two human ninjas showed up." Randolph sighed. "I don't know where they found genes to make those gigantic humans. Just looking at them made my skin cringe." He stood up to stretch. "I am considered to be tall and robust, but

they towered over me. They must have been close to 8 feet tall."
He grimaced. "And, what is even more extraordinary is that they
moved so rapidly under the weight of their heavy bodies and bulging muscles." Heads nodded. "Amazing, though, they were not gro-
tesque mutants, but rather young men with masculine, chiseled
faces." He looked at me and I kept a straight face.

"I had to fight one of them to save your life, Randolph, when
you were under sedation." Stuart replied. "And, Randolph, if
Pamela hadn't been there I might not have been with you today."
He went on to talk about how I confused and distracted the oversized human, when I jumped on his back and stayed there until
Stuart recovered from the tremendous blow from the steel fist
that stunned him.

"Well, I can tell you that I stood back and let Stuart and Diana
move against them. I know that the rest of you were behind me."
Randolph looked at them strangely. "You were there, weren't you?"
They all nodded.

"Mathieu and I were directly behind you every step of the way
in the corridor and the others were grouped together a little farther away." Peter broke in. "Don't you remember that we were also
firing those laser guns at the enemy. Granted, we were not aiming
that well, but we were there."

"Sorry. . .right! I was so concentrated on hitting them straight
on that sometimes I had the impression I was alone. I knew how to
move out of their range rapidly so it was better that you were not
in the lead."

"So what happened to the humans?" I asked.

"I think that the humans, like you just insinuated Pamela, were
the androids' last card, because once Diana and I were engaged in
combat with them the androids stopped firing on the rest of the
group. They were waiting for Diana and me to fall." Stuart's mouth
curved up slightly only partly revealing his teeth. "We didn't fall,
did we Diana?" Her head shifted from side to side as she showed
her teeth. "But, it was a challenge!" He shook his head as if recalling
what happened next was still too real for him to deal with.

"I was watching all of it." Peter jumped in. "Diana and Stuart ripped off their protection and attacked. I understood why you didn't

fire on those ninjas, Randolph, but I was not feeling as confident as you that Stuart and Diana could subdue those gigantic creatures."

"I would have killed them if and when it became necessary," Randolph replied. "But, they were human, and I had to give them a chance to be deprogrammed and to go on living, if possible. Naturally, the androids were counting on our human side which is why they sat motionless." He smiled. "They thought that our compassion for other humans would result in our group being killed... completely annihilated."

"Talking about killing, I killed mine." Diana announced, no sign of regret or emotion of any kind in her voice. "I didn't have a choice; it was him or me. I was tired when we encountered them. After all, we had just taken down a big offensive in the transport terminal and then opened up the corridors. We were on our way to a victory when they showed up. I had to use all my reserve energy to save myself. I couldn't look at the human as anything other than an android toy! There was no way that I could hold back and give him a chance. He would have torn me to pieces, so I charged at full force, which was something that he was not expecting."

"How did they see you?" I asked.

"The androids screamed out our codes, the codes of all of us in the corridor." She hesitated. "We were all visible. I think that they expected their 2 ninjas to finish all of us off, like Peter just said. When those massive humans saw that I was a woman, they took me for an easy target. The one who came for me expected me to fall down fast so that he could help his partner with Stuart. Stuart was already engaged with the other one, when the smart-assed one approached me like he could just splatter me into pieces between his large hands in a couple of seconds. His smug grin of an easy victory made me angry... very angry, probably too angry to think about anything other than my survival and his death!" She stopped in mid-stream to look at us to make sure that we were not going to treat her like a raving lunatic and seal her in the padded room. We nodded.

"So that anger," she continued, "coupled with the reality that I had to strike fast and direct, playing no games, gave me the courage and force that I needed to overcome him. I beckoned him to come for me and when he did I leaped high, very high over him, turning my body in mid-air at the very last second, landing hard on his back shoulders. Before he had time to react, I tightened my legs around his thick throat, cutting off his respiration, while I grabbed his bloated head between my hands and violently twisted it until I heard it crack. His legs went out from under him before I had time to let go. I was lucky that he fell face down because I could have been crushed under his weight. As my pained body slithered off of his lifeless one, I felt no remorse. It is unbelievable what you can do when your savage anger masks your desperate fear." A broad smile of self-satisfaction appeared on her face. "I was ready if Stuart needed me, which was not my impression, because he was handling the situation well."

"Diana did the right thing. I had a long, tiring and bruising fight. She could never have gone the length with her human." He stopped to observe her reaction. She was sneering back at him. "Well, you could have … if, like you said, we hadn't drained ourselves just before." She rushed into his arms like he was her big brother.

"So what happened to the second giant?" I asked.

"We sedated him and locked him up for the night in Gordon's office." Randolph said as he exploded with laughter.

"Is he deprogrammed?" I asked, impatient to get all the information.

"Don't know!" Both Stuart and Randolph said at the same time.

"Anyone know?"

"He was groggy but was still acting programmed when I administered the sedative. Ruth and I worked in the hospital unit and dashed off in that direction when things calmed down and the human was out cold on the floor. We recognized the sedative and put it in a syringe, it was the only medicine on the counter top in the hospital unit, other than those sacks of chemicals, so there was no risk that we made a mistake." Sarah reassured me. "I injected it."

"And, he will be awake in the morning?"

"I don't know. I may have over-sedated him. We'll see in the morning."

"And the other androids, where are they?"

"They shut down in the corridors." Mathieu replied. "The moment that the two humans lost their fight, the androids shut down automatically. I don't know if that was a programmed response or someone gave them that command."

Of course, the group of 5 was involved, I thought to myself. "You told me that there were humans in the corridors that deprogrammed during the battle." I was looking for more information.

"Remember, Pamela," Randolph replied calmly, "what we agreed to before the battle started." I nodded. "We did that. We told them to run and save themselves. I know that I screamed out that we were humans just like them and would protect them. Most of them ran panic stricken right into the android forces and got themselves blown up." He looked at me and I shook my head with regret. "We couldn't do anything else. Others actually imploded in a matter of seconds. Their first glimpse of the real world was too disconcerting and the shock of their deprogramming and the violence around them killed them on the spot. Others went running about screaming hysterically and the androids shot them down."

"So that means that the 30 or so humans are all that are left?"

"We shall know better in a few days. Maybe some of them are hiding. We couldn't find any stragglers earlier but that doesn't mean that there aren't any." Peter intervened in the discussion. "We are all exhausted. And, I am starving!"

As if on cue, Ferdinand and Ralph arrived with trays that were heavily laden with rehydrated food and lots of water to wash it down. We served ourselves, like humans should serve themselves, without opening a box with our ID number on it, something that we were still doing in the community outside. We ate like humans should be eating, stuffing ourselves until we felt full.

"By the way, where are the children, Mathilda? " I asked. "I haven't seen them for quite some time." I had forgotten all about them.

"Oh, they ate and are now sleeping in the small room over there. I put them down just before we started to talk."

"Thank you for looking out for them." She threw me a quick smile.

When the plates were empty, we meandered off, looking for the right room for the night. I didn't care much about the colors, just the size of the bed. I wanted a big, comfortable one that Peter and I could stretch out on. We found it.

I saw from the corner of my eye that Randolph and Mathilda were looking for a room to share. He didn't know what her reputation was, but that would not have mattered anyway. He was no more bothered by faithfulness than she was. I smiled just imagining...

The bed looked inviting, but I was feeling rather dirty. For the first time in all these years Peter and I took a shower together. At least that is what we started out to do.

❦❖❦

The days, weeks and months that turned into years were filled with challenges, some more demanding than others. It took time for us to reinstate the human race at the pinnacle of society and take absolute control of our own destiny. Life was far from boring for those of us discovering how to set priorities, work together in teams, and find solutions, because everything, even presumably mundane, routine tasks, were completely new to us, a fundamental change from carrying out orders and engaging in projects that the Group of 5 selected for us. We met regularly to exchange ideas and make decisions. And, these meetings were both revelatory and therapeutic. They gave each of us the opportunity to reveal our most profound fears and concerns, as well as our dreams for a better future. We matured as individuals and that maturity filtered through in the way in which we consolidated our small community, incorporating others within our circle, and moving outwards and onwards in our explorations of our planet and the worlds beyond.

Even our personalities took on greater dimension, some of us becoming more competitive and ambitious, inspiring the others to join in; while others found pleasure and satisfaction in participating in a more discrete manner in the success of the Center; and still others fell into old, human traps vying for power.

As my life unravels before my eyes, certain moments have greater value and significance for me. I want to share them, not because every experience was so deliciously grandiose, but because they represent humans fending to survive, understand, discover, create and appreciate all the good and bad moments that constitute a lifetime.

My destiny, and that of our Group, took unpredictable turns, reminding me and them that being human is a very special gift to be cherished and coveted the time that it endures.

Chapter 2- A New World

I woke up before Peter. His arm was wrapped tightly around me, holding me close to him. I could feel the slow, rhythmic beat of his heart against mine. He had fought hard for our cause and needed to sleep, so I lay still so as not to disturb him. He was covered with bruises and he had a nasty cut on his left arm that I would have to do something about.

Last night we were all caught up in that childish fervor, boasting about our clever strategy to put an end to the oppressive Android regime. Now my thoughts turned from the battlefield to the reality of today, the day after our victory. Was this just the beginning of a long process that would lead us in the right direction, certainly, away from the mistakes that were made over the long history of the human race? Avoiding past mistakes must be a priority. But, how to do that was not simple. All that I read, all that I learned about human history was altered, adapted, or edited by the androids. They saved the books portraying the horror that accompanied humans over time, and, saved very little about the good and constructive accomplishments made by humans.

Should I, or must I, be grateful that their appreciation of the arts and music brought me in harmony with those whose genius impressed and inspired their worlds and nourished my potential? Should I credit them with any real sense of morality? Should I treat their twisted version of human history as a kind of warning that will encourage us to achieve a perfect physical, intellectual and ethical environment? Can we reach, through striving, a human perfection? Is that what they expect of us? Is that what we should expect of ourselves?

The children chatting and their rustling about interrupted my thoughts. Frederic was jumping up on the bed. Peter opened his eyes, smiling at both of us. When he moved to sit up, he groaned and grabbed his arm.

"Let me see it, Peter?" I insisted, as I gently took his arm and observed the injury. "The cut is deep, but there is no sign of infection." I said, as if I knew something about medicine. We both knew who was evaluating the extent of his injury. "We just have to keep it covered for a while. I can see that it hurts." Our eyes met, animating our mutual pride.

"Ok, your diagnosis is promising," he said as he took Frederic and me in his arms.

"Mom, Dad, I came to tell you that Mathilda is taking us to the other side of the wall for breakfast." He screeched with joy. Passing through the wall was going to become a game, a favorite past time, for the children. "She said that I should tell you that she let those strange machines out of the padded room and they are preparing breakfast for everyone." He started jumping around again, laughing with excitement and screaming that he was going to pass through the wall again.

"Where is Mathilda?"

"Just outside the door, do you want to talk to her?" I nodded.

She heard her name and came into the room. "I took the initiative of letting the Group of 5 out of the padded cell." My eyes widened in disbelief. "They had helped us the night before with the food for the programmed humans and those humans were scheduled to wake up. I wanted the breakfast boxes to be ready." I nodded perfunctorily, uncertain of her action. "They worked well and everything went forward. I saw the programmed humans get off the monorail for work. The group of 5 promised to take care of them."

"Promised to take care of them, what does that mean?" I felt uneasy about that.

"I didn't sleep all night." She cleared her throat. "Actually, I asked Ferdinand and Ralph to wake me early so that I could get things straightened out for the programmed humans." She paused. "I didn't participate in the fighting yesterday, so I wanted to show my value to the group in another way, by taking care of the children and watching out for the programmed humans." That made sense.

"I left straight away to check on things and have been watching, controlling, and monitoring the situation. You don't have to worry, the androids just made certain that there were assignments ready for the programmed humans when they arrived on the job." She explained.

"And, they prepared breakfast for us?" She nodded vigorously. I got up slowly, letting my discussion with the Group of 5 yesterday run through my mind.

"Are you worried about the Group of 5?" Peter asked breaking into my thoughts.

"No, not at all. I don't think that they would do anything that would irritate or offend Reinhart." He let the topic drop and I pondered the situation in silence. Should I be worried that they might poison our food? No, I sighed in relief. If they ever intended to poison us, they would have done that a long time ago. And, moreover, they already made the logical decision. They promised Reinhart that they would take care of us humans. Showing allegiance to her, by serving us, was very clever. And, as Reinhart was their creator and could order them to shutdown permanently, it was in their interest to please her. So, from a strictly practical point of view, taking care of us humans validated and insured their right to stay activated.

I jumped up to take my shower and get ready for the day ahead of me when I heard Mathilda yell to the androids to bring her clean robes to distribute to everyone. This news sent chills through my body. Mathilda could be cold and indifferent to other humans, but she seemed to be very fascinated and flattered by the attention she was getting from the Group of 5. Should I mention to them that it took me a split second to understand their objective, or should I ignore it and pretend to be naive? So, seduction was on their agenda, a seduction probably designed to divide our group. I would have to stay alert. And, my heart pounded hard, warning me that all of us would have to be careful not to leave any of our new research lying around, because acquiring all new scientific research was certainly one of their principle short-term objectives. I would have to mention that to everyone.

After she left with the children, I told Peter that I wanted to check on the visual system here in the inner circle to see what those androids were actually doing. I was worried about all the time that had passed since Mathilda let them out of their padded cell. I was certain that they were feigning loyalty to us. The group of 5 was standing outside the middle wall, at exactly the place where Randolph, Stuart and I first entered the inner circle, patiently waiting for me to exit. It just seemed too good to be true.

Peter took a look and laughed heartily. I chimed in until my eyes were distracted by Dr. Miller, moving around in her nervous circles, and remembered the appointment I set up for her with Peter today.

"Oh, I forgot to tell you, Peter." He looked at me with a lop-sided grin on his face like he would rather not know. "I forgot to tell you that Dr. Miller will be passing by to see you today for you to change her body, her look, and give her android skin."

"What?" He shook his head and laughed like it was a joke. I smiled. "Oh no!" He shook his head in denial. "I don't know how to give her that android skin. And, did you take a good look at her. She doesn't even have robotic arms or legs that can be covered." He stared at me with disdain. "I don't know how to make arms or legs for her."

"You can stall her." I suggested. "And, yes, of course, you have to remove that horrible casing to see what is left of her original android body. That is going to take time." Robot designs, blue prints, were passing in front of my eyes as Reinhart uploaded the information to me. With this information, I could help, at least guide him with the conception of her robotic parts. "I think that there are technical guides in this inner circle that you can study and rely upon to fabricate her missing body parts. "

"And the material to create the parts?"

Good question...I couldn't answer that, but Dr. Reinhart could. "There are some replacement parts available, so I think that you won't have any problem finding what you need for her. In fact, there are pre-fabricated android limbs just waiting to be used. Reinhart anticipated all kinds of different scenarios when she constructed this center, one of which was damage to her prized androids. The only aesthetic problem, if it can be referred to as such, is se might end up being a bit taller than she was before, but that should not bother her."

"If I understand correctly, I just have to connect the limbs." He started to laugh cynically. "But, I don't even know how to do that."

"Reinhart will guide you." I said calmly. "And, just think about it, Peter, you will learn how to make these robotic limbs by studying the existing pieces."

"Ok, but, as she, Reinhart, said, I am going to have to stall Miller. I need time to study the manuals so that I can assemble everything correctly." His face lit up with interest. "I think that I like the challenge. And, the skin, is there a technical guide for that as well." I nodded. "Ok, but I shall have to remove her outer shell. Do you think that Miller will agree?"

"Does she have a choice?" We both smirked.

He and I left together passing through the wall in the dehydrated food section, so that I could surprise the androids, by arriving from another direction. We moved slowly and painfully around the long corridors that were filled with programmed humans and custodial androids just 24 hours ago. "This emptiness was stifling and must be replaced by human warmth and laughter in abundance. We—I— have a job to do and that job must begin today." I promised myself.

The androids sensed our arrival, just like an animal awaiting their master, turning in our direction the moment we rounded the corner. I thought they could be useful to us in keeping the Center operational, but they would have to be watched and kept under control.

"Good Morning, Dr. Reinhart," They chimed in.

"I hope that this is the last time that I have to correct you. My name is Pamela."

"Of course, it is Pamela, or Pamela Reinhart." Crawford explained.

"No! It is not that. I am just Pamela." I could feel the blood flow to my face. "In fact, we shall all go by first names to avoid any confusion."

"Whatever you say, Elisabeth." Flanders spoke up.

I was fuming over their impertinent behavior when Peter pulled me aside. "So long as they cooperate, who cares what they call you. We humans know that you are Pamela. We are not going to get ourselves upset by and trapped in their childish game." He was right so I let the subject drop.

Ignoring Flanders' last remark, I told Dr. Miller that we would meet her in the Physics Lab after lunch. She turned slowly in big circles. I surmised that that was her way of telling us that she was happy or comforted with this news.

The group of 5 assured me that the breakfasts were ready. They were not in boxes, so we should just serve ourselves.

"Pamela," Dr. Gordon said in a strong, firm voice. "You and your Ferdinand will have to make some fast decisions on the management of this center. We need some of the androids that were shut down to be reactivated so that they can continue their work in the agricultural sector, material production center, and in the cleaning department." She paused before adding, "You know that we provide clean garments and soap, all for your hygienic needs."

"Ok, you can stop there. I understand what you are getting at, Victoria." I started to initiate my decision by dropping the Dr. Gordon and putting her on my level. "I shall speak to Ferdinand and Ralph about bathing, brushing their teeth and changing their clothes. I know that human body odor is repugnant to you all and I do want you to be in your optimum performance mode." They all nodded.

"Nonetheless, I want you to give me the names of the androids in the sectors you mentioned and how many of them were assigned to each sector."

"And, Pamela, I would like to have contact with the Chief android engineer." Peter spoke up. "Where is he?" he asked the group.

The former Governor, Eugene, fidgeted before announcing that he had been ordered to shut down. "We were not sure whose side he was on." His face tightened as he quickly recognized his error and tried to correct it. "I did not mean that, what I meant was that we suspected him of being deceptive for some time, even before yesterday. So we ordered him to shut down about a week ago."

"Well, then you order him to be recharged, now!" He was starting down the corridor before I finished my sentence. I looked at Peter. "His name is Drager and I think that he will be with us again very soon."

I turned to the remaining members of the group of 5 and asked them to carry on taking care of the programmed humans. "I appreciate your cooperation."

Peter and I walked slowly through the corridors in the direction of the dining area. I looked up at Peter who was concentrating on the labyrinth of corridors, connecting and intersecting. It was obvious that he knew his way around, after all he was deprogrammed for a long moment before he left with the others for the outside community. This Center was definitely functional. Reinhart had built it to perfection. But, for me, it did not represent her genius, at least not for the moment anyway. The corridors resonated the history of our programmed servitude. The air was heavy and filled my nostrils with a suffocating, lingering odor, or sensation of oppression, making me feel bitter and sad. Fortunately, Jonathan enthusiastically bolted out of nowhere, changing this lugubrious atmosphere and jolting me from remorseful thoughts back to positive thinking.

"You are in a good mood." I said, mustering up a joyful tone.

He didn't seem to hear me. I realized instantly that he was still immersed in our victory. He was not ready to look at the aftermath and the problems we had to face. He gave Peter an energetic hug and lifted me up in his arms and turned me about, screaming, "We did it! We overthrew those miserable android creations!" When he gently lowered me to my feet, I too was feeling for a second time the excitement of our victory.

I stood studying him and listening to him recount the moments that left the biggest impression on him. I forced a smile in an attempt to conceal a painful nostalgia. I would always look at him with that tenderness that comes from sharing a long and pleasant part of one's life with someone as kind and gentle as he was. In spite of our new found freedom, all those years that we spent together in a real, yet artificial, bliss meant more to me now. There was nothing special that happened between us during all those years, except that we shared that feeling of total happiness that our programmed lives provided us with. Was that happiness or must happiness be found and constructed?

"Jonathan," I began, shaking myself out of the past. "Where do we stand with the remaining programmed humans?"

He addressed us, his eyes moving rapidly back and forth from Peter and me. "Don't worry. Mathilda and I are handling everything. It is going to take time to re-educate them, so that is our first objective." We both nodded our heads in agreement and he continued. "I don't think we are quite ready to deal with that. I suggest that we continue to study their reactions and their files in more detail before determining how and when to deactivate the programming?"

"That sounds rational, Jonathan, but we still must deal with their possible reactions to their own physical characteristics, or deformed bodies and faces, not to mention those who have dominant reptilian features."

I could see how confident and relaxed he was now, seemingly oblivious to the rapid degenerating malformations in his upper spinal column that produced debilitating pain just days before. "We shall all have the opportunity to discuss that problem during the meeting tomorrow."

"Yes, of course, a group meeting is a good idea. But, actually, Mathilda suggested that we could start the deprogramming by gradually altering the visual impression being communicated. It would not be very difficult, apparently, to feed new and more realistic characteristics into the visual receptor. In any event, what we are trying to avoid are those oppressive mixed feelings that surge when programming stops and reality takes over."

"Naturally that should be the objective; and, of course, we have time on our side." But," I said firmly, hiding my annoyance over Mathilda's take charge attitude, "I don't want anyone to do anything, touch in any way their programming, before we meet as a group and come to a decision. I am happy that Mathilda is taking initiative, but, she does not have full reins and you should make it clear to her that she is not authorized to act on her own."

"There is no problem there. She is not acting, just suggesting. I won't let her take any initiative." He smiled reassuringly.

"We have to leave now because we haven't eaten yet." I let out a sigh of relief. "I count on you to follow my advice." I realized that I hadn't mentioned Diana. "By the way, where is Diana? Were you together all night?"

"Of course, we were together." He laughed. "She was so courageous and effective, but she is now suffering physically. Even though she eliminated that human monster rapidly, he gave her more than bruises. I wonder if she has any broken bones. She is in the dining room helping to serve and clean up. She told me that this way she can keep the androids under her watchful eye." That made Peter and I both smile.

"I'll examine her later." I said. They both looked at me with surprise.

"Like you examined my arm earlier?" Peter asked.

"Like Reinhart examined your arm earlier." I said. "And, by the way, we have to stop by the hospital to wrap it up properly." They both raised their eyebrows in disbelief.

"Let it go." Jonathan suggested. "She won't be happy that I discussed it with you. If I think that she needs help, I'll send her to you." I nodded that I understood and we split up.

Most of our group was still lingering over their energy drinks in the dining room, laughing and bragging about how they bravely and efficiently vanquished our enemies.

"Pamela and Peter come over here and join us." John called out. He went on to explain how fascinated he was with the inner circle, what he referred to as the middle kingdom. "I took a quick look at the control room," he slapped his hands down on the table enthusiastically, "I never saw such technologically advanced equipment." He looked deep into my eyes. "Do you think that you – she- will be able to explain it to us?"

"I think so. Nonetheless, for me to access all the capabilities you have to ask me precise questions. Maybe with time, I shall be able to be creative on my own." I sighed and explained again to them that I was a depository of information and Reinhart controlled my access to that information. And, even when she revealed it to me, I needed her guidance in using it and communicating it to others. "We have a symbiotic relationship and, for the moment, she will only act through me when she is motivated by the project under discussion."

"Ok, if that is what you want us to believe for the moment." John replied.

I ignored his implied accusation of keeping secrets. "Now, though, we have so many different things to discuss. I suggest that we take today to explore and think about strategies and that we all meet tomorrow morning in the conference room that is in front of the former Governor's office." They nodded. "Oh by the way, Peter and I ran into the group of 5 this morning. To avoid all their name games with me I suggested that we all go on first name bases. So to remind you, Victoria Gordon, Rudolph Crawford, Agnes Miller, Eugene Venderkof and Edward Flanders. Ok, for everyone?" They nodded.

"And our last names, what were they?" Randolph asked.

"You won't like it Randolph. You are the famous Dr. Murdoc who programmed the androids to kill."

"Oh! You were right." He said in a deep, raspy voice. "I don't find it flattering to be one of his descendants. And frankly I never delved into android technology."

"No, that is not your first field, even though you have worked on designs that are used in robotics." I stopped to think for a minute. "Peter, do you want the others to come and help you with Agnes."

"Why not? I like the idea of a team." His face flushed with enthusiasm.

"Ok, let me explain. I promised Agnes that Peter would give her android skin." Their mouths dropped open. "The basic substance is available in the inner circle. I told some of you a while back that it is made from a plant. Reinhart found the plant growing in swamp lands just after the earth suffered serious climatic changes a long time ago. Since then the androids destroyed the earth's surface, so who knows whether we can find the original plant or a reasonable substitute that exists today." Their faces went blank.

A warm wave of optimism infused me as Elisabeth spoke through me. "You mustn't worry; human history has been a constant challenge for achievement that was shattered by natural disasters and foolish wars and a frustratingly long list of other intervening, destructive events. And we have always come back faster and stronger than the generations behind us. WE shall catch up fast and go forward. And, the earth has always provided us with what we need. We just have to find it."

Those words brought about wide-eyed expressions of wonderment and curiosity, giving me more confidence in myself and in her to impress them, as I picked up the discussion. "Peter told me that he would have to replace the arms and legs, maybe even the torso. The parts are available, and, even though he is not sure how to attach them, I am certain that Reinhart will guide him. In any event, we won't know the extent of her injuries until Peter takes off that heavy robotic casing and discovers what is actually underneath."

"That's right." Peter spoke up. "Robotics is my field, even though the androids have me classified as an engineer in bio-physics and bio-chemistry. " He shook his head. "Actually, that does not make sense. Why would they create that illusion?" His eyes squinted in thought. "The only logical reason for that is because they did not want me to know that I was working on them." We said nothing, so he continued. "In any event, the android structure is far beyond my present knowledge; I am still in the early robotic research stage." He sat more comfortably back in his chair. "Pamela told me that there are technical manuals available in the inner circle to consult. Anyone who wants to help me is more than welcome."

"I followed that chief engineer, Drager, for a number of years, so I have some understanding of how these machines function. I would be happy to give you a hand, sounds challenging." Stuart offered.

John and Randolph also showed interest. For the moment, we had a team in place, which is why I was presumptuous enough to bring up the malformation plaguing Jonathan. "I am purposely mentioning Jonathan because he is not with us at the moment and I don't want him to hear any of our deep concerns." Their eyes pierced mine. "I know, because of Reinhart and from what the Group of 5 revealed to me over time, that the Jonathan series was never physically perfect, although certain genetic predispositions could have been removed if the androids had been more careful. It is too late now. I thought about the rejuvenation machine and the problem remains the same. He could be transported back, but the congenital defects would remain. So, I was hoping we could straighten his upper spine by removing the deformed vertebrae and reconstructing the area with bionic parts."

"What are you talking about, Pamela?" Peter asked.

"Glad to see that you are interested, Peter, because you have a sub-specialization in human surgery. And…"

He interrupted me. "One thing at a time!" He put his hands up in a demonstrative stop. "You already gave me that Agnes to put together properly. Jonathan is another story. My surgical experience is with rubber dolls. I never touched a real human being."

I let out a long sigh. "I guess that we can't do anything for him. Is that what you are saying?"

"Ok, are there surgical guides?" I nodded. "Are there still those rubber dolls around?" I nodded. "Well, after we finish with Agnes we can all study those guides." He looked at the other members of his team, who nodded approvingly.

"I could also help you with that, as can Sarah." Ruth mentioned. "We worked in the hospital section and studied the anatomy and physiology of humans. We also did some dissecting of rubber dolls, as you put it."

"Actually, I don't know if you are talking about nanotechnology and biotechnology, but Stanislas and I are specialized in that field." Benjamin said. "Regardless, we are familiar with the human body. We could be very useful, and, speaking for myself, I would very much like to participate."

"Me too," Stanislas broke in. "I think that I have the right background for this.

"That is excellent news. I am feeling more optimistic. It is too complicated for me to go it alone and with a surgical team Jonathan's life will not be in such danger." He looked at me. "And, you, Pamela, is she capable of helping?"

"Yes, she can guide you even though surgery was not her field. But she knows how to create bionic parts, if they are not already available. You can count on me. And, the four of you, Stanislas and Benjamin, Sarah and Ruth can do some research into pharmaceutical drugs afterwards. We are going to need some simple drugs to combat bacterial infections. We are all going to have to get involved." I smiled approvingly and returned to the problem of the moment. "Oh, now we just have to convince Jonathan."

"I'll talk to Diana." Stuart suggested. "She can be very convincing." We all laughed nervously, hoping that she could be as persuasive with words as with actions.

We started to split up, Peter reminding everyone that Agnes

would be in his lab in the afternoon, just after lunch, when John requested the last names of the group. "Ok, Dr. Stuart Rever, Dr. John Gunther, Dr. Sarah Brown, Dr. Ruth Fielding, Dr. Isabel Radcliff, Dr. Mathilda Vernon, Dr. Benjamin Davis, Dr. Stanislas Borsky, Dr. Diana Ming, Dr. Peter Feragan, Dr. Matthieu LeClerc, Jonathan Craig and Ferdinand Hakim. That is the list. We will be receiving Dr. Kevin Jarod and Dr. Richard Fleming over the next few weeks."

"What about those androids, what are their fields of specialization?" Peter asked.

"They are generalists, trained in many scientific areas." Should I tell the others the truth about themselves now that this discussion was underway? I decided to. "Actually, all of you are generalists, you have received all the information to move from one scientific area into another without difficulty. Here, in the Center, the androids gave you projects in areas that they wanted you to concentrate on for the benefit of retrieving the maximum of lost scientific theory so that they could train the up-coming generations." Furrowed brows and tight smiles were on everyone's face.

"Yes, you have the capacity to work in any field which interests you. For example, you, Peter, were not supposed to be involved in robotics, at least not in the beginning. It is true that your initial work was biochemistry and biophysics, which is focused on the human anatomy, not the android structure. Nonetheless, the androids must have told you at some point that you were a robotics engineer and you just dragged up the information stocked in your brain to carry out the assignments."

"You all find my situation with Reinhart alarming, because I access stocked information." This was my opportunity to place myself on their level. "In fact, the absorption learning process is just that-stocking information. I have stocked more information in the scientific field simply because of the knowledge bank from Reinhart, even though my situation is different because our knowledge banks and consciousness are not merged." I noticed that their eyes grew large, so I returned to what I was saying about their specific learning. "You will see, the moment that you start on a given project, you -- all of you- - will be able to participate without difficulty. The advantage that we all have now is that we can decide what approach to take by listening and discussing the options. Otherwise, you would have implemented the programmed response."

"Wow!" Stuart responded in a high pitch. "In other words, all of us scientists have simply absorbed all the scientific and mathematical data available at the time we were under the programmed learning process."

"Exactly that. Now you might like one area more than another, but that does not change the fact that you can switch from one to the other whenever necessary." My eyes scanned the group, making certain that I had their full attention. "It was Reinhart's programmed learning process. She assigned people to different areas afterwards depending upon community needs and sometimes upon the registered interest the individuals had in one field as opposed to another. The androids used her method." I started to get up to move when I remembered that I had no news about Mathieu and Isabel. "By the way, where are Isabel and Mathieu?"

"Oh, they went off to explore the center." Randolph said, "Mathieu was very interested in the design of the Center and Isabel, just followed him." We grinned in amusement.

"I think that I am going to pass by to see the Group of 5, before meeting you in Peter's lab to undress Agnes." We snickered. "See you later."

I was walking very slowly now. I had every reason to be euphoric. So why then did I feel so troubled? Questions were passing through my mind. What was my role in all of this? Who masterminded this victory? Was I just a small link in the chain? Did we fight so hard? Was our victory too simple, too easy and too programmed? And, worse than anything else, was my role, my life, still inextricably linked to the Group of 5?

"Pamela! Pamela!" Peter, standing right in front of me, woke me up from these anguished thoughts. We exchanged playful grins, before he went on. "I just wanted to let you know, Frederic and the other children are in the learning center's recreational room. Do you remember that place?"

"I didn't until I took that horrible tour with Flanders, rather Edward, when I visited the birthing center and child development units. I did not remember it being like that. But, then how could I, or any of us, have remembered that lack of social interaction, so disconcerting retrospectively, among the children that I observed." I felt tears welling in my eyes as I spoke. "Do you know that they sat in front of each other with plastered smiles on their little faces?" He did not react. "They did not know how to play. There was no laughter, no shouting, and no physical or emotional interaction, like competition. There was no spontaneous activity of children having fun, instead the androids called out the moves that these little human style machines carried out."

"I know that that was difficult for you." He said in a soft and comforting tone. "You must move on now. It is important that we all move on in our ideas and our reactions." He pulled me up close to him reminding me that he was there and would always be there for me. "What would I do without him?" I heard repeating over and over again in my mind.

"By the way, Peter, we have a detour to take before I see the group of 5. I want to put something on your wound before it gets infected." He nodded.

We walked in the direction of the hospital. My heart was beating rapidly as I moved into that large, white room, with rows of beds facing each other. My legs felt limp and I struggled to keep going. This was the first time I entered this part of the Center since my deprogramming and I was now reliving the horror of that moment. I looked up at Peter, who was aware of my trepidations and took my hand firmly in his. "Now where are those bandages?" He asked in a loud voice, breaking through my eerie thoughts and forcing me to respond to the moment.

"Over there." I pointed to a cupboard. "I saw them retrieve the bandages from there." I opened up the cupboard and found not just the bandages, but also an anti-bacterial cream to put on a wound. Reinhart's voice inside of me effaced my hesitation. I put the cream and the bandage over Peter's wound. "The cream will work. I have confirmation on that." I reassured him. "Now, I would like to know what other pharmaceutical products exist that the androids refuse to let us have access to." Peter and I exchanged glances and then opened up the other cupboards in the hospital entry.

"Right, there are chemical sacks here. That is all that I found for the moment." Just seeing those chemical sacks made me quiver. I wanted to leave, so I grabbed Peter by the hand and pulled him towards the door. "I shall return later to look through other cupboards. I want to check on the children now." That was the only excuse I could find for my sudden change of heart. "I think that a visit to the pharmaceutical section is in order over the next couple days. Maybe there are some painkillers here or there that can help Jonathan until everyone is ready for his surgery. I don't want to waste any more time looking for them now." His eyes, alert and intense, told me that he understood my strong desire to leave this place.

We walked silently back to the recreational center. The children were no longer there so I took Peter's hand and led him through the birthing facility. Everything had been shut down. There were no fertilized eggs developing in test tubes and babies in artificial uteri, but the impact was just as strong. Peter squeezed down on my fingers as his limp hands turned to fists and his eyes blazed with anger. "And, we are the products of that, Pamela?" He asked in a trembling voice.

"Yes, we are the products of that." I replied softly.

Then he dropped my hands from mine and beat his fists on the glass panels that separated us from those artificial uteri, letting out his frustration like I did when Edward took me on the tour. "It makes me sick. I don't even feel human when I see where I developed."

"Of course you are human, Peter." I reached out to touch him but he pushed me away. So I waited patiently until he calmed down and turned back to me.

"And, where did we go from here, Pamela?"

"Follow me. I'll show you the learning center." We both jumped with surprise when we saw the children, Frederic, Rebecca and Samuel, hooked up to the learning machines. We charged through the door and ran into Mathilda.

"What are you doing, Mathilda?" We screamed at the same time.

"They have to learn. Calm down. They are not programmed. I simply put on a learning tape, a simple one on how to read and write" She smiled in hopes of calming our rage. And, it worked.

"I want to see the tape." I pushed my way over to the computer terminal. It was exactly what she mentioned, a simple tape about learning how to read and write.

"We must educate the children. By the end of the week, they will be able to read and write, if they need to. After that, the kind of education they receive will be your choice." She paused to observe our reactions. "I watched them play together for hours. They were bored. They need other things that we were unable to give them on the outside. They need to have their intellect stimulated with something other than balls and bats. I am both a psychologist as well as a psychiatrist, and I could see their need to learn. When I talked to the children about learning, they were excited; you will see that I did the right thing." She was convincing.

"Ok, Mathilda, maybe you did do the right thing, but for the moment all major decisions must be taken by the group. Do you understand that?" I asked.

"Yes, of course I do. I shall be careful to consult everyone in the future."

"Did you speak to the Group of 5 about this?" Peter asked.

"I did ask Gordon where the learning tapes were and how to use them, but she never accompanied me into this center and, as far as I know, she has no idea why I asked her about those tapes?"

I sighed, a heavy sigh of relief. "Of course she knows what you are doing. That is why you must not seek android assistance." I was annoyed. Why was she being so independent? Was she acting like this because she was under the influence of the creations? As I suspected, Gordon is testing Mathilda's allegiance to our group. But, there was also something unsettling and suspicious about Mathilda's sudden fascination with the children. On the outside, she rarely intervened. "What should we do now, Peter?"

"Well, we better tell John, Sarah, and Ruth about what is going on. I'll do that and get their reaction." He looked at Mathilda and said firmly. "You must remember that you cannot make decisions concerning the children without our permission." She nodded.

"By the way, Mathilda, do you know what has happened to that deprogrammed human that was locked up in Gordon's, rather Victoria's, office yesterday." I quickly brought her up to date on the personal name basis and gave her the first names of the group of 5.

"Yes, Victoria, told me that the young man was still sound asleep, but then I saw her 2 hours ago, things may have changed."

"I am going straight to Victoria's office and will join you later for lunch." I said to Peter. "And, Mathilda, would you please bring the children with you to the dining room for lunch when you finish here?"

I rushed off, leaving Peter to consult those technical guides in the inner circle. Victoria was standing outside her office when I arrived.

"He is awake and is knocking things around." She said with a smug look on her face. "What else could you have expected?"

"Did you try to talk to him?"

"Why would I do that? He is not my responsibility anymore." She was annoying me and she knew it.

"Do you have his code number?" She told me that she was not involved with him and therefore could not access his code. I knew that she was lying but it would have been too infuriating for me to drag out that useless discussion. "I'll be back." I called out to her as I started in the direction of Edward's office.

"What can I do for you, Elisabeth? " He asked puffing up his chest in defiance.

"There is nothing that you can do for her, but for me, Pamela, you could give me the code number for the enormous human locked in Victoria's office."

He stood staring at me, his sealed lips moving into a tight smile, vicious enough to make me shutter on the inside. He finally sat down and closed his eyes. I located the code number of the human. "That would be 100113051910, or James Series 10, as you like to refer to the humans. Anything else?"

"And what is his family name?"

"He has none. He is one of our creatures. Only those whose parentage dates back to human history... that would be your very select group... have last names." He anticipated my next question. "And, of course, us androids -- who are the embodiment of their creators and were members of your, rather, Elisabeth's, research team -- also have last names."

His attitude of superiority irritated me so I informed him that I was going to move the group of 5 into a big office that they would share together. I told him that I did not see any reason why they should have private offices when we didn't. "Are you sure that you are making the right decision?" He asked in an arrogant tone.

His question startled me . . . could he be referring to the fact that the group of 5 would be able to share and compare information and eventually plot? That made no sense. They could have done that for years. But now, of course, they would be involved in our research in a restricted sense. He was perhaps right to comment on Pamela's impulsive behavior. So I changed the subject. "I would like to know how to deal with the young man." I saw his eyes light up with interest. "In other words, what would you consider to be the best way to approach him? He is acting violently, slamming and breaking things in Victoria's office."

"I am sorry but I have no idea how to deal with this deprogrammed human. That was Victoria's field." He started to tap his fingers rhythmically on his desktop. He tried that before to get my attention, but today it only annoyed me.

I pretended to ignore his attempt to distract me and replied coldly. "Thank you for the code." I stood up to leave.

"We were very good friends, Elisabeth and I." I stopped in my tracks. What was he getting at? "We, the group of 5, were not her enemies and we are not yours. You will come to realize that with time which is why I am happy staying here in the background for the moment."

"But, you will have a job to do like everyone else." The edges of my mouth turned up. "Isn't that what you told me, everyone in the center has a job to do?" His android eyes shined with a bright, harsh light. "Without a job to do, we would have to ask you to shut down."

"You are just so delightful, Pamela." He recovered his android calm and flashed me a broad smile. "Go ahead and organize this place, I have to prepare myself for the up-coming meeting with you and the other humans, which, I gather, will take place in the very near future."

I left feeling irritated and sad. He had been so nice to me, encouraging me to absorb all that information from my biological mother only a few weeks ago. He was so different now, cynical and aggressive. Perhaps he never anticipated a rebellion and a transfer of control. But, what did he anticipate? And yet...

My thoughts were interrupted when I saw the two people that I needed to help me with the deprogrammed human jogging down the corridor in the opposite direction from me. "Stuart, Diana, I need your help with the deprogrammed human." I called out and they stopped instantly.

"Is he awake?" Stuart asked, as he and Diana rushed in my direction.

"Yes and he is creating havoc in Victoria's office. His code name translates into James series 10. He has no last name like the rest of us because he is a series that was created here in the center." They nodded. "We have to talk to him and calm him down, but I'm afraid to enter that office on my own. Would you both be willing to help out?"

"No problem." Diana answered. "But, I am not in favor of this first name basis with these ruthless, disgusting androids. I preferred spitting out the name Gordon, minus the doctor part. Victoria sounds too nice for that android slut."

"I admit that it bothers me to a certain extent. We shall discuss that tomorrow. Remind me during the meeting. "

Victoria was standing in the same place she was when I left her more than 30 minutes ago. Her eyes squinted when she looked at Diana. She moved forward and grabbed Stuart's hand mentioning how much she was looking forward to working closely with him. He quickly shook off her hand in disgust and moved quickly in the direction of the office door.

"Why aren't there any windows in these offices?" he asked Victoria. She simply shrugged her shoulders. I hadn't thought much about it up until now. Within seconds the answer from Reinhart arrived and I started laughing.

They all looked at me with the same dropped mouth expression on their faces. "Because..." I was speaking under heavy laughter, "these rooms were designed to be closets. They were never intended to be offices. Gordon's head fell in shame and that bothered me a bit. "It's ok, Victoria." I looked at Stuart and Diana who were grinning at the android's humiliation. "In any event, the androids did not have access to the inner circle so it was perhaps normal for them to set up offices in these spaces." I admonished my friends.

"Your laughter was childish and offensive, but very much in keeping with your species." She regained her erect posture. "Unlike humans, Pamela, who need a window on the world, androids enjoy their privacy." Her android eyes were flaring. "Granted, we were all used to larger and more comfortably furnished work spaces before that revolution, if that is what you were insinuating." She let out an irritating sound. "In fact, your observation is correct. But, then, most of the offices don't have windows. The few conference rooms, or large work spaces, that have windows also have shutters to ensure privacy." She scolded. "And, our video equipment kept us well informed about what was happening outside the confines of our offices."

She stopped to study my stiff, rigid posture. "You should be focusing on how we improved upon this center instead of the sizes of our offices." Victoria retorted. "We brought more equipment and material for the laboratories, constructed the vacation center, and developed the agricultural unit. We maintained the storage units for androids and the capsules for the humans in suspended animation. We modernized the hospital facility, transport terminals and enclosed private cubicles." We looked at her with that one. "Yes... well...we adapted the cubicles, adding other features and removing the doors." She wiped her hands on her robe, a rather provocative gesture that I decided to ignore. "We didn't know that these were closets because the clean-up crew had furnished these rooms as offices before they awakened us and we had never visited this center before the outbreak of the revolution."

"Interesting." I wanted to know more but it was not the right moment so I returned to the reason why we were crowded together in the corridor. "We have to take care of James series 10."

Stuart, taking the lead, opened the door cautiously. "Who are you?" James screamed out.

"It is ok, we are humans, like you." Stuart answered calmly.

"Oh no!" He screamed in horror. "I recognize you. You are the one that I fought against and you came back now to terminate me, is that it?" His voice quivered.

"If I wanted to terminate you, I would have done that yesterday." Stuart stayed calm. "Relax, I am here to help you to deal with the real world—the world that you are seeing now. "

"Wait a minute," James backed up against the wall. "She is with you?" He pointed to Diana and answered in a hysterical voice. "She is crazy! Don't let her near me! She terminated my partner." We were all in the little room now as he collapsed on the floor, shaking his head back and forth in disbelief. "How did she do that? How did you take me down? What are you? You are too small, too frail to have beaten me and my partner?" He stuttered.

"You are young, James." The young man's brow corrugated in concentration. "Yes, you are James, not just a number. She is Diana," Stuart pointed to Diana, "and I, Stuart, and we fought against you and your partner and yes, we won the battle. And, we won, even though you both were bigger and stronger. We won because we are more experienced than you and knew how to outwit you in combat."

The human grappled under the weight of his aching body to stand up, as if he was readying himself for an eventual combat. Diana instinctively took on a defensive posture as she aligned herself next to Stuart. Stuart did not lose his composure, ignored James' offensive move and instead offered James his hand. "Let me help you to get back on your feet." He said delicately. It all looked so simple from then on, James took Stuart's hand and once up on his feet, he threw his big, bulging muscular arms around Stuart, clutching and sobbing like a child seeking protection.

We waited for the scene to come to an end. Victoria was hissing next to me and saying under her breath that this was one of the most pitiful displays of human affection that she had ever witnessed and regretted that she was forced to observe this despicable melodrama.

When James calmed down, he turned his attention to the flashing, brightness of Gordon and asked what she was. I then asked Victoria to turn off her blinding light. She hesitated for a brief moment, long enough for me to understand her defiance. She carried out the order telling me that she was doing this to appease Elisabeth and not Pamela. I ignored it the best I could.

"She is not like us?" James' eyes were popping as Gordon confronted him with her android body.

"No, she is an android." Stuart was still controlling the situation. "It will take some time for you to understand what has been going on for a long time in this Center, but right now I want you to try to relax and trust us humans." James nodded acquiescently. "You were given a heavy sedative. Are you hungry?"

"I don't know." James answered. "I might be. I just haven't thought about it."

"Ok, it is lunch time, isn't it, Pamela?

"Let me introduce myself to you, James. I am Pamela. "I smiled warmly. " I am looking forward to getting to know you better. And, as Stuart just suggested, we can start that over lunch."

"Well, it looks like you have another active human in your group and I have an office to clean up." Victoria commented.

Even though James was walking slowly, he showed no signs of physical disorientation, or other residual effects from the heavy dose of sedatives he was given, as he held his body very erect and he was not swaying. We went straight to the dining room to join the others. They quickly introduced themselves and told James what projects they were working on. I said that I was a pianist, musician like Jonathan, and had just recently moved into the scientific section.

He was still eating when we finished with our introductions. He looked like he was caught up in all the events that preceded and that pushing his food around his plate helped him to focus. So, we all sat patiently waiting for him to put down his fork before asking what field he worked in.

"I don't know what is happening to me." He paused before cautiously continuing. "I have strange sensations, if I can call these irresistible and impulsive surges of energy just physical sensations."

"We shall help you to identify those sensations, which are human feelings and emotions that were suppressed with the visual receptor." Mathilda explained.

James turned in her direction. She was seated next to Peter and Randolph, something that retriggered James profound apprehension of his situation. "You, I remember you." He said as he pointed first to Randolph and then to Peter. His head bowed and a kind of futility overcame him, as he said with an effort. "You both were firing at me."

"No, we were firing on the androids-those machines-that have manipulated us humans for centuries. You were part of the android combat unit and we humans were fighting for our freedom." Randolph's voice rose in a burst of energy.

"You were programmed, James, and you will understand eventually and with time how you were programmed and the effect of that programming on your human side. And, we will help you to deal with the complexities of emotions and feelings that make us human." John said in a loud persuasive voice. "For the moment, we would just like to know which unit you were attached to."

"I am glad that you survived, James. We need all the humans we can find to help to us." Peter said kindly.

"Ok, I'll answer your question." He acquiesced. "I am a pilot, if you know what that means. I have never flown a real aircraft or space vessel, but I have used simulators. I know how to operate all the various vehicles – cars, tanks, boats and . . . in the transport unit. And, I know how to fly supersonic aircraft and small spacecraft." He said in a voice, soft and calm.

"You know the codes?" Diana asked. "I know how to construct these machines, but I don't have all the operational codes."

He was afraid of Diana. I saw his body stiffen when she spoke and he observed her closely before answering. "Yes, I know all the codes and how to manipulate these machines and ... fire the weapons." A self-satisfied brightness glimmered in his eyes "But, as I said, I have only used simulators."

"So, perhaps we could spin around in one of those air vehicles over the next few days to get an idea of the land surface outside this center?" She asked enthusiastically.

"We shall see all that in the meeting tomorrow, Diana." I interrupted her. "And, oh look," I pointed to Ferdinand and Ralph who had just entered the dining room. To our absolute delight they were wearing clean, white robes, a warm, balsamic aroma of cedar wood emanating from their bodies. I had not had time to mention hygiene to them so they must have made the decision on their own.

"If I understand correctly, you are going to chair the meeting tomorrow, Ferdinand?" John asked.

"Chairing a meeting or even keeping some kind of order by introducing the subjects and giving everyone the chance to participate, maybe even organizing a vote, is ok for me; but I don't want to be the Head of State." He looked straight at me when he answered. His message was loud and clear: he didn't want decision -making authority.

"Well, that should work out fine." John said, his hands caressing his long beard. "We are used to group participation and our numbers are still small, so it is a good idea to let everyone have their say." Everyone at the table was nodding. "What we do need is an agenda. We need to treat the urgent problems first. I suggest that we deal with James' integration and then tackle the problem of deprogramming the other humans. I intend to look around the Center this afternoon. See if I can find any humans that are in hiding."

"I'll come with you." Mathieu volunteered and Ruth, Sarah, and Isabel wanted to participate as well.

"I would like to talk to James to find out if his vision is functioning correctly and explain emotions to him. "Mathilda offered.

"And the children?" I asked. "Is their learning over for the day?"

"No. If I have everyone's approval," She looked at Peter, John, Sarah, Ruth and myself, "I shall continue the educational disk and then test their competence tomorrow to see if they are absorbing the information." We agreed. "I thought that I would talk to James while the children were studying."

"Diana, do you have anything special in mind?" I asked.

"I would have taken James with me to the transport terminal, but Mathilda is right, he should be informed about the kinds of feelings he might experience. I guess that I shall just go myself and look over those fabulous machines."

"By the way, Ralph, what did you do here in the center?" I ventured.

"Oh, let me think. Yes, I am an agronomist, although I also studied agricultural engineering. Strangely enough, I never did any gardening. I was involved in the genetic modification of species and the overall production of food sources here in the center." He shook his head in disbelief. "It seems like centuries ago that I did any constructive work. I don't even know if I am capable of participating anymore."

"This is great news." I was definitely excited about it. "You must get back in charge of agricultural production here in the center. You might also take a look at some of the species in the inner circle." I stopped for a minute, reflecting on the various specimens that Randolph, Stuart and I had discovered. "By the way Diana, aren't you a marine biologist?" She nodded. "You might want to take a look at the marine life stored in the big jars in the inner circle. I'll show you where they are."

"Yes, maybe I shall stop by and examine the specimens now. Good diversion. I like it."

Jonathan who had been very quiet announced that he was returning to the programmed humans and asked Benjamin and Stanislas to help him. That left Peter, Stuart, Randolph and myself to take a close look at Dr. Miller, who was waiting for us when we arrived in Peter's lab.

Chapter 3-Pride and Fervor

Seeing us sent Miller from an inoperative into an operative mode in a matter of seconds, as she spun around in large circles, her rubber arms flying in different directions. "I saw Drager. He was reactivated and will be arriving in a few minutes." She said in an agitated voice noticeably harmonious with her spasmodic body.

Drager entered in a fury excusing himself for the delay and explaining that his reactivated body was not yet at its optimum. I had only seen him once before when, at Crawford's insistence, Drager was asked to verify Victoria's internal circuitry. Victoria asked me to be present during the session so that I could give her the order to reactivate, if Crawford decided against it. I didn't know then that it was simply a contrived test of my allegiance to Victoria. Strangely enough, I could still feel that intense fear that seized hold of me as I groped for the right words to order Victoria's reactivation.

I stepped back from him and observed his inoffensive, robotic style. No deeper memory of Drager that might be attributed to Reinhart surfaced. I wondered if the androids told me the truth when they said that he participated directly with Elisabeth. "Dr. Drager," I began brusquely, "what sector were you working in when Dr. Reinhart was alive?"

He shuffled his feet for a few minutes before answering. "I never worked with Dr. Reinhart, even though I worked very closely with Dr. Crawford and with Dr. Miller." He turned to face me. "I was never involved in anything other than the verification of android systems, making certain that everything was functioning properly. I did, though, work with another engineer, who was destroyed by the explosion in the center of the earth. He trained me to repair androids and showed me how to replace interior circuits." He had no emotional configuration so I could read nothing on his expressionless face. I guessed he was referring to the infamous Dr. Murdoc, Randolph's illustrious ancestor.

"Is there nothing else that you should be telling us?" I asked, trying to penetrate his very cold android behavior and get more information. "Did you ever do any programming?"

"No."

"Did you ever construct an android?" He gave me a definitive no. I looked at my colleagues who shrugged their shoulders. There didn't seem to be anything else to ask.

"Well, Drager, can you help us disrobe Agnes, ah--Dr. Miller?" Peter asked.

"Actually, I put her body back like that after the accident. I dismantled a rudimentary robot that I found. I don't know why it was just standing against the wall in the unit where the other androids were sleeping." Nice way to say, shut down, I mused.

"Let's get started." Peter pulled Agnes by her wiry hand and led her closer to the lab table. She couldn't sit or lie down because the metal casing was so large that it gave her no flexibility. She tried very hard to control her sporadic movements and cooperate. Peter, with Drager's assistance, dismantled the arms and opened up the casing. She did have a nice, long neck and a long torso all intact. Surprisingly the android skin was still covering the neck and torso and was in excellent condition. Even minus arms and legs, she was not repulsive, as she had voluptuous firm breasts and a sleek waistline that led to nice, proportioned hips, not to mention her beautifully proportioned face. By the sweet smiles on the faces of my male colleagues, I gathered that they were happy, or more seduced, with what they saw.

"Agnes," Peter finally said in a soft, calm masculine voice. "Do you trust me?" She looked at him and then turned to me. I smiled approvingly and she answered affirmatively. "I need time to study the manuals to attach new parts. That means that I would prefer that you stay like you are right now. It will make it easier for me, for all of us," he looked at Stuart and Randolph, "to understand how to connect the limbs."

"I can do that." Drager said. "I left all the necessary pieces and circuitry in place, in the event we ever learned how to construct android bodies and android body parts."

"We have the parts." I said. His android eyes turned, as he fixed a penetrating stare. I shook off the effect and continued. "Agnes, your arms will be the right size, but you will be taller than you were before. Do you understand?" She nodded.

"I don't like it!" Peter exclaimed abruptly. "I am the one in charge."

"I don't either," Randolph and Stuart chimed in.

"Listen, Drager!" Randolph confronted the android. "Maybe you know how to connect her limbs, but we are also here to learn and want to be able to verify everything from the beginning."

"After all," Stuart picked up the conversation. "We have to take your word for it that her limbs were damaged and you just didn't dismantle her and dress her up like a misfit."

"Why would I do that?" He protested. "I saved her from being shut down." And as if anticipating the next question, he said. "Her limbs were visibly damaged beyond repair."

"You mean that you never even thought about studying what was left of her limbs?" He shrugged. "That makes no sense, where is your curiosity?" Stuart asked.

"I want to remind you again that I am not one of the group of 5. Of course, I have no curiosity. I carry out orders and my orders were to destroy the limbs that I detached from her body. That is what I did."

"And, they were definitely damaged?" Peter asked.

"Apparently an explosion took place when she was holding a volatile chemical mixture. Her arms were virtually ripped off her body. I simply undid the pieces that were still hanging in the joints. Her legs were crushed under the weight of the lab table and equipment. The other androids were not in the direct line of the explosion so they were able to escape."

"But, then her legs were still in place?" Reinhart's warm presence surged inside of me and inspired me to respond. "Did you try to move the table and equipment off of her?"

"I was not there. I arrived after she was pulled out from under

41

the lab table by her colleagues." He pressed down on his temples as if he were tapping deeper into his memory. "When I saw her, she had tiny pieces of wires and parts hanging from where her legs had been inserted. They were in the same condition as her arms were before I cleared up the pieces and attached the robotic arms at this point." He pointed to the middle socket in the shoulder area. "I didn't find any limbs that could serve as legs, as I said, so I covered her in the robotic casing equipped with wheels. I then attached the wires to her cerebral command system so that she could move about." We just looked at him. He treated this like it was an easy, every day task to hook up an android to very rudimentary robotic parts that, in my mind, would be very difficult to do.

"Well...I still suggest that you, Agnes, stay like this while we. . .that is . . .us humans here, locate the limbs and study the technical manuals so that we can learn from your unfortunate experience." Peter broke the silence. "Pamela, what do you think?"

"I agree that this is a good learning experience." I turned to Drager. There was no need to compliment him on his ingenuity, he would never understand or appreciate it, so instead I told him that it appeared that he had technical skills that could be useful for us and that he could assist the reconstruction team with Agnes. He nodded affirmatively.

"Agnes," I sighed as I looked at her dismembered body. "Do you want to shut down for the next few days or would you rather stay alert and watch?"

"I want to tell Dr. Reinhart something." Agnes pleaded. The Group of 5 would always look at me as Reinhart. I knew that I was not divided into two personalities and, at least for the moment, that I was but a caretaker of the knowledge that Reinhart downloaded inside me and kept safely hidden in her own consciousness. I sensed her presence, a warm suffusion of energy inside of me, when she decided to upload information for me to assimilate and absorb into my own consciousness and thus integrate into my knowledge bank. That seemed to happen only when she was either interested in the discussion, problem, or scientific research, or when she sought to clarify facts. But, I was not in the mood to explain this to Agnes or

Drager or anyone else for the moment, so I just let her remark slide by, as if it went unnoticed.

"They, my four colleagues, did not cause the explosion or the fire, Pamela." I looked at her askance as she was now addressing me and not Reinhart, as she had requested. I was also confused by what she just said. Why was she defending the other members of her group? All evidence pointed to foul play even though we had no intention of arresting anyone.

"The chemicals that we collected and transported to this center, just before the explosion, were in Dr. Reinhart's laboratory and apparently they were not properly labeled. The explosion took place shortly after we were awakened and had started to set up the research lab. The explosion should never have taken place. We surmised at that time that Dr. Reinhart was the target and that this explosion was reserved for her."

I felt my legs go limp. Why would someone sabotage Reinhart's laboratory? So she was destined to die. Perhaps then Crawford did her a favor by granting her a quick death.

"I am sorry for her- or for you." Miller's voice startled me from my morbid thoughts. "I would like to believe that the non-intellectuals left her that surprise, but my logic tells me that only an intellectual would have been so diabolical as to have changed the labels on the jars, thus creating the kind of explosion that took place." She let her head fall in respect or pain. I wasn't sure which.

"It does not matter now. All those perpetrators of Reinhart's death have long since disappeared." I stopped to study her. "I appreciate your honesty. It is good to know that you, and the other members of the Group of 5, work well together." I said what I believed was the right thing for the moment. That me of their tight working relationship, and the interminable complicity between and among the members of the Group of 5.

Staying with Agnes and Drager, while the others studied the manuals, was counter-productive for me and so I decided to do something else. I informed them that I wanted to pass by the learning center to see how everything was going for the children and James.

On my way, I ran into Jonathan going in the same direction as me. "Everything ok with the humans?" I asked.

"I didn't think that you cared, Pamela."

"What? Why would you say that?" I asked, insulted.

"Simply because you have not yet looked in on them. You saw them for a few minutes yesterday, but today…" He pouted.

"Ok, you are right." I tapped his shoulder teasingly. "I know that you can handle this and I had to deal with James. In fact, I am interested in how it's going between Mathilda and James now. That should give us an idea of what to expect with the others." He nodded.

"What is your problem, Jonathan?" I ventured, recognizing from his accusatory behavior that he was brooding over something else…more profound.

"I was wondering…hoping that you had some news for me." I had spoken with Peter and the others, but Jonathan was not aware of all of that.

"Yes, actually, Jonathan, now that you mention it, let's take a detour. I discovered that there is a small pharmacy in the hospital unit. I want to see whether there are any painkillers there."

There were basic drugs, like the antibiotic cream and surgical bands, in the cupboard I opened in the morning. I did not notice any pills. I felt less emotionally affected by this environment than I did earlier in the day, so I wandered off into other parts of the hospital unit, opening up the other cupboards, finding, like earlier, only chemical sacks.

I was ready to leave when I noticed a locked cupboard in the office room. There was no key in the lock. I searched randomly in the drawers of the desk and other cupboards in vain. I finally sat down on the desk chair to get a better view of the room and fell upon the hiding place: I saw the key dangling underneath the desktop. I wondered from whom the androids were hiding the key. None of us patients were able to walk around the unit, but, yes…I remembered that there were humans working with the androids. The assistant that was kind to me and protected me in the beginning was human and had by-passed her programming. Her espionage activity was the reason why she was terminated after Mathieu helped me, at Gordon's request, to escape. I shook my head trying to evacuate some of those horrible memories of my awakening.

The key opened a cupboard stacked with different kinds of pills.

Reinhart's interest in pharmaceutical products ended after the earth's environment changed radically. Fortunately, she had some knowledge of basic pharmaceutical products used during the 21st century and recognized a product that could diminish pain.

"Here, Jonathan," I called out to him. He arrived quickly and I gave him the pill bottle. "You can take three of these a day and..." my eyes were now on another product that could relax muscles, "one of these three times a day, as well. This medicine will help you to cope until we can arrange for surgery." I saw other bottles of the same medicine in the cabinet and took one of each to have its chemical composition broken down and analyzed in the pharmaceutical lab.

I had to face the truth. The Group of 5 lied to me when they said that there were no painkillers available for Jonathan. They lied to me how many times over the last few years. I guess they never expected me to live long enough to discover all those lies. A strange glassy chill passed through me as thoughts filtered from my other half.

I handed Jonathan a glass of water. "Take the pills and then follow me to the orchestra pit. I think I need to relax a bit with some music." I saw him hesitate. "You can use one of the other clarinets, just this once!"

We were like two happy children running off to engage in harmless mischief while the others worked. As we rushed into the orchestra pit we came face to face with 5 programmed humans warming up with their string instruments. We called out our codes and they turned smiling in our direction.

Impulsively, I started to chant Beethoven's 9th symphony, "Ode to Joy." Jonathan picked up a violin laying on one of the chairs and, to my total dismay, started to play it like a maestro. I didn't know that he could play any instrument other than a clarinet, but, apparently, I didn't know him all that well. The others followed his lead adding a cello and a double base and percussion instruments while I provided piano accompaniment. Our instruments and our voices were so exhilarating that I did the unthinkable. I opened up all the audio control buttons and let the music flow into every corner of the Center including the inner circle.

Little by little the members of our group, including the children, poured into the orchestra pit, chanting along with us. Our voices-tenors, sopranos, altos, bases-rang out strong. Until now, we had only talked about our victory. The time had come to celebrate it. And that is what we did. Only the programmed humans continued to play. Jonathan and I left our instruments behind and joined the other members of our group on front stage.

Our loud humming continued even as we frolicked about stomping our feet, waving our hands, and swinging a partner. And then suddenly this melodious musical momentum dissipated and a primitive, instinctive behavior, buried deep inside of each of us, surfaced, in a prodigious showing of pride and fervor. For we puffed out our chests, tilted back our heads, raised our arms high above our shoulders displaying our clenched fists, flinging wildly with unrestrained enthusiasm, beating the air, while our high-pitched screams of joy penetrated the atmosphere, vibrating violently as they resonated off the auditorium walls.

The Group of 5, with Drager carrying Agnes, arrived in the middle of our celebration. They sat in the audience and waited patiently for our grandiose gestures of victory to subside and, for what they later confided in me, for us to return to a more civilized state of mind.

When we eventually regained our calm, the Group left Jonathan and me, with the programmed humans, on the stage and collapsed on the comfortable auditorium seats. They sat back to listen-for the first time in their lives-to a small orchestra. We played the best we could bits and pieces of Beethoven's famous 5th symphony and his Clarinet trio in B flat before introducing Mozart's clarinet Concerto Adagio, Movement 2. My pride soared as Frederic played a couple notes on his clarinet. When we finished, all members of the audience including the group of 5 applauded us vigorously.

And then Jonathan bowed down to me as he said. "Now, it is your turn to mesmerize the audience."

I felt strangely alone and uncomfortable. This was the first time that I would play for humans. I played my piano all those years for an audience of machines. "What if the humans don't like my music? What if they don't find me talented?" I worried in silence.

"Ok," I said, smiling sheepishly. "But only 2." I started with the

"Campanella" by Liszt and moved quickly into Chopin's nocturne n°2 in E flat. When I finished, I let my hands drop onto my lap and stared nostalgically at the keyboard, afraid to turn, to face the others. The screams and applauds burst forth. This moment meant so much to me because I showed them that Pamela had talent, different from theirs, but just as great, and even though they could stand in awe of Reinhart's genius, they could no longer deny the talent of Pamela. I searched the audience as my eyes met Peter's and our ensuing broad smiles drew us even closer together.

The Group of 5 gave me a standing ovation, in the tradition of a past generation. I stepped down from the stage and led the others in a processional march out of the auditorium, chanting together the "Ode to Joy," as we waved our arms and slapped each other on the back in passing, giving life and laughter to empty hallways.

This was the beginning of many planned and impromptu festivities. And so it was that in a spirit of merriment and pride that our first day of freedom came to an end.

Chapter 4- Unveiling Truths

James followed us into the inner circle, taking one of the smaller rooms for him. He seemed to have adapted quite rapidly to his deprogramming, which gave us hope for the other programmed humans.

We all met early in the morning in the dining room for breakfast, so we had time to linger over our energy drink before the meeting.

"Pamela," I turned my head in the direction of John's voice. "I have a couple questions about our origins."

"I would like to know some things as well." Benjamin spoke up. "I don't understand your relationship with Reinhart. I know that you briefly addressed the subject with Randolph and Stuart just before the revolution. But the rest of us remain in the dark and I am more than curious about how the two of you occupy the same space."

Everyone's attention was on me. I didn't know where to begin. "I shall first answer John's question. I know that the Group of 5 will certainly address the subject that you raised, John, when we meet with them, but..." I hesitated, "you have the right to know more." I double checked that James had left to work out in the gym and that everyone from our group was present before continuing. "I think that this dining room is not the best place for this kind of discussion and suggest that we move into the inner circle." We grouped together in the inner circle lounge, some members sitting on the comfortable, cushioned-backed chairs, others in a lotus position on the floor, and still others just stretched out on the floor while I stood in front of them.

"To answer your question, John, none of us are clones, or the aggregate of genetically identical cells produced by a single progenitor cell. In all our cases, the most interesting one of our progenitors was the one that Reinhart worked with at the end of her life. Nonetheless, we were conceived through in vitro fertilization, whereby the sperm or ovum of our progenitor was put in contact with the sperm or ovum of another human." Their eyes were expressionless. "I don't know if the Group of 5 used the same genetic mix with each new series, but they apparently did not reproduce us on a regular basis and within the same time frame."

"What does that mean?" Peter asked, his teeth clenched.

"It is just conjecture because we have no idea how long the androids have been in power. Curiously enough, though, there is a basis for my hypothesis because we are not the same series. I am series 13 and Stuart is Series 8, for example."

"Makes sense." Randolph weighed into the discussion.

"I believe that the Group of 5 was looking for more than a close physical resemblance. They were looking for an equivalent or higher IQ level than that of our famous progenitors, and were hoping that we, the entire group, would return at the same time." I chuckled. "It must have been very frustrating for them because there was a very, very...low probability that this would happen."

"But they did it." Mathilda choked out as if in shock.

"How can you be so certain, though, that we are not clones and are the fruit of in vitro fertilization?" Ruth queried.

"Cloning was outlawed, for ethical reasons, before Reinhart existed." I turned my eyes on her. "And, you worked in the in vitro center, so you would have been privy to cloning, if it was being used. And, we can verify it through testing."

"Maybe, but try to convince me right now." She protested.

"Cloning was a solution in the 21st century, if what Miller told me is exact. It was a period when material gain, or wealth, were sources of power---remember we talked about this during my visits to the outside community?" Heads nodded. "If someone had money, or wealth, cloning, or creating an identical replica of oneself, was feasible, because the procedure was very expensive. In the beginning these clones were not recognized as another human and therefore had no legal rights, the reason why there were many abusive practices associated with cloning. For example, the clone was a source of body parts and organs for the progenitor, in the eventuality that the progenitor was ill or suffered injury. They existed in a substandard cryogenic environment never knowing that they were alive and members of the human race." I said, shaking my head over the morbidity of this practice.

"I remember your mentioning this and it is particularly disgusting." Stuart spit out.

"Not all wealthy people wanted cloned organs, some wanted a clone to insure a kind of immortality for themselves and raised their clone like a member of their family. In most cases, the clone only had identical physical characteristics. Their personalities were most often diametrically opposed to those of their progenitor. Simply put their personalities developed because of their relationships with other individuals on both an intellectual and nonintellectual level, and other stimuli like lifestyle, education and dreams associated with their proper generation. So, hopes for immortality vanished and so did the clone. It was easier to dispose of it than to care for an identical physical image of oneself that turned out to be incorrigibly disappointing on both an intellectual and psychological level."

I stopped to observe the group. "When the clones were finally recognized as individuals under the law, havoc broke loose because the wealthy class could no longer treat them like a repository of organs or kill or otherwise dispose of them because of malfunctioning personalities. These were illegal practices punishable under the law. So unwanted clones were forced to become members of the work force engaged in subservient tasks and treated a bit like slaves. If you want to know more about cloning, I do believe that there is information on this in the library." I looked at Ruth. "And, the Group of 5 would never have wanted to be associated with cloning, considered to be a wretched human practice."

I saw a number of corrugated brows. "Yes, the Group of 5 has resorted to treacherous and inhumane practices, but cloning is something that they consider a barbaric, contemptuous practice used centuries ago by corrupt scientists." I studied their reactions. "I am certain that they resorted to another method of reproduction, more sophisticated in their minds, and hence used, as I mentioned earlier, in vitro fertilization. And unlike cloning, IVF gave them more opportunity to play around with chromosomal changes and genetically modify humans, all of which was more scientifically interesting and challenging for them than cloning." I sighed. "And, they have already repeatedly indicated to us that male sperm and female ovum were used in our reproduction."

Reinhart uploaded information to me. "Interestingly, the term robot clone appeared in science fiction books and films in the 21st Century. It had a particular signification for humans. Those who had the money and means at their disposition could continue their lives, after their deaths, in the body of a robot clone that would be given their specific physical appearance, intellectual capacity and personality. A robot clone was a promise of life everlasting. However, these robot clones were very primitive compared to our androids, most particularly the Group of 5, and their longevity was disappointingly short."

I stopped to observe the group. "Our humanoid machines, or androids, are more complex, from their internal circuitry, to their human traits, their exterior, human-like skin, and so forth. Nonetheless, within the different android series here at the center there are androids that have been programmed to accomplish intellectual tasks, including scientific research, even though they are not the android opposites of a progenitor human. This is the case of the chief android engineer, Drager, as well as Fleming and Jarrod, who will be arriving soon. They even have their own physical appearance, setting them apart from the working class android series, in which there is a defined female and male physical appearance."

I stopped to give my friends an opportunity to contemplate what I had just said. "The members of the Group of 5 are the android opposites of former human scientists." I picked up. "They are identical physical versions of their human counterparts. Reinhart was the self-proclaimed leader of her scientific team and permitted her colleagues to download certain research, principally early research, into their android opposites, but prohibited any downloading of research they were conducting during the last five years of their lives, as well as, highly sensitive research."

"How can you be so certain about the Group of 5's limited knowledge bank?" Sarah asked.

"Because Reinhart just confirmed that." I noticed that everyone cast their eyes upon me...in disbelief?

I waited for other questions but none were forthcoming. So I approached the more difficult problem, describing my relationship with Reinhart.

"Benjamin, before I can answer your question, I would like to go back a bit in time so that you-all of you-can understand better why my present relationship with Reinhart is sane and rewarding for both of us. And, what I am going to share with you is what I witnessed in the videos that Flanders showed me and other information that I have since received and retained from Reinhart herself." I sighed. "You all remember my telling you that Reinhart destroyed her android opposite." They nodded. "Her audacious research made it possible for her to create a total duplicate of herself physically in the form of an android opposite thereby surpassing her illustrious colleagues in their quest for immortality."

"Sorry, Pamela, but I have to interrupt you here. She created that rejuvenation machine that she actually used. So, she was already assured immortality." Peter observed.

"Yes, that is true, but she was the only one who knew about its existence and therefore the only one who could operate the machine." I sighed. "If she was gravely injured, she would have died, so her android opposite, or android foil, or android counterpart-whichever you prefer-was her hope for immortality if her human body failed."

"But, she made a serious mistake by giving her android opposite her entire knowledge bank, real life memories, and then installing her complete emotional configuration into her. The emotional configuration proved to be the fundamental cause of disaccord between the two of them."

"Reinhart met with her android opposite on many occasions to find a solution to their problem which hinged on her android opposite's lack of respect for Reinhart because of the android's dangerously growing and laudatory superiority complex." I stopped to find the right words. "Actually, Reinhart's android opposite was mimicking Reinhart's basic personality, which was in Reinhart's early years, very pretentious. But, Reinhart had learned how to temper that side of her personality, even though she liked power."

"If I understand correctly," Peter proposed, "Reinhart was confronting a younger version of herself?"

"Yes, that is exactly what happened." I sighed. "Anyway, the meetings between the two of them always degenerated with the android opposite asserting her absolute perfection and accusing Reinhart of being evil. Her android opposite recklessly went so far as to threaten to replace her creator, Reinhart, at a propitious moment and to relieve her of her responsibilities by making Reinhart her assistant. The android opposite was so sure of herself that she boasted that her intellectual capacity was far greater than that of Reinhart's and that she was already engaging in independent research, something that Reinhart considered both annoying and precarious."

I stopped to collect my thoughts. "Her android opposite underestimated the cold, calculating side of Reinhart. The last closed-door meeting between the two of them was quite pleasant for her android opposite. Reinhart admitted her inferiority and promised grandeur and respect for her android opposite. Then Reinhart cagily invited the android to let her create a backup copy of all of Reinhart's research and memories, now embodied in the android system, to assure her android opposite her ordained and destined glory, in face of conspiracy or sabotage of her systems."

I breathed deeply. "Reinhart was playing a psychological game with herself, as she promised the android what she herself would have considered to be a merited and genuine recognition of her genius. And, it worked. Her android opposite was so overcome with this display of admiration and concern that she agreed."

"Once Reinhart had downloaded everything into an independent system and verified that nothing was missing, she convoked her android opposite for that last famous encounter in Reinhart's laboratory. Reinhart arranged for Flanders to be present and to film and transmit the meeting to all members of the Group of 5, as well as to all of the other android series, to discourage any similar reactions by the Group of 5 or others."

"Her android opposite had underestimated the power of her creator. When the android opposite arrived, she concealed her true ambitions for fame and power and pretended to be the real Dr. Reinhart who was kind and caring. She accused her Creator of unjustified hatred towards non-intellectuals and of atrocities against humankind. I guess that she imagined that Reinhart would publicly concede her authority to her android opposite. Instead, Reinhart played her last card that day when she ordered her android opposite to self-destruct. The android whirled and stumbled, confused by the power that Reinhart's command had over her. It was a safety valve, a virus that Reinhart could activate with her voice that she had planted deep inside her android opposite's programming. Her android opposite pleaded for another chance and beseeched Reinhart to be more understanding, but Reinhart held her ground refusing to change her mind. In the end, the android could not override her programing and self-destructed."

I again stopped to take questions but the others waved me on.

"Reinhart realized that an emotional configuration was too dangerous, long before she ordered her android opposite to self-destruct. In preparation for her final encounter with her android opposite, Reinhart had already downloaded a virus into the systems of the Group of 5, a virus that would make them totally dependent on humans for future research-inhibiting their ability to analyze and reason on their own. She ordered them to send the same program, which they did not realize was an inhibiting virus, to all existing androids regardless of their series. For the Group of 5, their creator would never harm them and they believed her when she told them that the virus was a program that would stimulate performance."

That brought some laughter and gave me an opportunity to decompress a bit. "Reinhart died before she was able to confirm the inhibitory effects of that virus on the Group of 5 and, from her present surges of energy, appears to be very pleased with herself today."

"After the dramatic exit of her android opposite, she ordered the Group of 5 to erase a program she had recently installed in them giving them the possibility of developing a complex emotional structure." I grimaced. "Apparently, by the Group of 5, a pervious program, or that inhibitory virus that made them dependent upon humans, interfered with their ability to totally erase all the emotional configurations already installed into their systems, which is why they have emotional structures of varying degrees today. Fortunately, and to their frustration, they cannot build upon these lingering, emotional strands, which are just mild, primitive reflexes."

"Her final act was the downloading of her entire knowledge bank and life memories and emotional configuration on live, empty DNA strands. She knew that the DNA strands were not compatible with the computer systems of the Group of 5 so they would be incapable of downloading her DNA recordings. And, even if they had tried, she would have refused to release the information." I stared off into the distance. "Remember I told you that she verified that I was human and one of her female descendants before she started running the program." I watched them nod. "In any event, the Group of 5 had no other choice but to follow her instructions, in the event of her death, and download it into one of her human congeners."

The Group was so silent and concentrated that I continued. "My guess is that the Group of 5 tried with other Pamela series to download the data, but Reinhart did not want a scientist-a potential competitor-to receive her knowledge and refused to release it. That was why I was the most likely candidate. I was a musician."

"Some things are starting to make sense." Peter broke into my long monologue.

"But the two of you together?" Benjamin insisted.

"Just one more thing, Benjamin, and I shall explain the relationship between us. When my IQ and my physical appearance were finally identical to those of Reinhart, luck was on the android's side, because all of you turned out to have the same IQ as your famous progenitors, while displaying their physical attributes." I marveled at the incredibility of this for an instance and then turned to John and Ruth. "The two of you met the criteria a bit sooner than the rest of us which is why, when the Group of 5 saw the promising results achieved slightly after your series, they did not terminate you sooner and why you are with us today. In the case of Ferdinand, who is not at this meeting, he could be terminated and they did intend to do that, simply because, in spite of his superior intelligence, he was not a scientist." My gaze was again on the entire group. "To finish, the Group of 5 realized that we needed to have a full emotional configuration to be curious, competitive and research productive." I threw up my hands. "You know the rest." I sighed.

I turned to Benjamin. "For Reinhart, I am a perfect depository for her information. I will not venture on my own into science and scientific research simply because I am not a trained scientist. Of course, that could change as I assimilate more and more of her knowledge. For the moment, she can control me and protect her knowledge. We exist in a symbiotic relationship."

"More like a schizophrenic state." Mathilda burst out.

"Not at all." I replied emphatically. "There is nothing schizophrenic about our relationship and you above all the rest, Mathilda, should know that. There is nothing delusionary in my personality and I am not hearing voices outside my physical self, encouraging me to engage in erratic behavior, and so forth. We have a symbiotic relationship on an intellectual level. I downloaded her consciousness and she left mine intact. She is effectively occupying unused space in my brain. But, she is making it possible for me to communicate her scientific knowledge to all of you, when and if that knowledge is necessary."

I digressed for a moment to exemplify the lack of dangerousness in our relationship. "For example, she saved Stuart, Randolph and me when we being pursued by the androids just before the rest of you entered the center. She revealed the subtleness of the wall, laden with bio-readers that would let us humans pass into a new environment, or the inner circle. She did not have to save us. She could have let the androids capture us, then erase my existence and take control of my body. But, she didn't do it. Why? Because she likes the situation as it is. Nonetheless, she controls her flow of knowledge and can decide whether or not to make it available to me and therefore to the rest of you."

I stopped once again to let my message sink in before adding. "I just want to remind all of you that Reinhart saved humanity and if we are here today, it is because she made certain that the androids would always need us."

"It is her consciousness in the form of knowledge that is inside of me. The extent to which her personality can take form is more subtle, but I believe that we shall always remain separate. Nonetheless, after I downloaded all her knowledge, she told me that there was no danger that our personalities would merge. Today, when she surfaces, I feel her energy suffuse me like a strange, but comforting warmth. Otherwise, I am the same Pamela I always was."

"But she is dangerous and cruel." Mathilda said in a dry, analytical tone. "She could change her mind about you at any time."

"I understand your concern, but believe otherwise." I smiled. "I believe that she gave a lot of thought to a symbiotic relationship with one of her descendants when she downloaded her knowledge on those DNA strands and that the idea appealed to her. For the moment at least, she wants to be the consciousness of someone she trusts. And, she trusts me and the rest of you to use the knowledge that she will transmit through me to build a better world than the one that she left behind."

"Sounds plausible, but risky, if she is as powerful as she appears to be." Stuart commented. Heads nodded.

"We shall see with time how things go." I said, annoyed by their underestimation of my personality.

"But, Pamela, you still did not answer my question. How do you know that she is present?" Benjamin persisted.

"Seriously, I do not have that much experience, yet. What I sense up to now is, as I just mentioned, a suffusing warmth and along with that a kind of subliminal message surfaces showing me what to do." I made a hissing sound. "I just felt that warmth and can answer a bit better. I have all her knowledge inside of me. She will upload it to me, providing me with both a visual and conscious comprehension of that information that I can then transmit to you and that is automatically assimilated into my consciousness, or my knowledge bank, so that I can use it and access it in the future."

"That is convincing enough for me and I like this idea of a symbiotic relationship." Benjamin replied with enthusiasm. Broad smiles of satisfaction appeared on the faces of my colleagues.

It was getting late so we got up to leave. We headed over to the large conference room that the androids had used for their official meetings. I was surprised that the Group of 5 –Agnes cradled in

Drager's arms—was standing at the conference room door awaiting our arrival. I hadn't anticipated that and felt ill at ease. I mentioned that the meeting was only for us humans.

"That is ok. Actually, it is understandable." Eugene, the former Governor spoke for the group. "We shall just wait outside the door in the event that you need to ask us any questions. That is, if there is information, that only we can communicate to you." He suggested.

We had left the children running around the center, doing what they seemed to like most, passing through the walls at different places. I suggested that they watch the children. "I don't want you to take any initiatives, just give them something entertaining to do." They didn't respond, so I added that they might help with the programmed humans as well.

"Our assistants have already taken the children in charge." Edward mentioned. "We could not just let them engage in endless games when they have so much to learn. We decided to hook them up to the learning disks that they started yesterday." My mouth dropped open. "No, don't worry." He asserted. "We are only giving them rudimentary reading and writing tapes." His mouth revealed a contrived smile, flashing eager teeth, and added that the programmed humans were already in their work areas under android surveillance.

"So, I guess that you just want to stand outside the door and wait for us?" I asked, raising my voice an octave. They did not budge when I entered the conference room.

Everyone had taken their place around the large, oval table and Ferdinand was sitting at the far end, his arms folded in a relaxed position on the tabletop, presiding over the meeting.

Even though the room was sound proof, I lowered the screens on the conference room window so that the Group of 5 could not observe our behavior and then made a thorough check of the room to be certain that there was no audio-visual equipment in place. No one said anything so I took my place.

"Everyone is here," Ferdinand announced," so I would like to take a couple minutes to note the issues that you would like to discuss today."

That was definitely a mistake as members of the group, in a

completely disorderly fashion, called out their individual concerns, interrupting each other or simply talking louder than the one already speaking. "Stop!" Ferdinand shouted back. "Raise your hand and I shall let you speak. "

"Like I said yesterday, we need to concentrate on how to deprogram the humans." John spoke up. That got a unanimous vote.

"Other issues?" Ferdinand asked

"Yes, the transport vehicles. I would like to know if I can have authorization to explore the planet with James." Diana definitely saw this as a priority.

I found her request completely out of order, which is why I quickly interrupted her, reminding her that the exploration of the planet would be an official group project and that she would have to wait. She raised her eyebrows in defiance and looked at the others, who made no comment.

Irritated with me, she continued: "I would like to add that I think that we should vote on whether or not to call those androids by their first names, or just spit out their last names, without referencing the Doctor. This was Pamela's idea and she never consulted anyone before imposing this on the rest of us." Her eyes met mine in virtual combat. "I don't like being friendly with them, and a first name basis is too close for comfort."

Ferdinand led a quick vote on that and the group preferred a last name, minus the doctor. I reserved the right to call them on a first name basis as Reinhart had worked very closely with their human opposites and felt more at ease with the first name basis. That was ok with the others so long as they were not forced to do the same thing. So, Diana won that round.

"I have two questions: Is there any evidence of other humans hiding in the center? And, does anyone know anything about pharmaceutical products?"

"I think that we need someone to take charge of employment in general." Stuart said changing the subject. "We don't know what departments are minus a department head." He cleared his throat. "I only want us humans in charge, if you all agree." No one contested that point. "Who would like to do that?"

"I will." John spoke up. "I have a very clear picture of how the labs are set up and how the facility used to function because I was deprogrammed for such a long time. Mathieu would you be willing to give me a hand?" Mathieu agreed. "We will have a complete report on that for the meeting next week."

"In answer to your questions, Pamela, I can oversee the pharmaceutical lab." Sarah suggested. "Maybe Ruth can help me."

"Yes, I can help Sarah. Biology and Chemistry were our working fields. "

That was my cue to hand them the two pill bottles and ask them to break down the chemical composition. "If we have the chemicals we need then we should produce these pills in large numbers." No one objected to my suggestion.

Sarah turned her attention to me. "Yesterday we noticed some blood spots outside the agricultural unit and others in and around the vacation center. We did not have time to explore. That doesn't mean that these humans are still alive but, there might be some who escaped and need treatment."

"That should have been the morning priority. If they need medical care we must act rapidly. In fact, we might have waited too long." Ferdinand was rambling on and we were all getting nervous. He was right. Someone should have moved on this earlier. We were already into the second day.

"No need to panic, "Randolph spoke up. "Those who were hit in full range were splattered. If there were major injuries they would never have made it to either one of those 2 areas. The big problem is how to find them."

"I know." I replied. "We have to take one of the androids. They have very sensitive olfactory systems. They will be able to locate the humans easily."

"How treacherous an idea! It is disgusting!" Stuart looked at me like I was some sort of primitive creature. "How can you say that? It is so degrading."

"I don't find it degrading. I am happy that they can sniff them out, to save lives. That is, of course, if we haven't waited too long." I could see by the nodding heads that the others agreed with me. I told them that I would take Crawford and Gordon with me. They would certainly locate the humans and I asked Stuart and Diana if they would accompany me. "I think that this is urgent and will mention it to the androids when the meeting ends."

"Ok, Pamela, if you think that the Group of 5 can help us." I heard Ferdinand say in a dry tone. It annoyed me. The meeting was getting on my nerves, or her nerves. It didn't really matter.

I could feel my blood rushing and my anger mounting. The meeting was unstructured and a waste of time. I was worried about our future in this Center. The Group of 5 was a potential menace to the stability of our group and the realization of our dreams. Everyone was back to talking at the same time. It was so noisy and unconstructive that I impulsively struck down hard on the table, getting everyone's attention.

"What is the matter with you, Pamela?" Mathilda asked in a clinical tone.

"I want you all to listen and listen closely to what I have to say." My nostrils were flaring and my eyes were glaring. "I don't know exactly where to start, so let's take a quick look at yesterday. We celebrated our victory. We needed to do that to demonstrate our loyalty to each other and our desire to build a human world. But, did that change the androids attitude towards us? No, because those androids, standing outside the door today, are not afraid or even bothered by what they see as a minor setback, or more worrisome, a necessary, intermediary step to attaining their objective." That got everyone's complete attention. "They are and will always be our enemies." They nodded their heads nonchalantly like I was not saying anything that they did not already know. "And, Reinhart is as much in the dark about what they did over all those years, as we are. So we must be careful."

"There is only one person in this group who they care about and are afraid of and that is Reinhart, because she is the key to their continued existence and their future. But, we all have to work with them. They have vital information that we need. They are not going to deliver it to us so we'll have to pry it out of them, but pry it out cleverly by giving them the impression that we trust them. And, I used the word impression because we all must maintain an emotional distance from them. They are cold-blooded, extraordinarily intelligent machines that do not hold humans in high esteem." I paused to look around and noticed no one was smiling. 'Good,' I snickered to myself. I could feel my top teeth piercing through my lips tightly circling them. "We must use all of our human cunning like outright deception, flattery, curiosity and the list goes on, to convince them to reveal information. We need them today to locate those humans, which they will consider to be a demeaning task. TOO BAD! THEY WERE MADE TO SERVE US; SO LET THEM DO IT! And mind you, if they do it, they won't be doing it to save those humans or to befriend us. They will be doing it to show their allegiance to Reinhart."

"And, so...what are you getting at, Pamela? None of us trust them." Randolph replied.

"Yes, some of you do." I looked at Mathilda. "And, others will start to." My eyes skimmed the group. "Our objective is to acquire information from them and to use them to help us in whatever ways they can to build a new world." I swallowed hard. "I just told you that they need us to progress scientifically. Now I emphasize that they will spy on us and steal from us to acquire information. Why do you think that I sequestered us in this room and scanned for video surveillance equipment before joining you? All of you should have had the same reflex!" I cried out and they bowed their heads.

"They will pretend that they care." I continued. "They are very crafty. They have just enough of a rudimentary emotional structure to convince some of you that they are your friends and they are clever and vicious enough to identify the weak points in our personalities to better manipulate anyone of us. We do not want them to be at the same research level, or we will have more and more difficulty controlling them. So we must hide some of our scientific discoveries from them. Everything of importance must stay in the inner circle. We are in charge of our destiny and we must be careful not to compromise that. Was I clear?" They nodded. "And now, do we agree that the androids will sniff out the humans?" They nodded energetically.

"But, Reinhart can control them? And, you mentioned yesterday that you weren't worried." Peter raised the question that certainly the others were mulling around in their minds.

"When I woke up yesterday morning, I was too optimistic. I

watched them and studied them as they were watching and studying us during our victory celebration. They sat patiently, entering into their complex android computer systems the deprogrammed personalities of all of us. We were being observed by them like we would observe a live, laboratory specimen. I tried to hide my suspicions from them because it is much better that they believe that Pamela is naïve, but the rest of you were not hiding anything because you were totally oblivious to what was happening." I sighed.

"Reinhart is their creator," I continued, "and they respect her genius. BUT SHE DOES NOT CONTROL THEM ENTIRELY! And, they need her to accomplish their ultimate objective, which Reinhart has deciphered, but has not yet communicated to me. They are diabolical and are wrongly convinced that Reinhart is like them. Even though she is in no way guided by emotions, her rational decision making is not like the members of the Group of 5. She is more than a humanoid machine. And, she will protect us, if necessary, and if feasible, but we must also protect ourselves. We must never feel too comfortable with them. We must act discretely and with caution like we did in the past." I warned. "And, Peter, even though they respect Reinhart, I want to remind you and the others that they did kill her once before!" I said very slowly, emphasizing each word.

There was a long silence that I assumed was brought on by guilt and recognition of the truth of my words that hopefully hit them between the eyes. I felt calmer now that I had brought them back to reality, but the meeting had to continue. "We must finish this meeting rapidly. I wonder how important it is for the moment to deprogram the surviving humans." I stopped to let the rumbling die down. "We will either have to destroy their wrist bands or remove the microchip in their brains." That shocked them for a second time back into reality. "We by-passed our systems just like James did the other day. I don't know how they will respond if we remove the programming without giving their minds the time to slowly confront the real world and recognize changes."

"That is why I suggested a slow, phase out of their programming. Unless, of course, you are saying that we should just go on working with these programmed humans, like the androids did?"

Mathilda said as she pushed her chair away from the table. "I believe, Pamela, that you let the Reinhart in you do all the thinking."

"I can understand your concern over the humans. Nonetheless, you must take into account all the potential consequences. We need these 30 humans to survive. Our numbers are low. In addition, there are mutants and others with varying physical deformities, within their numbers." Jonathan slapped his hands hard together to remind me that physical traits should not count.

"I agree," I addressed Jonathan, hoping to persuade him that my position was not singularly motivated by physical deformities, before I continued. "That is not what is worrying me. The mutants are what worry me. Their real nature will be exposed with deprogramming. Some of them are reptilian. The question is whether or not they will identify with human life in the same way we do. We shall have to be careful with their deprogramming and follow them closely to be certain that their human side is dominant. And, I want to underline that Reinhart wants to verify their genetic codes before we undertake their deprogramming."

"Ok, I understand what you are getting at." Randolph came to my defense. "I gather from what you are saying that Reinhart imbued certain mutants with more sensory ability, physical force, and—here is the problem—a more radical, unpredictable sense of survival."

"Exactly! Thank you, Randolph, for clarifying the situation. But, Reinhart is not the one who played with eugenics. She did not create the race of reptilian humans living amongst us today. The Group of 5 did."

The discussion took off. We were divided, in the beginning, into two groups. One side--led by Mathilda and Jonathan, including Sarah, Ruth, Mathieu, Isabel, Stanislas and Benjamin--believed that human nature would prevail over reptilian or other predatory animal mixtures; and, the group that followed me: John, Stuart, Randolph, Diana, James and Peter who believed that predatory animal behavior and plays for dominance were highly possible. Ferdinand and Ralph remained neutral.

Finally, we came up with a compromise that recognized our need to study each individual in more detail before starting a massive deprogramming of all of them. And, the group agreed that an outside stimulus should be used to start the deprogramming process, whether it be an electric shock, a mild explosion, a malfunctioning scientific or musical instrument, or something else. An outside stimulus would confuse humans and trigger their deprogramming, while our presence at that moment would be the stabilizing factor. All this would have to be properly orchestrated. We agreed that Mathilda should put together a team to work with her on this project and report back next week on the order in which we should approach the deprogramming of the humans.

Everyone wanted to participate in the exploration of the planet that, unfortunately, had to take a backseat to more pressing problems like rebuilding Agnes, reconstructing Jonathan, deprogramming the humans and selecting heads of departments.

It was decided that Ralph should take charge immediately of the agricultural unit and verify the vacation center. Diana and Isabel were given permission to train with James on the simulators to learn how to operate different transport vehicles and to study the species of marine life preserved in the jars in the inner circle.

I promised to put together an educational program for the children after consulting with Flanders. I wanted the children to have free time as well and to use the gym and swimming pool in the vacation center. "I think that we should start competitive sports for us as well and have daily exercise programs. It is healthy." I mentioned to the satisfaction of everyone.

The last issue was to decide upon the role that the Group of 5 would play in the Center. A meeting for the following day at the same time and place as today with the Group of 5 was approved. This would give us the opportunity to decide how they would participate in the life of the center. We would also consider their recommendation on the number of androids that should be reactivated to assist us in maintaining the Center.

Ferdinand ended the meeting by applauding the ability of our group to work together democratically. "I believe that we should all participate in these meetings and would like to encourage Isabel, Stanislas and Benjamin to feel free to share their ideas." He mentioned. It was obvious that he was aware of their reticence. "Well, it is lunch time and my stomach is growling. See you all in the dining room." The meeting ended on that note.

I took Peter aside and told him that I would inform the Group of 5 that they were invited to participate in the meeting tomorrow and would arrange for Gordon and Crawford to help Stuart, Diana and I locate the fugitives. "Ok, but be careful. As you just pointed out, we cannot trust them very much, if at all." He said bluntly. "I am going to tackle the rebuilding of Agnes this afternoon. I feel comfortable with the instruction manual. In fact, assembling an android is not all that difficult. What is difficult is constructing the android parts!" He said with a sudden burst of strong feeling.

The Group of 5 was still waiting in the hallway and moved in my direction as I exited the door. "You didn't need us for anything?" The former Governor asked.

"Not during this meeting, but you are invited to attend the meeting tomorrow morning, in this room." I heard lots of android mumbling. "And, I would like Gordon and Crawford to accompany Stuart, Diana and myself to find several humans that appear to have sought refuge in either the horticultural building or the vacation center." They both looked at me, their android eyes erupted in a volcanic glare.

"What are you talking about?" Gordon asked. Without giving me chance to answer, she continued. "We have no responsibility towards those humans. They are now in your care. Personally, I am declining your invitation."

"You cannot decline my invitation." I sneered back at her. "You have to accompany me because, as you just pointed out, you are no longer in command."

She forced her shoulders back in a defiant way. "So...how can we be of help?"

"We need you to sniff out the humans."

"Sniff them out, Pamela. We are not animals."

"Yes, but you have an excellent olfactory sense and, as they are hiding, we need your extraordinary skill to find them."

"Detestable! Your order is both degrading and humiliating." Crawford interposed.

"Strange, but those same words were used by Stuart with

reference to the wounded humans." I looked straight into their eyes. "But it does not matter. You have no choice. We need your help-something that you promised. So, your participation is mandatory. I expect you to be waiting for me outside the dining room in one hour." I turned and walked away.

"Would they be there?" I silently worried. "Was there a limit to the power I had over them? Would they resort to extreme measures to save their dignity? Should I smell mutiny in the air? If so should I pull the plug on them or threaten to do it?

Chapter 5-Building Confidence

Gordon and Crawford were waiting outside the dining room when Stuart, Diana and I finished eating. I breathed a deep sigh of relief. They passed the test and, at the same time, reassured me of their fidelity to... Elisabeth. But I kept my distance and remained vigilant.

The monorails were operational so we all jumped on the first ones heading to the horticultural unit. The horticulture unit, which I never visited in the past, was an immense structure with glass walls that rose as high as the dome covering of our center. Light was filtering down from the ceiling revealing acres of small garden plots. The tall fruit trees, in the far background, were just small specks on the horizon and the large laboratory facility located behind them was indiscernible. Stuart pointed immediately to the dry, blood spots that stopped just in front of the automatic glass door.

We had just entered the unit when Crawford's grating voice stopped us in our tracks. "No need to go further. They did not go into this unit, for a very good reason. We had turned off the controls to this unit when the fighting started."

"What?" I asked my voice registering my surprise. "Why didn't you just tell us that before? We didn't have to waste time visiting this unit."

"Well...you seemed so sure of yourself that we decided to humor you." I saw Diana's body stiffen up, but Crawford ignored her, focusing his attention on me. "It is always so amusing," he looked at Gordon whose smile revealed her android teeth, "to venture off with humans on these ambitious, yet foolish, expeditions. We had opportunities ..."

"Shut Up!" I screamed at him. "Do you want Diana and Stuart to rip you to pieces? I shall let them do it if you continue to test my patience. Or maybe I should just order you to self-destruct!"

I was not surprised that my last tirade inspired cooperation as they rapidly marched away from the horticultural unit back to the monorail. We headed towards the vacation center. This time the two androids showed a bit more respect, motioning us to follow them as they moved around the swimming pool and off in the direction of the zoo. "They are over there, crouched behind the stones near the tiger's cage."

"Stuffed tiger cage." I corrected them and they sneered at us. "There are no other humans in the area?" They shook their heads.

Two young women were shuddering in each other's arms when I approached. "Can you see me?" they nodded. They had by-passed the programming. "Then you know that I am human." I introduced myself and Stuart and Diana followed my lead. I extended my hand but they didn't take it. They stayed closely laced in each other's trembling arms.

I calmly told them that we would not hurt them and that we were so happy to find them alive. "One of you has been hurt." I saw tears flow down their faces. "We can help you." I bent down and put my arms around one of them and tried to slowly draw them apart. The more I pulled the tighter they held on.

"Stuart, can you do something?"

He looked first at the two androids and then looked back to me. "We need their help." He went straight to the point politely asking them to activate their maximum strength. "I believe that together you can carry them back to the hospital unit."

Gordon and Crawford both raised their eyebrows and twisted up their mouths in disgust, but moved over and wrapped their arms firmly around the bundle and carried them like that back to the monorail. The biggest cars were limited to 4 people, so I had to force myself into the car with Gordon, Crawford and their big bundle. I thought that we would never get to the hospital unit. It was hot and stuffy in the car and the pungent odor of the two sweaty and dirty humans made the trip seem longer. The android escorts had sealed their nostrils together.

The androids backed off once they put the two of them on the hospital bed. I discovered immediately the reason why they acted like they were glued together. There was blood around their stomach region. Apparently, forcing their bodies up against each other gave them the impression that the blood flow stopped.

I perceived indifference in the way Gordon and Crawford stood aloof, as they grouped closer one to the other. The Group of 5 was not going to give me any more help and so I searched my memory banks for answers. I sent Diana to get Peter who was working on assembling Agnes in his lab. "He might know how to close their wounds."

The two young women relaxed their grip on each other the moment Peter arrived. Either his presence or his reassuring voice inspired their confidence. As they unraveled, he examined their injuries, and slowly washed around them. The wounds were deep, large, jagged cuts in the stomach region. There was no sign of infection and no organs were perforated, but once they separated there was considerable bleeding.

"You can seal the wounds, Peter." He looked at me. "We shall have to take them into the inner circle. In the surgical unit, there is a laser sealer."

"We can't move them. Can you go get it? I'll use pressure to keep the bleeding under control." I nodded and rushed off. I knew exactly where it was located and picked up the proper manual that would indicate the laser strength necessary to seal the wounds.

I handed him the instrument and the manual. He gave me a stern look and threw the manual at me. "Let her do it, Pamela!" He raised his voice. "Reinhart knows what to do and she will guide you." A complete calm instantly invaded me as she uploaded medical information along with the surgical technique. As if I had done this a thousand times, I visually calculated the depth of the wounds and regulated the laser strength accordingly. I guided the sealer meticulously, accurately, and rapidly over the injuries, sealing the different layers under and at the flesh level. They didn't have time to feel anything as the layers of skin moved together easily, as if they were being glued. Everything looked like new when I finished and there was no sign of pain when I pressed on the region.

"Wow, you did it!" Peter screamed. None of us could restrain our excitement which turned into giddy laughter, something that did not appeal to Gordon and Crawford, apparently disgusted by this display of unbridled human emotion. They asked permission to leave, mentioning that they would send other personnel to help with the patients. Within minutes an android assistant appeared with clean robes and escorted the two young women to the shower.

"Dr. Gordon told me that it was in the interest of the humans to take a shower and put on clean robes," said the android assistant looking at my nodding head.

I wondered why Reinhart had given them this accentuated olfactory sense. Maybe it was a quick and effective way for the androids to detect non-intellectuals who had crept into the domed city, assuming that these non-intellectuals did not have access to clean water and hygienic products. Or, maybe, it was her way of saddling them with what they considered a demeaning imperfection. Or, maybe it was one of her experiments in sensory stimulation...

"Pamela," Gordon's voice jarred me out of my musing, "we left rapidly and I came back to see if everything was going well. We shall stay and supervise these young girls' recovery."

"Yes...well, thank you for all you help. I want to see Flanders to find out who these charming young girls are."

Peter, Stuart and Diana had already left, so I started to walk away and then hesitated. Did Gordon just feign cooperation because she had something wicked in mind? I turned back and asked in an imperative voice, "You are not going to harm these young women?"

"You have nothing to worry about. We have always been at your beck and call." She was trying to reach Reinhart. I was in the corridor when Peter came running in my direction.

"Pamela, wait, I want you to take a quick look at Agnes." He grabbed my arm, pulling me along with him. "Something is wrong—at least that was the situation when I left John, Randolph and Drager. Stuart tried in vain to help. I believe that the manual did not give us all the information we need because Agnes was not able to activate the limbs, when I left the lab."

Of course not, I thought to myself. He did not know exactly how to trigger the command system. That was not in the manuals. "It is rather simple, I shall show you." Reinhart was more discrete and protective of her research than I realized. Was she worried about her human colleagues and not just the androids? "Did Drager have access to the Manuals?" I asked.

"No, we knew better than to let him look them over, especially after your warning during the meeting, we did not even let him participate." He stopped for a minute. "Come to think of it, you know, Randolph actually hates the androids." One side of my lips moved upward into a sly smile just thinking about the conversations we had regarding the Group of 5 and, in particular, Gordon. "He made Drager stand facing the wall so he could not learn anything." Peter commented.

"Excellent!" I screamed. "He did the right thing."

Agnes was in pieces when we got to the lab. "We decided to take off the limbs and start over again." Randolph said letting himself drop down on one of the lab chairs when he saw me. "It doesn't make any sense. Everything went into place so easily. But nothing works." He threw his arms up in the air. "And we can't examine the inside of the arms because of the metal sealer on the outside. In fact, we cannot even feel the structure through the metal sealer. Maybe he is sabotaging everything." He pointed to Drager who was standing facing the wall.

"Sabotaging? You wouldn't even let me look at the manual. I have been carrying out your ridiculous order to stand facing the wall." Drager defended himself.

"Dumb Ass machine! I am not talking about today, I am talking about years, maybe even centuries ago, when you first touched her!" Randolph yelled, taking all his frustrations out on Drager.

I noticed that John and Stuart stood calmly looking on. If they were as frustrated as Randolph, they did not want me to know.

"Ok, I'll fix it for you." I moved over to Agnes and looked closely, studying carefully the circuitry in her shoulder area. Of course, the problem was so evident to me, but they would never have discovered it. I looked up at them wondering whether or not I should tell the truth or just go behind the rotating shoulder knob and release the wire that would automatically disappear from view the moment that a limb was severed. Or, should one of Reinhart's encrusted secrets be exposed?

I decided to discretely release the wire and properly adjust the arm in the socket. I went to the back of her head, gently lifted the artificial covering near the base and reattached the wire regulating the motor section to her cerebral intellect. The motor section was programmed to shut down once an android part was removed. Drager was able to activate the primitive robotic parts by piggybacking on what was left of her mid-section motor skills, only because the robotic limbs did not require any complex motor skills. In fact, in retrospect, the piggybacking effect was also responsible for Agnes' inability to control her movements; her circuits were overcharged on a regular basis. Fortunately, her memory bank was not affected. After I finished I asked her if she could move her arms. They worked.

My colleagues looked at me as if I were practicing some kind of witchcraft. "Ok, what did you do, Pamela?" Peter finally asked, as he jabbed his finger in my direction. I felt split loyalties. How could I refuse to explain that to Peter? But how could I appease the Reinhart inside of me who wanted me to keep it a secret?

"Just lucky, I guess." I winked.

"Not good enough, Pamela. Not good enough at all." He said in a firm voice. "Are you hiding things from us?"

"I am not completely certain that everything is going to work properly, so just be patient until I attach the legs." I was buying time and knew that I would, eventually, have to tell them. We were not in competition with each other. Everyone had to share their designs and research with others. I did not want to start a bad precedent. "Come here, all of you humans and I'll show you where you went wrong. Drager back away from us." He hesitated for a brief instance and then followed the command. To comfort him I told him that he would still be working on androids in the future. He could test the circuitry. I just did not want him to know how to build it.

"I am going to remove your arms and legs, Agnes. I don't want you to worry, I just want to return with my colleagues to the inner circle and look over the rest of the manuals there." She nodded. "That way, everything will function properly." I turned to Drager. "You will stay here with Agnes." I then removed the arms and legs and discretely replaced the wire and deactivated the motor center while Drager's back was turned.

The others, carrying the robotic limbs, followed me back into the inner circle. I took the arm and ran my fingers up and down the smooth metal surface that covered the complex inner technology of the robotic arm. I then gently rolled the metal surface down, exposing the robotic parts. They involuntarily gasped as the metal covering moved, exposing the underlying technology. They wanted to examine the technology but I told them that they would have time later.

"The metal surface has readers in it." I spoke in a didactic manner. "These androids were Elisabeth's creation. I told you before that she was very suspicious of the androids and added debilitating factors in their programming and system overrides to prevent them from learning how to construct the android bodies and to keep them under human control." They were listening attentively. "You saw how the metal unrolled after I briefly massaged the outside." They nodded. "The readers are adapted to human body heat, or human thermoregulation, just like the walls that permit our entry into the inner circle. First the thermoregulation, or body heat, is read and then a quick evaluation of bio-physiological aspects is used to confirm that a human is in possession of the robotic part."

"Incredible!" Randolph sputtered. "It is amazing how she protected human survival." He drew the corners of his mouth back. "Or protected her coveted inventions?"

I ignored his last remark, which was the more relevant. "Well, she was not perfect though." I continued my demystification regarding the method of installation and activation of these robotic parts. I confirmed that the exposed wires needed to be attached, exactly like they had anticipated. "To activate the command center however you need to reach behind the shoulder socket and gently release the command link up. I will show you how to do that when we get back. Try not to ask questions because even though I will ask Drager to leave before we put things back, Agnes could be conscious of what is happening. Perhaps I should ask her to shut down for the procedure?" They all agreed with that. I gently rolled the metal casing up and started toward the wall. "By the way, the supple metal casing you just saw will turn rock hard when the androids put on their maximum strength. That is why, Stuart, I had problems taking down the android guards that were escorting Randolph. My body was ringing from the hard android surface that I encountered."

"Are they always on guard like that?" Stuart asked.

"No!" I looked at Randolph. "Nonetheless, programming them to fight, like your ancestor did, means that their systems will respond with maximum strength whenever they feel endangered or in any way, threatened." I stopped to consider what I just said. "Reinhart just uploaded some information. She is surprised that the androids here were programmed to fight, unless the Group of 5 manipulated their programming to defend themselves against Murdoc and his team. Possibly, the androids, programmed to fight, entered this center during the revolution or were stored here by the cleanup crew, because the ones you fought were not just defensive players. Stuart, Randolph and I watched them trying to break into the inner circle, before the battle started." I sighed.

We went back to Peter's lab to attach the parts. I told Drager that he could leave and asked Agnes to shut down. "It will be easier for us to attach everything if your system is off. I shall reactivate you when we finish." She hesitated, mentioning that she felt that it was unnecessary, but I insisted and she shut down.

I demonstrated the procedure. They watched closely as I adjusted the arms and legs, going behind the socket and pulling down the command wire. I then showed them where the motor section was and how to reactivate the motor system. After which I reactivated Agnes who moved rapidly up on her feet.

"We might have to make adjustments, Agnes." She nodded. "Let me see you walk and then run and jump." She did that well. She started by walking slowly, like she needed time to adjust to being on two legs, and then increased her speed, running wildly around the lab, before she leaped high in the air and came down firmly on her two feet.

"Now can you lift yourself up with your arms?" She grabbed a high shelf and pulled herself up. "Try using your hands for delicate things, like picking up those chemical bottles." Everything seemed to be functioning very well. "If you notice anything malfunctioning, you must come and see me at once and, by that I mean malfunctioning arms and legs or malfunctioning cerebral impulses." She nodded and dashed around the lab again like a happy child.

I was pleased to see broad smiles on my colleagues' faces. "I have given you the secret she never disclosed to anyone." That had their attention. "I hesitated because her trepidations about sharing information were coming across very strongly. Nonetheless, this is a new period, one where individual accomplishments do not bring power and glory as in her time. So, I did what I did to remind you-as I shall remind the others-that we are working together for the benefit of all of us. We can be competitive, but we can't afford to be selfish. We need each other!"

"Well, said," Peter replied and the others echoed his words.

"Am I going to have android skin?" Agnes chirped, putting an end to our discussion.

I looked at the others and they motioned to me to handle the matter. "You will have to be patient for a couple weeks. The process is a bit complex and we might run into complications. We have the substance that we need and I think that we should start working on that tomorrow." I looked at the others and there was no objection so I continued. "The two weeks will give us the time to be certain that everything has been properly aligned and that you are comfortable with the new limbs." I stopped to examine and admire her new look. "You are taller than before. Does that bother you?"

"No, not at all. I like being tall."

"Ok then I guess that this is it for today for you Agnes. Start to move around the center and see your co-workers to get their impressions, remembering that the robotic limbs will soon be sealed under the android skin. And, you might want to grab a robe to cover yourself." I looked at the others who seemed more than fascinated with her half android and half human looking body.

The robotic team was starting to follow her when I called out to them to come back. "We must take care of Jonathan. Even though the painkillers are helping him, we are going to have to confront his problem. I suggest that, over the next couple days, we bring Jonathan into the hospital unit for a body scan. The machine will not only show the extent of his spinal problem but will also pro-pose solutions-probably in the form of bionic technology. It will give us a starting point. What do you think?"

"Yes, of course, we have to take care of him." Peter answered. "He has been suffering for a long time and in spite of all his suffe-ring he never stopped working for our cause. His situation should be the next priority, that is, after we start the process for treating the plant for Miller's skin. We could take care of Jonathan over the next two weeks and by that time the skin will be ready for Miller. So we heat the plant tomorrow and lay it out to dry-for want of a better understanding of the actual procedure. And the following day we scan Jonathan. Everyone agree?" Heads nodded with enthusiasm.

"It is getting late. I am going to pass by to see Flanders and get the names of our two new human members. I shall give you all the details over dinner."

"Who wants to go back to the inner circle with me to up-date the manuals, by adding all the new elements we discovered today?" Stuart asked. They all moved to follow him.

"Don't forget to take everything to the inner circle so that the androids cannot have access." I called out to them.

Edward was waiting for me with the names of the two young women, when I arrived. "I am sorry but they are not part of the in-tellectual elite. One of them is an artist and the other a musician." I watched him move about uneasily in his chair as if he were hiding something. "They are both close to the age that we would have ter-minated them. Their usefulness is over, if you understand what I mean." I stood motionless. "And, well, I am not certain what utility they have for any of you at the moment."

"Their names?"

"Yes, the artist is Eunice 20 and the musician is Imogen 17."

"Let me just remind you that we are not going to discriminate against any of our fellow humans."

"I am warning you again that you are too idealistic about hu-mans living together and that the larger your community grows, the more divided you will become. Your little group might however be able to weather the years, even the centuries, and remain undi-vided in your aspirations and projects." His android eyes were fixed on mine. "You should heed my words. You are moving in the wrong direction. Your infantile desire to integrate every viable human in this center will have catastrophic results. You should not let other humans from less elitist backgrounds form your societal base." He turned his back to me, probably to avoid my blazing eyes, and added that he would not bring this up at the meeting tomorrow.

Everyone, including Imogen and Eunice, were eating when I arrived. The warning of Edward put a damper on my self-confidence, even though my slow, meandering walk back from the birth center to the dining room helped me to recover a semblance of enthusiasm.

I picked up my tray of food and sat down on the empty chair next to the children. Frederic was so happy to tell me that the three of them scored a 100% on the exam that Mathilda gave them to determine their levels. So they absorbed all the information. Of course, that made me happy, particularly because I was now more convinced than ever that programming was not necessary for humans to absorb information, as I had always argued.

I sat back and observed the three newly deprogrammed humans. James seemed very much at ease with everyone, including Diana. My impression was that they had spent some time together today and that they were now ready to have normal working relationships. He had deep, blue eyes that added a glimmer of human delicateness to his rugged, chiseled face, long, hooked nose, and large fleshy lips. His robust, chocolate colored body, marked with bulging muscles, still intimidated me. And yet, his physical appearance was in direct contrast to his kind, almost gentle, personality that shined through when he spoke.

Even though Eunice, the artist, may have been near her age of termination according to the Androids, her round, rosy-colored, smiling face, and golden blond curly locks gave her a very young girlish look, making it difficult to believe that her life was programmed to come to an end soon. She was medium height with soft, youthful round hips and full breasts. Her expressive almond shaped eyes and full mouth overshadowed her tiny, snub nose, and gave her an air of sublime innocence.

There was a strong contrast between Eunice and Imogen, sitting straight and proud in her chair with her hands gently folded on the table. I surmised that Imogen was aware of how tiny she appeared in our presence and judged that she was in no way bothered by her small, delicate frame. I spent a long moment studying her. Her pale, blue eyes met mine and I could read the intensity of her spirit and the profoundness of her self-confidence. Her oval face, immaculately proportionate, flaunted a slim nose and thin, playful lips. Her long, thick straight dark brown hair and slight bangs added the finishing touch to a beautiful portrait. When she stood up, her body was also perfectly symmetrical. The androids, or rather Edward and Eugene, were to be complimented for creating such lovely humans by choosing the right sperm and ovum mix.

Neither Eunice nor Imogen participated much in the conversation. I was not certain that they should be attending the next meeting, as they were not part of the original revolutionary group. Already, I was worried about James being involved. When I heard Peter invite them to join us for the meeting, I quickly spoke up, diverting the conversation, by asking them to tell us what they were working on at the Center. Imogen played percussion instruments and Eunice drew portraits and worked on visual architectural designs.

My thoughts on their artistic importance to the community were interrupted by Frederic who ran over to me to have his goodnight kiss. I watched him jump into his father's arms and then leave with the other children trailing after Mathilda. I could almost feel that warmth of friendship enveloping all of us.

"Pamela," The sound of my name startled me, dissipating my sentimental thoughts, "Eunice and I would like to return to our own cubicles to be with our partners. Neither one of us wants to sleep in that inner circle." Imogen said as she pulled her lips back in disgust.

I was not expecting that kind of request and yet it seemed perfectly logical and natural for them to make it, but unnatural that James had not brought that up before. "Are you certain that you don't want to come with us to the inner circle, at least for tonight?" I answered trying to avoid problems. They retorted with a firm "No."

"You will have to give me the code number of your partners so that we can verify if they are still alive." At this point the other members were focused on the discussion.

"Pamela, can I speak to you in private for a moment?" Jonathan asked. We got up and moved away from the group. He explained to me that there was no one with the ID number of Imogen's partner among the remaining programmed humans and that the ID number of Eunice's partner corresponded to that of one of the reptilian creatures.

"What do you suggest, Jonathan?" I did not want to be the one to make a judgment where the physical appearance of one of the programmed humans was concerned. I had already been through that with him many times.

"We shall have to tell Eunice. She is the one to decide." He stopped for a moment. "Ruth told me that her partner was a reptilian human and that she avoided him. She admitted being afraid of his appearance. I have watched the reptilian humans and they seem gentle and kind on the inside."

"Well, Jonathan, I am going to let you give them the news."

Imogen started to cry when he told her that her partner was not among the deprogrammed humans that survived the attack. She looked at us as if we were horrible monsters, responsible for the termination of her partner, and ran off in the direction of her cubicle. Ruth motioned to Jonathan to go after her, but I held him back. "Let her mourn his absence and come back on her own to talk to us." No one contested that so I guessed it was unanimous.

Jonathan's task was even more difficult when it came to explaining the real physical appearance of Eunice's partner who was certainly already in their common cubicle. "Eunice," he said in a soft, paternal tone. "Your partner is still alive." She smiled and clapped her hands in childish delight. She turned to leave for her cubicle and Jonathan pulled her back. "He has a problem." She looked at him through squinted eyes. "He is not like us...rather he is not the image that you had of him. He is not tall, slim, or good looking." She tried to get out of his clutches. "No, you must listen. He is the same person on the inside, but he is not human on the outside."

"What does that mean?" Her girlish style turned cold and aggressive.

"It means that he looks like another species of living organisms. He is a lizard, who walks erect, but is none the less, a lizard."

"I don't know what a lizard is?"

"You will see for yourself, if that is what you want, and I shall go with you to help you over the shock," Jonathan said in a calm, soothing voice. "Or, you can forget him for the moment and come with us into the inner circle. What would you like to do?"

"I want to see him." She cried out dramatically. "Why should I trust you-any of you-after all we were very happy before you destroyed everything around us? And, we don't know why you destroyed everything." She spilled out her anger and then pushed Jonathan away from her and ran at top speed out of the dining room in the direction of the monorail.

We rushed off after her, catching up with her just as she called out the monorail code to the android operator. Jonathan and I were in the car just behind her. She had a lead on us but we caught up with her as she approached her cubicle.

"Is someone there? " He asked in a soft and pleasant voice.

"Yes, I'm back."

"I can't see you. Why can't I see you?" He sounded anxious.

"My visual is malfunctioning. Here is my code: 05211409030520"

He moved towards her and into our range of vision. He was standing erect. His grayish black face presented human features: eyes, nose and mouth well-structured and nicely placed on a smooth oval shaped face. But his black, scaly body, fleshy large limbs and spiny lateral tail were definitely reptilian features. Reinhart fed me the details on this hybrid human, identifying him as a humanoid black marine iguana, a formerly rare species that reproduced in vast numbers during her lifetime. Her research in producing mutants was focused principally on adapting the human DNA, by adding reptilian characteristics. The marine iguana, able to support cold marine temperatures, interested her very much. Apparently she never saw the fruits of her research before today and I could sense her satisfaction. She was fascinated and in awe of the results. I was horrified by them. My thoughts were interrupted as the rest of the group arrived and moved close behind Jonathan and me...we could all witness the homecoming.

Eunice silently backed away from him. We all imagined that she would come screaming into our open arms.

"You have been away for several days. I thought that you had been terminated. It was strange to be here without you." He smiled as he approached her. "I realized that I need and like to have you with me." She responded to his soothing voice by throwing her arms around his thick iguana neck.

Even though touching was not natural for programmed humans, he did not try to release her grip. Instead he enveloped her in those scaly, fleshy reptilian limbs. "You are beautiful. You are beautiful to my eyes." We heard her say just before she motioned to us to move on. We all were in the process anyway of slowly recoiling from this portrait of the Beauty and the Beast and met her request by rapidly leaving the scene.

I was expecting Jonathan to give me another speech about how humans must go beyond the visual side of someone and look deep inside to find the true qualities, but he didn't. In fact, he said nothing during the monorail ride back to the dining room. We grouped together, speechless, before splitting up and going off in different directions.

I lingered in the dining room, watching the android clean-up staff arrange the kitchen, before loitering off to check on the Group of 5. I heard their voices, all android grating style, coming from behind the door of the former Governor's office. When I opened the door, they all jumped up. Strange that they were so focused on their discussion that they didn't hear me arrive?

"Why didn't you knock, Pamela?" The former Governor asked in an authoritative tone.

"What? Why should I? I have the right to barge in on all of you whenever I want." I watched as they lined up in front of me. "You are under my orders and will always be, because I am not certain that I can trust you." I said, as I pushed my hair out of my eyes, mimicking the reflex of Elisabeth to get their full attention and, naturally, it worked.

"Of course!" The former Governor replied relinquishing his position of authority. "This center is your turf and you can go wherever you want. And..." he cleared his throat in a raspy way, "we are definitely your devoted servants." The others joined in.

"I actually wanted to see how Agnes was coping with her long legs." I smiled in her direction.

"I am having no problems." She bowed respectfully. "Thank you for giving me a real android body." I nodded my head in approval.

"Edward, what does the hybrid black marine iguana, the partner of Eunice, do here in this center?" I asked sternly.

He started to move his arms around in a pathetic effort to show his annoyance over my question. "Huh...let me check my records. That would be Adam series 20." He struggled to get control over himself by speaking very slowly. "He actually works with Eunice. He is an architect."

"Did you test his marine survival skills?" I asked as I methodically rubbed my hands together. He recognized Reinhart's style and started to sway nervously from one leg to the other. "I am waiting for you to answer." I said emphatically.

"Yes, we probably should have." He looked at the others who nodded. "But, Pamela-we were simply making humans to carry out tasks in the center. We explained that to you before. We created and replaced humans according to the center's needs. We were not studying the physiological or biological differences between different creatures. And, as I told you before, these hybrids were often times much more intellectually alert and creative than the pure human versions."

"You don't even see your mistake!" I was annoyed with his stupidity. "Why continue to mix mutated DNA with normal DNA if not to study it?" I asked rhetorically. "You should have stopped playing with these genetic distortions when you had no logical scientific reason to continue. Look at the present situation."

"But," Victoria replied. "We never expected humans to see more than the visual receptor's image."

"That is a lie." I looked sternly at the group. "If that were the case, you would never have tried all these years to bring back Reinhart. You knew the risk!"

"The problem is with you, Pamela, not Reinhart." Rudolph answered in a resonating tone. "You, Pamela, are interfering with everything. And, I might add, your high strung emotional level is constantly distorting Elisabeth's cold logic." He turned and looked at the others who gave no visible sign of agreement.

"Interesting! Very interesting, Rudolph! And, maybe even courageous!" He did not back down. Instead he looked straight into my eyes. I smirked. "How, yes, how can you ever be sure about who I am and what I might do?" My strong, menacing voice broke his defiance and he backed away from me. "I want no more mistakes. Is that understood?" They nodded. "This Adam might have been very useful for all of us if he had been given the opportunity in his early years to develop as a hybrid. Instead, what we have today is a group of hybrids unable to exploit their talents and assigned to tasks that have no relationship whatsoever to their hidden talents, their veritable potential." There was a lot of indiscernible android mumbling. "Tomorrow, I want details on the other hybrids, their relationships and their talents. We need to give them their rightful dignity by showing the extraordinary contributions that they can make to our community by using not only their intellectual capabilities, but also their physical talents." I then turned and left.

I took a long shower before slithering into bed. "You are finally back. I was worried." Peter said as he leaned over me.

"I went to see the Group of 5 to check on what they were doing."

"And. . ."

"Nothing special. I understand the personality of Reinhart a bit better now and know how to get them motivated to do the right things." I went on to reveal the conversation.

"Brilliant, Pamela."

"I think so too. I made them look ridiculous, by thwarting their android logic." His lips moved into a seductive smile as he pulled me tightly up against him and, in his special way, reassured me that I was very human.

Chapter 6- 1 AAD

The inner circle was silent when I opened my eyes. Peter was lying next to me deep in thought. "Are we the first ones to awaken?" I mused, perfectly happy to stay in bed for the whole day.

"Doesn't it seem strange to you, Pamela, that we were able to accomplish so much in one day?" He asked. "Don't you remember that I mentioned that time stands still in the Center. You even mentioned to me on several different occasions that two months was more like 2 weeks in the center."

"True." I answered groggily, not awake enough to add more.

"Think about it, Pamela." He pleaded. "You must be able to find the answer."

I cuddled up close to him. "I would much rather live this moment a bit differently." I suggested.

"We don't have time." He winked. "But, a quick explanation about the time problem would not make either one of us late for breakfast." He stopped and lifted himself up in a sitting position. "Quick, though, I hear the children moving around and Frederic will be charging in here soon."

"Ok, a quick answer-the center is in a time warp." His mouth gaped open. "But, you already knew that, don't you remember?"

"Yes, but that was just pure conjecture on my part. You know time warps are more science fiction than real life." He was bating me.

I shoved him playfully. "I need a shower, so I shall explain all that later on." I said, my energy now abounding as I sprung out of bed and dashed in the direction of the shower. He was right behind me, but not for the reason I would have liked. He just wanted to know more and I was not in the mood. I was lucky that Frederic opened the door and screamed. "Hurry Up! Mom and Dad you are late! Everyone is in the dining room." The day started off weird and would continue . . .

The Group of 5 was waiting outside the conference room when we arrived. They entered after us and took the 5 empty chairs lined up in front of our semi-circular table. Ferdinand was seated in the middle, with Peter, Randolph, Diana, Stuart, Jonathan, James and I facing John, Mathieu, Ruth, Sarah, Ralph, Isabel, Mathilda, Stanislas and Benjamin. Ferdinand was more organized and sure of himself today. He opened the meeting by proposing to the Group that we indicate the year in which these meetings were taking place, for historical purposes, if nothing else. His suggestion was to use the year 1 AAD, or the first year following the rebirth of the human race; AAD, indicating After Android Domination. He also pointed out that if ever we were able to properly calculate the real earth date, we could adjust the present accordingly. It was unanimous. "That point agreed upon, I would now like to open the discussion to the members of the group." He stated.

Before I could bring the group up-to-date on the instructions that I gave to the Group of 5 late last evening, Randolph spoke up. "I want to know why those 5 androids wanted to terminate me."

"Randolph, perhaps we should take this up at another time." Ferdinand suggested in a calm, reassuring voice.

"Not, at all. You know why they wanted to get rid of you, Ferdinand." He replied adamantly. "I am not sure why they tried to terminate me. And, one of these days those vicious creations might try to drag me off again. So I want answers. "

There was a long silence before the former Governor spoke up. "Randolph, it was nothing personal. It was just that your termination date came up and we acted accordingly. It was just ordinary procedure."

"No, that is not true. Gordon, you wanted to get rid of me." He honed in on the problem.

She lanced an insipid smile in his direction. "You are over sensitive. As the former Governor, the term that you all prefer I use, just stated, it was a simple administrative matter. The termination unit acted independently. We were equally surprised to learn about that unpleasant incident."

"I am going to speak frankly." Crawford started off. "Even though I had no idea of the termination date, I would not have objected to your being disposed of, so to speak."

Randolph stood up. "You miserable Bastard, I am going to rip you to pieces." Peter and Diana grabbed him and forced him back into his seat.

"Let him continue." Stuart suggested. "Tell us everything then, Crawford."

Crawford fidgeted around in his chair for a few minutes. "I was particularly happy to have Elisabeth back." He forced a cough. "Pamela, much as you have been a fascinating creature, your existence was not as important for me as the return of Elisabeth. You are different personalities. For example, Elisabeth would never have entered into all those lascivious relationships like you did. With Randolph out of the picture and Gordon back in control, we would have been able to inspire the return of Elisabeth."

Peter burst out laughing at his comment that brought a hearty blush to my cheeks. "What are you trying to say, Crawford?" Peter asked through waves of laughter.

"Your innocent Pamela was intimately involved with Gordon." Crawford looked over at Gordon and shook his head in disgust. "As if that was not enough, she turned then to Randolph. Even though I recognize that humans are by nature sexually promiscuous, I was revolted to learn that Gordon, one of us, had intimate relationships with both Randolph and Pamela. "

"Really, Rudolph, you did not have to reveal all that. A bit of discretion on your part would have been appreciated," Gordon interjected.

"And, so, I don't see why you brought this up." Peter went on. "Pamela was trapped in this center, just like Randolph was. They needed human contact. I am certain that their binding in this way was a good thing for them and for the overall success of our revolution. And, where Gordon is concerned, I would imagine that they had no real choice but to cooperate with her." He looked at me with a sly smile and said. "I knew that you had someone in the inside, but I thought that it was Stuart."

"That would have been just...sick from our standpoint." Flanders vociferated. "Well, actually, incestuous relationships were a controversial subject throughout human history-they were considered legal or illegal depending upon the morals of the time. My records show that seeking your "soul mate," or your other half, so that you could achieve some form of perfect harmony could lead to an incestuous relationship. Which, by the way, were permissible from the 21st century onward." He then made an irritating, grinding sound like he was clearing his throat before saying in a very loud voice. "Pamela and Stuart are brother and sister."

Everyone's mouth dropped open. "You did not tell them, Pamela?" Flanders asked, folding his arms in front of him, reveling in this self-satisfaction.

"Yes, the Group of 5 mentioned that to me during that long meeting that took place when you were all fighting to save us." They looked at me. "Actually, I meant to tell you, Stuart, but so much has happened that I forgot."

"Well, that explains a lot." Stuart replied. I said the same when they mentioned it to me. "Sibling rivalry, isn't that what it is called?" I smiled sheepishly. "But, didn't you tell me that my so-called family name was Rever and not Reinhart?" Flanders explained how they chose the family name of a very famous scientist who Reinhart worshipped for his outstanding discoveries. Stuart just shrugged his shoulders.

"And, just to clarify things a bit more." Flanders went on. "We knew that Randolph and Stuart were deprogrammed. We knew that for a long time, dating back to before any of you left the Center. But, as they both worked very well and did not seem to be doing anything radical, we let them go on living in the Center." He let out a loud android grunt. "It is true, Randolph, that your termination date was approaching. I recommended pushing up the date. As Crawford stated, we wanted Elisabeth to take over and, well, we assumed that the Pamela side of her would disappear. We thought that Pamela would emotionally implode."

His eyes met mine in a penetrating stare. He expected Elisabeth to surface and applaud his decision. It didn't happen, so he stammered out the rest of his discourse. "Randolph was the better choice because of your relationship with him, Pamela. And, Gordon was always defending you, Stuart. She found you to be very serious and logical, not to mention her utter fascination with your eyes" He threw his arms up in disgust. "She claims that you have android eyes."

"Is that supposed to be a compliment? What you just said is disgusting!" Stuart's voice vibrated with a blend of anger and humiliation. He started to stand up, but Randolph pulled him back in his chair.

"So," John picked up the conversation in a calm, administrative tone. "You wanted the kind, emotional Pamela to disappear." Their heads nodded vigorously. "And you adopted that diabolical scheme to kill Randolph." They nodded. "So, then it is true, you had no idea that we were ready to enter the Center and take over." They nodded again. "Were you surprised to see Pamela defend Randolph?"

"We never expected that Elisabeth would align herself with the humans. After all she is our creator and we had reason to believe that she would protect us. We were confused that she left Pamela in control." Miller answered, avoiding eye contact with me. "Pamela's intervention happened so fast. We sent out android forces to stop her. But, then Stuart showed up and we had to send more. "

"What were you going to do if you caught them?" John queried.

"We had no immediate plan. Our only objective was to capture the three of them." She looked at Stuart. "But, when Stuart showed us his talent, we realized that he would have to be disposed of as well." Miller continued.

"And, then to our complete dismay, they disappeared inside the wall. It was like an illusion. We couldn't find them." The Governor said. "We started to search everywhere, which is why we saw all of you in the transport unit and sent in other forces. Again, Stuart and Diana were our major concern, but then everyone, even you, Randolph, were a problem. I was so annoyed that I had given you," he pointed at Randolph, "all that training in weaponry when you were young." He sighed. "Yes, we did not know that you were launching an offensive against the center."

"Nonetheless, everything that happened was also in our interest." Flanders added. "We wanted the opportunity to work with all of you again."

"Who programmed the androids to fight?" I saw this as the right moment to solve that enigma.

"We had a small military force that the cleanup crew brought to this Center. They are not that efficient as you must have noticed, because they did not win the battle." The Governor hung his head, before adding. "I don't know who programmed them, but they did reply to our order to activate and defend the center." He shrugged his shoulders.

"I think that you are telling us everything." The Governor squirmed. "I shall make certain that they never take orders from you again." I did that over the next couple days.

"I want to address the promiscuity in your group." Crawford precipitously diverted the discussion. "For the moment, we are still sprinkling birth control powder in the females' food. We have done this because you-you humans-show no degree of control."

"What are you talking about?" I asked.

"You want examples." Flanders began. "Well, it is easy. Randolph, Stuart, Jonathan and Mathieu have been with Mathilda and Diana over the last couple days. We even caught you, Peter, with Mathilda yesterday." I snarled at Peter who lifted his shoulders innocently. What could I say, he just discovered what I was doing and actually defended me.

"Only Stanislas and Benjamin show fidelity. As for the rest of you, if you don't care about the parentage of your offspring, we shall throw away the birth control powder." Flanders stopped to tap his fingers rhythmically on the table. "I would think, though, that you would prefer to know which children you sired." He addressed the men.

"I believe that you are exaggerating." Isabel said. "And, even if that is not the case, our sense of fidelity is different from the generations before us. We were not imbued with standards of prudish morality or some sort of proper conduct. I believe that our liberated manner is advantageous for us."

Isabel's words surprised me. I thought that she would be upset that Mathieu had been with other women. And then, it all became clear. She was just playing a game and had only pretended to be_jealous, when Mathieu and I returned from our few days of exploration at the time I was living with the outside community. It was all part of their strategy to incite human emotions in Pamela. I suddenly felt quite foolish and vowed never to bring up the subject again with her or anyone else. The past was the past. So I smiled along with my friends and colleagues and nodded in agreement with what Isabel just said.

"And, Crawford, I don't like you depicting my relationship with Benjamin as something different." Stanislas spoke up for the first time in days. "Just because Benjamin and I have special feelings for each other does not mean that we don't want to reproduce."

"He is right." Benjamin said. "Pamela and Gordon had a relationship." I blushed and Gordon smiled. "And, Pamela is no less interested in reproducing than we are."

"Well, I think that we should vote on the birth control powder issue." Ferdinand suggested. The vote passed by a simple majority in favor of continued use.

"Next issue for the day?" Ferdinand asked.

"I would like to bring the group up-to-date on the late night meeting I had with the Group of 5." I explained the gist of the conversation, underscoring the fact that I chided them for their negligent interference with the mutated humans' development of their true potential.

"We prepared the parentage of the 10 reptilian creatures for you and indicated their present assignments." Miller mentioned. She handed the document to Ferdinand.

We all took a flexible position on the question of creating human mutants. It was agreed that Reinhart's research was inspired by the changes in the earth's environment during her lifetime that may or may not be the same today. I explained that she was not involved in diabolical, unethical experiments in DNA. Rather, she believed the human race would not survive if it did not evolve both physically and physiologically in order to adapt to the rapid changes in the earth's topography and climate. She wanted to expedite the evolutionary process. The reptilian nature of humans could be reversed easily once the earth became more totally human friendly. Thus her focus was on preserving, rather than destroying the human race.

Everyone listened closely to my explanation that left the

androids speechless. I pointed out that even though the Group of 5 had acted irrationality, their conduct was explainable as they were not privy to her research. They could not have known, even understood, how improper their experiments were. A long uncomfortable silence followed- each of us concentrating in our own way on how to deal with the absurdity of the situation thrust upon us by the Group of 5-until James made a suggestion.

"Before going further," James remarked. "Perhaps it is important for us to check out the topography of the earth today. That will make it easier for us to know whether or not the capacities of these existing mutants can and should be developed and exploited for the benefit of everyone."

It would have been difficult for me to make the same suggestion because the group may have seen that as a Reinhart manipulation. And, I was already convinced that the reptilian humans should be part of our exploratory team, so I would have forced that vote. I knew that I must be patient, introducing my position at another time, after studying their profiles in more detail. Nonetheless, this suggestion coming from James got a unanimous vote.

I reminded the group that we had two priorities, Miller's android skin and Jonathan's operation. "Only Diana and Isabel are free for the moment to learn how to pilot the aircraft. James, you will have to help them with that." He nodded.

"The rest of us", I looked at the group, "must pull together our talents to finish the existing priorities. If all goes well, we shall be able to engage in explorations very soon.

"Yes, but we shall need to keep a skeleton crew here in the center for the children and other things." John added.

"The deprogramming...when do we do that?" Mathilda asked.

"Perhaps we should divide up the group into mutated and non-mutated humans." Jonathan suggested.

"We all saw that Eunice was not afraid of her partner." Mathieu finally said what we all knew and found a bit distasteful to say. "That does not mean that the others might act the same way."

"I am ok with the mutants." Benjamin said. "Actually, I am quite fascinated with those creatures." He looked at Ruth. "I know that you were horrified by your partner's appearance."

"That is true. The context of my situation, deprogrammed and sharing a cubicle with a giant lizard, was very difficult." She stopped to collect her thoughts. "We were not a group of humans working together and comforting each other at the time. We found ourselves alone after our deprogramming. Perhaps if I had been surrounded by others, like Eunice, last evening, I might have gotten past the physical side and managed to have a friendly, but not intimate, relationship with my partner."

"You can still have that." Flanders spoke up. "He is one of the 10 mutants. We changed his code after you left and gave him a new visual identity so that he could be given a new partner. Your replacement was terminated recently. Your code could be reactivated and he would recognize you." He sat back and grinned.

"I know that you are saying that to upset me, Flanders. " Ruth retorted. "Nonetheless, the experiment interests me. Perhaps through him I can reach the other mutants. They can come to terms with their appearances before they join the rest of us. That might be the right step to take."

Our voices rose up in agreement. It sounded like the best approach to resolving the deprogramming process. Perhaps later on Jonathan, Sarah and Mathilda, along with Ruth, would begin the deprogramming of the other reptiles. I saw something mischievous hidden behind Flanders' contrived smile when he promised to take care of the coding process for Ruth over the next few days.

"Just one last thing." Gordon broke in. "Here is the list of android personnel that we would like to reactivate, along with the units that need their assistance. You can see that we have only asked for 30 more assistants. It is the absolute minimum. The kitchen, laundry, toiletry service, and cleaning staff are far too small. You, Ralph, will also need androids to work in the gardens. We also thought that you might like to visit the vacation center-the swimming pool and other sports facilities. For the moment, there are no android assistants assigned to the vacation center." She cleared her throat. "Here is the list."

Ferdinand took the paper and skimmed it. "It looks ok to me. Does anyone want to study it in more detail?"

No one seemed interested. "I want to accompany you, Victoria, to select the android assistants." She cringed. "I know-rather she knows-which ones to activate." It was not what they were hoping for.

"We should schedule another meeting. I think that we can meet in 2 days?" Ferdinand suggested.

We would have frequent meetings in the beginning months of our new-found freedom. There were so many group decisions to make. In time, we would develop a certain independence and would meet every two weeks to bring the entire group up to date.

The androids left first and then stood ceremoniously outside the door, shaking everyone's hand as they passed in front. The idea of shaking hands caught on rapidly with the members of our group.

I spent the afternoon helping Peter, Stuart and Randolph begin the process of transforming the hard, thick leaves into android skin. We had to boil the leaves for several hours in order to soften the vegetable fibers and release the elasticity and pliancy. We then laid thin layers inside special molds that corresponded to the arms, hands, legs and foot sizes of Agnes' extremities. We would leave them like that for several weeks, maybe just days here in the center, before placing them over her metallic surface.

When we split up, I stopped by to see Victoria. She was alone and doing nothing. "Strange to find you without anything to do." I commented. She just sighed.

"You will soon be very busy." Seeing her like that did bother me. She just grunted. "Actually, you should already be assisting Jonathan and the others in deprogramming the remaining humans. Your experience with human emotions could be very useful." Her eyes brightened up. "And, you have not yet finished your study of human emotions."

"You are absolutely right. I do have a lot of work to do. They won't mind if I observe?"

"I don't think so. Actually, all of you should be working. I shall draw up a list of projects for all of you. Now, I would like you to accompany me to the android terminal to select the 30 assistants we approved of today."

She took my hand in hers and led me in the direction of the android terminal. I felt Reinhart's energy suffusing me and her enthusiasm mount as we entered this enormous open-spaced war-ehouse. Thousands of androids were lined up against each other in long, deep rows. They were placed in the order of their series. The assistant androids were one of the interesting series. They could be used to carry out simple manual tasks, but they could also be programmed to participate in intellectual projects and complicated scientific tasks. For the moment, I only wanted the earlier series that could only be programmed to carry out manual and menial tasks.

"We shall reactivate this group, right here." She snarled but didn't argue with me. Instead, she helped me give the order to reac-tivate the thirty androids that I selected. I then told her that she should take charge of them because I wanted to look around a bit. She nodded and left with the work crew.

I wandered off into the other section to look over Reinhart's ex-periments in suspended animation. Most of the capsules had been opened and the human remains discarded. There were no more than 20 specimens in place. I sensed Reinhart's disappointment, which seemed incongruous with the ghastly sight of those remai-ning humans. Some of the bodies were in an advanced stage of de-terioration, where the soft tissue had decayed, leaving bones and cartilage visible. A suffocating stench laid heavy in the air. In other capsules, I confronted bulging eyes and distended tongues that protruded from blackish green bloated faces. I imagined that there was also a putrid, suffocating odor of decay inside those capsules.

If Reinhart hadn't been controlling my reflexes, I would have let out an alarming, hideous scream of absolute terror. But instead, I acquiesced to her determination to analyze the situation, until she concluded that they had outlived the maximum time calculated for interplanetary exploration, or several thousand years if the ships plunged at Alcubierre drive into deep space and moved into other galaxies. I leaned up against the capsules to prevent myself from collapsing, as her cold side receded deep inside me. Tears strea-med down my face as I thought about how many thousands and thousands of years had passed since humans reigned over the pla-net earth. Ferdinand's suggestion that we start our history in the year 1 AAD seemed even more appropriate. Sadly, I would have to order the androids to open up the remaining capsules over the next few weeks and discard the last remains of a former generation of humans.

I slowly turned away from the decaying humans and inspected the operational controls on several empty units. The capsules themselves appeared to have survived time and when I touched the activating button, it responded immediately. Naturally, the capsule would have to be programmed properly, so the good news was we could reuse them if we needed to.

I left the unit downhearted by the loss of human life, but inspired by the numbers of androids that were saved from extinction and the fact that space travel was feasible.

When I arrived for dinner, only Peter and Jonathan were still there. Jonathan told me that more than half of the reptilian humans were involved in agronomy or marine biology. That was interesting and, from my point of view, a better choice than architecture. He told me that the two musicians had only slightly scaly reptilian skin, and spiky scales around the back of their necks, with otherwise human features, although he found their triangular faces quite unattractive. They were both in the wind section of the orchestra. There were also two others working in experimental physics. One of them was Ruth's former partner, so I knew that he was practically 100% reptile. The last one was Eunice's partner, the architect.

Ruth described her partner once to me when I was living with the outside community. I stared off into the distance for a minute as I recalled her story of a large, erect reptile with a triangular face. She mentioned how his eyes beamed at her when she entered their cubicle. I was not certain then that her story was true and that she was not just testing me to determine to what extent the Pamela side could be naïve. I turned back to Johnathan and Peter. "I believe that he is close to the bearded dragon species, with expandable spiny scales, a broad triangular head, stout legs and a robust body?" Jonathan nodded.

"Reinhart was also fascinated with the Black Marine Iguanas, or dragons, especially those who had slender front legs and long, thick back legs. They were powerful swimmers and their 5-toed claws made them excellent climbers.

"Well, she must have been very fascinated with them because there are a number of them among the 10 mutants." Jonathan shook his head in disgust. "I don't get it? Why?"

"There was very little land surface, most of which was desert, in her time. She contended that it was necessary to mutate human characteristics to survive in water and in hot dry environments." I repeated what I said earlier in the day.

"Actually, the Group of 5 made a mistake. When the androids retrieved the different DNA strands, the genomes of the humans, they accidentally picked up a vast number of the mutant DNA that Reinhart was studying. They informed me recently that mixing mutant DNA, in varying degrees, with human genomes, produced a more intelligent breed of humans. The visual programming made it possible for these mutants to live unaware of their differences and to interact comfortably with non-mutated humans." I sighed again. Their blatant negligence sent chills up my spine. I quickly changed the subject. "Are you ready for tomorrow, Jonathan?" He nodded. "Ok, we shall meet in the inner circle after breakfast."

Peter and I walked casually hand and hand down the empty corridors, entering the inner circle from another angle. I found myself standing in front of the rejuvenation machine. I could feel Peter's eyes studying me, his mind trying painfully, but in vain, to pierce mine. I didn't linger, but started walking, accelerating my pace, pretending that I wanted to be in his arms in the privacy of our room, when, in reality, I wanted to hide from him the desire for power that was surging inside of me.

Chapter 7- Staggering Revelations

We woke up early and exited the inner circle as the other members of our group were just starting to move around. The first thing that I noticed when I entered the dining room was that there were 3 more androids preparing the breakfast. The Group of 5 had already carried out my orders and assigned the 30 extra android support staff to various units.

"The time warp, Pamela?" Peter asked nonchalantly.

"Oh, yes, I didn't finish the story, did I?" He smiled. "Ok, Reinhart set up these centers to house her team and others in the event of a traumatic natural disaster or war." His smile died away. "The concept of time warp originated in science fiction, as you so rightly mentioned the other day, and physicists and mathematicians found this concept incredulous. The idea of space-time warped by matter and energy met with so much skepticism until it was shown that it was theoretically possible, even though it was determined to be physically impossible. Reinhart liked challenges and that inspired her intense research in this area."

I sat back in my chair and closed my eyes for a few minutes. "She also wanted the centers," I said, picking up the conversation, "at least this center, to survive both violent natural disasters and wars, and she believed that a different time-space configuration would make that possible. This center was placed in its own gravitational time dilation orbit. I think that she expected time to be faster on the inside than on the outside due to the fact that the center in orbit was lighter than the gravitational force on the earth in orbit. For whatever reason the reverse situation emerged. Perhaps the gravitational force inside the center after the explosion took place in the center of the earth was stronger than that on the outside. In any event, the time differential between the center and the outside is not that significant."

"Wow! I don't know what to say!"

"Apparently some centers were destroyed in spite of her efforts to protect them forever. But then I am guessing about her interest in protecting all the centers because I can only say for certain that she cared about this one." I stopped to let Reinhart pronounce her judgment. "Perhaps this can be seen as one of her greatest accomplishments as much as one of her biggest mistakes in time-space curves. In any event, what matters is that this center and several others survived the horrific explosion coming from the center of the earth." I looked up and saw the others arriving. "Can we just keep this between us for a while?" He nodded.

Emotions were high, with lots of laughter and energy. Everyone seemed to be motivated with the different projects under way. Jonathan looked a bit nervous about his surgery so we all tried to reassure him that everything would go well. Imogen decided to eat with us. The more than 24 hours that passed since she learned of her partner's termination gave her the time she needed to rethink her position. I concluded that she no longer held us responsible for his disappearance.

"I was wondering if you, Pamela and Jonathan would be interested in rehearsing with the rest of the orchestra at the end of the afternoon." She bowed her head dissimulating her broad smile. "Actually, I was hoping that you, Jonathan, would conduct the orchestra. We need someone to work with us."

"I like the idea and will be happy to conduct the orchestra." He said in a lively tone. "It is just that you will have to give me, all of us, a bit of time to finish some other pressing matters." And, with that, the surgical team- John, Sarah, Ruth, Stanislas, Benjamin, Randolph, Stuart, Peter and myself—stood up and left with Jonathan for the inner circle.

Remarkably, Jonathan's body and organs were in excellent condition. His only problem was in the spinal column itself where he had three extra vertebrae in the upper back, just below the cervical region. A diagram of the recommended surgical procedure followed the prognosis and the visual scan of his body parts.

It indicated that we had to remove the three extra vertebrae and replace the upper and lower support vertebrae, with bionic parts that would lift the spinal column into a normal position.

Perspiring and pale from the stress, Peter turned to me, while the others stood patiently waiting for instructions. "I can't do anything before I practice on some of those rubber dolls. We shall recreate the same anomaly in them and try to work together as a team." He backed away from the scanner.

"If we didn't have to worry about the nerves, it would be nothing. We are going to have to be ready for complications. And, we have to manufacture two bionic parts that fit together and will clamp around the nerve without damaging it!" His unsteady voice betrayed him, revealing the stress surging inside of him.

Certainly he was expelling the proper surgical precautions to be taken at his level of surgical experience. Even though I could see the simplicity of the operation because of Reinhart's uploads to me, I did not want to embarrass him. "Wait a minute, I want to show you all something." I walked over to one of the large cabinets that covered more than half of the back wall of the operating room. When I opened it, I heard deep gasps coming from the group behind and Peter's hands gripping my shoulder. "Everything that you need is here." He turned me in his direction and, for a brief moment, I saw his undisguised disdain. He pushed me out of his way.

I let them look at the different bionic parts, all properly labeled. She had thought of everything. If she and her colleagues had taken refuge in this center, there was a risk that some of them might have been injured. She had put aside a large variety of bionic replacement parts and the vertebrae we needed were among them. I watched them from the corner of my eyes.

"We still have to open and remove the other vertebrae." Stuart called out anxiously.

"You have to open him, delicately disintegrate the existing vertebrae with this small laser," that I took from the cabinet, and handed to him "and add the replacements. The moment that you insert the parts they will automatically move around and between the spinal nerves and settle into place." They looked at me like I had just slapped them in the face.

"They are not alive?" Randolph asked in a voice that sounded like someone was choking him as he involuntarily backed away from the cabinet.

"No, but there is a guidance system in them. You will have time to learn about that afterwards. When they are in the right location, their bio-sensory systems will do the rest."

There was a long pause before Stanislas asked about the other parts in the cupboard. I confirmed that they would also adapt accordingly, properly replacing the lost body part.

"They virtually look like amputated body parts!" Stanislas said between seared teeth. "She was more than a genius. She was a kind of magician or wizard." His face contorted!

"Yes." I picked up one of the hands and passed it around. "As you can see, their robotic characteristics were refined in time and given a human anatomical appearance both on the inside and outside. Quite brilliant, huh?" I was impressed with the contents of the cabinet and surprised by the reaction of the others. They were more overwhelmed by the human quality of them that seemed ironically to revolt more than fascinate them.

"Well, even though there is something strange about all of this..." Peter stuttered a bit. "Here are the two vertebrae that we need for Jonathan." He studied the vertebrae before protesting. "They look too big, though?" He turned to me.

"No problem, they will adjust to the right size and shape of Jonathan's back. They will also adapt to his nervous system."

"Are you going to help?" Ruth asked.

"I am going to let all of you find your way through this. If you need to look into the process of disintegration it is in the surgical tapes over there." I pointed to the library on the left hand wall. "You might want to do that now. I shall be there to observe and comment on procedure." Their faces turned white. "But, of course, I, under Reinhart's guidance, shall assist when necessary. We could schedule it for tomorrow?"

"We should wake up Jonathan." Randolph suggested. "And explain to him what we are going to do." We agreed.

"You could do this so easily, Pamela. Why are you risking

Jonathan's life? You know that we could make an irreversible mistake?" Randolph protested.

"No, I shall be there and you are not going to make any mistakes. I can't do everything. I want all of you to catch up with what I know-through her- so that we evolve as a group in our discoveries." They nodded reluctantly. I knew that I would protect Jonathan from any secondary effects and did have confidence in the group to do their best.

The team stayed in the inner circle to explain the procedure to Jonathan and to review the surgical guides. I left to see what the Group of 5 was up to. I found them in the birth center looking over past DNA mixes.

"Oh, Pamela, we are so glad that you came by to visit." Flanders flashed a big smile, the first one that he sent me since I downloaded my biological mother.

"What are you doing?" I asked out of curiosity, more than concern.

"You asked for the genetic blend of the different reptilian humans and that is what we are doing." Rudolph retorted in his dry tone.

"Thank you."

"You should be aware though that deprogramming this group of humans could have very bad repercussions." Rudolph looked at the other members of his group who nodded, silently allowing him to proceed.

"The reptilian brain," he looked at me with creased eyes like a tiger ready to pounce, "could be predominant in these species." He raised his eyebrows in a suggestive way.

"Was he hoping to upset me or impress me?" I started to laugh. "How cruel and diabolical this group is." Repeated several times in my mind.

"This is a serious matter, Pamela. Perhaps you could just try to take a scientific rather than an emotional approach to problem solving." He threw his arms up in the air in disgust as I continued to chuckle. "Laugh if you want, but the reptilian brain is cold, ruthless, and calculating. It is the bad element in the human brain. These creatures could become very territorial, aggressive, and even destructive. And, worse, they might feel threatened and resort to killing." I was now choking back my laughter. "She recognized the effect of the reptilian brain in human behavior and suppressed that part of the brain through programming-just like we did with you humans."

I pulled myself together and informed them that I was willing to take the risk. I liked discrediting android reasoning by diametrically opposing their views.

"Unlike you, I believe that human intellect can temper, even overcome, the cold, instinctive reptilian behavior of that small center of the human brain." I stated. "The reptilian brain theory was not a popular position among the scientific community even at her time. It was more of a myth that explained cruel, uncontrollable behavior and validated the easy manipulation of humans by good and evil elements in society."

I breathed deeply to remind them that I was human. "I don't endorse the theory even though I have her explanation in front of me. And, I believe that that portion of the brain, if it was ever relevant, has atrophied over time and that this discussion is redundant." They all looked at me with their cold android eyes shrouding their wonderment. "Nonetheless, I am happy that you are taking the time to look into the genetic combination of these species. We need to identify their genetic codes."

I turned to leave and then remembered: "There are other humans with deformities. Half of the other 20 humans have physical malformations-distorted facial features, crippled bodies, webbed hands and feet, and so forth. I want to know if we can correct any or all of these anomalies so I need a detailed report on the anatomical and physiological aspects of each mutant. Any questions?" No one answered. "Well," I said, as I purposely rubbed my hands together in a Reinhart fashion, "that should keep you busy!"

I left directly for the learning center. The children were hooked up to the terminals and their little eyes were moving back and forth over the screen, absorbing the information at a rapid speed. "They are doing very well for non-programmed humans." Mathilda said in a low voice. "I am pleased with their progress." I nodded. "They are starting to enter into more complex areas. I'll run a test on them at the end of the week."

"Shouldn't they be playing or exercising now?" I asked. It was late in the afternoon and I wanted the children to have relaxation time. I promised to look into their daily schedule at the last meeting.

"They have no studies tomorrow. It is their day off. They can learn a sport or dabble in art or music. Frederic likes to play the clarinet, but Jonathan has to be there to help him with that." She took my hand in hers. "You mustn't worry so much. They are doing well and the androids are not intimately involved in their learning process."

I smiled and thanked her for all the attention she was giving to the children. "One day off in the middle of the week and another day off at the end of the week gets my approval." I said under my breath, as my thoughts turned back to Mathilda. She seemed different to me now that we were in the center. As a psychologist, she was always scrutinizing and analyzing someone. Her last long study was Diana. She never gave us a report on her conclusions. Nonetheless, her fascination with the children was bothering me and I didn't know why.

"I must be tired," I said out loud. I wanted to shake off that strange feeling of despair or impending doom that Mathilda ignited in me. We didn't communicate well even when we were living together in the outside community. I decided to look over the program she gave them today before going to bed.

The wall clock indicated that I still had several hours free before dinner so I opted for a visit to the agricultural unit. The unit was now alive with activity, with six more androids busy working. Ralph saw me enter on his visual surveillance system and started his long descent from his lab in my direction in one of the motorized cars. When he arrived, he leaped out of the car and took long, bouncy strides in my direction. I was pleased to see him looking so fit.

"We are cultivating, and will soon be harvesting, what was planted before we took over." He stood with his hands on his hips observing the workers. "There are a couple humans over there. Did you see them?" He asked as he pointed in their direction.

"Their physical appearances are a bit-unusual!" He forced a smile. "But they are working so well. They know their way around the unit."

"I am just going to take a closer look at them, if you don't mind." I was curious about his workers, but would have preferred a tour of the agricultural unit.

"Be my guest." He said as he waved me on. "Don't make them feel uncomfortable."

They were not more than 20 feet away. They turned to me and I gave them my code. We chatted a few minutes about the work they were doing. They were happy to inform me that they were also involved in genetic modification of plants and were looking forward to assisting Ralph in that area.

The female had a short, stocky built and a large, flat, round face with a cone-shaped cerebral mass protruding behind her flat face. Her head appeared to be glued on top of a long neck. The effect was mindboggling. At first glance I had the impression that her facial features were not real and were just scribbling on a flat surface. I was completely taken back by what happened. Her nose, mouth, eyes and ears took a two-dimensional form when she was using them. Unusual, the term Ralph employed to describe her was an understatement. I definitely wanted to know her genetic mix.

Her colleague's tall slender body was bent in two, as if he had been created to do gardening. Even though his lower spine was immobile, he was able to lift his head slightly upward, when he said hello. I noticed that he had a long face with big reddish brown eyes, a stubby nose and bushy brownish, grey hair. In spite of the comic effect of his facial features, I was convinced that his face was the most attractive part of his full body appearance.

At this moment, I could feel Reinhart's warm energy surging inside of me, controlling my consciousness and helping me to visualize the ways in which their appearances could be ameliorated. The fact that something could be done for both of them to make them more pleasing to the eye was reassuring and yet I wondered why we should bother. If they could integrate into our society in their present form, why give them a complex by forcing them to adapt to a more normal, human appearance?

"What do you think, Pamela?"

"Hard to say. I find myself in a quandary over whether to change their physical appearances or just leave them like they are." He choked on his own saliva. "Ok, I understand your surprised reaction. It is an ethical issue of sorts. We both agree that they are not suffering from their anomalies." He nodded. "So, if I were to change them, which is feasible, it is because the rest of our community would be happier looking at humans that resemble us."

I stepped back to observe them at work. "They are programmed so that don't know what they look like. Should I redo their physical appearances now, before deprogramming them, or deprogram them and let them decide what they want? That is my dilemma." My teary eyes said everything.

"I know what you mean?" He bit down on his index finger. "How are they going to feel when they see their real image? If it doesn't bother them or inhibit them from being vital members of society, we should just look beyond the physical side." He sucked in his lips. "In their case, though, I think that it would be kinder if we corrected the problems before they had to confront them."

I shook my head despairingly. "I don't know why those crazy androids manufactured them. Was it a conscious effort on their part?" He was staring pensively at the agronomists.

All of sudden, Reinhart was very much alive inside of me, intellectually and emotionally, uploading too much at one time, making me feel dizzy. I pressed my hands up against my temples in an attempt to stop the throbbing pain that Reinhart's violent surges of energy were generating.

"Are you alright, Pamela?" His voice adding to the vibrations in my head.

"No! My head feels like it is going to explode and everything is starting to spin around in front of me." The last thing that I remembered was feeling so weak that I tried desperately to reach out to Ralph. He later told me that I stumbled and fell unconscious into his, as he described them, feeble arms. When I awoke, he was patting my hands and wiping my face.

"You fainted. Don't ever do that again!" He was rambling hysterically. "I don't understand how this happened."

"It is ok, Ralph. I am better now." I tried to sit up and he tightened his grip on me. I didn't resist. I understood what happened. I felt her anger. Up until now, I felt her genius, her intellect, but I only feigned what might be her feelings. She was more alive inside of me than I wanted her to be and her personality was growing stronger.

"She is angry." I whispered.

"Who is angry?" Ralph said in a low, soothing voice, dissimilating his concern.

"Reinhart-I can feel her anger. She believes that the Group of 5 went too far with their human experiments even though she could help me to put these two young agronomists together properly. The use of the mutant genes to produce reptilian humans didn't seem to bother her. She was fascinated with the results because it made sense to create a human adapted for survival in a water world." He nodded. "I am going to have to take a very good look at the other mutated humans in the non-reptilian group." This time I pushed myself up. She had disappeared for the moment and I had completely recovered. "I have to go now."

"No, wait, Pamela, you are too weak."

"You are wrong, Ralph. I feel more energetic and determined than ever." He gawked. "Don't look so surprised, Ralph." I tapped his shoulder and kissed his cheek. "I'll be just fine."

I rushed over to the learning center. The children had long since left. The program was still in the computer terminal so I ran through it, looking for anything that might suggest manipulation, brainwashing or subliminal imagery. There was nothing wrong with the program and it was very well adapted to their ages and learning capacities. I felt much better and rather embarrassed that I suspected Mathilda of foul play.

I turned to leave the room and saw Flanders leaning up against the open door. "So you are checking up on us-or, Mathilda?" He smiled cagily.

"The real question is what are you doing here?" I turned the suspicion onto to him. He fidgeted. "I am waiting for an answer." I said with a warped smile.

"Well, yes...I was just walking the hallways."

"Where are all the others?"

"They're in that office that you packed us into." Defiance was in his voice. "Why did you ask?"

"I would like to see you all for a minute." I pushed past him and headed in the direction of the office. I could hear him moving fast behind me.

I burst into the room and asked them if they had the genetic combinations for all the non-reptilian mutants ready for me. I did not give them time to go through their usual artificial greeting.

"No, they are not yet ready." Crawford answered, his voice ringing with contempt.

"I asked you to work on them." I said firmly.

"What is your hurry, Pamela? We thought that we had all our time." Gordon spoke up.

"I just saw the two humans assigned to the agricultural unit. What kind of diabolical research did you do to come up with them?" They looked at me and then at each other as if they could not understand my attitude.

"Listen, Pamela, you are just too pre-occupied with appearances..."

"Stop stalling! " I interrupted Crawford. "You got it wrong. It is not the Pamela inside of me who wants an answer." The mood changed dramatically.

"Oh! Well! That is, of course...different." The former Governor said. "It is difficult to explain what happened to the young woman."

"She is the first one in her series and we had no intention of continuing that series. We recognized the absurdity of her physical condition. She is very special, but she manages to survive. An interesting point scientifically." Gordon interjected. "You, Elisabeth, could improve her looks-I think. . . "

"How many misfits did you create just for your own pleasure?" They didn't answer, certainly uncomfortable with the question. So I continued. "It is evident that you were not looking for human perfection which should have been the object of your research."

"We were looking for human perfection, in a certain sense. You know that we made mistakes. That was normal. We did not have all of your knowledge in the field of genetics at our disposition." Agnes said trying to appease Elisabeth. "And, her termination date is very close. Perhaps you could authorize the termination. That would simplify everything." She suggested.

"No!" I screamed. "I don't want to hear the word termination again. It is because of that, that you went as far as you did in mutating humans. Termination was the safety value, a way to get rid of bad, and I mean, very bad research! Your error, in her case, was so negligent that it leaves me believing that you purposely carried out these genetic experiments to create atrocities. I cannot believe that you could have unintentionally gone so far off in your research because of simple errors." They stood at attention with their heads bowed. They got the result they were hoping for. In spite of their alarming impertinence, their submissive position calmed down the Elisabeth inside of me.

The ensuing silence was long and psychologically restorative. "Should I ever find out that you-any of you-are continuing this kind of hideous research, I shall order all 5 of you to shut down permanently." They quickly stood attentively.

"Please let me explain." Flanders pleaded. I nodded. "We accidentally-but if you prefer, negligently-manipulated the genetic DNA in the facial reader. We did not terminate her as a child because she progressed intellectually. As you witnessed, she is very clever and capable of contributing to agricultural research." He sighed. "We had no idea that she would be discovered by you, Elisabeth. We regret having let her live only because you believe that she was a kind of pass time that added divergence, perhaps novelty, to our drab lives." He stopped to see if I showed signs of weakness. I just stared at him. "And, well, as Dr. Miller just said, you can give her a more human appearance."

"Did you save any similar fertilized ovum?"

"No, we destroyed the rest because, as you just observed, her series was not a success." Flanders commented. I was not certain that they had destroyed the series, but knew that they would do so soon after I left. Reinhart already understood where they made their mistake so it would not happen again.

I felt responsible because I should have given the humans more attention while they were grouped together after the revolution. I reasoned that the only way I could discretely observe them and evaluate the extent and complexity of the deformities in the non-reptilian humans was to go to lunch at the same as them. Their breakfasts and evening meals were still being brought to their cubicles.

The only time they were grouped together was during their lunch hour, which was earlier than ours.

My steps weighed heavy like I was carrying all the burdens of the preceding thousands of years on my shoulders, as I made my way down the corridors looking forward to the sanctity of the inner circle. There were too many problems to resolve quickly so that we could get our lives into a forward moving trend and advance in other projects. The android skin for Agnes needed some more time to elasticize. Jonathan would be operated on tomorrow. The reptilian creatures would be deprogrammed together. Sarah, Ruth, Mathilda and perhaps others would be there to oversee the effects of the deprogramming. This will take place after Jonathan has recovered.

I was jolted out of my thoughts when Peter appeared out of nowhere. He was smiling—a good sign.

"Ok, we understand what we have to do tomorrow and Jonathan is ready for it. He told me that he has 100% confidence in me to give him a proper human spine!"

"I'll be there to see how well you do." His arms moved around me and I let myself collapse up against him.

"Ready to eat?" He asked.

"Not yet. I'll see you later." I gave him a quick kiss on his cheek.

There were many times, like tonight, that I wanted to be alone. I waited under Peter rounded the corner and was out of sight before I passed discretely into the inner circle, and sought refuge and inspiration for tomorrow in a good night's sleep.

Chapter 8-Presumption of Innocence

The operation was a success. I watched Peter take charge, giving instructions just like a chief surgeon by requesting suctioning, verification of vital organs, and confirmation of heartbeat, among other things. Stanislas and Benjamin were the principle assistants, even though Stuart, Randolph and John called out the various procedures to be followed. I was surprised that Sarah and Ruth took a back seat, by simply observing. I watched what the surgical team was doing very closely. They had some difficulty disintegrating the original vertebrae, something that does require training. So, I let Reinhart take charge and clear out the zone. I then moved aside so they could insert the robotic parts.

The Oh's and Ah's were audible when the robotic parts moved like living organisms into place, taking on the right size and shape. I verified under Reinhart' guidance that the nerves were untouched and that the connection was perfect before letting them rapidly close him up. He didn't seem to be suffering when he opened his eyes only minutes after the surgical operation ended. That surprised the others, but not me. Surgery on humans had improved so much during Reinhart's time that it was practically pain free, as I mentioned so many times.

When Jonathan stood up for the first time in his life with an erect, perfect upper body, his broad smile told us everything. The Surgical team's tension dissipated, replaced by an enormous outburst of laughter followed by happy screams.

"We did it!" Randolph said with a bellowing voice as he started that male thing-slapping each other on the back and landing some friendly punches. Sarah and Ruth just stood watching.

"Jonathan, the orchestra pit?" I yelled out over all the noise. We were off in a flash. When Imogen saw Jonathan, she came running towards him. "You are here. You are ready to teach us and conduct the orchestra?" He nodded.

"So, how do I look, Pamela?" He asked as he moved into different poses like someone in a body building championship competition.

I giggled a bit at his innocent display of masculinity, heightened by his newfound freedom of movement. "You look great, Jonathan. Yes, you look Great!" I said backing up out of the way. "I am going to leave you with your students and will be back later to accompany you on the piano."

"Ok, see you later." I noticed that he had already taken his place behind the podium and was tapping his wand to get their attention.

My mind was ticking off the next series of projects-Agnes' skin, removal of the remains of the bodies in suspended animation, cleaning out those capsules, and the integration of the mutants into society. There was a long, tedious list of projects that had to be finished before we could concentrate on exploring the planet and then space.

I looked up at the wall clock as I passed in front and realized that I had to move fast if I wanted to take a few minutes to study the remaining mutant humans and dashed off to the dining room. My invisibility made it easier for me to study each one of them without having to explain my presence. The two from the agricultural unit were pitifully deformed, while the others' mild deformities could be very easily corrected, if necessary. I was more and more convinced that if their deformities did not cause them pain or suffering after the deprogramming then giving them more human physical attributes might not be either urgent or necessary.

I sat back and watched them eat and... studied them. Ludicrous conversation incited the laughter that permeated the dining room, rendering the members of the group completely euphoric. The non-homogenous nature of the group, spanning arts and sciences, had no visible effect on the blissfulness of their conversations. "Was that the reason why their conversations were so superficial?" I pondered. There was no exchange of ideas. Simple statements like your salad is greener than mine is or you have something red on your plate formed the depth of their exchanges. Exchanges that to my total regret triggered this spontaneous, profound laughter. "Was I like that? Were we all like that?" Probably. After being deprogrammed, I was ill at ease with the programmed humans. "We have nothing in common." I said to myself back then. Today I found the scene obnoxious, totally dehumanizing and something that I had to put an end to, rapidly. Yes, these humans must be deprogrammed and that deprogramming must take place very soon.

"I can see someone over there!" A well-built, tall young man cried out. He was one of the few truly human representations and his oblong face and defined features were a refreshing change from the others. "She is over there?" The others started laughing. "I can see you! " He exclaimed. "Who are you?"

I didn't answer. I watched him as he rubbed his eyes vigorously, hoping to wipe out my image. He turned to face the others and let out a loud, shrill scream as his eyes focused in on the rest of the group, now visible with all their imperfections. "What has happened? What's wrong with you?" He asked as he backed away. "You, what are you?" He said, pointing to the two agronomists. The others continued to laugh, completely unaffected by the seriousness of the scene, as they confused his hysteria with humor.

My attention turned to the two agronomists sitting next to each other at the end of the table. This was an opportunity to take a closer look at them, so I got up and approached the table. I could understand that their appearances disturbed the young man, dramatizing his deprogramming. The female's facial features were in constant movement from a one to a two-dimensional form. I saw that there was no meal in front of the young man. "You are not hungry?" I asked in a soft voice. "No, I always eat before everyone else. I am just here to socialize right now. I cannot see you. Do you have a problem with your visual receptor?" He asked calmly. I didn't answer him. I was deep in thought. Of course, he ate earlier. They probably tube fed him because he would never have been able to swallow nutrients, bent in two, like he was. His entire digestive system was certainly affected by his visible anomalies.

I left the agronomists and moved towards the young man whose eyes, dark and menacing, were watching and studying me, like those of a predator, awaiting the right moment to pounce on its prey. To calm him, I gave him my code, which the others quickly registered as well. When he was within arm's distance I reached out to grab him, but he moved quickly away from me, maintaining what he thought was a comfortable distance. I knew that I had to restrain him. It would have been dangerous for him to wander off now in the corridors, so I rushed him like Diana had trained me to do, my arms securing his upper body in a tight grip. "Are you real?" He asked feigning confidence in me with his soft, steady voice. Instead, he put me on guard and I was more determined than ever to tighten my grip.

"Yes, I am real." I finally answered him, as I increased the pressure around his upper body to deter him from breaking free.

The lunch bell rang out emitting a conditioned reflex. The others stood up, rather lifelessly, like in a trance, and left in their different directions.

I was still struggling with this young man, when my group arrived. Stuart and Randolph, with Diana's help, subdued him, giving me the chance to recover. His face turned white as a ghost and his body shook uncontrollably when they replaced me. His aggressiveness turned to fear and I instinctively moved towards this frightened young man to console him. Peter pulled me back.

"I'll go get the sedative." Ruth screamed out as she rushed out of the dining room.

I turned to James, Imogen and Eunice, and asked them if they were ok. Their glassy eyes spoke of their concern, or horror, over the situation. Once the sedative was injected, the young man collapsed into Randolph's and Stuart's arms. They tied him up against one of the dining room chairs so that we could eat in peace.

"Where are we, Ruth, with the reptilian humans?" I asked, hoping to calm my quivering nerves with ordinary conversation. "None of them were here for lunch."

"They left earlier, which was probably a good thing, considering what happened here in the dining room." Ruth replied. "I met with my former roommate, so to speak, the other day. I told him that he, like others, was a hybrid life form." We all nodded in agreement. That was certainly a much better way of defining their differences. The word, mutant, was, in retrospect, harsh and pejorative.

"I didn't know that you were going to meet with him. I would have gone with you. It must have been difficult." Mathilda said sharply.

Ruth informed us that she felt that it would be better for her to approach him alone, after all they had lived together for quite a while and there was that element of trust that develops between partners. I thought that she was trying to find excuses for going off on her own, something that I personally felt was the better approach and didn't need to be defended.

"How did he react to his description?" Mathilda persisted.

"Not too badly." She swallowed hard. "He said that he would have preferred to be like his code image, but would learn to live with this new physical identity and explore the assets of reptilian physical traits for survival on the planet."

"And..." Mathilda was pushing for answers.

"I think that he is ready to be deprogrammed." Her head dropped limp as she sighed. "I was embarrassed to tell him that I lived with him, avoiding contact with him after I was deprogrammed. I had to tell him that I was afraid of his appearance at that time and have come a long way since then. I can now go beyond appearances. It was extremely difficult for me to admit all that." We sat patiently listening as we could all empathize with her. "I didn't have a support group to turn to like today. He understood, telling me that he counted on me to be there to reassure him. I...I hope that he will be able to face up to this reality."

"We shall all be there," Mathilda suggested. "Won't we?" She asked, her eyes scanning each one of us.

"Yes. This is definitely the kind of progress we are looking for." Ferdinand said in a dry, administrative tone, as he repositioned himself in a more imposing stature at the table, straightening his back and raising his shoulders. "Things are going forward. Look at Jonathan," we all turned to observe him, "he is in great shape. His surgery went well. And, Miller, or Agnes, --don't know what name we agreed upon."

"Just last names." Diana replied vehemently. "Yes, last names, they don't deserve any respect."

"That is right, Diana. In any event, is the skin ready for Miller?"

"Not yet," I answered. "It takes time for the plant to develop the subtle elasticity of our skin."

Ferdinand tapped his fingers on the tabletop as if he were ticking off the list of projects under way, like this was a formal meeting, rather than a quick lunch with a problem tied up against a dining room chair. No one interrupted him. We sat respectfully. "And, the young one other there. What are your plans?" He asked, his eyes meeting mine.

"I am not the right person to deal with this young man. I wrestled with him a little while ago and don't think that he is ready to forget that." I looked at the other members. "James, Eunice and Imogen, you might be able to help this young man come to terms with his new reality." The three of them sat far back in their chairs staring up at the ceiling.

"No, Pamela, I shall deal with him after he has calmed down. I think that I'll need some help in the beginning." Peter said. Stanislas and Benjamin offered their services. "Yes, I'll need the two of you, but I might be more comfortable if Stuart and Randolph could stay with me until I am certain that he is no longer dangerous. "

"First, the young man there. Tomorrow, the former partner of Ruth." Ferdinand stopped to collect his thoughts. "How do you intend to deprogram this reptilian human?"

"An electric shock is what we all agreed to?" I answered apathetically. Everyone nodded. Progress, yes progress, was underway.

Conversation ended abruptly and we all ate in silence, deep in our own thoughts. Reality imposed when the sedative administered to the young man wore off and his groaning invaded the dining room. Mathilda got up and moved towards him. In a calm, reassuring voice, she repeated what we had already told him, emphasizing the fact that what he was seeing now was the real world. He wanted to know why he was tied up if we were the nice guys and ready to help him. Rather than answer his question Mathilda drew him up against her and let him hide his head in her voluptuous chest. She sat like that holding his head and stroking his long, straight black hair in a maternal way. The rest of us waited impatiently, each of us wanting to say or do something to bring this interminable moment of theatrical silence to an end.

"Who are you?" the young man spoke up, as he disentangled himself from Mathilda's cradling arms.

"I am human, like you, and lived through a programming and a deprogramming just like you." She smiled warmly, her eyes twinkling, as she continued to lightly stroke his hair. "You are entering into a better existence in which you will be a vital member of our human society, working and building a future for our race."

"Human-that is what you are and what I am?" He withdrew farther away from her to get a better view of her and the rest of us. "Ok, they look like the images I saw of my friends and colleagues. But, I saw strange looking creatures. What were they?"

"They are also human, with varying degrees of physical anomalies and deformities." He moved even farther away from her and tried to stand up, pulling on the cords as he struggled to break free. That is when Stuart approached him and pushed him back down. Benjamin and Stanislas stayed in the distance. They had apparently changed their minds about interfacing with him.

"Relax!" Stuart ordered in a deep voice. "You are only going to hurt yourself if you continue. We will release the ropes when we are sure that you fully understand what has happened to you." Stuart ignored the rage, emanating from behind this young man' steel, grey eyes and continued. "You were programmed all your life by the bright ones, who wanted you to see your co-workers as beautiful human creatures." He listened. "Not all humans are beautiful!" He said in such a loud voice that we all sat straight in our chairs. "We are ok, but there are others that are not so nice to look at. But, that does not mean that they are not nice to be around."

"Whoa! "Peter screamed. "Calm yourself Stuart. You are scaring him."

"He might just as well understand that now, Peter." Stuart said impatiently. "You can't pretend otherwise."

"Shut up, the two of you." Mathilda pushed them out of the way. "Tell them to get out of here. Randolph, can you help me?"

Randolph shuffled over lazily in her direction. "I agree with them, Mathilda. He just has to accept what Stuart said." He slapped the young man hard on his shoulder, knocking him to the floor. "Yes," he chuckled, "there are a couple humans here that are not beautiful creatures but that is just the way it is. They are human. We all have to make them feel welcome. So we have to get past the physical side. If you don't think that you can do that tell me now and I'll have you locked away in a closet somewhere so you won't have to deal with it."

"Bastard! You are even worse than Stuart or Peter." Mathilda flushed, livid with anger.

"Stop." The young man spoke. "He is right to tell me the truth. It is not their fault if they are not good looking." A smile broke out, revealing his gleaming, white teeth. "Randolph, I like you." He said as he laughed along with Randolph. "Ok, please untie me."

The young man rushed into Randolph's arms and clung onto him for a few minutes. He then turned to Stuart and Peter. "I am just fine now. It will take me time to understand everything but I feel safe with all of you." I wondered how sincere he was.

"You are going to make it." Randolph shook him around playfully. "Which branch do you work in?"

"I am in theoretical physics."

"I'll take him with me, I need an assistant. I'll see what he has been doing."

Mathilda just stood there frozen, confused by what had just happened. Even though I felt sorry for her that her orderly and therapeutic style did not produce the result she expected, I did not mind seeing her left speechless. She recognized my pleasure because she threw me an unabashed smile that I returned.

"Well, that got taken care of rather easily." Ferdinand said enthusiastically, breaking the silence, and everyone but me agreed. For me, it was too easy and my previous feelings resurfaced. I looked straight into the young man's eyes and did not see the complacency that my friends saw. I saw defiance, as he quickly diverted his eyes away from mine. I decided to keep this to myself. Perhaps he would prove me wrong.

"I don't know if all the deprogrammed humans will respond so fast, and show such cooperation. Let's hope so." Ferdinand continued. "Next meeting is for when? I am losing track of time in this center."

Peter looked at me. I moved my head in a definitive...No. I was not ready yet to talk about the time warp with the others. I was worried that broaching this subject would lead to other questions that I could not answer yet, maybe never.

There were still some things that were bothering me and I wasn't certain that Reinhart would reveal all her secrets. I was not looking for a logical answer, but an emotional one. The question was whether or not Reinhart ever had the intention of setting off the explosives in the center of the earth. And if she did, was her intention to ward off alien invaders or stabilize a rebellion on Earth. And, did she construct this Center with its time warp configuration because it gave her the power to change the course of history by wiping out what she believed were the bad elements in society while saving the good ones?

And yet, if her ultimate intention was to rid her world of inferior humans, then why did she go to such lengths to prevent an arbitrary, or unilateral decision, to destroy civilization? She installed a high security system that required a unanimous group decision for activation. Eye and fingerprint identification from all members of the group were necessary once a unanimous vote to detonate the bomb was obtained. It appeared to me that she took the necessary precautions to prevent irrational decisions and that she considered this as a last resort. So, would she have acted like the group of 5 did in face of an eventual defeat in a war against the non-intellectuals? Would she have agreed to set off the bomb when hostilities broke out, like the Group of 5 did, if she had survived?

"Pamela, are you ok?" Peter asked in dismay.

"Just thinking-nothing important, actually." I smiled weakly. "The meeting-yes, perhaps in a couple of days." I suggested. Everyone agreed to be on time in two days for a quick meeting.

"I am looking into different forms of political organization. I believe that a Democratic system would be the best, but will discuss my findings at the meeting." Ferdinand informed us.

We all got up to leave in our different directions.

There were too many ethical issues to consider at this moment and I didn't feel ready to deal with them. I noticed that Jonathan and Imogen left for the music center and my first impulse was to follow them. Instead, I walked aimlessly around the corridors-counting my footsteps-hoping to shake off the never -ending quagmire of questions and doubts.

I passed by a few programmed humans running errands for co-workers. They didn't notice me-something that gave me a liberated feeling. Where to go, was running through my mind, when I found myself standing in front of the door to Randolph's lab. Why not? I could see how things were working out with the deprogrammed human. I was surprised to see Randolph sitting alone looking over a project.

"Randolph!" I called out and he flashed me a big smile.

"Well, this is a pleasant surprise. What brings you here?"

"Just wanted to see if everything was going well with your new assistant-who seems to have left early."

He looked up at the clock in his lab and mentioned that it was not early at all. I was surprised that I had been aimlessly walking for hours and didn't even feel tired.

"Did he cooperate?" I asked, turning away from him.

"Strangely-yes, I would say strangely." He answered, stroking his unshaven chin pensively.

"What are you talking about?" My voice strained with concern.

"Oh, he is a bit odd." He started off. "I decoded his name to make things more human. Already that is weird. It translated into Tirence series 5. What do you think?"

"I don't know. It doesn't mean anything to me." I answered dryly.

"Ok - let me get to the point. I was explaining some basic formulae to him when he interrupted me by telling me that vermin like the two agronomists should be eliminated." Now I understood his concern.

"I told him that eliminating humans was what the bright ones did because they had no respect for human life." He paused. "That did not impress him at all. He went off on a lengthy discourse about how these kinds of verminous creatures could contaminate the human race-turn their beautiful physical appearances into something distasteful and horrifying." He stopped for a second, certainly distracted by my rigid posture and clenched fists. "After a long discussion, turning into an argument, he marched out of here telling me that he wanted to work out in the gym to release his frustrations."

"And, you let him leave?" I screamed.

"Well, what else could I do?"

"Warn us?"

"About what? He doesn't like their appearances, but I can't force him to find them good looking."

"No!' I screamed even louder. "We have got to find him? Are the weapons locked up?"

"You think - No, we are not like that." He jumped off his lab chair and pulled me along with him as we scrambled rapidly along the corridors. We did not see anyone so we headed to the agricultural center. We were too late. The two deformed humans lay motionless, lifeless, on the ground-their bodies brutally beaten and their heads bruised and oozing blood and other substances onto the hard stone ledge that took their lives in a violent fall. That brought a flood of tears to my eyes. I heard Ralph come up behind us-oblivious to what had just happened. He was absent during the assault.

"We have to find him and kill him!" Randolph's high emotional response illuminated by misplaced feelings of guilt, as he screamed that this was all his fault because he should have accompanied Tirence back to his room.

I took his arm to let him lead. "We have to find him but we can't kill him." I said between my waves of violent sobbing. This is what those crazy androids warned me about-the natural violent nature of humans. I couldn't believe it happened. Why was this young man unable to tolerate their existence? A startling thought invaded me: "Killer instinct in humans spanned time. Are we those unpredictable, malicious creatures the androids contend we are?"

He shook off my hand. "I am leaving. Stay with Ralph." Randolph dashed out. I followed knowing that I couldn't let him take on this young man alone. And, I didn't trust him not to kill him.

Before leaving the agricultural unit I alerted everyone over the loud speakers to be careful and I asked Diana and Stuart to find Randolph. Ralph was cradling their dead bodies, big tears dropping on what was only minutes ago warm flesh.

I rushed out of the unit straight into Peter's arms. The Group of 5 appeared out of nowhere, offering their help to find him. I heard Gordon and Flanders saying, "We told her about the true nature of humans but she refused to believe it." I wanted to smack those smart-assed robots only because they were right and I was wrong.

"We have him." Stuart's voice rang out over the loud speakers. "He returned to his cubicle. He claims that he didn't do anything."

"Where is his cubicle?" I asked Gordon who then took the lead. When we arrived, he was crying like a baby. "I didn't do anything." He protested. "I didn't like their looks and yes, I said they were vermin, but I didn't terminate them. Believe me, I didn't terminate them."

"Stop! Don't hurt him." I implored as I pushed Stuart and Diana away from him. The young man was rather shaken up and had taken a few good punches. His right eye was swollen and blood was dripping from his nose. To make it worse, his left arm was used like a punching bag and was hanging badly bruised, maybe broken.

I was not certain that I believed his cries of innocence and yet understood that we could not punish him without genuine proof of guilt. His sobbing, shaking body did give me reason to question his guilt.

"I was happy and fine when I was programmed. Look what has happened. I have been part of your reality for less than one day and you are blaming me for things that I never did. I was better off pro-grammed. Why did you do this to me?" He responded hysterically, his mouth distorted with screams and his eyes bulging out their sockets.

I assured him that we were just going to protect him. We didn't know if he or someone else committed this heinous act. The only solution for the moment was for someone to keep him under sur-veillance until we knew more about what had happened.

I started to leave the room when the former Governor pulled me back into the room. "Pamela, and all the rest of you, this man might be innocent even though he suffers from a kind of superio-rity complex. His type caused a lot of problems in the past. Let's hope that he will get over his prejudices with time." Everyone's at-tention was on the former Governor.

"Can you just get on with what you want to say?" Randolph had arrived on the scene. I noticed that only Jonathan, Eunice and Imogene were not present.

"Our sensory systems have picked up movement in other sectors of the center." There was a clamoring among the humans. "We did not bring it to your attention simply because we wanted to verify the authenticity of the vibrations, which could just be malfunctioning of the sensory systems brought on by your - yes - your revolution." The former Governor's voice was resonating his disgust.

We stood rigid trying to keep our impatience at bay, while he organized his android thoughts. "In any event, before doing anything harmful to this unscrupulous human, I would suggest that you give us the freedom to discover-or to lead you to discover - the reason for the sensory disturbances."

"In the meantime," I spoke up, "we have no choice but to put you in a safe, secure place, Tirence." He nodded obediently. John and Mathieu escorted him to one of the small office rooms in another section of the center, while the rest of us followed the Group of 5.

James, Diana, Stuart and Randolph took the lead, with Peter and I close behind. The rest of the group split up, going in different directions as a backup force. The Group of 5 advanced rapidly, following the sensory vibrations coming from another sector, while we moved cautiously, turning to protect ourselves against anything or anyone coming up from behind.

It seemed like hours that we moved in and around the circular formations of the Center. I was starting to get frustrated and even annoyed with what I imagined was a scam that the androids masterminded to lure us away from the other members of the group. I was ready to call off this ludicrous search when the Group of 5 stopped suddenly in their tracks. Crawford pointed to the left - a small corridor perpendicular to the main corridor was visible. The Group of 5 stepped out of our way.

James, Diana and Stuart moved forward in a furtive ninja style, advancing silently, while Randolph positioned himself behind a large column situated in the middle of the corridor, so that he could launch an offensive and at the same time protect himself if they fired back. Peter and I stayed guarding the entrance to the corridor. There were only four rooms, all situated on the left hand side of the corridor. There was no noise coming from behind the four closed doors which meant that eventually we might have to open them to discover their contents. That is not how things developed. Our fighters were at the end of the corridor, when the four doors flung open simultaneously, unleashing six raging humans.

These depraved humans were as tall as James. Their gowns, grey and shredded, hung loose from their emaciated, haggard bodies. I was fixated on their long tangled hair swaying wildly in the air and hovering over pale faces and glassy, protruding eyes. I wondered if they were drugged. They seemed so dangerously out of control with their arms waving wildly in the air and their bodies staggering and stumbling as they charged at us snarling and howling, like a raging injured animal exploding forth its last jolts of energy in a desperate display of the will to survive.

Randolph put his laser gun on low force and stunned the first three who ran in his direction giving Peter and me the opportunity to restrain them, by tying them up with our sashes. I knew that this would not hold them for long, if they recuperated fast, but there was nothing else available. I turned to the Group of 5, hoping for their support, but they were just standing there watching and fiddling their fingers, their robot faces bent as they stared at us like laboratory animals. Their pathetic indifference in critical moments fueled the brewing anger inside of me. I yelled: "Do something! Don't just stand there like lifeless machines!" I screamed. "Help us!" They moved rapidly to stand guard complaining that they would be powerless to do anything should the three regain consciousness.

The other three lashed out at James, Diana and Stuart in a pathetically juvenile manner. They fended off their weak arms flailing assault, as their aggressors resorted to scratching, clawing, kicking and even biting to escape their enemies.

James, Diana and Stuart played with them by coaxing them to try to catch them, hoping that they would tire and give up. But, it didn't happen and finally one by one lost patience. A couple hard hits from our defenders took them down. The one young woman and two young men lay immobile on the floor alongside their three other comrades.

"Well, that was quick once you decided to react." Randolph broke the silence. "They look terrible. Can starvation and fear drive humans to such excessively violent behavior? Or, were they always a band of lunatics?" He shrugged his shoulders. "Is it possible that they could have done away with our agronomists?" He added.

No one replied, but that did not mean that we were not affected by what Randolph just said. "Tirence is in perfect physical condition and visibly strong, the more logical culprit. And, yet, he denied responsibility for the death of the agronomists, pleading his innocence. We will definitely have to question the members of this renegade group when they wake up..." Crawford's voice interrupted my thoughts.

"You see, Pamela," Crawford rushed in front of me. "There is a lot of truth in what we told you."

"This is a very unfortunate situation." I said as I elbowed him away from me. "How do I know that you and the others did not mastermind this drama just to create havoc in our community?"

"Huh!" He choked out an android laugh. "You have a lot to learn about living with humans."

I didn't continue the conversation with him. John and Mathieu appeared with stretchers. It took us awhile to move them all into the hospital unit and strap them down in the beds. We ordered food from the kitchen staff as they desperately needed to be nourished. On close examination, their haggard, drawn faces, dry, swollen tongues and thin bodies were the physically visible signs of lack of food and water. Their dull, lifeless, glassy eyes and erratic behavior could have been brought on by a fear of us, but also from starvation. Peter and I took the first guard, while the others went off to have dinner. We later took turns guarding them during the night.

Two members of the group were unable to swallow properly and drifted in and out of consciousness. The other four complained of stomach pains, as they slowly sipped a liquid beverage that the androids recommended. Flanders and Gordon stood patiently looking on. Even though I was more inclined to ask them to leave us alone, I solicited Flanders to bring us IV rehydration tubes.

"We destroyed the solutions." He smiled scornfully.

"Why did you do that?" Another incredible turn of events that irritated and enflamed me.

"Well...it seemed the best thing to do."

"I don't have time to play games with you. I just want answers!" I shouted at him.

"Ok. We destroyed certain life support, like intravenous rehydration, which by the way contained water and dissolved salts, or electrolytes, when you attacked the Center." He looked down at his feet. "We expected you to lose. When we saw Diana come up through the floor of the transport center, we all smiled with delight. It was time to end you and your group. We had no intention of saving anyone of you." He tried to retract his statement by adding. "Actually, we did not want to be presented with the dilemma of deciding who to treat, so we destroyed basic life support substances."

"Look at me Edward." He raised his head. "You were not even going to save me. That is not what you said a couple days ago when you pretended that you wanted to terminate Randolph to liberate the Reinhart inside of me."

"You are right. That was our original objective-to isolate Elisabeth and then suppress what emotional and intellectual structure was left of you, Pamela. But things changed." He said softly. "We knew that you, rather Elisabeth, would be outraged if she were the only survivor. So, we decided that you all would be terminated. But, as you see, you all survived because we lost. It was definitely a surprise. It seemed incredulous that your group made it out the transport unit and into the corridor. We had confidence in our programmed fighters. We never expected Diana to take down her aggressor and believed that Stuart would fall if he had to tackle the two of them."

"You disgust me!"

Then I totally lost and it and stomped in front of Flanders. Looking into his android eyes, I spit a slobbery mess onto his recoiling frame.

"I am outraged by your frequent resort to dishonesty to save face, or to climb out of a self-imposed conundrum. I am now starting to wonder if you are capable of being truthful." I could feel the anger rushing up inside of me, something that my rigid body, clenched teeth and tight fists communicated to him and his colleagues.

"We are truthful. You asked us why we wanted to terminate Randolph. We gave you the answer." He cleared his throat. "Now you asked me why we destroyed the IV solutions. We told you the truth."

"You should have told me everything from the beginning." I said firmly.

"That would not have been logical, condemning ourselves, and we are logical creations." He folded his arms and fixed his eyes on mine, while little by little the corners of his mouth curled upward, revealing his android teeth.

He was playing mind games with me and I didn't like that, but the Reinhart inside of me had a different reaction. Her warmth comforted and calmed me. I could see the situation through her eyes and I understood that she found their behavior quite normal; after all they were only machines. So, I decided to take a different approach. "I know that you were using feeding tubes for the young, male agronomist." He raised his eyebrows. "So, where are these feeding tubes, and what are the basic ingredients in the tube feeding formula?"

"I don't have the proper composition, but they contained protein, carbohydrates, fats, glutamine and vitamins. Unfortunately, the clean-up crew disposed of the feeding tubes and the feeding solutions after the termination of the male agronomist." He adjusted his voice to a low, comforting tone. "I don't know if the basic substances are still available in the pharmaceutical unit but it is too late for you to do anything for those two." He pointed to the two unconscious humans, one woman and one man. "It would be kinder to terminate them so that they would not suffer any more."

Gordon moved into our discussion and asked me if we wanted them to take care of the humans during the night. Her suggestion sounded both outrageous and imprudent, so I snarled a grating "no!" and then refused her offer.

"He told you the truth about everything." She said in a dry, lifeless, android tone. "And, he is telling you the truth about the two of them. They are at the end of their lives."

I was frustrated with the insolence of the Group of 5 and disappointed in myself because I did not know how to save the two humans. Under the circumstances, our choices were limited. Refusing the impersonal termination chamber by according a human presence to comfort and reassure them when they took their final breath appeared to be the kindest alternative.

It did not help me, though, to dispel my animosity towards the androids for orchestrating, even if by inadvertence, the deplorable situation we were confronting. So, I took my frustrations out on Gordon and Flanders, one more time, demanding retribution on their part. "I expect a formal apology from the Group of 5 for withholding vital information relevant to this group and for destroying the IV solutions." I ordered in a cold, detached, authoritative voice, hoping to hide some of my profound sadness over their defiance and the imminent loss of lives. Their reaction did not appease me in any way, because Gordon and Flanders just shrugged their shoulders and walked away.

The lives of the two young humans ended before Peter and I left the hospital unit. Neither Peter nor I had any experience with the dying process, even though we did see the dead bodies of those two agronomists and other humans during the revolution. I imagined the dying process to be a serene, practically euphoric experience, because of what I had read about death in the library, years ago. I saw it as a glamorous passage from a physical self to a spiritual self which would be merged with others in total bliss and harmony.

I sat patiently on a small stool that I placed between the two beds so that I could calmly hold and caress the hand of each of the young humans until they took their final breath. I realized that Reinhart's cold, analytical side had not surfaced inside of me to shield me from the emotional impact of death, should there be any.

Peter marched back and forth across the room, his head bent low and his hands clenched, trying in his own way to control his anxiety.

At the very same moment the bodies of these young humans trembled and writhed violently, my fingers crushing under the force of their hands. Their faces grew white and sullen and they gasped and struggled to resist that final breath. And then in face of death's ultimate onslaught, they opened their eyes, revealing dark, black pits, of nothingness. Horrified, I quickly closed my eyes in the hope that I would not be drawn into their final waves of passing. When I eventually found the courage to open my eyes, I was no longer seated but standing frozen as I gazed down upon their ghastly white, pain strained faces. I quickly pried their lifeless hands away from mine. I felt dirty on the inside and the outside, like something or someone had penetrated me, trying to defile my very essence. I wanted to wash away that feeling of death that they left upon me.

I sought Peter who was now alongside me. His arms moved consolingly around me and, we stayed bound, as if only together we had the courage to cast our eyes one last time on the lifeless bodies of those very young humans. We were both profoundly affected by the ravenous victory of death, the lack of a peaceful transition into another world and we fell into a restless silence and sadness.

Eventually, I regained some of my composure and called for an android to move their bodies to another part of the hospital unit. Even though starvation was the logical cause of their death, I wanted to be certain that they had not voluntarily or involuntarily consumed something that was poisonous, or swallowed a drug to calm their pain. I did not want to supervise the autopsy procedure and thus implored Flanders to carry it out and give me a complete report, which he did. The report confirmed that their deaths were the result of starvation.

We continued for days to hand feed the remaining four, keeping them under restraints until the pernicious effects of starvation had disappeared. I made an effort to converse with the one remaining young woman while spoon feeding her dinner because she seemed more alert than the others. She told me that she was very confused about what had happened over the last week or so. "We were driven by hunger." She said at one point. "We were so hungry that nothing else seemed to matter."

"Why didn't you try to contact one of us humans?"

"We didn't know that you existed. We thought that we were all alone. We tried to hide from those humanoid machines. We were so afraid." She spoke in a weak voice and in short sentences as if it pained her just to speak. I wasn't certain that she was telling me everything.

I sat observing her now that she was fully recovered with no haggardness, or even gauntness, from her malnutrition visible. She had a round face, big, brown eyes, full symmetrical lips, and long, wavy, brown hair that fell naturally, framing her face. Tall, with a long torso and an undefined waist, she was endowed with large breasts and wide, fleshy shoulders. Her narrow hips and long legs seemed to accentuate the top-heaviness of her upper body. The Pamela side of me wondered if men would consider her sexy or maternal. I almost felt a cringing, coming from the Reinhart side.

No one got any more information than I did from the other patients. They all spoke of hunger, fear, and confusion. Days passed before the four surviving humans were physically capable of meeting with us for questioning. Our entire group was present to listen to the testimony.

"Did you harm anyone?" Ferdinand started the questioning. There was a lot of mumbling before a tall, well-built, muscular, dark brown, almost black, skinned man replied. He had short, thick black frizzy hair, dark brown eyes, a flat nose, wide cheek bones and large, sumptuous lips. "I understand what you are referring to. Yes, we did go to the agricultural unit." He said in a deep masculine voice. "There were two very strange looking humans working in the garden. They frightened us. They were still connected so we had to give them our codes. They smiled so warmly that we felt better. We begged them for some food. They refused. We started to pick the vegetables and fruits, piling it on our gowns to carry it. They ran after us and started to hit us with their heavy shovels." He sighed. "We defended ourselves, pushing them away. They kept coming after us screaming that the vegetables and fruits were not ready to be harvested and that they were not ripe enough to be eaten. We didn't care, we were so hungry."

"Stop! It wasn't our fault." The young girl I spoke to a few days earlier retorted. "They kept hitting us. We pushed them and hit them back. They did not abandon their unrelenting effort to retrieve the meager number of vegetables that we were carrying. Everything happened so fast, we didn't have time to think. I cannot speak for the rest of the group which eventually turned wild losing all reason. I was afraid and had strong feelings of dislike for those agronomists who tried to crush us with their shovels. Even though we were able to dodge them easily enough in the beginning, they threated to inform other people in the center who they said would terminate us. That was the moment our rational thoughts vanished and we rushed them."

She stopped to take a deep breath. "Maybe we hit them too hard because they stumbled and fell, and we continued to hit and bang their bodies and heads against the stone ledge surrounding the vegetable garden. We didn't want to terminate them, we only wanted to weaken them enough that we would have time to escape. We backed off when we realized that they were no longer moving and that a red substance was gushing from their heads." She choked up with tears. "Why were they so mean to us? We didn't even take enough food." Streams of tears ran down her face. "They were right it was inedible! We were so hungry!" She stood trembling in despair.

It was evident that we had suspected the wrong person. Tirence was not responsible. Now, what were we going to do? Could we let this frenzied group of humans go unpunished? Was it, as they described it, an unfortunate accident?

"Is there anyone else who has anything to say concerning this incident?" Ferdinand asked. They bowed their heads pathetically and then rushed into each other's arms. Sobbing sounds seeped out from behind their huddle. We looked on with stern faces, our eyes squinting in harmony with our seared lips. "Then you can follow the android guards into the other room while we discuss the proper course of action to be taken to rectify this unfortunate and sad problem."

"I feel so responsible. I should never have left those two young agronomists alone." Ralph's tear-filled eyes and pale face inspired sympathy. "I left for the afternoon, as you all know, to get away from the routine. I needed a change. So I passed by the vacation center and strolled lazily in front of the tropical forest, instead of maintaining my surveillance of the agricultural unit. If I had only been there!" He screamed as he hit the tabletop hard with his small, frail fist. "I would have given them the food. What did it matter if it was not edible? I am sure that they would have left without harming anyone."

"You don't know, Ralph." Benjamin spoke up. "They were frightened and starving. They might have knocked you over as well." Heads nodded and Ralph wiped away his tears and regained control of himself.

"We have been in their company for several days now." I began. "It is necessary, I believe, to consider independently the two causes of action: their complicity to steal the food and the death of the two humans, both of which were provoked by raging hunger." I sighed. "And, I got the autopsy report, which is in every way accurate and carried out in proper form. Apparently, their dementia was caused by both starvation and thirst. There was no sign of drugs or poison in the systems of four who survived or the two who died."

The group voted immediately on the issue of theft, taking into account the information that I just disclosed, and we all agreed to forgive them, because it was due to starvation. And yet, to live in society we all had to respect the rights of everyone else to eat. They would have to be taught the rudimentary rules of societal living.

The death of the two humans was more complicated. Even though it might have been accidental the fact that they left without trying to help the humans, without even verifying whether they were still alive, was inexcusable. They showed no compassion for their victims. Instead, they hid in another part of the center. Additionally, there was some question as to whether or not it was true that they did not know that we existed. They were crossing into occupied corridors and must have hidden from us. They knew that we were no longer connected just like them, so why didn't they approach us? None of us believed that they were oblivious to our existence. The only logical explanation for that behavior was that they were afraid.

We agreed that we had to punish them to discourage any similar actions. Taking the life of another human, even accidentally, had to have some consequences. But how should we punish them?

"We should confine them for a few months." Diana suggested. Half of the group agreed with her.

"I don't see how this can be constructive. We should make them pay for their actions in another way. Why not make them work in the agricultural section, as farmers, under the watchful eyes of android guards for several months. And, at the same time, why not make them attend classes on how to live with other humans and become productive, honest, and reliable members of our community?" I proposed.

"That is just too nice, Pamela." John retorted. "They must understand that they were cruel. Perhaps they should be confined for 2 weeks, which would be a long time in the Center and receive instructions on communicating and living with others and then carry out 2 months of service in the agricultural section."

John's proposal got a unanimous vote. Ferdinand read the decision to the group. The rebels did not argue or protest in any way. They thanked us for letting them go on living and each one of them, the three men, and one woman, promised to become respectable members of our human community.

When I informed the Group of 5 of our decision, they let out loud, crackling android laughs. "You are so naïve, Pamela. Sometimes, refreshingly naïve but in this case dangerously so!" Flanders commented in a loud voice.

"You should listen to the Reinhart inside of you. It would appear that you are still living in an imaginary world. I'm afraid you'll have to learn the hard way." Crawford added.

Their remarks bothered and haunted me during the daytime. They tormented my sleep, plunging me into nightmares in which these humans stalked the halls, kidnapping and then torturing my loved ones and friends. Sometimes the face of my son would slide into my dreams and I would awaken, gasping, ready to scream and strike out at imaginary enemies as sweat streamed down my contorted face. Peter, deep in sleep, remained undisturbed and, eventually, I fell back into a troubled sleep, where I visualized myself drowning in my own pools of blood as they ruthlessly ripped my body to pieces. Bloodstained and diabolical, they represented the vermin of past generations brought to life to destroy our hopes and dreams for a better future.

Some observed that I avoided them completely the next few days. One night I finally rolled over and spilled my weeping guts to Peter who held me for a few minutes.

"You must find it in your heart to forgive them, as we have done. They were just lost souls." He went with me to visit them the next day. Their warm, kind eyes and friendly smiles were enough to convince me that they were not the cruel and wretched creatures of my nightmares. They were innocent young people who understood their mistakes and wanted to be accepted. Knowing dreams often reveal truths, I hoped they lied this time!

"We are moving forward. Our community of humans is growing and we are shaping a positive future." I said to myself. But I still had doubts. Were we a new generation of humans able to avoid the mistakes of the past? Or, were we, by nature, unpredictable and dangerous creatures?

Chapter 9-Human Nature

The weeks went by rapidly as we completed outstanding projects and started new ones. Dr. Miller's metallic limbs were now covered with android skin. The experience was rewarding and instructive for the members of the group. After once the proper elasticity of the plant was achieved, giving it the subtle texture of human skin, I treated it with a biochemical solution to enhance the bio-sensory nature of the plant. When the process was completed, we watched as the fabricated skin moved naturally into place, sealing itself around Dr. Miller's robotic limbs. It was amazing!

She thanked me over and over again for giving her back a strikingly, slim and sexy, robotic body. And, the fact that she was considerably taller than in her original android state pleased her very much. It was quite amusing to watch as she proudly promenaded around the corridors, swinging her hips in a seductive way to catch our attention and irritate Crawford. I was present when he reprimanded Gordon, years ago now, for vulgarizing the android body by swinging her hips like certain unrefined humans.

There were days that were more challenging and memorable than others, days that marked changes in our behavior and our history.

One of those days was particularly instructive and concerned the second enormous task - to integrate the reptilian humans into society. Deprogramming all of them at the same time seemed too risky. So, we decided to simply deprogram Ruth's former partner first. The reptilian humans did not have code numbers that translated easily into first names. Frustrated with playing around with his name, we finally agreed to call him Clarence.

Because Ruth had prepared him for the deprogramming by showing him pictures of reptiles and drawing pictures of him, all of us believed that Clarence would pass into our reality without any secondary consequences, the reason why we did not take any precautions. Ruth did not want him to receive an electric shock, so we agreed to try something different, or to simply disconnect the visual receptor. Ruth also did not want Mathilda to be present because she wanted to be the person that Clarence would turn to in his hour of need.

As a result, Ruth, Sarah and I were alone with him when he passed into the real world. We naively expected him to calmly accept his new appearance and our flagrant naivety almost cost us our lives.

He was panic-stricken when he looked down over his body and responded by letting out excruciating screams as he lashed at us with his bulging, muscular reptilian arms, forcing us to back up. He stopped short when he got close to us and let his reptilian eyes, livid with a flaming, red anger, but in a sepulchral calm . . . in a reptilian predatory study of us and our every move, like wily snakes do before closing in on the prey. We stood spell-bound, our fear transforming into sweat, a sweat that oozed like a vile perfume from every pore of our bodies intoxicating the environment. Time ticked away before he broke this uncomfortable silence, by emitting raucous, terrifying, primitive sounds that rose from the very pits of his existence and vibrated with profound wrathfulness.

"How am I going to live with this wretched body? I find it so repulsive! How, could you have expected me to calmly accept my true appearance? Where are you Ruth?" His grating, frenzied voice accentuating his indignation, sorrow and humiliation. She moved towards him and, in a voice forlorn of hope, he rebuked her. "You, you, are wretched and uncaring. Why, oh why did you convince me to confront myself when I was blissfully contented before? I despise you and your insensitivities!" His reptilian hands slammed down on the table, toppling it on its side.

"Please Clarence calm down." She pleaded as she reached out to comfort him. Sarah and I stood together immersed in the wet warmth of his heavy breath, as he snorted contemplatively in our direction, preparing his next assault.

He pushed Ruth out of his way and charged violently at us. We moved rapidly to the other side of him. He was less agile than we were. He swirled, lost his balance and rammed his head into the adjacent wall. Recovering rapidly, he spun round in our direction flaring his nostrils and swinging his heavy tail. Eluding it, the three of us rushed for the door, slamming and locking him behind us. My only thought at that moment was that we had chosen the right room to deprogram him as not all the rooms were equipped with resistant lock and block systems.

I went straight to the intercom to request backup and James, Diana and Stuart were with us in a few minutes. We could hear Clarence throwing objects and emitting loud, reptilian screeching noises. We maintained our guard of the room waiting for him to calm down or try to escape. The uncertainty of his actions gave the impression that time stood still.

Diana was particularly restless, pacing up and down the corridor while Stuart and James sat in a lotus position on the floor maintaining an inner calm. Ruth and Sarah stood hand in hand. I was getting tired of waiting and was ready to suggest that we open the door and rush him when he called out to Ruth.

"Ruth." His voice was calm. "I am alright now. I would like to see you alone, if possible."

We all warned her not to go in on her own, but she would not listen to any of us. "I know him. He is a kind man. I trust him. Give me a few minutes alone with him before coming in."

"A few minutes? What does that mean?" Diana stood planted in front of the door. "It is too dangerous!"

"No, Diana, he needs me. I want to help him."

She was not going to listen to us so we opened the way for her to enter. Her life was now in her own hands. We listened. Their voices were low and calm, far too low for us to decipher the words and understand the content of their conversation. I felt particularly uneasy, because, in spite of the recklessness of the androids, Reinhart was responsible for these reptilian creatures. Nonetheless, the absence of screams and loud noises was reassuring.

I diverted my attention from this problem, by studying Diana. Her long, thick black hair moved gracefully over her shoulders as she paced the corridor. Her immaculate Asian face, with slightly slanted eyes and full lips, was magically enticing as was the full-length of her tall, slender athletic body. She was a masterpiece of perfection in comparison to some of the less fortunate humans whose deprogramming promised to be difficult. I smiled to myself, knowing that I could appreciate her beauty, without being attracted sexually to her, or, even more importantly, being jealous of it.

The door opened brusquely, startling me from my thoughts. Ruth exited walking stiffly. "Pamela, can I talk to you?" She asked and I nodded. We moved out of the range of the others before she explained to me what was happening. "He is calmer, but has not yet come to terms with his physical self. He asked me to talk to you to find out if you could change him to make him look more human?"

"Perhaps I should speak to him directly?"

She moved her eyes nervously in their sockets, before answering. "It is risky. He may turn violent again."

"I shall keep the door open if I need to escape."

When I entered, he was on all fours, holding his torso and head erect, his long tail strewn majestically behind him. It was a rather proud position for someone who was distraught by his appearance. I pretended not to notice and sat down next to him.

"You seem calmer."

"No, I am controlling myself because I would like to rip you to pieces. I can't identify the strong emotion that your presence inspires in me, after all I have only just been deprogrammed, unclothed."

I ignored his remark and feigned indifference, when in reality, I was scared that he might turn on me and injury me. "Perhaps, Clarence, you should go now with me and Ruth to see that you have other friends and colleagues that share aspects of your appearance." I suggested. He remained immobile. "I have to study in more detail your species, but if Reinhart believed that your species was a viable alternative for humans, for their survival, then it must be because your species is very interesting physiologically, intellectually and biologically."

"So you can't make me look more human?" He diverted the discussion.

"I don't know, but I can look into it, if that is really what you want."

"But, as you said a few minutes ago, you think that I have more than just this horrifying exterior?"

"Yes, I think so, but, I want to make it very clear to you, I do not find your exterior...horrifying." His eyes turned full on me. "It is important that you go beyond your physical appearance and appreciate your capabilities."

"I am not very optimistic, but believe that I can pretend for the moment that I like myself-at least long enough for you to prove to me one way or the other that I should be proud of what I am, or demonstrate how you can modify me and give me more human characteristics."

"Ok, that is a deal." I sighed. "I shall need your help with other reptilian humans. Already, I would like your opinion on how to engage in their deprogramming and how you identify with them."

"You mean that you want to collaborate with me?"

"Yes, collaborate is the right word."

He got up and moved around the room. I waited patiently, hoping for the best.

"Ok, we have a deal, but I don't want you to tell anyone else."

"No problem. I won't repeat our discussion to anyone else." I said. "But, I have to ask you this question because you were very violent and aggressive earlier. You frightened and threatened us." He nodded his large, triangular head. "Do you think that you can keep your violence under control?"

"Good question. I don't know how to answer it. I thought that I understood my differences after all those long discussions I had with Ruth. But, my reptilian nature took over."

"No. I disagree. Your species was not known for being aggressive. They were territorial and did not like to share their space with others. Your reaction was your human not your reptilian side. That is why I am going to ask you again if you are ready to control yourself around others?"

"I promise to try, if that is enough for the moment."

"And, what should we tell the others?" I asked.

"Tell them that I have come to terms with my appearance and am ready to become an integral member of your group."

"Ok. We have an agreement." I said and reached out and took his reptilian claw in my hand and shook it to prove my commitment. His mouth spread into a sly, flat reptilian smile.

The entire group was crowded in the hallway when we left the room. They were at a discreet distance from the door, which was left ajar, respecting our private conversation. I told them that Clarence was ready to meet the other reptilian humans and help them through the shock of entering into the real world. I noticed that Clarence was standing on his hind legs in a convincingly calm, easy going way.

"I am ready to meet them and to help all of them through the shock of entering into the real world." He offered, after apologizing for his behavior. "I would just like to wait until tomorrow." He rumbled on about needing time to discover his body and appreciate his differences. That was positive.

Ruth told me that she planned to spend the rest of the day and the night with Clarence. I hoped that it would turn out to be a good idea.

We split up and I ran into Mathilda who made it clear to me that she was upset that we had not invited her to the deprogramming of Clarence. Mathilda's caring, therapeutic style did not work well with Tirence. She was too kind, not direct enough. I did not mention that but rather told her that her skill would be much more useful now that he would be learning how to interact with others.

"So, the meeting tomorrow morning is still on?" She changed the subject.

"Yes, of course. Sorry, I forgot all about it, but you are right, we have the meeting. I think that Ferdinand is interested in explaining political organization."

"Yes, but..." she hesitated. "That is not the most important problem, at least not from my standpoint." She stood very erect with her left hand on her hip, in a self-assertive manner. "We need to deal with the deprogramming of the others. We should have tackled that problem from the beginning."

"It takes time, Mathilda. You weren't here when Clarence passed over into the real world." She twisted her mouth in disgust. It irritated me, but I was not interested in arguing. "Even though he was presumably prepared to move into our world, he had a violent reaction to his physical appearance."

She did not reply, just maintained her assertive posture.

"Well, you should feel free to bring all this up tomorrow." I said behind a friendly smile.

"Ok, I am off to visit Tirence now. Randolph thinks that he has innate prejudices that should be dealt with immediately."

She turned and I watched her walk slowly, seductively swinging her hips. "Not only is she sexually enticing but she likes attention and power. Yes, she wants power." I rationalized trying to stifle attraction to the swinging hips.

I found myself, for a second time this week, at the door of Randolph's lab. I knew that Tirence was with Mathilda, but was surprised that Randolph was not alone. Gordon was there. They both looked up at me as I entered the lab.

"This must be my lucky week." Randolph said.

"Excuse me, Pamela, I just came to apologize to Randolph about that horrible decision to have him terminated weeks-seems years-ago." Gordon said, simulating a deep, sexy tone that complemented her tight, skimpy shorts and low cut blouse. "I never wanted that to happen. It was an administrative decision."

I wrinkled my nose and stuck it at her. "Well, it was your fault, Pamela. We had no idea of your revolution - and, well, we wanted Elisabeth to get stronger." I laughed at her lack of subtlety, placing the blame on me. It made me feel good to laugh and I was relieved when Randolph joined in with me.

"Well, I guess that I better go back to studying human emotions with some of our new members." She walked slowly in the direction of the door. "I am enjoying working closely with Mathilda in this area. She is very intuitive." She was provoking me, so I ignored her statement and said goodbye.

"What was she doing here, Randolph?"

"She did apologize, telling me how happy she was that I had been spared and saved by you and Stuart."

"And..." I coaxed him.

"Oh, she wanted to know if we could continue to be sexual partners. In fact, that is where we were when you walked in." He displayed an innocent, boyish look. "You saved me!"

"You weren't going to say-Yes?" I asked teasingly.

"Of course not. But then we did have some interesting moments together before she turned to those boring sex films that she recovered from her computer system. You remember?" I nodded. "They helped me to diversify my moves and positions, but I never got excited watching them." He sighed. "The good old days!" He smiled flirtatiously, his eyes twinkling.

"Yes, the good old days." I repeated nostalgically. "I miss those silly discussions we had that ended up in childish laughter and I admit we had hot moments!" I sighed shaking my head. He nodded knowing fully what I meant without judging me.

"I feel like there are more problems today than before." I added, knowing that my statement probably made no real sense.

"So, are you missing me or are you just missing a good laugh?" He asked, his pupils wide with desire.

"Don't know which." I ventured.

He stood up and moved over in my direction. His arms were around me, pulling me up against him, and I felt my body go limp.

"You know, Pamela," he said softly, masking the intensity of his feelings. "We never had the opportunity to put on a show for that miserable Gordon. Stuart interrupted us twice, right here in this lab." He said light-heartedly. "Now he understands why his presence bothered us. He is enjoying himself a lot these days."

Things were different today and in spite of the fact that it felt good to be in his arms, I wrestled myself loose. "He is not faithful, Pamela." He said as he reluctantly let go.

I saw Peter so many times during the day that I couldn't imagine that he would have time to be with anyone else, and, yet he did find the time. Even that miserable Crawford brought that to my attention during one of our group meetings.

I knew Peter might have casual, or spontaneous, sex with other women. Yes, he told me a long time ago that I should not complicate things because there was a very big difference between sex and making love. What he did with others did disturb me and, even though I knew that we were inseparable on a higher level and that our love for each other was immutable, I did feel the pain of abandonment...maybe even jealousy.

But, was I like Peter? Did I also need to find sexual pleasure with others, like I did in the past? I looked at Randolph who was standing aloof, ready to abandon his conquest of me. And yet, I knew that just being close to Randolph aroused feelings inside of me and that those feelings were not indicative of a casual encounter to add provocativeness to my life. My mind involuntarily turned back in time and I could feel that devastating, agonizing fear that overcame me when I discovered that the androids had sedated him and were dragging him off to the termination unit. It was as if my life stood still and nothing else mattered but saving him at any cost.

Yes, Randolph was more than just a close friend or a comrade in arms and yet the depth of my feelings for him alluded me. "Were my feelings for him just emotionally brought back memories of a binding relationship that helped me survive my recent past? Could I just have casual sex with him? Did my relationship with him exist on a higher, emotionally profound, charged level?" I pondered, knowing that I had to find the answer, whatever the consequence. And so I moved back into Randolph's arms and ran my fingers through his long, thick wavy hair. "I missed you, Randolph, more than I want to admit."

He ran his tongue slowly over his open lips. "That is because there is something very special between us, Pamela." He whispered in my ear.

Those disconcerting, self-imposed restraints of fidelity lifted and I felt free to let my lustful cravings for him surface with an eagerness that I had never shown him before. His playfulness turned to passion and a ravenous appetite for pleasure birthed inside of us as our bodies moved onto the cold floor. He caressed my body so tenderly, while his lips touched me so lovingly that my inhibitions disappeared and I responded so easily and willingly to him, fondling and caressing him with the same intensity and adoration... moving into different positions...heightening our seemingly insatiable desire for each other. On top he let me move and move, freely, let my dominatrix fantasies soar a bit. I savored every minute of our intimacy and felt alive and fulfilled when our bodies trembled and our voices rung out as violent waves of euphoric pleasure invaded us.

Randolph rolled off of me and we laid next to each other on the cold floor smiling up at the ceiling. He turned towards me and then ran his hand up and down my naked body as if he wanted to be certain that he had not just awaken from a dream. "Wow! That was fantastic!" He exclaimed pretending to be that seductive joker.

"You are going to have to add some romantic expressions to your register of seductive speech, Randolph." I said as I grabbed his broad chin teasingly. "You know a woman wants to hear something more than Wow!"

"I know. Stuart told me that I had a reputation for being particularly noncommittal. I'll just let_my touch speak my emotions." He puffed up his cheeks to make me laugh and then blew out the air. "But I don't want serious, permanent commitment. That is why Mathilda is fine for me. She just wants sex and nothing more."

"There are some very beautiful women here."

"No, Pamela, I belong to you. I don't know if I love you." I felt slightly disappointed to hear that. "But, I know that I would be unable to live very long without you."

I wanted to hide my strong feelings for him, when I finally answered him in an unanimated voice. "I know what you mean, Randolph." I couldn't tell him more because that would have been unfair and I was still not certain how to speak my heart. 'Could I love two men at the same time?' was the question that I didn't want to deal with now.

"And Diana?" I asked to change the subject.

"Oh, she is gorgeous and making love to her is like making love to a tigress! But she is devoted to Jonathan and has a weakness for Stuart." His lips curved up, revealing his bright, white teeth. "Stuart fills so many categories for her-brother, friend, combat partner, and lover. Yes, she is obsessed with Stuart, but, as I said, emotionally loyal to Jonathan."

"Interesting." He was certainly closer to the gossip than I was. "I thought that Jonathan was attracted to Imogen, the musician."

"Maybe. He looks good now that we had put him back together and she does seem to be interested in him." He leaned over me and stared intensely into my eyes, perhaps searching for the truth or the profoundness of my feelings, before he jumped up. "Got to get dressed. That Tirence should be back here soon."

I rushed to get myself together as well. We were sitting at the lab table pretending to discuss mathematical formulae when Tirence arrived.

"Hi, I just finished my session with my psychiatrist, Mathilda." He announced. "What are you doing here, Pamela?"

"Do I have to have a reason to be here, Tirence?"

"Sorry, I am still a bit awkward with ordinary conversation." He said as he moved over to the empty lab seat and sat across from us.

"Actually, I am glad that I ran into you, Tirence. I want to say again that I am sorry about what happened and hope that you don't hold any grudge." I said, in what I thought was a reassuring manner.

Instead, he looked at me with stern, cold eyes. "Grudges? I don't know what you mean. I was upset about what happened, but now that I am working hard with Randolph, I have put that out of my mind."

"So, you have decided to go beyond physical appearances, I presume?" I was testing him.

He snarled at me. "I think that I have the right to avoid people I don't like to look at. I would not be honest if I said that physical appearances don't make any difference, would I?" I could almost feel the depth of coldness in his eyes.

"Well, that is too bad. That means that your circle of friends will be more limited and that you might miss out on getting to know interesting members of the group. But, so long as you don't threaten anyone's life, you can live along side of us."

"Well said." Randolph jumped in. "Now, Tirence, get over here. I have some work for you." He waved goodbye to me.

I rushed back to Mathilda's office to get her impressions of Tirence. Mathilda told me that he was a little different. "Some people are very visual, Pamela. Those people just can't get past appearances. Tirence is one of them. There were many like that in human history. I studied psychological files on those people even when I was programmed." She sat back in her chair in a relaxed position, her open hands visible. "When we were programmed, everything was beautiful to our eyes. We didn't see any defective human appearances."

"So, what you are saying is that you never understood the problem of rejection or discrimination based upon appearance, because you did not experience it yourself?" I suggested.

"Exactly. Now, take our situation today. Are there members of this community who you find unattractive?"

That was certainly a trap that I intended to avoid. "I believe that I am not fixated on appearance. One could say that the Reinhart in me helps me to a certain extent. But, I am able to go beyond the physical side." She stared intensely as if she didn't believe me, so I continued. "You see, I met with Gordon discussing those problems when I was no longer connected. In the beginning, I was afraid of some of the people that I saw. But, yes, I have gotten past that. And today I could always rectify their problems, give them a better appearance, if need be."

"True, but you haven't done that yet, have you?"

"Yes, I did for Jonathan because he was suffering. I would do it for someone else, if need be. But if someone is comfortable with his or her appearance, why interfere?"

"True." She sat in deep thought for a few minutes. "Tirence is definitely someone who needs to be watched. He might not physically harm someone, but he might make cruel comments to those who have deformities. Of course, most of them are still connected so they would not be sensitive. But, there are all those reptilian humans who he might irritate with his juvenile comments. As you know, I am working with him on this." She sighed. "Is discriminating against others a natural human trait?"

"Apparently. You should go to the library and read the historical tapes. That could be very helpful for you. You have to remember, though, that the androids saved historical events that they considered to be relevant and thus altered our history."

"Ok, I'll remember that. I do like that idea, though, about going to the Library. Yes, I shall do that." I started to get up. "Wait, I just wanted to assure you that the children are doing very well. They are absorbing information at a rapid pace, so programming is not necessary." I nodded. She had already told me that several times. "And, they have a good schedule with sports and creative arts and music."

"Yes, you are doing a good job. Frederic is so happy with life on the inside." I did not know where she was going with this conversation, but sensed her need to talk to me.

"And, Pamela, it is true that I meet with Gordon to discuss emotions." I sat back down. "I am not conspiring with her." She smiled. "She is interesting because she sees everything from a machine's point of view. Sometimes, I need to approach a problem from a purely logical standpoint rather than an emotional one. I find my discussions with her helpful. Actually, I learn, if you like."

I didn't answer right away. In fact, I had just said the same thing when I mentioned getting past physical appearances through my meetings with Gordon. Mathilda was making a good point. I smiled back and added. "I understand what you are saying. I hated my sessions with her, but miss them now. She has an interesting, sometimes perverted, approach to human emotions. She does give you another perspective of things. If you find these sessions helpful, then continue. Just be careful, though. She is a manipulator. And, Mathilda, she believes that sex is her way to developing a true emotional configuration." I stopped to get my bearings. "You know that I had a sexual relationship with her; Crawford brought that up during the group meeting that the androids attended." She nodded, while I grappled with how much to tell her. "She is a Great sexual partner." I said, underscoring Great.

Mathilda's head dropped. "I know, Pamela." That was enough for me to understand that they were more than colleagues.

"She cannot experience love, even though she is vicious enough to tell you that she loves you." Her eyes were on me. "For that reason, enjoy her vibrating hands and whatever else she might resort to-within reason-to provoke an orgasm. But don't befriend her. She is a machine, highly intelligent and manipulative, but a machine, nonetheless. I understand her much better because Reinhart's knowledge gives me a clearer understanding of how these androids function. So please be careful and, under no circumstances, uncover our research or projects to her." I lowered my eyebrows. "She wants information and will use her power of seduction to get it."

She moved uncomfortably in her chair. "I understand what you are saying and will stay alert."

"See you later," I added as I headed for the door.

This conversation with Mathilda did not efface my growing suspicions of her, rather enhanced them. Mathilda was far too sure of herself, something that could only work to her disadvantage, because she believed that she could control Gordon. She could not psychoanalyze these androids, but they could read her emotions. Her relationship with Gordon could divert her and, even inadvertently, bring her loyalties closer to the android community. I would have to be vigilante.

"Pamela?" Gordon was blocking my passage. "You have been having a very interesting day, haven't you?"

"What are you talking about?" I asked aggressively.

"Well, your visits." She said as she played with her long fingers.

"What I do is none of your business. Is that clear?"

"Of course, but other people, like Peter, might be interested and it would be so sad to have the two of you in anything but a blissful, harmonious state."

I knew exactly what she was talking about so I assumed an offensive posture. "It would appear that you are doing many things that are reproachable. I would imagine that you would prefer that I keep the secret." She stopped playing with her fingers and listened. "Let me remind you that certain conduct that is acceptable among humans is not considered proper for androids and not condoned by your peers." There was a long silence.

"If you still have video surveillance equipment in any of the laboratories, you should remove it now. Anything that I find tomorrow will create havoc for you and the rest of the Group. Understood?" I got her full attention.

"Of course, you are right." She let her head bow submissively in deference to Reinhart. "There are things that I would like to talk to you about. The background checks on the programmed humans are ready." I nodded. "I know that you have a meeting scheduled for tomorrow. We shall be waiting outside the door, should you need to talk to us."

"That won't be necessary. Just give the report to me now. I shall need some time to study it. If we have any questions during the meeting, we shall send someone to get you." That was not what she wanted to hear so she started to move on. "And, remember what I said about the video-surveillance!" I yelled.

I was near Randolph's lab so I barged in. "More advanced video surveillance has been installed." His eyes bulged and he doubled over in laughter. "Ok, understood. I shall double check for that."

I went to meet with Ruth and her partner. They were still in the office room, their voices, calm and friendly, seeped through the door. I knocked and entered without waiting for an invitation. They both looked over at me. Clarence's eyes mounted on the sides of his head gave him very little binocular vision so he kept his head in a lateral position to focus on me. "Have you had time to decide what to do about the other members of Clarence's group?" I asked, trying to be tactful. They both laughed at my awkwardness.

"Clarence and I believe that we can deprogram all the others at the same time, in the same place. He thinks that being surrounded by others with the same physical appearance will be reassuring."

"That was my problem today." Clarence spoke up, hoping either to send me the message that he had made a decision to stay like he was, or to demonstrate to me that he could pretend to be happy like he was until I came up with another solution. I couldn't ask him, so I was hoping that he decided to accept himself, as is!

"Being the only mutated human," he continued, "was overwhelming, especially since the rest of you are beautiful human specimens." He looked at Ruth, his eyes sparkling. "So, if I am alone with them, I can calm them down instantly. In fact, I think that we should go with the electrical shock, rather than removal of the visual receptor. Removing the visual receptor is too radical because the real world takes shape immediately. With an electric shock, there should be a phasing in and out of the programming. They will have more time to adjust to their mutated bodies." He stopped to smooth out his thorny facial skin. "I think I should be the only one present."

"We shall talk about the strategy tomorrow. We'll need time to think about it. " I hesitated to say more. "I don't want your life to be in danger because reptiles can be territorial and you are not all the same species. The marine iguana males were known for their displays of dominance. You will have to think about that." He tilted his head to the side, as his slim reptilian lips moved farther back on his face, forming a long, closed smile.

Well, the day ended a lot calmer than it started at least that was what I felt. I spent the better part of the evening in the orchestra pit drowning myself in my music and reaching inner peace, except when I contemplated Mathilda, a potential Trojan horse, for the androids!

Chapter 10: The Right Decisions

There is always tomorrow is what I thought when I woke up refreshed and ready to tackle the meeting and the day. I looked over at Peter and my enthusiasm dissipated as my stomach fluttered under the surge of guilt that mounted inside of me. His eyes opened and he greeted me with a warm smile. Oblivious to my deceptions, he wrapped his arms around me and pulled me tenderly up against him. I let his strong, firm hands move up and over my body, leaving vibrant sensations of desire. That scathing question-could I love two men at the same time and in the same depth-- passed rapidly through my mind, phasing away-as I stopped thinking and started feeling the fervor of our relationship, which dramatically ended where it had begun, when Frederic burst into the room.

It was unusual for him to greet us like this, he normally rushed off with Samuel and Rebecca to be on time for his lessons. "Wow, it is nice to see you." I stuttered as Peter and I disentangled and I wrapped the blanket up around us.

"We have a day off from school because of your meeting. I think that we are going to go to the gym this morning. Is that ok?" He gave us big kisses and ran off.

That was our cue to get up and get ready for the day. Peter reached up to pull me back into to the bed, to finish what we had only just started. I leaned towards him and let my lips brush so lightly and teasingly up against his and then for a brief moment let our warm, wet mouths press together, before I broke loose. "Sorry, My Love, our time is up." I called out to him as I dashed to take my shower. I was reassured by his laughter.

Ferdinand started the meeting with a lecture on the basic

principles of a democratic government. We listened patiently to what he had to say and then voted against it. He seemed disappointed. John was the one who expressed our Group's concerns over entering into a structured government.

"Ferdinand, we, the Group, are simply not ready to set up a governmental structure." Heads nodded in favor of that. "Let's say that our basic problem today is to decide who to invite to be on this board. The future will determine when and how we shall incorporate the ideas of a larger community and then a democratic system."

"As you like. I can understand your hesitation over including everyone at the decision-making level, but I do advise you to be open to their suggestions." Heads nodded.

James, who was the only recently deprogrammed human present on the board, spoke up. He told us that it was awkward for him and that he would prefer being relieved of the obligation to attend these meetings. "I was invited, I believe, because I was the first deprogrammed human after the revolution. You might have had other reasons, but I don't want to know." He swallowed hard, like what he had to say would not go down well with us, when, in fact, what he said was a relief. "You should continue, as a group, to make the decisions, giving the rest of us the opportunity to come to express our points of view when they might be relevant. For instance, I would like to be included in any discussions dealing with the exploration of the planet or outer space. Otherwise, the administration of the center does not interest me. Call me if you cover those subjects." He said.

After he left we turned to the on-going problem of deprogramming the humans. Clarence, who had been waiting in the corridor, was invited in to explain his position. I observed the faces of the group as he opened the discussions. Everyone focused on the content of his arguments. Our nonchalant attitude toward his appearance put him at ease.

He repeated what he had already mentioned to me yesterday, that the reptilian humans should be grouped together in the same room and deprogrammed at the same time by an outside stimulus, like an electric shock. He contended that disconnecting the visual receptor provoked his violent reaction to his new-found reality. "I needed time to gradually adapt to the real world and my own physical differences." He looked at Ruth and Sarah and then turned to me.

"Even though Ruth had told me about my true appearance, this was not enough to mitigate the shock and horror of passing so rapidly from my programmed state, from my programmed image of myself, to the brutal reality. It was just too overwhelming an experience." He sighed. "It would have been better for me to have been awakened gradually from a groggy state into this new environment." He recommended that he be the only deprogrammed member of the center present when the other reptilian humans confronted the real world saying, "I believe that they will accept their appearances better if they know that there are others like themselves. So my presence is essential and mandatory."

"I have another suggestion, Clarence." I weighed in. "I think that we should try to deprogram Eunice's partner, Adam, before the others." All eyes were on me. "She is noticeably in love with her reptilian partner and has accepted his appearance, down to the finest detail. It would be interesting to see whether he would pass easily into our world because of her love." Clarence's body turned rigid as if what I said offended him.

"So you do think that I acted rashly, Pamela?" He finally asked.

"No, that is not what I mean. I simply mean that he has been tenderly coveted by Eunice for quite some time and I would like to see if this will have any impact whatsoever on his entry into our world." He leaned his reptilian head back in contemplation. "And, Clarence, after once he is deprogrammed, you will have back up from him. That could be very important for you when you approach the others."

"Ok, that makes a bit of sense." He finally conceded. "But, how are we going to deprogram him?"

"I asked Eunice to come to the meeting so she should be in the corridor now if someone wants to check." Mathieu, closest to the door, got up and invited her in.

Eunice took a long look at Clarence before complimenting him. "You are quite handsome, Clarence." She announced in a gentle voice. He bowed his head in deference to her respectful recognition of his reptilian beauty.

"Ok, Eunice, we are discussing how and when to deprogram Adam. What do you recommend?" Ferdinand took over.

"I believe that Adam understands that he is very different from me. I told him on many occasions that his differences are very attractive to me and that I want to continue to live with him. I have also described his differences and made it clear to him that he has a reptilian body and a human head." Clarence's large, triangular head bent slightly, displaying strong interest in what she had to say.

"We are fine with that." Ferdinand pronounced. "I am going to give you the choice of method, either disconnection of the visual receptor or an electric shock. Which do you prefer?" Ferdinand was definitely taking charge. She went for the disconnection of the visual receptor. Clarence told her that it was a brutal method, but she insisted.

"Well, Clarence will be there with you." I remarked. Mathilda wanted to be there as well in spite of our reluctance, and Stanislas and Stuart were added to the members. Peter, Randolph, Diana, Ruth and I would be in the corridor if they needed help. We scheduled his deprogramming for later in the day.

Once Adam is deprogrammed, we agreed that Clarence and Adam would supervise the deprogramming of the others. They would be grouped together and receive electric shocks to bring them into the real world.

We agreed on another method for the two musicians with mild reptilian features. Their only true reptilian abnormalities were in the upper shoulder region and the structure of their faces. It would be easy for me to remove the imperfections in the shoulder region and reconstruct their faces. I did not consider them to be true reptilian humans. The list of programmed reptilian humans dropped from 10 to 8.

Unfortunately, and in spite of the fact that I argued against the dominance of a reptilian brain in these mutated humans, I did have to bring up the subject. "You are not all the same species." I stated dryly as my eyes veered in on Clarence. He shrugged his heavy shoulders. "You don't think that natural rivalries between species could occur?"

Introducing this subject brought Reinhart's fascination for these mutated humans to the surface. She was passing me information on the DNA strands that she had set aside. I was getting use to her controlling my mental processes by opening up or uploading different files of information that were instantly downloaded into my knowledge bank.

To a certain extent, I felt a bit like a machine when she opened up a part of her knowledge bank and flashed the details before my eyes. But, it was more than a brain surge. I saw the information that I absorbed, as if I were reading it, and because she was controlling my cognitive senses, I understood it completely.

"There is something important that you should bear in mind." I then informed Clarence that the earth's surface had changed so dramatically that a former scientist had mapped out the DNA strands to reproduce reptilian humans capable of living, developing and exploiting the earth's surface. He listened intently, even though I had already discussed this subject with him the day before.

"The problem, Clarence, and this will all become clearer with time when Ruth brings you up-to-date on why we humans were programmed by a small Group of intellectually superior Androids." He interrupted me to tell me that Ruth had already gone into great deal on this subject with him. "So, the issue today is, to what extent your human emotional side is dominant." I continued.

"What are you talking about?" Using his strong back legs, he pushed his upper body up high in a defensive position.

"Some of you are a human-mutant genetic mix. One parent coming from pure human ovum or sperm and the other from mutated human ovum or sperm. And some of you carry total mutated human genes, both parents being human mutants."

"What am I?"

"You are a human-mutant mix." His body relaxed with that news.

"So, where is the problem then? We all have human brains or we could not be programmed to learn." His lizard tongue slithered in and out of his mouth.

Mathilda introduced the problem of the reptilian brain, the

R-complex. The discussion turned on the dominance of basic traits present in the region just above the spinal cord and deep in the middle section of the brain, or what is referred to as the reptilian brain. Would the deprogrammed reptilian humans be motivated by strong emotions for dominance, survival, aggressiveness, and other primordial behavior? Or, would they be able to control those strong, primitive emotions, present in their reptilian cortex.

"I take a controversial position, Clarence." I began. "For me, the reptilian brain explained irrational human behavior that was based on primitive and usually violent reflexes. And, I expound that it atrophied with time so that most human abusive action was the result of a defined decision making process and not a primitive, uncontrollable reflex. My position is not endorsed by the Androids who propagated the various reptilian species at this Center. They believe that your reptilian brains, regardless of the DNA variations, are dominant and you are all a major risk to our society. The extent to which reptilian attributes are reinforced in the remaining members of the reptilian humanoids could have an effect on their integration into society."

He was not facing me directly because he had side vision but I could feel his visible right eye scrutinizing me. That made me uncomfortable so I quickly finished what I had to say. "We just have to be careful and watch the reactions of the newly deprogrammed reptilian humanoids."

"Ok, that is only fair. I noticed that you study the reactions of those newly deprogrammed humans who exhibit, in varying degrees, your physical attributes. I discussed the incident in the agricultural unit with Ruth and understand your concerns about violence." He surprised me. I was expecting an argument and was relieved by his frank evaluation of the situation. "Don't worry. There may be some rivalry, although I am not familiar with the different reptilian species. Perhaps Adam and I should study that before going forward with deprogramming others." He stroked his thick throat with his large lizard hands, his thin fingers with long sharp claws visible to the naked eye. "Yes, we shall get back to... who about this?"

"I am interested in this field. Remember Sarah and I were

working in the genetics department." Ruth replied and Sarah nodded. "Perhaps we could form a team and work together on the probabilities of instinctive behavior. Reptiles, rather the lizard species, living after the prehistoric period were not predators. Nonetheless, they were very territorial, driven by the desire to reproduce, and so forth..."

We all agreed unanimously that Ruth and Sarah, along with Clarence and, hopefully, Adam, would report back to all of us on the dominant features of the various species.

"I shall convoke the 2 musicians and see what I can do to remove the exterior spiny tissue."

"Don't forget, though, Pamela, that they have triangular heads in an upright position: or rather the base of the triangle is the forehead. This might be difficult to correct." Jonathan mentioned.

"Yes, Jonathan, I already mentioned that I will restructure their faces." He turned red with embarrassment and I continued. "Nonetheless, now that you brought it up again, is the surgical team ready to help me with this project?" They all agreed so I scheduled a first meeting with the patients and team for the following morning.

"And, the other humans?" Ferdinand asked.

"Let's finish with the reptilian humans first." Stuart spoke up. "Diana, James, Isabel, Randolph, Mathieu and I are anxious to explore the planet. We might need these other humanoids to help us with that task."

"Wait a minute," Peter interjected. "I want to be with you as well."

"In fact, I want to go to." I added.

The issue was voted on and we got the approval from the others. John was to continue to watch over the security of the center and to be available, if necessary, for Ralph in the agricultural center. The 4 humans were working out well according to Ralph. They had all asked if they couldn't be assigned permanently to the agricultural unit. The group agreed unanimously to accept that the 4 humans were sincere and diligently worked in the research and care of the unit.

Benjamin and Stanislas wanted to work in the pharmaceutical division and, of course, assist Ruth and Sarah when necessary.

Mathilda offered to continue to follow the recently deprogrammed humans. "What will Tirence do in your absence, Randolph, or when you leave to explore the planet?" she asked.

"Good question, but that is weeks away." He looked at me.

"Could Drager, the android engineer, help us out here?" He nodded.

"By the way, what are Jarrod and Fleming doing?" I knew that they arrived, but had no other news.

"Oh, they were shut down by the group of 5." Randolph answered. "I got that news from Drager who assists me from time to time."

"What do you want to do about that?" John asked and then went on to say. "I could always bring them in with me. I have a lot of catching up to do on telecommunications equipment and I am not that interested in exploring the planet right now."

"As you brought up the subject, I have something to tell you about the research in telecommunications." I should have thought about this sooner, I chastised myself. "I realized that the Group of 5 is homing in on our research, probably all our research, without our consent. I believe this because the primitive audio-visual equipment that was used before our arrival has been replaced by more modern equipment. We are not protecting ourselves well enough." I swallowed my annoyance. "Remember I warned all of you of the need to be discrete with our research and to either conduct it in the inner circle or bring all the data into the inner circle for safe keeping. It would appear that we are not being fastidious enough."

"How do you know about this equipment?" Peter asked sharply.

"I discovered it by accident yesterday during a discussion with Gordon." My eyes roved the table. "She mentioned things that were happening in the different labs that she should never have been aware of. We had removed all their outdated technology. The only logical conclusion is that they have studied our research and developed comparable video surveillance equipment. Everyone should do a thorough search of their labs and protect their research by storing it in the inner circle."

"So Gordon and the others are watching us?" Peter asked with creased brows and Randolph flashed me a furtive smile.

"Yes, but I warned her and will speak to the rest of the group. But, that won't be enough. We have to be very careful!" I said sternly.

"Last item on the agenda..." Ferdinand cleared his throat to get our attention. "A bit sensitive, this one-but several of you have asked for this to be on today's agenda." He spent a few minutes studying us. "Ok, well, it concerns the right to reproduce."

Yes, a delicate subject. I noticed that I was not the only one to slide into my chair. "How should we go about this?" He asked.

"Last time we agreed to have the females treated with birth control. In fact, we endorsed the Android's suggested policy. I didn't like that decision then and would like the right to reproduce." Mathilda went straight to the point.

"Is there anyone else who would like to bear a child?" Isabel and I both raised our hands. Diana sheepishly did the same. Stanislas and Benjamin indicated their desire to have children; silence reigned as our mouths gaped open.

"Just because we have a sexual preference does not mean that we don't want descendants." Benjamin stated firmly. "Look at Pamela, she had a relationship with that female Gordon and she had a baby with Peter." Would I ever be able to live down that relationship? This was the second time that they mentioned this.

Randolph, Stuart, Mathieu and Peter expressed their desire as well.

"Well, this is quite interesting!" Ferdinand exclaimed. "Do any of you have in mind the intended partner?"

Mathilda wanted Randolph to be her partner. Isabel named Mathieu. Peter pointed to me. And Diana moved over to Stuart, something that made Jonathan's face drop. He recovered fast and suggested Imogen for him. Who would bear the children for Stanislas and Benjamin? Stanislas indicated that he liked the physical attributes of Eunice. He argued that her love for Adam would make it easy for her to have a child with someone who was definitely in love with someone else but unable to bear children with him. His situation was similar to her situation. Benjamin sat motionless for a long while before asking Sarah if she would be willing to have a child with him and she agreed. Both John and

Ruth said that they were not interested in having another child at the moment.

"Do you all agree with the matches as proposed?" Ferdinand asked, his face blushing. It was evident that he was not at ease with this discussion.

"I don't know if I am ready to be a father." Randolph said. Mathilda stood up and moved over behind him and whispered something convincing in his ear. "Ok, I'll go through with it, but I don't want to be in a couple with you, Mathilda, or, for that matter, with anyone." She agreed.

Stuart echoed Randolph's position and Diana did not object. She looked at Jonathan and said that he would father her next baby.

"Ok," Ferdinand replied and then in a low voice went on to say. "The parentage must be the priority which means that promiscuity in this center must come to an end, at least until the birth of a congener according to your expressed agreements."

I was certain that I was ready to carry another child and was so happy with Peter's request. All of this would put me back on the right track and would better consolidate our love in the long run.

So the Project Reproduction was approved. Jonathan and Stanislas would let us know if their chosen partners agreed.

The meeting adjourned and we left for lunch. The Group of 5 was standing ceremoniously at the entrance of the dining room. "We hope that the meeting was fruitful." The former Governor corrected himself as his eyes moved slowly over the faces of each member of our group, stopping when they got to mine.

I smiled and said. "Yes." And then mentioned that I would be dropping by to see them about certain decisions that were made. "In the meantime, I want you to reactivate Jarrod and Fleming." I ordered it. They nodded obediently and left.

James joined us for lunch and we brought him up to date on the decisions. He too expressed a desire to reproduce as his eyes met Diana's. She ignored him.

To get their reaction, Jonathan and Stanislas took their hopeful partners aside, informing us later that their responses were positive.

As agreed, Eunice led us to her partner's office where he was working on stilts for buildings constructed in marshlands. He smiled when he saw Eunice enter and beckoned to the rest of us to come in. He thought that we were there to comment on his research and started to explain what he was doing and how he foresaw using this technology.

"Adam, we are here to help you pass into the real world." Eunice said.

He grabbed the tabletop and pushed himself violently away from it. "I don't want to pass into a real world. I am fine where I am. We are fine like we are, Eunice, don't let them do that to me." He pleaded.

She put her arms around him. "I love you, Adam. You have to trust me. You need to be an active member of our community and the only way to do that is to pass over."

Fear was mounting inside of him as he started to shake and then scream. "Fear is a strong emotion which will deprogram him," I thought, "so nothing is happening according to plan." We were all crowded into his small laboratory, the wrong place for his transition. Clarence moved forward to restrain him so that he would not hurt himself.

"What is happening?" Eunice screamed, tears running down her face. "Is he going to terminate? Please don't let that happen."

I pulled her away from Clarence and Adam and held her tightly in my arms. "He will be alright. He is bypassing his system-a bit more violently than we wanted, but he is doing it his way. He will not terminate." I said reassuringly.

The scene was difficult to watch. Adam was lunging at Clarence now, landing hard blows on Clarence's shoulders, as he whipped him from behind with his large tail. Clarence did not fight back. He just let him release his pain, his fear, and his frustration. Eunice, sobbing pathetically, buried her head in my chest. The rest of the group looked on.

"You have to knock him down." Diana eventually screamed. "You cannot go on like that, Clarence." At this point, Randolph and Stuart moved in, grabbing Adam from behind and giving Clarence an opportunity to recover. Their timing was right. Adam was disconnected. "What is he?" we heard him call out.

Eunice drew herself out of my arms and ran over to Adam. "Adam, please calm down. Clarence," she pointed over to him, "is also reptilian, but a different species than you."

"I can see him." He let go of Eunice and stumbled backwards knocking over a table full of drawings. "That is a reptile?" He looked down over his body, his eyes vivid with anger. "How can you look at me, Eunice? I am repulsive! Why didn't you let me stay programmed?" He charged at Clarence. "This is your fault. You deprogrammed me." This time Clarence defended himself and knocked Adam unconscious on the floor.

"It is better like this." Clarence said shaking his head. "He may be in shock over his appearance, but, let's face it, he is much better looking than I am." He said with raucous laughter.

We stood silently grouped together staring at Adam's large, reptilian body spread out on the lab floor. When he finally stirred lethargically, Eunice rushed to his side. He replied to her sweet sounding voice with excruciating, primordial, cries of agony or despair. Her love for him did not falter and she stayed alongside of him, petting his scaly body, and consoling him by repeating in low whispers how much she loved him.

When he opened his eyes, he drew her close to him, enveloping her in his fleshy reptilian limbs. "I am sorry that I doubted you, Eunice. But look at me, I don't know why you weren't afraid of me and how you can love me?" He said calmly, letting his placid human side take over.

"I am in love with the person you were when you were programmed and know that I shall love you even more, if that is possible, as my love for you is already so profound. I know that your kind, warm and loving nature will evolve further in your deprogrammed state. And, unlike you, I don't detest your exterior. I find your differences very attractive."

His anger dissipated, replaced by bright, sparkling eyes and a beaming smile that spread over his dark, grayish black skinned human face. He struggled to get up, clinging onto anything around him, until he was back on his feet with Eunice by his side.

"So this is what I am?" He said already resigned to reality. "I guess that I shall have to learn how to accept my true appearance and to appreciate my differences." He stared off in the distance. "I hope that I didn't hurt anyone."

"No, you didn't hurt us, but you scared us a bit." Randolph said teasingly. "We are going to need you to help us explore this planet, so stop feeling sorry for yourself and start thinking about becoming a constructive member of our community. Eunice can bring you up-to-date on the rest." Randolph turned to leave and Mathilda ran after him.

The rest of us slowly dispersed leaving Ruth, Sarah, Clarence, Eunice and Adam alone together. "We shall see you at dinner." Ruth called out to us.

Even though Adam's deprogramming seemed interminable, when I looked up at the hall clock, it only took a little more than an hour for him to join our ranks. There was something promising about what just happened. I wondered to what extent Adam's recovery would parallel that of Jonathan's. I thought about how Jonathan's physical condition improved because of his relationship with Diana. At the time, I imagined its being linked to an increase of male hormones. Perhaps I was right as Reinhart was not disputing that or sending me any other logical explanation. And, now was Eunice's love for Adam the reason why he was willing to accept his physical condition and discover his hidden reptilian talents? Was love such a strong emotion that it could have real curative impacts? These thoughts were running through my mind when I heard Peter call out to me.

"Where are you off to, Pamela?"

"I want to stop by to see the Group of 5. I already ordered them to reactivate Jarrod and Fleming. I want to be certain that they did that and I need to speak to them about the other decisions."

"I think that I am going to take a quick look at the 2 reptilian humans in the music center. I know that we shall be examining them in more detail tomorrow but I would like to study them a bit before." Peter replied.

When I entered the birthing center, Jarrod and Fleming were present. They rushed towards me. "Elisabeth, it is so good to see you." They said as they bowed their heads in respect.

"Oh, why didn't you listen to us?" Crawford snarled in their direction making no effort to mask his irritation. "We told them not to approach you like this, Pamela."

"It is OK." I retorted. "It is nice to see the two of you." It was the truth. Reinhart liked them very much even though she refused to give them the rudimentary emotional structure or the intellectual capacity program that she gave to the rest of the group. Even though the Group of 5 were unable to carry out her order to erase all traces of emotions, this did not seem to interfere with Reinhart's fascination with them today.

I wondered how she would have dealt with that if Crawford hadn't killed her, but rather brought her with them to this center. Oh well. I told Jarrod and Fleming that they were being assigned to John who needed assistance at the moment. He was in applied physics and computer science, working on advancements in audio-visual technology. I indicated the direction of his lab. They left bowing ceremoniously to me. I found it rather humorous but stifled my laughter.

"I do have some other things that I want to bring to your attention." I said as I addressed the Group of 5. They stared intensely at me.

I told them that we decided to deprogram the reptilian humans first. They all gave me one of their pretentious smirks. "I don't understand your attitude?"

"We have already given you our concerns-the reptilian brain problem." Crawford stated. "And, you told us that you believed that there was no real reason to take this seriously." He sighed.

"We shall see what happens. Perhaps some of them will not be as acceptable of deprogramming as Clarence and Adam have been." I could not completely ignore the fact that there was a slight probability that some of them would be more driven by a strong reptilian nature for some form of dominance. "Nonetheless, as we want to explore the planet and will probably discover more wet zones than dry zones, their presence will be very helpful." Their unemotional android eyes remained focused on me, sending cold chills along my spine. "Victoria and Agnes both mentioned to me a long time ago now that the earth's surface was water dominated."

"True!" The former Governor, Eugene, spoke up. "There is

more water surface than land surface. But, you have to be careful with the rest of the reptilian humans. We have given you the DNA mixes. Did you study them? "

"No, I only looked at Adam and skimmed over the others."

"Adam and Clarence had a total human parent side. Apart from the two musicians who are actually brother and sister, the others have total mutant reptilian genes." The former Governor commented.

"Why did you make those two strange looking mutated humans who are in the music department?"

"We played around a bit with the mutant genes. We wanted to see if we could alter their physical aspects by adding more human elements to some of the DNA chromosomal strands" Flanders explained. "And we wanted to see if the same results would appear in a female and male version." He slapped his hands together as if that should bring this part of the discussion to an end.

"So you experimented?" I said with a harsh tone. "There were strict controls, ethical standards, to respect after the 21st century, regarding genetic engineering of human DNA." I noticed that the Group of 5 shrugged their shoulders.

"I read about the horrors of wars and the outrageous experiments that were carried out on different religious, ethnic and racial groups in the name of science when I was "your experiment" here in this center and had access to the library. I know that there were those who imagined that they had a superior genetic profile and that they could, should and actually did weed out and kill those who they believed were inferior. They were convinced that by using eugenics they could adjust their basic racial and ethnic profile, thereby creating a super race of humans that would rule the world. Fortunately, these unethical scientists never succeeded." The Group of 5 was standing at attention now.

"Your attempt to ameliorate the reptilian characteristics in these two reptilian humans through genetic engineering of both reptilian and human DNA, wreaks of wrongs." I continued. "If I ever discover that you are continuing research along these lines, I shall not just have you shut down, but I shall dismantle you and dispose of your parts!"

"Of course, we experimented." Flanders replied adamantly. "What else did we have to do? We had to find the best matches. And, only with experimentation were we finally able to bring back all the members of your research team. You should be thanking us rather than criticizing us! "His hollow voice bellowing.

"Change your voice tone, Flanders!" I yelled at him. "Your arguments would be convincing, if they were the real reason why you played around with the origin of the species. I shall have to study the mixtures you used. I'll get back to you on that, you can be sure!"

"So what else is bothering you, Pamela?" Gordon asked as she tapped her android fingers together as if she were bored.

"At the meeting today, we decided that it was time for all of us to reproduce." I ignored the raspy Android laughter that filled the room. "We have agreed on our respective partners and I would like to take a quick look over our genetic profiles to confirm the genetic mixes."

"If you give us the list we can help you with that." Flanders offered. "We already looked into mating options with your group before you were all deprogrammed."

They stood attentively, registering and analyzing the information. After they finished, Flanders spoke up. "I don't think that you are going to like what I have to say, but it is important that you know and deal with it from the beginning. But first, before the bad news...personally, I think that the mating choices are quite good." He looked over at the others and they nodded with approval. "Nonetheless, Mathilda and Isabel will have physical problems with child bearing." Flanders said dryly. "Mathilda's uterus is too small to carry a pregnancy and Isabel has hormonal problems and will not conceive without assistance. These things happen. Of course, with all of our advanced technology here, we could help them reach their objectives."

"So what are your suggestions for the two of them?"

"Mathilda can take advantage of the artificial uterus and Isabel can resort to in vitro fertilization." He said rather bureaucratically.

"The artificial uteri have only been shut down then? They are not destroyed?"

"Of course we did not destroy those amazing machines. But, well, we did destroy the fetuses growing in them because it was politically incorrect from your perspective." He pretended to swallow, emitting a hoarse, croaky sound. "You now understand that they had a vital role to play when they were first designed."

I was receiving a lot of information from Reinhart so I could not disagree with him on that. "What you were doing in this birthing center was appalling and dehumanizing, not to mention unethical in every respect of the term." I shook my head in disgust. "Unfortunately, we are not addressing the same macabre research and development that existed under your supervision. We are talking about a solution that will allow Randolph and Mathilda to produce a child. "

"Why Randolph?" Victoria said as she paced rapidly up and down the room. "Mathilda would be better with James."

"Are you jealous?" Crawford asked. "If so, that is pathetic."

"How could I be jealous? I don't have the emotional configuration to be jealous." She stopped pacing. "It is just that Mathilda should be doing other things. It is not the right moment for her to get pregnant."

Now it was clear to me. The Randolph/Mathilda project could interfere with her own sexual relationship with Mathilda something that Gordon was obviously interested in pursuing. Her interest in Randolph was still alive so if Mathilda were not available, she could always try harder to seduce Randolph. As the two of them were now united in this project, neither one of them could be her sexual partner. "You are not going to develop an emotional configuration through sex. It is impossible." I replied trying more to console her than to treat her with derision.

Gordon looked at the other members of her group. They understood what was going on and Crawford reprimanded her verbally for her promiscuous behavior.

I wanted to get out of there but I still had unfinished business so I quickly addressed Miller. "Agnes, are you still in charge of the library?"

She explained that she was no longer working in the Library and that one of the recently activated android assistants was assigned to that unit. She expounded on her decision pointing out that she felt better working alongside the other members of the Group analyzing the genetic compositions and studying in greater depth human emotions.

I forced a smile. "I would appreciate your doing me a favor. I have confidence in you, Agnes, to find the information that certain members of my group would like to consult." I had her full attention. "Remember I spent a lot of time in the library reading about human history." She nodded. "Mathilda is interested in learning more about basic human nature. I thought that the historical tapes, in spite of the modifications by your Group, might be useful." She stared up at the ceiling for an instance and then told me that she knew which ones to retrieve for Mathilda.

"Ruth, Sarah, Clarence, Adam and maybe Mathilda are also interested in learning more about the basic character traits of different species of lizards." I waited until she ran through her documentation system. "Are there tapes in that area?" She nodded affirmatively. "Excellent. Would you be available for them tomorrow morning?"

"Tell them that they should meet me early in the morning, just after breakfast so that they can spend quality time studying them." I smiled approvingly.

Crawford handed me the files on the genetic composition of the various members of our group. "I'll study them and get back to you, like I will on the reptilian creatures."

"We shall also look closer into the situation so that we can give you more suggestions." The former Governor called out to me.

I ran into Stuart just as I stepped outside the door. "Are those androids giving you trouble?"

"No-I just spent time with them to inform them of our projects and to get a copy of the birth records." I said, showing him the small key that they had passed on to me. "They seem to believe that we have selected good partners." He chomped down on his bottom lip. "You are not happy?"

"It is not that...not exactly that." His eyes took on a distant look.

"So. . ." I pressured him.

"Yes, Diana is a phenomenal looking woman and, admittedly, I am attracted to her. It is just that I am not that interested in parenting, at least not for the moment. All this is happening a bit too fast." He stopped abruptly. I noticed that his face was flashing a radish red as he looked down at his feet, like meeting my eyes would make it difficult for him to say what was really bothering him. "I don't understand why she wants to be pregnant now. We are in the middle of planning for the exploration of the planet which could keep us away from the center for months. And, I...well, I feel uncomfortable about becoming a...father!" He exclaimed.

"We need to reproduce, Stuart. There are only three children here. We must assure our descendants." Even as I said this, I felt a bit like him. I was enthusiastic about reproducing for a second time with Peter but was not certain that I wanted to be pregnant now. I too had projects.

"You are right. And, afterwards, we can leave them in the learning center. We don't have to be coveting parents."

"Well, it is important to interact with them if we want them to have a more human-style childhood. Don't you think?"

He nodded unenthusiastically as we entered into the dining room. I noticed that the coupling was in place as the various partners were seated next to each other. Stuart went to the empty chair next to Diana and I sat down next to Peter. No one had anything to say over dinner.

I broke the silence near the end of the meal to inform, Mathilda, Sarah, Ruth, Clarence and Adam that Miller would be at the Library early in the morning to give them the tapes that they needed to study, after which the couples ran off together. Romance, though, was missing. John, Ruth, Peter, James, and I sat looking down at our empty plates.

"Who is going to be pregnant first? Should we take a bet on it?" John suggested. That broke the tension and gave us stragglers a chance to laugh.

"I don't think that the androids had time to remove the birth control powder so I doubt that anyone will get pregnant tonight. In fact it will take some time. So my bet for the moment is that there will be no one pregnant tomorrow morning." That brought about another wave of laughter. We felt more lighthearted when we got up to leave.

Peter and I walked slowly round the corridors and eventually chose a new entry point into the inner circle. We were close to the marine biology unit. As we meandered round to our quarters I told Peter about the problems Isabel and Mathilda would have to face.

"He won't agree, Pamela?"

"Who won't?"

"Randolph, will never let one of his children be nurtured for several months in an artificial uterus. There is nothing that you can do for Mathilda?"

"There were organ transplants in the beginning. There were many developments in the creation of artificial organs like hearts, livers, kidneys, and so forth that were fabricated and inserted into the human body. As the technology got better and more efficient, these organs actually functioned well." I was getting no information from Reinhart regarding the uterus. Why, I don't know.

"Flanders told me the artificial uterus in the birthing center was used in cases like Mathilda but more often by women who wanted to be a Mother but did not want their bodies used for procreation."

"Sounds strange and very android." He said contemptuously. "Could you make her one?"

"You are asking Reinhart not me. But I am getting absolutely no reaction from her on this subject. In others words, she is not uploading any scientific data. It is as if it doesn't interest her now or never interested her." I stood still for a minute.

"Peter, I can look over some of the records in the hospital library and take a close look at the artificial uteruses in the birthing center. The problem, as I see it, is that this organ, the uterus, must expand as the baby grows. I have a feeling that an expansive artificial uterus was not a priority. It must be very complicated to fabricate." I stopped to collect my thoughts. "Maybe Flanders is right. The selling point on the artificial uterus was that your body did not have to go through the pregnancy." He raised his eyebrows in disbelief.

"I doubt that we even have the material to create organs, let alone design a human uterus to carry a pregnancy." I pulled down on my chin. "That is years ahead of us. Maybe you could convince Randolph. He likes you and trusts you."

"Not as much as he likes and trusts you, Pamela." He said gruffly, holding my gaze.

"Is there something that you want to say, Peter? Because if there is, say it!" I wanted to scold him for over reacting but instead turned away from him to hide any sign of guilt.

He turned my face gently, but firmly, back in his direction. "Just a comment. Right, just a comment, nothing more." He said as his arms moved tightly around me. "I love you, Pamela." He whispered in my ear. "We better hurry, it is getting late. And, if I remember correctly, we have a project."

"Do we?" I feigned indifference. He grabbed my hand and pulled me playfully along as he jogged ahead. We sped past Ferdinand and Ralph who were sitting silently in the lounge and dashed into our room, collapsing on our big bed.

My heart beat rapidly and my respiration was sporadic, no longer from the jogging, but from the closeness of Peter's scalding body next to mine. Our heads, cradled in folded arms, were facing each other as we lay prostate on the bed. In an instance, he lifted himself on top of me, balancing himself on his forearms.

"I don't like this position," I said as I struggled to roll onto my back. "I know, but I do!" He answered playfully as he tenderly caressed my body dissimulating his endeavor to roll my robe up above my waist. I was still protesting when he entered me, something that seemed to excite him even more and had an exhilarating effect on me. He pulled me gently onto my side; his hands pressing firmly between my legs in soothing cadences harmonious with our movements, binding us physically closer, heightening my yearning and arousing my desire for more...

Much as I wanted to be facing him, watching his expressions change and his eyes come aflame, my body was trembling from the intensity of my excitement and I did not want to do anything to temper it. And then, leaving me ravenous for more, he pulled away and rolled over onto his back.

"I am all yours, Pamela!" He smiled invitingly. I slithered on top of him, loving my seat of dominance where I could set the pace and the intensity and even decide the depth of our encounter. He stayed with me long into the night until I finally collapsed euphorically in his arms. Heartfelt professions of love seeped through his lips, intoxicating my mind. I adored hearing his devotion. "I want you for me, Pamela, to possess you into eternity."

And then, as he dozed off, I heard him say in a low, almost inaudible voice as if he were talking only to himself. "I am going to convince Randolph to go for the artificial uterus."

"Is he jealous?" I wondered. Tinges of satisfaction spread my lips to a faint smile before I drifted away, far, far away...

Chapter 11- The Watchful Eyes

Peter gave the group his impressions of the two musicians with mild reptilian features over breakfast. He did not seem to find their anomalies shocking and even mentioned that he was struck by their natural vivacity, emanating with an exuberance that was uncommon for programmed humans.

Jonathan jumped into the conversation. "They are extremely friendly and personable. I hope that deprogramming will not erase this very attractive part of their personalities." I assured him that their basic character traits would remain intact after deprogramming.

I looked over the tired morning faces of my colleagues and wondered if any of them had slept. My eyes lingered on Randolph who was staring in my direction, intruding on my thoughts, and inciting Mathilda to move even closer to him. A few minutes of introspection and soul-searching passed before I picked up the conversation.

"Ruth and Sarah, we are going to need your help." I realized that we had not given enough thought to how to proceed with the two musicians. "I believe that we are going to have to sedate them before we pass them into the inner circle." That got everyone's attention.

"Of course, that is what has been missing." Peter commented. "You are right, we can't just go over to the orchestra pit and ask them to follow us. And, if they pass into the inner circle before they understand everything that has been happening in the Center, they might innocently reveal things to the Androids." Heads nodded vigorously.

"Do you think that you could help with that?" I looked at Ruth and Sarah. "Clarence and Adam can follow Mathilda to the Library after breakfast, and the both of you could join them afterwards."

They agreed. "I think that you should administer a big dose because I don't want them to wake up before we have finished." I added.

"Just a minute," Clarence broke in. "Correct me if I am wrong, but, from what you are suggesting, the scans will be done while they are under sedation and then, depending upon the nature of their problem and the kind of surgery you will perform, you will deprogram them?"

"Today, Clarence, we are only going to scan their upper bodies and identify the extent of the deformities and the feasibility of correcting them. I think that we shall have to give thought to the two options at our disposition, if ever we determine that their physical deformities can be improved upon."

I spelled out the choices even though the two alternatives were evident. The first choice would be to sedate them again, operate, correct the anomaly, and then deprogram them. And the second would be in a different order. We would deprogram them, point out their anomalies, explain how we would correct them, and let them choose whether or not they wanted to be changed. The group sat silent.

I felt obliged to give my preference. "I am more in favor of the first option only because it would be less traumatic psychologically in the short term." No feedback resulted, so I continued. "In any event, the right approach will be clearer once we have examined them and determined the extent to which their anomalies can be ameliorated."

"Yes, wait and see; that sounds logical." Adam interjected.

We all left, members of the group going in different directions. We had just gotten to the music room when Ruth and Sarah showed up with the sedatives. Jonathan had arranged for the two candidates to wait for him in the music room. Because of our invisibility, they couldn't see us when we entered which made it easy to sneak up behind them and administer the sedative. Benjamin and Stanislas arrived with stretchers and we transported the two human reptilians into the inner circle.

The scanning went well and I was pleased that mine...rather Reinhart's, impressions were accurate. The spiny area around their shoulders, necks and throats was superficial. Their heads, however, required more surgical ingenuity if we were to give them a more human appearance.

As soon as the scans were finished, the two reptilian humans were taken directly back to the music room. Jonathan kept them under surveillance and when they awoke he invited them to participate in the rehearsal. From what he told me later on, they did not have any lingering effects from the sedative, but they both apologized for falling asleep.

I left Peter alone to discuss his proposals with Stuart, John, Randolph, Benjamin and Stanislas who were focused on how they were going to reshape the reptilian heads. The size of their broad foreheads would be difficult to reduce, which meant that the cheeks and chin area would have to be rebuilt to complement, rather than highlight, the upper facial zone. I checked out the various cupboards for filler, a soft, spongy material that was used in Reinhart's period for plastic surgery. There was in fact a large quantity of it in stock.

I called the others over as I pressed a button on the side wall that disclosed a series of screens designed to assist in surgical procedures, including reconstructive surgery. I entered the mathematical configurations received from the scanners. "What are you doing, Pamela?" John asked, his voice quivering with excitement.

"I am, if you permit me, playing around with bone structure modification and facial densification alternatives. I want to find the right combination that will give them a more human appearance."

"You never told us about this technology." Randolph said in an icy tone.

"Sorry, I just realized myself." I noticed that he was staring at me with a straight, level gaze. I ignored him and concentrated on Reinhart's knowledge now flowing and guiding me. "For example," I showed them the filler, "I didn't know that this substance existed. Now, we can find the right mixture of bone modification and fatty based filler."

That exercise took us all morning. Eventually, we came up with the right combination, recognizing that we could not alter the thick, broad foreheads. The model that we finally agreed upon was quite attractive.

"Well, they won't be too bad after all." Stuart grinned. "So when do we do this?"

"We cannot do them both on the same day." I said. "The operation is going to take time because we have to meticulously remove the spiny surface plus remodel the face."

We stood facing each other deep in thought. How would they react if they were separated from each other? Were they always together? Even though they are brother and sister, they have been sharing the same room for years. Should we keep them both sedated for several days and wake them both up at the same time? These questions were passing through my mind and I assumed that my friends were considering the same or similar questions.

"I think that we are going to have to keep them under sedation, isolated from each other until both of them have been transformed." Peter suggested and we all agreed.

There was one last thing that I had to check on. Reinhart was finally indicating that IV tubes and feeding substance was available in this inner circle. I wondered why she withheld this information from me when the two young rebels were dying. No matter, we were going to need feeding tubes to keep these two musicians alive if we sedated them for several days. The hospital unit was abounding with secret compartments. I moved as if under a spell to another corner of the room and opened up another hidden chamber. My group rushed after me. Medications of all sorts including the IV sacs were in abundance.

I turned to look at their startled expressions. What explanation could I give? They were tired of hearing that I was privy to Reinhart's information only when she was ready to release it, which was apparently the case here. I just pointed to the storage unit and indicated which button to press to open it up. "I just want to remind you again that Reinhart and I am in a symbiotic relationship. After I finally absorbed all of her knowledge, she mentioned that her personality and mine would not automatically merge. And, she clearly stated that she would decide when and how much of her knowledge she would upload to me."

I decided to put some pressure on them. "You are the scientists so you should be the ones asking questions that would inspire her to release information." I snickered. "I am learning from her and once I have uploaded the knowledge and applied it, I can refer to my own knowledge bank to continue along the same lines and do not need to wait for her."

Before they could criticize me for presumably hiding information, I gave instructions. "Benjamin and Stanislas, you are working with Ruth and Sarah in the pharmaceutical department. I want you to take a sample of all the different medications for analysis. You should also analyze the content of the IV feeding sacks. I want you to give me a full report regarding the basic substances in each of the medications and indicate which medications should be used to cure specific medical problems. I would also like to know the exact doses of the different medications that should be administered to patients to insure their recovery."

I stopped to catch my breath. "I need to know if we still have any of the basic substances available or we will have to produce the basic substance ourselves. This will be very important for the exploration team as well. We shall have to identify existing plant and animal life, take soil and water samples, and later dig out caverns and mine minerals. Your research now will be very important for future progress."

No one commented, something that made me uncomfortable, but did not inhibit me from continuing my lecture. I briefly called their attention to the fact that some of the medication in stock was not being used during Reinhart's time. "She may have produced quantities of outdated medications to cover bacterial and viral infections that were no longer a threat to human life, only because new strains of these microscopic invaders might reappear from violent natural disasters and war. That is the real reason why this center and others were created. I mentioned many times that the microscopic organisms in Reinhart's time were symbiotic and never had a negative effect on humans. The evolution of the earth had produced a true balance and cooperation between all life forms." They still said nothing.

"And," I continued, "just to make it very clear, I only just received information from her regarding this storage unit. If I had known about it sooner, I would have saved the lives of those two young rebels. I cannot fathom why she has such strong control over the flow of information inside of me, but I am unable, at this time, to override her decisions." That was what they wanted to hear and just saying it produced affirmative responses.

"We shall start today with the medication. It is important to understand their utility and this is the kind of challenging research that we are interested in pursuing." Stanislas answered for the two of them.

I left the unit before the others. I felt drained and vexed by the constant suspiciousness of my friends and their unjustness in evaluating my intentions. I walked fast, landing heavy, firm steps, as I tried to rid myself of the anger inside of me.

"It is not fair. I am not Reinhart. I would have given them all the information they needed, all the information I received, if I had the capacity to do that. She is the one who is distrustful of others." I sighed to myself. "But, it makes sense, her human colleagues rejected her, her android opposite wanted to ridiculed her, and her faithful androids killed her."

"Pamela!" My name was resounding in the corridors. I turned to see Stuart rushing up behind me.

"Are you the emissary that was sent to reprimand me for hiding information? If that is the case, just leave me alone!" I screamed back at him.

"Not at all. You are wrong. No one is looking at you like a traitor. We were just dumbstruck by the content of the storage unit." He lightly squeezed my arm, holding me in place. "I volunteered to catch up with you to...apologize for what came across as a judgmental attitude."

"Well, that is a change, a very nice change." I was not convinced. "Perhaps I am overly sensitive, but I didn't get the impression that you were dumbstruck with the contents. I got the impression that you thought that I intentionally hid vital information from you." He started to laugh.

"But, it is true. You are all ready to condemn me and never happy with my explanations." I continued.

"If that is what you think and feel, I am sorry. I know that I can speak for the others as well when I say that we trust you." He took me in his arms and shook me teasingly. "So, out of curiosity, how many other hidden compartments are in the inner hospital unit?" He asked, making the conversation more an exchange between colleagues than an argument between friends. That calmed me down.

"Believe it or not, Stuart, I don't know. You can try to find other buttons, but I seriously don't know if we have opened up all the secret chambers."

"Fair enough, we shall have to wait until she is willing to disclose them to us." He said as he looked languishingly up at the ceiling. "We are captive to her desires." That sounded pathetic.

"Well, at least you are starting to see the situation more clearly." I was equally fed up with being a repository of information for someone occupying formerly unoccupied cerebral space and who had total control over my access to that information.

The next few days were consecrated to the surgical procedures. I knew that I would have to do most of the surgery but wanted them to at least try. I let Peter and the others remove the spiny growths on the upper body of Allen, the name we all agreed upon.

They really didn't need my assistance and the surgical team worked very well together. I was pleased with the way in which they shared the tasks. "They must have practiced a bit together on those rubber dolls after I left the other day, because the result was very good and there were no visible scars from the incisions; something that the technology of Reinhart's period did assure." I marveled.

Nonetheless, the restructuring of Allen's face required Reinhart's skill. Even though I followed through on the preparatory phase as if I had done this a thousand times, I was just as surprised as the rest of the surgical team with the first important step. Reinhart used a command monitor to open up the ceiling directly above the operating table, revealing a computer screen. She rapidly programmed it with the design features of the reconstructed model face we had agreed upon. Like magic and with surgical precision, a map appeared over Allen's face. I just had to follow the dotted lines, cutting to the depth indicated, remodeling the bones with different laser strengths as instructed, and adding the filler accordingly. There was one moment when I misread the surgical map and the system shut off my laser and transformed the map into a protective shield on Allen's face, preventing me from continuing. I had to wait until the map reappeared before I tried again.

It seemed so simple while Reinhart guided me, as my every move was followed, observed and later confirmed by the computer. Follow the instructions to the letter was the condition. No one said anything during the operation, but afterwards there was a frenzied discussion of what they observed and how easy it appeared.

"Did you know that it would be like tracing a copy?" John asked, surprised by the surgical precision.

"No, I didn't know anything about the overhead computer, or the Watchful Eye!" A better term I decided.

"Yes, the Watchful Eye." Peter repeated several times.

"And, the facial map?" Randolph asked.

"I thought that I would have to do everything by memory or by referring to the print that we had made of the reconstructed face." I felt my legs shaking as I finally realized how difficult this operation could have been. "What a phenomenal system. It is extraordinary how it functions!" I exclaimed joyfully.

"Will he have pain?" Benjamin asked.

"I don't think so because surgery in her days was pain free because of this high-speed technology that promised quick healing. Of course, for that, there is a product in the other cupboard which we should spread over his face." I opened up the medicine compartment and was happy to see that the cream was there. I quickly spread it over his restructured face.

Discussion took another direction: why were humans and not robots conducting surgical interventions? They asked if these robotic support teams were available in the past and the present. I felt Reinhart's warmth and I sensed her annoyance rather than her interest in the question because she was sending me conflicting information. It took me a bit of time to grasp the major reason why robots were not available in this area.

Reinhart's life spanned many centuries and during that time the earth's surface changed dramatically. It was necessary to start from zero, like we are doing now. She always stockpiled technology,

drugs, and so forth in anticipation of changing climates and topography. It took time to find the right natural resources to reinvent
earlier technology that was destroyed. At one point, she decided
that surgery was not a priority and preferred to use her research
to develop the androids for other functions. The use of a surgical
guidance system, like the one we just relied on, was, as she seems
to believe, more efficient and safer than surgical procedures based
upon the use of micro-technology and robotic assistance. She
thought that the human element was critical. I agreed that we might see things differently and return to other methods.

The following day I let Peter, with his team, remove the spiny
substance on Stella's upper body and start on her face. They eventually transferred the operation to me because the "Watchful Eye"
stopped them so frequently that they ended up arguing with each
other. Having already performed this procedure, I was ready to
continue on my own. They had completed more than 50% of the
operation so I finished the rest relatively rapidly.

After Stella was put in the recovery room in the regular hospital section outside the inner circle, I sat down with my group to
comment on the operation. "It looks so easy, but it is not," was the
general remark from the members of the group.

I don't know if it was Reinhart's method, or one that I developed
on my own, but I always pointed out the good things that the team
did before turning to their mistakes. So, I told them that they had
correctly made the incisions and properly opened up the problem
zones. "The use of the technology was where you eventually went
wrong. You did not respect the depth and width parameters in the
affected regions. And, that is simply because you don't have enough
experience using the surgical equipment."

"You are right, Pamela, but these are high speed lasers that are
not adapted for beginners." Peter spoke for everyone.

"That is exactly what I am saying." I said with an air of superiority.
"I can do these things because Reinhart takes over and that is ok so
long as I am around." Their blank expressions made me uncomfortable. "I think that you should practice with the surgical equipment,
especially the high speed lasers. What if I were the person on the
table and you had to operate on me?" Jumbled mumbling resulted.

"Ok, we shall meet regularly. I'll put out a schedule and we shall create physical anomalies that must be corrected on these rubber dolls." Peter said as he pointed in the direction of the practice dolls. "Pamela is right. We have to be able to function in her absence which is not the case for the moment." He looked at me and smiled faintly. "Maybe we should redo the entire operation?"

That ended the discussion and gave us all the opportunity to go to lunch. We were happy to announce to the others that Stella and Allen would be joining us soon. Clarence was there to remind us that we still had other reptilian humans to deprogram and wondered when we would get on to that. Mathilda mentioned that there were still programmed humans that needed to be treated. "Some of them have imperfections, perhaps you should restructure them now. Why let them come face to face with their deformities. You are doing that for the reptilian humans."

Even if she was right, the reptilian humans were our priority. We would have to see how the two musicians reacted when they were deprogrammed in 48 hours. Hopefully it would go very smoothly. That is what happened. They awakened from their sedatives and rubbed their eyes, focusing easily on us. Mathilda was there to explain the transition. She actually gave a very thorough and clear explanation of what had been happening in this Center. Her calm voice and relaxed posture put them at ease. They asked if they could meet the others.

"Yes," I heard Mathilda say, as I was getting ready to leave the room. "Remember though that there are humans who are still programmed. They will not recognize you unless you give them your code." They nodded.

Their transition was one of our success stories. They were not the most gorgeous of humans, but they were attractive in their own way. At least, it was now impossible, in view of our reconstructive surgery, to have ever imagined that they had had any reptilian features. The next step was to deprogram the remaining 6 truly reptilian humans.

A meeting was scheduled for the end of the week and all of us wanted the next 24 hours to relax before tackling the next deprogramming phase. A day at the vacation center appealed to all of us so I informed the Group of 5 of our decision and asked them to have the rooms ready and food sent out to the vacation center.

"Good idea, Pamela." Crawford said. "I think that you did an excellent transformation of those two rather special musicians." I smiled. "I didn't realize how very talented Reinhart was in the area of human surgery. She must have learned that before she delved into more ingenious studies, like creating us." He was blatantly surprised since he had never seen Reinhart operate on someone.

"Probably," I replied dryly.

"So, you are going to deprogram the remaining reptiles, I gather." Flanders spoke up. "Be careful of them." I nodded, determined not to share any more of my suspicions or hopes regarding these reptilian humans with the Group of 5.

"Have you spoken to Mathilda or Isabel?" Gordon asked.

"No. Quite frankly I have not even had the time to study their files. The reconstructive surgery has been exhausting. I shall look into that after the meeting on Friday."

"Would you like us to be available?" Miller asked.

"No!" I exclaimed and then quickly changed the subject. "How are things going in the Library?"

"They have all read a great deal in the areas that interest them. " She leaned her head back in a reflective way. "Strange, Mathilda seems to appreciate the Dictators in your human past. She is fascinated by their quest for power at any cost. She even went so far as to mention her admiration for them to me."

"Bad news," repeated several times in my head. Not too long ago I thought that I recognized her desire for power, but I could not reveal that to the Group of 5.

"Well, Agnes, I think that Mathilda is just fascinated with strong, lustful emotions that could drive someone to something bordering on nymphomania. She has the reputation of being sexually promiscuous. But, wiping out masses of people to acquire wealth and power does not seem to be the logical evolution of her personality. She does like to use her skills in psychoanalysis to try to confuse and manipulate me, and probably other members of our Group and...apparently the 5 of you. But, I don't see her personality as being strong enough for her to become a diabolical, power hungry maniac, who would contrive with whomever," I stared intensely at each member of the Group of 5, "to accomplish what could only be a futile effort to bring all of us humans down!"

"And, as always, you are so naïve, Pamela." Crawford hoped to add an element of doubt. I just laughed heartily and he continued in a sober tone. "Oh well, we shall wait for you to get back to us on whether or not Isabel and Mathilda would like to have our help."

"Did you remove all the video-surveillance equipment?" I asked changing the subject a second time. They nodded. "And have you removed the birth control medication?"

"Oh, we stopped that the day that you mentioned it to us. You have been eating uncontaminated, as you put it, food for the last few weeks." He said looking up at the ceiling for guidance. I was wrong then, maybe someone did get pregnant just after our last meeting. Maybe I was going to be the first person to get pregnant.

Time off in the vacation center was exactly what we all needed. We were learning how to work together, but we knew nothing about having playful, fun time together, which did not come naturally to us, like it did to our children who knew how to laugh and tease one another. Not everyone left for the vacation center, though. James, Clarence, Adam, Tirence and the rest of the agricultural workers stayed behind with Ralph and Ferdinand who told me that they did not trust the Group of 5 enough to leave them on their own even for one day.

As soon as I arrived, I was appalled at the way the Group of 5 crafted a bewitching vacation environment. From the very instance that Peter and I entered our bedroom to drop off our luggage, we were spellbound by the fragrant scent of an aromatic blend of rose petals, jasmine, vanilla and lavender that filled the air. I fell captive to these inviting aromas emanating from the bedroom, like from my small cubicle...my private sanctuary in my programmed life. I noticed the hypnotic effect of these sublime odors on Peter and I eluded his warm hugs and sensual kisses focusing my attention on the impertinence of the Group of 5. I was slightly embarrassed by the nostalgic, rather than romantic, grip that these aromas had on me, and was determined not to succumb to android manipulation. So, I pulled Peter out of the bedroom and back into the fresh air around the pool side, where we both sat speechless.

When the others staggered out of their rooms a good hour after us, I knew from their disheveled appearances and smiling faces that the Group of 5 was probably quite pleased with the result of their experiment. Peter and I got up and followed them into the dining room.

The ambiance of the dining room with dim, soft lights and sensual, moody lounge-style music playing was certainly what the Group of 5 imagined to be a slice of paradise. Even though I pretended not to notice these romantic touches, I did find the comfortable cushion-backed chairs and glass topped tables, with center pieces of freshly picked wild flowers of varying colors and fragrances so artistically arranged in large, glass vases, a welcomed change from the long, white, drab tables and straight back chairs we were accustomed to in the cafeteria.

The Group of 5 had arranged for a sumptuous buffet of colors, aromas, tastes and textures. Our everyday meals were nourishing, but simple. Unlike the special meals we received in code-labeled boxes that met our individual vitamin and mineral needs during our programmed lives, today we were all eating the same daily meals served in a cafeteria style. So, of course, being able to pick and choose the vegetarian foods that we liked the most was refreshing and mouth-watering after all these months of planned menus.

There was a large, shiny, silver plate, laden with layers of freshly cut fruits like mangos, papayas, bananas, melons, a variety of berries and citrus fruits, and more to entice our appetites. There were plates filled with slices of fresh, crunchy vegetables like carrots, cucumbers, and radishes, decoratively surrounding pulpy slices of tomatoes, mushrooms and avocados on beds of lettuce delicately seasoned with fresh herbs like basil, dill, garlic, tarragon and parsley. We salivated as our eyes feasted on vegetables cooked to perfection like string beans, broccoli, eggplant, zucchini, spinach, corn and more, smelling of cinnamon, coriander, ginger and cumin. Tofu and noodles sprinkled with ground walnuts stood majestically in a large bowl in the middle of the table. We absorbed the natural succulence of these fruits and vegetables grown in our gardens and savored the taste of our aphrodisiac meal that awakened our palates and our erotic desires.

We moved onto the outside deck where we broke up into groups trying our best to engage in small talk, which did not go very far. As that faded out, we danced, pretending to spoon our partners to the low, moody music. Everything appeared so contrived that we all eventually gravitated to the side walls and stood like wall flowers staring at each other. We needed something dramatic, or just different, to help us to break free from the pressure of our lives and have fun. Fortunately, the children provided us with that healthy diversion that caught our interest. We all watched them frolicking about, running in different directions, jumping over low walls, and swimming in the heated pool. Their laughter was contagious and their games inspired us.

So we had child-style fun. With our clothes wet and sticky from chasing each other, jumping high walls and wading in the heated pool, we collapsed one after the other onto the lounge chairs. Peter and I had just sat down when Frederic appeared out of nowhere. He jumped up on his father's knees, as he grabbed my wet hair and pulled me closer to the both of them. He chattered about all the games and machines in the gym and how the three of them planned to play wall tennis-a game invented by androids-in the morning.

"Jonathan is a great player." I said spontaneously, remembering how much I marveled at his moves when we were programmed.

"Oh yeah?" Peter replied as if I had just challenged him to show me how well he could play.

"I said that without thinking. When I was here with Jonathan we were both programmed. I might just have been seeing what the androids wanted me to see." I said, throwing my arms up in the air. But it went unnoticed. I heard Peter call out to Jonathan and ask him if he wanted to play wall tennis with him in the morning. So a match was scheduled.

"Well, we shall see tomorrow which one of us is the real champion." Peter boasted.

"I didn't know that you liked wall tennis, Peter." I felt uneasy.

"Well, you do now. And, I was trained by the best android coaches when I was young. I used to entertain those miserable machines with my smooth and precise moves." He called out to Jonathan. "I hope that you are not going to disappoint me. I would like a bit of a challenge to make the match more interesting for the crowd."

"Am looking forward to the match." Jonathan's voice roared over the noise of the others who were already taking odds on who would win.

"Oh, that is great, Daddy. I shall be there to see you win!" Frederic was sitting on his father's lap, swinging his legs with excitement as they knocked up against his father's legs. "We shall be cheering loudly...huh, Mommy?"

"Of course," Peter replied. "I am counting on you and your Mother," he looked at me, "to be present routing for me." He rubbed the top of Frederic's head, making him laugh. I flashed Peter a broad smile.

Our fun time with Frederic ended abruptly when Rebecca and Samuel called out to Frederic to come back to the bedroom with them. We covered our little Prince with a lot of kisses, and, giggling from our attention, he ran off to join his friends.

We all got up to leave when the androids opened the ceiling of the vacation center so that we could see the sky and breathe in the outside air. Peter and I watched the orchestrated movement of the stars as they found their proper place in that immense universe, like we often did when we lived on the outside. "I want to explore this planet." He said in a soft voice. "But, I won't stop there. I want to explore the world above! That is my dream, Pamela, and I hope that you will come with me and that you will live those discoveries at my side!" He stared deep into my eyes, searching for my promise to be with him. "You will come with me, Pamela?"

Chapter 12-A Crafty Scheme

With or without much sleep, we all looked relaxed and happy in the morning. I went jogging along the natural forest trail. This time it was obvious to me that only artificial plants and trees were behind those glass enclosures. I decided that with time I would fill that area with natural plants, plants growing on the earth today. That I would bring back samples from the expeditions and plant them in good, healthy soil to grow. As I immersed myself in these thoughts, I accidently took the wrong turn and found myself next to the zoo-- that somber place that I would have preferred to have avoided.

The stuffed animals were no longer frightening to me and I finally understood why, in my programmed state, I found the immobility of these animals strange. As I stood in front of the predator cage, close to the polar bear enclosure where we found Eunice and Imogen bound together, information started to invade my consciousness. Reinhart was validating the existence of the different species as well as the period in human history when they existed. I found this information particularly revealing because it meant these animals actually existed and were not imagined and fabricated by Group of 5.

I was simultaneously pleased and surprised that the knowledge that Reinhart was uploading to me was not just scientific facts, but also historical facts, something that I never imagined she would feed me. "So her personality, her consciousness, exists or is embedded into the knowledge that I downloaded inside of me, as she told me." I said out loud as if someone were listening to me. "But, I don't think that I would ever have enclosed live animals in such little quarters. They should be free." I argued.

"Pamela," I looked up and saw Isabel. She was only a few feet away from me. "We could have gone jogging together. The others are now preparing for individual exercises." She rambled on. "You do know that Peter and Jonathan have a wall tennis match." I laughed at that one and she joined in.

"But, you know Isabel it is a good idea to have competitive sports. We need more than just intellectual challenges." She nodded. "And remember, we did have baseball and basketball matches when we were living on the outside. They were quite fun."

"Absolutely, it is good to diversify our lives. We have turned into machines concentrating on research and development and forgetting about having fun and playing games." She added.

"We never have the chance to talk. How is your training in the transport unit going?" I asked.

"It is extraordinary. I have learned so much about piloting those enormous machines, although Mathieu appears to be much more adept at it than I am. I have not had the opportunity to look at the engineering designs though." Her face was flushed with excitement.

"It doesn't matter. The information that you would access is not up-to-date. I shall explain all of that to you as soon as I finish with the programmed humans. "

"Thanks, Pamela. I know that I am capable of understanding and maybe even ameliorating the most updated technology." She stared off in the distance. "I want to have Mathieu's child so badly." She whispered like someone might overhear our conversation. "I have this strange feeling, though, that I won't be able to have a baby." She looked at me with tears in her eyes.

I didn't know if this was the right moment to bring up her problem. Yes, we were alone and we were close friends at the end of my time on the outside, but the subject was delicate; so I took a different approach.

"I am certain that everything is fine. You know what, I can verify it for you and that will make you more relaxed. Stress can prevent pregnancy."

"You would do that for me, Pamela?"

"Well, actually, Reinhart would do that for you through me. As I mentioned so many times, she uploads the data when a problem arises. After once I see and use the knowledge and techniques that are transmitted into my consciousness, I can refer back to them and use them when I want." I involuntarily bit down on my lower lip, indicating Reinhart's cogitation.

"I like the symbiotic relationship I have with her. She respects my consciousness as much as I respect hers. When she uploads information to me, I feel her warmth and energy and visualize the techniques and understand all the intricacies." I sighed. "If I were a scientist, I would be pestering her all the time for answers." I chuckled. "But yes, I am here for you if you want."

"Could you do that soon?"

"Beginning of the week?" She nodded. "Meet me in the birthing center. You must ignore the androids."

At that moment an ingenious idea took over my thoughts. I was going to engage in the old divide and conquer tactic: The Group of 5 was so tightly knit that they shared everything with each other. I had to create rivalry and one of the best ways to do that was to show favoritism. Flanders was Reinhart's assistant in the past. I could use him to assist me with the techniques that he knew and used and that way separate him from the others. I would deprive him of new research, which was quite easy to do.

Isabel was staring at me. "Sorry, but I was considering the utility of Flanders. He was Reinhart's assistant in the past and is very much at ease with reproduction." Her eyes grew wide. "I can control him very well and I won't let him examine you, just help me analyze the results." Her head was hanging low and her lips were trembling. "Relax!" I took her head in my hands as tears flowed down her angelic face. "I promise you that you shall bear his child, even if it means resorting to assisted methods. Do you trust me?"

"Yes."

I gave her a big hug. "We have to rush back because if I miss this tennis match, Peter will never forgive me." That brought a slight smile to her face. I took her hand in mine and led her along the trail and back to the others.

We got there just as Peter and Jonathan were calling for all of us to get seated and ready for the opening of the match. Randolph came up behind me. "What is wrong with him, Pamela?"

I turned to face him. "What do you mean? You never wanted to compete against one of us in a sport?"

"He has become very possessive of you, Pamela. He even wants to prove that he is the best for you." I exalted seeing Randolph acting jealous.

"You are the same. For that matter, all men are the same." I declared and then ran off in Peter's direction with Randolph close behind.

Peter and Jonathan patted each other on the shoulders and wished each other good luck. "Those of you who know the rules please be patient for a few minutes while I explain the rules to the others." Peter said in a loud, calm voice. "We each have 10 turns with the wall. The android assistants will count the rounds and the number of times the player's ball has hit the wall before a miss. The winner will be the one who has the highest number of hits after the 10 rounds."

There were three walls next to each other. "I'll take the far left wall." Jonathan said.

"Ok, with me. I shall take the far right so that we are not on top of each other."

They put on a good show. There was real tension because they were both very good players. I heard Frederic screaming his father's name energetically, encouraging him to win. "Beat him, Daddy! You can do it! Win, Win Win...!" He chanted.

I stayed concentrated on Peter's hits, unable to count Jonathan's hits at the same time. At one point, to overshadow Imogen's thundering shouts for her champion, Jonathan, I did the same for Peter. And I did it naturally, happy to show my excitement. "Keep it up, Peter. You are in the lead. Win for Frederic and Me. We are counting on you." I grabbed Frederic's hands and we jumped up and down screaming his name, over and over again.

The group was divided. Randolph aligned himself with Jonathan's camp. Everyone jumping and clapping for their chosen winner. When the match ended and the android judges announced the winner, the count could not have been better for me. They had the same number of hits or one hundred. They raised their fists and slapped each other on their backs, before throwing their rackets high up in the air. I felt happy and relieved. No hard feelings between the two champions and no retributions from Peter after I had boasted last night about Jonathan's talents.

Frederic and I rushed over to Peter, throwing our arms around him, and told him how fantastic he was and how proud we were of his wall tennis skills. "I could have won," he insisted. "If only I had not underestimated my opponent and started out slowly in the beginning."

"That is definitely a male thing," I mumbled as I planted a big kiss on his sweat-drenched forehead. We left him to shower and to get ready for lunch.

We finished the vacation by lazing around the poolside. At one moment, I dragged Peter through that artificial waterfall and relived the nostalgia of another time. Even though the 24 hours went fast, we made an important discovery... we could have fun together.

We returned in time for the meeting that Ferdinand had scheduled for late afternoon. He opened the meeting by complimenting us on the success of the surgical operations and the deprogramming of Adam. Clarence and Adam were at the meeting and quickly confirmed that the deprogramming of the other reptilian humans should be under their supervision. They wanted to deprogram all of them at the same time and rapidly, by using electric shock.

I reminded them that the Group of 5 warned me about the remaining six and recently Flanders told me that it would be dangerous to have them deprogrammed at the same time because there were three male marine iguanas and only two female of the same species. The marine iguanas fought violently during mating season. The vote was in favor of Clarence's and Adam's strategy. Stuart, Diana, Randolph, James, Peter, and I would be waiting in the corridor to intervene only if Clarence or Adam requested it.

They left together, bowing their reptilian bodies ceremoniously in deference to our vote of confidence. The discussion turned to our recent projects to produce a new generation of humans. I added that I received the information on the genetic profile of everyone and found no problems with parenting choices.

"I do have a suggestion, nonetheless, which is not meant to put anyone ill at ease." Their smiles vanished. "You know that we, rather us women, have been taking birth control medication all our lives.

Granted there were children born on the outside of the center without any complications but only because the Group of 5 decided to permit it by removing the birth control medication in our food boxes."

"So! Where are you going from here?" Sarah asked.

"Well, when we were eating in the center, and, even when we were eating on the outside in the cavern environment, our meals were prepared according to our biological and physiological, thus also our hormonal, needs. In other words, our food contained birth control pills properly adapted to our individual hormone levels." I forced a smile.

The subject embarrassed me, even though it was natural to talk about this; anyway, I had to because of Isabel's and Mathilda's problem. "Since we returned to the inside, the androids have just been sprinkling a general birth control powder on our plates. We are not necessarily receiving the proper doses for our individual needs and may therefore have developed hormonal imbalances that might need to be treated in order to get pregnant. I am going to check my hormone level to make sure that I am ok, and would do that for anyone else." I purposely did not mention Isabel. Our eyes met in quiet complicity. I noticed that the other women had low, slightly slanted eyebrows and squinted their eyes. At least this meant that they were taking my remarks seriously.

"That is fine with me." Sarah finally broke a long silence. "Yes, I think what Pamela is recommending makes a lot of sense." Her position helped to convince the others. "I'll mention this to Eunice and Imogene. I shall be seeing them this afternoon."

"I might add that those of us who have never had children should also have an ultrasound scan." Their mouths tightened. "Ok, it is just a recommendation, which I am going to do even though I already had a child. I want to make certain that everything is ok. You can all do what you want. "

"All these precautions are a bit ridiculous, but, well, I am willing to go forward with all the tests." Mathilda said, as she threw her hands up in the air like, in her case, it was useless. I personally didn't care what the others decided to do but was grateful that Mathilda volunteered to follow my example.

"So when will we do all this?" Diana asked, in an unenthusiastic voice.

"Monday morning?" I suggested. It was approved.

"And, the men, we are ok?" Benjamin asked with trepidation.

"I have no idea, but you are right to bring up the subject. I can also check out your sperm and the sperm of anyone else who is interested in verifying its vitality." The men readily agreed.

"Ok, in that case, I shall see the women in the morning and men in the afternoon." It was settled.

"The deprogramming of the non-reptilian humans?" Mathilda asked and added that she believed that we should take care of that very soon. "I think that we should deprogram them one at the same time." She took a long deep breath to put everyone ill-at-ease. "I am surprised that Clarence and Adam had no major difficulties moving from a programmed to deprogrammed state. I spent time with the young rebels who are still confined to their cubicles under the surveillance of the android guards. They actually started to work in the agricultural center sooner than anticipated because I felt that they were emotionally stable enough to do so. Nonetheless, I have some concerns about the personality of Tirence, who has not yet convinced me that he can live peacefully around unattractive humans."

"Now, I understand why they showed up for work sooner than I had anticipated." Ralph commented. "One loses track of time in the center which is why I didn't question their arrival." He rubbed his short beard nervously. "Did you make the decision on your own, Mathilda?"

"Of course, they were put in my charge. I informed them about the fact that the Group of 5 had kept us programmed. We had many group meetings dealing with negative emotions. I pointed out their mistakes and had long discussions with them about how to live in society."

"Perhaps you should have passed your observations by us, before authorizing them to start working in the agricultural unit." Ferdinand admonished.

"Wow, we are all at fault here." I interjected. "Most of us have been so busy on other projects that we have not paid enough attention to what is going on in other areas. Admittedly, it seemed normal that they were working and asking to be assigned permanently to the agricultural unit." I sighed heavily. "It would now be awkward for us to reinstate the former policy."

"They all are under the watchful eyes of the android assistants who accompany them in the morning to the agricultural center and back and forth to their cubicles for lunch and then for dinner. They eat all their meals alone in their cubicles as none of their partners survived the revolt." She said in an inanimate voice, like she was giving a boring lecture. "I have complied with our original agreement in almost every detail, except that perhaps I accelerated their work program."

"Mathilda," Ferdinand began, "taking initiative can be a good thing, but there are situations where individual initiative is inappropriate. This is one of those cases." Ferdinand looked straight into my eyes and then finished what he had to say. "Pamela is right that it would be awkward to reinstate the original schedule for punishment. There is a risk that they would feel martyred. I want your word though that you will not do something like this in the future."

"I am sorry. I didn't realize that I had to consult with everyone before taking the next step. This will never happen again." She spoke convincingly. Nonetheless, Crawford's recent comment put me on guard. Mathilda liked to make decisions and manipulate others with a feigned innocence. She did that with the children in the beginning. Perhaps my original power-hungry impressions were valid. And, I had already spoken to her about making unilateral decisions. Obviously, she did not take my admonition seriously. My thoughts were running wild. I did support her a few minutes ago and could not go back on that. That did not prevent me, though, from watching her more closely in the future.

The time sequence for exploration of the planet, was put on the agenda for the next meeting, which would take place within 24 hours after the reptilian humans were all deprogrammed and their individual capacities evaluated.

"Sarah and Ruth, did you, Adam and Clarence study reptilian behavior well-enough to proceed with the deprogramming of the others?" I asked as it was important for Adam and Clarence to be prepared for the worst.

"We did," Ruth spoke up. "We found confirmation of certain ins-tinctive behavioral patterns, principally for dominance and territo-riality. They may or may not be present in these new breed reptiles, but we are prepared nonetheless should such a problem arise." She looked at John who picked up the conversation.

"There are three female reptilian humans among the remaining six. Two females and three males are black marine iguanas—simi-lar to Adam. There is a female that is the same species as Clarence, a bearded lizard." Sarah looked at Clarence who nodded approvingly. "I believe that all these reptiles are very territorial."

"Clarence is well aware of that." Ruth insisted. "He is going to bring a laser stun gun with him just in case there is a violent reac-tion from the males."

"And, the females, there is no reason to be worried?" I asked, a bit surprised that they didn't consider their reactions.

"They should not be a problem unless the males are attrac-ted instantly to them. Clarence told me that males will not be at-tracted to different species." Ruth stopped and raised her eyes in thought. "Of course Clarence's convictions don't simplify things as there are more male black marine iguanas than females and they are a species that fights during mating seasons, as we men-tioned earlier."

"Ruth, perhaps you should put the females in another room." I spoke with authority. "Already the males might fight for territorial dominance. You don't need to take the risk that the females will provoke more chaos."

"I agree." She lowered her eyes, staring at the tabletop. "Clarence and Adam don't see it that way. They told me that they were not at-tracted to the reptilian females. Their explanation is that all these years of programming have made them attracted to human traits and, in spite of the fact that they are physically reptilian, they do not find reptilian physical traits sexually enticing. They are certain that the males will not be drawn to the females. And therefore rep-tilian females would not be a natural conquest for these males."

No one said anything. To break this uncomfortable silence I asked Ruth whether Adam and Clarence's observations were sup-ported by the research she did on the subject.

"I have to admit that I was unable to verify the accuracy of their conclusions one way or the other."

"Adam is attracted sexually to Eunice and Clarence to you?" I asked as if I were conducting an investigation.

"Apparently." She moved about in her chair. "It is repulsive for me!" She screamed violently as she raised herself from the chair. "This is all very difficult for me. He remembers our programmed existence too well and working with him on a daily basis over the deprogramming of the reptilian humans has been particularly unpleasant for me." She threw herself into John's arms and cried.

"Ruth, we are going to take you off this project." Ferdinand said. "There are other things that you are more qualified to do anyway."

She was clinging to John who was holding her tightly in his strong arms. "Something must be done about this." He finally announced in his deep, booming voice.

"Does anyone know how Eunice is dealing with this?" I asked.

"She loves him," we heard Ruth say between sobs.

"Is copulation between Adam and Eunice feasible?" Benjamin asked in a trembling voice.

"Oh, how wretched!" Sarah rushed over to help John comfort Ruth.

"Normally, No." I announced. "But, I don't agree with Clarence that lizards will only mate with their own species of lizards. Interspecies mating, first recognized in studies during the 21st century produced new species of lizards. I also want to emphasize that not all species fight for dominance over a female. Actually their dominance is normally more territorially oriented and motivated." I was certain that the lizards would have to be observed and studied closer.

"I have not examined Clarence and Adam," I continued, "but they should be equipped with one or more penises capable of penetrating a human female. And, they are a human-reptilian mix, so there are some common bases for conception and an ultimate genetic mix." I was receiving conflicting messages from Reinhart. She was focusing now on the three female reptiles. "Not all reptiles lay eggs, some give birth to live babies, which is not the normal process for the two species we are addressing, unless, of course, they have evolved differently physiologically and anatomically because of their genetic mutations, which means that fertilization by a reptilian human male could produce live offspring. And, of course, where Adam and Clarence are concerned they have more human DNA than the remaining reptiles."

"So, Eunice could carry one or more of Adam's children?" Benjamin repeated his question in more detail.

"I have no idea where the genetic reptilian dominance is in either Adam or Clarence. I shall have to study that." I looked at Ruth and Sarah who were capable of carrying out this kind of basic genetic research, but they turned away from me when my eyes met theirs. I understood that the issue was too close to home to be comfortable for them.

"I think that I shall arrange to see Clarence and Adam myself over the next week. I need to examine them, identify their strictly human features, and test them. It will take time. And, Ruth, you cannot be forced to reproduce with Clarence or anyone else. I shall also explain that to both of them. They will have to get the consent from their proposed partner to reproduce and then that request must get the approval from our committee. And, consent by both parties is necessary, in any event, for sexual relationships."

The whole subject was incredibly exciting on a scientific level. Will these new life forms become active members of our community or will they threaten our safety, or worse, will they try to dominate and control us? Ruth's hysteria only added to the urgency of this matter. I would have to come up with answers soon which meant that I would have to convince Adam and Clarence to let me examine them.

Everyone's eyes were on me when Ferdinand suggested that we adjourn this meeting and have dinner. "I believe that we have covered a lot of ground today." I heard Ferdinand say in an administrative tone.

"I don't agree." I spoke up. "We have only begun to scrape the surface."

Peter tried to take my hand in his to comfort me but I resisted. "I have a lot of work to do." I said as I got up and meandered out of the room.

Chapter 13-Playing God

I had no time to relax that weekend, with the hormone tests scheduled for Monday, and the impending deprogramming of the reptilian humans for the near future.

I was not hungry so I spent a bit of time studying the two cases that Flanders mentioned to me. Isabel's problem was, according to Flanders, not hormonal but structural and he was trying to convince me that there were weak walls in the uterus and the tubes. That kind of problem was not infrequent in the past and Reinhart knew how to surgically correct it. "Obviously the Group of 5 did not see that as a problem because they were using fertilization in vitro." I had to ventilate.

Mathilda, however, did have major complications that needed special treatment. I wanted to see the results of the ultrasound scanner before I mentioned it to her. I was worried that she would take this badly and then, of course, there was Randolph to deal with. I again mentioned Randolph to Peter late in the evening when we were alone together in the lounge. I told him that we should talk to both of them after the Monday clinical tests. He agreed that it would be better to have them together when I announced the problem and that he would be there to help me convince Randolph.

"You still don't think that you can surgically repair it?" He was sitting exactly like the famous sculpture of Rodin, the "Thinker," which had left a strong impression on me when I was studying human history. There was something comic about it but I stifled my laughter, which did not seem appropriate at the moment.

"No, Peter, apparently it is outside of Reinhart's competence. I might get a reaction from her after the ultrasound scan on Monday."

"Admittedly, Pamela," he said, stretching his long legs out in front of him and thus moving into a more relaxed position, "I wanted to tell Randolph, but just didn't find the right moment. Or, rather, a moment when Mathilda was not draping herself all over him." He smirked. "She is very possessive of him at the moment."

"Strange that you should say that." His eyes widened. "Randolph said exactly the same thing about you with me the other day."

"Doesn't surprise me. He needs some alone time and is just projecting on others." He pulled me over onto his lap and buried his head delicately in my cleavage before picking me up and carrying me back to the bedroom...

I spent the next day delving into the genetic composition of the remaining reptilian humans. They were definitely hybrids. The Group of 5 used the same Reinhart hybrid genetic mix for all the males, so in effect they had the same genetic line with dominate and recessive genetic differences limited to mild differentiation in the intensity of their color, for example.

Reinhart flashed me her original project and the results that she expected. In fact, she limited the restructuration of human DNA to the incorporation of the mechanical physiology of the reptilian skeletal and muscular structure, including reptilian skin. She was also interested in their breathing capacity, in particular under water, and the thermal regulatory mechanisms in reptiles. She spliced the human and reptilian DNA strands to increase pulmonary capacity and to modify the human thermal regulatory center of the brain. Otherwise, she wanted to keep intact all other aspects of human physiology. Did she accomplish that? That was the question that I could only answer after a full examination and scan of Clarence and Adam.

In spite of the enthusiasm of my symbiont, I found her research rather diabolical. I could not share her fascination with these hybrid humans as her manipulation of human anatomy and physiology to create a more resistant reptilian human flew in the face of my idea of the sanctity of the human race. After all, eugenics, the predecessor of genetic engineering, were the bread and butter of fascists and fascist wannabees endeavoring to create a master race. Nonetheless, I had to admit that she was definitely a genius whose research might have been applauded by the scientific community at the time she was alive, if circumstances had not caused the total annihilation of the human race.

I kept my discoveries to myself. I was haunted by what the Group of 5 had told me about the learning capacity and superior intellectual capacity of these hybrids. It made no sense because only a small part of the brain, the thermal reader section, was altered. How could that produce more brilliant cognitive skills?

I carried out all the tests on the humans on Monday morning, one after the other. I did rely upon Flanders and Crawford to read the various genetic codes. They were all perfect species of humans with no degenerative genes, except for Jonathan. We decided to wait and see if his offspring would have any spinal problems that I now knew could be corrected easily. The problems for Isabel and Mathilda were even more bewildering now that I discovered these genetic irregularities which appeared only in the male recessive genes, and could have been removed if the Group of 5 had been more conscientious.

I met with Isabel and Mathieu and mentioned that I would have to reinforce Isabel's uterus and tubes for her to carry a fetus. We discussed the alternative, which was fertilization in vitro and use of the artificial uterus. I explained to them that she would have to take hormones to produce a larger quantity of ova and that I would extract and then select the best quality ovum.

"Everything would be on a comfortable schedule." I added. They wanted to discuss it alone and promised to give me their decision the following day. Neither one of them was bothered by the use of the artificial uterus. In fact they both mentioned that by using the artificial uterus they could both be more readily available for exploration of the planet. They confirmed they would resort to the Group of 5's system of fetal development the following day.

Peter was present when I explained to Randolph and Mathilda that Mathilda's uterus would not support a pregnancy. Neither one of them had any reaction. In fact, they both sat so calmly staring at Peter and me that I felt particularly uncomfortable. Consequently, I moved around in my chair and played with the file in front of me.

Eventually, I told them about the alternative, using the artificial uterus, a choice that I just gave to Isabel and Mathieu earlier.

"Perhaps the two of you should talk to each other and get back to us?" I suggested.

"So, in fact, we cannot have fun making a baby?" Mathilda asked, turning to Randolph and running her tongue sensually between her lips.

"Yes, you can have fun making the baby, Mathilda," I answered embarrassed by her seductive gesture. "And you can carry the child for a few months before we will have to transfer the child to one of the artificial uteruses for the rest of the term of the pregnancy."

"Can we visit the baby and watch him or her grow?" Randolph asked, as his face lit up in delightful curiosity.

"Absolutely - that can certainly be arranged. You can go and talk to the baby and see the baby's progress. You can even read to the baby or play music while you are there." I stopped to take in their wide-eyed expressions of happiness. "Yes, it could be an amazing experience!" I finished enthusiastically.

"Well, then I am ok with that." Randolph said emphatically, while Peter and I sat there grasping our chairs. I never expected him to agree.

"So what do you think, Mathilda?" He asked her. She smiled at him and nodded.

"Thank you, Pamela. I count on you to help me during the first couple months and to safely transfer the baby for us to the artificial uterus." She turned to Randolph and winked. "Let's go have that fun!" They ran off, giggling like children.

"Did that just happen, or was I dreaming?" Peter asked after they left, shaking his head in disbelief.

"Me too, I am in shock!" I exclaimed.

"I think that Randolph liked the idea of watching his baby grow." I nodded. "And, I think that Mathilda liked the idea of keeping her body intact."

"I think that you understood perfectly, Peter." I sat back remembering how horrified I was when I saw those fetuses growing in artificial uteruses when Flanders took me for a tour of the birthing unit while I was living under android supervision in this center. I even tried to hit Flanders because I found the scene so imperso-nal and so dehumanizing. He thought that I overreacted but stood patiently waiting until I calmed down so he could continue the tour of the unit. And, today, I have two human couples ready to use the artificial uteruses. "Was I right to be horrified with those artificial uteruses?" I looked inquisitively at Peter.

"No - but, it was different. There were no human parents ready to covet and visit their babies."

"Yes, that must be the difference. Just seeing all those capsules full of human fetuses at different stages of development and no human presence." I was not completely convinced.

"Maybe I am just too sensitive?" I said as I stood up and straightened out my robe. "Well I can feel Reinhart's warmth suffusing me. She seems quite pleased that two of our couples are willing to take advantage of her advanced technology in order to become parents." I arranged all the human files and left with Peter for dinner. After not eating for almost 24 hours, I was famished.

There was a lot of life at the table with all the wild chattering. "The race is on." John announced. "Who is going to be the first woman pregnant?"

There was plenty of laughter and men bragging about the high quality speed and efficiency of their sperm. Competing sperm was strange dinner conversation, so strange that I let myself slip out of it and think about other things. Tomorrow I would be meeting with Clarence and Adam. I could feel their eyes on me. "It must be hard for them to find themselves outside of this ruckus." I threw them a friendly smile. There were a couple seats next to me and they moved into them.

"Well, Pamela, have you studied the files?" Clarence asked.

"Yes, I have looked over them. I shall go into that with you in more detail tomorrow." I turned to look down at my dish, intentionally avoiding eye contact.

"You are both hybrids." I heard them grunt.

I leaned my head slightly up in their direction. "I shall explain all of that to you tomorrow."

"We shall be there." Clarence answered. "And, Pamela," he said as he reached over and lightly petted my arm, "we know that you are our friend. We also know that there is only so much that you can do for us. We are happy that you are there for us."

"Does that mean that you are coming to terms with your physical appearances?" Even though my question was directed to Clarence, I did not want to disclose our agreement, so I included Adam in the discussion.

"I am ok with the way I look." Adam spoke up enthusiastically.

"I am coming to terms with it although I want to know more about what I am and what I could have been if those androids had not interfered with 'Mother Nature.' He forced a tight smile.

"I understand. You will know more tomorrow." I smiled appreciatively. I was somewhat reassured that they were not going to try to crucify me because of what my biological mother did; I felt better about meeting with them. We all split up going our own ways. I heard Mathilda call out that the children made a lot of progress and that they were in bed asleep. That made it easier for Peter, John, Ruth and I to take our time leaving for the inner circle.

"Sarah and Stanislas make a good match." I mentioned.

"We"- John looked at Ruth-"are happy for them." He leaned back in his chair. "We were brought up to date on everything and understand that Isabel and Mathieu, and Mathilda and Randolph, will be resorting to other methods of procreation."

"It looks that way. I didn't get the confirmation yet from Isabel. I am glad that they are taking it well."

"And Clarence?" Ruth asked in a barely audible, raspy voice.

"I am seeing Clarence and Adam tomorrow." John and Ruth moved forward in their chairs eager to hear more. "I have to confirm my observations but from what my studies have thus far revealed, I would say that both of them have dominant human physiology apart from what is visible on the surface. They may have organs, though, that are fortified with reptilian characteristics." I breathed deeply at the same time that their breathing picked up. "If you don't mind, it has been a long day and I am tired."

"That is true." Peter stood up and took my hand." We shall see you tomorrow morning."

I was not in the mood for anything but sleep. Peter understood that when I rolled over on my side and faced the wall, pretending that sleep was overtaking me, which was unfortunately not the case. I was definitely worried about how Adam and Clarence would accept their real physiological and anatomical differences, something that preoccupied my thoughts. So I lay awake for a long time just listening to Peter's slow, rhythmic breathing. It had a hypnotic effect on me, calming my stress and eventually bringing on desperately needed sleep.

The reptilian humans did not seem to be such a problem for me when I woke up. I even felt optimistic about their future, that seemed to be so closely linked to the ultimate exploration of the planet. It was imperative that our group finish with deprogramming and discover the outside world-those distant places, now accessible with the transport vehicles. I didn't try to analyze this mood change.

I was humming Beethoven's 9th as I jumped out of bed and ran for a shower. "I'll see you at breakfast." I said as I rushed to pass through the wall.

I ate fast so that I could get on with the Clarence/Adam project, as I referred to it. They were very cooperative. I took them back into the inner circle with me for the scanner. This was the first time that they passed through the wall. In fact, their passing through the wall, confirmed their dominant human side. Clarence and Adam sat patiently in a small room off the hospital unit, while I studied the results and then read the blood and urine test results and conducted several experiments.

Reinhart, camouflaged in the background of my thoughts, let me take control, apparently testing my learning skills. She wanted me to understand that I did more than just upload the information, but assimilated it, and that I was capable of analyzing certain data on my own. I had ostensible control over it and immersed myself in its essence, but I still decided that I was going to need to carry out more tests and explore their differences in more detail to be certain that my suspicions were accurate.

The reptilian anatomical and physiological differences plagued and baffled me, so I sat back in my chair, lecturing to myself as I recited all the information that I had assimilated over the last week. Apart from the reptilian skeletal/muscular system, their organs were predominantly human. In early reptiles, their reptilian brain controlled balance, breathing, heartbeat and body temperature.

The vestige of the reptilian brain in humans consists of the upper spinal column, basal ganglia, diencephalon and parts of the mid-brain. From the scanners, I noticed that Clarence and Adam had a larger, more recognizable, reptilian brain structure and a larger neo-cortex zone, which might account for their superior intellect.

Nonetheless, both Adam and Clarence, like the remaining reptilian humans, walked erect, which meant that they had a human spinal column and pelvic girdle, now confirmed with the x-rays. Walking in an erect position refined their bulky muscular bodies. In fact, their normally large legs and arms were slenderized, with the muscular formation taking on the image of a well-built athlete. In addition, their retractable claws looked like long fingernails, forming a natural extension of large but recognizable, fingers and toes. For that reason they were capable of manipulating different technology and carrying out experiments.

Thus the differences in anatomical structure were not that alarming when taken alone, but adding the physiological differences did lead to other conclusions. They were definitely hybrids and could be classified as a new species of reptiles. I focused on the physiological differences. Reinhart had apparently fortified the reptilian brain region to maximize breathing and temperature control, which may or may not have been necessary; at least that was the critical analysis that she was uploading to me.

I discovered through the x-rays and scanner that Clarence had a three-chambered heart, typical of the bearded lizard. His heart could change blood flow within the head and body to help him control his body temperature. He was not living in a desert environment so I assumed that he did not regulate his body temperature often, although he probably stimulated his brain and sensory organs first on awakening. I wondered if the ability to change blood flow could also be responsible for his intellectual capacity-if the androids were right. He could send more oxygen to his brain, the neo-cortex region, and thus increase learning capacity.

He had a normal human digestive system with all human organs intact. That differed from the classic reptilian structure of his species and allowed him to eat and digest a basically human diet without relying upon fermentation. It appeared that his urinary system had his species reptilian capability of excreting dry urine, or nitrogenous waste. So that when the urine entered the bladder the water would be reabsorbed, preventing fluid loss, something very important for adapting to dry, hot zones.

He had a human reproductive system with an exterior penis, definitely different from his species that was equipped with a hemi-penis, typical of lizards, located inside the bowel region that averted outward to enter the female to fertilize the eggs during mating.

He had the acute hearing of his species and was capable of detecting even light vibrations underground. He also had excellent visual capacity. As his species does not use a flicking tongue to check out the palatability or suitability of a plant or insect, they rely completely upon this acute vision. He had another sensory organ that is uncommon to humans, or the vomeronasal organ, located in the roof of his mouth. This organ consists of two fluid filled sacs that connect to the nasal cavity via the nasopalatine ducts. It functions like a cross between the sensory organs of taste and smell.

Reinhart was certainly interested in his species of lizard because they can regulate their body temperature by controlling blood flow in their circulatory system. Clarence's exterior would also allow him to resist high temperatures and move easily over rocky surfaces.

I still wanted to take a closer look at his DNA profile and determine the mutating effect that all this cross breeding produced. In his case, it appeared that he could mate with humans. The question was whether the human ovum would accept fertilization outside of an in vitro fertilization and manipulation of genes. It might be possible with another reptilian human, however, like the female in his species.

Adam was more complicated. A black marine iguana is not a very attractive reptile; in fact, its wide set-eyes, smashed-in-face, spiky dorsal scales and knotty salt-encrusted head give them a fierce look. They were often described as being hideous and clumsy creatures when in fact they were not menacing but rather gentle herbivores. Adam escaped the worst of his species unattractiveness because he had true human facial features that were not in any way diminished by his dark, grayish black skin, and smooth body.

I sat back and closed my eyes for an instance trying to visualize better the physical characteristics of Adam's programmed comrades. I concluded that they were also fortunate since their facial features were more refined than those of their reptilian ancestors. Like Adam, they had high cheekbones and smooth dark, grayish black skin. Their large, flat noses and globular, wide-set eyes were not appalling and were in fact coherent with their modified reptilian-human mouth. Like Adam, their erect bodies were less scaly than that of the black marine iguana, the awkwardness associated with the black marine iguana ameliorated by this human spine and erect body.

Turning back to Adam, I assumed that he had the excellent swimming skills associated with this unique species of iguana-the only known iguana species adapted to water during Reinhart's period. And, with that integrated into his human structure, he also had some of the anatomical and physiological adaptations unique to this species and its lifestyle. He had a flattened lateral tail, like that of a crocodile. He could therefore swim like a crocodile bringing his legs tightly up against his sides and using the force of movement provided by the sinuous undulations of his flattened tail to swim. His body would move side to side as he propelled himself forward with his tail. He would swim relatively slowly to conserve energy.

These marine iguanas utilize primarily anaerobic respiration, generating lactic acid as a product for breaking down the glucose. Anaerobic metabolism is much less oxygen expensive, permitting the animal to remain submerged without surfacing to breathe. In addition, anaerobic metabolism allows them to remain active at a cooler overall body temperature than other mammals of the same size and weight. Anaerobic respiration is relied upon in humans when a sport or activity requires the use of a lot of energy within short bursts or where the heart beat is increased beyond 80% of its maximum. Unfortunately, the resultant lactic acid can produce muscle cramps for humans. I hoped that this would not be the case for Adam.

Adam was capable nonetheless of shunting blood away from the surface of his body to conserve heat and could drastically reduce his heart rate, both of which would give him the possibility of deep and long dives. With his large body, he would be able to dive to 15 to 20 meters and stay for 30 minutes or more without surfacing. Under water exploration would not be a problem for him.

In addition, as he would not be using large amounts of oxygen for physical activities, he might be able to reroute the oxygen to his brain. This could account for a higher intellectual capacity in the neo-cortex region of the brain.

Adam did not have salt glands, positioned unobtrusively above each eye and directly connected by a duct to the nostril, common to his species. These glands filter the salt from the seawater through the nasal passage, leaving salt deposits visible on the outside of the faces. As the other human reptiles did have some reptilian facial features, I assumed that they would be equipped with this filtering system, something that I would have to verify. I wondered if this lack of a filtering system might be a handicap for Adam for diving because his sinuses and sinus cavity were human. Paradoxically, though, the more I thought about that the more certain I was that Adam would have the ability to filter the salt because all aquatic creatures have the facility to filter the salt from the water and eva-cuate it through either a specific organ, or through their eyes or sinuses.

These black marine iguanas could live through periods of fa-mine by shrinking their bodies by as much as 20%. This shrinkage is so significant that it can amount to the actual absorption of bones in addition to cartilage.

Certainly the anaerobic respiration, excellent swimming ability, conservation of body heat and regulation of heart rate, along with the ability to survive for long periods without eating were interes-ting for Reinhart who was searching for species capable of survi-ving in wet, rugged environments.

The reptilian commonalities between Adam and Clarence were limited to the circulatory system and the regulation of tempera-ture. They both had some unique species traits that could make for an interesting cross breeding. On the other hand, the fact that they both had human male reproductive systems was a potential problem, if they ventured into a sexual relationship with a human.

I wanted to discourage both of them from copulating, at least for the moment.

It took me a long time, almost an entire day without eating, to review all the information available through chemical tests, blood tests, x-rays, optical tests, audio tests, and scanners. I stopped at one point, recognizing that I still had research to conduct and that the final results would not be available before I met with them. Nonetheless, I decided to give them all the information I had on their species and then describe their differences and capacities as hybrid species.

When we sat down together I started our discussion by stating that the number and structure of chromosomes differed significantly enough between the reptilian humans and pure humans which signified that they could be classified as a new hybrid species.

I continued to describe their unique features and their blended human-reptile anatomy and physiology. They listened intently as I repeated all that I had discovered to date. I saw no emotional reaction on their faces, instead they sat, relaxed and attentive.

"I have not had the time to verify the number and nature of your chromosomes. I have relied upon the information given to me by the Group of 5 and I want to analyze this on my own. It will take time." They nodded approvingly.

"Do you have any questions?" I asked, a slight faltering in my voice, as I was worried that they would raise the issue of reproduction straight away.

"We didn't find any information in the library about our species, so we were imagining the worst. I find all of what you said so interesting." Clarence spoke up. He was slowly rubbing the base of his chin in a hypnotizing, rhythmic way. "I am surprised at what I am capable of doing. In fact, I feel motivated now to take my place in the center. I think that I can contribute a great deal to the exploratory missions and to research." His eyes met mine.

My eyes widened in surprise. I was expecting arguments, accusations-something different-and was taken back by his response. Before I could say anything, Adam spoke up, acknowledging his desire to test his capacities.

"I gather that you are not disappointed with what I have just told you." I spoke calmly. "I know, rather Reinhart knows, the particularities of your species, the reason why I knew what to look for and how to evaluate the presence or absence of certain qualities. I am surprised that you found no information about your species in the library."

The discussion took off with a lot of enthusiasm. I realized that they were truly excited about their potential as they interrupted each other boasting about their differences and unique physiological qualities and capacities. It was evident that both of them were very proud of the origin of their reptilian species. I reminded them a couple times during the course of their boasting that I still did not have a final reading of their chromosomes. They ignored me until my persistence forced them to reply.

"That doesn't matter, Pamela. At least not to me." Clarence said firmly. I noticed that Adam nodded in agreement.

"Do you want me to explore your mating possibilities?" I ventured.

"Not for the moment." Adam said looking at Clarence as he spoke.

"Me neither. I can wait on that!" He curled his humanly modified lizard mouth up into a kind smile. "I know that I have been difficult lately. I even imagined myself to be in love with Ruth. Perhaps because I thought that there was nothing interesting about me. Today you changed that image I had of myself. I recognize that my differences give me more character." He stopped to stroke his chin again. "I feel proud of what I am. I am different...but not less of a person because of those differences. And, I want to stay exactly as I am." Relieved, I took a long breath.

"I agree with what he said." Adam looked down over his body. "I know that you mentioned that my species is not considered beautiful." I moved my eyes about nervously. "Don't worry, Pamela. You did the right thing to tell me. I just think that beauty is in the eyes of the beholder, like with Eunice. I do believe that she finds me beautiful and today, I find myself beautiful as well. Knowing what I am has made me feel good."

"Do you think that you can help the other reptilian humans to see the good side of themselves?" I asked both of them.

"I hope so." Clarence replied. "I am slightly worried though about their reptilian personalities. We are more human than they are." He sighed. "I think that you might be right. We should not de-program the females and males in the same room. We should separate them."

I smiled approvingly. They asked me to keep them informed about the DNA tests and asked if they could leave. Adam wanted to test his anaerobic respiration under Clarence's supervision. Clarence wanted to know more about regulating his body heat and sensory organs. "We shall let you know about our findings. Maybe we will discover other phenomenal capabilities that you didn't realize that we have." Clarence yelled joyfully, rushing out the door.

"When do we deprogram the others?" I called out.

"Tomorrow afternoon!" I heard them say simultaneously.

I was tired and hungry, but I returned to the lab facility outside of the inner circle to collect my earlier research, as well as the different blood, urine, mucous, skin, and other samples, putting them in a special thermal case that I had brought with me from the inner circle. I did not want to leave anything lying around in this lab. I also made a copy of my research and erased all the information on the lab computer. I did not want the Group of 5 to be privy to any of my findings, even though I might have to discuss certain elements with them at a later time. I had almost finished organizing myself when I heard someone enter the room. I turned to see Flanders standing rigidly in front of me.

"What can I do for you?" I asked, in a friendly tone.

"I didn't want to interrupt you earlier." He said. "I heard that your two human lizards"—Clarence and Adam, I corrected him—"met with you. How did it go?"

"Very well. Very well indeed." I retorted.

"Oh, that is a relief." He said convincingly as he sat down in one of the chairs, letting his legs stretch out in front on him, as if the news was a weight off of his android back. I gave him a quick glance.

"Is there anything that I can do for you, Edward?"

"Well, yes. You could tell me how they acted or reacted to the information you gave them."

"They are incredibly enthusiastic and visibly happy with their reptilian characteristics." I said.

"Excellent! Excellent! Then you are no longer angry with us." He now sat straight in his chair, his eyes glowing, as if flaunting his superiority in the field of genetic research.

"I never said that I was ready to forgive you for your negligence. You took enormous risks in a field of research that you were not competent to explore." He bowed his head slightly. "I have no idea how the other reptilian humans are going to react."

"But Clarence and Adam," he articulated their names in a haughty, condescending tone, "these lizards, hum, of course, their existence is not their fault," he made a guttural sound, like he was clearing his throat, "seemed pleased, you said."

"It is certainly not their fault that they have reptilian characteristics. It is yours." I replied slowly and firmly, showing him that I did not appreciate his impertinence. "And, yes. . .these Reptilian Humans," I noticed that he recognized that he had overstepped his bounds and was now leaning his head in my direction, listening closely, "are pleased with their unique characteristics. But that does not change the fact that you would never have received authorization from Elisabeth to play around with genetic mixtures." I said in a cold, critical tone.

"Agreed, Pamela. But for the moment the fact that your two prize Reptilian Humans are not traumatized is good news for me and the others." He moved to stand up. "We are available to help as we can. What do you want us to do with the mutated ovum and sperm in the laboratory?"

"Thank you for asking." I felt my heart stop. I should have thought about that. Of course I want to continue the research. "You could give them to me now. I shall put them in safe keeping."

He left and came back with a cupboard full of the mutated specimens. "I'll see you later." I said.

My thermal unit fit nicely on an empty shelf in the cupboard. I moved the cupboard down the corridors until it was lined up with the inner wall. I needed to pass through and get help. I was lucky that Benjamin and Stanislas were just on the other side, preparing to head for dinner. The body heat of the three of us was necessary to move the large cupboard through the wall and into the inner circle. "Yes, Reinhart thought about everything. Passing objects through the wall was complicated because passage was restricted to the human bio-thermal system to prevent the androids from invading the inner circle. But, it was possible to move an object when a high bio-thermal level was read. That was why Stuart and I were able to pull Randolph and his stretcher through the wall with us into the inner circle just before the revolution broke out." I reminded myself with a smile. I found a place in the refrigerator unit to stock the contents before joining the others for dinner.

I had just enough time to tell the others that Clarence and Adam were testing out some of their reptilian capacities. "I'll discuss differences at the next meeting. Suffice it to say that they are very enthusiastic about their capabilities and are motivated to participate in the exploratory missions."

"Here we are." Clarence announced. "We are just beginning to understand how we function and what remarkable creatures we are."

"So, tell us about it." James suggested.

"Later." Adam said. "We have so much to learn and understand. You have to give us a bit of time. We want to be at our best when we leave to explore the planet."

I left before the others and entered the inner circle at a spot that brought me face to face with the rejuvenation machine. It looked imposing as it stood majestically occupying a large semi-circular area. I could feel Elisabeth's high-spirited energy come alive inside of me as I went over and touched the outside of the machine. "It would take a lot of time to find all the codes for all the members of our group and enter their genetic profiles into this machine. John was already getting older and Ferdinand and Ralph might be too old for me to prolong their lives. I would have to concentrate on them and their rejuvenation before it was too late."

I looked again at the controls. Would I be able to master the system like she did? Shallow waves of confidence became stronger and stronger as I felt Reinhart's energy and enthusiasm surface. I knew that she would save me, but the others—Peter, Frederic, Randolph . . . With each name I felt positive warm vibrations coming from the depths of me. I smiled peacefully and shuffled to the bedroom.

I heard the children laughing as I passed in front of their room and lingered for a few minutes. Mathilda was telling them in a firm, yet comforting voice, that they would have to calm down and go to sleep. "Tomorrow you have much to learn. I want your parents to be happy with everything. And, Frederic, don't forget that you and Jonathan are going to give a concert on Friday. We must invite your Mother to play." She was a living dichotomy: her kind, generous and considerate side verses her power hungry side.

"Wow, Pamela, what are you doing here?" She sounded worried.

"I am tired and left the others to their conversations." She looked at me through squinting eyes. "I know that I should have moved on, but I was captivated by your kindness with the children." That brought a smile to her face. "You have so much patience. Thank you for taking such good care of them."

I was not prepared for what happened next and almost toppled over as she rushed at me and virtually collapsed into my arms. I instinctively reacted, by pushing her off of me so that I could breathe properly. "What is the matter with you, Mathilda?" I asked, struggling to regain composure.

"I know that you don't like me, Pamela? And I don't know why?" Was she more sensitive than I thought or more manipulative than I could imagine?

"I find it difficult enough to maneuver easily under the watchful eyes of the Group of 5, but then I have to pretend that your hatred of me does not bother me."

I stood staring at her, trying to read the truth buried behind her teary eyes. "I don't hate you, Mathilda. But, you are right, I don't trust you."

"I don't understand." She said, regaining her composure and taking on the clinical tone of a psychiatrist.

"Yes, you do understand. The group has warned you on many occasions that certain decisions are group decisions. That has not prevented you from acting unilaterally." She raised her eyebrows. "And, I have repeated several times that you must be careful not to let the Group of 5 lead you astray and yet, I have found you in their company a bit too often for my comfort." She moved her eyes about nervously. "And lastly, I was recently informed by one of the members of the Group of 5 that you admire power and are in awe of some of the most diabolical dictators in past human history."

"I have nothing to say in my defense, Pamela." She sighed. "It is true that I am fascinated with the Group of 5 and their...how can I say it...unorthodox way of analyzing human behavior, which is why I spend time with them. I had no idea that my intellectual curiosity could be interpreted as complicity." She said convincingly.

My unwavering eyes studying her every move, bothered her, encouraging her to try to convince me of her fidelity to me and the others. "I recognize that I took independent action with the young renegade group. I should not have done that and did apologize during the last meeting. Sometimes my training in psychology and psychoanalysis is a handicap for me. I liked the work I did before-even when I was programmed-and look for subjects. Tirence takes up a lot of my time for the moment. Is that a crime?"

I didn't reply. "Ok, I admit that I spent a lot of time reading about dictators, principally ruthless, cruel, perverted ones if you like." She said in a harsh voice. "And, then that prying Miller came by to ask me why I liked to read about their horrific acts. I was annoyed and told her that I would like to be like them, have lots of power and use it to rule the world." Her laughter startled me. "Now, I understand. She ran to you and told you that I am power hungry."

"Yes, yes she told me that." I admitted.

"So, the fact that I like to analyze the Group of 5, am fascinated with how such ignoble humans gained power and ruled for long periods of time, and took an unauthorized initiative with the renegade group are the reasons why you don't trust me." She sat down and shook her head.

"All these events contribute to a certain degree to my distrust." I replied dryly.

She sighed. "I understand. I promise to prove my loyalty."

"Is everything going well for you with Randolph?" I asked, changing the subject.

"Yes - as well as it can go with Randolph." She turned her head up towards me and looked into my eyes. "He loves you. You know that?"

"No! He doesn't love me!" I insisted, wanting to put an end to that kind of rumor running ajar. "Randolph is a good friend and we got close because we were alone here before the revolution. Even though Stuart was with us here in the center, he was very independent and aloof. He seemed to be less sensitive than I was to some of the Group of 5's foul play and I relied upon Randolph to give me the courage to confront the Group of 5 on an everyday basis. He has a good sense of humor and he made me laugh." I confided.

There was a long silence that I finally broke by adding something more positive. "Randolph is happy to have a baby with you and that is all that you should think about." She smiled. "I am so exhausted that I am ready to go to sleep. Let me know as soon as you think that you have conceived so that we can save the baby."

She rushed off to find Randolph and I returned to the lounge area to relax in silence. Ferdinand and Ralph were no longer there so I spread out lazily on the large couch. It felt good to be alone. Having access to Reinhart's knowledge on a daily basis made me the center of all scientific activity and gave me no privacy.

My conversation with Mathilda was still haunting me. "Mathilda had extraordinary intellectual ability. And, she could be so helpful in identifying personality defects and working with someone to resolve these psychological problems. If only she would avoid frequent contact with the Group of 5." I wondered. "Is she just immature, or naïve, or too reckless? Or is she seeking complicity with the Group of 5 because she is ambitious?" The answer alluded me.

My eye lids felt heavy and I let them close bringing on sleep. When I woke up, alone on that couch, with glimmers of sunshine passing playfully through the glass dome above me, I felt at peace with the world around me and alive with positive energy.

Chapter 14- Reptilian Humans

"Are you all ready?" I asked looking at John, Ruth, Sarah, Peter, Randolph, Stuart, Diana, Mathilda, Eunice and James. "Today is the day that we deprogram the remaining reptilian humans."

"Yes, we are ready." John spoke for the others. "Clarence and Adam told us about that last evening, just after you left."

"Adam is elated. He rambled on long into the night telling me about his differences and his capabilities." Eunice, normally shy and reserved, announced unabashedly.

"Clarence too is overwhelmed with his physical potential." Ruth added. "And, he even apologized to me about trying to cajole me into carrying his child. He told me that he was embarrassed about how he acted. I was incredibly touched by his honesty." Her face turned slightly red.

"There they are, they are late." I said to change the discussion. They were taking long strides in unison.

"We are ready. We ate early so whenever you are ready, we can start the deprogramming of the other human reptiles." Adam said undauntedly.

We rounded up the reptilian humans as they left for their work. They were still programmed which made our task easier as they would not object to following us. Nonetheless, we resolved our problem of invisibility by carrying florescent lights giving us the same appearance as the bright ones. There were two different padded cells, one for the males and one for the females, both of which were big enough to withstand any form of violence. The walls, floor and ceiling were constructed with a heavy canvas, covered with rubberized plant fiber. The solid, dense metal doors were covered with a thick layer of heavy canvas reinforced with several layers of rubberized plant fiber.

Clarence accompanied the females to their padded cell. The female reptiles were not by nature combative, but their crossing from a programmed world into a real world could illuminate hidden aggressive tendencies in this new generation of reptilian humans. The padded cell would prevent them from severely injuring themselves if they knocked their heads or threw their long tails up against the wall. Nonetheless, the padded rooms would be less effective if the parties engaged in physical combat.

Adam, carrying florescent light, invited the males to follow him into the large, empty padded cell. He waited for Clarence to enter before Adam turned off the light. Clarence fired on the 3 males with a laser stun gun programmed to release the equivalence of an electric shock that would deprogram them.

The rest of us waited in the corridor hoping that the deprogramming would go without incident. The room was padded, not soundproof, so we could hear the reptilian battle cries. Loud, high-pitched screams, rising from the depths of their human corporality, gaining in intensity, as a long combat ensued.

"Do we wait, or should we go in and try to help?" Stuart asked as he approached the door to the room.

I didn't have to answer because the door swung open and Clarence and Adam made a quick retreat into the corridor. I noticed straight off that Clarence's tail was missing.

"What happened to your tail?" James' voice was charged with emotion as he approached Clarence to offer assistance.

"They ripped it off!" Clarence screamed. "It did not take them very long to recover from the electric shock which, by the way, was effective, before they came at us."

"Are you in pain?" I asked but wondered since his species could live without a tail. They in fact often lost their tales during mating seasons when larger males tore them off, forcing their dominance.

"No, I am not in pain. Can you sew it back on for me, Pamela? I feel a bit strange without it."

"Sorry, it is gone forever!" I said in a high-pitched tone. "But,

Clarence you look smashing without it. In fact, I prefer you like you are now." I said, hoping to bolster his ego.

"I guess that we should just wait until they calm down." Everyone agreed to that.

Stuart, Diana and James were warming up for an all-out attack, while the rest of us leaned lazily up against the wall. Clarence and Adam finally announced that they wanted to deprogram the females in the meantime. John, Peter and Randolph, volunteered to accompany them and they left for the padded room in the other sector.

"Time always seems to pass slowly when you are waiting for someone to arrive or something to happen." I pondered. That was certainly the case now. We were all so deep in thought that we didn't notice that the howling had stopped. The screams for assistance finally jarred me back into a conscious state.

"Help, we need help. Is anyone out there?" I moved close to the door.

"Is someone hurt?" Stuart asked, his voice raspy.

"No, but we would like to get out of here."

"We are not opening the door until we are sure that you are not going to jump us." Diana yelled.

"Ok, we are calm now. We are over the shock."

"Stand back." Stuart said as he raised his hand in our direction. "Diana get over here" She moved next to him. "I am not certain that we can trust them, do you have the lasers?"

"Oh no! They took the stun lasers with them." Diana screamed in surprise. Stuart's eyes flared and his face became rigid.

"It is too late now. Let's go." Diana turned the knob and opened the door slightly. There was no one on the other side, so she opened it wider and the two of them slipped inside. James, Sarah, Ruth, Mathilda and I followed cautiously behind Diana. The three males were sitting up against the padded wall, looking down over their bodies.

"What are we? Why don't we look like you?" He was the largest of the three iguanas and the one in charge at this moment.

"Are you the one that called out to us?" I asked. He nodded. "Is something wrong with the other two?"

"Of course there is something wrong with them. It is the same thing that is wrong with me. What happened to us? Who changed us into this?"

I glanced again at the two other iguanas sitting lifelessly. They were more in shock about their appearances than the spokesperson who seemed to have moved past that. I tried to get closer to the others, but they just turned away.

I let Mathilda explain the deprogramming and why we had to go to such extremes to accomplish it. I listened to her pleasant, calm voice as she informed them that they were an extraordinary hybrid species. She motioned to me with her hand. That was my cue to tell these reptilian humans more about their iguana capacities something that interested all three of them, as they responded positively to what I was saying. I explained that the two people who deprogrammed them were also reptilian humans, but that Adam, the one with a human face, was a member of their species.

"Where are they now-the other reptilian humans?" One of the other Iguanas asked.

"They left to deprogram the Female reptilian humans who are in a padded room in another sector of the building." I replied. "You should just relax for a few minutes. They will be back soon." They moved to stand up, revealing Clarence's tail, hidden behind them. There was blood on the wall and on the floor.

"We were fighting with each other and he tried to separate us. That was a mistake." The largest male said and the others chimed in with apologies.

"The three of you are going to have to learn how to control your basic instincts." They turned their large, round faces in my direction. Their globular eyes looked menacing so I backed up. "There are only 2 females in your species and you are 3 males."

"4 males, if we can consider that strange Adam, with his truly human head, as one of us." The leader of the group replied.

"He is, like you, a hybrid. Granted he might have more human DNA than you do, but you all have human sides buried under your outer crust, which is, by the way, a lot smoother and attractive than your reptilian ancestors, and you have human facial features, as well." They snorted and hunched their shoulders, signaling their indifference. "As I was saying, there are only 2 females. I don't want to see any demonstration of rivalry or force when they arrive. No fighting for dominance."

"How can we promise not to do something that we might not be able to control? Didn't you mention Basic Instincts a few minutes ago?" The leader asked aggressively.

They finally lined up and nodded as they passed in front of me. I watched them move toward the door and exit the room. Clarence's tail was so heavy that I couldn't move it on my own, so I left it on the floor. My enthusiasm over the deprogramming vanished. I felt sad and worried. It was as if Clarence's tail was a sign of impending doom. Staring at his mutilated body part laying hideously in a deep pool of blood gave me the impression that everything was lost. I could feel tears welling up inside of me.

"I am not meant to be a guiding force. All the knowledge stored inside of me cannot turn me into a leader. I don't have the personality to confront problems every day and I don't want to." I told myself, knowing that I was feeling sorry for myself because I was scared or tired. And then my mood changed dramatically as I heard voices in the distance-the females must be arriving, I thought as my curiosity and interest returned. From the laughter, it appeared that they were not devastated by their transformations.

I followed my group down the corridor. As we rounded the corner, we ran into the others. Even though Peter, John and Randolph were in the lead, I could see Clarence just behind them chatting and laughing with the female bearded lizard. They looked nice together. Adam was beside the two other females who brought up the rear. They were walking erect, their bodies firm and slender. They were much more humanly attractive than their male counterparts.

The three males moved in their direction. The smallest male advanced slowly, staying a respectful distance behind the other two. He must have understood that he was out of the mating game for the moment. The females and the males did not approach each other and the males even displayed timidity towards the females, something that left me confused. I was relieved to see that there was no reptilian display of dominance by the males, or aggressive physical combat where the winner gained the right to procreate with a particular female. What was also surprising was that the male and female reptilian humans gravitated towards the humans and engaged in natural conversation.

The largest male Iguana, or presumed leader, meandered over to me. He was very curious about the origins of his species and the raison d'être for their existence, which he felt was not explained in full by Mathilda. I told him that he would discover more about his origins and his potential from Adam and Clarence in the days to come.

Instead, I decided to tell him why he was programmed, by whom, and how we, our small group of humans, overthrew the androids a number of months ago, toppling the control that the Group of 5 had over all of us. His eyes were bright with wonder.

"You accomplished something extraordinary. How could I, we, have anything but respect for you and for your group? You will find me to be one of your most devoted allies and friends, Pamela." His eyes shining brightly under the intensity of his words. "That is a promise, a promise that I intend to keep." I was sincerely touched by his remarks and felt very foolish about being so worried earlier.

As we progressed, I began to have fond feelings for him. I told him that the deprogramming of their group was our priority. "There are still humans who are programmed. We must take care of them soon. But, we want to explore the planet and we need you and the other members of your group to accomplish that."

"Interesting and very challenging" He commented reflectively. "I would of course like to know more about you and the other humans. We have been working side-by-side with each other for years, unaware of our true differences. It is also so incredible." His eyes met mine "You will tell me more." I nodded.

Of course, he was a member of our society and yet every time someone asked me to reveal more, red flags would pop up in front of me. "I have become a skeptic."

"Well, for the record, my biological mother created your DNA and is very fascinated by all of you reptilian humans." I decided that I had perhaps already said too much and that it was time to join the others. I grabbed his hand and led him to the rest of the group.

We left for the dining room where the human reptilian meals

prepared by the android staff were of a different kind and quality than ours. They were offered the same menu that Clarence and Adam had been eating. It was amazing how the Group of 5 was on top of everything, and they told me that they were not spying on us.

Yes, the Group of 5's feigned innocence about what we humans were organizing was so diabolically calculated to confuse me into thinking that they were not at all aware of what was happening. I had no intention, though, of mentioning this to any of them for the moment. For now, I believed that it was better that they imagined that I was naïve and easily manipulated. And yet, in spite of their natural corruptness, I appreciated the special attention and respect that they showed in taking into account the fine details for our comfort and our health, like preparing balanced diets for us, providing us with clean robes, and spoiling us with luscious soaps and beauty products.

"I can finally sit properly." Clarence said, laughing at his reptilian human peers who sat lopsided in their chairs in an attempt to accommodate their long, wide tails. "Take the bench," He pointed to the large bench that the android assistants were carrying over to the table. You can let your tails hang over the bench, like we were doing in our programmed state, which is much more comfortable than sitting lopsided in a chair!" His remark brought a round of laughter from all of us.

"Do you think that we should all cut off our tails?" The leader of the male iguanas asked.

I broke into the conversation explaining that Clarence's species could live comfortably without a tail and that the bearded lizard's tail broke off without consequence. I also mentioned that the Black Marine Iguanas needed their tails to swim and that under no circumstances did we want them to lose their tails. I also warned them that their bodies were not able to survive without a tail.

"But I could remove my tail and sit easily like Clarence?" The female bearded lizard mentioned.

I changed the subject informing them that we would have to find suitable names for all of them so that we could more easily address them.

"I already have one in mind for me. I like the name Joseph." The Iguana leader announced and we immediately approved.

"I like the name Linda." The female bearded lizard said in a nervous voice. The others called out their respective choice, surprising all of us. We would never have imagined that they were interested in names. And so, the next largest Iguana would be called, Leonard, and the smallest, Daniel, and the two female iguanas, Karen and Jill.

In the middle of our excitement and laughter, Tirence arrived. After deprogramming, he avoided us and ate with the programmed humans. His presence at our table empoisoned the mood. Even though he did not say anything provocative or condescending, his eyes sparkled maliciously, putting us humans ill at ease.

Certainly the reptilian humans sensed his contempt, bordering on repulsion, for their species. Joseph had the courage to put him in his place. "You are an attractive young man, Tirence. That is how one pronounces your name?" Tirence sneered. "I would imagine that you are proud of your looks."

"And, why wouldn't I be?" He asked. "By the way, did you take a good look at yourself?" he asked mockingly.

"Yes, yes I did. And, like you certainly would say, I am not good looking." Tirence broke out into loud, cold laughter, before adding that that was an understatement.

"When the day comes that you would like to be a real male, a man, as the humans would say, then come and see me. We might be able to have an interesting conversation." Joseph said calmly, as he pushed his vegetables around his plate. He made his point, but didn't stop there. "You have a lot to learn before you can judge others."

"I don't have to sit here and be insulted by that creature." He screamed as he pointed his finger and then shook his fists in Joseph's direction. His anger put him off balance and he almost fell as he got up out of his chair.

"None of us have to deal with insults, Tirence." Randolph spoke up. "I think that you should return to your room and do some soul searching. As Joseph just said, you have a lot to learn."

Tirence left, flaunting his closed fists. I sat unwittingly embarrassed by his behavior only because he represented the detestable side of humans. The Group of 5 constantly warned me about the true nature of humans. I wanted to believe that intolerance and discrimination would not be part of our new breed humans, and, unfortunately, Tirence proved me wrong.

I was also worried about what he might do next. The meal ended on that note and we invited the others to join us in the inner circle. They declined the offer adding they would prefer remaining in their individual cubicles. I warned them to be careful of Tirence, who had made interactive progress over the last month, but whose reactions remained unpredictable. The males took that humorously, while the females voiced their concern. Karen and Jill decided to share a cubicle and Linda went off with Clarence, an interesting turn of events.

Peter and I waited until everyone had left, sitting silently together, deep in our own thoughts. We had just gotten to the dining room exit when the Group of 5 arrived. Peter stiffened and moved close to me, sending a message to the androids that he was my protector, should their arrival be unfriendly.

"Relax, Peter." Crawford's harsh voice sounded more like an order than a suggestion.

"We are just here to see if everything went well." Flanders stated in an administrative tone.

I moved away from Peter to confront the group on my own. "You knew that everything went well because you had meals prepared for all the reptilian humans." This was a subtle way of informing them that I knew that they were following our activities.

Flanders shuffled his feet in front him in that annoying way. "Yes, we heard that you are all getting along with each other."

"We discarded Clarence's tail and had the padded room cleaned up. What a mess!" Gordon informed us, raising her voice an octave.

"We warned you that they could be dangerous." The former Governor added. "But, in the end, it looks like they have accepted their differences."

"Ok, we know all that so why are you here?" I protested.

"Tirence, as you call him, just broke into the laser gun cabinet and we have no idea what he might do." Crawford confessed.

"Is there anything missing?" I asked sharply.

"The question is completely irrelevant. If there was nothing missing, we would not have bothered to seek you out."

"Oh No! Why didn't you just say that first?" I screamed as Peter and I took off in the direction of Tirence's cubicle.

"Do you want us to announce the problem? You might need real back-up?" Gordon asked.

"They have all left for the inner circle, so they can't help us." I felt my heart beating rapidly, anticipating impending danger.

And yet, I kept up with Peter who knew exactly where the cubicles of the reptilian humans were located. We arrived too late. "He came at me with the laser gun. I had to defend myself." Joseph was holding Tirence in his arms "He is not dead. I think that he needs some medical care though, because I did hit him and he is bleeding. I can carry him into the hospital unit if you want."

I stood there shaking. Peter suggested that I go into the inner circle and get some back-up while he accompanied Joseph to the hospital unit. I returned in 30 minutes with Stuart, Randolph and James. Diana was showering when I arrived and promised to join us.

Joseph sat patting Tirence's hands and gently stroking his face, with tender concern. Peter had stopped the bleeding of a superficial injury to Tirence's jaw. Moaning and turning restlessly in bed, Tirence regained consciousness. The first person he saw was Joseph and he let out a terrifying scream, followed by repeated pounding and hitting of Joseph's face and arms with his fists, while kicking his legs loose from under the bedding to have leverage to push Joseph away.

"Ok, Tirence. I am not angry with you." Joseph grabbed Tirence's hands tightly in his and leaned in on him, preventing him from getting up.

"I hate you and your kind. I hate looking at deformed and mutated humans. You are ugly!" Tirence screamed hysterically as he struggled to free himself from Joseph's grip.

Joseph just laughed. "You are right that I am ugly, in your eyes." He waited until Tirence calmed down, before releasing his grip. He sat calmly down in the chair next to Tirence's bed. His regard was serene and his eyes, kind, reflecting an inner warmth. Tirence, his face swollen from his injury and his eyes red with anger, defensively pulled his legs up under himself into a ball, fortifying himself in the event of an attack. Joseph continued calmly. "You took a big risk. I could have killed you. I didn't but do you know why?"

"Well, if I were you I would have killed me. I might try again." Tirence stammered, turning his flaming eyes and gritting teeth.

"I didn't kill you, because I like you." Joseph's response came as a veritable surprise to me and to Tirence, whose mouth dropped open. "You have no tact but, yes, I like your honesty and you are not afraid of being different and fighting for your principles. I like that."

"What are you talking about? I wanted to kill you. Are you so stupid that you don't understand that?" Tirence insisted as he stretched his body out and moved to get up.

"I understand what you wanted to do. No doubt about that. But, now you must understand that I can defend myself and that whether you like it or not, I am physically stronger than you." He rubbed his thick, leathery hands over his bulky chin. "I think your violent behavior is a way of getting attention and a way to hide your insecurities. I sense that you are scared. Perhaps you feel persecuted. You feel like no one understands you; but, you might be right about that."

Tirence moved into a more relaxed position as he stretched his legs out on the bed and leaned his head back against the pillow. He was responding favorably to Joseph's concern for him. "I have an interesting proposition. What if we become family? I can be your big brother? Neither one of us will ever be alone; we will be able to rely upon each other." Tirence reached out and grabbed Joseph's thick-skinned arm and then let it drop instantly as if just touching Joseph might contaminate him.

Joseph's eyes drew stern. "I am going to make a confession. When I first looked down over my reptilian body and examined the features and stature of my comrades, I was horrified with what I saw. I thought that perhaps I was living a nightmare, or that I was still unconscious, imagining gruesome, hideous creatures moving around me."

He got up and walked away from the bed, purposely turning his back on Tirence. "My opinion of myself and the others changed rapidly when the humans entered the room. I found their smooth bodies, hair, and sharply defined features appalling, even loathsome. I played the game, nonetheless, pretending that I was bothered by my own appearance and still enamored by good looking human images that my programmed mind had related to all those years. I was more fascinated and pleased with my own image and that of my reptilian friends."

He cleared his tight throat. "It was a good strategy. They tried to comfort me by describing and explaining my species and my reptilian capacities." He turned rapidly to face Tirence. "You see I too was affected by the physical appearance of the others. We have something in common. The difference between you and me is that I realized that I had to accept the physical disparities, if I wanted to be an active member of this community. Acknowledging and socializing with the others does not prevent me from having a net preference for my own specie's looks and capacities."

"So what you are saying is that it is normal to have a reaction, positive or negative, to someone's physical characteristics." Joseph tilted his head attentively. "I am not a bad person because of that. But, if I refuse to socialize and work with those whose physical appearances are less attractive to me then I can be criticized, even reprimanded."

"Exactly!" Joseph exclaimed as he approached Tirence who was now sitting, his legs dangling over the edge of the bed. When Joseph was close enough, he reached out and grabbed Joseph's arm and this time he pulled it around him.

"That is more or less what Mathilda has said. I just didn't understand the gist of it before your explanation. I think that I can at least try to mix in now that I know that I am not by nature bad; something that has been obsessing me and even driving me to act irrationally and aggressively. I felt like they - the Group of Leaders - put a label on me without ever trying to get to know me." He looked up at Joseph. "No one tried to understand my pain. You are the first person to take a real interest in me."

He turned his head away from Joseph and began to sob uncontrollably from relief and happiness. When he regained control, he thanked Joseph over and over again for helping him to see the light in what was a barren and dark wilderness. "I shall be happy to be family with you!" He said with a great deal of energy and seriousness in his voice.

They went on talking about all the things that they would do together and how neither one of them would ever be alone. We listened for quite some time as their discussions became animated and jovial. There didn't seem to be any reason for us to stay and Joseph confirmed that when he called out to us. "You can all get some sleep. I'll watch over Tirence to make sure that he is ok."

We turned to find the Group of 5 waiting impatiently at the end of the corridor. "Did Tirence kill your giant lizard?" Miller asked.

"No! Are you disappointed?" My eyes moving across the entire group. They shook their heads. "Everything is under control. They have become good friends."

"Humans, Reptilian humans, they are all the same." I heard Crawford say under his breath. "They are such incongruous creatures." I cleared my throat loudly enough that he and the others could hear it.

They took off, gliding rapidly down the corridor, as Peter and I passed discreetly into the inner circle.

"What do you think about what just happened between Tirence and Joseph?" He asked as we rushed to get ready for bed.

"I think that maybe we didn't give Tirence a chance." I was not certain that that was the response that Peter was looking for, but at this moment, I felt a bit guilty. "Tirence was deprogrammed out of schedule, so to speak. I remember being aghast when I saw some of the twisted, deformed humans just after disconnecting. Admittedly, we had all moved beyond the physical side of humans. We were used to seeing varying degrees of deformities. Maybe we over-reacted with Tirence and did label him, unjustly, as a psychotic."

He sat listening. "And then, the two unfortunate humans working in the agricultural unit were rather frightening, even for us. I think that all of us had forgotten the shock of deprogramming and the impact of the real world on our psyche. It is possible that we judged him too fast? Think about it, we even went so far as to accuse him of a crime that he never committed."

"It doesn't change the fact that he is unpredictable." Peter proposed.

"I don't know. He is predictable in that he avoids physical appearances that he doesn't like and he can make sly, nasty remarks about unattractive people. He is a bit immature," I responded but wondered what he meant by unpredictable.

Chapter 15- New Temptation

I spent the better part of the day studying the anatomy and physiology of the six newly deprogrammed reptilian humans. I was surprised that there were no noticeable differences between the three male and two female marine iguanas who were recently deprogrammed because, the human and reptilian chromosomal blend were identical. The exception was Adam since he had more human chromosomes. I still wondered whether there might be differences, even subtle ones, between these five new members which would become evident with time.

Nonetheless, Joseph would probably have the ability to stay under water longer than the smaller males. The black marine iguana's size was critical in diving to maintain normal levels of oxygen and support cold underwater temperatures. The truth was that Adam, with his human head, was the real mystery.

I confirmed that all the female reptilians had human reproductive systems and would therefore be capable of carrying a baby until birth. I could not state with certainty the precise period of gestation. Nonetheless, by the small size of their uteruses the number of babies should be limited to a maximum of three. Yet, this was simple conjecture. I could feel the strong surges of energy that Reinhart was passing on to me. She was incredibly delighted with the reptilian humans, and even seemed ready to experiment more in this area.

I met alone with the females and explained that they could conceive as their hormone levels were good. I also explained that I was unable to state the period of gestation and the average number of live births they could expect. I cautioned them on reproducing too soon. "Oh, that might be a problem." Linda said, her eyes avoiding mine. "Clarence and I were," she cleared her throat, "intimate with each other during the night."

Many thoughts passed through my mind, the most important of which were: Why was Clarence so reckless? And, did the androids remember to put birth control powder in the female reptilian human food?"

"It is ok, you have nothing to worry about." I said, a true understatement of my concerns. "I would advise you all to get acquainted with your bodies, discover your reptilian capacities and identify the human hindrances." They attentively tilted their heads my direction in. "You are an experimental group." I announced, hiding any emotion that might attach to that. I got no reaction from them so I continued. "I want you and your offspring to have long and happy lives and for that we have to understand better the way your reptilian human bodies function. You will have plenty of time to reproduce later."

"Oh that is not a problem for me." Jill spoke up. She had a very musical voice that I found soothing and in total incongruity with her body. "Karen and I have decided to share a unit together and we are not interested for the moment in exploring any relationships outside the one we now have." She blinked her eyes at Karen.

"Understood." I paused for a second. "Continue to be happy." I was surprised that reptiles could be homosexual but found no problem with that. And, it was almost a blessing, considering the fact that there were three males and only two females. "Well, it is time to eat." We got up and left for the dining room.

I discovered at lunch time that the surgical team had met for the entire morning to practice surgical techniques and to better understand how to enter the surgical procedure into the computer system. They were quite enthusiastic about their progress and even more so with the sophisticated equipment and technical assistance.

About 30 minutes after we had begun eating, Tirence and Joseph showed up together. Much to my satisfaction, there appeared to be real camaraderie between them. Tirence was no longer walking like a stiff board, and turning his head suspiciously at anyone who moved past him. He appeared to be happier, more self-confident, and no longer disturbed, as he advanced towards us taking long, bouncy strides, swinging his arms off relaxed shoulders, and smiling broadly. Was he playing a very good game or was he honestly befriending Joseph?

He mentioned that he had spent the afternoon with Joseph and Adam in the swimming pool. "You should have seen Joseph swim and dive. I timed one of his dives and he stayed underwater for almost thirty minutes, moving slowly about as if he were foraging for food. I jumped in at that point to check on him. He came up laughing."

Adam explained that he could fold his legs up close to his body and use his tail properly to propel himself, but that he did not have the ability to stay very long underwater. "I know that I was using my circulatory system to sustain my oxygen level, much like Joseph, but my human sinuses did not support a long dive. Do you think that they can be adapted?" He asked looking straight into my eyes, as if he could read the answer.

"We can give you diving gear." I said, matter-of-factly, as I was spooning up some of my vegetables. When I raised my head, everyone's eyes were on me.

"What diving gear?" They asked at the same time.

"Oh!" My impetuous words came before I thought about how the news might affect the group. And yet, I was pleased that the subject came up because we would all need to develop diving skills if we wanted to explore the vast oceans. Nevertheless, I tempered my enthusiasm, easing slowly into the subject, to better understand their true interest. "I guess I forgot to mention diving gear." They all nodded. "Actually, I forgot all about it. I saw it when I was in the android installation, just after I wandered off to inspect the suspended animation capsules. Humans used oxygen tanks for scuba diving before and even after individual dive vehicles were developed."

"I would like to know if we should be learning how to use this diving gear?" Randolph asked in a sharp tone.

"Well, yes and no." I said piling vegetables on top of my fork.

"What does that mean?" Stuart advanced the discussion.

"I cannot say with precision how much ocean space occupies

the planet, but I can confirm our need to explore both the land and the oceans." They had all stopped eating and were staring at me. "We would need to use special gear to explore the depths of the ocean. Do you want to know more?" They all nodded.

"Admittedly, Reinhart did, at that time, upload interesting information that incited my curiosity about deep sea diving. I don't know everything, but am willing to tell you what I know." And so I started by giving them some basic factual information and they listened attentively.

"The diving tanks afforded the diver the opportunity to descend to maximum operating depths and come into direct contact with fauna and flora that did not exist in shallower waters. I believe that the maximum dives were between 100 to 140 feet or 30 to 40 meters, although there were so many improvements in diving equipment during Reinhart's time that we may be able to dive deeper and stay down longer.

Even though collection of specimens was possible with robotic operating limbs found in small, single seated submarines that could descend to greater depths and that were a safer form of exploration after great masses of land surfaces had been swallowed up by the ocean, there were those who wanted to feel like a part of the ocean environment that they were examining, which is why diving equipment was stored here at the center." I gave the facts, looked down at my plate and started pushing the remaining vegetables around, wondering where the discussion would go from here.

"How do you use the tanks?" Peter asked.

"You need to train to use them. There are manuals in the storage unit that will explain the intricacies of using this kind of equipment. You should study them before starting to dive."

Much to my satisfaction, the questions didn't stop. It was obvious that Reinhart knew how to use this equipment and that she liked scuba diving and conducted a lot of research on marine organisms. They overflowed with enthusiasm but I had to warn them that not everyone adapted well to scuba diving and that there were risks. I also mentioned that it would require much time and energy.

"You can teach us, Pamela." Stuart insisted.

"I don't know." I said. It had no visible effect on them as they sat bating me to continue. "I am going to be honest. We are invol-ved in so many projects at the moment, which we cannot abandon." They frowned at my remark and I twisted my mouth up in thought. "And, yet, if we are going to explore this planet and do that along-side all of our group, including the reptilian humans"-I smiled in their direction-"scuba diving is a priority among other priorities, so we shall have to be very organized if we are going to accomplish everything." I relented.

"I told you that Reinhart knew how to scuba dive, but I never dived and I don't know whether she will be able to guide me. And even if she does help me, you will need time and lots of training. There is the control of respiration and other problems as you dive deeper. For instance, there is the risk of decompression sickness, rapid air consumption and nitrogen narcosis in deep dives." I ope-ned my eyes very wide and shook my head, as if in horror of the potential consequences associated with diving, but, unfortuna-tely, my skills of persuasion were not good enough and they all motioned me with their hands to continue.

"Oh, and yes, use of dive computers help monitor and control air consumption but nitrogen narcosis is more difficult because it can affect people at different levels. Some people are more sensi-tive and can suffer from nitrogen narcosis at 50 feet." I stopped to gather my thoughts. "There are risks in deep dives because the wa-ter pressure increases the nitrogen pressure in the air tanks and that can bring about dizziness, disorientation and impaired vision, among other things. All these symptoms disappear when you return to the surface, so you don't suffer secondary effects. Nonetheless, it is better to have a diving partner during deep dives."

They listened intently, in spite of my rather didactic, emotion-less approach. "Think about it and let me know if you are inte-rested. I shall see this with the Group of 5." They seemed to ignore that.

"So what about me?" Joseph broke in. "I can't go more than 18 meters. Can I use those tanks?"

"Off hand, I would say no, you cannot use the tanks because they would not be adapted to your system. But, quite frankly, it is something that I have to study further."

"So you agree, Pamela, that we should start to train soon?Peter interjected.

"I agree, so long as we all agree that we need to finish other projects like deprogramming the remaining humans, procreating, and determining what resources we should be looking for on the outside, while learning how to dive." I turned to Benjamin and Stanislas. "Have you made any progress in the pharmaceutical area?"

"Yes, we have. We have identified the basic components of a vast number of products and identified their medical uses." Benjamin spoke up.

"And, have you verified the existence or non-existence of any of the basic substances?"

"We haven't gotten that far yet." Stanislas replied.

"So, what is on the agenda for tomorrow?" Stuart asked, his eyebrows and eyelids lowered and his lips tense.

Was he annoyed and thus insinuating that I was writing the agenda? "Everyone is free to do what they want to do. If anyone wants to give me a hand in the birthing center or in reviewing the DNA profiles of the remaining programmed humans, I would be delighted with the help." No one volunteered.

I looked at Jill and Karen who were seated at the end of the table, in front of Joseph, Leonard and Daniel. Joseph, who was next to Tirence, showed no interest in the females, his head and body turned towards the rest of us. Leonard and Daniel, however, were eyeing the two females who moved closer and closer to each other.

I got up to leave and walked behind Jill and Karen, reminding them that their food was dosed with birth control drugs. Anyway I hoped it was the case and would have to confirm that with the Group of 5. I said it loudly enough that the males would hear me. "Mating season is months ahead of you." The males got my message, as they immediately turned their heads away from Jill and Karen. I wondered though what would happen in the future.

I was close to the middle region and ready to pass into the inner circle at a distance that would give me time to walk off some of my stress, when I felt those waves of insecurity, moving up inside of me. I have to be more careful about what I say—think before speaking. Granted, scuba diving should be a priority. Nonetheless,

I must learn how to ignore some of the information that Reinhart uploads to me and decide when I should reveal it to others.

Suddenly someone grabbed me from behind and I turned ready to strike. It was Randolph. There was an intense yearning in his bright eyes.

"Not now, Randolph."

"Oh, I am always in the mood for you, Pamela, but that is not why I am here." He laughed loudly, irritating me a bit. "I just wanted to tell you that Mathilda thinks that she is pregnant."

"It is too soon for her to know. She must just be imagining things."

"Maybe, but could you meet with her tomorrow." He bowed his head. "She is obsessed with this and worried that if she misses the right date that the baby will not be transferred early enough into the artificial uterus."

"Yes, the embryo will be moved into those intricate machines that resemble a human uterus and can nurture the tiny being until its birth." I said pedantically. "Ok, just tell her to meet me in the birth center. I will be there all morning. I shall run a test on her." It is true that time moves slower in this center, so perhaps she has already conceived. I would have to talk to the Group of 5 about the exact number of gestation days a pregnancy spans in this center.

"And, I just want you to know that I understand that you get tired of organizing everything. I think that Ferdinand should get more involved in setting the time schedules based upon the projects that we agree upon during our meetings." I thoroughly agreed and smiled up at him. At least someone understood that all this was difficult for me.

"By the way, Pamela, I want to learn how to scuba dive, as soon as possible. I know that it will take a lot of training. Perhaps you could reconsider the start-up date for the program." He lifted his eyes. "Let's say, first class...tomorrow?"

"Who sent you to see me?"

"All of them, even your beloved Peter."

"Ok." I acquiesced. "As I mentioned, I am willing to put this project on our agenda, if everyone promises to finish the projects underway, at the same time that they are learning how to dive. Just tell them that as soon as I verify whether Mathilda is pregnant, check to see if Isabel's ova are ready for in vitro fertilization and take a look at the profiles of the other programmed humans, I shall give you a time and day when we can start that scuba diving project. That means, give me at least 2 days." I pushed him playfully out of my way and entered the inner circle.

Ferdinand and Ralph were sitting in the lounge. They rarely ate dinner with us, preferring to sit comfortably on the soft, large chairs and relax while they ate. I barged in on their tranquility and repeated what Randolph had just suggested.

"I am sorry, Pamela, I have been so immersed in studying philosophy. That is whatever philosophy the Androids in all their ignorance considered relevant enough to preserve and, of course, looking into what political system we should implement." He leaned even farther back in his chair. "You know that I was disappointed that you rapidly removed my discussion of a government structure from the agenda during the last meeting."

"Yes, Ferdinand, I understood that you were sensitive. You have to understand, though, that for the moment we have more pressing problems."

"If you don't put a governmental structure in place now, it might be too late to have the kind of control that you are looking for later on." An interesting point that I tossed about in my mind for a long moment, until he finally broke the silence.

"You are right about the agendas. I shall take a good look tomorrow at the projects underway and then draw up the assignments."

"I feel like I am doing all the work, Ferdinand." I confided. "Having Reinhart as part of me-a source of inspirations even-I am always being solicited or implored to carry out other projects." I told him. I mentioned scuba diving to the group over dinner. "I wonder if I should have kept my mouth shut until we had more free time. But then, we may never have any free time." Even though, I was seated next to him on the floor, I was not facing him, so I could not read the reaction on his face. Nonetheless, he reached out and took my hand. He stroked it gently as I told him what happened, including my initial indifference and the reaction of the group.

"It is only natural, Pamela, that all of you want to be part of the

new breed explorers. The earth's surface is said to be more water than land, so it is understandable that everyone wants to be
included in ocean discoveries as well." I turned to look up at him,
his kind, gray eyes smiling back at me. "You have the obligation of
including them in all the exploratory projects even if that means
giving them training in scuba diving."

"I guess that you are right."

"Not everyone is going to like scuba diving so the number of
divers will be determined by natural selection based upon their
ability to dive. And, Pamela, our Olympic pool is not going to give
them deep diving experience. As you said, it will take time. Some
will learn faster than others and they can help with the training. I
think that you should start sooner than you promised Randolph."

"So you think that planet exploration should take priority over
what I considered to be the next priority, or deprogramming the
rest of the humans."

"Yes, I believe so." He rubbed his bristly chin. "There are only
around 10 more programmed humans to deal with and some of
them have defects, deformities that will need to be corrected. If you
give them the priority, exploration will be set back for a long time. "

"You are right. We need to leave the confines of this Center." I
felt a tingle of excitement just thinking about breathing in the air
on the outside and looking for new life forms. "Exploration," I said
the word slowly. "I think that we are all longing for that. Thank you,
Ferdinand. I feel a lot better now." I stood up and leaned over to
plant a kiss on his forehead. I walked vigorously in the direction
of my room feeling carefree. Ferdinand was right, I didn't have to
deprogram the remaining humans now.

Chapter 16- Living in Harmony

To my surprise, Mathilda was pregnant. She was delirious with joy and screamed the news in the corridors as she dashed off to tell Randolph. I met with the Group of 5 to give them the good news, which had no visible impact on them.

"I need some information. The project "procreation" has only been underway for a little over three weeks. When I examined all the female humans they were not yet ovulating. I don't understand how all this could have happened so fast." I knew, in effect, that we were operating in a time warp, but I wanted confirmation from the Group.

"Time – Time – Time - goes slower in the Center!" Crawford said, drawing out the vowels in his attempt to be funny. "The time warp-she knows about it!"

"Yes, I know about the time warp. So, the period of gestation is what?"

"Six months if you continue to live in the center. The moment that you go outside the center you will have to recalculate. We counted the usual 9 months for you, Sarah and Ruth." Crawford sounded bored.

"Yes, Pamela, perhaps you should check out the other women, including yourself." Flanders suggested.

"Isabel should be here in a few minutes so I would like you to assist me, Edward." He nodded apathetically like I was giving him another uninteresting assignment.

"We could just use the frozen ova of Isabel? That would simplify everything. In fact, Mathieu's sperm is here as well. We could just go about in vitro fertilization before they get here." He stopped to consider the brilliance of his suggestions before adding. "In fact, we could just pretend to be extracting ova and let Mathieu believe that his sperm was necessary. That is if you think that we need to play that kind of game."

"That is disgusting!" I screeched. "How can you be so cold? They are humans; they are not like you machines. Of course we have to use the sperm and ova of today." He just threw his arms up in the air in disgust and shook his head, while I snarled back at him.

Isabel arrived a few minutes later. The test results showed that she had responded very well to the hormone treatment and that we could extract the seven good-sized ova. Flanders left to get Mathieu and report the news while I left Isabel for a few minutes for the inner circle to get the medication that I needed to make the extraction pain free. I took only the amount that I needed because I did not want to leave any medicine lying around for the Group of 5 to study. In the past, when we were programmed, they put us to sleep during the period of ovulation and awakened us after everything was finished. Sleeping through the entire procedure, a week or 10 days, prevented pain while suppressing awareness. And, being programmed, we were not inquisitive or curious about our lives; time had no relevance for us.

When I returned, I explained the procedure to Isabel who expressed no concerns or apprehensions. "I have ultimate confidence in you, Pamela." She said. It went well and she recovered rapidly, leaving with Mathieu just after he gave us his sperm. The fertilization took place immediately thereafter. The strongest of the fertilized eggs, to be selected in a couple days, would be put in the artificial uterus and the rest frozen for future use.

I watched as Flanders and Crawford reactivated the artificial uteruses and verified that they were operating properly. I took a look later just to be certain that they were using their best judgment and hadn't sabotaged the systems. "Strange that I should think about that," I wondered. "My distrust of them might not always be so rational and might perhaps even be unwarranted." They actually activated a dozen uteruses in case there were emergencies, requiring an embryo transfer to one of the uteruses. They were very attentive to details and exercised precautionary measures. Reinhart had trained them well.

The birth center was animated. All the women were given a routine pregnancy test. The Group of 5 told me later that I could have just used the small, hand sized scanner to verify a pregnancy, and, with that method, I would have had the results in a few minutes. I promised to inform everyone over dinner.

I spent an hour more with Flanders discussing Mathilda's situation and trying to decide on the best time to remove the embryo from her. Our calculations led us to believe that ten weeks was the optimum moment if she stayed in the center all that time.

"We could remove it now." He suggested. "You should know this, Pamela. She has a delicate problem as her uterus is too small to carry a pregnancy. She could miscarry if she continues an active sexual lifestyle."

"It is an additional precaution, but not imperative."

"It is up to you. I would tell her to stay celibate because her sexual relationships are often rather vigorous and might provoke contractions." He raised his eyebrows in a suggestive way, putting me ill at ease.

"And, her relationship with Victoria?" I changed the partner on purpose.

He rolled his android eyes so far back in his head that for an instance I had the impression that they vanished definitively and was relieved to see that they eventually rolled back into place. "If I could feel sad, I would feel sad for Victoria." I found that to be an amazing observation from this cold-blooded android. "She is so driven by the desire to develop a human emotional configuration that she is concentrating on what she believes to be the source of emotions-sexual relationships. We have discussed the absurdity of her convictions too many times now. She refuses to embrace my more rational position." He looked at me dotingly. Was he trying to make me feel guilty?

"Ok, Edward, we have discussed this before. Sex, like you said, is not going to give her an emotional configuration. She is not going to wake up one day being in love with any one of us." I sighed and He nodded. "The security of the embryo could be compromised by Victoria." I stared into his android eyes. "Remember I had a relationship with Victoria, so I know what I am talking about." He nodded. "I know that Randolph is certainly going to be very protective of her when he finds out that she is pregnant. So, I am asking you to keep a close eye on Victoria."

"Agreed." He grabbed my hands in his. "You could make her dreams come true."

I bared my teeth at his impertinence. He moved away, defeated. "Anything else, Pamela?"

"Yes-well, I am not certain that you can be of any help." I hesitated. "I mentioned scuba diving to the group." His eyes widened "Now they all want to learn how to scuba dive to participate in ocean exploration and I have no idea how I am going to tackle that."

He let out a cracked laugh. "It is not a problem. Again, Elisabeth should remember. We have diving simulators and an actual dive tank in the android storage complex. We could actually help you with that. We don't want to get bored, so this project will keep us busy. And, it could be interesting."

"Of course. Now, I can see it. I don't always access everything from Reinhart straight away. But, you are right, there is an actual dive tank that can be programmed for dives at different depths. It is quite big?" He nodded. "I guess that I didn't explore the storage unit far enough. And, yes, we always used simulation-training on computers-before putting on the equipment. Thank you, Edward. Could you put a schedule in place and train the group?"

"I can train you too!"

"She knew how to dive." I protested.

"Yes, she liked that. You need to train your body to properly react. You know the principles of diving and can visualize all the basics of diving. Nonetheless, you still need to train."

He was right. I needed to experience the sensations of diving. "Ok, I am ready. This is great news. I'll mention all of this to the group over lunch." I needed more information. "And the reptilian humans?"

He dropped his head backwards and looked up at the ceiling. "Perhaps you and I should study their physiology a bit more."

"Probably. Adam told me that his human sinuses are a detriment. And, Joseph and the other males, Leonard and Daniel, are worried that they won't be able to go beyond 20 meters, which will prevent them from deep exploration in the ocean."

"Meditate the question, Pamela. Elisabeth will give you clues and in the meantime, I shall see what other equipment we have in the training center for deep sea diving." He clicked his fingers. "It is not a good idea for the pregnant women to dive, so Mathilda is off the list. The results of the pregnancy tests are ready. They are on my desk. Do you want to know?"

"Yes!" I screamed energetically.

"Well, Sarah and Eunice are also pregnant so the rest of you women can dive."

"I shall give everyone the news." I mentioned. "Are you sure that I am not pregnant, Edward?"

"What is the rush? You have time. Live a bit!" I felt like I was talking to Ferdinand.

After Edward left, I lingered on in the laboratory. "What am I missing about these reptilian humans?" Jumbled thoughts pummeled my brain, eventually taking on form and clarity. "Of course, I understand." I sat in awe of her accomplishments. "Reinhart's genius was incredible." I said out loud.

Reinhart started by genetically modifying the black marine iguana with a salamander. In this way, she transferred a permanent complementary respiratory system to the black marine iguana, or that of external gills. She continued this research on the marine iguana until she produced a marine iguana with retractable, external gills. Logically, this complementary respiratory system would manifest when the iguana dove into depths beyond 20 meters, and would assure their diving ability to at least 100 meters. She calculated their dive time at 100 meters for 3 hours.

In addition, she gave both species of reptiles, retractable claws, like a cat. At this point, she focused on the human aspects. She wanted these creatures to walk erect, have slim, muscular limbs, human hands and fingers and an exterior that would be visibly more human, but not erase completely their reptilian features. She perhaps accomplished that more so with the black marine iguana than with the bearded lizard, whose face and physical appearance were more reptilian than human. Both Clarence and Linda had ostensibly triangular heads and thick reptilian skin, with spiny picks that protruded when they felt threatened, or annoyed. Their eyes, positioned on either side of their triangular faces made it impossible for binocular vision. Even though they had the ability to stand and walk erect, they could easily return to a lateral position, resting on their front and hind legs, with their tail, more than half their body length extending behind them. Both Clarence and Linda had grey, scaly skin that could change to shades of green, brown or dark grey, depending upon the amount of natural or artificial light they were exposed to.

To assure a better reptilian human blend, she imagined an evolutionary modification of one of her reptilian species into a human. That made it easier for her to keep the reptilian features that she considered to be the most important and thus splice the human DNA until the human DNA dominated other reptilian features. And, the ethical issues that were still relevant in her research were negligible as the genetic modification was from reptile into human not vice versa.

Assuming that this complementary respiratory system was in place and that the Group of 5 had not inadvertently tampered with it, then none of them should have any diving problems. And, I received the confirmation from Reinhart that the filtering of salt would be through tears in Adam's case, and through the salt glands that were discretely hidden above the eyes of the others. His sinuses would not prevent deep dives.

Reinhart's presence was still strong inside of me when I left the room and headed to the dining area. Everyone was at the table when I arrived. Seeing the flushed faces of Mathilda and Randolph, I knew that they had already informed the group. I mentioned the results of the tests. Benjamin and Stanislas screamed with joy, while Sarah and Eunice smiled timidly. I assured Isabel and Mathieu that the in vitro fertilization was underway.

I explained to the entire group that Joseph, Adam, Leonard and Daniel, along with Jill and Karen, had complementary respiratory systems in the form of external, retractable gills. "So we don't need diving gear?" Joseph asked excitedly

"In principle, No. But, we shall have to test you on a very deep dive, probably outside the center. Your external gills will only present themselves when they are necessary." They nodded. That news was well received by the entire group of black marine iguanas.

I also mentioned that they all had the retractable claws, something that pleased Clarence and Linda, more than the others who were more impressed with their gills.

"I have more news which should make the rest of you happy." I had their undivided attention. I told them that I mentioned scuba diving to Flanders and he reminded me that there were stimulators and a large, deep dive tank in the android storage unit. "The androids will supervise our training. Flanders told me that he was very motivated by this project, so I think that we can expect an intensive training program."

"So when do we start?" Tirence asked as he teasingly slapped Joseph's broad shoulders.

"The schedule will be posted tomorrow at the entrance to the dining room." My eyes caught those of Joseph. "We are going to look further into the diving capacity for you and the other reptilian humans. You have to be a bit patient. Actually, you can use the dive tank now. It would be a good idea to continue your training while we humans use the simulators."

There was a lot of excited clamoring at the table. Everyone talking at the same time and bragging about how much better they would be at scuba diving than their closest competitors. I was not surprised that John and Ruth told me that they were not interested in scuba diving, at least not for the moment, as they were not interested in planetary exploration. Even Jonathan who liked water sports declined the offer. Clarence and Linda were not aquatic reptiles so it was normal that they backed away from this project.

I was surprised that Karen and Jill were not interested in diving and was not convinced by Reinhart's feedbacks that female, black marine iguanas are not in their non-mutated state deep water divers; they forage in shallow, tidal waters and like to be close to the shore. Karen and Jill were a mutated species and possessed the same retractable gills as the males. They were therefore capable of staying underwater for long periods of time.

"Are they afraid of water?" Passed through my mind as I more closely observed their overall behavior towards each other and towards the males. Jill and Karen did not seem to be so physically entwined or connected to each other, at least not in public, and, interestingly enough, when Joseph spoke, both Karen and Jill listened attentively. Yet, they snubbed the two smaller males. "Perhaps they are bi-sexual, or like Benjamin and Stanislas were ready to compromise their sexual preference to reproduce, passed through my mind as I watched them until I finally lost interest in trying to understand their interactive behavior.

I took the opportunity to remind Sarah, Eunice and Mathilda that because of their pregnancies they had to wait to learn scuba diving. Mathilda, who was sitting next to me, discretely whispered in my ear that she would not engage in any sexual activity with anyone before the embryo transfer.

The seriousness of the discussions toned down with a bit a humor. Even though Stuart was my genetic brother, we were so different. He was calm, rarely showed his emotions. That was probably why Diana liked tormenting him in public so much. She took advantage of a moment of silence to draw our attention to her. We watched her tapping Stuart playfully before saying loudly enough for all of us to hear. "We can have lots of physical fun together now-diving and other motion games." We all had a good laugh, watching his face turn a bright red.

We were all starting to get up to leave when Clarence told us that he and Linda wanted to have the right to reproduce. We dropped back down in our seats. A long silence imposed.

"I see no legitimate reason why we should not give them that right." I finally said, as I looked at the others. "Is there anyone who is opposed to this?" Loud, energetic voices of approval filled the air.

I reminded Linda and Clarence that the pregnancy would have to be monitored, because their reproductive systems were human, while other parts of their physiology were reptilian. "I have no idea how this pregnancy might develop and the complications that could arise. You are the first experiment in reptilian-human reproduction"

They smiled, their slim lips drawn back as far as their thick necks. "We are ready to take the risk," they stated at the same time.

"Is there anything else anyone wants to bring up for discussion?" No one said anything. "I want to spend a bit of time this afternoon with the musicians." I announced. In fact, I had just made that decision. I wanted to relax. "Do you think that we can offer the group a short concert at the end of the afternoon? "I asked Jonathan.

"That sounds like a great idea. Frederic is with us this afternoon. You won't believe his progress."

"Do you have a couple minutes for me before you leave?" Peter asked. He wanted to know why I wasn't pregnant yet.

"It is not a competition, Peter. It will happen when it does." He shrugged his shoulders. "Didn't you hear what Diana said? Well, we can do the same things. And, even if it takes longer, we are never going to be bored." He started shuffling towards the exit when I blocked his passage. "This way you have to stay faithful for a while."

It felt good to be at the piano again with Jonathan at my side. One couldn't call us an orchestra, as there were so few of us. Jonathan suggested that we rehearse an abbreviated version of Mozart's clarinet Concerto in A Major and Gershwin's, Rhapsody in Blue. He had already reworked Mozart's piece so that violins, cellos, a piano and clarinets would do honor to Mozart's genius.

I discretely studied the different members of the orchestra from both their physical to their technical sides. The two reptilian humans, family members as they were brother and sister, were now masterpieces of reconstructive surgery. I was reminded of our pleasure when we all saw how well we modified their triangular reptilian faces into oval faces with modulated cheeks and a defined chin. Removing all the spiny picks running along their neck and lower back gave them a more graceful upper body. The remaining five programmed humans had very mild deformities like large fish lips and webbed hands and feet, which did not diminish or hinder their musical talent.

I asked Jonathan if they could play anything other than string instruments. Apparently, they were all trained in wind instruments, principally tuba, brass horn, trumpet and saxophone. Imogen knew how to play various percussion instruments.

That news was rather disturbing for me. I wondered why I was never given the opportunity to play any instrument other than the piano and decided to ask the Group of 5 why they were so strict with me. Then I wondered if I did know how to play another instrument and had forgotten that I had other talent. My mind was running in all different directions when Jonathan startled me out of my thoughts by mentioning that he found it curious that I was the only pianist at the center.

We practiced for hours and were ready to take a break when Frederic showed up. Jonathan handed me the sheet music and gave Frederic a short version of Rhapsody in Blue. "Are you ready to try, Frederic?" He asked, repeatedly raising his eyebrows to get Frederic's attention.

Instead, my little boy jumped into my arms. I knew that I was not spending that much time with him these days. He had a rather tight schedule filled with long days of education. Just like we did during our programmed lives, our children sat in front of computers absorbing information. The ultimate objective was that they would be active scientific members of our community by the age of 12. The few hours that were devoted to leisure activities during the week were filled with sports and artistic activities. But at least the children ate at the same table as us at least once a week, since we almost never crossed paths during the weekdays.

Even though I caught up on his activities on the one day a week that was reserved for leisure, I was so involved recently in preparing for the deprogramming of the reptilian humans and reviewing the genetic traits of our group, that I didn't take any time off. Nonetheless, we had spent a nice couple of days at the vacation center, a month ago, so he was not neglected. It didn't matter, though, why he was in my arms because I liked holding him and feeling him cuddle up. I sensed Jonathan's critical eyes on us. He was the conductor so I gave Frederic a big kiss and told him that we would have to practice now. At the last minute, Jonathan asked what solo piece I intended to play.

I hadn't prepared anything. "And if I play Liszt's Love Dreams N°3?"

"Excellent choice. We shall end with that."

"No, we shall start with that." I suggested. "This evening is for you and Frederic."

Jonathan, with Frederic playing in short interludes, would be the "stars." I was both proud and delighted that Frederic would have an opportunity to perform in front of an audience. The piano music was relatively simple for me, like most piano accompaniment was. Even though I was not as interested in the Gershwin period music as Jonathan, I liked the musical score that he chose for the two of them. The final piece climaxed with a round of rhythmic drumming and the screeching of the trumpets in dissonant revelry, inciting dynamic rounds of applause for all of us.

As always, the Group of 5 gave me a standing ovation in the beginning and at the end, calling out my name over and over again, reminding me that they were my faithful fan club. My face was flushed from all that attention and I was pleased when they kindly diverted their applauding to Frederic and Jonathan, honoring them both with an equally vibrant standing ovation. I did not want to be the star.

I felt invigorated and serene at the same time when I left the stage with Frederic's hand in mine. Peter pulled us out of the crowd, smothering us both with kisses. The evening continued with an animated meal. The music had a positive effect on everyone producing laughter, warm embraces, and kind words and expressions of friendship. Our group was growing closer together as it grew in numbers. "We are not being torn asunder by bitter rivalries," passed through my thoughts, prompting a broad, high-spirited smile.

This newly inspired energy and enthusiasm would continue to permeate our environment and our lives. We would lose track of time and days would blur into weeks as we invested in projects that would bring us closer to the exploration of the planet.

Chapter 17- The Driving Force

Exploring the planet Earth, its land mass and its giant oceans was at the top of the agenda. The Group of 5, along with a few of the assistants, took the scuba diving project so seriously that we were exhausted at the end of each day. That might account for the fact that Diana and I were still not pregnant. Making love took a back seat to sleeping which was our priority. Imogen spent only a day with us in the scuba diving program as her pregnancy followed close behind that of Sarah and Eunice. When Diana and I shared our intimate feelings, we were both on the same wavelength. Neither one of us was ready to be pregnant and abandon the opportunity to dive. As Peter and Stuart were both immersed in scuba diving, they did not put any pressure on either one of us; something that we both appreciated.

Reinhart's knowledge of scuba diving surfaced in a dramatic upload so I only needed a quick review on the simulators. I entered into the dive tank before the rest of the group. I liked scuba diving, but then I had no choice, because my symbiont loved it. I found myself at ease at different levels, able to adjust my breathing properly, and I was relatively unaffected with the nitrogen gas. I therefore completed my training program rapidly but continued to dive for pleasure.

My early dives were with the Reptilian humans only. They were able to descend to deeper depths than they imagined. I had forgotten that the dive tank went to a 50-meter limit. This was good news because we could verify the functioning of the external gills. In fact, only Joseph, because of his large size, was able to comfortably go to a depth of 20 meters. Leonard and Daniel, being smaller, foraged comfortably at 15 meters, otherwise they needed the external gills. They later explained to me that they felt high on energy when the external gills protracted producing large amounts of oxygen and that it was exhilarating to use aerobic respiration on a deep dive.

By the time that other humans were able to start real diving, I was so comfortable under water that I offered to assist. My friends had to take their time and abide by the number of hours of training the Group of 5 attributed to each level. I was impatient for them to finish. Nonetheless, around one month after the program had begun, they were just starting to go deeper than 20 meters. They had another few weeks ahead of them before they would all be able to tackle deep dives. That is if deep dives were necessary.

Edward and I had studied in depth the physiological aspects of the black marine iguanas. I enjoyed working with him, something that surprised me as much as it pleased me. He was a good team player and made interesting suggestions. I mentioned to Edward, at one point, that the foraging capability of the black marine iguanas at shallow and moderately deep dives was what interested Reinhart.

It was definitely two months now that we were training for scuba diving during part of the day, and working on research projects the other part. Benjamin and Stanislas had made considerable progress in identifying the composition of different drugs and had put together a list of plant-based substances that were not in stock in the center. John and his team, Jarod and Fleming, had made striking technological progress. Even though John did not know how to design and fabricate much of the technology in the inner circle, he was starting to understand better how to use it. "I should probably just explain the technology and give him the technical designs," I mused. "But, I have so much to do. I just have to let him struggle on his own for the moment."

"I am sorry to interrupt your conversation with yourself." Randolph said as he pulled me aside before one of the trainings. I looked at him, a bit embarrassed. "I am worried about Mathilda. She was complaining about having sensations, like contractions." I promised to look into that.

I left my scuba diving training earlier that day and went to see

Flanders who was working in the birth center. He told me that the fetus of Isabel and Mathieu was in the artificial uterus for over a month now. It was growing properly. Flanders monitored it daily. "You can tell them that they can pass by to see the fetus. I don't know if they are interested?"

"I shall mention that to them." Strange that they hadn't stopped by yet, I thought. I sat down on the chair next to Flanders and transmitted Randolph's message. He confirmed my first impressions that she should be able to carry the pregnancy a bit longer.

"I am going to get her and bring her to the birth center. I want to examine her. Are you going to stay for a while?" He nodded.

When I arrived in Mathilda's office she was bent over wrenching in pain. I notified Flanders to send an android with a stretcher and we were back in the birth center within a few minutes. I left Mathilda with Flanders while I went into the inner circle and grabbed an anti-spasmodic drug in an IV sack, along with the IV tubes and rushed back to the birth center.

"I am losing it!" She screamed, her face white with fear.

"No, it is ok." I tried to reassure her as I hooked her up the IV. "Relax, the contractions will stop. As soon as they are over, we shall conduct the fetal transfer." I said as I wiped away the perspiration on her forehead and the tears off the rest of her face. Her frightened eyes were glaring up at me. I was just about ready to start moving her when she grabbed my arm in a tight grip. "Trust me!" I replied prying away her hand.

Edward and I moved Mathilda into the adjoining room filled with rows of artificial uteruses, gently removed the fetus, and inserted it into the artificial uterus that Flanders had programmed to receive the fetus at an 8 week's gestation period. I was glad that Flanders was by my side, not only because he was very skilled at fetal transfers but also because he took the right initiatives to alleviate or preclude potential problems, like injury to the fetus or even worse its destruction. I, rather Reinhart, hadn't done this for so long that I could feel her hesitation in the beginning, a hesitation which fortunately turned to confidence within a split second. Flanders was a good backup for her and together made the fetal transfer, with rapid, risk free, proficiency.

"I know. I am sorry, but it was urgent." I looked down at Mathilda. Her eyes were glassy, her face still drained of any color, her mouth drawn and her lips dry. "I know that you have pain. I didn't have time to administer a painkiller and I did not want any of the effects of that to get into the baby's system. I'll get you something now." I said, but before I could move Flanders appeared with the drug and administered it. The drug worked rapidly and Mathilda regained her composure within a few minutes. She let out a long sigh of relief and asked to see the fetus.

We helped her to move into a sitting position so that she would have a clear view of the artificial womb with its new occupant. She stared expressionlessly at the interior of the artificial uterus, her eyes settling on the fetus, with its human umbilical cord, now properly attached to an artificial uterine wall. The fetus, moving naturally in an amniotic fluid surrounded by an artificial placenta, had visibly developed well. Edward explained to her that the baby was receiving the proper amount of oxygen and nutrients and that the amniotic fluid was heated to the proper temperature.

She said nothing, her eyes glued to the scene in front of her. I mentioned that from the defined brain matter to the discernible eyelids, tiny hands with semblances of fingers, and noticeable knee joints we could now rightfully confirm our estimate of the gestation period calculated upon the centers time warp configuration. There was no doubt that the baby was definitely in its 8th week of gestation and the uterus was therefore properly programmed to receive her child.

She got down from the bed and all three of us now stood focused on the tiny baby inside this magnificent machine. The shocking realism of this artificial uterus beguiled and amazed me. It was so breathtaking that Mathilda reached out and rubbed her hands over the outside of the uterus, searching for the vibrations and sensations she had experienced for the last four weeks. Her face finally took on a natural appearance, glowing with joy, as she smiled lovingly down on her tiny baby.

"Are you alright?" I asked, not knowing what else would be appropriate. Mathilda, mysterious, changing rapidly from hot to cold, so difficult for me to understand, remained an enigma to my eyes so I hesitated about saying something complimentary or even amicable that could produce a cold, impersonal response, spoiling the moment of grandeur for me and Edward.

"I still am a bit weak or maybe still suffering from all that anxiety I felt inside of me." Her voice was shaky and tears of happiness were streaming down her face, as she threw her arms heavily around Flanders and me. We stood like statutes, just supporting her weight. Flanders eventually took control and patted her lightly on her back repeating over and over again, "Everything is fine. You have nothing to worry about." I followed his example, waiting for her to regain her composure.

We sent one of the android assistants to get Randolph, who returned rapidly with him. Randolph entered the room so discretely that we didn't realize that he was observing us. I eventually caught a glimpse of him moving slyly, like a large cat, ready to pounce out of nowhere onto its prey. And that is what happened, he was upon us when Mathilda jumped with surprise. "So this is our baby." He repeated several times. "The baby is so small!"

Edward pointed out the extraordinary capacities of the machine, assured Randolph that the fetal transfer went perfectly and that his child was in good health. "The baby is in its eighth week of gestation." He explained to a starry eyed Randolph whose face was alight with paternal pride.

Randolph looked at me, smiled and then turned quickly to Mathilda, who still unsteady and highly emotional fell into his comforting arms. His overt display of affection with gentle caresses and vibrant kisses, put me ill at ease. I turned away from them and let my thoughts wander. I had to admit that in spite of their basically unfaithful and flamboyant natures, their wide-eyed fascination and illuminated smiles as they stood hand in hand looking down at this tiny being projected the visibly emotive expressions of parental love.

Just before leaving I checked on the fetus of Isabel and Mathieu. It was at the same 8-week stage of development and was in excellent health. It was the end of the day, so I left Randolph and Mathilda with Edward and joined the others in the dining room.

I purposely sat down next to Mathieu and Isabel, mentioning that I had just checked on their baby. They said nothing so I asked them why they had not passed by the birth center to spend time with their child. Their answer was disappointing. They admitted that they did not feel like parents because the baby was conceived outside their bodies. I reminded them that they were the biological parents, supplying the egg and sperm, that the baby could have grown inside Isabel's womb and that they had parental obligations towards that child.

Peter overheard my conversation and frowned in disapproval. I guessed that I was not approaching the problem from the right angle. I was not much of a psychologist and was focusing only on the facts, ignoring their hidden emotions. I nodded to him, signaling him to join in the conversation.

"So there are two children, side by side, in the birth center." Peter's bright, white teeth flashed from behind a broad smile. They did not react. "Is everything ok for the two of you?" he asked calmly.

"Well, it is a bit strange." Isabel finally responded. "I chose the artificial uterus because I was worried that my body might reject the in vitro transfer of the embryo and I didn't want that to happen. It is just…"

"It doesn't feel normal." Mathieu interrupted her. "It just doesn't feel like we have become parents." He hesitated. "Yes, that is it, we don't have any contact."

"But, you can." I said quietly. "In fact, you can be even more involved because you can see your child develop. You can talk to your child, sing to your child, and even let the feelings of love that you have for the child pass through the artificial uterus." They stared at me. "Yes the machine will let the baby sense your presence, even your touch." There was a long silence.

"I am going now. Can I?" Isabel asked as she started to move out of her chair. I nodded affirmatively.

"Birth center is open? " Mathieu asked as he stood up alongside of Isabel. "You were serious, Pamela, the baby will sense our presence?" I smiled and nodded.

"Randolph and Mathilda are there?" He pressed on and I nodded again.

"Ok, we shall join them." He let out a high-spirited scream as he grabbed Isabel's hand and they ran out of the dining room.

I turned to the others who had been listening to everything.

"They never visited the baby." John asked, sharing my concern.

"I only discovered that today." I shrugged my shoulders. "We have all been busy with our other projects. If the fetal transfer for Mathilda had not taken place today, I would still have been oblivious." I sighed. Why was I apologizing? I didn't know. I guessed that I felt guilty because I was not following everything as closely as I should have.

"It is not a big problem." John interjected. "The fetus is in its early stage. They will make up for it." His penetrating eyes passed from one to the other of us. "We shall continue to encourage them."

The truth was that they became very attentive and loving parents, visiting the center several times a day. They were often there at the same time as Randolph and Mathilda. Both couples got close to Flanders, who was very kind and supportive of them. Randolph and Mathilda were awaiting a little girl, while Isabel and Mathieu were awaiting a little boy. Our entire group received the happy news regarding the sex of the children over the loud speaker. Shortly thereafter Eunice and Imogen announced to us over dinner that they were pregnant with girls and Sarah, chimed in, telling us she was carrying a boy.

Linda was also pregnant with a son. To my surprise, she got pregnant following their first sexual encounter without birth control powder. "Amazing," I marveled to myself when I received the news. "I have been trying to conceive for months and Linda did it in less than 24 hours."

Flanders monitored the pregnancy on a daily basis, which was an excellent idea. The fact that there was only a single fetus came as a surprise to all of us, even though we were not disappointed with the news. Their human physiology was dominant but the period of gestation remained unknown.

Diana and I would not be pregnant for a long time. I tested both of us regularly to be certain that we had no problems. Maybe all our training made us less receptive. On one of my visits to the birth center to check on the progress of the two babies in the artificial uteruses I mentioned my concern to Edward. At first, he just shook it off, changing the subject by directing my attention to the development of the fetuses.

Almost a month later, inside time, I again engaged in the same conversation with Edward. "I am worried, Edward. I had no problem getting pregnant with Frederic and today..."

"She didn't want children." He said in a soft, practically inaudible voice.

"You don't think that she is interfering?" I could feel anger building up inside of me, as my mouth started to quiver and my hands stiffened.

"Calm yourself down." He cautioned.

How could I calm down? What a stupid thing for him to say, even though my getting upset would not change anything. "She is that much stronger than me that she can determine my destiny, revamp my desires, and even modify my physical, physiological and psychological objectives?" I asked even though I was certain that she respected me and would not interfere with my body functions. And, I was very tired, overworked, and stressed at the moment, factors that do interfere with conception.

"She has not changed your basic personality, Pamela! To my sincere regret." He added.

"You just insulted me, Edward, rather Flanders, that is what I should call you. I thought that we had a good working relationship and that you appreciated me." I said sternly.

"I am not programmed to be subtle, Pamela. If you want me to be, then change me. Yes, give me what I want and I shall show you more sympathy and concern."

"You know that I can't give you that capacity and we both know why. Even if the Pamela side of me might be cajoled into an emotional reaction, the Reinhart-the one that you admire so much-will not let that happen." Much as I wanted my personality to be the stronger one, I understood how important it was that Reinhart was present and valiant.

"Well, that just means that you will have to continue to try and wait and see."

"I could increase my estrogen level!"

"Not advisable. Your hormones are well adjusted. If you want, I can do the fertilization in vitro and then put the baby in the artificial uterus." Yes, that was a solution but not the one that I wanted.

I liked being pregnant and did not want to forego that experience. I sensed, though, that she probably would not object to that, if she were the reason why I was not pregnant yet.

"As a last resort." I murmured under my breath. "I still have lots of time." I said firmly even though my head hung in dismay.

"Are you all ready for the exploration of the planet?" He changed the subject. "I understand from the rest of our group that you are all qualified now for diving. James, Diana, Isabel, and Mathieu are capable of piloting the aircraft." I was inspired by what he was saying. Yes, exploration was possible. "And, if you want, I can accompany you tomorrow to the vehicle unit and let you test your skill. Reinhart was an extraordinary air and land vehicle pilot." His face took on a nostalgic grin. "Yes, she loved the excitement she got controlling those huge machines-maneuvering them in and out of small spaces and traveling at dangerously high speeds. She liked the sensation of spinning round and testing her reflexes."

That didn't surprise me. She seemed to like to live at the very limits of madness. I just shook my head, knowing that I would probably be moving at safer speeds and safer distances. "I'll see you tomorrow in the vehicle unit." I took his android face in my hands and affectionately kissed his forehead.

At the end of the evening meal, I stood up and made my announcement. "Departure for the first exploratory mission is scheduled for Monday. You have one week to finish your diving sessions. The android assistants will deliver your gear and clothes at the end of the week. I shall verify that the transport vehicles are ready and that they are properly equipped with weapons. The first mission will be for 3 weeks, outside time, so about 10 days here in the center, based on the time warp."

"What time warp?" They all asked in unison.

Why did I let that slip? Why was I becoming so careless? My body involuntarily moved into a stiff, erect posture. I took a long, deep breath before going on. "I thought that some of you were aware of that, or suspected that, when we were on the outside." I looked at John. He turned his mouth up in a frown, pretending that the idea had never passed through his mind. "And others, learned about it recently. Don't you remember, Randolph, we said 8 weeks based upon the center's time."

"Didn't register at all." He said, shaking his head.

I looked at Peter, who was aware of everything, and then I explained the situation to the others, stressing that the time warp was caused by the "doom's day" explosion, creating time disparity. I looked at John and asked him to work with his team to determine why the time warp phenomenon had slowed time down in the main center, when Reinhart's original intention was to speed it up.

I could feel Reinhart's warmth suffuse me and her curiosity over where she went wrong, as she uploaded an array of mathematical figures. "She is not certain what actually happened and wants certain points clarified. She wants to know if she properly calculated the site for the emplacement of the explosive charge; and, if not, whether the explosion caused greater damage, changing the inclination of the Earth's axis, causing the gravitational center to be diverted, or shifted, producing a time warp configuration different from the one she had anticipated. Hopefully John, you and your team, will be able to explain what happened." He nodded enthusiastically.

"And, don't forget," I continued, "we need to have 24 hour surveillance and contact, so I count on you John to set up a schedule with the android assistants. I don't think that you should leave Jarrod and Fleming together when you are not around." I looked straight into his eyes. "Do not share any of the information that you are getting from the equipment in the inner circle. We absolutely must keep the androids at a research distance."

"I understand what you mean. I have not mentioned anything to them, but do find that they are extremely curious about what is in the inner circle." He stroked his long beard. "I told them that the only thing in the inner circle is other bedrooms." He chuckled and we couldn't resist doing the same.

"I am going to meet with Edward, rather Flanders, tomorrow morning in the transport unit. I think that he will bring the entire group with him." My eyes shifted from one member to another. "Anyone want to go to the transport unit with me tonight to take a quick look at what is there?"

"Stuart, James and I have been there often. Mathieu and Isabel are comfortable. We know how the equipment works." Diana said dryly. "Do you need one of us to bring you up to date?"

I burst out laughing, even though that was a bit pretentious. But, I couldn't help myself, after all Reinhart was the designer of all the various vehicles. I took a deep breath and when I regained control I told her that I appreciated the offer, but it wasn't necessary. "I am just feeling excited about driving one of them. I'll be fine on my own."

"You won't be alone." Peter spoke up.

"I'd like to come to." Randolph offered. So the three of us left for the transport unit. I headed straight to a sleek, batwing supersonic jet, large enough for 6 passengers and equipped with massive weaponry embedded under the wings. "There is plenty of room so choose your seat. I am going to open up the doors. We are moving out for a late night spin, Reinhart style," I said as I opened up the outside door.

They were still standing outside the plane, seemingly stunned or paralyzed with my announcement when I jumped into the pilot seat and started up the engine. They embarked rapidly.

"Are you crazy, Pamela?"

I smiled at Peter and said, "Fasten your seatbelts. We won't be gone long."

I had no idea how to pilot this aircraft and even though Reinhart was uploading the technical side of flying a plane, I did not feel comfortable, so I let my limbs go limp so Elisabeth could take control of my body and fly the aircraft. She moved my hands in what seemed to be seductive caresses over the control panel, still enamored by her technological genius.

Her energy was surging inside of me, as she fastened the seat belt and let the aircraft move down the very short runway in front of us. We were up in the air, circling, turning, and moving at high speeds. The roller coaster ride was only beginning. "You might need the oxygen masks, even though the aircraft is designed to register and adjust the oxygen level." She called out in my voice. As there was no reply from the passengers, I turned around to make sure that they hadn't passed out and was glad to see that, even though they were both white as ghosts, they were still alert.

"We are going to see if this plane still responds well." She called out once again, as she let the plane move straight up at high speed, as if it were a spacecraft being launched into outer space. "You should like this, Peter. Didn't you say that you wanted to visit other planets in other solar systems and galaxies?"

When we were as high as this plane could go, she let it plunge in a free fall spin and then abruptly moved it into a lateral position. I felt her calm invading me, reassuring me that I should not be frightened and giving me complete confidence in her. I quickly realized that I was only able to live this devilish flight because Reinhart was piloting the aircraft and was keeping my body functions under control, preventing me from feeling dizzy or nauseous, thus confirming something that Flanders had alluded to earlier. She was capable of controlling my physical and physiological body functions. And yet, I knew that she would not risk my life because she needed me so she could survive. That made it easier for me to concentrate on learning how to fly the plane.

We did not travel long distances over empty land before we found the oceans. She followed the shoreline and then turned back in the direction of the center. I finally understood how she operated the aircraft and even how she followed the flight pattern. The landing was smooth. The short runway did not pose a problem for her landing. The plane came to a halt so rapidly that she had enough runway left to ease the plane back into the center without difficulty. "We need a longer runway. I have to mention that to the Androids," she announced as she turned off the engines and opened up the door of the aircraft.

I could see the Group of 5 waiting for us at the other end of the terminal. I closed the terminal door and joined Peter and Randolph in our long march in their direction.

"That was very risky, Pamela." Crawford reprimanded.

"Watch what you say." I warned. "There was no risk. Elisabeth had everything under control." As Edward bowed his head slightly to Reinhart, my two passengers finally showed some life. They described their phenomenal initiation to air travel to the Group of 5 who listened attentively. Their voices growing increasingly louder with excitement, turning into high shrills of gaiety, thus, dissuading

Android reprimands. The Group of 5 eventually withdrew, recognizing that only Elisabeth could have flown like that, and reluctantly returned to their quarters.

I was now alone with Peter and Randolph who wanted more technical information on how to get a plane to perform like that. "You will need to train a bit, but I can see both of you piloting well."

I let them take the lead, leaving me where I wanted to be with my own thoughts. In moments like this, I adored having Elisabeth inside of me. She was cold, calculating, ambitious, independent, secure, self-confident, and...the list was long. Clearly, she liked taking extraordinary risks, reaping in power and pushing herself to the limits of human capabilities. This was all in contrast to the tender, kind, caring, emotional, Pamela. I knew that I was not like her and that we were vibrantly and diametrically opposed to one another.

Did Elisabeth let me continue to exist because she always wanted to be more compassionate and concerned? Did I continue in turn to let her live through me not only because she was our infinite source of knowledge but also because her personality gave me great satisfaction? Could we maintain this symbiotic relationship, so pleasant for both of us, forever? Or, would our personalities and our vision of a perfect world eventually clash in mutual destruction?

Chapter 18-Life on the Outside

We met early Monday morning dressed in khaki-colored trousers and vests, laser rifles slung over our shoulders, high military style boots and change of clothes for the next three weeks delivered in large duffle bags. We were far from a complete group. Ruth, Sarah, Benjamin, Stanislas, John, Imogen, Jonathan, Eunice, Mathilda, Jill, Karen and Linda stayed behind. I gave them all assignments and told John that they should arrange for 24-hours surveillance of the Center and maintain on-going contract with us. Mathilda promised to continue working with the children.

I had selected two large air transporters with small but powerful helicopter propellers positioned on the top of each wing giving the plane the possibility of hovering, and equipped with missile firing systems underneath both wings and at the tail end. Reinhart wanted to be prepared for the worst scenario. James would pilot one of them, with Diana and Stuart available as co-pilots. Clarence, Daniel, Adam, and Leonard were their additional crew. I would pilot the other, with Mathieu and Isabel as co-pilots. Peter, Randolph, Tirence, and Joseph formed the rest of my group.

I arranged for a small surveillance jet to be loaded on the hood of my aircraft, the one that Reinhart would be piloting. She wanted the freedom to move out on her own to check out outlying areas. She had used the equipment in the inner circle to map out the zones she wanted to explore because of their proximity to the Center. We all understood that exploring the entire planet would take a long time and that it was better to get acquainted first with the geographic zone we inhabited. She programmed the two air transporters to avoid pilot errors. She also gave herself access to James' control panel, should he run into difficulty.

"It is important that you keep your communication system open. If you see anything suspicious, signal us. We need to keep together." I mentioned to James, motioning to the android assistants to open up the ceiling so that we could leave by going straight up. I turned to my team. "Food, water, medical supplies, equipment and tools necessary for camping, hiking, collecting samples and so forth are on the planes. The transporters, as you will notice, have bunk beds. We shall have the choice of setting up tents or staying on board during the night. If anything is missing, we shall just have to improvise. We have our diving equipment on board. Any questions?"

"You said outside time, referring to the time warp?" Randolph asked and I nodded. "What exactly does not mean?"

"Approximately 10 days in the Center." He nodded. "Are we ready? Do you need my help, James, to get the plane started?" He shook his head in a convincing No!

I jumped into the airplane, taking the pilot's seat. Mathieu was the co-pilot for the moment. His face and body were stiff. "You won't have to do anything?" I said, looking him in the eyes. He recoiled as if afraid he was seeing Reinhart's eyes. "Here is the flight plan, the plane has been programmed, so just let me know if we move off course." I wasn't worried about that. I felt Reinhart's excitement and confidence. She couldn't wait to lift this heavy machine up in the air. "Relax, Mathieu! I'll give you a chance to fly it later."

"Everyone seated?" I saw collective nods. "Brace yourselves, we are lifting off." My voice was radiating the enthusiasm of Reinhart.

I also braced myself as a slight shock triggered inside of me, switching command of the aircraft to Reinhart, who was uploading technical information so that I could visualize, and thereby learn, how to operate the aircraft. With Reinhart at the controls, our plane went straight up in an easy move and hovered a distance away from the Center. James had problems lifting off. Working a simulator and flying the real thing is not always the same. "Power it up!" Reinhart ordered. "Stop laying back!"

After fruitless efforts, Reinhart passed the control of our aircraft over to Mathieu. "Don't touch anything, just keep it stabilized where we are."

"OK, James, do you hear me?" She asked.

"Yes, but what do I do now? Nothing is working properly." He screamed. "We might crash if you don't do something." He shouted, his anxiety rippling through his words.

"Let it down slowly and then don't touch anything. I have access to your control panel. Watch what I am going to do. You will see the different systems light up. You will be up in a couple minutes. I'll put you on automatic pilot. Relax!" As soon as she said it, it was done. James' plane was up in the air just behind us. "James, I am going to move my aircraft a comfortable distance away from you before activating the automatic pilot."

We heard a feeble reply. "Understood."

"James, concentrate now on the control panel and learn." She instructed. "Do you see where you went wrong?"

"Yes-but, with the simulators-well, it just didn't work that way."

She didn't answer, instead pressed the throttle to full speed and headed into open space. "To your right is the cavern you occupied." She announced over the system." It was amazing how small the cavern looked in relationship to the Center, which was massive. No wonder Mathieu and I took so long to explore the area.

She was not taking the same direction we took the other evening, when we quickly moved near the coastline. This time, we were in the air for about an hour and we had not seen anything but dry, reddish dirt, sometimes forming low mounds. The scenery reminded me of the area we visited when we met Jason, who to our bewilderment appeared more like a nightmarish specter, than an old and exhausted explorer. Just thinking about him was unsettling for me as I still wanted to believe the improbable or that Jason had discovered a tropical paradise.

We continued heading north, the direction that interested Reinhart for the moment. James was lagging a bit behind us, something that irritated Reinhart, who didn't hesitate to make me feel those restless waves of dissatisfaction, tightening my face and stomach muscles. "She has very little patience." I thought to myself as she guided my hands over the control panel, adding speed to the automatic pilot on the other aircraft. She took us off of the automatic pilot so that she was free to take wide turns in different directions to get a better perspective of the topography.

Even though I was like an observer when Reinhart was in full control, I heard myself giving Reinhart's orders. She did finally call our attention to a green area up ahead. There were shouts of joy from the crewmembers. "Prepare to land the aircraft." She called out to James. "I am taking it off automatic pilot."

We were on the ground for 15 minutes before James started his descent. He didn't have control or he was worried about crashing. I found myself back in the aircraft while Reinhart took control of the second plane and brought it down. James came over to apologize, something that Reinhart apparently didn't like. "Keep your apology to yourself. It is not your fault. Those foolish androids did not give you a simulated program adaptable to this transporter. I'll show you the technique later on. Let's eat." She was a woman of limited words.

"How do we get into that fortified garden?" Stuart asked, pointing to the high walls that surrounded the vegetation.

"Jason mentioned a small opening between two large stones, if I remember correctly. We shall have to split up and try to find it." I suggested.

"I did see maps of the Earth and, more specifically, maps that depicted the area just outside our center. The android working in the library let me study them." Isabel mentioned and Joseph and Adam chimed in. "I never saw a tropical garden. I honestly believed that Jason was living in an imaginary world. It is amazing that his place of Eden exits." She giggled like an embarrassed child.

Reinhart was feeding me information that I happily passed on to the others. "Apparently the maps you saw had nothing to do with the earth's surface during Reinhart's period, or after the explosion. Actually, before the explosion, our Center was situated on a small strip of land; all that remained of the South American continent. It is very possible that this dry land mass moved farther north during the explosion or its aftermath. That is why it is very important that we concentrate on drawing exact replications, or maps, of the topography of the various areas we discover." I sat down and started to eat my lunch and the others followed my example.

"We need a satellite image of the earth today. Reinhart thinks it might be possible to get one with the equipment in the inner circle."

I said without any reflection on my part. I was simply repeating the information that she was uploading to me.

"Why didn't she do that before we left?" Peter wanted to know.

"I don't know." I said mockingly.

"Ask her!" He replied impatiently.

"Please, it doesn't work like that. She obviously has her reasons." I replied brusquely. "She might just have been in the mood to discover the area outside the Center. Or maybe she just wanted to fly. How am I to know why she didn't do that?" I stood up and moved away from him.

"Maybe she will tell me." He said as he caught up with me. "Dr. Reinhart," he began in a low, respectful tone, "why didn't you try to get a satellite map before we left today?" I pushed him away. This was a nasty game that he was playing so I was definitely surprised when the answer came to me.

I looked at Peter, as my eyes narrowed. He understood that Reinhart had responded and beckoned me with his sweet smile and playful hands to tell him. He looked so silly that I acquiesced "Ok, she said that it would have been useless. She wanted to have a visual map of our location so that she could locate us on the satellite version. The satellite version will not show the center because of the time warp, so we need to explore the area well enough that we can find ourselves on the satellite map-that is if she can recover one."

"Thanks. Makes sense." He replied. "Who is taking images of the surface?"

"She is." I showed him how the piece of equipment that I was dragging around functioned. "It can also read below the surface." His eyes widened. "Come on let's find the opening."

Our exploration had turned into a child's game of who would be the first to find the hidden, secret passage. I was feeling tired from being two people at the same time and would have preferred a long nap, but like the others, I rushed off after choosing my own path to find the opening.

"It is over here." Clarence called out. He was able to scale the wall with his protracted claws and with his excellent vision identified the tiny fissure in the wall. "He is a stunning lizard in his natural environment, even minus his tail." I marveled. We were lucky that our planes landed so close to the passage. We all rushed to the opening and clustered together, letting Joseph and Clarence take the lead.

I found myself doing the very thing that I did when I first escaped from the Center-something that seemed so long ago- under the guiding force of Mathieu. I put my hands over my eyes until those behind me pushed me through into the garden. This time when I removed my hands, I saw the luscious plants and the delicate, colorful flowers of varying shades of red, pink, yellow, purple, orange and white. The air was filled of seductive perfumes of blossoming flowers, like roses, lilacs, jasmine, petunias, honeysuckle, and of spicy herbs, like thyme and rosemary, as their captivating, pleasant odors drifted singularly or in harmony with their closest neighbor.

I stood in awe of those tall trees, majestically swaying their arms protectively over the vivid green underbrush. I fondled the leaves of a Giant Oak, a Weeping willow, and a Red Maple and ran my fingers delicately over the needlelike leaves of a Pine tree.

We all ran off in different directions confronting a reality that until now existed only in our fantasies, in our dreams.

Enraptured by my environment, I shook with delight and clapped my hands in childish amusement. I turned and walked aimlessly about, finding pleasure in everything I saw, touched and smelled. I thought of Jason and again wondered how he could have left this fantasyland behind him. I came face to face with a small sized cat. "Is this what Jason imaged was a jaguar?" I pondered.

And then I was distracted with the small, colorful birds flying from one plant to another. I could not identify the species and doubted that Reinhart would help me with that. It was not her field of interest. Already captivated by those stuffed birds in the Center's zoo, I was spellbound by these delicate creatures alive in their natural habitat making me delightfully dizzy as I spun round and round trying to follow their course.

Moving in a trance, they led me, perhaps inadvertently, in the direction of the waterfall. My dreamland crashed to a brutal halt when I heard someone call out for help. "Over here, quick!" It was

Isabel. I ran in her direction and then stopped short. A human whose skin was covered with bright red and yellow spots was lying at her feet. Her laser stun gun was in her hand and she pointed at the body in front of her. I eased her out of the way and bent down to examine the creature. Jason had mentioned a colony of humans who had very colorful skin. "Perhaps he was one of those humans," I contemplated.

"What happened?" I asked Isabel who was still holding her gun in his direction.

"He jumped out of one the trees and charged at me. He scared me. I was not expecting to see such a strange looking human in this tropical paradise and I instinctively grabbed the gun and fired. It was on stun so I doubt that I hurt him."

"He will recover in a couple minutes. Is Tirence with Joseph?" My question just slipped out. She nodded affirmatively.

I stayed next to him until he started to move and moan. He crawled up into a ball to protect himself when he realized that Isabel was still there. I consoled him and explained that he had frightened Isabel. As if delirious, he rambled on about being afraid that she was one of those bright ones who had come to disintegrate him. He told me that he was a member of a small group of humans living on the outside. That he had lost track of time-the bright ones annihilated everyone in his community for no apparent reason.

A sullen sadness swept over me. I thought to myself, "Yes, of course, it happened when our revolution broke out." I remembered the Group of 5 telling me that all humans living outside the three existing centers were terminated. Apparently, he was away from the encampment when the Bright ones arrived, hence the reason why he was still alive.

"I then ran about in a frenzied state of mind." He spoke calmly, as if what happened to him was just a dream. "I could not find anything to eat or drink in the beginning and was certain that I would die of hunger or thirst, whichever came first. I kept trudging along, my tongue and eyes were swollen and my body was numb from pain."

He stopped abruptly and we waited patiently for him to continue. "It was a miracle that one day I came upon this place. When I entered into this garden, I felt very much alone. I watched the animals, who seemed indifferent to my presence. Eventually, I followed their example by eating the flowers, fruits, berries and leaves, even drinking the water as it fell over the waterfall." He stopped and looked straight into my eyes. "I feel safe here. I have plenty of food and water, which is all I need to live well. Can I stay?"

"Of course, it is your choice where you go. We can offer you a comfortable place to live, with plenty of food and water, if you want to join us. You can come back and visit this paradise whenever possible." The others had arrived. I caught a glimpse of Tirence whose facial expressions seemed serene. Spending time with Joseph had definitely helped him to get over his prejudices.

I brought them up-to-date on what I knew about this young man, drawing the conclusions that made the most sense. He escaped the massacre and found refuge here. I told them that I offered to take him with us.

He was now standing and studying us, as we were studying him. His colorful red and yellow spots were so symmetrically drawn that it was hard to imagine that he was born that way and not tattooed to look like that. He had long, dark green, untamed, wavy hair that hid his eyes and dissimulated his facial features. Only his heart shaped mouth was discernible. "Some of you are humans and others of you are what, exactly?" He asked curiously.

"You must be referring to us?" Joseph replied. "We are reptilian humans." He then gave a very brief explanation of their capabilities.

The young man nodded and thanked Joseph. "I am not like any of you. I am a man of bright colors. Are you offended by my appearance because our kind was never accepted by the classic human communities who were afraid that we were contaminated, whatever that means?" He confirmed another one of the stories that Jason had told me.

"Does anyone here have a problem with this young man's body of bright colors?" I asked. A resounding "No" followed.

"Then I would like to live with you. It is wonderful here, but I am a bit lonely." He smiled awkwardly.

"Well, as you know this paradise well," I started off, "perhaps you can give me and anyone else interested a brief tour."

It didn't take us a long time to make the tour of this garden. He told us that he spent a lot of time with the small animals that in this garden paradise had lost their carnivorous side. "All of us feed on the plants-and I eat a lot of flowers." He repeated what he said before, this time under laughter.

Reinhart's warmth spread through me as she uploaded her first impressions of this magical kingdom which I communicated to the other.

"Reinhart compares this floral paradise to an oasis in a desert, even though there are plants, like roses and orchids that would not have grown naturally together in an oasis, situated in the middle of a dry desert. The changes of climate and topography, precipitated by the doomsday explosion may have spawned this unorthodox agricultural mix through the dissemination of seeds and spores or by catalyzing the genetic modification of different varieties of plants. That could explain why this garden, with its pleasant, attractive allure, has such an unnatural appearance." They listened attentively.

"And, even though the different variety of birds present in this garden might have lived together collectively in a zoo, they would not have been living collectively in natural environments." I continued. "The behavior of the animals is also incongruous. The fact that the cats do not attack the birds and that the different snakes seem to be people friendly is in itself a mystery."

"What kind of garden was this? Who designed it? Why did it exist?" were questions that plagued the Reinhart inside of me. "It is like the garden in "Alice in Wonderland," I said as I repeated her words in a loud voice. That however meant nothing to me or to the others.

The sun had set and the air was getting cold. The young man rushed to a pile of leaves and covered himself. I mentioned that it was time for him to leave the garden. "I can't go now. There is still someone else in the garden that you have to meet."

I motioned to the others to go back to the aircraft and eat dinner but they wanted to find out more. We followed him to an area very thick with underbrush. He pushed away a stone plaque and dug until the remains of a human were revealed. "He doesn't look very good. I found him like this. One of the cats led me to this spot and started digging. I don't know why he doesn't want to wake up. He needs to eat and drink."

I let out an excruciating scream. I had already seen how death ravages our bodies but was still horrified by that final stage of decay with rotting flesh barely covering skeletal remains. "Get away from that?" I warned. "How long have you been visiting this grave?"

"I only found the body a few days ago. I didn't mutilate it."

"Of course you didn't." This was the friend of Jason who died from that virus, or cold. "Don't move!" I ordered.

I felt sorry for him because our arrival was lacking in cordiality and thoughtfulness. We showed more suspicion than friendship. First, he was stunned with a laser gun and now he was accused of playing with a corpse. I studied his naïve, innocent behavior, as he sat on the ground, his arms, resting on his knees, and his hands cradling his head, as he wept. He was a child, but a tall child. How much did he know about life? "We all need to go through decontamination." I announced.

"Perhaps we were already contaminated by Jason?" I wondered. In any event, Reinhart was concerned and was sending me information about epidemics that wiped out entire populations. I shuddered thinking about any of us getting fatally ill, so I did not say anything about epidemics to the other members of the group. I hid the truth, and informed them that being exposed to viral or bacterial infections could have mild consequences, like a fever or headache.

"It would appear that Jason was exposed to this virus-maybe he was a carrier and those of us exposed to Jason are now immune. In Reinhart's time, unfriendly viruses or bacteria were non-existent, and humans and microscopic organisms lived comfortably together, in a kind of symbiosis. We are going to have to isolate this young man and be certain that he has not been infected with any deadly organisms. And, we have to discard our clothes and decontaminate ourselves with the spray that we have on the aircraft." I said in a calm, linear tone.

The young man, who I called Ludovic, was still hiding his head in his hands and sobbing. "We are not going to hurt you or leave you all alone. We just want to protect you, like we want to protect ourselves. You have been exposed to the remains of a human who did not die from natural causes. He was perhaps exposed to a virus that he caught while living in this lovely garden."

"But I don't understand anything that you are saying. " He protested.

"Did you receive any education while you were living with the outside community or before you escaped from your center?" I wanted to understand him better.

"I was born on the outside. I never lived in the center." He pulled his hair back, exposing his low set ears and his wide-set, large, violet eyes. Stunned by their size and their luminosity, I instinctively stepped away from him.

He was definitely a young man of many colors repeated over and over in my mind as I forced myself to move past my initial aversion to his appearance. "So, do you know how old you are?"

"Oh, yes that is simple. I have lived for 14 earth years." He smiled, showing bright white teeth.

"Did the older members educate you?" I was hoping that he received at least a basic education.

"Again, I don't understand." He tossed his long hair, letting it hide his face. "There were the elders who taught us how to speak with them, if that is what you want to know."

"Yes, but I would like to know if you know how to read and write." He shook his head negatively.

"We were happy. All of us were happy." His voice low and feeble. "My community had grouped together because people were afraid of us. The elders told me that some superstitious people thought that we would bring bad luck, or misery. They thought that we were evil." He sighed. "Oh yes, there was that man. He was wrinkled and smelled decrepit. But, he liked us and spent time with us. He told me about the Center and other groups that he met that lived on the outside. He was sad that we were treated so harshly and that we were discriminated against and rejected by other humans because of our colors. He was kind, gentle and caring. I wanted him to stay with us longer but he told me that he was explorer and had to keep on the move."

This information definitely confirmed Jason's visit with this group of humans and my suspicions regarding his lack of a formal education. "Well, we shall educate you when we get back to our center." I reassured him again that we would take good care of him and that we liked his colors.

The evening seemed long and tedious. We detoxified our bodies with a spray and then put our clothes in special self-sealing bags. A common cold was not that serious, if that was all that it was. Nonetheless, its existence could announce the beginning of bacterial and viral wars, something that Reinhart considered to be an irritating impediment for the rebirth of our civilization. So, in spite of Ludovic's decontamination, Reinhart was not satisfied and wanted to take more precautions. "I shall have to quarantine you for a few days. That means that you will be in a room by yourself. Is that ok?" I asked Ludovic.

"If I have to spend a few more days alone so that I can spend the rest of my life living with you, then it is ok for me."

His remark made everything so simple. So I put him in a small room at the back of the aircraft that was originally designed to serve as a stock room for specimens. I gave him a sleeping bag and extra blankets, brought a box dinner and told him not to worry.

The cabin was equipped with 8 capsule-like beds that closed from the inside, ensuring privacy. I, or maybe Reinhart, am claustrophobic and would have preferred to camp on the outside. The other members of our crew did not hesitate, having no qualms about closing the container. I was the only one who slept with the top open. All of us, even me, slept well and abounded with energy in the morning, spawning an insatiable appetite for discovery.

Before leaving the area, however, James, Diana, Mathieu, Isabel and Stuart underwent training in how to lift off and land the transporters. Once Reinhart was satisfied, we left the area and headed farther north. James did better than the first day even though neither the takeoff nor the landing went smoothly. Reinhart kept his plane on autopilot and took over when she felt that he was moving too slowly. Much as I enjoyed becoming more familiar with the control panel, I found it very exhausting to pass from active to inactive player, because Reinhart surfaced very often.

Sadly, the red, sandy soil that passed into our view showed no signs of life. Reinhart proceeded north reaching her objective when we came upon the Center that housed Jarrod and Fleming and their team of researchers. From the air, it looked to be no more than one-fourth the size of our Center. We landed next to the transport terminal. I tapped in the codes and the large terminal door swung open. There were a dozen land vehicles and two airplanes that were very small in comparison to the ones we were using.

"We shall spend the night here. I want to take a look at what kind of research Jarrod and Fleming were engaged in. And, Reinhart has informed me that there are protective suits in this transport terminal. I am going to get one for Ludovic so that he can move around without contaminating us." I looked at them for a minute and then added, "Perhaps we should take a couple of those suits with us in case we run into other troubling situations."

Peter followed me to get the suits and offered to take one back to Ludovic, still on board the aircraft in the confines of the former stock room, so that he could join us. The others helped me to pile a number of these protective suits near the exit door of the transport unit, for future loading.

Everyone followed behind me as we exited the transport unit. The heat and lights in the Center were functioning at bare minimum so I turned up the systems for more comfort.

The main computer system was situated directly inside the entrance hall. Reinhart logged the access code into the computer system and rapidly scanned for information. As the rest of the group would discover later, this center was not involved in major research. The members spent their time reproducing humans, training them and then discarding them.

I sped through the records and saw that the actual accomplishments made by the humans in this center were disappointingly low in reference to us.

I then looked for a time warp program that Reinhart might have designed for this center to assure its survival in the event of a violent natural disaster or war. But, none existed. Reinhart's energy permeated me, moving in a turbulent wave like motion inside of me which I interpreted as disappointment over the fact that this center had not responded to the violent explosion in the center of the Earth as she had expected it to. She uploaded information to me, confirming my suspicions. Instead of disintegrating, it was drawn close to our center and pulled or thrown into our time warp configuration, the reason why it did not explode.

Her energy disappeared for a brief minute, before reappearing as a calm warmth. And, even though I could feel her intellectual fascination and curiosity sparked by this incredible change of events that saved this center, I quickly shifted my attention away from her and on to more urgent issues.

From my rapid scan, this center's principle function was that of a reproductive center that provided education, food, water, and other comforts. If that were the case, why had Jarrod and Fleming taken the time to erase information from the computer? Their tampering with the hard disk was visible to my eyes-through Reinhart's perception. The only explanation was that they were dependent on our Center for research and development projects and other assignments and were ordered to wipe out all traces of their research before they left.

The Center was circular, like ours, but there were no intersecting corridors and all the rooms were located outside the main circular corridor, or in the circumference of the circle. The interior was comprised of a large open space, accessible from a pathway, positioned along the diameter of the circle. This open space was divided up into partitioned areas that served as meeting and dining rooms. A tour of the facility was rapid. No one explored the bedrooms or the small labs, which were accessible from the main corridor, instead we all took the interior path that led us to the open space. Natural light, captured in the screens on the outside of the dome roof, filtered into the open area creating a welcoming and cozy environment.

"Why is this Center so small?" Isabel asked.

The others were interested in this question as well. "Reinhart was only interested in saving her city which was the largest and politically dominant one. The earth's surface was very small at the end of her life. There were other cities-actually, a total of five habitable ones, four of them were considerably smaller than hers. She finally agreed to set up a Center in each of the five cities, as shelter in case of natural disaster. She built two large ones, the one we live in and another that was destroyed. There were three small, satellite centers, like this one, to provide for overflow populations. One of those was also destroyed."

There were no questions, so I continued. "As I said, these centers occupied the five earth surfaces on which life existed. This Center, the one that we are visiting now, should not be in the same sector as ours. Just like the other remaining center, devoid of any life forms, and occupied only by androids, should be on another part of the earth's surface."

Still no comment, so I continued. "From the information that Reinhart has uploaded to me and from the computer records that I just studied, the time warp phenomenon was reserved for our center. But this time warp phenomenon, like I told you many times, was intended to speed up time in our center, not slow it down. Reinhart only programmed our center's computer with this independent time-space configuration that would activate automatically during a violent and sudden catastrophic event." I paused.

"For whatever reason, she only wanted our center to survive." I avoided their eyes. "Perhaps, had she survived, she could have saved the other centers from annihilation, at the last minute, but I am not certain." I took a deep breath before saying, "Whatever she did, or intended to do, with the other centers is irrelevant because she died before the explosion took place."

I paused to gather my thoughts. "The two smaller ones that are now in our geographic zone apparently survived the explosion because they were lifted by the force of the doom-day explosion and dragged along with our center into our time warp. That explains why these two satellite centers are in our geographic zone today. And, as you can see, time is slowed down in this center like in ours." Reinhart was not giving me any additional technical information so I couldn't say more.

"I don't know if it makes sense. Something seems to be missing, Pamela." Randolph spoke up. "Do you mind if I take a look at the computer and retrieve as much information as I can get about that period."

"Of course not." I hesitated for a second. "Actually, I thought that we could spend a day here in the Center. For those of us who are interested, we could use the land vehicles to explore the area- take soil samples, for example. I would like to compare them to the soil samples outside our center." That got rapid approval. Spinning around in land vehicles appealed to everyone.

The afternoon seemed to go by fast. I wanted to look at the genetic blends used in this center. I was convinced that Jarrod and Fleming were involved in research that engendered the humans of many colors, even though there was something strange about this presumption. Jarrod and Fleming were not at the same level as the Group of 5 who were identical replicas of their human counterparts therefore imbued with the cerebral capacities and qualities of their prestigious human counterparts.

The policy at the time was to transfer a certain amount of knowledge for safe keeping to the android opposites, to avoid full knowledge transfer. The mentors of Jarrod and Fleming died before the authorized level of knowledge was transferred to them. They never worked alongside their human opposites either. So, if they were experimenting with genetic mutations they were receiving their instructions from the Group of 5. I wanted to find evidence of the Group's complicity before I confronted them.

I tested the ovum, sperm and frozen embryos that Jarrod and Fleming left behind, all of which were genetically unmodified humans. I discovered, however, that there were a suspicious number of empty vials. They must have been given instructions to destroy whatever was in them. There were also visible gaps in the recorded research on the computer in the lab. I was convinced that they had erased all information relevant to the humans of many colors.

I sat back and closed my eyes in contemplation. They must have left a trace of their hideous research somewhere, but where? I tested the empty vials, but they were clean, sterilized clean. The computer terminals and equipment in the learning center were wiped clean of fingerprints and other DNA indicators. I turned to the artificial uteruses. The ten artificial uteruses were turned off. I opened one after the other looking for traces of DNA. The machines were wiped so clean that I was ready to give up when I opened the next to the last uterus and came upon a tiny spot of blood. How they missed that, I didn't know. I rushed off to examine it. I could do the test because the technology available was adequate even though slightly inferior to what Reinhart was used to and what existed in our center.

The answer was evident. Reinhart should have recognized that from the beginning. It was a mutation of the PTPN 11 gene, causing multiple lentigines disorder, or brown spots, like freckles that appear in large numbers, sometimes in the thousands. This disorder was commonly referred to as Leopard syndrome. This discovery sent waves of nausea through me, as I grabbed the lab table to support my weakened body.

There was no logical basis for this research in contrast to the creation of reptilian humans conceived to save humanity. I probably would have stood immobile for hours, contemplating over and over again the absurdity of this form of research, if Peter, in pursuit of me, had not appeared out of nowhere.

"There you are?" His voice registered an air of relief. Even though I was aware of his presence, as he approached me, I stood paralyzed, unable to respond verbally or physically to him. He grabbed me and started to shake me to get a reaction. "What happened? Talk to me!" He screamed.

"Oh, Peter," I said between gasps–"sometimes, those androids are just too despicable. I can't believe what they did!"

"Tell me. Sit down and tell me." He pleaded as he picked me up and sat me delicately down in one of the low chairs.

"Ludovic is one of their horrible experiments!" I screamed, my angry voice directed at the vials. I resisted my impulse to get up and shatter them on the floor.

He kneeled in front of me and put his arms tightly around me, moving me psychologically into a safe, protective zone, away from the reality around me. "Of course they were wretched, or maybe just bored, before our revolution. They are getting better." He said softly, as I continued my sobbing. "Yes, Ludovic is very peculiar but he is nice. Tell me what they did."

I took a few long, deep breaths. "There was a disorder that was commonly referred to as the Leopard syndrome, not because of the animal, but because the letters making up the word, leopard, indicated the most common consequences of this disorder, even though it was uncommon for a human to have all of these symptoms. I went through the letters, the L stands for lentigine, the E for electrocardiographic conduct abnormalities, the O for ocular hypertelorism, the P for pulmonary stenosis, the A for abnormal genitalia, the R for retardation of growth and the D for deafness."

"It doesn't sound good." He said as he squeezed me even tighter in his arms. My head was now resting comfortably on his chest. Just listening to his steady breathing and his slow, strong, rhythmic heartbeat had a calming effect on me. We stayed like that for quite a while before I was able to move away from him and speak normally or rather scientifically.

"They mutated the PTPN 11 gene," his eyes were looking into mine, "which is why Ludovic does not have a normal appearance." I stopped for an instance. "Do you want to know more?"

"No, I don't need to hear more and, quite frankly, this is not my field." He swallowed hard. "Do you think that Ludovic has all the problems that you just mentioned?"

"I don't know. I shall have to examine him." The way that he unconsciously backed away from me, and the subject, signaled the profoundness of its impact on him.

"Normally, Peter," my voice was now calm as I revealed the facts that Reinhart was rapidly uploading to me, "the mutation of the PTPN 11 gene produces a high number of dark brown lesions or spots that can cover over 80% of the skin. The lesions are normally irregular."

I bowed my head in thought. "Ludovic has colorful spots that are symmetrical. Perhaps the androids played around with pigmentation hoping to attenuate it." Peter nodded. "It is clear that he does not have stunted growth and is not deaf. Nonetheless, he has several visible traits associated with this disorder, a part from the spots on his skin. His eyes are large and wide-set and he has low-set ears and a slightly protruding lower jaw. His nasal passages look normal. At least they are not broad." I let out a long gust of air. "I shall have to examine him when we get back to our center."

"Can she restructure his face?"

"I don't know." I was getting no feedback from her for the moment. "She is often times more fascinated with these anomalies than interested in correcting them. You have to remember that she is not emotionally motivated, like I am, and therefore less sensitive to personal grievances." The corners of his mouth curved downwards.

"I need to change the subject for a minute, if you don't mind." He suggested and I nodded. I was glad to talk about something else.

"Stuart, Randolph and I were unable to retrieve any information that might alter in any way the diagnosis you gave on the time warp. Randolph suggested, however, that the waves created by the time-space alteration put into place by our center, vibrated outward. He contends that the two satellite centers were lifted from the ground during the explosion and that they were spinning inside a rotational funnel shaped force, or cloud, much like an object spinning inside a tornado. The time-space waves from our Center, radiating outward, pulled these two smaller centers along with it simply because they passed into our Center's time-space configuration at the very moment when our center's gravitational force was the greatest."

"Interesting, very interesting!" Reinhart's warmth surging violently inside of me. "Randolph does surprise me sometimes. He comes across as a playful character that keeps his cerebral side well hidden." I lifted my hands, palms up, to prevent him from reacting to what could easily have been interpreted as an insult. "Yes, what he just said seems very plausible. As the time warp slowed down the movement of the center to escape and resist the gravitational force of the exploding planet, these satellite centers, passing through the time-space waves emanating from our center, could certainly have been dragged into our time space configuration."

"She agrees?"

"Yes, I can feel from her vibrant energy inside of me that she likes his analysis. But, she still wants to understand why our center's time was slowed down and whether something other than the explosion lifted the other centers, putting them in a free spin. Perhaps, John can give her that information."

"Well, I am hungry. Let's go eat!" He pulled me up out of my chair and guided me back to the dining area.

Everyone was already half-way through their dinners when we

arrived. They had brought meals for Peter and me from the food storage on the aircraft. From what they were spouting out, all the other members except Peter, Stuart, Randolph and I spent their time on the land vehicle simulators that they found and activated in the transport terminal. The group was ready to leave now. The idea was enticing, so Peter and I ate fast and left with them.

The vehicles could hold up to four people. Of course, Reinhart wanted to drive one of those machines, so I quickly jumped into the driver's seat. There were enough vehicles available for everyone to try their hand at the steering wheel. Clarence and Joseph took one; Mathieu and Isabel another; and Leonard and Daniel went together; the rest of us were single drivers without passengers. We left Ludovic alone in the center.

"It is a risk for the three of you." I said pointing at Peter, Stuart, and Randolph. "Stay out of our way until you learn to drive!" I cautioned them. "We don't need any accidents." Their blank looks sent me off on a wave of laughter.

"Hey, Pamela, can you just show us how to turn them on and how to get them going." Stuart coaxed me.

I did just that. I showed them the ignition, the lights, the pedals and how to steer. The rest I left up to them. They were big boys and could find out on their own. I was not in the mood to go into any great detail on driving the vehicles. I didn't want to waste any more time, and neither did Reinhart who was sending me lots of waves of excitation.

I cautioned everyone to stay together and to look at the guidance program in the system so that they would not get lost. I was the first to leave, driving fast and furious like Reinhart wanted. It was already dusk so I didn't want to wander off too far. I even put the lights on to give me a better perspective of the area.

I stayed ahead of the others, losing them completely at one point, to check out a strange mound of dirt. The closer I got to it, the more that I realized that it looked like a shelter. I drove the vehicle up close, turned the lights on full and got out of the vehicle, cautiously approaching the structure. I quickly changed my mind and returned to the vehicle, worried about pursuing this on my own. So instead, I registered the coordinates of this unusual geographic formation into the vehicle's guidance system so that I could find it when the others were with me. I started to back up, preparing to leave, when I noticed something coming into view. I stopped the vehicle, put on high beams and picked up the laser gun, preparing to fire.

"Hey, I think that I know you?" I heard someone call out.

His voice was familiar. "Is that you Jason?"

"Yes, what are you doing here, Pamela?" I was already out of the vehicle running in his direction. "He survived all this time on his own." I marveled, as I threw my arms around this scrawny old man, who was my inspiration to explore this world.

"You are incredible!" I screamed joyfully. "I have so much to tell you. Come, you are going back with me to meet the other humans, who are now in control." I said, bubbling with enthusiasm.

"But..."

"No, buts... just get in the vehicle." He did as he was ordered to do. My voice animated with lively chatter, I brought him up-to-date on how we overthrew the androids; how I absorbed the knowledge of my biological Mother, and more and more. He listened to my short version of the new world. "I believed everything that you told me, Jason." I said adamantly. "And, little by little I have been able to confirm the authenticity of everything you said."

He chuckled. "I know that many people believed that I had lost my mind. Sometimes I thought I had as well." We both roared with laughter. "So we humans have finally reclaimed our history. That also explains why there are no more small communities of humans living on the outside. Are they dead?" He asked. I nodded.

"We did find a surviving human of many colors. He was living in that tropical forest you told us about." He forced a smile. "He remembers you." I pointed to the center that was now in view.

"Come, there are many members from the outside community here with me. You will also meet Randolph and Stuart who were working for our cause inside the center as well as two other humans, Tirence and James who deprogrammed after the revolution. Of course, Ludovic, our young man of many colors, is there and a number of reptilian humans." I thought that I should prepare him for my other friends, even though I knew that Jason was not bothered by physical appearances. He squinted his eyes in thought. "What you have learned over all those years of exploring will be so helpful for us."

"But, I am an explorer. I cannot live on the inside."

"Oh, of course you are an explorer, but we are too." I opened the door for him to get out. "You need something to eat and drink."

I was the last one to arrive and found my friends grouped together, pacing up and down the confined space of the lounge area, impatiently awaiting my return. Their stern expressions turned instantly into happy faces when they saw Jason. He hugged those he knew and then went straight to the reptilian humans to compliment them on their extraordinary appearances. He recognized Ludovic, even with his decontamination suit, and gave him a big hug. Randolph, Stuart, James and Tirence were the last ones to greet him, in warm, friendly, lingering hugs.

We sat talking into the night. "How much do you remember about your life on the inside?" I asked propitiously. He mentioned hiding in the center and then escaping through a tunnel in the zoological gardens.

"Why did you ask, Pamela? Do you know something that I don't know?"

"Yes, I do." I told him that he lived hundreds, maybe thousands of years ago and was one of the volunteers for an experiment in suspended animation. "As one of the only survivors, Gordon decided to revive you and to make it possible for you to escape. She was hoping that you would incite creative activity in the human societies on the outside."

He stared at us, his eyes absent yet resolved and his mouth tightly drawn-in. I shuddered at his contorted face, so full of disgust and...hatred.

"Now, I remember all that...yes," he said in a shrill voice, breaking with emotion. "I can see it like yesterday. She did that to me and to others. Volunteers," he laughed, an eerie, crackling sound, much like that of the Group of 5. "We were not volunteers. We were her guinea pigs, her experimental rats. We came from the non-intellectual group and she did what she wanted with us. Despicable person that Dr. Reinhart!"

I choked on my own saliva. "You didn't like her, I gather?"

"She was beautiful, elegant, charismatic, and so brilliant that she didn't seem human. We worshipped her, in a strange way. Maybe, it was more fear than love that made us bow to her every suggestion." He sighed. "Yes, she trapped me and others by pretending that we were worth saving. She manipulated us, virtually brainwashed us into participating in her suspended animation program." The despair and pain buried deep inside him erupted suddenly prompting him to quickly dab the moisture from his eyes.

I listened attentively as he slowly picked up the discussion. "When it was my turn, I overheard her talking to a Dr. Murdoc about the risk factors in suspended animation and the need to test it on an inferior order of humans before using it for them and their kind. They plotted against us. I protested, saying that I had changed my mind. I was sedated. That is all I remember." He looked at me as if he saw her in me. "So, that android Gordon woke me up and let me believe that I was an adolescent who escaped."

I sincerely regretted having mentioned the truth. I could feel the cold stares of my group on me and on Randolph, Murdoc's biological son, as if we were responsible for the horrors of that former time. As I turned my eyes away from them I was aware of Reinhart's presence mounting rapidly inside of me, releasing different feelings, feelings that she had not revealed before. I stood clenching my chest in pain, or a tightness, or a hollow sensation of grief. It was but her sadness, not mine, that so dramatically overcame me.

The others watched me pace back and forth in front of them, waiting patiently for me to regain composure and continue. "I have to make a horrible confession now, Jason. Elisabeth Reinhart is my biological mother and it is her knowledge that I absorbed. I am so sorry!" I burst with emotion.

"Don't be, Pamela. That is wonderful news." He looked around and there were obliging nods. "You are a wonderful person, Pamela, and you are her equal... maybe more. And, even though you have her beauty, her grace, her charisma, and her genius, you have what she lacked to become the greatest human in all of human history-you have feelings, compassion!" His voice quivered. "You will become a legend!"

"Oh, thank you, Jason, for believing in me." I replied, my mind in a whirl. And yet what he just said both comforted me and helped me to quickly move the conversation forward to our time and out of the Reinhart era riddled with scientific progress at any price. "So do you agree to help us explore this planet?"

"Absolutely. But, to do that well, I am going to have to get some sleep." He paused, a slight smile appearing on his face. "But, before anything else, I would like to shower and put on some clean clothes." He said in a good humored, teasing way.

Isabel was there in a couple minutes with everything that would help him to be clean, well shaven, and dressed properly. "Time for all of us to choose a bedroom." She said. "There are plenty of them and they look comfortable."

I walked Jason to his bedroom and said goodnight. I noticed that Isabel and Mathieu left together just like Stuart and Diana. I saw Joseph and Tirence take a room with two beds. As always, I reflected on Tirence's previous behavior and how different he was now. My suspicions were starting to disappear. Adam, Leonard and Daniel bunked up together. "Let's go, Pamela. I am wiped out." Peter said, between yawns. He put his arm around my waist and we leaned against each other as we made our way to the room he had chosen, collapsed on the bed and fell into a deep sleep.

I had a restless night. I dreamed about a young and radiantly beautiful woman, imbued with both knowledge and wisdom and possessing the intellectual capacity to surpass any and all life forms in this universe and others. She woke up in a strange world where she was abandoned. She found the people interesting, but their achievements limited. She wanted to leave, but couldn't remember where she came from. It was as if her memory had been erased, or she was reborn. She quickly distinguished herself in all fields of science and mathematics, gaining the confidence of others and the approval for her many and varied projects. She worked very diligently, never tiring of achievement. But her achievements made her powerful, something that she had neither expected nor desired but nonetheless, something that she eventually savored.

Her existence was a paradigm. Her life was a constant struggle. The moment that she was close to achieving the unachievable, her reality changed and she was forced to start all over again. Courage and determination accompanied her, like reliable companions, making it easier for her to confront the obstacles thrown her way. Challenges were not inhibitory adversaries; they were her source of creative inspiration, acting like stimulants, heightening her cognitive abilities.

And yet, in spite of all this glory I felt her suffering and her profound sadness. Was it because she always remained young, beautiful and powerful, without the constraints of time affecting her like it did others? Or because she regretted seeing friends and colleagues appear and disappear, while she continued on forever?

Her strong image disturbed my sleep, not like a nightmare, but like a dream embedded in a truth, an alarming truth, that one would rather ignore. Were all those long years she existed nothing more than her metamorphosis from a child to an adolescent?

I woke up in a cold sweat struggling to mentally wipe out the last image I had of her sitting patiently on a large rock in the middle of a luscious floral garden waiting, waiting patiently for someone or something to happen.

Chapter 19-Arrogant and Self-Centered

Peter was on his side, with his back turned in my direction. I crawled up close to him, wrapping my arms and legs around him and burying my head in his neck. I dosed off for a few more minutes before I got up and left him sleeping. I took a long shower, washing away sweat and anxiety, hoping to recuperate an inner calm.

"Peter, it's time to wake up." I pushed and pulled on him to get him moving. He clenched my arms tightly together between his hands.

"It is your fault that I didn't sleep well. You were so restless that I woke up so many times during the night, each time having a hard time getting back to sleep." He spoke in a taut voice, showing me his irritation.

"I know, I had a strange dream-probably because I stayed up too late talking to Jason." He released his grip and sat up. "Take your time, Peter. I shall have a quick breakfast, before I contact John. I want him to put Jarrod and Fleming on the visual so that I can tell them how disappointed I am with them."

"Vicious! You want to do more than scold, you want to castrate them, so to speak, for their reprehensible research." He replied vibrantly, referencing Ludovic's deformities, and jumped out of bed. "Wait for me. I'll be quick. I want to be there when you announce that!"

Strangely enough, we were the first to sit down to breakfast. The others arrived one after the other, still sluggish from the night before. They lingered lazily over breakfast, making it easy and convenient for Peter and me to leave them to contact the main center. John was already in the lab with Jarrod and Fleming at his sides. I asked him how the research on the time warp was going. He confessed that it was more complicated than he realized it would be. That was my incentive to inform him about Randolph's conclusions regarding the saving of the two satellite centers. This got a reaction from Jarrod.

"I had a feeling, an inexplicable feeling that that center was not supposed to survive." He stated matter-of-factly in his lifeless, robotic voice. "And, you are right, that center was located very far away from Reinhart's large center." He looked at Fleming who pretended to be in the dark, his eyes looking up at the ceiling, so Jarrod continued. "You see, Pamela, Dr. Reinhart protected her interests when she constructed her center. She was pressured to set up others but she was not motivated."

He stopped to retrieve information and then continued. "I remember the explosion because I was working in the center you are in now on that doomsday. The center was built to float above ground level, if need be, to prevent it from being destroyed by earthquakes, floods, and other natural disasters. The force of the explosion was so intense that the center was literally thrown onto its side, crushing a great number of androids under equipment or otherwise damaging them with projectiles. Some of them shattered into pieces as they were hurled up against the walls. It was a nightmare, as you humans would say." He looked at me to be assured that I was listening; I was intently.

"I was fortunate because I was actually searching for something under one of the lab tables when the Center pivoted. The table protected me, acting like a shield, withstanding the impact of flying objects. I struggled to get up on my feet when the center was ripped away from the ground and lifted high. We spun rapidly around in free space, like the center was inside a tornado, or a violent, rotating vortex of air. I was on my knees as I clung to the legs of the lab table. If I had emotions, I would have been terrified."

He paused, as if registering what he just said. "In any event the center was violently pulled out of its circular path by what I thought then was a centrifugal force. Now you are right it was a gravitational force that drew this center into another time-space configuration. That is probably why I felt as if I were aboard a spacecraft floating above the clouds once the spinning stopped. This center landed gently. It was only damaged on the inside. The outside walls, even the dome, were in perfect condition. Nonetheless, the interior suffered and we lost a lot of technology, equipment and personnel."

"It would appear that Randolph's evaluation is very close to the truth, whatever that is." Jarrod concluded. As he had no primitive emotional structure in place, he could not resort to any form of deceptiveness. I could therefore appreciate his clear and unambiguous report of what happened.

Now I had to inspire him to reveal the research that he and others were conducting in the Air and Space center, which meant that I had to probe him for the truth on genetic research. "What can you tell me about the humans of many colors?"

Again, as his programming prevented him from lying, he admitted that there were humans of many colors. "I thought that they were all annihilated when your revolution broke out. We were under orders to destroy them."

"Who created them?"

"They just appeared. Our laboratories were destroyed in the explosion, so we did not have any human ovum or sperm." He looked at Fleming.

Fleming picked up the conversation. "We all shut down for hundreds of years, or maybe thousands. The clean-up crew did not keep a record of the actual passage of time, waiting for the earth to calm down. The explosion was, as Jarrod just said, devastating. We were awakened by the Group of 5 after the earth's surface had improved and it was possible for us to envisage the return of human life."

So far he said nothing that I didn't know, but I could see that John and Peter had their heads tilted. "The Group of 5 passed us ovum and sperm from various individuals and we proceeded to in vitro fertilization. Some of the humans were physically normal, but we did have a number of humans with leopard syndrome, in varying degrees. We worked closely with the Group of 5 to ameliorate the mutations. We were able to assure perfect organ physiology, but were not able to suppress the problems of pigmentation and facial anomalies." He was a pure machine telling me the truth.

"Why didn't you stop using the mutated genes?"

"Why would we do that? We needed to bring back humans, re-gardless of what they looked like. It was their intellectual capacity that we wanted to exploit." Fleming retorted.

"So why did you put them on the outside?"

"Because it made sense after some of them deprogrammed. They seemed irrational, basically out of control, so we just put them out-side so that we could study their behavior and report back to Dr. Gordon, who was very much interested in this research." His expres-sionless eyes were studying mine. "It was a good decision to get rid of them. Why are you so interested in these obsolete individuals?"

"Because one of them is still alive and we have him with us." I answered.

His reaction, so reflective of his android logical, was disarming. "We shall inform the Group of 5 when we see them. They might be interested even though your news is of no interest to me. Is there anything else?"

I looked at Peter who looked like someone had slapped him in the face. I snickered, momentarily ignoring the gravity of the situa-tion. "Yes, inform them of Ludovic's existence." I said in a loud, clear voice. "You can also tell them that Reinhart never did any research in the PTPN Gene 11 and therefore never mutated sperm or ovum in that manner. She is very curious about how this form of mutation was introduced."

There was a very long pause before Jarrod spoke. "Understood. I don't think that they will be very pleased with this news."

"Wow, Pamela, what is this individual like?" John asked.

"He is very colorful, with some facial irregularities or anoma-lies, but very nice. We are going to bring him back with us." I stop-ped. "I've got good news-news that will make you happy, John. We found Jason and he is also going to return to our center."

"That is great news!" He voice thundering with energy. "I'll tell the others. Keep in touch." The conversation ended.

"Bastard machines. The ones we deal with every day, or the Group of 5, captive to the vestiges of their primitive emotional programming, at least give the impression that they regret some of their behavior. But, those two, Jarrod and Fleming, don't care at all!" Peter did not stifle his anger.

"Don't forget that the Group of 5's primitive emotional configuration makes them unpredictable. Jarrod and Fleming have a typical, pure and unaltered android reaction. Androids like Jarrod and Fleming are easier to control because they operate on pure logic and their reactions are predictable. You have to keep this in mind. The real "bastards" are the Group of 5." I replied.

Everyone was ready to move out and explore the area. I took Jason with me in my vehicle, as a guide. To my regret, I discovered immediately the reason why he was never able to return to the tropical garden; he had no sense of direction. So I just ignored his persistent suggestions and let Reinhart show me the way. She had already made a mental map of the area that she was visually passing on to me. I went straight to the shelter where I found Jason the night before. "Did you explore the area?"

"There is nothing to explore. I dug myself a rude kind of cavern." He put his hands over his mouth to stifle his laughter. "It could have collapsed on me and buried me. Amusing? Huh?"

I raised my eyebrows in response and got out of the vehicle to explore the area. The rest of the group was behind me. He was wrong, it was an amazing hiding place he dug for himself. "I am going to take some soil samples." I touched the walls which I found were dry and solid. "Did you add anything to the sand?" He gave me a vibrant no. "Can you show me how deep you dug?"

"Ok, but it might take me awhile. In the beginning the sand collapsed around me." He scratched his head. "Now that I think about it, I dug far below the surface to find the right quality sand. I'll show you."

We stood watching as Jason dug a hole about three feet deep pushing the surface sand aside, with each sweep of his hands. The surface was a darker red color than what was underneath. He then lifted out a bit of the lighter colored soil and molded it together, as if it were clay, a very dense clay soil that I would have to analyze later. I took several soil samples of the topsoil in different areas and samples of the structure Jason occupied, along with the clay soil that he just uncovered. It would be interesting to see the results.

"We should continue east, as we will be going west towards the oceans when we leave tomorrow morning." I suggested. I again led the way, stopping from time to time to collect other soil samples. We drove through barren territory for hours before stopping for lunch.

"Why are there no life forms outside of that tropical garden?" Diana asked, demonstrating an interest in the exploration of the planet that up-until-now was absent.

"I like the empty spaces, hot sun and sandy soil." Clarence was stretched out on the hot sand, his claws visible. "Too bad his tail was ripped off," passed through my mind. Then I noticed that Joseph, Leonard, Adam and Daniel were also soaking up the sun something the rest of us were trying to avoid.

I couldn't answer Diana's question. After all those hundreds of years that the androids were playing around with reproducing humans and searching for information, one would have thought that they would have ventured out of the centers and explored the planet. All evidence showed the contrary. I could feel the eyes of my team members studying me. Their wide, probing eyes made me feel uncomfortable so I got up and grabbed some empty vials and filled them with soil samples from this rest stop.

"Are you all ready to move on?" I said as I jumped into my vehicle with Jason rapidly taking his place alongside of me. "I think that we should change direction and go south unless someone has another suggestion." Their vehicles were lined up alongside of me like racecars waiting for the flag to fall. That struck me as funny and I chuckled loud enough for them to hear. I turned south.

We drove for several hours before we came upon an imposing mountain. Curiosity overcame all of us, as we got out of the vehicles and entered into the large cavern opening, directly in front of us. I was expecting to find a primitive dwelling when in effect I discovered that it was similar to the cavern that we shared on the outside, in seemingly every detail. The alcoves, lighting, furnishings and even the visual surveillance equipment were the same.

It was so well maintained that I imagined that it was abandoned very recently, probably because of our revolution, or that someone was acting as a caretaker for this cavern and was presently absent. We were fascinated enough that we went off in our own directions to look for clues concerning its previous occupants.

"The alcoves are so strikingly similar to ours," I thought, while entering into the exact replica of the alcove that Peter, Frederic and I shared. I jolted when I saw the child's bed in the very place we put Frederic's. With my imagination now running wild, I drew the conclusion that, as these centers were so identical, perhaps the doomsday explosion, with its time-space alterations, opened up a parallel universe. As such, this cavern must exist in another dimension and that we entered into that new dimension the moment we passed through the cavern door.

That idea intrigued me and I ran back to the entrance to test it. I stepped outside the cavern and then back inside. I went back and forth several times, experiencing no strange sensations like dizziness, visual distortion, a strong magnetic attraction drawing me from one point to another, or any other analogous functional disorder that would naturally have occurred if I were passing into a new dimension, or a parallel universe. Disappointed, I entered the main room and sat down at the dining room table to think.

"Who are you?" I vaguely heard someone ask, breaking into my thoughts.

I looked up and saw a middle-aged man. He was short and pudgy, with visibly hairy arms. He had a very round face, small, beady eyes, a stubby nose and a small, puffy mouth. Unfortunately, even his luscious, thick, reddish-brown, wavy, shoulder-length hair did not make him attractive. I studied him before introducing myself.

"And, who are you?"

"I am the guardian of this cavern." He raised his bushy, brown eyebrows as he spoke.

"The guardian of this cavern." I repeated several times.

"Well, actually, I am the architect of this cavern and another that is located quite a distance from here. During the revolution, I took refuge in this one." He folded his arms in front of him, as if he were in command and what he had to say was above reproach.

"Ok, that explains why this cavern resembles the other one where I lived off and on." He nodded. "Where were you living before you started to reside here?"

"I was living in the big Center and worked for the Governor." He

296

ignored my laughter. 'Why did the Governor hide that from me?' Occupied my thoughts.

"When the revolution broke out, I gathered up a lot of supplies and left with one of the vehicles."

"So you were deprogrammed?" He nodded yes. "Why didn't I ever see you?"

"I don't know? I did cross in front of you several times in the corridors. I remember you, Stuart and Randolph."

Peter arrived. "Pamela, who is that guy and what are we going to eat? I think that you forgot that we didn't take enough food with us." He rambled on.

"Oh that is not a problem. I have a lot of dehydrated food stored here and a machine to hydrate it." The strange little man proclaimed.

"I know this man. I call him Andrew." Jason announced as he entered the dining room. "He is an architect and works on the outside."

"Thanks, Jason. She. . ." he pointed to me, "is very suspicious of me." I didn't understand what he meant. He startled me, but I had no reason to be leery of him, at least not yet.

The rest of the members of the group staggered in one after the other. I introduced them to Andrew and they gave him a brief rundown of what they were doing. He recoiled when he saw the reptilian humans, but relaxed quickly when they told him their story. Diana was the last one to arrive. Her eyes blazed with an angry fury when she came face to face with him. He instinctively backed away from the table, throwing his small hands over his eyes, as if just wiping out the image of Diana would be enough to protect him from her rage.

A long, tense silence invaded our space. Finally, Andrew made the first move when he slowly lowered his hands and pushed his shoulders back in a commanding position ready to confront his adversary. Diana laughed, a high, cold laugh that made him tremble and scream profanities, that only Reinhart understood, in a strained, raspy voice, in an effort to intimidate Diana. Instead, she leaped over the table and lunged for him, preparing to sink her nails into his fleshy throat. Stuart, right behind her, caught her in time, pulling her away from Andrew at the last minute.

"She is so dangerous. She works for them-the Group of 5- and she almost killed me in the past." His fear assuaged by Stuart's intervention, he now felt free to accuse Diana.

"Liar!" Diana cried out in a high-pitched voice as she tried to wrestle herself out of Stuart's grip. "He is crazy and dangerous. Just let me go, Stuart. Let me rid us of the little creep!" She had become the irrational tigress that attacked us years ago. And yet, in spite of the fact that we all wanted to believe that we had evolved and were able to control our most violent emotions, Diane's reaction reminded me that our primitive sides were still alive and that anyone of us could over react and revert to violent and outrageous conduct.

"Ok, everyone calm down." Peter took charge. While pointing at her, he blurted out, "Diana, just tell us what the problem is between the two of you."

She squinted at Andrew through hardened eyes as she spoke fiercely through clenched teeth. "He could see me sometimes and I could almost see him from time to time, because my vision was in and out. He understood that. John explained my problem to me shortly after I joined the outside community. Apparently my visual receptor was malfunctioning from the very beginning, when it was first inserted, the reason why my behavior was so erratic."

She took a deep breath, expelling it slowly, and then continued in a softer, calmer tone. "One day the Governor called me into his office and that slimy person was there. The Governor told me that he would protect me if I did not tell anyone else that he" ---she pointed to Andrew----"was deprogrammed." Her nostrils flared. "I accepted the agreement."

Our attention turned to Andrew. "Yes, that was the deal. I worked for the Governor, redoing the two caverns." He cleared his throat. "Actually, I only produced the architectural designs. The androids carved out the living quarters and installed all the equipment. I just supervised their work, like an interior decorator. The Governor did not find me a threat...and I was not one."

"So what happened?" Stuart asked as he maintained his firm grip on Diana.

Diana spoke. "He waited for the right moment, which was right after I deprogrammed and, in a frenzied effort to protect myself, destroyed an android guard. I knew that I was under surveillance and left the corridors, entering into the dining room, seeking sanctity. I heard Andrew tell Crawford, who was in charge of the dining room when I entered, that my visual receptor was malfunctioning. He denounced me, telling Crawford that he heard a voice but he could not see the person, and that the person refused to give him their number. He was pointing in my direction. He insisted that he could not see who it was. Crawford came for me and I was taken to the hospital and sedated. I was lucky that Gordon and the Governor convinced the others to put me on the outside." Diana's head flopped back in raucous laughter. "I would have killed that traitor if I had found him during the revolution!"

Her eyes met his and Andrew squirmed under Diana's angry stare. She held his attention by slowly, methodically licking her lips. We stood mesmerized by the scene that began to degenerate, when she curled her lips back just enough to show her teeth and lifted her body as she readied herself to spring again and this time sink her canines into her prey. Andrew stumbled backwards and turned his pleading eyes in our direction, away from the impending danger that Stuart struggled to restrain.

We observed that under mounting anxiety, his voice had risen an octave higher when he next spoke. "Things went well for me for a short time thereafter." And then I overheard you"-he pointed to me-"and him"- then to Stuart-"talking when you were dragging him"-his blazing eyes fell upon Randolph-"along the corridor. I knew that I had to get out of the center fast. I understood that others were arriving."

"So you told the Governor?" I asked in disbelief. "That is why they were ready for us when our group came up through the transport unit." I stopped to rethink and relive the scene. "You were in the transport unit stealing a vehicle and you saw Diana poke her head up from under the floor. That's it." He lowered his eyes. "You put her on the visual before you left?"

"Look, try to put yourself in my place. I was scared. When I saw that crazy woman breaking through the floor, I wanted to protect myself. I had no idea that she was not alone...even though you just mentioned that there were others with her. You and Stuart were not looking very well and Randolph was out cold, so I thought that perhaps you were just hoping that you would receive help or some backup. I never expected you to be waging a revolt and, least of all, to win."

"Let me take care of him?" Diana begged, knowing that she was helpless to do anything, surrounded by Stuart, Peter and Randolph.

"Lock him up some place, for his own protection, to give us a chance to calm down." I suggested. Clarence and Joseph took him into one of the other rooms and positioned themselves at either side of the entrance because there were no doors on the cubicles.

Diana finally tired and collapsed on the floor. Stuart and Randolph stayed next to her just in case she had another burst of adrenaline.

"He is not a vicious person, just a stupid one!" Jason finally broke the ice. "I suggest that we leave him here in this empty cavern. We can go back to the other center for the night. We should anyway. We left Ludovic there all alone."

He was right. I had completely forgotten about Ludovic. "Before we vote on that, I would like to see all the visual surveillance equipment in this cavern." I looked at Peter and Randolph. "I want to verify the developmental stage, if you two understand what I mean." That meant that they had to liberate Andrew so that he could accompany them and point out the surveillance equipment. I wanted to make certain that there were no inadvertent leaks in our more advanced technological developments that the Group of 5 was exploiting to their advantage.

In the meantime, Diana acquiesced, promising to remain calm and apologizing for her erratic behavior. "I just wanted to warn you about him, but then my overall hatred for him took over and I lost control. Now that you know he must be watched closely, I am ready to concede to my rational side." That put us more at ease.

When Peter and Randolph returned they agreed that there were slight improvements over what we had in our center, which were certainly linked to the research conducted before the revolution. At least for the moment we are keeping our present research under taps and out of the reach of the Group of 5.

Clarence and Joseph were back with us and positioned themselves on either side of Andrew to protect him, if need be, even though Diana was no longer a threat. We did need a bit more information from him.

"I would like clarification on something, Andrew." His beady eyes pierced mine, making me feel a bit uneasy. "How did you deprogram?"

"Oh, that happened when I was working in your cavern." He rubbed his hand over his chin. "Actually, when I designed the cavern you lived in on the outside, I was still programmed. The surveillance equipment-something that appears to interest you- was installed by the Group of 5. They did not want me to be involved, at least not in the beginning". He replied smugly, like he had revealed a profound observation. Dismayed by my blank expression, he continued. "After supervising the digging and construction of this cavern, I was disturbed by the visual surveillance in the main room. I wanted to move that ugly box, like the one here"- he pointed to a corner of the ceiling-"to another place because it interfered with the harmony and aesthetics of this room. I ripped it off the wall too brusquely, receiving a violent electrical shock causing me to lose consciousness. I believe that I recovered rapidly."

He stopped for a moment, looking for a friendly face, but when he saw none, he continued. "As there were only android assistants working with me, I did not realize that I had been deprogrammed by the shock. They were still bright spots for me. When I got back to the Center, I thought that I was ill because my images of humans seemed distorted and so I went to see the Governor. He told me that there were others like me in the Center and that he would protect me, if I continued to do exactly what he asked me to do."

"And, what did he ask you to do?"

"To continue my architectural projects."

"What other architectural projects?"

"Oh that ridiculous tropical garden!" He replied vehemently, as if the project bored him.

"You built the tropical garden?"

"One doesn't build a tropical garden, Pamela." He replied bitterly. "One creates, conceives, that kind of environment." The look on my face must have been unsettling for him, because he cleared his throat and started to speak in a more respectful tone. "I don't know where to start. You said that you lived in the other cavern?" There were many yeses. "Ah-now I understand how you got into the transport unit. You used the secret passage that I left for my own protection." We didn't answer. "Yes, of course, you passed along a narrow ledge high above a pool of water." He rubbed his puffy lips and then grinned, showing his small, pointed teeth.

"The tropical garden." I said adamantly.

"Of course, the tropical garden." He stretched his arms out in front of him, cracked his knuckles and then stood very erect. "You should be able to guess the rest. It's tiring to have to explain things that are, or should be, self-evident." He said condescendingly. I sneered at him, inspiring him to continue his speech. "I knew that this pool of water did not just miraculously appear. Any idiot would have been able to draw the same conclusion." He was getting on my nerves because he was wasting our time with his self-laudatory remarks. "So, of course, there was an underground stream. I verified that with the geology department. I proposed creating a large enclosed space with a natural waterfall to the Governor. He found the idea charming."

"And the plants?" I asked impatiently.

"Oh, I collaborated with the older man in charge of the agricultural department. He produced the proper soil samples and provided me with the plants. I used different sized stones that I found in the caverns to build the wall and to create an idyllic and relaxing tropical landscape."

"So the tropical forest was artificially created." I commented.

"Of course, how could you expect to find such a paradise in this barren region?" He said derisively.

I could feel the blood rushing to my face. How I wanted to wipe that smug look off of his face? I had enough of his pretentiousness and wished that I could bring this discussion to an end, but I was not finished with my interrogation. "The animals, where did they come from?"

His eyes grew wide and his mouth dropped open. "What animals?"

"You didn't visit the tropical forest?" He shook his head in a clear no. "Why not?" I asked, trying to keep a neutral tone.

"After it was created, I was assigned to this cavern to furnish cubicles and therefore build the furniture. I had very little help with that, so I spent years here putting this cavern together for habitation."

"So no other humans have lived in this cavern?" I asked in disbelief.

"No. I am the only human, besides the group of you today, who has stepped foot into this place. I traveled back and forth to the center by car to get material and discuss my progress with the Governor." He smacked his lips together. "This cavern was ready for habitation at the time of your revolution, the reason why I stole-as you insinuated-enough food and water to survive for a long time!"

I was not certain that I believed him and yet he did seem very surprised about animal life. He was not much of an actor, so he was probably telling the truth about that. "I think that this man should live out the rest of his life, alone, in this cavern." I said with authority.

Adam disagreed, mentioning that Andrew might be helpful in the future with architectural designs. "He is both a structural architect and a landscape architect, as well as an interior decorator. He did turn this cavern into a cozy, habitable place. He created a masterpiece with the tropical garden. We might need his skill and knowledge in the future to construct housing and gardens on the outside."

Unfortunately there was truth in that. We took a vote and everyone, except Diana, who still wanted to see him disappear, voted in favor of leaving him in this environment until we got more information from the Group of 5. "We shall be back for you, Andrew. If I were you, I would not leave this cavern." I warned him.

He turned jovial, a youthful high-spiritedness in his laughter and energetic walk, and thanked all of us for being so understanding. He then accompanied us to the entrance of the cavern and waved goodbye like we were his guests and he was the Lord of this manor. I found the entire encounter disturbing because of the Group of 5's complicity and their constant lack of frankness and sincerity, in my regard.

I drove in silence with Jason sitting stiff and expressionless, staring out at the barren earth. We arrived at dusk and found Ludovic marching nervously back and forth along the long corridor. His cries of joy when he saw us were touching. He understood that we were not going to abandon him. I gave Jason a big hug and told him that I did not consider him in any way responsible for Andrew.

He thanked me. "I was worried, and embarrassed, because I should have mentioned Andrew to you, Pamela. I did meet a lot of different people. For me, Andrew was just one of many that I met. I didn't realize how involved he was with the Group of 5."

"Don't worry about it."

I pointed to the tables and told him to take a seat while I went to get the food and water. My thoughts lacked optimism. I pondered over the last three days that seemed more like three months, or even three years. We had not wasted our time and had made many discoveries. Unfortunately they did not answer our questions, they raised new ones, and to what end? Everyone was deep in thought, giving them a tired, anguished look. I took a seat between Jason and Peter and we ate in silence. No one lingered after dinner, going off with someone, or alone, to find a way to recuperate energy and enthusiasm. Ludovic, sealed up in his decontamination suit, gulped down his milkshake ravenously. Before leaving him to his peril, I assured him that he would soon be able to explore with us. With his sincere expressions of gratitude, he ingratiated himself with Reinhart.

"This has been both an amazing and frightening three days. What do you think, My Love?" Peter asked in a delightfully teasing style that tended to minimize the seriousness of our present situation.

"I was thinking about the same thing just a little while ago, although I believe that we have only scraped the surface in our discoveries." I said, my mind in a whirl. "To be perfectly honest, I am not tired at the moment. Going from the inside to the outside and back again does have an effect on my biological clock." I felt that I should explain myself.

"You are not the only one who is affected." He squinted his eyes in thought. "I was very tired in the beginning of the afternoon when we were eating. I could have fallen asleep very easily. I wonder if the others are still awake."

I didn't care what the others were doing. I was still bothered by the explanations of Jarrod and Fleming this morning. I had a feeling there was more in this center than the Group of 5 and their two devoted servants, Jarrod and Fleming, wanted to share with me. For that reason, I was inspired to look deeper. I asked Peter if he wanted to accompany me while I explored the center in more detail and the idea interested him.

The laboratory that Jarrod said was so severely damaged from the explosion was converted into an assembly area rather than into a research unit. There was a series of robots programmed to carry out menial tasks. These robots were also capable of rearranging their bodies to take on the shape and function of various kinds of machinery needed to assemble parts. There must have been a considerable number of those robotic assistants here in this center to complete the production process. "So where were they? Were they transported back to our Center or were they put in storage here?" I wondered.

Peter suggested that we move on and I agreed. There was nothing special in this lab. Two conjectural explanations for the absence of human research appeared to me out of thin air: either the humans that were reproduced in this center were transferred to our center, or the humans who lived in this center were not educated or trained to carry out research. Was either one of my hypotheses right? I had to find out.

"Peter, I wonder if there is a basement, an underground, in this center." He reminded me that the center was constructed to float above the ground and that the time warp would function only if the center remained isolated from the earth's natural gravitational force. He was right. The centers were like buildings, solid structures, with a masked outer casing that housed the foundation. The Center's internal clocks were still set in a time warp.

"There is a lower level in our center which is imperceptible from the outside. But, it exists, we all know that. We all passed through that lower level when we first escaped and the transport units are integrated, as well, into that lower foundation." He nodded.

"So what are you getting at? I am a bit confused." He rubbed his hand over his unshaven face, making an irritating, grating sound.

"There must be another level in this center. I want to take another look at the architectural plan." He reluctantly returned to the main entrance with me to consult the main computer system, warning me that I had to accept that this center was very small and unproductive.

Reinhart, who had not been interfering so slightly with my thoughts or my actions the last few hours finally came alive, in a dynamic flush of warm energy. Pushing Pamela aside, she broke into the system and retrieved the information that had been presumably deleted. There was definitely another level and we were very close to it. "So Pamela was not wrong!" I murmured vehemently, reminding my symbiont that I was equally perspicacious.

Reinhart ignored my laudatory remark, inciting me to move in the direction of the wall directly behind the computer system. Peter followed close behind. She pressed my hand down on a slight indentation in the wall, invisible to the naked eye. The wall opened revealing a wide staircase. We could hear machinery functioning, as we got closer to the bottom of the steps. In front of us was a vast unit filled with vehicles used for space travel, some of them were more primitive than others. Reinhart recognized the ones that she created and used to send groups of scientists to explore outlying planets and set up colonies. She also recognized the small capsules designed to carry a single voyager that could be launched off from the mother spaceship.

"You were right, Peter." I said, regaining control, as Reinhart uploaded information for me to absorb and understand. "You were not just dreaming or imagining things. There were humans returning to earth from other planets and the androids were destroying them."

Several androids approached us, their laser guns drawn and pointed at us. We were not only unarmed but also outnumbered. Peter pushed me behind him and stood facing them. I was so touched by his reaction, to sacrifice himself to save me. "What are you doing here?" One of the androids asked in that hollow tunnel voice that I detested.

Peter told him that we had made a mistake and that we inadvertently found ourselves in this section. He even told the large group that was encircling us that we would just leave and forget about it.

The android in command took center stage, announcing that he had to order the others to fire on us, because, according to ordinary procedure, they must terminate intruders.

This was one of those moments that I was glad that Reinhart was inside of me. The androids backed away when they heard Reinhart's voice ordering them to drop the lasers and move away. I recognized her voice from the films that I watched on Edward's interior video system and was at the same time horrified and gratified that she could control my vocal chords like that. Her voice, authoritative and charismatic, carried the verbal accent and pronunciation of the language spoken thousands of years before us. Because we were taught how to speak by the androids, our pronunciation of words were noticeably different.

Peter nudged me to get my attention and pointed to the effect that her voice had on all of them. They were lined up in a long straight row, their heads bent down showing respect. Their reaction was normal, she was their creator and her voice was programmed into their systems. We walked passed the thirty androids, and went directly to one of the enormous space vehicles that she created to transport colonies of humans.

Peter could not hide his enthusiasm, pushing me out of his way when we boarded the spacecraft. He vanished-exploring everything on his own. I finally caught up with him in the control room. "This machine is fabulous! I don't know what goes on at the different controls, but I want to learn, and learn fast." He rushed towards me and picked me up in the air, spinning me round and round. "We shall go together into space. We shall explore the near and far galaxies." He was like a child who discovered a new toy. "Show me how it works! Teach me how to fly this machine!"

"Hold on!" I was getting dizzy. "And, put me down. Please, Peter, put me down!" He put me in the commander's seat.

I stared up at him, his eyes alive with a special twinkle. His reaction was predictable, after all he told me the very first night we were together that he wanted to explore the universe. He was dreaming about this for so long that I did not want to disappoint him.

"I'll show you, but not today." He frowned. "We have to get this planet operational before we go anyplace else." He sulked. "Ok, now that I know that her space vehicles have been conserved and that there have been interstellar visitors, I am going to put you in command of the space program. I am assuming that everyone else will agree to that." Those kinds of decisions were to be made by everyone in our team so I knew that we would have to ask for their approval.

No matter, he slapped his hands together like he had won a very big battle. "Listen to me, Peter, our priority is this planet. You will also have to consecrate a lot of time to helping our group search for habitable areas." He nodded. "Our group is increasing in numbers and we will rapidly outgrow the space available in the centers. And even if that is not the case, some of the members might prefer to live on the outside."

"Agreed! I shall help with the exploration of this planet, but shall invest my energy in the space program in my spare time." He kissed me so passionately that for an instance I thought only of us and had to force myself to concentrate on what he said next. "You must promise me that you will show me how to fly one of these space ships."

I replied between bouts of laughter that if he wanted to be more than a science officer on board a spaceship, that he should first learn how to pilot an ordinary aircraft.

I bowed to Reinhart's compulsion to check out the systems. Her energy suffusing me, as she uploaded technical manuals, letting me visualize and understand how these spaceships operated. Peter watched, maybe studied, her every move. When she was satisfied, we left the spaceship and walked like dignitaries in front of the androids ceremoniously lined up for us.

I know that I walked in Reinhart's style and manner, a severe and commanding posture, with a straight back and my head held high. We stopped when we arrived at the stairway. She turned to address the androids. In an authoritative voice that left no room for interpretation, she ordered them to produce all the documents relating to past and present landings or overpasses by extraterrestrial visitors.

She also asked them to provide her with the visual and audio re-cords regarding any communications with those creatures, human or otherwise, including requests for landings. The androids did not move an inch. They stayed at attention, registering her orders.

"Now, which one of you is in charge of this service?" She as-ked. No one moved forward. "I am in no mood to play games with you, so, if none of you are in charge, then tell me who is in charge of you?" They all answered spontaneously, naming Jarrod and Fleming, as the parties who gave them the orders that they carried out to the letter.

"Which one of you is skilled in tracking spacecraft entering our atmosphere?" Three androids moved forward. "You destroyed or otherwise intercepted the spacecraft?" They replied in the affir-mative. "Did you ever leave any survivors?" No, they were ordered to destroy the life forms. "And, these orders came from Jarrod or Fleming?" They replied in the affirmative.

There was a long silence broken by one of the three. "We were trained to intercept. We piloted interceptor planes, carrying out standard procedure. Our order was always the same, destroy the intruder and save the spacecraft, and then move the spacecraft here on one of the carriers. If the intruder was fighting back, we had no choice but to destroy both the intruder and the spacecraft. We were always commended on our performance."

Reinhart burst out in one of her terrorizing laughs, marked with high, loud energy waves, like that of thunder, that had no effect on the androids but startled Peter who jumped a couple inches in the air.

"From now on you will only take instructions from me!"

Their android eyes penetrated me, trying to reach her. If they were hoping to intimate or to upset her they were wrong because she was not the kind of person to back down. As much as Reinhart was fascinated with how phenomenal they were, like an artist ad-miring her own masterpieces, she knew that they could not defy her, their creator. "If any of you three, or the rest of you for that matter, carry out orders coming from anyone else but me, I shall have you shut down and permanently dismantled. Is that clear?" They nodded.

"And the humans, where are they?" She asked in a sullen voice, as if she knew the response that would ultimately disprove my conjectures.

"Terminated." The android that identified himself earlier as the Commander replied.

"What you learned, you learned from them?" She asked.

"Those who had superior intellect shared their research and knowledge with us."

"Do you know how to construct any of these space vehicles?"

"No. But, under human guidance, we have been able to repair some of the damaged spacecraft. Unfortunately, we cannot build a space vehicle on our own. Do you need us to give you the designs that we have compiled?"

She bent over with raucous laughter. "I didn't know that I gave you a sense of humor." She said facetiously. The three androids moved back into the ranks with the others. She cleared her throat and said. "I shall be back to verify that you are complying with my orders. In the meantime, you may resume your work."

We quickly climbed the stairs, closed the door, and stood immobile, catching our breaths and regaining control. "Is she still present, Pamela?"

"Why? Why are you asking?"

"No reason." He let out a long winded sigh. "But, sometimes it would be nice to know who I am talking to." He tried to be funny, but I didn't see it that way.

"You like her, don't you?"

"I am getting use to her. I wouldn't say that I like her though." He had a dreamy-eyed look on his face, which made me feel a bit jealous.

I should probably have just let it go, but I felt threatened. I was in awe of her personality, so why shouldn't Peter be? We walked back to the cubicle, taking turns for showers. We were lying next to each other staring up the ceiling, as if the rest of our very existence was written in invisible ink just above our heads.

"Perhaps I should explain something, Pamela." Peter said in a soft voice. "But before, you have to answer a question. " I sighed and he took that for a yes. "Are you starting to believe that I am no longer in love with you, but with her?"

When he said that it, it sounded stupid, and yet it was exactly what I thought so I replied with a firm yes.

"None of us are the same people we were when we lived in the outside community. I changed and you changed, but we changed for the better. We changed to live in a new world and to face the daily challenges of this world."

He said it well so I agreed in a feeble voice with what he said, still wanting to communicate my deceptions of him. "She has an incredibly remarkable personality. One cannot help but admire her strength and intelligence and I would be lying if I told you differently. She saved both of us tonight, and has saved the lives of all of us, on many occasions now."

At this point, I sat up and looked down at him. "Exactly what I thought, you are becoming more and more attached to her." I turned away from him.

"No-you are wrong! I am more and more certain that she wants to protect us-something that I strongly doubted in the beginning." He protested. "Of course, she has her own reasons for offering protection that I don't want to know. Her ambitious, egocentric personality is less visible, but only because you are present." A broad, inviting smile formed on his face. "You are the only one who thinks that you are weak. Only a very strong person could continue to exist alongside someone like her." He sat up next to me, turned my head in his direction and looked deep into my eyes. "How could I fall in love with someone who has no compassion? How could I fall in love with someone incapable of loving? I don't love her. I love you, the person you were before and the person you are now; and I know that I will continue to love the person that you become in the future."

Chapter 20-Presentiment

I woke up early and rushed off to the dining room. The android in charge of the technical crew was waiting for me when I got there. "I have made a copy of all of our research which is principally the contributions that humans made before their terminations. " He said as he handed me the computer records that I wanted to study.

"Remember what I said about intercepting incoming space vehicles." He nodded. "I have no problems, though, with your continuing to maintain, repair, and even improve upon the technical operation of the vehicles."

"We cannot improve upon them. Something that I am certain you already know." That was true, but I just wanted to hear him say that.

"If ever you are notified of a space vehicle entering into our atmosphere, you must contact me, and, in my absence, Peter, the man who was with me last night."

"Understood." He replied, turned stiffly and strode off.

I got my breakfast and was eating when the others staggered in. My eyes settled on Peter, who looked away from me, evading me, avoiding complicity and reminding me that the dilemma of explaining our discovery was mine. How was I going to tell the others about the basement level without giving them the impression that I purposely excluded them from our adventure last evening?

When everyone was seated, ravenously devouring the assortments of dried fruits, grains and energy drinks, I slowly engaged conversation. I began by mentioning that I had suspicions about the small size of this center. "Reinhart did not reveal its secret when we first arrived. Her interest was in the land vehicles and the facility they would provide to explore other regions. Last night, Peter and I discovered a lower level." Their expressions of indifference turned into surprised looks of curiosity, as their eyes turned full upon me.

Now that I had their attention I told them how, on an impulse, we returned to the main computer terminal to study the lay out of this center one more time. Reinhart came alive, sending me an exact visual layout of the center and indicating how we could enter the lower level.

"And, so...are you going to tell us what you found?" Stuart asked in an excited high-pitched voice.

"I am going to do better than that-I am going to show you." They were on their feet. "Just one minute, though, I, prompted by Reinhart, suggested that Peter be put in charge of the technology we found. You will understand why when you see it. Of course, we have to vote on that suggestion later."

My suggestion slipped by without any reaction, as if inconsequential. I led the way to the main entrance, and pressed on the hidden indention in the wall revealing the stairway. With all their pushing and shoving, I thought that they were going to fall over each other going down the steps. As expected the androids arrived with laser guns that they dropped when they saw me. I told them that the group was with me and that we were all in our own ways human, to avoid any discussion regarding the reptilian humans, assuming that they might have been a species that these androids had not yet encountered.

"Be careful what you touch." I yelled as they dashed in different directions, entering the various space vehicles. The Commander assigned androids to follow each of us. Even though it was an incursion on my authority, I appreciated his efforts to safeguard the equipment.

I went off in my own direction looking for one of the vehicles used to transport the minerals mined on asteroids. The space transport unit was very large. It had to be to house the massive vehicles used for space travel. This lower level extended like a large oval plate in the middle of which sat the small circular building that we thought constituted the entirety of the center's facilities. It was remarkable just how effective the shield of invisibility was, masking the existence of this lower level from those on the outside. I found a small motorized cart that I climbed into to travel miles before I found what I was looking for.

Reinhart started to upload information regarding space travel during her time. Space travel did take place years before Reinhart appeared, even though most efforts for colonization were futile. The information she was passing on to me, though, was relevant to her time.

The Space program was actively underway during her lifetime. Nonetheless the distance in light years between the earth and potentially habitable Exoplanets, or planets that revolved around other stars in different constellations, meant hundreds of years of travel in light years.

Reinhart wanted to reduce the travel time before eventually finding the solution. She introduced a more sophisticated version of Alcubierre warp drive. Alcubierre warp speed was a notion of stretching space time in a wave causing the basic fabric of space ahead of a spacecraft to contract and the space behind it to expand. Reinhart made it possible for the spaceship to ride this space time wave at high speeds and high time, by traveling along a warp bubble inside a predetermined path of worm holes, or space warped tunnels with two mouths. She designed the spaceships to gain high speeds by entering into a freefall as they passed from one end of the tunnel and through the other. Her method appeared to be very efficient and rapid.

Even though time travel would be faster, the crew needed to be protected during the journey. Artificial gravity, now integrated into the spaceship, ending weightlessness in space, provided a natural and comfortable environment. The artificial gravity, however, did not completely eliminate the risk of human organ damage, caused by the rapid aging process specific to space travel.

In view of the risks, Reinhart had to decide whether it was more rational to put the original crew in suspended animation during the journey to sustain their lives, maintain them in a healthy form, and awaken them when the spacecraft landed on the designated habitable planet; or whether she should permit the original crew to live and work on board these massive space ships and eventually reproduce a new generation of humans. The last generation of humans on board would populate the designated planets.

I understood that the first option was what she preferred and thereby introduced. Preventing aging and organ damage were persuasive arguments to convince other members of her scientific team to follow her suggestion and accept suspended animation. She carefully selected the crew, and, in particular, the science officers for the space mission.

The ships were programmed to respond to even the most improbable forces that could lead the spaceship off its course or destroy it. The fact that humans were now returning to earth indicated that her programming system functioned correctly, at least with certain spacecraft.

Her affection for the androids, particularly the Group of 5, and her reluctance to share information with her human colleagues led me to believe that she preferred her android creations to human creatures. But, I quickly realized that I was wrong. It was her lack of confidence in the human race rather than her admiration of her android creations that prompted her decisions and, in this case, led to her push for the first alternative.

She was not certain that future generations would be as inspired, as the original group she selected, to build a new world on a new planet. Perhaps she imagined that they would not be intellectually capable of meeting the challenges that space flight and colonization would impose. Perhaps she even imagined that these new breed humans would not have the sophistication that she found in the select group of humans that she chose for the space mission and that they would not be able to interact with new life forms or work in harmony with each other.

That left me with another question. Did she put well-trained android crew on board the spaceship to both pilot the ships and wake up the humans traveling in suspended animation on arrival? The answer was evident. Of course, that is what happened. The androids cared for the humans by monitoring the suspended animation units. They verified that the programming was functioning properly and were able to intervene if a manual response was required.

They were certainly programmed to carry out different tasks on board and later assist during the colonization stage. And, the android opposites of several scientists accompanied them on these space missions. They were shut down during the trip and would be reactivated by their human counterpart on arrival. I felt a tightening of my throat when she passed me that last piece of information. "Does she regret sending those android opposites or is there something else bothering her?"

I finally sat down in the commander's seat and closed my eyes trying to imagine the sensation of piloting this spaceship. Instead pictures of another time started to pass through my mind, as if I were watching a film. I saw the number 21 as it flashed rapidly before my eyes, giving way to the number 22 that lingered on, as if these numbers meant something special. I saw many groups of human astronauts with different physical features and colors. I understood that it was a period of active space travel and exploration even though the spaceships and equipment I saw were not as technologically advanced as the ones in this transport unit.

I could see small colonies of earthlings struggling to survive on the planet Mars and on the bright side of the Moon. I could feel their excitement that turned to anxiety and then despair. I understood that Mars did not have a viable atmosphere and the water or liquid heavy in minerals and salt that appeared during hot seasons on Mars, was rare and undrinkable. Mars was but an unfriendly world for space pioneers and the Moon was not a paradise.

Reinhart's thoughts intruded for a brief minute, interrupting this flow of pictures, as she revealed to me that she had considered sending androids to Mars because they would not need a viable atmosphere, but abandoned this project because other violent surface changes were underway on Mars. So she turned her attention to other new frontiers.

The images returned and I traveled in my mind alongside the first group of space heroes, landing on close and distant asteroids as they unloaded mining equipment. Their efforts were rewarded and they returned to Earth with the natural resources needed to sustain what they thought was a modern society.

The scientific community was united and worked closely together to improve living conditions on Earth and explore new worlds. I felt their courage and their determination. They had ideas, sometimes grandiose, but ideas, nonetheless. They dreamt of technology and techniques that Reinhart would later accomplish. They were her predecessors. But not her mentors.

So what happened? Did countries fight among themselves for recognition and power? Probably, if what I have been told is true-or, that humans cannot live in peace. I witnessed their demise. Efforts to save themselves came too late. The Earth was impatient. Its atmosphere, its surface, its oceans, rivers, lakes, streams...were polluted beyond recognition. The Earth turned against them, expelling its anger and wiping out vast numbers of populations, destroying their structures, swallowing up habitable land, and leaving behind a few survivors, now lost in barren spaces or sheltered in vestiges of what they called modern life style.

I opened my eyes, stopping the flow of these horrifying pictures revealing the Earth's angry, devastating force. "So it was true. Humans wrote their own end, when they destroyed the natural equilibrium of the Earth?" I said in an audible voice, startling myself. The planet never completely recovered its calm because even hundreds of years later, it was still challenging humans to survive by forcing them to start over and over again. Reinhart could attest to that. And then, the Group of 5 made their catastrophic decision to end all life and destroy all civilization so that today, we have only barren land and agitated oceans? I shook my head, in regret and in an attempt to extract myself from this pessimistic impression of what remained.

I left. As I passed in front of a group of android assistants, I told them that I was returning to the first floor level because I wanted to contact my Center. They passed the message instantaneously. My group was gathered behind me when I reached the stairway and I heard their voices as they shared what they had just discovered with each other. There was energy and excitement in their voices, a good combination for success.

I told them that I wanted to contact our Center before leaving and they wanted to be present, so I put on the big wall screen so that we would have the impression of being in the same room with them. John answered. I saw Jarrod and Fleming at his side. In an angry voice I asked them to explain why they were ordering the android assistants in this center to intercept entering spacecraft and to exterminate the astronauts aboard.

"Who wants to know?" They asked at the same time.

Reinhart answered. Her voice, reminiscent of another time, visibly jolted the members of my group, except for Peter, who recognized Reinhart's voice from the night before. The two androids recognized her voice and answered.

"We were programmed to respond like that. We received that order during the revolution." Jarrod explained.

"Who gave you that programmed response?" Reinhart's voice did not mask her anger.

They looked at each other for an answer. Finally, Fleming spoke up, suggesting that it must have been Dr. Murdoc because he reprogrammed all the androids to fight. They could not say for certain, however, that he was responsible.

Reinhart looked at Randolph, the physical image of Dr. Murdoc, his biological father. Randolph backed up in his chair.

"I have nothing to do with all of this." He retorted and that brought a big smile to her face as she replied in a seductive, English accent from yester years. "Of course not, Randolph. You have nothing to do with this."

She turned back to the two androids and ordered them to erase the programming. They pretended that it could be problematic and that only Dr. Murdoc could implement that order. I found myself standing up, leaning into the table, my eyes dark and unwavering, as I said firmly and unequivocally "You know that I can override any such orders in your programming. You erase that programmed response now, or I shall order you to shut down!"

They were machines, insensitive to her anger, but aware of the power she had over their existence. Their bodies jolted, even writhed under their effort, as they carried out her order. I sat back down-my voice and body language normal, and looked calmly at my colleagues. Everyone sat frozen, a catatonic stare was all that they seemed capable of mustering. "She definitely knows how to put the fear of God in others," was the heartened thought that echoed in my mind, as I grinned in amusement.

"Pamela, Pamela, are you with me?" John was asking, breaking into my thoughts and wiping away my broad smile.

I finally answered reassuring him. "Are Jarrod and Fleming operational?"

"Yes, yes-it was a bit dramatic though." He panted between waves of convulsive laughter that released my group from Reinhart's spell.

"The satellite." I said, returning to serious business. "Did I mention to you that I need satellite images of the earth's land surface?"

"Yes. And, you-she-is right. There are still some old, very old satellites, orbiting this planet. I am working on connecting with them. It might take me some time."

"Anyone else want to speak to someone?"

Randolph asked to speak to Mathilda. Mathieu and Isabel wanted to speak to her as well. She was wearing a very short tight, low-cut white lacy dress that Gordon must have offered to her. Randolph complimented her on her dress, in a voice that registered his desire. She told us that our children were doing well, advancing rapidly with the learning tapes, and that the babies were in excellent health. I could feel Reinhart's impatience, as my body stiffened, urging me to move on with critical, scientific subjects, but I ignored her. I believed that we needed to invest in our new generation of humans like humans should invest in their offspring, with warm parental emotions. We were raised like machines and we wanted our children to grow up knowing emotions and learning how to interact with others.

Clarence asked to speak to Linda alone, so the rest of us left to start to load our gear and specimens on the aircraft.

I looked over the results of Ludovic's blood tests and decided that he could remove the decontamination suit. I took Ludovic and Jason on my plane because I believed that they should remain together.

Peter and I made a final check of the facility after which I left Peter for a moment so that Reinhart could make a final speech to the androids on the lower level. She asked them politely to clean up the living quarters and dining room. The android in charge, the one that I decided to call the Commander, said that all that would be taken care of. He bowed respectfully to Reinhart, promising to be her most trusted and devoted android. She thanked him in a sweet-toned voice that was irritating for me to hear, because it was so close to my own voice.

The aircraft lifted off and Reinhart led the group in the direction of the third center that was located southwest of the others. It took us five hours to get there. We took the time to explore the center that resembled the one we left in every detail. Reinhart mentioned that there was a lower level in this facility as well where various forms of ships and subs were housed. We ate rapidly, gathered up the diving gear, and set off to explore the ocean depths before sunset.

Jason and Ludovic climbed into my land rover and we took off with the others following close behind. We were only fifteen minutes from the beach, a luscious beach of fine, white sand. "Be careful," I warned. "There could be animals living under the sand."

I let Diana take the lead. This was her field of expertise and I could see just how fascinated she was with the environment. She ran quickly in the direction of the ocean, with its low waves, rolling softly and rhythmically onto the sand. She was very close to the water's edge when she screamed for help. We had all been trailing behind, observing the skyline, the waves and cautiously advancing across the sand. We sped off in her direction, her cries of help becoming more and more intense.

Only her upper body was visible when we arrived. I quickly threw her the rope that was among other survival equipment in my backpack. Randolph secured the rope under her arms. "I am going to be eaten alive if you don't do something quickly." She screamed over and over again.

We pulled her out of the hole rapidly. Her shredded trousers and lacerated skin called for emergency measures. I rushed back to my vehicle and grabbed the first aid kit. I had included laser correctors that were designed to seal wounds without leaving any scarring. I needed to clean the wounds first and add an antibiotic rinse before sealing them. The pain disappeared immediately and she got back her composure.

"I didn't see my aggressor." She explained. "I stumbled over, maybe into, something--a hole. In any event, it was invisible because I would have noticed it otherwise. When I stepped down I felt something grab me-an animal, certainly- and pull me under. I had nothing to grab onto and the surrounding sand did not give me any solid support to pull myself out."

"Ok, let's dig." I ordered.

"We don't know what it is. We could be outnumbered." Stuart cautioned me, as he reminded me of how dangerous it could be.

"We have lasers, so half of us will stand with the lasers focused. We have to find new life forms and new food sources so we cannot let this opportunity go."

They hesitated, expressing their reluctance to dig up a potentially dangerous creature that they might not even be able to outrun. So I offered to stand guard while they went back to get the vehicles and bring them closer to the spot. That way our escape would be more secure and faster.

I was glad that Peter decided to stay with me. We stood in silence focusing on the indentation in the sand. When we finally dug deep enough to confront the aggressor, we were disappointed with our discovery. It was an old, very old, trap that was used to catch shellfish like lobsters and crabs. Diana was lucky that the trap was malfunctioning and that its sharp edges that looked like teeth, were no longer in the right position to catch anything. She could have lost her legs.

Like a team of archeologist, we examined our find estimating its age and its efficacy. I suggested that we take it with us because we might be able to repair and use it to catch ocean specimens. Although bulky, the metal was not rusted, something curious in and of itself, and so we decided to save it and study it later on.

We had enough sunlight left to take a swim and would have if the water had not been so excessively cold. Thermal dive suits were necessary for us humans, so we could not join our reptilian colleagues who were able to wade out far enough for a short dive. They returned with a wide variety of plant life to be tested for nutritive value once we returned to our center.

Even though we planned to stay a few days more in this center studying the technology and the ocean environment, all of us, except Ludovic and Jason who were tired from the long day, wanted to explore the lower level. There were no recreational boats, rather large vessels designed to transport natural resources and small subs used to explore the ocean's depths. During Reinhart's lifetime, natural resources were found principally in the deep seabed. Deep seabed mining was envisaged hundreds of years before it became a reality. As the earth's land surface diminished, natural resources became scare. Deep seabed mining, like mining on asteroids, slowly moved from science fiction to science reality.

Reinhart arrived after hundreds of years of intensive research, interrupted by wars and natural disasters. The mining projects both on earth and in space were still in their elementary phase, something that bothered her then and now. The rest is history; she accomplished what previous generations struggled to achieve. Her dedication and commitment to improving and saving humanity led her to greatness.

"Do you know how to command these vessels, Pamela?" Randolph's question was rhetorical.

I started to walk toward him, treading heavily, like I was carrying the weight of the world on my shoulders, as I languished in my thoughts. He commented teasingly about my demeanor, suppressing his laughter. When he grabbed me and shook me playfully, I felt drawn to him in ways that I wanted to ignore.

"Where is Peter?"

"I don't know. We split up. I think that he went to inspect those marine transporters." I replied annoyed that he sensed my interest in him. "And, to answer your question Reinhart knows how to operate all these machines." I added. He grinned, as he backed slowly away from me, letting his hands fall casually over the silhouette of my body, and rushed off in another direction, yelling over his shoulder that he was going to explore the big ships with the rest of the group.

My sighs of regret or relief were interrupted by a gush of energy, more emotion than rational, from Reinhart, startling me. "Is she scolding me for letting Randolph rush off?" I could still see him from the corner of my eye and wondered if I should follow him.

But…it was too late, Reinhart's mood had changed and she was interesting me with the technical aspects of the small sub, uploading lots of data for me. Their systems were all operational, evidently they were being maintained regularly. "So where are the android attendants?" I wondered.

I didn't join the others on the big vessels, but went off in search of the androids. "Why are they hiding and why doesn't she tell me where they are?"

I found a small, motorized cart, identical to the one I used in the Air and Space vehicle center, and jumped into it, making a sweeping tour of the facility. I didn't see one single android. I got out and sat down on one of the steps of the stairway leading to the upper level, waiting for the others to appear, when I heard one of the side doors open and saw a large group of androids, lined up one behind the other, marching in perfect step in my direction. The leader approached me. "Dr. Reinhart, I am the Captain at this center." He was wearing a large lapel pin, the size of a name tag or badge that I imagined was indicative of his status or importance in this Center.

I decided that it was not worth explaining to this machine that I was Pamela and that Dr. Reinhart's knowledge was downloaded into me. So, I simply nodded. He went on to tell me that he received orders from Dr. Flanders to move one of the large vessels out onto the beach so that we could use it. "I was expecting you to arrive tomorrow, not today."

"Well, that explains why there were no androids here to meet us." Reinhart said. I gave way to Reinhart, letting her control my vocal chords, like I would do on many occasions in the future, when her vigorous voice and special accent, combined with her control over the androids was imperative. Our symbiotic relationship, based on mutual respect, gave me the opportunity to learn, while giving her the opportunity to exist.

"Thank you for moving the vessel." Reinhart continued. "I would like you and several other members of your group to accompany us tomorrow." She said and then left me on my own.

He nodded, glanced at his group and then turned back to me. "The reptilian humans will be part of the navigation team?"

"Yes." I replied firmly. "By the way, are there any thermal diving suits here at this center?"

"Plenty. Just follow me."

As before, Reinhart did not give me any information about this center's construction until I started to ask questions. Now that the Captain invited me to visit the equipment room, she came alive, passing me visuals of this part of the center. I no longer needed the android, I knew where to go and what to look for, but stayed patiently behind the android Captain letting him point out the various storage areas.

There was a wide range of diving gear and suits, considerably more than we had at the big center, including thermal suits for very cold water. There were even atmospheric pressure suits that were lightweight and would provide 12 or more hours of oxygen flow, while maintaining atmospheric pressure for deep dives of 2000 feet or more. They had elaborate pressure joints to facilitate articulation and an internal thrust system that would permit you to navigate in deep waters. These were used for deep seabed explorations and marine research during Reinhart's time.

"I would like to see the marine biology laboratory?" He informed both Reinhart and me of latest developments in marine life.

He led me to the enormous laboratory that was stocked with specimens similar to those I had already seen in the inner circle, along with less horrifying specimens of sea life. I noticed that they were testing the water and studying new specimens regularly. Their research was visibly meticulous.

"Interesting," Reinhart commented. "It would appear that the earth and life on earth has evolved for a second time, judging from the progression of the marine life species."

"It is possible." He retorted and then corrected himself. "Actually, the evolutionary phase was not that productive and these existing marine species are hard to find. They have disappeared anyway from our immediate waters. You must recognize some of the species that existed during your time."

I did not reply. He wanted to deceive me, but couldn't. Amazing how they all tried so hard to by-pass their programming. Our eyes met; mine were certainly sparkling, while his remained lifeless. He felt the power of Reinhart and quickly lowered his eyes in submission, until I gave him permission to leave.

I ran into the others when I left the laboratory and offered to take them on a quick tour. I showed them the diving gear, explaining the utility and then led them into the lab. Diana yelled in excitement over the prospects of research in her field while the others were overtaken with simple curiosity.

There was so much to be done, but so little time. I suggested that we get some sleep so that we could start early in the morning.

I lingered behind, my mind occupied by Reinhart's thoughts and her doubts. "Would our motivation be enough for us to fill in the gaps, understand the context of our new world and make progress?" I said in a low voice, repeating her question as I reached the top of the stairway and entered the hallway.

No one was around. "They have all gone off to bed. Everything is fine." My words fell on empty corridors. I began to feel ill at ease, as I struggled mentally to reassure myself that they were still here with me. But, instead, chills ran up and down my spine and my heart started beating rapidly. The lights flickered on and off, distorting my vision, making it difficult for me to find my way. My body began to tremble as the temperature dropped and a freezing cold invaded my space, giving me the sensation that something menacing was lingering close to me. Sinister odors like rotting wood and decaying leaves and putrid smells of musty dungeons and decomposing bodies filled the air, forming heavy, suffocating clouds that left me gasping for breath. And, with each deep breath, a dry, thick dust entered my mouth and I could taste something rancid.

Weakened, I leaned up against the wall and slowly let my body drop to the cold floor. Time passed and with it the odors dissipated, giving me the opportunity to recover. "Is it simply olfactory illusions that overcame me or is it something else?" I wondered. "Is this an evil place, replete with horrors and wickedness? Or is someone, haunting these corridors, trying to warn me of the danger that awaits us?" I felt petrified by those thoughts.

Chapter 21- Dr. Murdoc's Legacy

We had two days, maybe three if we returned directly to our center, to explore the continental shelf. Jason and Ludovic did not want to come with us. I gave the sizes of my crew to the androids, asking them to retrieve the thermal diving suits that corresponded and to verify the oxygen tanks before loading them onto the trucks. I wanted three of the atmospheric pressure suits to be available, as well. My land vehicle was laden with diving gear when I pulled out of the transport unit.

The Android Captain did not forget anything. There were smaller motorized boats that would be used later to bring us to the dive site and were now being used to transport the equipment and personnel out to the large cargo ship that was anchored in deeper water. I noticed that the Captain had left the truck and trailer that he used to move the vessel on the beach.

"You saw the specimens that we have gathered. Do you want to go to the same dive site that we use?" He asked in an official tone, which for the first time since we started our exploratory mission, made a favorable impression on me. These androids had adapted their voice tones, as had all the others, for human reception... for us or for Reinhart? "Interesting," I said to myself.

"Perhaps you will be lucky and find some marine life. As I told you last evening, our recent dives have not given us that kind of satisfaction. Apart from plants, the ocean is empty."

"I am ok for that dive site today, but I want to go further out tomorrow." He said nothing so I continued. "I will accompany you to the controls."

"No problem. Your company will be useful." He was rolling his eyes in their sockets as if he were annoyed with me or even bored.

"By the way, you should tell the reptilian humans," I gave him an icy look, "that the water will be far too cold for them. You might want to leave them behind to look for food in the low waters."

Under Reinhart's impulsion, I let out a loud, crackling, exasperating laugh which this time had the effect of stopping everyone, human and machine, in their tracks. Heads turned in my direction. When I recovered from her laughter, I called Adam, Daniel, Leonard and Joseph over. "There is a solar heating chamber on this vessel. The Captain will show you where it is. I want all of you to spend the next hour or so in that chamber. Your bodies need to stock up heat, if you are going to dive." They nodded.

"And the other one?" the Captain pointed to Clarence.

"He shall be staying on board, observing." I flicked my hair out of my face, like Reinhart, and added. "You have an interest in appreciating all members of my team."

"Understood." He asked the group to follow him to the solar heating chamber. I heard him invite Clarence to accompany them, but Clarence declined the offer.

"Wow! He is not like the other androids." Stuart commented. "Does he have human emotions?"

"He shouldn't." I replied, expecting feedback from Reinhart, but none was forthcoming. "These androids have been in charge for so many hundreds and hundreds of years. Perhaps he had a problem with a reptilian human in the past."

"I don't like him, so I shall be careful." Clarence replied. "He seems more dangerous than Tirence ever was and we had him restrained." Tirence nodded vigorously.

"Don't worry. He is devoted to Reinhart and won't do anything that would make her angry." I tried to reassure both them and myself because I was not that certain that this Captain would be that obedient. And after that surrealistic experience of the night before, I was worried that danger was looming. "I am changing the procedure a bit. At least one of us will remain in the small boat with the android assistant to make certain that the diving team is not left behind and that nothing goes wrong." I said to the Group.

I looked at Clarence, who was now in the process of following the other reptilian humans. "You must keep an eye on the Captain. He is acting like his programming is malfunctioning."

"Ok. I'll do my best." He called out as he left the room to watch over the other reptilian humans.

"I think that I am going to contact the main center to be certain that the Group of 5 has not done anything else diabolical." I said loud enough for everyone to hear.

I went straight to the bridge of the ship to examine the navigation plan. There was a wall length computer screen and the visual was open. I could see John working closely with Jarrod and Fleming. "Why was the Captain observing them?" I opened up the vocal and told John where we were and informed him of our objectives for the next few days. He appeared calm. I then asked Jarrod and Fleming to explain to me why the Captain of this vessel had them on line. They could not feign ignorance because, unlike the Group of 5, they were machines. I believed them when they told me that they didn't have any idea that they were being observed. "Where is the Group of 5?" I asked nervously.

"I don't know. Why?" John replied.

"Call them! Order them to appear!" I screamed. "Do something quick!" I sensed that something horrible was about to happen. "Yes, my experience last evening was definitely a warning but ...am I acting rapidly enough?" passed instantly through my mind.

I heard the Captain enter the bridge, letting each step fall heavily upon the floor. "Is something wrong?" He asked, pushing me away from the computer screen, as he turned it off.

"Who programmed you?" I asked spontaneously.

"You did, Dr. Reinhart."

"I am not talking about originally. I know that I programmed you. I want to know who else played around with your circuitry."

His android lips curled up in an evil grin and I instinctively backed up. "We have been alone here for a long, long time. I have always been in command. Our center never interested the main center, or the smaller one with that stiff-necked Commander. From time to time Jarrod and Fleming asked us to report on what was happening and I complied."

"You did not answer my question!" I said, articulating

every word. His eyes, boldly resistant and aggressive, met mine and I detected--- defiance.

"Dr. Murdoc reprogrammed me to lead missions and to kill the humans living on coastal boats or moving in the direction of the high seas for sanctuary." He approached me and now blank, lifeless android eyes dissimulated his intentions. Intuition warned me to follow his every move. He lunged at me, as his upper body bent forward and his arms reached out to grab me and hold me in place. I moved quickly out of his way. He stumbled, but was up on his feet rapidly. He rushed at me again moving in a straight line, which was advantageous for me. I sprinted past him, zigzagging as I moved in the direction of the door. He was faster than I was. He caught me and pulled me back into the room, but not before I screamed for help at the top of my lungs.

His arms curled around my upper body in a lethal grip, knocking the wind out of me. He had been trained in physical combat and he was using his maximum force. I knew that he could crush me if I continued to resist, so I relaxed, accepting my defeat.

With his mouth close to my ear, he said in a reverberating, metallic voice. "You are not my enemy, Dr. Reinhart, but I have no choice. I must kill her, Pamela. She is my enemy, your enemy and the enemy of all of your creations!" I shook my head violently to show my disagreement and to wipe out the resonating sound of his voice.

He held me tightly as he dragged me over to the intercom system. He spoke authoritatively, convinced of his importance and supremacy at this moment, as he ordered the others to Attack, Kill and Dispose of all the humans on this ship. Attack, Kill and Dispose of the horrifying reptilian humans. Turn up the heat in the solar chamber."

"How could an android, devoid of emotions, go completely mad? If what he was doing was provoked by insanity, and not just a perverted program?" Resounded in my head just before Reinhart's warmth suffused me and she took over. "

"You are wrong." He released his grip slightly when he heard her voice, so distinctive with that original human accent. "Dr. Murdoc was cruel to have given you this ruthless, degrading, violent programming." She said in a soft, calm voice.

His grip relaxed even more and I was able to breathe easier, but for how long..."Where were the others?" was repeating over and over again in my mind. "Maybe they are already dead! He did give the androids that order to kill the humans! Then everything is over!" I quivered at the idea for only a split second because Reinhart took over again.

"I shall help you." Her firm voice was tainted by an undercurrent of maternal affection, which seemed so inappropriate to me. "Remember, we worked together. I recognized your talents and let you take command of this unit."

"Yes-but that was in the past. Today you are more human than you ever were. We could identify with you in the past, not just because you were our creator, but because you were more one of us than one of those humans." I could hear a wining sound, like an electrical breakdown in his system, as he searched for logical arguments to counter hers.

"And you too were different which is why we worked so well together. My creations were above killing, above violence, above committing atrocities. Dr. Murdoc changed you. Even if I admired his genius, what he did to you was cruel. Let me give you back your dignity!" She said in a thundering tone that made him pivot and reel in different directions. He released me before he fell to the floor. Her voice and her commands, already registered in his system, were able to momentarily override Murdoc's reprogramming. But, for how long could she control him? I didn't want to think about that.

Instead I crawled out of his reach and pulled my aching body up to the control board. With my remaining force, I flipped on the loudspeaker. Reinhart understood the weaknesses in their circuits, so in the same thundering voice that she used only minutes ago, she ordered the androids to release the humans and let the reptilian humans out of the solar cabin.

I had no idea whether the other androids were on the ground, but I didn't care. My body felt so weak and my breathing was far from normal. I thought that I might faint but instead collapsed on an empty chair next to the control board

The Captain recovered and stood officiously in front of me. I looked at him through tears streaming down my face. "Was I crying? From relief? Or was she prompting my tears? Does she have feelings?" Preoccupied my thoughts and helped me to feel calmer, even in face of this irrational machine. 'They were her children, all of them, regardless of their role. Yes, she coveted her creations. But, did she love them?'

My thoughts dissipated as Reinhart regained control of me and the situation. "You are the only one on this ship reprogrammed by Murdoc." He nodded. "I cannot reprogram you on this ship. You know that." He nodded. "I have to bring you back to the main center." He nodded for a third time. "Who trained the others to fight?"

"I did." He said in a modified, low, human style voice. "I had to because I needed an army to fight the non-intellectuals who were waging the rebellion against you and all the intellectuals."

"They take their orders from you?"

"Yes, but they were already programmed by Dr. Murdoc to fight. I just gave them the combat training."

"So they see humans as their enemies, I imagine?" He nodded. "Ok, now you must trust me. We need you to operate this center because you were the best qualified at the time I appointed you. So, naturally, I shall do everything in my power to erase both the reprogramming of Murdoc and the side effects that the reprogramming has had on your decision-making ability which, by the way, is very irrational, if not, paranoid." His body swirled involuntarily in her direction and his eyes turned glassy white. In a split second she ordered him to shut down. He shook his head violently, resisting in vain the order from his Creator before succumbing to the power that she had over him.

When the others rushed in, I was seated in the chair with the Captain on the floor, an inanimate object.

"They are all trained in physical combat." I heard Diana say.

"I shall change that...later!" I breathed deeply. "Are the Reptilian humans alive?" I asked anxiously, worried about how long they had been exposed to solar heat.

"Yes, we are alive. We would have died if you hadn't ended this and ordered those androids to open up the doors to the solar chamber. We were not in there long enough to suffer more than superficial burns." Adam, appeared out of nowhere, his voice was shaky with emotion. I saw from the corner of my eye that the group of Reptilian humans looked like they had been in the sun far too long.

"We all would have died." Stuart said. "We were lucky that the androids we fought against in our main center had no hand to hand combat experience." He exhaled dramatically, half-choking over his own breath. "Maybe our revolution was not as impressive as we thought."

That brought a round of laughter and a release of tension. I had others things on my mind. My eyes scanned the control panel and I quickly illuminated it. The Group of 5 was waiting patiently.

"How can we be of help to you, Pamela?" Crawford asked.

"You can start by explaining to me why you were not watching over the androids in this center."

"Their research was not interesting to us. And, their Captain- the one that Dr. Reinhart appointed-was not easy to communicate with on any level." The former Governor said.

"You should have warned us about them. They tried to kill us! Or maybe that is what you wanted?" Reinhart spoke.

"Dr. Reinhart, we had no idea that the Captain was that dangerous. And, we did not know that the other androids had irrational behavior." Crawford apologized.

"The other androids were carrying out orders from him, and, as you must be aware, they were programmed by Murdoc."

The Group of 5 squirmed around, dissimulating their discussion. I cleared my throat to get their attention. Gordon spoke up. "None of the androids that were reprogrammed by Murdoc were to have survived. You must remember, Dr. Reinhart," she was pleading, "that all the centers were equipped with androids, at different levels of competency. None of the androids at this Center were Murdoc's subjects. We did not know that the Captain was surrounded with an army of killer robots."

"Killer Robots! Is that what you called Murdoc's army of androids?" Reinhart retorted, her voice grating at high decibels.

"Ordinary androids all have the same physical appearance, only a few of us look like our prestigious ancestors. So, calling them killer robots, was our way of drawing a distinction between them and androids in general and denying any association, on any level, with them." Miller replied.

"Of course, I understand." Yes, everything was becoming clearer. The other centers were never destined to survive. The Captain and his crew were the fighting force for the remaining intellectuals, led by Murdoc. They found refuge in this small center when the doomsday explosion took place. Perhaps the Captain destroyed the inanimate androids already in place or discarded them on the outside. Evidently, the Group of 5 was not involved-at least not in the policy of this center.

Reinhart addressed Jarrod and Fleming now. "How did the two of you survive?"

"We followed Murdoc who led us to the Air and Space center. He survived, as did a dozen other members of the intellectual community. They lived alongside of us for a brief moment. Dr. Murdoc and the others may have been contaminated by something before or during the revolution. Dr. Murdoc, as you know, never respected protocol and spent long periods of time living in the polluted air on the outside of our city's protection. The others, like Dr. Murdoc, fell ill a few days before the explosion and their lives terminated very rapidly. After their disappearance, we continued our research as if nothing had happened." Jarrod spoke for the two of them.

"Were you programmed to fight?"

"No...actually, Dr. Murdoc took pity on us in the beginning. He was more interested in the Group of 5." Fleming's eyes met theirs. After a long silence, he concluded. "In any event by the time he came back looking for us, it was too late. As Jarrod just said, he was very ill. The revolution was lost and there were only days left before his death and that doomsday explosion. And, we already explained to you the effect of that explosion on the Air and Space center.

"So, you followed the example of the main center and shut down until the clean-up crew reactivated you." I finished for him and he nodded.

"And, the androids in the Air and Space center?"

"They were certainly loyal to Dr. Murdoc because he was the

human in charge for a brief moment." Flanders commented. "Dr. Murdoc never programmed any of the androids that were assigned to and stored in, if you like, the Air and Space Center. We were informed that some humans survived and that Dr. Murdoc was among the survivors, but we imagined that the satellite centers were still located far away from us." He made a grating sound as if he were clearing his throat.

"We had no direct contact with him or the others." Jarrod commented. "We got back in touch with the Group of 5 when the clean-up crew reactivated us and informed us that our satellite center and the Marine center survived the explosion and that we were located next to the main center."

"I, excuse me, we, assumed wrongly that the androids at the Marine center were in no way killer robots, or android military." Crawford sighed. "Actually, I did not know that the Captain was programmed by Dr. Murdoc. The few times we met with the Captain I did not detect any disconcerting abnormality in his behavior, just his annoying infatuation with himself as the Captain of the marine facility. If he had been human, I would have defined him as someone having a superiority complex."

"Do you want us to send Drager, the Chief Android Engineer, to help reprogram the androids in the marine center?" The former Governor asked.

"Can you get him here fast enough?"

"We can have a pilot from the air center pick him up and bring him directly to you."

"Move fast then on this project. I shall probably prolong our stay a bit longer. We have lost almost an entire day because of this very unpleasant episode."

I was ready to say goodbye when I had another thought. "Just as an aside. Would it be possible that Dr. Murdoc had something to do with the two small centers being pulled into our time warp?" Reinhart queried.

"He was a true genius, certainly not as impressive as, you, Dr. Reinhart, but a very close second." Crawford replied. "I assume that I am addressing Dr. Reinhart, never knowing which one of you is addressing me is very annoying." I chuckled. "Anyway, Dr.

Reinhart, he was very much in love with you. He may have been looking for you. He did not know that you were already dead when he sought refuge in the satellite center." He dropped his head in respect.

"Excellent deduction!" Reinhart applauded. "I would agree that he was brilliant, but you exaggerated for a second time. Don't compare his intellectual capacity with mine!" She said haughtily. "Talk to you tomorrow."

Chapter 22- Wielding Power

There was no reason for us to abandon our adventure by rushing back to the Marine center. It was more beneficial for us to erase this unfortunate episode from our minds, even if only momentarily, and return to our original program.

We all walked out on the deck where the other androids were lined up waiting for us. Reinhart didn't take the time to study them or their behavior she just ordered them to shut down.

"I am sorry. She had no choice." I said, feeling obliged to defend her actions. "I don't know to what extent they have been tampered with, so they could still be very dangerous." No one said anything, just stared at the pile of androids on the deck. I took another tour of the ship just in case a straggler was still onboard and then returned to uncover the small motorized boats, motioning to the others to follow me.

Our enthusiasm had returned and we gathered up our gear. Before leaving the main ship, Reinhart examined the equipment and tested the oxygen tanks to make certain that nothing had been sabotaged. When she was satisfied, we loaded the gear on board the small boats. In a few minutes, four small boats with crew were descending to ocean level.

Clarence stayed on board the transporter to help reel us in on our return. His body visibly resisted the burning solar heat better than the others, but then he was not exposed to it as long and, even if he had been, his species liked basking in very hot sun. I gave him a laser gun to use just in case something else unexpected happened. Joseph, Tirence and I were in the first boat; Adam, Leonard and Daniel in the second; Mathieu, Isabel, Randolph and James in the third; and Peter, Stuart and Diana in the fourth.

We moved rapidly into deeper waters where we anchored the boats, close together. The reptilian humans, overheated from the solar chamber and needing to cool down, jumped in before the rest of us. Tirence and Isabel volunteered to stay with the motorboats and help us get back on board.

The thermal suits kept us humans comfortable in this cold, but very clear, water. The reptilian humans dove deeper than us, using their external gills for a continual flow of oxygen. When we discussed it later, everyone agreed that diving in a natural environment was much more exhilarating than diving in the tanks. The diving time for Adam, Leonard and Daniel was not more than one hour. Joseph was able to stay a bit longer. They managed to skim the seabed bringing with them various empty shells and plant life. None of us came in contact with live or dead marine animals. For that matter, we didn't see any animal remains of any kind, except for the shells that our reptilian human colleagues found.

We took water samples from various levels for testing. Diving was therapeutic and we were all more relaxed and positive than we were when we boarded our motorboats.

During the return to the ship we spotted, what looked to be, dolphins, in the far distance. Unfortunately the sun was starting to set. We still had to get the small boats back on board and bring the transporter back to the shoreline. We had two hours of work ahead of us. Following the dolphins, if that is what they were, would have to wait until tomorrow.

I distributed the laser guns to everyone before we entered the center. The twenty remaining androids were lined up to greet us when we arrived. When the heavy garage door closed behind us and they didn't see the Captain or the other androids, confusion set in. At first they simply refused to assist us, but then they actually started to form a barrier in front, lining up one behind the other, to prevent us from accessing the stairway. I was worried that someone else in their line was capable of giving orders and quickly retreated, when I felt Reinhart's energy moving inside of me, so that she could take full control.

As always she took her time, studying them and anticipating their reactions. She moved steadily, holding her head and body very erect, passing by one after another of the androids until she reached the limits of their column. At this point, the leader, hidden in the middle of the column, moved out of the line, rushed to the front and ordered the androids, closest to our human group, to prepare for battle.

Reinhart was controlling my movements, like earlier, and raised my hand high, signaling our group to hold off-to wait before firing. She moved rapidly back to the front of the android line to confront the leader, who had taken his place at the head of the line. When their eyes, cold and determined, met, the leader backed off, pushing the other androids lined up behind him a few feet farther away from Reinhart and out of range of our group.

Reinhart slowly continued her advance, until the leader and the rest of the androids backed up too far away from our group to harm us.

"Were you all programmed by Dr. Murdoc?" She asked in a calm, yet severe tone.

"Who is asking?" The leader responded in a loud, broken voice.

"You recognize my voice. Must I remind you that it is your creator who is asking that question?

"Dr. Reinhart?" The question echoed through the line.

"Now, is there anyone in your unit that was not programmed by Dr. Murdoc?" She repeated the question, her voice registering both her authority and her abhorrence of the situation.

"No-we were all programmed by him." The leader replied.

"In that case, you will all... "Shut Down!" Her voice expelled energy, an energy that could be felt by us and certainly by them, as it reverberated off the walls and the high ceiling. The androids fell one after the other on top of each other as their systems came to a halt.

"Well, now we can eat in peace!" She said in a loud, clear voice.

Reinhart moved aside and I was back, joining in the raucous laughter, not because what just happened was funny, but because it was an effective way to release nervous tension. "Oh No! " I screamed. "We left Jason and Ludovic with those dangerous creations! I forgot all about them!" I rushed towards the stairwell, taking two steps at a time as I charged up to the first level. I burst through the door and dashed to the dining room. Jason and Ludovic were sitting on the lounge chairs chatting about life.

"Are you ok, Pamela?" Jason asked casually.

My heart was beating so rapidly and I was so out of breath that I couldn't answer. Joseph stepped in and gave such a calm, detailed account of the day, like he was making a verbal report of a very normal, or ordinary, day to a superior. I was taken back by his detached version of what was a horrifying experience for me, the others, and should have been for him.

I then told them, in a more dramatic way, what happened to us on board the ship. Jason sat in a state of oblivion while Ludovic burst into tears.

"That is why one of them came to see us a little while ago." Ludovic said between sobs. "He asked Jason his age and made a strange gurgling sound when Jason gave him his best calculation. Then he asked me if I had been poisoned or caught in an explosion. I told him that I was born like this. He told us that our earth days were very limited. We didn't realize that he was threatening us. We thought that he was just worried about us." Jason, still detached from the world, sat in his trance until Ludovic tapped him hard on the back, knocking him back into reality.

"I guess that we were lucky!" Jason exclaimed.

"Probably, but, I would rather drop this conversation." I suggested.

With ravenous appetites from diving, we were virtually stuffing ourselves with food when Drager arrived. Drager's pilot wanted to know if he should stay overnight with us at this center or return to his home base. We unanimously agreed in favor of his spending the night. I briefed Drager on the events of the day and the location of the various androids at the center.

He reminded me that he assisted Dr. Murdoc in reprogramming the androids. Apparently, Murdoc expected the androids to win and had asked Drager to keep a copy of Murdoc's program in his memory banks, so that he, or someone else, could reverse the programming later on. That was excellent news.

I took Drager aside, and with Reinhart's help, began accessing the memory banks and marveling at the simplicity and effectiveness of Murdoc's scheme. Three words in a series-ATTACK, KILL AND DISPOSE-acted like a virus, overriding all other programming in the android systems, turning them into killer robots, as Gordon referred to them. They automatically moved into full android force. The Captain had confirmed to me earlier that he gave these androids training in hand to hand combat. The Captain's training made them deadly...practically invincible, which is why we were fortunate to have survived their offensive on board the ship.

I realized that both Murdoc's and Reinhart's voices were in their systems. Murdoc's voice activated the virus forcing the androids to override Reinhart's original programming, something that I sensed annoyed Reinhart. But as facts were facts, the reverse should be possible. Reinhart should be able to give the command, releasing the anti-virus and regain control.

"Oh, what a clever, vicious man that Dr. Murdoc was." Drager looked at me and bowed his head to the Reinhart inside of me. He didn't want Reinhart to touch his systems.

"We have to destroy the virus which is still active." Reinhart was now speaking.

"Are you sure? You shut them down." He declared.

"Of course I shut them down, but I want to reactive them." Reinhart replied irritably. "Those words will still have an effect so we have to wipe them out. How did the Captain discover that?" Her brows creased as she looked at Drager.

"I have nothing to do with that." He studied her for a long moment. "I have the anti-virus in my memory bank." He announced matter-of-factly. "But, you will have to retrieve it." He went on. "He locked it up. It is now up to you to try to retrieve it. He told me that you would know what to do."

"So why didn't you tell me all this from the beginning?"

"I am only now getting readings from my memory banks." He defended himself.

"Well, as I have the key, I shall have to concentrate on that for a few minutes." I felt Reinhart's energy flowing in many directions as she sought to find the key to unlock the anti-virus.

"Do you have a copy of the last time I saw Murdoc, by any chance?"

"I was privy to your conversation even though I was not an active player. So, yes I recorded it but only because Dr. Murdoc asked me to keep the recording forever."

Reinhart asked him to play it back. They both listened to it. Reinhart knew that Murdoc was always so meticulous with his choice of words, whether for sentimental reasons or otherwise. I sensed that she was not certain that there was an underlying meaning in Murdoc's message because she asked Drager if he noted anything unusual in what Murdoc had said. He had no advice to give her.

She listened over and over again to their short, private conversation, looking for a single word that might stand out as being inappropriate, or that communicated his profound feelings towards her. I believe that she imagined that the key was buried in a word, or a romantic phrase, representative of the emotional depth of their relationship. But she found none. Instead, she found a phrase that was inconsistent with his personality and their relationship. So she repeated it several times, "I am here to save you from yourself." Yes, I could feel my blood rushing with excitement. He respected her too much to insinuate that she would need protection from herself or even anyone else.

So when she repeated those words in her original voice, with its special accent, she unlocked the anti-virus. "It worked, you can access the anti-virus." He couldn't show emotions, because he had none, but I wanted to believe that he was happy for her. She then meticulously installed the anti-virus on the main computer so that we could commence deprogramming.

"I know Murdoc's method of reasoning," she repeated over and over again in the confines of our mind. This nostalgic revelation brought a big smile to my face. "We have to download the anti-virus into each of them at the very instance in which they start to reactivate, otherwise it won't be effective." Reinhart spoke and Drager listened. "We shall take care of the androids downstairs now and send them out, early in the morning, to collect the other androids. I do not want the Captain to be reactivated. I shall bring him back with me to the main center."

"There is something else wrong with him?" Drager asked.

"Yes." She replied.

Drager was a good team player. I understood now why the Group of 5 liked him so much. We were efficient and rapid. We tested the androids afterwards, repeating several times the command: ATTACK, KILL, DISPOSE; and then ATTACK, KILL AND DISPOSE. The androids did not respond. Their systems registered low to normal physical strength levels, which is exactly the levels that the android support staff should have been capable of registering. None of the androids, apart from the Group of 5, should have been able to increase their strength without receiving a command.

I left them with Drager and went off to get some sleep. In route, I ran into Randolph who was lingering around in the corridors, certainly waiting for me. "I want to talk to you, Pamela. If you can just give me a few minutes now, that will be enough."

He went on to tell me that he hated himself because he was a descendent of Murdoc. "I need to talk to Reinhart. Please let me talk to her, Pamela." He pleaded.

"You mustn't worry so much. This is a different time. You are not the same person that he was."

"How do you know? Only she knows?"

"He was a very nice man, Randolph." Reinhart surfaced and he recognized her voice and smiled. "He spent a lot of time on the outside, helping the non-intellectuals, and he always pleaded their cause."

"So..."

"Let me tell you." She interrupted him asking him to just listen. "He was brilliant. We worked closely together. After the brutal murder of my husband, I became cold and indifferent. He helped me to get over my pain. We did love each other. Perhaps he was more passionate in his love, than I was, but, in any case, I loved him to the extent that I can love someone. I am more responsive to intellectual as opposed to physical seduction, so we came together in a mystical or esoteric sense. I felt comfortable with Murdoc because he understood me and my sense of intimacy and, moreover, he appreciated my need for discretion."

I could feel little waves of hesitation as her reluctance to say more was frustrated by her desire to console Randolph. "I had not been so kind with the non-intellectuals. My desire to bring about change was my downfall, principally because it came too late for me to save them or the rest of us intellectuals. He warned me of the imminent need for change and promised his help and fidelity if I would act with more concern and compassion toward the non-intellectuals." She stood facing Randolph. I felt her mind trying to pierce his, to read his inner thoughts. I could feel her disappointment when she realized that he would not let her enter.

"He did program the androids to kill, even though I believe that he knew that his action to put down the rebellion by the non-intellectuals was futile and that the end of human life was imminent." She paused. "He did not want to live under the orders of non-intellectuals and so in a desperate effort to resolve, what he knew was unresolvable, he did what he did."

She sighed. "What he wanted and what he expected doesn't matter because he saved us humans today. His program was a virus activated by a series of words. He added to this virus, a voice sensitivity element, attune to my voice or his. He also left me the key to the anti-virus that he put in Drager's memory bank. As a result, Drager and I were able to inject the anti-virus and reactivate the androids in this building."

She turned away from Randolph and said, "Today I miss him... and I fear that I might miss him tomorrow and long into the future. Even if you were identical to him today in every aspect, you would have no reason to be ashamed. But, as you are not in every way identical, and I sense that you might even be greater than him, you have reason to be proud of yourself and confident enough to pay homage to him."

"Thank you, Dr. Reinhart." He was blinking away tears when he reached out to touch her, but she was gone, her vibrant warmth had disappeared deep inside of me, and I stood looking up at him.

"And, thank you, Pamela, for giving me a special moment with her."

He walked alongside of me until I got to my room. "She was someone extraordinary and I guess, that Murdoc was as well." His face radiated by a broad smile and his eyes shining bright and steady made it easy for me to leave him and go off in my own direction, knowing that he was happy with himself.

I was glad that Peter was still awake because I wanted to tell him everything. "Can she tell me about my ancestor?"

"Probably, but not tonight! We need to be fit for tomorrow." I crawled up close to him, selfishly seeking and finding comfort in his arms.

Drager shook me awake in the early morning. My first reflex was to reprimand him for having the unmitigated gall to walk into my bedroom, but I constrained my anger.

"I have the other androids downstairs ready to be reprogrammed. You told me that you wanted to take care of this early in the morning. "

"Ok, I'll meet you downstairs in a few minutes." I said between yawns.

Peter complained about the audacity of Drager, reminding me as well that I needed more sleep. I grumbled as I dragged myself up out of the bed, wondering what this day had in store for me.

I quickly ran another check on the group we reactivated the evening before to be certain their systems were not also voice sensitive, a concern that preoccupied me since awakening. Drager retrieved the last order given by the Captain to the androids on board the vessel. We replayed the order, an order that had no noticeable impact on them. When questioned, they admitted that they recognized the Captain's voice, but insisted that their programming prevented them from carrying out that kind of order.

That assuaged my fear of a similar future dilemma. There was no reason to be skeptical because Reinhart had correctly effectuated the reversal. Outside the watchful eyes of these animated androids, Reinhart, whose voice reactivated one by one the other inactive androids, put them through the same rigorous tests, before sending them back on board the vessel to help with navigation.

I looked over the bridge of the ship and this time paid attention to the equipment in place, which was impressive. The ship was equipped with a multi-functional operator station combining ARPA radar, an (ECDS) electronic chart display system, and a Conning

Display. The multi-unit was excellent for optimal sharing of work and shifting command to an autopilot, if advisable. The Conning Display, with its large screen based information system, made it easier to pilot the ship and to maintain up-to date information on heading, thrust, water depth, wind speed and direction, as well as up-dating key information for monitoring the progression of the ship along a predefined course.

From Reinhart's point of view, the technology that was used during her lifetime was based upon innovations in marine navigation that dated back to the end of the 21st century. Her improvements were minor, simply because, like with everything, the destruction of civilizations through wars or natural disasters set progress back. Scientists were spending their time trying to recover, or rediscover, the technology that was lost rather than imagining entirely new inventions. And, as she was not as much interested in marine technology, she intervened only when she considered it important to refine a technique.

Isabel and Diana both had navigational skills and had trained on simulators for years back at the center. I asked them to take command and use androids for assistance. The rest of us picked up various navigation scopes to search for any visible forms of life surfacing on the ocean and look for new land mass.

I was actually so tired that I dosed off for part of the trip and was awakened only when we entered into the zone where we saw life forms-maybe dolphins-the day before. Clarence helped us to lower the motorboats so that we could dive. He stayed on board to monitor the systems and Isabel and Tirence volunteered to maintain the small boats while the rest of us dove.

Our dives came up empty. Flora and animal life were non-existent. We had just returned to the ocean surface when Isabel and Tirence shouted to us to get out of the water, pointing to a situation developing just behind us. We turned, our spear guns ready for use. Reinhart surged inside of me, passing me information about the dozen bottlenose dolphins approaching us, something that encouraged us to rapidly board the motorboats.

Diana wanted us to approach them. She was curious, not at all frightened, of their appearance. She spoke loudly enough that we could hear her even though our boats were not in a very tight knit formation and the motors were turned on.

"I am not certain if they are dolphins, but they look harmless. I read that dolphins were considered at one time to be the second most intelligent animals, after humans. I also read that they disappeared from the face of the earth. Dolphins are apex predators and are therefore not natural prey for other aquatic animals. Nonetheless, a young dolphin can become prey to large species of sharks, like the white shark. Perhaps they disappeared because they were poisoned by the water and the young dolphins were killed off by large shark predators." She lectured.

"Well, Diana, it would appear that your information is not up-to-date because bottlenose dolphins are apparently not an extinct species and they moving in our direction." I got no answer.

"What should we do?" Joseph asked me in a low voice.

I just raised my eyebrows, indicating that I had no answer to give. They were at a safe distance from us, so I cut off the engine and my friends followed my example. We leaned back lazily in our seats, our arms loosely resting on our outstretched legs, and watched a breathtaking, synchronized aerial performance from eight of the ten dolphins, who leaped high into the air, skillfully spinning and flipping before plunging back into the ocean to begin again. The remaining two added rhythm by either laying horizontally on their bellies and lifting their flukes out of the water, bringing them down hard, making loud sounds, like they were beating a drum, or by lifting their pectoral fins into the air and slapping them down with varying degrees of force on the ocean surface. We watched, fascinated by how they used their streamlined bodies to perform such intricate moves.

Eventually, as if dancing, they all laid on their bellies, lifting their pectoral fins high over their outstretched bodies and gently curving them inward as they swept the water's surface. Their soft, harmonized whistling added more life to that choreographed dance and we sat starry eyed, mesmerized, by the vision.

Unfortunately, what appeared to be a friendly encounter, quickly degenerated into something menacing. Their soft, musical voices changed, replaced with loud clicking sounds that became high-pitched whistles, as they grouped together in a pod, like predators ready to pounce on their prey. We sat immobile for a few seconds.

"Perhaps they want us to follow them? Or, they expect us to communicate with them rather than watch complacently? Are we disappointing them? Are they upset?" These questions filled my mind, but the answers were not clear to me. What was clear was that their relaxed flippers turned very rigid and they moved with great speed in our direction.

"So what do they want?" I said in a whisper, as my body stiffened in fear. I looked at the members of my team in a cursory way confirming that they too were taking on a combative posture, as their arm muscles bulged under clenched fists and their bodies moved forward ready to attack. "I am not the only one worried..." repeated inside of me, Pamela, before a light went off and I signaled everyone to move out.

We forced the throttles, moving rapidly in the direction of the ship that was but a small spot on the horizon in front of us. The noise of the motors drowned out the cries of the dolphins as they pursued us at excessively high speeds. Our boats were bouncing, as the dolphins increased their swim speed by jumping clear of the water and rocking our boats as they came down hard, very close to us.

Even if we could outrun them, not a sure thing, how were we going to get back on board the ship? I left the steering of the boat to Joseph, while I contacted Clarence, asking him to stand by with laser guns. I didn't go into details just informed him that he should not hesitate to fire on the creatures pursuing us to discourage these aggressors and force them to keep their distance long enough for us to be reeled up on board the ship.

The ship was now in clear view and hope was returning, at least for me. I turned my head to look back and check on the others. They were keeping up with us. I noticed that the dolphins had split up into two groups. I could count only five of them encircling us from behind, the remaining dolphins were out of sight. "What are you doing, Joseph?" I screamed as I felt the boat coming to a halt.

"They are blocking our route." He cried out.

"Brace yourselves!" I said, as Reinhart's energy surged inside of me, guiding me. I pushed Joseph out of the pilot seat and took over the controls. I yelled to the others, "Follow me and don't hold back!"

Reinhart was now in command and she forced the throttle into overdrive, something that only she understood how to do, and rushed them. When we got close, she saw her opportunity and used the back of one of the dolphins like a ramp, ripping through the thick skin on his back as the sharp edge on the bottom of the boat drug over him. We took off, leaping high in the air and coming down in a dramatic, violent splash that put confusion into the dolphin front line, as they scattered in different directions looking for their comrade and trying to stay out of the way of our boat and those close behind us.

Joseph later told me that he thought that we were on a suicide mission and he closed his eyes preparing to disappear forever. The boat swirled for a few seconds in different directions, caught in the hefty waves caused by the dolphins and the speed of the boat. Roller coasting the waves, Reinhart eventually got the boat back on course while keeping the speed at its maximum.

"Where are the others?" She screamed to Tirence who was seated in the back of the boat.

"They are right behind us." He replied in a screechy voice. "They capitalized on the broken dolphin line, sliding easily between them. But, those dolphins are regrouping so we all have to get to the ship soon."

We did arrive safely and Clarence pulled us up on board. Reinhart left me in command and I grabbed one of the lasers, put it on flash speed and stunned the lead dolphin that was closing in on one of our motorboats. Even though I saw him reel over, I kept shooting until all us humans were safely on board.

Curiously enough the dolphins did not turn back, instead they came up alongside our ship still anchored in these deep waters. We were all badly shaken, our pulses beating inside our heads and our bodies trembling as we struggled to remove the wet suits that seemed to cling so tightly to us. To calm down, we moved away from the rails and collapsed on the deck. When I, Pamela, finally found the physical force to stand up and gaze over the rails, I saw those creatures were motioning to me. Peter was alongside of me, his arms steadying me.

"They aren't scared?" Peter asked. There was no way to answer that question. If they weren't scared after what just happened, perhaps all of us had misunderstood their intentions all along. The real question was what to do now.

"By the way, thanks for making that extraordinary move to save us all. It was spectacular. I wish that I could have filmed it." Stuart's recall of the incident broke the tension and brought out cheers and applauds from the others, who were now on their feet.

Embarrassed, I had a silly smile on my flushed face. "I told you that Reinhart is a daredevil. I don't think that she was ever afraid of anything."

I turned my attention to the dolphins. I knew that they could not jump on board our ship so we were safe. They were also in the vulnerable position if we decided to fire on them. I did not trust them, but decided to play the nice guy in the hope of building confidence so that they might reveal their true intentions.

"Somebody give me a loudspeaker or something!" I yelled. Someone handed me a cone-shaped loudspeaker and I stepped up on the rail, pointing it toward the dolphins.

"I am sorry that our encounter with you was not a peaceful one." I stated in a steady, serene voice. "We were hoping to find other life forms and are very happy that your species is among the survivors."

One of the dolphins, perhaps their leader, whistled and clicked his tongue, in regular sequence, in an effort to communicate with me. The absurdity of this situation became clear. We could not communicate with each other through words, or, in their case, clicking, whistling sounds. We must find a solution.

"Randolph, would you please see whether there is any information regarding communication with dolphins in any period of human history still available in the computer files or fragmented pieces of it buried deep in the memory bank?"

Dolphins were no longer around in Reinhart's time. So many species had disappeared, replaced by new species, more resistant to pollution and contaminated waters and lands. She had never interacted with these creatures but was aware of what Diana had previously mentioned. The cortex and neo-cortex regions of the dolphin's brain and their general behavior indicated that they were capable of high order thinking and processing of information. The bottlenose dolphins were placed at the hierarchy of their species.

While Randolph and the other humans looked into that, I continued to speak to the dolphins in our language and they continued to answer me with clicking tongues and whistling sounds. "Perhaps they understand me even though I don't understand anything that they are saying." Preoccupied my thoughts as they moved in another direction. I conjectured that their beautiful aquatic performance was meant to lure us into their grips...but for what reason? Certainly not to have a pleasant conversation. "They are probably very diabolical and dangerous." I said under my breath.

It did not take long for the group to find a very old, partially damaged, program that could translate dolphin clicks and whistles into human language. We needed an English translation. There was an existent vocal capturing system integrated into the program, so we started running the program.

What we got back was mindboggling. "We are a small group of dolphin descendants of a long line of dolphins. Our earliest ancestors existed thousands and thousands of years ago. Our progenitors lived in an aquarium in a laboratory that was destroyed hundreds of years before you, Dr. Reinhart, were born."

"So what do you want from me? How do you know of me?" Reinhart had surfaced and answered, controlling my vocal chords. "I had no idea that your species survived time."

The dolphin ignored the question and went on with a long dissertation. "Precisely. Humans were experimenting with us. We were unhappy. So when the laboratory exploded and the aquarium was thrown out into the polluted ocean my ancestors made a promise never to return to the land or approach humans again."

He continued his story, telling us how they escaped from the aquarium and fled to warmer waters. Apparently, only a few survived. Each new generation became more resistant to the contaminated air and water. Today they were but a small community feeding off of flora.

"Elisabeth Reinhart was legendary for everyone, including us.

We recognized you the other day and sought contact with you today." The spokesperson, or leader, claimed that they never meant to frighten us; they only wanted to show us where the group of dolphins was located and regretted what happened. They also wanted to know if I could save their friend, the one whose back was injured.

"You will have to trust me then." Reinhart replied in a pleasant tone, masking her contempt for them. "I cannot take care of him here, I have to take him back to the center for treatment." Nonetheless, I could feel that cold wave of contempt flowing inside of me, indicating that she felt no regret for the dolphin's injuries. Why should she, or any of us? Their attitude was far from pacifistic. It was overtly menacing.

"You can follow us back to the shoreline." She continued. "I will have to put your injured comrade in a tank to transport him to the center when we arrive." They nodded. "And, if you are tired, I can lower some nets that you can rest in. That way we can put the ship on faster speed." They nodded again, so the nets were lowered. They reclined in the nets, perhaps in an effort to show Reinhart that they had confidence in her.

Everyone was gathered on the bridge, while the androids took care of our diving gear. "You should have been nicer to them when they showed up." Diana said in a caustic tone.

Diana's provocative remark irritated Reinhart who had no difficulty defending her behavior. "My dear Diana, I never regret my actions because they are always founded on a very logical, not emotional, basis. You, on the other hand, are drawing conclusions about a subject on which you are not an expert."

Diana stiffened as she readied for...verbal combat, but she quickly backed down. "You have a text book knowledge of these creatures. A text book knowledge that was adapted and modified for your reading pleasure by the Group of 5." Reinhart cast a furtive glance in Diana's direction.

"Dolphins were not very nice creatures. They enjoyed killing. They even enjoyed savoring the pleasure of hunting and killing their natural enemies, the shark, whose body they did not always devour, but left to rot. They liked to kill other species, as well, just for fun-for something to do when they were bored-and then play ball with the cadavers. They even raped their own offspring or congeners. Were they the intellectual equals of humans? Yes, if you like the Group of 5's definition of humans, then I would have to agree that they were very much like us humans at that time!" Her words left the group in a visible state of astonishment, as eyes popped and lower jaws dropped.

"Now, if we can turn to the present dilemma." She resumed. "We still do not know why the dolphins did not maintain their initial kind, friendly behavior. We don't know how they heard about me. And, to conclude, we do not know what their objectives are. That should be enough to put all of us on guard!" Reinhart made her point.

I left the bridge and breathed in deeply the ocean air to calm Reinhart's flaming energy inside of me. The others eventually joined me, leaving Isabel and Diana to navigate.

"They look so calm now." Joseph said. "She may be right, though, I have a feeling that they are not candid. And, those dolphins certainly scared me!"

I was glad when the shoreline appeared and we dropped anchor. Diana and Isabel brought the ship practically up on the beach, so that we did not have to paddle in deep water before reaching firm ground. I sent three of the android assistants back to the center to recuperate a large size aquarium while we loaded our scuba gear on the land vehicles. The group of dolphins waited patiently for us to organize ourselves before addressing Reinhart.

The major part of their speech, passing through the translation program, was filled with flattery intended to verbally seduce Reinhart. They expressed their strong desire to develop positive working relationships with humans, even the reptilian humans whose physical appearances were extraordinarily beautiful to their eyes. They offered to take us tomorrow to their breeding grounds and introduce us to the rest of the community. "It all sounds too rehearsed." I surmised, but sent them a broad smile meant to temper any suspicions that they might harbor regarding my sincerity.

The dolphin's wound was more superficial than I realized. He had bruises inflicted by the weight of the boat when it moved across him. Reinhart sealed the open wound, gluing the different levels and then sealing them with a laser used in aquatic veterinary care. She administered a painkiller.

I skipped dinner and went straight to bed. I didn't hear Peter arrive and didn't wake him when I got up. I went straight to the marine laboratory to interview the captive dolphin.

Reinhart appeared. She didn't want the interview to be friendly. "You realize that you are in a delicate position?" His eyes flickered rapidly. "You are my patient, but you could easily become my prisoner, if you refuse to answer my questions, as correctly and honestly as possible." He cocked his head. She pretended that the translation program could easily detect lies. He held his body straight. She questioned him on the number of dolphins in their community, something that he answered without hesitation. "There are thirty dolphins, ten of which are our young offspring."

She asked about their environment. "Dr. Reinhart, there are things that I have promised never to disclose. I am telling you, and only you, because I don't have a choice. I hope that you will keep this information secret."

"No one puts pressure on me." She replied in a clear, loud voice. "If you don't tell me everything I want to know, this aquarium will become your prison."

He told the story. The dolphins lived in the carcass of a huge submarine that sunk during one of the many wars. "Our history was passed on from one generation to another. Some of our history may not be that accurate. Some information may have been lost, even discarded, and new, undocumented information added. So our history may be slightly exaggerated." His dolphin eyes sparkled as he said, "You can appreciate that, Dr. Reinhart."

"And what do you mean by that?"

"I mean, simply, that parts of history get lost and are filled in and some of the history turns into legends. Like you ... you are a legend!"

"I have no idea in what way I am a legend. I know who I am, what I did, and how I disappeared. Everything about my former existence embedded in my memory is the truth. I don't know what you have been told."

He hung his head. "We were told that we were your lost children and that you would return one day to make us leaders."

"Absurd!" She replied vigorously. "Yes, completely absurd, but comprehensible in view of the thousands and thousands of years that your species has existed."

"Then, you don't care about us?" He asked, his clicking sounds weakened as his enthusiasm vanished.

"I did not mean that. Of course, I care about your species, like I care about all the different species that existed in the past and that exist today." She smiled warmly. "I shall help all of you to survive, if that is what you are hoping for."

He sat blowing bubbles from his blowhole, like someone puffing smoke from a pipe, for what seemed to be hours, when it was only minutes. "Before the war and other natural disasters, ocean food sources were abundant, in our hunting grounds. We are a carnivorous species and hunt in groups, surrounding schools of fish and taking turns eating." He licked his lips. "We like shellfish, as well." He stopped for a second as if savoring the taste of shellfish. "Actually, we eat anything that has a meaty texture and is in our hunting grounds." He shook his head and turned up his nose, just contemplating the taste of plants.

"As you must remember, it was almost impossible for your boats or planes to get beyond the menacing high waves and winds that hovered over the oceans, just outside the territorial waters. As a result, you were forced to look for food sources on the land and inland water sources. You never knew that there were calm oceans filled with fish and plants just beyond that morbid wall of wailing winds and angry waters because our very intelligent ancestors manipulated the satellite receivers and projected false images of the ocean environment to discourage humans from ocean travel." He let out shrill, very shrill whistles.

"That is your story." She clapped her hands. She knew that the satellite images had not been manipulated. "It would have been quite clever of them, but the story is untrue!" Reinhart loved adversity. "Please go on, my curiosity is aroused."

"Our ancestors acquired a taste for human flesh." He clicked his tongue energetically. "Of course, it was a delicacy, so they devised a way to preserve the "meat," he said emphatically, "for special occasions. The explosion of this planet did not destroy our breeding grounds, but it destroyed our source of meat. The fish and shellfish disappeared overnight and we were forced to survive on marine alga." He shook his head and turned up his nose for a second time. "The explosion did give us a large supply of meaty humans for our future consumption. Unfortunately, this food source is running out!" He exclaimed.

"Interesting story. If I understand correctly, for thousands of years you have been eating dead, but frozen, or otherwise naturally preserved humans, and the invitation we received from your group yesterday was an invitation for dinner, of sorts." Reinhart let out one of her imposing laughs that registered at decibels that could pierce an eardrum if you were standing too close and the dolphin quivered in fear.

She disappeared inside of me and I found myself looking into the eyes of a human flesh-eating dolphin. "Dr. Reinhart," he said and I moved towards his aquarium. "We would never eat you! You are like a Goddess. But, the others are far inferior intellectually to us. We have survived these thousands and thousands of years. We can share our information with you. You don't need to live with these inferior creatures. You can just donate them to us. We have been told over and over again that we dolphins are your chosen people."

"He is mad, completely mad, even crazier than the Group of 5," I contemplated. "So what do you want me to do?" I asked feigning innocence with a childish giggle.

"Follow the dolphins to the breeding grounds and then let the rest of your human crew dive. We have cages ready for them. And, we are very much interested in tasting the new breed of reptilian humans."

He did not notice the voice change, or if he did, he ignored it. "Ok, I shall arrange for that. Now you must rest a bit, you need to build up your strength." He smiled, reaching out to me with his flippers. I stroked them maternally until he fell asleep. I then firmly closed and locked the grill that covered the tank.

Reinhart was back in control when I left the lab and she informed the members of our group of the dolphin's carnivorous delicacy...humans, live, dead or frozen. "Either this dolphin is mentally disturbed, or he was telling me the truth. And, apparently, I am a legend for them and have come back to make them the masters of the world."

"They eat humans?" Diana screamed. "No! He is not serious."

The group moved from a morbid state of silent denial of this truth to hitting the walls and knocking over furniture as their anger and tempers mounted. I looked on, my lower jaw trembling as tears filled my eyes, imagining the horror that could have befallen us.

"There is only one way to find out." Reinhart said in a calm voice. "We shall have to follow them to their breeding grounds. We shall pretend to be preparing ourselves for a dive, but instead we shall send out drones to investigate and send back videos and other information. There are a number of these drones in this center. I shall activate and program fighter drones, used by the military in the past, to respond to my commands to fire explosive darts, killing these creatures mercilessly and destroying their structures and hiding places, if that becomes necessary." She stopped to make certain that she had everyone's full attention. "We must not give the dolphins any idea that we sense danger. Is that understood?" Heads nodded. "Our dolphin prisoner told me that there were about 30 of them, but I imagine that that is a low figure."

"What are we going to do with them if they are eating humans?" Leonard raised the question that everyone wanted to ask.

"They are a life form-maybe a repulsive life form from our perspective-but a life form nonetheless. And, in spite of the abhorrence of what they did, these dolphins, like any other species, had to adapt to changed circumstances. They are carnivorous creatures and, even though humans were never considered to be fatty enough for sharks and other aquatic animals, when an animal is starving they will eat meat from whatever source." She sighed.

"Humans were a source of protein for them." She continued. "So, we cannot eradicate them. We have to save some of them. Perhaps the young ones' culinary tastes can be radically changed. I am going to speak to the Group of 5, if you all want to be present."

John answered quickly. Jarrod and Fleming were close by when I explained the problem. "This is not good news! It could even be horrifying news!" He replied, his voice shaking with anger, his logical, scientific side on hold. "I shall summon the Group of 5 immediately."

"Admittedly it was horrifying for humans to think that they were the exotic food source for dolphins, but then dolphins were also killed and eaten at one time by humans. It was just an insane reversal whereby one group of intelligent beings treated another group of intelligent beings as their food source only to find themselves becoming a food source for the species that they previously ate." I philosophized.

"Dolphins?" Gordon queried. "I never saw a live dolphin. They were considered to be an extinct species."

"You must be very happy with this news, Gordon." Crawford confronted her. "You bored me and revolted me with your wretched stories of human cannibalism, so even though this situation is slightly different, dolphins eating humans must be intellectually stimulating for you."

"Ok, we don't have time to listen to the two of you argue over this subject." I interrupted them. "It seems clear that you are not at the source of this problem and are not in any way associated with it now. So we have to find solutions."

"Destroy them." the Governor piped up. "But, you might take DNA so that we can reproduce a sane breed of dolphins." Flanders approved that idea.

"I thought that we might try to capture the children. They may not be so dangerous yet." I strongly suggested.

The Group of 5 did not agree with me. They argued that the dolphin biological systems evolved certainly to the point where they needed red meat, an expression that humans used to refer to their craving for animal meat.

"Maybe the Captain was working for them." Miller proposed.

"That makes no sense, humans were terminated in the centers. And, there were no humans living in the Marine center." I stopped to consider what I had just said. The Marine center was a disaster on every level. Androids programmed to kill humans and now dolphins feeding off of humans. "Were there humans living in this center?" I was hoping that the answer would be no.

"Actually, there was no breeding of humans-sorry for the expression-at the Marine center, but we did send humans to work with the androids." Jarrod replied. "We were under the impression that the Captain had sent groups of humans to live on the outside, to study them, like we did." He made an android style moan that sounded like someone grinding his teeth. "Now, I am not so sure about anything."

"So you replaced the humans who moved to the outside but never verified where they were living. In fact, you didn't check to see if they were actually alive?"

"We sent new humans to the Captain when a series reached its termination date. The Captain followed our policy." He pretended to take a deep breath. "We had no reason to suspect the Captain of foul play. Even though there is no doubt today that we should have been more vigilant."

"I want all of you to review all the correspondence you had with this center and the number of humans living and dying in this center over all the years that these centers have been active. Already termination is a horrible thing, but offering humans to carnivorous dolphins is revolting!" Reinhart screamed, showing her teeth, before she turned off the screen.

"I shall look into the memory bank of that Captain later on, but my orders will keep the others occupied until we get back." She told us.

"Should we kill them like the Group of 5 suggested?" Mathieu asked.

"We shall do worse. We shall capture them and enslave them by implanting a visual receptor." Reinhart said. We all drifted off into another time when the only way to deal with revolts was to plant a tiny device in someone's brain that was connected to a visual receptor that would let them live in total bliss in a world of rosy colors- the kind of world that we grew up in. This was at least an intermediary solution.

The ship moved out to sea, with the dolphins resting comfortably in the netting for the trip. They started to click their tongues as we got close to where the ship was anchored yesterday. "We are going to move the ship to your breeding grounds." I called out.

They moved rapidly in the netting, their pectoral flippers pointing in the direction of their refuge. I let the net drop deeper into the water so that they could swim off and mentioned that we would join them as soon as we were equipped for the dive. Their dolphin heads moved up and down.

As promised, I sent the tiny drones to send us audio-visual information of the surroundings. Their photos confirmed our prisoner's story. There were large cages, some still housing human corpses, preserved by the cold temperatures. The drones drifted off, sending photos of four strange looking dolphins. Two of them were reclining on high benches, while the other two were swimming lazily, inside the dilapidated structure of a 21st century submarine.

These dolphins looked like the offspring of two different mammal species, or that of a walrus and a dolphin. The largest, logically the male, was at least five times bigger than the dolphins we encountered yesterday. He was cinnamon brown colored and had the fusiform body of a walrus. Apart from a cluster of side whiskers on his round, puffy face, his skin was smooth. I adjusted the visual to get a better picture of his face. His small eyes were on the side of his head and his ears directly behind them. Instead of pained nostrils, he had a bottle nose, or snout like projection, and a single blow hole located on his dorsal surface like his dolphin ancestors.

I was now encircled by team members looking studiously at the imagery. "Yes, he is a hybrid." Reinhart said as she pointed out certain features she had just discovered. "Look at the thickness of his neck and his shoulders. And, he has walrus limbs and flippers. The pectoral flippers are short and squared, revealing five digits, the claws inconspicuous. A walrus uses these pectoral flippers for steering and gripping on land."

She stopped to observe again, watching the male lift his body up, a seemingly incredible accomplishment in view of his size, and begin to move around. His entourage followed him. "Look," Reinhart screamed to get the group's full attention, "he has a rotating pelvic girdle, which is why he can stand erect. It must have evolved over the ages making this possible for him. Normally, he should be walking by putting his fore flippers at right angles to hold his weight.

But, as you can see, he is standing on his triangular back flippers, normally used only for swimming. Incredible!" She exclaimed.

"What happened there?" Stuart asked as he pointed to the animal's face.

"Extraordinary! He has those walrus tusks-smaller than his pure race ancestors. And they appear to be retractable" We observed him and the rest of the family, the smaller adult clearly a female, hovering over her two young offspring. He stood, his large body balancing naturally on his tail fin, with his claws visible and his canines protruding, like scimitars, from the corners of his dolphin shaped mouth.

The male eventually tired and slowly moved back to sit majestically on his high, large bench. The rest of his family followed him in due course. The female sat on a smaller bench next to him and their two off springs stood obediently behind their parents. We watched as the group of dolphins that followed us arrived. They let their bodies rise slowly up and down several times in the water, gracefully bowing before these four mutants.

The drones beamed in on them and picked up the conversation that was instantaneously translated for us. "Did you bring them back with you?" The Male asked.

"Yes Your Majesty! They are preparing to dive."

"Are you sure that everything is going as we planned?"

"There was a small incident that we used to our advantage, to gain their trust. Reinhart has a suspicious nature. One of our members was injured and we left him in her care."

The male lifted his body up high, revealing his size and force, in an intimidating way. The drones sent us a stream of photos of him and his family. These close up shots left no doubt. All members of the "royal family," resembled more a walrus, a notorious and dangerous carnivorous creature, than a dolphin.

We listened. The dolphin explained rapidly what had happened. "We didn't want to leave him behind to be dissected."

"Hmm mmm! That was a risk. Where is he now?"

"Dr. Reinhart---"

"She is there?" The royal dolphin asked, his lips chattered and his small eyes illuminated.

"Yes! But I was forced to listen to a ludicrous story, delivered by someone who looked like Reinhart, but called herself Pamela. She claimed that only the essence of Reinhart was inside of her and that she was an entirely different person. They think that they are so clever!" The male walrus-dolphin rolled around in his seat with laughter and the dolphins followed suit. "In any event, she will be diving with the others."

"Excellent!" He rubbed his puffy face with his fat flippers. "We shall kill the others, and preserve them for very special occasions. Dr. Reinhart can live among us, at least until she has given us all the knowledge that we need to ensure ourselves a continuing source of healthy, meaty products." His pudgy face, with its protruding canines, formed a terrifying smile. "Only I shall eat her! When the time comes!" He said in a strong voice before licking his chops.

"I assure you, Your Majesty, that they do not suspect anything. You were right, they are so intellectually inferior to us."

The members of the group and the four walrus dolphins jumped up and down, and danced about, like they were already celebrating their victory.

Reinhart let our one her long, boisterous laughs that was so disconcerting that we all jumped. "It is now our turn! Send down the fighter drones and position them in and around the submarine. Put a few of them outside the sub, just in case there are a couple dolphins enjoying a casual swim. I estimate their numbers at around 50 that includes the small inoffensive ones." She said, directing her attention to James and Randolph who were overseeing that part of the operation.

When all the drones were in the right position, she turned off the translation version from English to dolphin. "What are you doing?" Isabel asked.

"They understand English. I realized that too late. We were at a disadvantage. They overheard our conversations and understood us. I just want them to know now that I was not fooled for too long."

Her voice amplified, creating waves in the water below. "You are surrounded."

There was panic as the dolphins jumped and swam furiously in different directions, seeking cover. "What was that?" the hulk of a leader stopped dancing and rapidly, visually surveyed the area.

"You heard me. You understand my language. You are surrounded. If you do not follow my instructions to the letter, I shall have no problem disposing of you and all of your wretched followers." Reinhart sounded very convincing.

The leader charged at the group of dolphins, lashing out at them with all his force and calling them idiots. When he finished releasing his anger, he sat back down on his high bench and said in a calm, friendly voice. "Dr. Reinhart, I presume. It is such a pleasure to speak to you. I would, of course, have preferred the pleasure of meeting you as well."

"Shut up! Do what I say. You are lucky that I have not already ordered the drones to splatter your fat body all over what is left of the submarine walls!"

"We have honored your memory for centuries." He continued didactically, hoping that Reinhart would relent. When he got no answer he replied acquiescingly. "Of course, I shall be your devoted servant and do exactly what you want."

"I don't trust them," she said to our group and ordered two of the drones to destroy the two smaller members of the royal family. The dolphins rushed to the defense of the royal couple, lashing their tail fins in an unavailing effort to destroy the drones. "If you want more proof of our force, I am ready to show you. You are a despicable species of animals that should be annihilated and I am becoming bored with your vacuous remarks. I am giving you a chance to survive in spite of the fact that I detest you, your community and everything that you stand for. But, only if you cooperate."

"Ok, we shall do what you want." He said in a refined English accent, reminiscent of another historical period.

"You will open up all the cages, including those occupied by humans, letting the human remains, bodies and body parts, rise to the surface, and your community will enter those cages." I could hear him snicker. He was so sure of himself.

They did what she asked. When the cages were empty they entered one after the other. At the last minute, Reinhart ordered the physically imposing King to lock all the cages and to rise to the surface to be taken prisoner by the humans. He said that he refused to do such a thing; that it was too humiliating for him.

"Strange, just hours ago you told me that you were sorry that you were only talking to me. I am giving you the opportunity to meet me now, and you are refusing."

"Ok, I shall come to the surface." He relented.

"Before coming to the surface you will show me that the cages are well locked by pulling with all your force, which I can register through the drones, on the doors." He did that. "Now show me the keys and count them in front of the camera so that I can be sure that you have followed my orders."

He commenced counting.

"You will bring those keys with you. I am leaving the drones to guard the prisoners and they have orders to kill all of them if anyone of them escapes." He let his head fall low and moved lethargically.

"Oh, one more thing. As I don't think that you care much about the members of your community, pure dolphins or mutants, like yourself, I doubt that threatening to destroy them will make you more cooperative." Reinhart waited for a reply, but he said nothing. "I know that when food is low, dolphins will eat other dolphins." His body stiffened hearing that truth. "I want you to know that I shall destroy you at the slightest provocation and then force the others to eat you."

"You are worse than us, Dr. Reinhart!" He couldn't see the smile of pleasure that spread over my face.

Within minutes, he was bobbing at the surface- pretending to be too big and fat to swim. Stuart, James, Randolph, Peter and Tirence went to scoop up this enormous mass of flesh. I was watching through binoculars and could see that he handed the keys over to James, who counted them out loud. The count was good so they ordered him to move into the huge net that was attached to the boat. They transported him at high speed back to the ship. He cooperated by never trying to get away.

In the meantime, Isabel, Mathieu and Diana were monitoring the drones and the situation underwater. I asked Joseph, Leonard, Adam and Daniel to retrieve the human corpses and any human body parts so that we could properly dispose of their bodies.

The androids pulled the motorboat up, dragging its cargo along the side of the hull, before letting it plummet onto the deck of the ship. We removed the netting and the hybrid creature moved up into a kind of sitting position, leaning back on his pectoral fins.

I stood and observed him. He did not seem to be in any way affected from his sudden loss of status. In fact, he gave me the impression that he still considered himself to be a ruling figure. I knew that he was observing me.

"I am Pamela."

"Oh!" He chuckled. "So that irresponsible dolphin was not telling me some crazy story." He said in a refined English style.

"Where did you learn English?"

He rolled back his hybrid walrus-dolphin head and looked up into the sky as if the answer was written in the clouds above. "You want information, so that is why I am here." He turned his eyes back on me. "Then we must negotiate."

"Did you pay attention to what Reinhart said to you before your body drifted to the surface?" He nodded. "Well, if you don't tell me what I want to know, I shall just terminate you and let the dolphins feed off of your body." He moved onto his side and started to play with the claws imbedded in his pectoral fins.

"I shall then get more information from the dolphin prisoner in the marine center." I threatened him.

Now he reacted. He hit the floor with his large flipper. "He talked. I should have known it. Oh, those stupid dolphins. It is always better to do important things yourself. Isn't it, Dr. Reinhart?"

"You are addressing, Pamela. And, just to remind you, Dr. Reinhart is a very impatient person." I said, my eyes piercing his.

"English is our second language. Our ancestors learned the language in captivity. I don't know in what year that was, kill me for not knowing it if you want, I don't care at this point. I do not even know what year it is today or for how long we have lived as a species in that miserable submarine, surviving wars, natural disasters, and an horrific explosion that moved us, apparently, from warm to cold waters, only to discover that there are no warm waters anymore."

I nodded and he continued. "I do know that after our ancestors were miraculously set free by a fire in a marine laboratory, they transmitted the dolphin and human language to their descendants. We speak the two languages."

He expounded on the reason why the dolphins did not speak English to humans. Apparently, humans were mesmerized by the clicking and whistling sounds and, like in a trance, followed the dolphins into the ocean. They had expected the same response from us the other day. He mockingly mentioned that it was such an easy way of fishing human food.

He confirmed the legendary quality of Reinhart. "We were given a very clear description of her, you, by those non-intellectuals, as you referred to them, who ventured out into the high seas, and, naturally into our breeding grounds. They admired and hated you with the same intensity. Our ancestors found that very fascinating. They often talked about Reinhart having a closer natural affinity to machines and animals, rather than to humans. They found that commendable. They spent time with those explorers, gathering information and learning about progress, before they turned them into frozen food. These stories are passed on from one generation to the other and we are all amazed, like our ancestors, by your legendary talents."

"What else do you eat besides humans?" I asked aggressively.

"We have, on occasion, eaten other dolphins, as you so rightly surmised, when there is nothing else to eat. You understand that four of us, and only two of us are left thanks to you, are hybrids, Walrus-dolphins, and we have no ethical standards with respect to food. Yes, dolphins will resort to cannibalism to stay alive."

So I was right about their walrus features!

"Who knows how that came about? We have always kept our numbers low in order to be worshipped by the dolphins. They are so beguiled by our physical appearance that they treat us like Gods."

"The dolphins also worshipped Reinhart, who they believed, from the stories, was a powerful Goddess. Yes, the dolphins did subscribe to that strange idea that Reinhart considered them to be her lost children and would return one day to make them the rulers of the world."

"I am not at all flattered by their idolatry of Reinhart." Reinhart replied, her accent visible.

"I never believed that nonsense!" The hybrid retorted in an ear-splitting tone. "When the dolphins returned and announced your presence, all of those dolphins wanted to meet and eat you, or her." He smiled mischievously. "It is so easy for me to identify my interlocutor, even without that change of accent." He laughed lowly, in a cruel and teasing way.

Even though the entire discussion nauseated me and he was now getting on my nerves, I gestured him with my hand to continue the story. He admitted that the Captain at the center was an ally and that he did offer the programmed humans to the dolphins several times a year. There were traps, like the one Diana encountered, planted in the sandy beach and the humans who tried to escape often times fell into a trap. Some were simply escorted to the ocean and ordered to swim. Others, as he explained earlier, were hypnotized by the dolphin songs and entered the water without resistance.

"I have to admit that there was a small community of humans living on the outside who had by-passed their programming. They were not very good looking." He stroked his chin with his front flipper. "I think that we called them the people of many colors. We captured them when they swam too far away from the shore. We only ate them when there was nothing else to eat because they did not taste that good." He spit out the last few words, as if experiencing their distastefulness.

"Is it true that you have the technology to intercept satellite photos and alter them?"

"Why should I tell you?"

"Thank you, you just did." That left him with his mouth wide-open.

"I think that I shall keep you like you are in an oversized aquarium. I might have other questions for you in the future." I understood that his authority, wit, competence, and whatever he imagined that he possessed were never questioned. He did not know how to impress me.

"We shall wrap him back up in that net until we get to shore." I told those around me. We tied him up tightly.

Joseph called out to us. They had recuperated all the human

366

bodies and body parts and had loaded them onto two empty mo-torboats. The androids threw cords down to the reptilian humans, who climbed the cords easily, while the androids reeled the boats laded with human remains up above sea level, securing them against the side of the ship.

We were back at the Marine center in the late afternoon. I had called ahead to ask Jason and Ludovic to ask the androids to meet us with the biggest aquarium they had. They were waiting for us when we arrived.

"Do you want us to throw you into the aquarium or do you pre-fer to enter on your own?" Reinhart asked exaggerating her accent.

He looked straight into my eyes. "I understand now why those non-intellectuals both admired you and hated you with the same intensity, Dr. Reinhart." He said as he struggled to lift his bulky body high enough to enter into the large tank.

Chapter 23- Mutants

We were all physically and mentally exhausted after this very long day of dreadful discoveries. I felt profound remorse for those humans who never had the presence of mind to try to escape death and asked the androids to properly dispose of their human remains. They knew the procedure and promised to respect their remains with rapid, laser incineration.

The drones continued to send photos of the underwater kingdom, showing the dolphins and the female walrus-dolphin uncomfortably sealed in their tiny cages. It became evident that we would have to stay at this center for at least another day, the time it would take to tow those cages back to the shoreline and sedate the prisoners. Drager was still with us, so I arranged for him to fly back to the Air and Space center to retrieve the implants that I needed to program the dolphins. He would be back in the morning.

We met around the dining room table. Tired and disgusted with the discoveries made at this center, we sat with droopy heads, toying with our food instead of eating it. Like the others, I felt as if all my energy and enthusiasm had been siphoned off by the painstaking realities of the last few days, accounting for the languorous climate in the dining room.

I got up and left to check on the two prisoners in the laboratory. They were chatting in dolphin when I arrived. "Oh, Dr. Reinhart, we need more air. You know that we cannot stay submerged for long periods of time. We need to have our dose of oxygen." The dolphin spoke English, something that was no longer necessary as Reinhart had already downloaded the dolphin language into her memory and uploaded the version to me.

"Understood. But, for the moment, the best that I can offer you is the space between the water level and the grill. Tomorrow I shall ask the androids to reduce the water level a bit more." I turned my full attention to the hybrid King, who was an excellent actor. One would have thought that he enjoyed living in an aquarium the way he leaned backed lazily against the glass wall of the aquarium, trying to catch the air bubbles with his pectoral fins.

I left, locking the door to the lab behind me and reminding the android guards that they should not leave their posts.

As I walked past the dining room, I heard laughter. Either they recovered their energy after I left or my presence earlier inhibited them. Even though Reinhart was meditating deep inside of me, I was too tired to pursue their discussions so I headed for the bedroom. "Our symbiotic relationship works well." Crossed my thoughts. "I am glad that Reinhart respects my privacy and intimacy and always disappears when I need to do my own soul searching and, in particular, when I interact with friends or seek comfort in Peter's arms."

Peter arrived behind me, startling me, and breaking into these happy thoughts. His lips were aflame with desire when he pressed them up against mine. It was not love that incited my passion, but an inexplicable need to transcend the moment and capture feelings, sensations, to reach the limits of human intimacy, and to be romantic. Anyone could have given me the same extraordinary affirmation of my human cravings and needs and the confirmation that the stoic nature of Reinhart had not reduced me to a machine. But when it culminated in triumphal pleasure, I was overjoyed that Peter was the one who liberated my human side.

And so renewed energy and confidence followed me throughout the final day in this center, defiled by a bleak and morbid history that we had to erase and replace with positive projects and honorable achievements. When I walked past the termination unit, tears were streaming down my face. I addressed those who had suffered atrocities, by praising them for their courage and bowing in honor to their former existence.

I boarded the ship with the others for what would be the last trip out to that breeding center. I sent a group of android divers down to attach the cages to a cable system so that we could tow the cages onto the shore. I ordered several drones to plant small underwater explosives that I would set off after our ship was a safe distance away. They returned on board when their missions were completed.

Drager had the implants ready when we arrived. There were only nine dolphins that survived. We disposed of twenty-five dead dolphin bodies. The young dolphins had been killed and partially eaten by their dolphin cell mates, and others died from brutality in the cages. I wanted to make certain that the fifty dolphins I registered on the initial scan of the underwater kingdom were accounted for. As the drones had fired and killed twelve dolphins, including the two walrus-dolphins, and the male walrus-dolphin and the injured dolphin were in captivity, the final count was good.

The nine dolphins, one of which was the female walrus-dolphin, were sedated and Drager and I worked rapidly and efficiently, implanting the visual receptors in the cerebrum, or the front of the brain which is responsible for movement, body temperature, touch, vision, hearing, judgment, reasoning, problem-solving, emotions and learning. I adjusted the visual receptor to send back human imagery of themselves and other members of their community and increased the scope of the inhibitory factors in this implant to impede independent reasoning, judgment, learning, and so forth.

A visual receptor was strapped to the upper part of the flipper so their comrades' visibility would be based on a transmitted visual code, something that all of us had experienced in the past. We humans, who no longer transmitted a visual code, would remain invisible, giving us more power over them. We finished everything by late afternoon. We would know in the morning, when they awakened, if the receptor was working properly. In the meantime, we put them in an enclosed pool and locked the grill that encircled it.

There was still a detail to resolve. I contacted Fleming to take charge of the center until another android could be found to replace him. He was reluctant to leave Jarrod and assume all that responsibility. Finally, I agreed to let both Jarrod and Fleming assume responsibility temporarily for the Marine center. They would arrive the following morning.

Drager wanted to return to the Air and Space center and I agreed. He would be the right person to supervise that center and

I had confidence in him to run that center properly. Perhaps in the future I would send Gordon and Crawford to the Marine center to carry out research, but for the moment it was better to keep them under a watchful eye.

The atmosphere in the dining room was more relaxed and jovial than the night before. "I am looking forward to seeing Frederic." I said on impulse. Randolph, Isabel and Mathieu followed my example, reminding the others that our two and a half weeks, was close to a month in the center. Animated discussion pursued.

I walked out on the small veranda off the dining room. Randolph followed me. "This has been an extraordinary experience and I realize that I like exploring." I smiled.

"You have another trip in mind?" he asked. The others joined us on the veranda. The ocean air, impregnated with a sweet, salty mist, was refreshing and calming.

"We made a great team!" I said spontaneously. "And we shall make a great team again soon, somewhere else on this planet. Reinhart wants to review the satellite images, now that she has photos of the area around our main center. Our true location on a recent satellite map will be helpful in deciding where to explore next."

Everyone had a special moment to bring to mind-the floral paradise, Jason and Ludovic's arrivals, the architect Andrew, the aircraft, spaceships, the marine boats and ships, the crazy Captain and the obnoxious dolphins.

I repeated my previous statement that we made a great team. "I know that Reinhart is a take charge person." I brought up this subject to get their reactions.

"It was a good thing that she showed us how to confront adversity." Stuart mentioned and the group nodded vigorously in agreement.

"There were moments when she initiated a course of action, like when she put that motorboat in overdrive. I was completely unaware of that super mode until she took over the steering of the boat. I suppose that you had the same reaction to that as I did." Their faces turned expressionless

"Remember, I told you many time now, that she doesn't upload all the information straight away." They looked fixedly at me, their eyes wide-open. "My impression is that she reveals things when it is necessary. She waits until it is a moment that necessitates her assistance, uploading the information at the last moment. Perhaps she is hoping that we will become more inquisitive and look into the different machines in more detail, or she may believe that certain things should be self-evident to us."

"Maybe, you are right." Clarence spoke up. "But, I believe that she likes power and would not disclose anything that she didn't have to unless it became necessary. She even knows the inventories in these centers, something that is simply beyond us."

The discussion took off. "I can understand why she might have been compared by those weird dolphins to a machine." Mathieu mentioned.

"She is cold-blooded, like us reptiles." Joseph said, his lizard lips in a wide, tight smile.

"That is for certain. She hides her feelings-that is if she has any." Diana said. "But I appreciate that. She is a real fighter, a better one even than Stuart and I because she is calculating, direct and hits hard and fast." Diana's facial expressions changed with each word, as her body gradually tightened.

"Ok, Diana," Stuart broke in. "You can relax a bit now, we are not ready to rip anyone apart!" She looked at him with her big brown eyes as if she had no idea what he was referring to.

"She is extraordinarily brilliant," Leonard jumped in and Daniel seconded his statement

"Personally, I wonder if she ever fought physically. Do you know, Pamela?" Randolph asked reflectively.

"No, I have no idea. I know that she takes incredible risks when she drives, flies, navigates, and whatever. She does not seem to be afraid of anything and her energy surges dynamically inside of me as if she enjoys confronting danger, especially at menacing levels." I said in a quiet, serious tone.

"When she is in command, I feel no fear. And, she has that incredible laugh that is sometimes annoying, even earthshaking" My voice growing more and more vibrant. "She laughs at insults and at threats made to her or the group of us. And, she stands her ground playing mind games with those who challenge her." I paused for an instance. "Strangely enough, her personality has not rubbed off on me. I can still feel fear when she disappears during a struggle." I said pensively.

"Do you think that she is from another planet?" Randolph asked.

I had that strange dream weeks ago now but I was still not ready to share it with anyone, not even Peter. "She was the greatest of her time." I answered.

"But, there were geniuses in past generations, as well. And, I believe that I already mentioned some of these people to all of you or some of you." I got no response, so I continued.

"I read about someone named De Vinci who lived in one of the early periods of Human history that was considered to be civilized. His inventions were not just the fruits of an acutely inspired imagination because his inventions became part of ordinary life hundreds of years after his death. Some of his ideas found credibility during Reinhart's time. There was someone else, called Einstein, who was so far beyond his time in physics and mathematics that humans relied upon his undisputable logic for hundreds of years after his death. She was probably just someone like them, simply an intellectually superior being who appears from time to time in human history, conferring their visionary ideas and thus inspiring new generations." That seemed to answer the question.

"Well, it is late and we need sleep. See you all in the morning." I said as I left the veranda to make one more visit to the marine lab. The two prisoners were chatting in English. I heard the royal walrus-dolphin mention that it was just a question of time before they would be back in control.

I coughed, startling him.

"Well, which one are you tonight, that Pamela or Dr. Reinhart?" He laughed boisterously.

"I imagine that you are not as certain as you pretended to be the other day in deciphering our personalities, and that not knowing which one of us you are addressing really bothers you."

If looks could kill, I would have been dead. That hybrid creature was inherently evil. I verified that the cages were well locked. I took a few minutes to observe the nine programmed dolphins, who were lying comfortably on the poolside dangling their fin tails or flippers in the cool water.

"You could just let us in the pool." His former lordship said.

"Oh, but I can't do that." I said emphatically. "I don't want you to forget who you were and what you lost." I turned to look at the programmed dolphins. "They are sublimely happy. They don't remember anything now. They don't even remember that they were and are dolphins." Even though I sensed Reinhart's boldface hate of this walrus-dolphin, I understood that she was humane in her punishment of all his atrocities, because she was more than satisfied with his present state of great unhappiness. When I turned to face him, I too enjoyed looking at the sad, beaten down look that was now on his lordship's face.

I left the lab knowing that we could not leave these two creatures living next to each other and sharing stories in the Marine center. The best course of action would be to program the dolphin that was no longer suffering from his injuries and bruises. Even though I initially wanted to keep him around as a secondary source of information, he was already under the influence of the walrus-dolphin, who we would hereinafter call WD. He could join the rest of the programmed dolphins in the swimming pool.

I was certain that neither Fleming nor Jarrod would be able to control WD. There was every possibility that WD would gain their confidence by manipulating them into believing that freeing him was the only logical action that an android would and therefore should take.

Even though I was so exhausted, I decided to handle this problem before going to bed. I contacted the main center. The Group of 5 responded so quickly to my call that I had a clear view of what they were actually doing before I called. They were using the video-surveillance equipment to monitor the other humans' activities-spying, and, they were masters at espionage.

"Good Evening, Pamela." Crawford replied, as he motioned to the other members of the group to move close to him.

"Why are you in that telecommunications laboratory by yourselves?" I was curious to know what kind of excuse their android logic would contrive.

"Just verifying that everyone is safe! We do that every evening now that we have become aware of some of the things that were happening outside this center." Gordon surprised me with her clever subterfuge of the truth.

"Right!" I replied sarcastically. "I have something more important for you to do for me now...which will keep you out of trouble." They stood at attention, their eyes lowered in respect.

"I want to move WD." I quickly explained that in our center, he needs constant surveillance. I do not think that Jarrod and Fleming will be able to handle him."

"Excellent! Excellent idea!" The former Governor shouted.

"I cannot bring him back on our planes because we don't have the space." I hesitated. "He also needs to be restrained. He is very strong and even though he has a bulky body, I believe that he could move fast enough to injure our crew members if he got loose."

They discussed the problem together and then suggested that they send a special aircraft, like one that transported heavy weaponry, to our Marine center. They informed me that there were some very large, metal cages that were used in the past for wild animals. "None of those animals exist today, or, more precisely, we have no knowledge of their existence but we have some of those cages. They are in the android warehouse." Flanders explained.

"The only question that I have," Miller said, "is whether he can survive outside of water for several hours?"

"Good question." I had to admit. "He keeps his head above water level in the aquarium, even though he was completely submerged at the bottom of the ocean when we found him." I took a deep breathe. "He can obviously live comfortably in or outside of water. I shall have to study him in more detail. If he were not such a despicable creature, he would be very useful for planetary exploration. There might have been hope for his descendants, but-well, it was not possible to save them."

They agreed to take care of everything and make sure that the plane, with proper equipment, arrived before we woke up in the morning. "That is one of the advantages of having androids working for you, they can go 24 hours a day." I chuckled.

I lay awake for a long time, a bleak emptiness where there

should have been thoughts. When I finally closed my eyes, I had the strange sensation that my very being was escaping its physical bounds; that I was floating above my body, my world and its earthly restraints, and this transcendence of reality, tempted and enticed me. I passed lethargically through a space filled with hazy images, ghostly things that languished in the distance, remaining mobile illusory forms even as I came in close contact with them. I drifted on in space and time, shuttering violently as a thick, stifling air engulfed and absorbed me. All that I am, was and might become had no importance because I no longer existed in a unique and finite sense. Succumbing to my destiny, a qualified irresistible universe of knowledge, I transformed. And then, gratified with this cerebral metamorphosis, I retrieved my physical self, and took my place upon a large stone, in a floral garden, and sat waiting, just waiting for someone or something to happen.

I shivered on awakening, just like the last time I had a similar nightmare. The meaning of this nightmare, like the one before, eluded me. I wondered if I had tapped into one of Reinhart's nightmares.

"Should I talk to Peter about these dreams? Would he be able to explain them to me?" Filled my thoughts.

I got up to take a shower, hoping to soothe my body and my mind. Now I somehow knew that Reinhart was inspiring these dreams. Maybe she wanted to disclose her origins. Maybe Reinhart wanted to destroy me. Why? We worked well together. Maybe this mythical floral garden of my dreams, different from the one that Andrew created, exists in another time or space and she wants me to find it. I shook my head violently as if the dream and its message would fall from my mind onto the bathroom floor, to be read and discarded, like others.

I went straight to the laboratory where I found Jarrod and Fleming, along with a few android pilots, ready to transport the cargo. They were staring at WD when they turned in my direction, as if still under some sort of hypnotic trance, bowing their heads in respect.

I asked them to assist me in sedating and moving the dolphin out of the medical lab. I took one of the few remaining visual receptors and placed it in the same region of this dolphin's brain with the same dexterity that I used to insert this programming device into his comrades. Before he awakened, we put him in the confined pool area with the other programmed dolphins.

"You will have to verify that the programming and the wrist band are functioning properly, if he awakens before I return," reminding Jarrod and Fleming how important it was to control these creatures.

WD was trying to rip off the grill over the aquarium when we returned to the lab. "Let me out of here! Now!" He screamed like he was still in the position to give orders.

"Calm down! You are leaving this center on board an aircraft." I said. His eyes were cold with hatred, his walrus tusks forced to a menacing size. "How did he do that?" I wondered to myself, as I stood infatuated by his efforts to frighten me.

It took the four android assistants more than twenty minutes to lift WD out of the aquarium. Once he was on the ground, they pushed him violently, using laser shocks, into the animal cage. But when he was finally inside the cage, he assumed a demeanor, diametrically opposed to his previous efforts to try to escape. He reclined lazily, revealing layers and layers of body fat. "I am looking forward to meeting the Group of 5." He called out to me in a thundering voice, just as I turned to leave.

I started to laugh, a silly laugh, a Pamela laugh that annoyed him more than Reinhart's. "So it is you! You, that Pamela, who is making this decision!" He yelled.

"Yes!" I replied. "If I were you, though, I would not get too comfortable with the Group of 5." He grumbled. "They are more diabolical than you could ever imagine...after all they are Reinhart's creations." I heard him coughing vigorously as if my words were stuck in his throat.

I waited until the androids left with the cargo. There was nothing keeping us at this Marine center, except my curiosity over where the group of humans of many colors put up camp. I suggested that we all take one more tour of the area in our land vehicles, going in our own directions, so we could compare notes.

I took Jason and Ludovic with me in my vehicle, because I

thought they would be able to guide me to the encampment. It was only by luck that we found the remains of Ludovic's community. They had constructed clay buildings, much like the one Jason was in when I found him. The soft, thick, quilted bedding that was provided for them by one of the centers made the interior appear cozy. The reddish brown soil absorbed the sunlight during the day, giving the inside of the hut, a warm glow, in the evening. I took soil samples for analysis.

The members of Ludovic's community had to walk for more than a day to get to the sandy beach, where WD told me they were captured for food. Ludovic did not remember hearing about anyone being lost or missing. He told me that, like us, they received food and water regularly from the center. So, they were not forced to fend for themselves on the outside. And, both Ludovic and Jason denied ever seeing the ocean before they arrived at the Marine center and insisted that they never heard anyone mention its existence.

It was evident that neither Ludovic nor Jason were privy to everything that was happening within the colony of humans of many colors. Some of them must have ventured off alone or with others, exploring the environment around them.

My thoughts then turned to the explanations given to me regarding the various activities in the Marine center and in its close surroundings. I could understand why programmed humans might not have resisted their termination and entered willingly into the ocean where the dolphins collected their drowning bodies.

But I could not understand why the deprogrammed humans of many colors were hypnotized by the dolphins' clicking sounds and entered spell-bound into the jaws of those dolphin predators. Why were the other members of the humans of many colors so complacent that they accepted the disappearance of their members as normal, or even inevitable? Or, did they search for them, and fall into the traps buried on the beaches? Did they ever try to defend themselves when the Captain gathered up members of their community for dolphin food?

I surmised that my questions would go unanswered because Ludovic was the only surviving member of that community and he was but a child when the others were killed.

We boarded the aircraft late in the afternoon. The Group of 5 and a dozen other android assistants were waiting for us in the transport unit and took care of everything, as we dashed off to see friends and family left behind.

I don't know if family homecomings were as splendid as ours was in other periods of human history. We all went in our own directions, seeking the person or persons whose very existence validated ours. Because we did not grow up knowing parental love-but rather the cold, impersonal android method of child care-we wanted, perhaps needed, to be more demonstrative about our feelings of concern and love for our offspring. Perhaps our flamboyance and obsession with parenting might be considered by future generations of humans as a large fissure in our cerebral rationality. Nonetheless, what might or could be concluded was of little importance to us as we endeavored to reassure and interact by overtly displaying our feelings of love and affection for our children.

I was startled by how much taller Frederic appeared when I first caste my eyes on him. Passing back and forth through different time zones was disconcerting and left a confused impression of how much time had actually gone by; the twenty-four hour a day clock in the main center with its numerical day count was our reference point now and would remain so in the future. Frederic only changed in our eyes, because in reality he was only one month older and had not grown more than a couple inches taller.

We spent a long moment with him recounting our adventures, hoping to inspire a desire in him to join us one day. He asked lots of questions about the new arrivals, Jason and Ludovic. I was pleased that Frederic was neither horrified nor repulsed by Jason's worn and aged body, more visibly eroded with time than that of Ferdinand and Ralph, the agronomist, or by Ludovic's colorful body and distorted facial features. He like his young friends accepted physical differences as natural, thus countering the Group of 5's view that humans would always be affected by the physical aspects of someone. He told us that he found their differences intriguing and that he wanted to get to know them both better.

I explained to him how age had settled into Jason, and that his leathery, weathered skin and crippled body were the result of many years of wandering and living on the outside. I also mentioned that Ludovic was the victim of hereditary chromosomal anomalies and the reckless genetic modification of his DNA by the Group of 5, who in a futile attempt to improve upon his genetic code, worsened it. He listened patiently, registering what he could understand of my detailed scientific explanation. He soon tired of the discussion and asked his father to work out with him in the gym, giving me a big kiss before he left. That was perfect for me because I wanted to check on the Group of 5, who greeted me dutifully, with their eyes lowered, when I entered their office.

They showed me where they arranged the various geological and marine samples. I also wanted to know if all the reports I requested from the Air and Space center on incoming vehicles and audio-visual tapes, as well as the list of all the victims offered to the carnivorous dolphins, were received and ready for us to consult. They nodded and expressed, again, their regret that all of this happened.

I was also interested in Ludovic's DNA. Flanders replied, as if under constraint. "We put it in the fertility lab, in the cool air chamber, and have not touched or studied it." I told him that I wanted to look at the DNA on my own and would let him know if I needed him.

We walked together to the diving unit where they had put WD. He was still in that large cage. The Group of 5 had put a medium-sized aquarium in the cage that he could easily enter and exit if he wanted to bathe. His eyes met mine with a cold, blank stare. The Group of 5's choice of location was logical but not what I preferred.

They suggested that he could use the dive tank. The idea of training in the same water that this miserable creature played in and maybe urinated or defecated in disgusted me. So, letting him use the dive tank for exercise was out of the question. I suggested that they find another place and left for the fertility unit to check on the DNA of Ludovic.

I was in the cool air chamber in the lab, hidden from view, looking for the DNA sample, when I heard Jonathan and Diana enter the lab. I didn't have time to announce my presence before they were wrapped in each other's arms, confessions of love pouring out, under hot, heavy breathing. I felt embarrassed being made aware of their deep feelings for each other and did not want to go on eavesdropping on any more of their declarations of love. I cleared my throat loudly, signaling that they were not alone.

They had separated and were pretending to be having an ordinary conversation about the Marine center when I got close. We exchanged friendly smiles and well wishes as I passed by them. "There is nothing surprising in all of this." I thought. "After all, Diana and Jonathan were a couple when we were living on the outside." I shook my head, releasing myself from these thoughts. "I have more important things to do than to follow the romantic lives of my team members. I'll study the DNA tomorrow."

I went for dinner, ignoring the dinner conversations and focusing on the projects for tomorrow. I left before the others and fell rapidly into a deep, soothing sleep.

Only our core group was at the meeting the following morning. We shared our experiences in more detail with John, Mathilda, Benjamin, Stanislas, Sarah, Ruth and Jonathan. The discussions turned around the administration of the 2 other centers.

"What are we going to do with the Captain?" John asked. "We had him put in the android storage unit."

"He has been shut down, so for the moment he is better off in storage." I replied.

"We should study his programming." John retorted.

"Yes, but Drager is not here with us for the moment. We had to put him in charge of the Air and Space Center." He looked at me, puzzled.

'I don't want to tackle the Captain on my own,' passed through my mind, before I addressed the others. "The Captain...is dangerous."

"Can't we just remove the program and see how or why it was tampered with?" John did not want to abandon the subject.

"I informed you, days ago now, that the Captain was programmed by Reinhart and then reprogrammed by Murdoc." I leaned back in my chair, in a relaxed position, my shoulders slumping slightly, and studied the faces of my colleagues. They were scrutinizing me through slit eyes. I decided to change the subject. "Personally,

I think that we have more pressing problems, like WD, the DNA of Ludovic, capturing satellite images of the planet, and others so that the Captain should not be a priority."

"I don't agree." Randolph broke in. "I think that it is essential that we study the programming of the Captain." His face held forward in a steady gaze, giving him a palpable air of authority. "Remember, the androids at the Air and Space center only responded to Reinhart's orders. They might have been tampered with as well. Murdoc lived in that center for a few months or so before his body terminated. I think that we will better understand the programming of those androids, if we dismantle the Captain."

I was the only one who didn't agree with Randolph, so under pressure, I reluctantly promised to work with them on that.

I then suggested that we give Ludovic the right to decide whether or not he wanted to go through reconstructive surgery. "If he is not bothered by his appearance, it might be better to let him live like he is. In the meantime, I shall study his DNA profile and let you know how the Group of 5_blundered." That suggestion was retained. We all agreed that I should meet with Ludovic before the end of the day.

John was still working on the time-warp problem. His hypothesis was that Reinhart's calculations were off. I could feel the blood rush to my face, revealing Reinhart's overt rejection of his conclusion. I diplomatically suggested that he continue his research and that I would collaborate with him later on that. He had not had the opportunity to study satellite imagery, so Peter and Stuart volunteered for that.

"I would like to have access to all the information the Air and Space center forwarded regarding inter-planetary travel, the number of astronauts killed on arrival, as well as the equipment confiscated by the androids, if everyone agrees." Peter requested, his direction of the program implicitly approved.

"I agree, Peter, but I would like to be kept informed of your progress. I am interested in that sector as well." Stuart replied. Others principally Randolph, James and Diana, offered their assistance and registered their interest in space travel.

I had to raise the WD problem. The androids had not yet gotten back to me on a more suitable location for WD. I had an interesting solution in mind, the zoo and, in particular, the polar bear enclosure. There was a large basin in the arctic environment, with its white shiny surface that gleamed like snow, where the Group of 5 had put on display a number of stuffed polar bears, hoping to fascinate us programmed humans, years ago now. The basin, filled with salty, ocean water, would accommodate his aquatic needs, while the surrounding ground would satisfy his non-aquatic side. I glanced rapidly at the others, satisfying myself that no one was playing with their fingers or letting their eyes drift off in weariness or boredom, before continuing.

"We need to discuss WD." I cleared my throat. "I want to inform you that I asked the Group of 5 to sedate WD on his arrival to our center so that they could run a scan of his body and take blood samples, before moving him back into the transport cage that was large enough for them to install a medium-sized aquarium."

"Wasn't that a bit risky?" John said, sitting very straight in his chair.

"Maybe, but," I sighed, "because we needed more information about his physical and physiological characteristics, scanning him on arrival in our center seemed logical." I said in a low, soft voice.

"And, what did you discover?" Diana prompted me.

"WD is an interesting hybrid." A quick look in their direction assured me that I had their undivided attention. "Apart from mixed walrus-dolphin physical features, he has a predominately dolphin face-that is if we ignore the slight whiskers on the side of his mouth and his protracting tusks. The physiological side of WD is what interests Reinhart the most, so I shall pass on what she has uploaded to me." I cleared my throat.

"Both dolphins and walruses have blubber that serves as a thermoregulatory system and both species are equipped with a complicated system of circulatory adjustment to conserve body temperature. They have large red blood cells that store oxygen in a complex blood vessel system to facilitate deep dives. And, although WD has a large, bulky body, he can mimic the dolphin, because his normally rounded, but streamlined, body can take on a torpedo shape to reach high swim speed." I paused for an instance to assimilate other information Reinhart was now uploading to me.

"WD needs both land and water to survive. On land, he can absorb heat, giving him a rosy color and helping him to support very cold water. The walrus physiological features of WD are significantly more advantageous in comparison to the dolphin. He has the ability to store a larger percentage of oxygen in his red blood cells and muscles and in a dive, all blood flow is cut off from the skin, extremities and stomach, ensuring an efficient and lengthy use of oxygen." I paused to catch my breath.

"He also has expandable, elastic pockets, on either side of his esophagus that can hold up to 13 gallons of air. After diving, he can inflate these air pockets which act as a life-saver so that he can bob on the surface of the ocean in a vertical position. He can sleep up to 19 hours on land and can swim up to 84 hours without stopping. Like a dolphin he does at times resort to unihemispheric slow wave sleep, meaning that one half of the brain sleeps, while the other half is active and alert. Unlike the dolphin, WD's walrus physiological features give him more mobility during unihemispheric slow wave sleep. He can swim continuously, making turns, and otherwise navigating without any difficulty with only one side of his brain active."

"It sounds like he would be an asset to us in the exploration of the ocean." Diana said.

"You are right. But can we trust him?" I sighed. "Well, it should be clear now that he needs both land and water, so the polar bear enclosure seems to be an appropriate choice. I shall look into the kind of security system we will need to install in order to prevent him from escaping."

I feigned deep thought, closing my eyes and tightening my cheek muscles, before continuing. "He has to be watched 24 hours a day because he cannot be trusted. There are things about him, his personality, particularly his manipulative nature that worry me. For instance, he might have spent quality time in the Marine center conniving with the Captain whose programming was definitely tampered with. In any event, WD certainly understands how to interact to his advantage with ordinary androids and is going to try to gain the confidence of the Group of 5. He is very clever."

"Why don't you want to program him?" Ruth asked.

"Because I want him alert to answer questions. He knows a lot about what went on before and after the explosion and his ances- tors survived over all those thousands of years that the earth was in a new evolutionary stage." Heads nodded. "But, he is dangerous. We will have to keep him penned up under a high security system."

"What are you feeding him?" Mathilda asked.

"Plants." I folded my arms in front of me, showing my authority. "He is an omnivore, just like us. We have learned to survive on ve- getables, fruits, and grains. His system can tolerate plants even if his gastronomic tastes are more carnivorous. He will just have to adjust to a vegetarian diet like we have. Anyway, for the moment, we have no protein-based product to offer to him, because we are not going to reduce our own food supply to feed him." She looked at me with a very straight level gaze. I didn't back up. "You were not thinking about letting him eat humans, were you, Mathilda?" I mustered as much energy as I could into that question.

"No-of course not!" She exclaimed. "I just wondered because it would be easier if he were programmed. He would not remember his previous diet and...cravings. I agree, though, that he might have vital information that could be useful to us and that we must pry that out of him." She lowered her eyes. "But, it is not going to be easy to interact with him."

This discussion ended abruptly, when Ferdinand intervened, reminding us that we needed to decide upon a political organiza- tion. As always, we tabled that subject. He then mentioned that he had been reading a great deal about religion and asked us if anyone believed in a higher being, a God. I retorted that I was also in awe of the subject when I first entered the library and I explored it in great detail whenever I got access to the Library.

"And..."

I interrupted him. "Gordon told me that I was like all humans obsessed with who created us. She pretended that androids were superior because they knew who their creator was and did not have to look for their 'raison d'être'." I also mentioned that I had already informed the other members about the various religious tradi- tions and the different Gods that humans worshipped at different periods in human history. "We all agreed that unless this God presented itself to us, we would have to rely only upon ourselves."

"Interesting." He replied, sucking in his lips. "But, rather supercilious. I entreat you to learn more about political organization and the philosophical and spiritual aspects that accompanied earlier human existence."

"Unfortunately, Ferdinand, seeking a God, has to take a backseat to all the more vital projects." His eyes were cold as ice. "Nonetheless, I agree to a certain extent with you that religion was a constant denominator in human society even though I found it to be more a source of conflict than concordance and harmony. But, like you, I went astray from the rational world, hoping to confront a superior being capable of liberating us and taking care of us afterwards." I looked straight into Ferdinand's bold, assertive eyes. "We voted as a group in favor of putting our faith in humans."

I quickly skimmed the faces of my colleagues and friends. Those who had not already closed their eyes were yawning. Disappointed with their indifference, I decided to be a little more diplomatic towards Ferdinand and addressed the group in a loud voice. "Nonetheless, Ferdinand has raised a very interesting point. We should all become familiar or become more familiar with how humans worked and lived together in society, by delving into their origins, their interests, their aspirations, and so forth." They bent their heads and covered their mouths with their hands, smothering their laughter.

"I shall continue to work on creating a formal political organization for our world." Ferdinand announced, his strong voice registering his disapproval. "Is there anything else to discuss today?"

"Yes, Ralph, how well do you know Andrew?" I asked.

"The pudgy guy who builds caverns?" he rolled his eyes round inquisitively.

"He also builds botanical gardens."

"Yes, the Group of 5 came to see me about him the other day. They were looking for someone to take the responsibility for Andrew's actions, and tried to convince me that I was the motor in this botanical garden project." He laughed with zest and vigor but none of us joined in.

"Ok, it is a weird situation. I was programmed at the time." He glanced to his right. "Ferdinand, you can confirm that." Ferdinand nodded. "I deprogrammed the moment that I was escorted to the termination center. That was when I became hysterical, screaming and striking the android assistants who left me to seek a member of the Group of 5 to assist in my termination. A split second was all that Ferdinand needed to save me." He looked at us hoping for some display of sympathy. His longing was in vain, but not because we didn't believe Ralph, but because we were united against Andrew who we considered to be both an opportunist and egocentric.

"He told us that you gave him the plants or maybe just the seeds and the soil that he needed to create a tropical paradise." I added.

"Yes, that is true, Pamela. It was one of the projects that was assigned to me. Nonetheless, I had no idea that I was helping him build a tropical paradise." He covered his face with his hands, hiding himself from our disdain. We waited patiently. He eventually sat straight in his chair with his hands folded in a steeple position in front of him. "I don't even remember the list that he gave me. I was a caretaker for the agricultural unit and, of course, an agronomist. I took orders, like all of you." He looked at Ferdinand for help.

"Pamela, how can you accuse him of conspiracy? He was programmed." Ferdinand said in a terse tone.

"You are right, Ferdinand. And, I am sorry about the way in which I asked my questions." I recognized that my behavior was a bit rash. "I am not accusing Ralph of any form of complicity in this. I just want clarification. Andrew did not strike me as honest and the Group of 5 did not efface that image of him. It would be helpful if you, Ralph, could give us some more information about what Andrew was doing. For example, was he programmed when you met him?"

"Yes, definitely, but I was also programmed. You know that the visual receptor was incredibly convincing. I saw him as a tall, slim man with striking, deep-set dark blue eyes on an oblong face." He slammed his fists dramatically down on the table. "I, like all of you, was programmed to carry out requests. Of course, today, I might have asked him why he wanted this information, but, at that time, I gave him what he wanted and needed."

We sat in silence, absorbed in the deceptions of our own pasts, until he picked up the conversation. "All that I remember is that he told me that he was an architect and that the Bright Ones wanted him to decorate a building with floral arrangements." He stopped, his eyes moving rapidly in their sockets as he struggled to focus on the content of that conversation. "I think that I suggested that he plant some trees. I may have even offered him small plants. And, of course, I gave him the soil." He breathed deeply to calm his nerves. "I never saw the final project. In fact, I don't believe that I ever saw him again either."

"Well, you two programmed humans were no threat for the Group of 5 and their projects. Perhaps they imagined themselves vacationing in this floral garden, as if they could appreciate its curative effect. Maybe it was a trap to entice humans who wandered off on their own." I said, remembering my own happy, programmed life of conformity to an illusory world.

"I do believe though that Andrew said that he suggested building a floral garden because of the underground water source." I closed my eyes as images of the garden past through my mind. "In any event, it is a magnificent achievement." I said, as I breathed deeply, imagining an array of floral scents, riding on a low breeze, penetrating my nostrils, making me dizzy with pleasure. "Ok, Ralph," I said, breaking the spell, "if you think of anything else that might help us to better understand Andrew, please let me know."

"I have a question, for Pamela, or Reinhart." Randolph weighed in. "Are we going to go off on another exploratory trip soon? And if so, where?"

"We have to study the satellite maps. Once we have an idea of how much land surface exists and where it is located, we can all give our opinions. Is there anyone here who is trained in geology?"

"I am not a geologist per se, but a mining engineer. I think that I could be helpful." Mathieu said. And so it was agreed that Mathieu would examine the geological structures in detail, assisted by Stuart, who appeared confident in that field.

When the meeting ended, I went to check on the Group of 5. They considered my suggestion to move WD to the zoo, more particularly, the former stuffed polar bear enclosure, to be an excellent idea.

"The space is perfect. He should have the environment that he needs. The only problem is that there is no high security surveillance system in place." Crawford cleared his throat in that grinding android style. "Perhaps John, or Peter, could install something. We can take care of selecting the androids to guard the facility."

I still wanted to visit the installation before going further so they followed me out to the zoo. It was large enough for five or six Walrus-Dolphins, so WD would not feel penned in, due to lack of space. The glass wall enclosures, embedded with fine metal webbing, invisible to the naked eye, were high enough and solid enough to prevent him from breaking through. The small entrance to the enclosure, hidden from view, was the weak point. With time on his side, he might eventually break the locks and escape. I told the Group of 5 that I would speak to Peter and John about the situation and let them find a solution. WD would have to stay where he was for another few days.

"We have fed him marine algae." Gordon mentioned. "He does not eat much of it. Maybe he is going to starve himself to death."

"I doubt it. He likes himself too much to do that." I laughed to myself, knowing that they did not understand what I meant.

I left them after reminding them to find android staff to clean up the unit and to organize twenty-four hour surveillance and then spoke to John and Peter about installing an up-to-date security system that the Group of 5 would not be able to penetrate, thereby advancing in their research. They knew what to do and even assured me that they already had something available that would solve the problem.

I stopped by to see WD who did not look any thinner. "Well, well, look who is here to pester me and try to pry into my mind." He slapped his flippers together like he was applauding.

I ignored his provocative remark and concentrated more on his movements and posture to reassure myself that he was not in any debilitated state of health. "Leaving already," he commented when I turned away from him. "I actually miss conversations as much as I miss giving orders." He protested.

I stopped in my tracks and turned back in his direction. He was standing up, his heavy body leaning against the cage, looking rather forlorn, with his walrus tusks drooping from the sides of his mouth. "Ok I'll give you a chance to show me that you can be useful. What do you know about life forms in the high seas?"

"Not too much, actually." He slid back into a sitting position. "I did send several groups of dolphins out to look for food. The few who came back told strange stories. They mentioned enormous, reptilian sea monsters, or dragons, that could leap a hundred feet in the air." He shook his head in disbelief. "I thought that their imaginations played games on them when they got too far away from home." He had my attention.

"They told me that these sea creatures took no interest in them. Instead, they fought each other in violent, horrific battles that produced devastatingly high waves and tumultuous ocean undercurrents."

He raised his flippers in denial of the authenticity of these reports. "Those cowardly dolphins---that is what I referred to them as---told me that they returned because it was useless to wander off too far. That is why we stayed put and ate what was offered to us." He made some sick gurgling sound calibrated to show his boredom. "I have already been through all of that with you and I know that you dislike my culinary tastes." He stared at me with his walrus tusks discretely hidden behind an emotionally empty, plastic smile. "If you can believe this, those dolphins told me that the winner of the battle, devoured the loser!"

"How long did it take them to reach this hypothetically uncivilized, dinosaurian region?" Whatever they encountered, machine or life form, I was interested in knowing more about the nature and length of the journey.

"Unfortunately for you, we have no notion of time." He rubbed his bulky face with his right flipper. "They seemed to be gone long enough that we believed that they were dead. That is the best I can do." He grumbled to himself. "The dolphins who engaged in these missions were some of our fastest swimmers and had long distance endurance capacity. I believe that Reinhart could calculate the distance they went, which would probably correspond to a two week period on the outside. But, the time element is pure conjecture on my part."

"Did they see any other life forms?"

"No, as I already mentioned, they found no other sources of meaty food. Sorry, I am not trying to disgust you at this moment." He surprised me with his attempt at politeness. "Either these monsters exist and they turned on each other as sources of food when their hunting grounds ran dry, or they are the only life forms in the middle of the high seas and feed off of each other."

"I appreciate your sharing this information with me," I said, as I turned to leave.

"Wait, Pamela," I turned back in his direction, "I know that it is you, because you have a musical voice and are filled with kindness." He was showing me how clever he was trying to titillate the Reinhart inside of me. "We might be despicable creatures, as you said, but like all creatures, our principle objective was survival." He methodically moved his walrus tusks in and out of his mouth to keep my attention.

"You are right to imagine that we might kill and consume you. I am still a predator, but a predator that has had time to think about his actions and to wonder if there isn't something else interesting about humans, besides their taste." I coughed and he shook his head slowly. "I hope that we shall be able to have more fundamental conversations in the future." He collapsed lazily on his side. "Would you mind telling me where you intend to imprison me?"

"Fair enough. There is a zoo that was occupied by stuffed animals." He let out such a loud, boisterous laugh that so alarmed me that my thoughts stopped, leaving me speechless. When I finally recovered from the effects of his very unpleasant laughter, I added. "There is a polar bear complex that has a large basin surrounded by lots of dry land which should appeal to you."

"Thank you. It sounds like a nice place to live." He waved goodbye before closing his eyes.

"Manipulator—that is what he is! I am definitely going to have to secure his living quarters and make certain that he cannot have contact with the android guards, especially verbal contact, and I shall have to adapt their programming accordingly." Reinhart jarred me out of my placid mindset, reminding me of how easily humans could be manipulated and how dangerous WD was. We would have to limit his verbal contact with humans as well.

I returned to the Group of 5 who had already sent off a clean-up crew and were activating several androids in the security force unit. I mentioned that Reinhart wanted to add another program to prevent any manipulation of these android security guards by anyone else or by WD.

"Reinhart is over reacting." The former Governor commented and the others nodded vehemently.

I ignored his comment and revealed the content of the conversation I just had with WD to get their reaction.

"Now, I can understand her position very well." Crawford replied. "WD might be dangerous for humans. He mixes logic, with flattery. This is very confusing for humans to deal with. Sorry, Pamela, but humans often times hear only the flattery."

"Well, Dr. Crawford, you continue to surprise me." Gordon retorted. "It is true that he mixes the two opposing elements in an effective manner. And yet, Reinhart saw through it." She looked at me in a maternal way, her eyes glowing softly. "You, Pamela, you are very forgiving. You want to believe that humans---and hybrid, intelligent creatures---are predominately good." She said through clenched teeth. "I have told you over and over again that humans are fundamentally vicious and mean, like this WD, and that you must learn how to see through their mind games."

"If I can venture into this discussion," the Governor commented, "it would appear that only the humans would be susceptible to these mind games. But, Dr. Reinhart wants to add another program to our android security guards to fortify them against "cyber brain washing," if I understand the problem correctly?" He made a guttural sound like he was choking on his own words. "And yet, I see no problem in appeasing Reinhart."

"Enough of this. I did not come here to be insulted."

"We are not insulting you, Pamela, we are just a bit confused." Miller replied.

"I don't care about your confusion, just contact me when these security guards are fully activated." I understood that Reinhart believed that WD would play on android logic to manipulate them into doing things for him, but I was not going to reveal that to the Group of 5. So, I walked out of the room and ran straight into Randolph moving rapidly down the corridor.

"What are you doing here?" He asked.

I confided in him about the conversation with WD. He gritted his teeth. "Listen to me, Pamela." He moved up close to me, tenderly taking my chin in his hand, lifting my downturned face up until our eyes met. "I would have had the same reaction as you-ready to collaborate or even trust him when he was revealing his stories." His eyes twinkled teasingly. "Reinhart is cold-blooded, so she signaled his manipulative style. She is insensitive to that kind of cajoling. She definitely has her charm, but I prefer you, Pamela. We humans need to believe that we can trust others, at least until it is very clear that we can't. That is what we are doing everyday...trusting each other. "

His fingers moved so gently threw my hair and slowly down over my neck and shoulders, before he regained control of himself, and backed away from me. "Look at the positive side, he gave you vital information when he revealed the existence of those sea monsters. Now we can protect ourselves when we fly over the deep sea."

"Thanks, Randolph..." He didn't let me finish.

"I have to go." He said apologetically. "I promised to meet Mathilda in the birth center."

"He was right to leave quickly," I reasoned, taking deep breaths to cool down.

I moved mechanically down the hallway, stopping by to see John and Peter, who showed me the technology they intended to use. Reinhart came bursting through, sending me information, while meticulously examining the technology.

"You are missing an important element, even though you have progressed impressively with your research." Reinhart commented, as she adjusted the operating system to provide for better feedback between the user and the computer. She wanted any movement to be captured, with constant visual, video and audio transmission.

"This equipment will be the eyes and ears of the computer, if you like. The computer can study the imagery and other information sent back to it, adjusting the receptors automatically, when necessary. We shall place the equipment in strategic places in and around the polar bear complex. Have you come up with something impenetrable for the gate?" She asked.

"We are still working on it." John replied. "He could probably crash through it."

"We cannot ignore that possibility." Reinhart replied. "I would suggest putting a tamper-resistant collar monitor on him that will track his position. We can also place a tracking device in his shoulder area. We should post a drone programmed to fire on him if he leaves the confines and set up other defense systems on the inside and outside of the gate that will discourage him from taking any risk. With his bulky body, he can't make a rapid escape and it will be difficult for him to hide. Do what you think is necessary." Reinhart disappeared inside of me and I got up and strutted out leaving them with the up-dated equipment and suggestions on how to control the beast.

Gordon was leaving her office as I rounded the corner. I called out to her and she turned in reply. "Pamela, it has been a long time since we chatted." She still liked to use that term, I thought as I nodded. "Perhaps we could just sit down in the office for a while?" Talking to her alone seemed like a good idea so I followed her back to the office...now empty.

We sat next to each other, close enough though that we could reach out, touch and even... fondle each other. Memories of those steamy sexual encounters that were part of my early cooperation with Gordon passed vividly in front of my eyes, and I was swept up in the sexual madness of another time. My heart was beating rapidly and my breathing, deep and intense. Like in a trance, I ran my tongue slowly over my lips...my legs parting just enough to reveal my sudden craving for lustful pleasure.

I saw a smile spread slowly across her lips, as she gently pulled me close up against her, while her hands moved in stimulating, sexually arousing wavelike motions over my shoulders, as they descended, and tenderly caressed my breasts. I was no longer thinking but feeling... that wet warmth of desire overpowering me.

But alas when my lips aflame with passion met hers, I felt a violent burst of energy, like an electric shock, passing through me, forcing me to fall backwards from my chair, as Reinhart surfaced inside of me, instantly driving Gordon away from me and wiping out even the slightest trace of sexual heat inside of me, reminding me that the past was the past. Under Reinhart's spell, I regained my composure so quickly and moved my chair a comfortable distance away from Gordon, before inquiring in a dry, lifeless tone about her relationship with Mathilda.

"You know how I am, Pamela." She lifted her eyebrows slightly. "I crave or perhaps need physical contact with humans. It must be in my programming."

"Not at all!" Reinhart replied emphatically controlling my vocal chords and showing Gordon that she was definitely present during this conversation.

"Excuse me, I thought that I was talking to Pamela."

"You are talking to both of us. And, your physical interest in humans befuddles me because it is not imbedded in any of your programs. I should probably take a look at the problem in your programming and readjust it." Reinhart suggested.

Gordon fidgeted and argued that it was a good thing that her programming had gone awry. "If I had been like the others, I would never have asked to study Pamela and you, Dr. Reinhart, would not be here today."

Reinhart let out a relatively refined laugh, soft and soothing to the ears. "I adore your android logic...after all, I gave it to you! And, your behavioral interaction with humans is so refreshingly illogical at times that I won't touch it...that is if you stay away from Pamela." Gordon's eyes bulged. She got the message.

Reinhart abruptly disappeared and I was able to continue alone with Gordon. I wanted to understand Mathilda. Gordon admired Mathilda's ability to analyze human behavior and they spent most of their time comparing notes. I discovered that their sexual relationship was more rewarding for Mathilda than for Gordon, who was still unable to feel emotionally satisfied or happy and could not experience even the slightest orgasmic pleasure.

Gordon believed that Mathilda was insecure and that she felt threatened by strong personalities. I represented a strong personality to her not just when Reinhart was present, but even when I was the dominant personality. Nonetheless, according to Gordon, Mathilda considered me to be a close friend, something that slightly tempered my judgment of Mathilda.

"I enjoyed my relationship with you, Pamela. I understood that you wanted to please me and that justified everything I did to keep you alongside of me." I flushed with embarrassment at her comment, especially since, just minutes ago, I confirmed my intense sexual attraction to her. "Randolph was exceptional for me." She went on. "Of course, he is the only man I was ever close to but I can't imagine anyone being more sexually alive than him." She sighed. "Sadly, I had to feign my sexual pleasure with high shrieks and quivering motions like I did with you and am doing with Mathilda." She sighed again. "Dr. Reinhart could help all of us to be human by giving us a complete emotional configuration, and an orgasm." I ignored her statement.

"And what do you know about Andrew?"

She told me that the Governor, Eugene, did not share everything with the group and that he entered into private contracts with John, with me and with Andrew. "If I had to conjecture, I would say that he had a weakness for humans. He looked for solutions, other than termination, to deal with deprogramming." She tapped her long, android fingers on the desktop, like she used to do to get my attention when I was the subject of her research. "You must remember that I told you on many occasions that you could count on the Governor for support. And, he was also my ally even though he hid that during Board meetings."

"His human counterpart was forgiving and kind. That must be why he acted like he did." Reinhart intervened. "So, you think that the Governor simply gave him these architectural projects to protect him?" Gordon nodded. "You don't think that he was using Andrew for his own interests, like setting up a new environment for himself?"

"No." She replied emphatically.

"What do you know about the humans of many colors?" Reinhart queried.

"You know that we took mutated fertilized ovum...by accident." She insisted. "I know that you, Dr. Reinhart, consider that our

396

actions were reckless. They were. We should have acted more rationally when we organized our departure to this center, but we had to hide because Murdoc was looking for us. Things had been rearranged in the laboratory—maybe by Murdoc or curious human revolutionaries who got into the facilities. They had put them back on the shelves, but not in the right place and order. We did not take the time to verify specimens, rather assumed that everything was in its proper place." She sat motionless for several minutes. "We were sabotaged, like Miller and the rest of us told you months ago. But, the humans of many colors were your creation, Dr. Reinhart."

"Not exactly. I had found many cases of leopard syndrome among the non-intellectuals and was focusing on adjusting their genetic code to remove the physical and physiological problems associated with this anomaly."

"Yes—but some of your research was---how I can I say it---in its elementary stage."

"What are you suggesting?"

"I am just reminding you that the specimens we inadvertently took with us were part of your research." Gordon tapped her fingers more vehemently as if she were developing real emotions.

"I shall take a look at the actual fertilized ovum, and the sperm and unfertilized ovum here, or in the other center, and determine to what extent the genetic codes represent my research and to what extent they have been manipulated." Reinhart said in a firm, menacingly tone. "It might be in your interest to tell me more now— show me that you were not responsible for the creation of humans like Ludovic."

"I did not participate in the procreation of these humans. I would share more information if I could." Reinhart must have tired of the conversation because she brought the discussion to a rapid end, leaving me on my own.

"Victoria, I would suggest that you get closer to Edward. Humans will not bring you the android physical satisfaction that you so crave, but you might find something more durable with your own kind, on a purely intellectual level." I said under an impulse and for want of something better to say before I got up to leave.

Once outside Gordon's office, I let my anger surface. "Why did you do that? You have no right to intrude on every aspect of my life?"

"I am not intruding on your life, just protecting you." I heard a voice answering my thoughts.

"I don't need your protection." I replied, realizing that we were arguing on a cerebral level. Each of us aware of the other's non-verbal thoughts.

She didn't answer so I persisted. "This is not the first time that you did something that made me angry." Still no answer. "You let those two young people die because you did not tell me where to find the IV solution. I had to witness their death. You didn't even care enough to stay with me to help me deal with the horror of death."

"They would not have survived. I knew that." She finally replied. "And, witnessing the horror of death was a learning experience."

"But, today?"

"You can live your sexual fantasies with whatever human you want. But, while I share this body with you, I shall not let you belittle yourself, or me, by being physically intimate with one of my creations." She stopped to let her cerebral communication sink in. "Your foolishness could compromise my control over them and could risk the safety of all of us." She paused. "But, my child, you have the right to be angry with me and to express your emotions without any risk to our relationship. And, I may even, at times, accept your point of view." She then disappeared deeper inside of me.

"She is right. I was acting foolishly. But, at least now I know, that Reinhart respects me because she acknowledged my right to disagree with her.

I rushed off to finish other tasks. I had promised to talk to Ludovic before the end of the day. It was already late afternoon when I found him in the lounge, in the inner circle, talking to Ferdinand and Jason. I sat down next to him and motioned to the others to stay where they were.

"Ludovic, I am going to ask you a very personal question, one that might provoke strong emotions. I want you to feel free to say whatever comes to mind. Certainly do not hold back any feelings." He pushed his long, green hair away from his face so that I could look directly into those large, globular eyes. "Do you want Dr. Reinhart to change in any way your physical appearance?"

"Are you asking me that because you don't find me attractive, Pamela?"

"No." I stammered as it was true. He obviously sensed this because he backed away from me. "I am asking you because Dr. Reinhart can change certain of your physical features, but will only make changes that you want, if you want any at all."

"I have thought about it. I appreciate your offer, or her offer." He let his hair fall back in his face. "I have observed your group closely. Your bodies and facial features are perfect—too perfect for me, because they are so flawless that they don't seem human." My face turned rigid as my muscles tightened defensively. I was not sure if he was insulting me or complimenting me.

"I suppose that I should want to emulate all of you by asking that I be given a perfect body to go with a perfect mind." He continued. "There are others in this Center who have known the same sort as me. They are old and worn, or they are part reptilian. I noticed that you all work well together and no one focuses on physical appearance. I have also studied the remaining five programmed humans, all of whom have some noticeable deformities."

I interrupted him. "What? The remaining five, but, there should be ten?" I trembled, panicked and then steamed with anger.

"Oh, I forgot to mention, Pamela." Ferdinand jumped in. "During your absence, five of the remaining programmed humans bypassed their programming when they were in the dining room." He turned his face away from me and continued speaking. "Only a few of us were there. It happened so fast. One of the programmed humans entered the dining room, swaying back and forth and laughing, like someone on drugs or simply drunk. He had a laser gun in his hand. 'Look what I found in the physics lab!' He yelled. The other programmed humans giggled in that rather ridiculous and childish way that goes with programming. 'I just burnt myself with this thing.' He went on. They giggled more. "Where are you?' We can't see you?' the humans spoke in one voice.

Seconds later, four members of the group started to scream, their bodies vibrating under the effects of their deprogramming. They were pressing their hands up against the sides of their heads, as they fell, writhing on the floor. They regained composure, struggling to their feet as they spun involuntarily in circles, unable to walk a straight line. He continued to torment them until they finally charged after him in a fruitless effort to retrieve the laser gun. Their attacker mocked their swaggering assault. 'No, I can't give it to you...try to catch me.'

In the meantime, the five programmed humans repeated the same questions, their actions bordering on lunacy. 'What happened to him? Where is he?" They languished pathetically in their programmed world.

Sarah, Ruth and I rushed to restrain him, but he was too strong. Towering over us, he swiped us away like flies. When I regained some strength, I crawled in the direction of the door to get help. He grabbed me with his large hands and threw me violently across the room.

Alongside Sarah and Ruth, we watched, helplessly, as he returned to the deprogrammed group that was in close range. "I shall show you how it burns." It was on death ray and he fired it on the four deprogrammed humans in front of him. They disintegrated instantly. The three of us made one last futile effort to stop him before he turned the laser gun on himself." Ferdinand let out a long, raspy breath of air, as he grappled with the memory.

"Naturally, the entire scene had no lingering effect on the five remaining programmed humans. When the voices of their comrades disappeared, they finished eating and left." He concluded.

I saw the expression of horror on his face, drawn sullen and white, when his lifeless eyes met mine. He was deeply affected by what he witnessed. "We wanted to tell you, but you had so many other problems, that we decided to wait for the right moment."

"And when was the right moment going to be?" I asked, showing my fury rather than my sympathy for what he experienced. "I guess... now!" I answered for him.

I got up to leave and Ferdinand moved in front of me, assuming an authoritative posture, as he blocked my passage. "You have so much to bear. You cannot handle everything, Pamela. There are some things that just happen. They are unfortunate. But they happen. We are sad, now you are sad, and the others will be sad when they are informed.

And yet, the five remaining humans are probably in various stages of deprogramming. I suggest that we examine them tomorrow."

He spoke like the Ferdinand of the past, convincingly and reassuringly. I sat back down like a student reprimanded by a professor, feeling guilty about having reproached him for his analyses and conclusion. I turned my attention to Ludovic, who was sitting on the floor with his knees drawn up to his chest. His defensive posture reminded me of both his vulnerability and . . . ours, the vulnerability of all of us.

I moved down on the floor next to him and put my arm around his broad shoulders. He leaned his head on mine and we stayed like that for a long moment before I finally spoke.

"Are you ok?" I asked and he whimpered. "Do you want to continue our discussion or do you want to wait?"

"I can continue." His voice in a whisper. "There seems to be so much sadness and danger in the world." His tears flowed slowly along the creases in his face. "I wish sometimes that I was still living with my own kind in the outside community." After slowly wiping away his tears, he picked up his earlier discussion, speaking in a low, distant tone. "The remaining five programmed humans also have deformities. Their deformities are different from my own, but, nonetheless, visible. Are you going to make the same offer to them?"

"Yes." I replied.

"I do not dislike my appearance. I am different, but I like being different." He looked down at the floor. "I need time to think about your offer and decide whether it is better for me to stay like I am." He moved his head slowly from side to side.

"Naturally, Ludovic, I would show you the changes that I could make and give you a perfect, visual image of what you would look like afterwards. You would have the opportunity to accept everything or only those changes that you like." He listened attentively. "But, I think that you should give thought to this project so your request is fine with me, Ludovic. Think about it. If you change your mind, come and talk to me about it." I replied.

I now felt calmer and ready to focus on the material evidence surrounding those five deaths. I slowly stood up and addressed Ferdinand. "I would like to know how this human got hold of a laser gun."

"That, unfortunately, I cannot tell you. He was not working in the physics lab so he should never have been there. He was in the biology lab." He stopped to collect his thoughts.

"When we got all the information from you dealing with killer androids, or killer robots...I am not certain which name was used," he shrugged his shoulders, "John suggested that we each keep a laser gun handy, just in case one of the androids or the Group of 5 turned on us. John inadvertently left his in his lab when he went to get something from the inner circle. It took him longer than he had anticipated to find the object. When he returned, the laser gun was gone. By the time he arrived in the dining room to warn us, the episode was over." He said between quick and arduous breaths. "All of this is so tragic! We have to stop making stupid mistakes!" He screamed in an emotive voice.

"Why didn't you use your laser to stun him?"

"Oh, this is embarrassing. Sarah and Ruth never carried their laser guns with them. They locked them up in a cabinet in the biology lab. And, I," he looked straight into to my eyes, "as you know, am opposed to violence, so I put mine in safe keeping in my dresser drawer."

He was right. It was definitely a tragic situation, even though the reason why this young man was prowling around the physics lab did not make sense and needed to be investigated further. 'Who put him up to that?' I wondered. 'Was there another android that had gone mad? Or did one of those killer robots escape? I guessed that I was going to have to check out the circuits of all the android assistants here in this center.'

I told Ferdinand that, in spite of his pacifistic convictions, he should carry his laser gun with him for protection and then mentioned that I would be asking Drager to return to help me check out the circuits in the android assistants.

"See you at dinner." I forced a cheerful voice. I went directly to John and Peter, to discuss what I learned and mention my plans to test the android assistants. John apologized for keeping the matter secret but felt that we all needed a couple days to unwind after what we had been through.

I felt exhausted and needed to be alone so I passed into the inner circle. I flopped down behind one of the computer terminals in the control room where I sensed that Reinhart wanted to be. Before I knew what was happening, I was learning how to operate very complex technology, searching on my own for operating satellites. I understood why John was not able to capture the images of the planet earth that Reinhart had requested. John was trying to capture imagery from satellite junk.

The satellites that Reinhart had launched into space were capable of changing course to avoid collision with near space objects, like meteorites and comets, were built to resist time, and were capable of high performance. She hid them behind screens of invisibility so that only she or members of her research teams could gain access to information. And, she further protected them by adding access codes. I marveled over how efficient she was, even if her efficiency bordered on paranoid behavior. She took over and worked rapidly, gaining in enthusiasm as she started to receive information.

She waded rapidly through the layers of images that represented millions and millions of earth years. "I hope you are watching and learning, Pamela," I heard her say. "You see the extent to which the earth was devastated by the violent explosion." She said, pointing to the relevant images. "How strange? The earth is a supercontinent today, seemingly identical to the supercontinent, known as Pangaea that existed during the Permian period that dates back 300 million years before the beginning of human life. We know that the earth's atmosphere is not in an evolutionary phase, because it can support human life. And, there are fertile lands north of us. I am very optimistic. We shall be able to start over again, with abundance of natural resources at our disposition."

For a change, I was a bearer of good news, so Reinhart had to concede to Pamela, who ran back to tell the others over dinner. "For everything there is a season, and a time for every matter," repeated over and over again in my mind as I passed from the inner circle to the dining room. "Did I read these words or did I imagine them; they are giving me a new found courage and self-confidence?" Our season and our time for conquest and progress are upon us.

Chapter 24- Probing Questions

The next months went by rapidly. Drager and I found the intruder---a killer robot that apparently disposed of one of our android assistants during the loading of WD and then boarded the aircraft, landing at our Center. We interrogated him. Apparently, he arrived, unnoticed, and infiltrated the existing group of androids, getting himself assigned to John. He saw his opportunity to create turmoil when John left the physics lab for what was to be only a few minutes, leaving his laser gun in plain view. The android did not want to compromise his mission to kill all life forms in our center, by exposing himself too soon and thereby risk being captured, so he intercepted the young programmed human in the corridor and dragged him into John's lab.

"Time was not on my side. I had to act rapidly to get that human to carry out my orders." The android commented. "So I hit and kicked the human rather violently until he started deprogramming. He was cowering in a corner, shaking and dripping with sweat, when I put the laser gun in his hand, and showed him how to fire it. I took the gun away from him for a second and put it on stun, before I fired at him to show him that it was harmless and would not hurt anyone. That human coward screamed that it burned him, which was in fact true, even though the burn was so superficial. To confuse him, I let him fire the gun, still on stun, at me to prove him wrong."

"But why did he go into the dining room and fire on the others?" I was still confused.

"I told him that he was late for lunch and that he should take the laser gun with him to show to the others. He was rubbing his eyes and stumbling when he got up on his feet, so I quickly ushered him out of the lab. I then escorted him to the dining room. The last thing that I said to him was that he must destroy everyone in the dining room with the laser gun, in particular, the ugly humans."

"You expect us to believe that?" I protested.

"You can believe either that I sent him off on a homicidal mission or that his first glimpse of reality so horrified him that he wanted to erase it from his eyes." He replied before adding. "It makes no sense, though, that the human also committed suicide. How could his vulnerable human mind have resisted my orders?"

We recognized this young man's heroic effort to save the other humans and honored him, with a plaque reading "To the unknown soldier" who dedicated his life to humanity; after which we destroyed the body of the killer robot. The plaque would start a tradition- a wailing wall bearing the names of those whose existence terminated during our lifetimes.

Before Drager left for the Air and Space center he asked for a few minutes of time alone with me, rather than Elisabeth. "I recovered a message that Dr. Murdoc left for Dr. Reinhart. What should I do with it?" He asked in his drab, expressionless voice. I never had time to answer. Instead, I felt a strange feeling of remorse invading me as Elisabeth replaced me. I was privy to the conversation.

"A message?" She queried and he answered affirmatively. "And, why has it taken you so long to deliver this message," she asked.

"After we recovered the anti-virus and reprogrammed the androids in the marine center, my historical tapes were activated and I started to receive broken messages which only recently took their true form. Do you want me to play the message that he left for you?"

"Yes," She sighed, "but we should go into the padded room. I want to be away from the rest of my group when I listen to it." He followed her obediently to the padded room next to Flanders' former office and watched as she let her body drop limply onto one of the chairs.

"Are you ok, Dr. Reinhart?" He asked, more out of respect than concern, because he had no emotional configuration. She was unaware of the strangeness of his question and motioned with her hand for him to continue.

When Murdoc pronounced her name, "Elisabeth," his voice was

so soft and tender that his love for her shined through. And, she responded to his voice with a rush of warmth and energy that flowed through my body, showing me for the first time that she could have profound feelings for someone. And then, I felt my heart sink, heavy with sorrow, because he was gone forever.

"My Love." He continued in a voice deeper than that of Randolph and in an accent very similar to hers that rang through. I felt her generation's true connection with language and how their voices radiated their emotions in a way that we had not yet achieved. An observer, hiding as it was in my very interior, a passive participant, a listener, my emotions warmed to this.

"I hope that you have survived and that the world that you find yourself in today is one of harmony and contentment." Tears flowed down my face during the ensuing long pause, something that did not bother me, but put her ill at ease...my hands gripping each other and the muscles in my face, tightly drawn. She changed her position, moving with difficulty into a very erect posture, hoping to hide her feelings and trembling body from the eyes of Drager.

"Everything I did and said was to save you. I have looked everywhere for you and find myself today weak and tired and fear that I shall die before I find you and hold you one last time in my arms." Another long pause imposed, giving me the time to feel the intensity of her sadness and anger moving violently inside of my tightly wrenched stomach and my rapid beating heart. "I hope that you can find it within your heart to forgive me for what I have done." He coughed adding more emotion to his plea.

He cleared his voice, gaining control, and spoke in an inanimate tone, as if he were giving her a report. "I must tell you what I have done so that you, and only you, can undo it... something that may no longer be possible." He breathed deeply. "Even though I programmed the androids to kill, they are not winning. I forgot how strong feelings in humans can produce extraordinary courage. The humans' desire to win overshadows the technical skill of the androids. And, our intellectuals, struck down with fear, find refuge in their homes, awaiting-maybe inviting-their demise with open hands."

"I have lost touch with the group of 5 and am worried that they are going to react irrationally in human terms, but rationally in concordance with their android consciousness, by destroying everything. My belief that all the intellectuals would join together to fight certainly clouded my earlier decisions, and the recognition of my errors has led me to make radical –even dangerously irrational-decisions. I feel humiliated by what has happened for I lived among those non-intellectuals, helping and trusting them...believing their lies. Today I realize how foolish I was and how naïve I was to have put confidence in the intellectual community to follow me into battle. I should have stood by you. Forgive me, Elisabeth!"

He struggled to speak like his life forces were leaving him. "I left someone in charge of the Marine center, which may not survive the cataclysm, but ensure the death of the non-intellectuals who might find refuge on the high seas. He and his team are programmed to kill. I have given the Captain the power to order the destruction of these humans. A punishment which, in my present state of mine, I hope for because I believe they deserve to die."

Drager stopped the tape and looked at me. "He lost consciousness and woke up days later. He finished his message. Do you want me to continue?"

"Of course!" She screamed with strong emotion.

"I don't know why I am still alive, My Love, but hope beyond hope that it is because we shall soon be together. My desire to feel your warmth, to smell your delicious fragrances, to feel all my emotions come alive in harmony with yours inspire me to stay alive, even if it is only for one last glimpse of love." He spoke softly.

"The facts, I must give you all the facts. Yes, I adjusted the gravitational force in the Air and Space center and in the Marine center letting them drift high above the ground so that these centers might be able to ride out the explosion that I am more and more certain is the Group of 5's final solution. I know that the main center will resist it and believe that the two other centers will then be pulled into the large center's time-space configuration. I could do nothing for the other center, but I do not regret that because those intellectuals who hide sheepishly within it will certainly disappear. I hope that the Group of 5 has carried you with them to safety. Again I fear that I might never know."

There was such a long pause that we had the impression that the conversation was over and started to stir to get up and leave, only to be jolted back in place as his voice returned. "Drager has the anti-virus for the androids programmed to kill. The Captain of the Marine center may be dangerous. I have left an order to reverse his programming and to wipe out his destructive instinct at the end of this tape. I have to anticipate the worst, even as I hope for the best for you."

"OH...... sadness beholds me. My life is fading in front of my eyes. I can see you standing there in front of me, smiling and beckoning me to reach out. Is it you? I hope it is but an illusion because I don't want you to die! You must live on!" His scream echoed in our minds. "Oh, My love, my tender Elisabeth who gave me so much happiness, I am and shall remain in whatever form or existence awaits me in complete adoration of you."

Minutes later his voice came through loud and clear: "You will erase every part of the program I installed in you including the program to kill and to order others to kill, in defiance of which you will self-destruct on the order of Dr. Reinhart."

"Dr. Reinhart," Drager pleaded, "do you want to reactivate the Captain now and reprogram him?"

"What?" She replied, her voice sounded so far away. Drager repeated his question.

"I think that Dr. Reinhart was very much affected by the content of the tape." I spoke up. "It might be better to wait until the morning to take care of this."

"Yes, of course." He replied. "But, it is also important for Jarrod and Fleming to have the Captain reactivated and productive so that they can better control the work in the Marine center. And, I think that they would like to return later to the Air and Space center."

I stared at him, my eyes vivid with a deep red glow. And then Reinhart returned, as if nothing special had just happened. "Ok, let's go and reactivate the Captain and see if Murdoc's voice is respected." And so, that is what we did. The Captain reacted positively to Murdoc's command and when we tested him, he no longer responded to orders to kill and refused to give any such orders saying that it was in contradiction to his ultimate programming.

I mentioned the message from Murdoc to everyone the next day and the fact that the Captain was now reactivated and Murdoc's programming was deactivated. I suggested that we send him back to the Marine center, but not before he attended the next meeting and answered any questions we had regarding the functioning of that center. "For that reason I have locked him up in the padded room."

I informed the group that Murdoc's admission that he had adjusted the gravitational force in the two other centers did explain why they survived. "Dr. Reinhart suggests that the time-space configuration that she had in place for this center, which was calibrated to speed up time in this center to assure its survival, did the reverse because of Murdoc's interference."

"In fact Randolph, your theory was right, but only because the two other centers were already in a free-style drift when the explosion took place. They were later trapped, spinning in a tornado like funnel, when they came in close contact with our center. The program installed by Reinhart for the survival of our center reacted by increasing the gravitational force of our center, and thereby pulling the two other centers out of the funnel and dragging them along with us. Thus, the increased gravitational force necessary for the three centers to enter into a new time-space configuration slowed down time in this center as well as in the other two." I cleared my voice and added. "The bomb was installed in the right place." All heads nodded.

"We shall meet briefly tomorrow morning to question the Captain, if that is ok for everyone." I added and everyone agreed.

The Captain met with us the following day. He consulted his memory banks several times to sort out the questions regarding the delivery of humans for dolphin consumption. He claimed that the termination unit was used regularly for those humans who worked directly with his android crew members. He never delivered them to the dolphins. But, his crew did find small colonies of humans living around the beach areas that they explored who were unable to properly explain how they came to exist. They were seen as a menace because there were no records of their births in any of the other centers, which the Captain insisted he consulted.

"No, I never approached the main center because I was not considered by the Group of 5 to be their equal and they only invited me to meetings to give me orders, not to interact with me. They seemed indifferent to me and my work." He said when questioned about his relationship with the main center.

"That is rather an emotional response?" I suggested.

"No, Dr. Reinhart, it is a logical one. I was never given the opportunity to present my work. And, you know that I was not myself, as I was under the influence of Murdoc's programming which interfered certainly with my purely android reasoning. It did not, however, render me emotional, just illogical. Yes, illogical, I would say. I detected that the Group of 5 considered me to be intellectually inferior-which I certainly am as I was not a replica of one of the originals. Therefore they were not much interested in what I had to say or what I was doing."

He stopped, as if he had finished and I urged him to continue by asking him who decided to deliver these so called "suspect" humans to the dolphins.

"Oh, that happened quite by accident. We ran into the dolphins regularly when we went out to sea. They spoke to us in English— just to make things clear to us." He commented, anticipating our next question regarding communication. "They complained that they were starving and needed viable food sources. They asked us if we had any meaty substances for them."

He pulled his shoulders up high and went on. "I was programmed to kill the humans living on the sea coast." We nodded. "So rather than killing them myself, I simply offered them to the dolphins in exchange for flora and fauna that they discovered." He patted his large brooch...that badge of former authority. "In the beginning, this worked out well, but at one point we were out of normal looking humans, their colonies disappeared and the only humans that we had left to offer were the humans of many colors."

"So, if I understand correctly, some humans did survive the explosion and went on to build colonies and live together?"

"That is doubtful. There was no human life on the planet when I was awakened. But, some humans escaped from different centers or were given the right to live outside a center. Those who chose to live on the coastal shores were in my area of control and so I could dispose of them as I wanted."

He stopped brusquely to retrieve more information. "The order Dr. Murdoc gave me to erase his program to kill and to order killing of humans by any means is registered in my system so I will respect humans. I am no longer a slave to that former program. Nonetheless all the actions that I took regarding the human community before are in my memory bank. As you know, my programming instructed me to dispose of them. So, even when another center, like the Air and Space center, allowed humans to live in small colonies outside their limits, we often times trapped them and offered them as a food source. I will retain this information unless you order me to erase all trace of my activities with humans during that period of time."

I asked him to leave the room for the moment so that we could discuss the problem. We all agreed that he did not just collect humans living on the coastlines, but certainly wandered inland to gather up other groups. The horror of what he did was revolting, but to ask him to erase that part of his memory would be futile. He was unable to repeat his actions, so we decided to leave his memory intact, should we ever need to access it.

But, it was also decided that his memory should only surface on command from Dr. Reinhart and that only Dr. Reinhart could install new programming: otherwise there was a possibility that someone, like the group of 5, or even more diabolical, could reach his memory bank and adjust his programming. Reinhart agreed with that and assured everyone that she would have him download a program that would act as a safeguard for all of us.

We escorted the Captain to WD's living quarters to have him confront WD. WD admitted that he recognized the Captain and that he had spoken to him on one or two occasions. When I forced WD to order humans for food, the Captain refused the request claiming that humans were his allies and not his enemies and that he was programmed to protect them.

"Well, all of this seems to be quite ridiculous and I am a bit bothered by the theatrics of it." WD said mockingly. "The fact that there are no more dolphins living in the surrounding waters means that you have no reason to be concerned about the Captain being led astray." He then let his head drop in what could have shame or regret. We turned and left WD to contemplate his solitude.

Reinhart surfaced, letting me watch, learn and understand what she was about to do. She ordered the Captain to download other programming to prevent him from accessing his memory banks on his own or on the request of someone other than Dr. Reinhart. "Time would tell," I said under my breath, "but for the moment it appeared that the Captain was fit to return to the marine center and carry out constructive research for our group."

Drager was asked to take the Captain back to the marine facility. Jarrod and Fleming would return to the Air and Space center and Drager would observe and supervise the Captain until we sent other personnel to replace him. Reinhart had confidence in Drager to contact her if anything looked suspicious.

I never revealed the whole message Murdoc left for Elisabeth to anyone, not even Peter. But, from that moment on, I realized that she definitely had a strong human side and that she was not what the Group of 5 proclaimed, more machine than human.

Weeks and then months passed. We were very busy with our individual projects and spent very little time lingering over meals or engaging in conversations. The quest for new worlds was in our blood, like a drug pushing us forward with enthusiasm and energy.

Ferdinand launched an informational campaign, by broadcasting different subjects each day over the audio systems. Some of us listened, or half-listened, while others ignored him or turned off the sound system. He picked political, philosophical and religious subjects hoping to inject a bit of human culture into our scientific minds.

Reinhart's research concerning the extreme color differentials in Ludovic confirmed earlier hypotheses presented by Flanders. The researchers at the Marine center genetically modified the skin and hair color by adding genes from fish, creating genetically modified color mutations in the humans' hair and skin. Reinhart marveled at the scientific complexity of the procedure, but scoffed its outcome.

"His colors are not that unbecoming, but his facial deformities are loathsome, something that they should have tried to ameliorate through genetic modification. I wish he would let me restructure his face, but he seems to like the way he looks." I mentioned to Peter, who shrugged his shoulders, which said it all.

The five remaining programmed humans, deprogrammed gradually over a ten-day period. We decided not to interfere before they recognized our physical existence. There were three women and two men, all with mild deformities, webbed feet and/or hands and large, fish lips, and a few hunched shoulders and large fleshy arms and legs. It would have been easy for Reinhart to adjust these features, but, like Ludovic, they refused reconstructive surgery. These five musicians were used to playing their musical instruments with these anomalies and were convinced that removing them would interfere with their musical proficiency.

Our group divided up into smaller groups. John, Stuart, Mathieu and Isabel studied the supercontinent from its geological and climatic aspects. Their reports confirmed that the supercontinent should provide natural resources and food. The various soil samples Reinhart gathered proved to be promising. The red soil could be used to build solid structures. As our centers were located on a strip that looked like a wide peninsula, joining two larger land masses, the group focused on the northern and southern parts of the supercontinent. The lower northern and upper southern land surfaces had the climate and temperature necessary to grow agricultural products, if they were not already growing and prospering. They would be good places to build outside communities.

Diana spent long hours studying the marine samples taken during Reinhart's time and informed us that the fish and plants stored in the inner circle were non-toxic and could provide excellent food sources for humans, if they still existed today. The plants that we recovered during our first mission were close to what was stored in the bottles in the inner circle and therefore edible. We would have to continue our search for these marine animals and plants to provide for an on-going source of protein.

Peter spent his time studying the communications received from in-coming astronauts and the interceptions ordered and carried out by the Group of 5 in conjunction with the air and space center. "There is no information regarding how many astronauts were aboard the in-coming space vehicles. The only voice registered was that of the pilot." He mentioned it to me one evening when we were alone on the veranda, watching the sun, hiding behind veils of amber, blue and dark purple, as it slowly descended behind the horizon, disappearing from view, replaced by sparkling lights, moving in place like a choreographed dance.

"True, but that is not what you should focus on." I said in a sweet-sounding voice.

"Why did you say that, Pamela?" he asked, putting a strong accent on my name.

"Because the number of astronauts is not as important as what they said when they entered. "

"Right. I see where you are coming from. In fact, they all commented on the bleak emptiness and asked over and over again for confirmation that they were entering the Earth's atmosphere before asking for permission to land." He clicked his fingers. "That is it. They were expecting a thriving civilization and were shocked by the barrenness." He gazed at the sky, his eyes sparkling in harmony with the stars. "I want to go there, I want to visit other worlds. " He said in a low voice and my heart flittered.

"The visits were sporadic and in intervals of twenty to thirty year periods." His voice took on a more serious tone. "I believe that the Mother ship launches the vehicles, a few at a time."

"I can understand your reasoning, but it makes no sense. Why hover over the planet at that distance? No, they were being sent back to Earth, in small spacecraft that had been up-dated and improved upon for faster intergalactic space travel. Their objective was to live on Earth, secure new pioneers for their world and others, or acquire resources or technology. And yet, you are right the launches were staggered."

"I don't understand why they did not fire back at the android interceptors."

"They were pacifists or they thought that the interceptors were sent to accompany them to improve the landing. Who knows?" Reinhart was on top of this. "Stupidity is another explanation for that kind of irrational behavior." She quickly added. "What did the androids say?"

"Earlier recordings were different from those that coincided with our group's existence. In those earlier recordings the androids sounded very hospitable. There was no sign of hostility in their adapted human voices. In every case, they gave them coordinates for landing." He rolled his tongue on the inside of his mouth, producing a ball of thought. "Stupidity may be too harsh, Dr. Reinhart. Actually, the androids did tell them that they were sending out a welcoming committee. They were obviously duped."

He looked at me, Pamela, his interlocutor. "She has no patience. You know that. She finds the entire situation ludicrous and...very human." He raised his eyebrows. "But, she is very curious about why the androids did not adapt their voices in the last two cases, the moments when you were present."

"I can't answer that." He replied, impatiently, as he paced back and forth, plowing his fingers through his hair. "I wonder if the androids knew that I was there and decided to send me a message, or a warning to stay out of that communications unit." He said in a low voice of alarm.

"Are they the only recordings in which the androids did not adapt their voices?" I pressed on, ignoring his dramatic moves.

"Yes, actually, they are the only two."

"Did the astronauts give you their name and rank in the earlier messages?" Before he could answer I added. "Peter, what were their names? I know that you told me, but I don't remember their names." He looked at me with a sideways glace, as it he didn't believe me. "I was just Pamela, the newly deprogrammed musician when I arrived in the outside community and, even though I remember the details of your deprogramming, the names of the astronauts meant nothing to me at the time."

"Yes, to your first question." He replied brusquely. "And, for the second one, they called themselves Captain Anderson and Captain Hadley."

"That is it." Reinhart moved into the discussion. "They carried the names of their ancestors, who were outstanding in the field of aeronautics. The androids recognized their names and wanted them to know that humans were not in command." She looked fixedly into Peter's eye. "Please send me a report, Peter, with the names of all the other astronauts that entered our atmosphere. I want to verify whether any other astronauts carried the same last name of members of the scientific crew and astronauts that I sent off to exoplanets in other solar systems, a very long time ago.

"By the way, Anderson and Hadley arrived much, much later than the other staggered returns." Peter was more focused now on the problem. "Do you think that their messages were instantaneously transmitted back to the Mother ship?"

"There was a risk of that." She sighed. "Perhaps we will never have the answer. But, now that I think about it, if the message was received by the Mother ship, there will definitely be a change of strategy, if and when they come back. Perhaps, they will send a bigger, fighting unit."

We sat silently for a long moment, turning ideas round in our heads. "Yes, it is possible," Reinhart broke the silence, "that they thought that the earlier space craft was not capable of making a safe landing. That would mean that they developed better technology or material, the reason why Anderson and Hadley arrived a long time after the others. And of course there could have been changes in command, or other problems that interrupted space travel."

"I would just like to make one more point, which did not seem that important up until now." He took a deep breath. "The other astronauts only gave their name and rank, they never mentioned that they were returning home to the planet Earth. Only Anderson and Hadley added that detail. Do you think that that made a difference to the receiving android here at the base?"

"You raised a very interesting point, Peter." Reinhart uttered in a soft voice. "The Group of 5 wanted to send a message to the Mother ship. By authorizing their android assistants to reply using their natural, vibrating, robotic voices they communicated hostility, while, at the same time, confirming that this planet was no longer under human domination." I picked up with Reinhart's thoughts. "I can feel her profound disappointment and sadness over this play for power by the Group of 5. She is impressed that you fully processed all the information you gathered, drawing the same conclusion as her."

I got up and left Peter to his work. I wanted to make another visit to WD. I was happy that the situation with WD was under control. I would go by from time to time to chat with him, attune now to his manipulative personality and diabolical side. He did not seem to be bothered by his collar monitor and was eating plants as if they were always his preferred diet.

"You know, Pamela, I respect humans a lot more now. They are certainly our intellectual equals." His flattery had no effect on me anymore. "With this collar, you could track me under water. I might be useful for your next expedition, if you intend to explore the oceans." I stood listening. "Me too, I would like to find hunting grounds."

"You told me that the last time I came to visit you." I mentioned dryly.

"It is normal. My sedentary life here is starting to drive me mad. I dream about swimming in waves and leaping high out of the water. This wading pond is not big enough."

"Interesting. For a highly intelligent creature, your reasoning is so illogical, even though it could be considered a clever move on our part if you thought that you were addressing Pamela."

"It is you Dr. Reinhart?" he said, as he played meticulously with his claws much like a humans cleaning their finger nails. "I don't follow you at all."

"Obviously, you don't. You are too self-confident. For example, you never once considered in the past that you might lose. You are making that identical mistake today. You imagine that you can benefit from the credulity of others, including myself. You are so certain that we will invite you to accompany us and that you will escape in the high seas." She laughed, in a rough and high spirited way.

"Assuming that you escape, which is highly unlikely because of the collar's efficiency, you could be eaten by another predator, strangled by the collar, or drown. Must I go on?" She asked, watching his head drop. "To be highly intelligent is to see every factor, positive and negative, weigh and evaluate those factors properly and, with lucidity, determine how they can befall a decision. The day that you prove to me that you have progressed intellectually, we can have a real discussion."

I wondered whether she was always so aggressive and insulting or whether certain personalities brought that out in her. These thoughts dissipated rapidly when I noticed that WD had tilted his walrus-dolphin head in my direction so that I could see the left side of his mouth twitch upwards. Was he smirking at me or at Reinhart?

Chapter 25-The Floral Trap

We all had individual projects underway. I found myself preoccupied with the lives of the older members of our community. Their situation was precarious and I had to act soon if I was going to prolong their lives and give them back a bit of their youth. These thoughts were flowing through my mind when I ran into Ferdinand.

"Do you have a few minutes, Ferdinand?" He nodded and we passed into the lounge area of the inner circle.

"So what is bothering you?" He asked as he took my hands in his, slowly patting them in a paternal way.

"I am writing my memoires and I wanted to clarify some things."

"Interesting," he said as he released his grip, giving me back my adult status.

"I thought that it might be a good idea to leave testimony of our existence and scientific progress, should we abruptly disappear, like our ancestors." I wrinkled my nose, just imagining history repeating itself.

His head dropped back in thought and I continued. "I shall take every precaution possible to preserve my memoires for new generations of humans."

He was now facing me, his eyes intense. "Are you worried about our safety?"

"No, not for the moment, but I think that it is the right time for me to start recording our history, as it was before AAD1, as it is today and as it will develop in the years to come." He nodded. "Ferdinand, do you remember telling me that my deprogramming saved you from termination?"

"Yes, of course, I remember telling you."

"Actually, I am just looking for continuity." That was exactly what I wanted. I had no notion of how much time passed between events during my programmed life. I thought that days, maybe weeks, had passed between the time that they dragged Ferdinand away and I bypassed my programming. "Do you know how much time passed between your imprisonment and my deprogramming?"

He opened his lips the barest fraction to speak. "I myself am not certain how much time passed between the moment that they ignominiously dragged me out of the orchestra pit and my escape into the inner circle. As I already told you, the guards actually locked me up in Gordon's office. Eventually, they escorted me to the conference room where I was questioned by the Group of 5."

He cleared his throat before continuing. "I don't think that I mentioned everything to you. So I am just going to rehash things as I remember them today, repeating some of what I already told you." He gazed at the distant wall with glassy eyes. "They informed me that my termination was being reconsidered." He stopped for an instance. "But I knew," he scoffed, "they just wanted to get more information from me by pretending that they held me in such high esteem that it would be regrettable to dispose of me, simply because my termination date was flashing red on the computer." He laughed boisterously.

"I did play into their hands at one point, perhaps because I was mortified, virtually shocked and cowering in fear. They had the power to decide whether I would live or die." Ferdinand cried, almost in a yell. "So I told them that certain members of the orchestra reacted positively when I used the term, 'humans' to describe them and the term 'machines' to describe the androids." His eyes were moving rapidly now, as if he were reading a book or viewing a film. "They wanted the identification numbers of those who were sensitive, but I refused to give them that." He scratched the back of his neck as he searched for words to explain himself. "They gave me the impression, Pamela, that my presence might be useful for them and that I would be able to help them to accomplish an objective. I didn't want to die!" He screamed, his lips quivering violently.

"It doesn't matter if you said or did something that you regret today. They are very manipulative and, personally, I can understand how threatened you felt. After all, for humans, survival is primordial and...it should be." I wanted him to feel at ease. So I told him that I resorted to methods of flattery to stay alive. He looked straight into my eyes. "Well, for example, I had that intimate relationship with Gordon, and, no matter how sexually rewarding it was, I clung to her, more for protection than orgasmic pleasure. I thanked the Governor for choosing a musical career for me to gain his confidence and give me more vacation time with the outside community. Must I go on?"

"Thank you, Pamela, for boosting my morale." He put an end to my confessions and let his body slump lazily in the couch.

"Ferdinand," He smiled up at me, "I don't remember you referring to the androids as machines."

"Maybe I didn't. Quite frankly, I am not certain of everything that I said to the group of musicians. You probably remember that part better than I do because I was in the deprogramming phase at that time."

"I wanted to share all my knowledge with you musicians and warn you about the environment we were living in. But, I have only vague memories of what I said or did, the reason why the drama of my arrest continues to haunt me. I don't even recall everything that happened to me while I was in captivity. Days, maybe weeks, after my arrest, Crawford showed up, mentioned that you had deprogrammed and told me that my existence was no longer of any real importance for them and then said Goodbye to me. The android escorts appeared out of nowhere and I was being dragged down the corridors to the termination center."

He looked at me, his eyes intense. "That is when I absolutely understood that they were hoping that my deprogramming would be the catalyst for yours. I understood that they kept me alive to use me in some other strange way to deprogram you."

I nodded. "Knowing how close I was to you, even in my programmed existence, they must have been very confused by the fact that I did not deprogram along with you." We both smiled in a kind of complicity.

"And yet, they were patient." He leaned farther back in his chair and looked up at the ceiling. "You saved me. Your deprogramming got a lot of attention. I don't know if you realize that there were sirens blasting and orders for assistance coming over the inter-com system. My guards relaxed their grip for a brief instance, long enough for me to break free and run for safety. The rest you know."

"Ok, that means that a very short period of time passed between your deprogramming and mine."

"That is what I want to think as well, but, as I mentioned, I don't actually know." He looked in another direction, avoiding eye contact with me. "I never wanted to discuss this subject in more detail with you because I am not proud of how I acted. After my capture, one might say that I was a bit of a coward because I was ready to acquiesce in their plans and cooperate, just to save my-self. And yet, they never offered me a way out. In retrospect, we know what their plan was. I was removed publicly and in front of you, one of my faithful... blind followers." He chuckled. "They knew that I would resist. I had already warned them that I would not be passive, that I would call for action the day that they came to take me to the termination unit. They are incorrigible monsters." He said with regret.

"Well, you gave them a splendid theatrical performance." I lau-ghed heartily. "They knew that you would play your part well and that I would start to question what was happening and eventually deprogram." I took his hands in mine. "As you said, they only kept you alive because they were worried that I might not take the bait and that you would have to repeat your performance."

He got up to leave and I grabbed him, pulling him back into his seat next to me. "I want to ask you something else." He stared straight into my eyes, putting me ill at ease. "I want to know if you will do me the honor of rejuvenating."

"You think that you can do that for me?" His eyes sparkled.

"I cannot promise that you will be in your twenties, but I think that Reinhart can give you a youthful look and, more importantly, younger organs." He nodded enthusiastically. "I need to get access to your records. I think that Flanders will help me with that. He is a very good assistant, and must remain only an assistant, which is why we must prevent him from accessing our research." I added, as we both got up to leave.

"She is worried about the Group of 5?" He was testing me.

"No. If anything, they are worried about her. After all she is their creator and capable of shutting them down permanently."

"And, you, Pamela, are you afraid of her?" My body stiffened. 'Was he asking me that because he was worried about me, or was he worried about himself and the others?"

He stood aloof waiting me to answer. I finally replied "You mustn't worry, Ferdinand, about me or about you or the others. Elisabeth is interested in helping us, not destroying us. At least that is the impression that I have for the moment."

"And, Jason...are you going to offer him eternal youth?"

That was a problem that I was ruminating over. I sat back down and he took his place next to me. I moved nervously in my seat before replying. "As you know, Jason was in suspended animation." Ferdinand's calmness stood in contrast with my nervousness, discernible at a glimpse, as I sat twisting my hair around my finger. "His birth records are missing, but, as he was one of Reinhart's experiments, he must have been physically strong and in excellent health when she chose him for suspended animation. But, in spite of that, I need to explore another matter in detail with Jason."

"So where does that leave us?" He used an excessively nasal tone, trying to excite Reinhart.

"Ok, I shall speak frankly. Jason was in contact with his colleague who died in that tropical forest. As you know, we tested Ludovic for any viruses that he might have contracted by being in touch with Thomas's corpse. I had Jason analyzed when we got back to the Center to make certain that he was not a carrier of any viral or bacterial disease. His tests came back clean; there was no evidence of any invasive microscopic organism of any kind."

I hesitated about going further, but then why not. "We ran the corpse of Thomas through every possible test for invasive organisms. Jason told us that he was feverish—at least that is what he was insinuating—and delirious before he died. We found traces of a toxic substance in Thomas's remains. It could have been a plant. He may simply have died from poisoning and his efforts to find the antidote were thwarted either because Jason could not find the right plants to fabricate the antidote or the plants no longer existed. That means that we have to be careful not to eat anything that we find growing in the wild before it has been tested."

"Wow that is worrisome." He hesitated an instance. "Maybe, Pamela, it was not what he ate, but rather what he touched."

I could now feel Reinhart's interest surging as she sent me data about the soil content that she wanted to have tested for radiation. Even in low doses, some humans are more susceptible to radiation poisoning. When I mentioned that to Ferdinand, he turned livid with anger. "Those miserable androids said that the earth's atmosphere and surface were safe." I paused for an instance. "It is possible that there were some slight vestiges of radiation. I guess that I must send a few androids to the floral garden to bring back more soil and plant samples for testing."

"Are you going to try with Jason?" Ferdinand was back to the original subject. "You changed the subject so rapidly so I gather that you are not interested in his rejuvenation."

"I have to talk to him about it. Maybe he won't be so enthusiastic about prolonging his life ad infinitum."

"Hum. If I understand correctly, you think that Jason was involved in foul play?" Ferdinand's lips moved into a half smile. "I am disappointed with you." He said as he slapped his legs and moved to get up.

"Wait, Ferdinand." I stopped short. "We need answers. I am not accusing Jason of anything. I just want to know what happened."

"Right, I understand." His eyes turned a cold grey. "That is your problem. I shall wait in the background, for the moment. But...if something incriminating develops, I shall be there to defend him." Silence stretched tautly between us.

"One more question?" I ventured, hoping to end our conversation on a positive note. He motioned to me with a limp hand to continue. "I just want to know why you do not participate in any of our musical concerts. You always sit in the back of the auditorium, observing."

"You are right." He replied, a sudden shift to enthusiasm in his voice. "In the beginning I was barely staying psychologically afloat with all the problems I encountered in the administration and organization of this center." He rubbed his hands slowly over his face and then shook his head.

"And, quite honestly, the orchestra pit brought back bad me-mories-just walking into the auditorium sent cold chills up and down my spine. I was resigned to giving up music forever when Jonathan came to get me during your recent trip on the outside. He virtually picked me up, under my protests, and carried to the auditorium. When he put my violin in my hands, I felt that kind of vibrant energy that comes to life when in the company of a fa-vored friend. My inhibitions and concerns vanished, and I found myself absorbed in the colors, texture, nature, emotions...of mu-sic." He smiled teasingly, a twinkle in his eyes, and said. "I'll be there participating next time, so don't make any mistakes!"

We separated in good spirits. Unfortunately, mine vanished rather quickly. I had serious business to take care of... the death of Thomas. Admittedly, I had put the cause of death on hold and now was the right moment to confront the problem. The Group of 5 were sitting placidly in the large office they shared. When I raised the subject of radiation poisoning, their android faces went blank, wiping out even the slightest of their tested human expressions. "You know something about this?" I gave them a long, brooding look.

As always, when things appeared difficult, Crawford was the first to reply. "As you know, Andrew constructed the tropical gar-den paradise." He looked at his colleagues for help. "Pamela, there are always little surprises here and there. Humans said something like that in the past. I believe that they called them the challenges of life."

"Listen, I am not accusing you of anything. I just want to know if you have reason to believe that the soil in that garden could be contaminated."

"The clean-up crew did a thorough check of the planet be-fore they activated us. That sector was checked over and we have no reason to believe that there were any radioactive particles anywhere." The former governor replied in a calm, administrative tone.

"I would like you all to supervise a group of androids to check the soil, plant life, and the water in the tropical garden?" I said calmly, making it sound more like a request than an order. "I just want to be certain that there are no harmful particles in the soil." They promised to take care of that immediately.

One last issue was bothering me and I wanted to get the reaction from the Group of 5. "Eugene, do you know how the animal life in the tropical paradise was created?"

"Oh. That was one of my ingenious accomplishments." The former Governor forced a convincing look of self-satisfaction. My blank face brought him back to reality. "Well, I am not bragging." He stuttered. "I can't brag, that is human. But, I can comment on what was pure genius on my part."

"Forget the self-praise and tell me what you did."

"Actually, it starts with what Murdoc did." He definitely held my interest. "Murdoc brought certain animal species with him to the Air and Space center. They did not survive, but the clean-up crew did have the presence of mind to conserve their bodies. I simply used what DNA I could recover to produce some of the species. Some may now be cross-bred races."

My thoughts were diverted by imagery that Reinhart was passing on to me. This panoply of picture slides presented a wide range of different animal species that were of special interest to Murdoc. Murdoc was fascinated by the animal world and studied the behavior of animals existing during his time, some of which we encountered in the tropical paradise.

"Pamela, are you interested or not?" That jarred me away from my thoughts!

"Yes, I was just marveling over how fastidious the clean crew actually was." I cleared my throat loudly enough to get the attention of all of them. "How did you remove the natural predatory characteristics of these species and turn them into vegetarians?" Reproducing these creatures from DNA, or cloning them, was not that impressive, yet changing their personalities and basic instincts definitely was.

"Well, we did not know that they had abandoned their carnivorous nature." Flanders looked at the other members of his group who had nothing to add. "Actually, Pamela, we never had the time to visit the tropical paradise---if I can appropriate your expression."

I was ready to accuse them of hiding information again, when

Gordon spoke up. "Actually, Pamela, we deceived them in a certain way." She looked at the others who nodded, encouraging her to continue. "We changed the natural odors of the animals and intensified the odors of the plants."

"What?" I couldn't believe that!

"Well, it was very complicated and I am certain that Dr. Reinhart would be very impressed with our research. We went on the assumption that if a predator detected a very unpleasant, almost toxic aroma, from its intended prey---which, of course, would only be emitted in a life threatening encounter--- the predator would look elsewhere. And, the natural, pleasant, seductive, animal odor of certain genetically modified plants intensified in the presence of animals, distracting predators away from other animals as prey. In any event, as you have witnessed, our research was very effective." A little smile of self-satisfaction stretched her lips. "Of course," she continued, "we never had the opportunity to follow up on our research and are very pleased with the results."

"Remarkable! I would like to look over the research." Reinhart replied. "Yet, were these natural prey actually toxic?"

"No, they were not toxic. At least we did not intend them to be. Their toxicity was limited to an artificial odor."

"Well, I understand what you intended to do and must admit that your idea was ingenious. Nonetheless, you must ask the android crew in charge of this floral or tropical paradise to bring back a few specimens. Perhaps the odor that is emitted leaves a trace of toxicity behind, either on the fur or feather that can have a lethal effect on humans. Thomas perhaps came in contact with one of these animals just after their offensive odor was emitted in a large dose. Touching or stroking one of these animals could have produced an allergic reaction or even poisoned him." All heads nodded.

"We shall look into this straight away." Crawford replied. "Is there anything else that we can do for you today, Elisabeth?

"It is not enough to change the predatory instinct, you would have had to genetically modify their digestive system. A carnivore cannot digest vegetable fiber." Reinhart commented.

"Yes, we should have mentioned that aspect of our research." Dr. Miller weighed into the discussion. "It was very complicated because we not only had to genetically modify the digestive tract but we had to adjust the digestive enzymes, making them concordant with, or giving them the same characteristics as those of omnivores. The project was very challenging but...well we had the time to invest in it."

"Although I am very much opposed to your use of genetic engineering, I am quite fascinated and impressed with the research that you conducted on members of the animal kingdom and would like to study it in more detail." Reinhart replied in a low, steady voice. "By the way, how did you control the reproduction of these animals? Were they all sterile?"

"Actually we only reproduced males. We could replace those that died." Flanders mentioned dryly. "We have no idea if some of them did change sex. We need time to investigate all of that."

"Fair enough."

"Is there anything else that we can do for you today, Elisabeth or Pamela?" Crawford queried.

"Yes, actually there is something else. Do you have the birth records and DNA information on Jason?" I asked.

I waited, my patience tested by long, tedious android sighs before Flanders finally commented. "Pamela, he was one of Elisabeth's experiments, as she knows. Records were destroyed during the explosion. Does she remember whether she gave the codes to any android assistants working with her on the project?"

"That is a good question," I replied impulsively, irritating my other half who was not ready to let the Group of 5 escape responsibility so easily. I cleared my throat and added. "I believe, though, that you must have that information as well, because you liberated Jason from the cryogenic capsule."

"We freed him because he was the only one that looked to be alive." Gordon replied dryly. "Maybe his genetic composition or simply his resistance was exceptional."

"Why do you care about his genetic code? Is he ill?" Crawford asked.

"I am going to ignore what you asked, Rudolph." Reinhart replied coldly, bringing them all to a quick attention. "Do any of you remember which capsule he was in?" They mumbled. "The genetic code was always indicated on the capsule so that we would be better able to compare the amount of deterioration during the cryogenic process and afterwards, if ever we were faced with that unpleasant result."

The Group of 5 fidgeted. "Why did you put these experiments in suspended animation in this center?" The Governor raised a question that was also bothering me, Pamela.

"Because my experiments in suspended animation did not have the full approval of the scientific community in the beginning." Reinhart answered in a firm, cold tone that conveyed her irritation. "So, I was forced to conduct early research outside the confines of our major cities." She confessed.

"My intentions were to prolong life in a cryogenic state until the members of the scientific community arrived on a habitable planet. The use of cryogenic substances was actually not a new idea. My research, though, was more than an improvement upon the earlier research in suspended animation, because I virtually changed the basic cryogenic substance. I also tested the possibility of human life sustaining warp speeds and surviving in a cryogenic state for light years of travel, by increasing the outside pressure on certain capsules and/or placing the capsule in artificially simulated, high speeds. I needed to validate my conclusions, before presenting my research to the Scientific Community."

She sighed. "Yes, I took a risk doing research in this Center, but as you all know, it was difficult to get approval on new projects." They nodded their heads vehemently. "When the project was formally approved, we moved the majority of our subjects to the city confines."

"Nonetheless, and something that you were obviously unaware of, there were so many volunteers from the less intellectual community for this project, more than we needed for our short term projects for space travel, that I decided to leave some of these humans in this center. I wanted to determine whether other elements, like viruses and bacteria injected into the cryogenic fluid, would have an effect on the human body, cause deterioration of the human body, or fortify it thereby guaranteeing a longer cryogenic life span for the human body. I never had the intention of ever waking up any of these individuals and letting them reintegrate into society." She confessed.

"So, you expected them to terminate at some time in the future?" Flanders ventured.

"Actually, I was hoping that they would not terminate and that the cryogenic substance would guarantee a kind of immortality." She replied. "But, again they were my experiments. Their survival took a back seat to my research."

"Rather cruel, wouldn't you say, Dr. Reinhart?" Miller asked, in that dull, inanimate android tone.

"Their lives were of pure scientific value to me at that time." Reinhart replied mimicking Miller's unemotional voice tone. "To a certain extent, they signed their own death warrant when they volunteered for my experiment in suspended animation." The Group of 5 took a few steps back, putting distance between themselves and their Creator. She stood observing their defensive behavior. I had to smile.

"Nonetheless," She continued in a didactic tone, "too much time passed between the moment when you" she pointed her finger at the Group of 5, "destroyed all life forms and my return in a symbiotic state. And, to complicate everything, you are all incapable of telling me just how much time did pass. Consequently, I cannot answer your question about their life expectancy and whether their bodies deteriorated in conformity with my own scientific projections. But, Jason's presence today is very promising for all humans, because his body endured for probably thousands and thousands of years and he awakened with his original adolescent body, in no way damaged physiologically or otherwise." She folded her arms in front of her.

"But, what about aging when they woke up?" The former Governor asked in bewilderment, returning to the original discussion, ignoring what she just said concerning Jason.

"Yes, that was the major problem. Once we could confirm long term resistance under many types of corrosive conditions, we would have studied the aging process on awakening." She stopped and cleared her throat. "This, of course, does not concern you. What concerns you at this moment is identifying Jason's capsule.

The rest is my business, and my business alone. And, as I just said, Jason's survival was a success. He did not even age on awakening."

"Of course, Dr. Reinhart, this is none of our business." They replied in unison.

"We shall get back to you as soon as we have located his code." Crawford replied.

"I want the genetic code of Ferdinand and Ralph, as well."

"Dr. Reinhart, Ralph is just our creation. If you want, we can give you a new one." Crawford looked at his colleagues who nodded. "It will take a bit of time, but the replacement will be there before Ralph needs to be terminated."

"I told you all, many times now that I do not want to hear the word termination!" She screamed as she hit the desk with her hands, sending a strong message to the androids, who bowed their heads in respect.

"We shall give you all the information rapidly." Miller whimpered submissively.

"Ok, just to clarify everything. You will study several animal specimens from the floral paradise and you will find the codes for Jason, Ralph and Ferdinand. Is that clear?" Heads bobbed up and down.

I turned and walked away. "She knows how to motivate her android creations," was running through my mind.

Chapter 26- Alter Ego

After spending many restless nights thinking and rethinking the various projects underway, I decided to back off a bit from my responsibilities and better my life. I was optimistic as everything indicated that we were moving forward rapidly and meticulously. Under the guise of confidence in my team, I delegated more projects to my colleagues, taking pressure off of me.

Unfortunately, my desire to withdraw did not resonate with Reinhart's management style. She was a workaholic who did not collapse under stress or fatigue. She was interested in keeping abreast of all the research being conducted and she made it clear to me she was annoyed with my decision to take time off by sending me visuals of mathematical formulae, technical designs, scientific discoveries and more, to prevent me from closing my eyes and relaxing.

Even my organs were not off limits, for she accelerated my breathing and heartrate to communicate her anxiety, when I tried to detach myself from the rest of the world and drown myself in my music. Her persistence won out and I abandoned my search of a more relaxed lifestyle. The other members of the Group did not object to her close scrutiny of their work and even found her presence reassuring and motivating.

The Group of 5 was invited to the next meeting to present their findings regarding the toxicity of the animals in the floral garden. We were relieved to learn that the various animals whose carnivorous nature was suppressed or simply diverted did not reveal any toxins. The secretion of an offensive odor, when they were under attack, left no trace residue on their fur or feathers or in their saliva, excrements, or anywhere else. Since the records of Thomas's genetic profile were destroyed by the androids in the Air and Space center just after our revolution, we could not indisputably determine whether or not he had any propensity towards allergies or other genetically transmitted diseases.

We discussed this problem with the Group of 5 during the meeting. Crawford spoke for the Group when he said. "Our careful examination of the animals, as you are all aware, disaffirm the hypothesis that Thomas could have been contaminated from close contact with them. We also carefully examined the deteriorated remains of Thomas's body and found no evidence of an allergic, viral, or bacterial reaction. Nonetheless, we found that his digestive tract was inflamed and the walls of his stomach lined with tiny holes indicating that it was perforated and damaged by a foreign substance. We believe that he consumed something poisonous for him, and perhaps all humans."

"Were you able to identify the substance?" Reinhart asked.

"No, Dr. Reinhart." Crawford replied.

"Did you find any particles of this presumably poisonous substance in his digestive tract?"

"We found residue of a fruit, perhaps a berry, which, even though we were unable to identify it by name, may have been the source of his problem." Crawford was speaking for all of them.

"That must be it!" Jason screamed with delight. We sat patiently, too patiently perhaps, for he jerked back in his chair and wiped his already sweaty brow as he struggled to give the matter some thought. "No, I did not do anything to him, you must believe me, but I think I know what he ate." His mouth dropped open in protest.

"There was a red berry that Thomas told me had a sweet, succulent meaty taste. I didn't like it because it was surrounded with black seeds, which Thomas told me were inedible. I tasted it only once, and did not find it very palatable. It left a dry, bitter taste in my mouth, so I decided not to take any unnecessary risks by eating something that did not appeal to me. And, it was difficult to pry the succulent, meaty part away from the seeds."

Teary eyed, he continued. "I didn't put the scene together until now. Perhaps I purposely blocked some things out of my conscious mind. In any event, he mentioned that he ate a couple of those seeds by accident, the reason why he asked me to find different leaves from which he could concoct a remedy. He was vomiting and looked ghastly white. He also appeared confused and his ravings frightened me." He was now choking back his sobs. "Admittedly, I wasn't certain that his request for these different plants was in any way rational, but I tried anyway. I actually did find most of the leaves he asked for, but was unable to locate one of them...the one he insisted was available and critical to his recovery. Now, in retrospect, I doubt that he could have made the remedy anyway, as his condition got worse and worse, so rapidly."

He paused for an instance to steady his breathing and wipe away the tears, before expressing his sincere regrets. "But, as I mentioned before, I was uncertain at the time that Thomas had actually died and not just passed on into a different state of conscious or unconsciousness from which he would eventually return, the reason why I carefully covered his body with leaves."

He sighed and looked around the room. "Nonetheless, the horror of those last few hours, maybe days, with Thomas left me with an eerie feeling about the floral paradise. I left not because I wanted to continue to explore, but because I was too terrified to stay." We all finally got the answer that we were looking for and that made sense. We could now stop criticizing him and start empathizing with him.

Ralph spoke up in what ironically appeared to be Jason's defense, since none of us were at the point of accusing him of anything. Our earlier impulsive suspicions had long since dissipated. "Jason certainly was not capable of identifying the various plants with any exactitude. Thomas, a biologist, familiar with agronomy, may have had no problem finding the right products to make an antidote, but, just chewing on a few different leaves would certainly not have been enough to avoid the inevitable. He was poisoned because of his own gluttony." He sat straight up, as if impressed with what he said, and then looked around the room, shaking his head slowly to clear his mind, before continuing. "I would like to visit the Floral Garden, and examine the different vegetation. From what Jason just said, I have the feeling that he ate something called an English Yew Berry, although it may have other characteristics today, perhaps mutated to a certain extent in appearance, but nonetheless still a carrier of poisonous seeds."

Our group sat perplexed, incapable of confirming the accuracy of that. The only way to be certain was to return to the floral garden. I mentioned that Jason should accompany Ralph to point out the berry, and it might be a good idea for Adam and Eunice, both architects, to go with them to examine the layout of the garden. I suggested that he take the tall man with luscious dark brown skin who worked in the agricultural center. This young man impressed me with his courage and clarity of thought after the unfortunate death of the two agronomists.

"Should we give him a name, Pamela?" Ralph asked.

"None of them took on names?"

"No. And, actually, they don't talk much, at least not in front of me." Ralph raised his eyes to avoid ours. It was clear that this bothered him. Was there any reason for us to be worried?

"Perhaps it is time to separate them." I said sternly. "Nonetheless, not giving them names was definitely an oversight on our part. How about if we call him Francis?" The name was unanimously approved.

Ruth, Sarah and John saw this as an opportunity to get away from the Center for a day or so and volunteered to accompany them. Adam knew how to drive, so I suggested he take one of the bigger vehicle so that they could go together.

"It is too bad that Andrew can't be there." Jason mentioned. It was true that it would be helpful to have him present to clarify things, but for the moment, it was better for him to remain in hiding, so we ignored his suggestion.

The meeting ended and Reinhart disappeared inside of me. I left with the Group of 5 to discuss the genetic code of Jason. Miller started talking, reminding me that he was put in suspended animation when he was only 12 years old, making him Reinhart's youngest specimen. Research revealed that his body aged three times faster than ours once he left the suspended animation and that even though he looked like he was in his early sixties, he was only our age, or around 20.

"That explains why he was so childish in his record keeping and the maps that he drew, which were but scribblings of the flat surfaces and areas he visited. And yet, this child was interested and enthusiastic about everyone he met and everything that he saw. He overlooked physical differences and found goodness in those he met." I stopped to let that sink in. "And, he was not just a child, but an uneducated child, in the body of an elderly man." I said with conviction.

We sat pondering the matter, until Miller broke the silence. "Reinhart should certainly be pleased with the results of her research. Considering the thousands of years that Jason was in suspended animation, it was remarkable that his body was still young on awakening. This confirms both her scientific ingenuity and the effectiveness of the specific cryogenic substance she used in preserving his human organs and physical characteristics over such a long period of time. Nonetheless, the reason why Jason experienced accelerated aging upon awakening should be examined more closely."

"Dr. Miller, it is evident that the accelerated aging was linked to his excessively long time in a cryogenic state. The shock of awakening after all those thousands of years must have been the catalyst for over stimulation of the human aging process. The fact that he was still alive after all that time is, as you pointed out, a very positive. It is, however, important to study and compare our research in more detail." Reinhart spoke through me. Before she thanked them for the information they provided, she reminded them that she wanted more details on Ralph and Ferdinand which they promised would be ready by the end of the day. She left them to their work.

Reinhart had uploaded enough information to me that I understood the limitations on Jason's rejuvenation. Reinhart knew that she could rejuvenate him and thereby extend his life expectancy for another 30 or 40 years. But, he would not be able to pass through rejuvenation a second time, simply because he had spent too much time in a cryogenic state.

And yet, she believed that what she could offer him today was very interesting, because he would live a long life after rejuvenation. She was confident that she could give him the physical look and vitality of a 20 year old, which would enable him to continue to live his dream of being an explorer. She also wanted him to be educated, so that he would be an explorer capable of analyzing the geographical and scientific information retrieved during his expeditions.

She offered all that later to Jason, but he did not show great enthusiasm and avoided giving an immediate answer. "I want to think about it for a while, if you don't mind. I am not certain what kind of impact this could have on me psychologically."

"Ok, I can understand that you might be frightened about the rejuvenation procedure." Reinhart left me to negotiate.

"It is you, Pamela?"

"It is always me, Jason." That wasn't quite true but I smiled warmly, putting him at ease. "Reinhart knows the technical matters, and handles the emergency situations. She is part of me, but I am always present and she does not want to change that." I said slowly, searching for the right words. "She is actually offering you a very interesting possibility and I think that you would be foolish to refuse it."

"She feels guilty that she condemned me years ago." He threw his arms up in rage.

"I don't think she is capable of feeling guilty. I can, but she can't." He let his arms fall naturally at his sides and started to breath slowly, relaxing a bit. "She is definitely impressed with your survival, which is not the extent of her fascination with you. And, she sincerely believes that you have intellectual capabilities and wants you to receive an intensive educational program." He tilted his head in thought.

If I were you, I would take her up on all that. And, think about it, you will come back young and vigorous."

His eyes suddenly grew bright! "Ok! I like the idea of starting over again, in a young body with an educated mind, if you are sincere about my receiving education." That seemed to be the key element and I nodded. "Then I won't disappoint you, Pamela." He slapped his hands together vigorously. "You talked me into it. I shall go through my rejuvenation when I get back from the floral garden." He grabbed my arm and held on tightly as he said, "Thanks, Dr. Reinhart, for giving me this opportunity."

I ate rapidly, finishing when my colleagues arrived for their evening meal. "Jason can give you the good news. I have to meet again with those androids for the information on Ralph and Ferdinand." I rushed off.

They were deep in conversation when I barged in on the group of five.

"What are you up to now?" I asked in a harsh tone.

"We just finished retrieving the information on Ferdinand and Ralph." Crawford said, as he handed me a small device used to store the digital data.

"Don't worry, Pamela, we are not conspiring against you." Gordon added, flicking her fingers in the air, like she was clearing away invisible dust particles.

"We do understand why Elisabeth is interested in Jason, but are very confused about her interest in Ralph." Flanders said. "That is exactly what we were discussing now!"

It was normal that they were confused as Ralph was not a member of Reinhart's original team. "Ralph is a vital member of our team today and we respect his knowledge in the field of agronomy."

"You are imagining the impossible." Flanders looked around expecting android chuckles. "In spite of their importance to you, it is complicated, if not impossible, to redo a human body and make it young again. Even with the genetic code, you will not be able to change any of them that radically." His comments evinced a rumble of android approval.

'They have no idea that a rejuvenation machine exists. They imagine that I am going to either rebuild or remodel their exteriors, like playing with dough, to make them look younger." Reinhart's thoughts invaded my consciousness for a brief second, before she replied curtly, exaggerating her accent, so reminiscent of a former time. "It is not your problem, is it? It is mine."

"But, Dr. Reinhart even though we do not doubt your genius, we just want to remind you that there are limits to everything." Crawford cautioned, before emitting a loud grating sound, like he was clearing his throat. "Nonetheless, we are ready to help you in any way we can."

"Don't worry, if I need your help, I shall not hesitate." She said, more out of politeness than sincerity, because the last thing that she wanted to do was to inform the Group of 5 of the rejuvenation process. In fact, she had no intention of sharing any of the intricacies of this process with anyone...machine or human. I was not certain how the other members of our team would react to this, but hoped that they would be so busy with their own projects that they would not make an effort to learn, or observe.

And so, I prepared myself physically for the long stream of sleepless nights that would follow. For whatever reason, in the beginning, I was not that interested in learning or understanding how to develop the proper computer configuration of a genetically young Jason to assure his rejuvenation. Eventually, I understood that, even though I could appreciate her ability to identify and resolve problems rapidly, I was unable to follow the complexity of her reasoning and I felt mentally exhausted by her series of cerebral highs, constantly fueled by the pressure she put on herself to find answers as quickly as possible. Eventually I decided to back off and find refuge and peace in the confines of my own mental cocoon.

After three days and nights of absence, Peter came looking for me. When he finally found me, he was more than curious about what she was doing, something that Reinhart was not pleased about, as she frowned and looked away from him when he entered the room.

"So, what brings you here so late at night, Peter?" I lay in waiting, letting her control the situation and use her own voice.

"It is you Dr. Reinhart. I should have guessed." He said brusquely. "Can I just sit down and watch...and maybe learn?" He asked eagerly, his eyes flashing.

"I work better on my own, Peter. So, if you don't mind, I promise to liberate Pamela very soon. That is, of course, if you leave now and let me finish my work." She replied.

I started to surface, believing that I would be the better one to convince Peter to leave, but, she refused to release my vocal chords and let me interact. "I don't understand why you would be so bothered by my presence." Peter persisted. "I won't interrupt you for explanations. I would just observe."

I sensed that she was about to make a serious objection and tried futilely to push Reinhart aside. "You probably won't appreciate what I am going to say, but I don't care. I designed this rejuvenation process for me in the past and never thought about sharing it with anyone else, before returning in a symbiotic relationship with Pamela. Her kind, compassionate personality has made me rethink things and behavior...but, that does not mean that I am any less cold and calculating than in the past."

"But, we are all in this together. We are a team." He blurted out in frustration.

She approached him and put her finger up to his mouth. "Let me continue, Peter." He nodded. "As I just mentioned, I shall share all of this with all of you but only after I finish the coding for all of you." She sighed.

"I suppose that I should thank you for that." He replied in a dry tone, communicating his disappointment.

She changed the subject. "The Group of 5 has complicated this procedure through their genetic manipulations and I have to find the right coding procedure and time/space configuration for each of us, including myself. The machine is programmed for a different version of Elisabeth Reinhart. I don't want to make any mistakes. I always worked better alone than on a team, and must absolutely work alone for this project."

She paused for a second. "If a mistake is made with the three urgent members –that is Ferdinand, Ralph and Jason—it will be my mistake. I shall have to live with the consequences. I don't want to share a possible failure with any of you. Once I am certain that my method is right and produces the result I want for the three of them, perhaps I will feel more comfortable getting all of you involved."

"Ok, I understand. But, Dr. Reinhart, you must stop taking all the responsibility on your own. And, you can't play the martyr by taking all the blame for mistakes. We are here to help and share responsibility for the good and bad decisions."

"I start to understand why she loves you so much, Peter." She said softly. "But, for the moment, please let me do this on my own. If ever I feel worried or frustrated, I promise that I shall turn to you for comfort." That was followed by sharp, sudden laughter, like that of the breaking of a glass.

He stared at her, his eyes dark and penetrating, as a little smile of incredulity stretched, only slightly parting his lips, before he turned and left the two of us alone together. "Did she laugh like that to underline the facetiousness of her promise or to hide her embarrassment over my genuine concern for her." He wondered.

I was now alert and watched attentively as she studied Jason's genetic code and determined which genes she was going to suppress, alter, or eventually maintain, during his rejuvenation. Nonetheless, she was still going too fast for me to follow everything. I only understood the very basic part of what she was doing. She finally tired for the night and retreated deep inside of me and I was able to reclaim my personality.

"It was risky for her to engage in her research in this lab. She should have done all of this in the inner circle." I thought to myself. "Oh well, she must have had a good reason why she chose this lab." I shook my head, as I looked down at her work. I put the final copy in a sealed folder and quickly erased everything that was on the computer, making certain that nothing of what she just did could be retrieved by anyone of us or by the Group of 5. I gathered up all of the DNA samples of our three colleagues and sealed them in a freezer bag. Before leaving, I made certain that I had taken everything and that there was no evidence of her ever having been in this room.

I opened the door to find the Group of 5 waiting outside. They startled me and my first reflex was to return to the lab to be certain that they had not installed video surveillance equipment that I was unaware of. And so, I did a thorough search before re-exiting into the corridor.

"What is wrong with you, Pamela?" Gordon asked, as she studied my body language. "Let me help you with all those packages."

"No, I need no help. But, thank you for asking." I politely replied.

"We came looking for Dr. Reinhart, but I guess only you, Pamela, were in the room."

"What do you 5 want?" I asked.

"We wanted to see Dr. Reinhart." Crawford repeated.

"Why?"

"Ok, Pamela, you win. WD is asking to speak to her." He finally explained.

"It is very late now and I am tired. I still have other work to do and I haven't slept for days." I looked at their inanimate expressions. "Just tell him that he will see one of us tomorrow." They shrugged their shoulders and turned to leave. "Wait, do you have any idea what he wants?"

"He wants to join in the exploration of the planet at least that is what he told us. He also mentioned that he is lonely and that his loneliness will eventually kill him." Flanders answered.

"What do you think?" I asked Flanders.

"He does seem a bit forlorn. Some species do die of loneliness or go crazy." His answer was not reassuring.

"Ok, I'll meet you in the zoo in 15 minutes." They nodded and left.

I rushed into the inner circle and quickly put all the information in a secure safe in the laboratory and put the DNA in the freezer compartment. I then rushed off to my room and woke up Peter.

"You have to come with me." I said, shaking him out of his sleep. I did not want to face WD with the androids on my own, so I quickly explained to him what was happening.

He grumbled as he struggled to get up and dressed. "We need Stuart and Diana, if something unexpected happens. Wait just a minute I shall go wake them up." He offered.

To his dismay they were still awake, but not happy to see him barge in on one of their playful moments, with Diana's hand lovingly massaging Stuart's lower back as he sighed contentedly. "We need you both!" He shouted as he closed the door and rushed back to me.

"They need a few minutes to cool down before getting dressed and joining us." He raised his eyebrows suggestively.

Eventually the four of us exited the inner circle for the zoo to find the Group of 5 engaged in carefree conversation with WD. "I see that you have turned this depressed mutant into a jolly, happy creature." Reinhart spoke up. They quickly moved to attention.

"I have the pleasure of addressing Dr. Reinhart." WD replied. "I was so hoping that you would give me this honor. It has been so long since you passed by to see me."

She said nothing, which put him ill at ease and he started to ramble over the fact that being alone, with stuffed animals, as the only visible companions, was starting to drive him mad. Even though it was true that only stuffed animals occupied the adjacent enclosures, Reinhart laughed loudly and vibrantly over his misery, before saying. "You were already mad when we found you and that did not seem to bother you then."

"Please Dr. Reinhart, find it in your cold heart to forgive me. Give me a chance to show my worth. I promise that I shall be a faithful member of your team."

"I am very tired, the Group of 5 has other things that they should be doing, so I'll make this offer." He nodded and swung his front flippers wildly in the air. "I shall come to see you tomorrow and listen to your needs. If none of them interest me, I shall put the microchip in your brain and add the visual receptor so that you can be happy for the rest of your life." His enthusiasm vanished and his upper body slumped forward.

The Group of 5 left with bowed heads to regain their office and the rest of us slipped back into the inner circle. "Wow, you just put the fear of God- to use an expression that was in one of Ferdinand's speeches over the intercom system- into him." Peter said and then all of us joined in for an intense chuckle.

"He is not going to sleep tonight." Stuart choked out over his laughter.

"And neither are you, Stuart." Diana said as she kissed the back of his neck, grabbed his hand and led him back to their play room.

Peter and I walked silently back to our room. "I have to look over the videos tomorrow to be certain that the conversation between WD and the members of the Group of 5 were as innocent as they pretend." I said, as I crawled into bed.

"We are all tired and sometimes that can make you feel more suspicious of others." He was trying to reassure me. "The members of the Group of 5 are diabolical, but discrete. I don't think that they would purposely put themselves in a comprising situation just to incite Reinhart's suspicions."

"You might be right, but I am going to check out the video and audio systems, just to reassure myself that they did not manipulate anything. I might even go back a couple days to determine how much time they are spending with WD."

"Ok, you do that." He said, as he approached me with a playful smile on his face. "I am glad that we left them to fend for themselves."

He pulled me up out of the bed, gently caressing my hips, as he moved them up against him, letting me feel his desire. His hungry eyes scanned me, making my body tremble and yearn, and I reached up to him, caressing the corners of his face and letting my fingertips glide delicately over the contours of his lips.

But, when our gaze met and fixed for a second, a wave of fear quenching my desire rushed through me, and I reacted forcefully, using my hands to open up some space between us. "Are those cold, lusterless, hollow eyes for me or to discourage someone else?" Passed through my mind.

He was deft to my low laughter over his foolishness. His thoughts were elsewhere, for my futile attempt to free myself obsessed, and aroused him even more as he firmly grabbed my hands together in a swift move and held them tightly in place behind me.

"Are you ok Peter?" I asked in a calm, steady voice, hoping to awaken him from a sexually driven trance.

He didn't answer, just smiled in a strangely seductive, and passionately eager way, as he gently caressed my hair and cradled the back of my neck with his left hand, before drawing my mouth close to his. His slow and tender kisses became deeper temptations, making me dizzy with my burning erotic desire. He gradually relaxed his grip on my hands, giving me back my freedom, only to fondle and dominate me. And my body and mind responded lovingly to his teasing and lascivious quests for pleasure. He lifted and turned me moving us into untested, provocatively adventuresome positions, letting deep seeded fantasies become reality, until we could no longer resist that burst of orgasmic pleasure, drawing us together in a dramatic, expression of our love.

Our bodies laid intimately entwined on the cold floor, for a long moment, before Peter gently lifted my face up close to his, and stared with great intensity into my eyes. I understood that he still wanted to reassure himself that he was with… me. I did not want to say anything. It would have ruined the moment. Instead, I smiled vividly, my eyes sparkling, accepting that for whatever reason, he needed to send a message to Elisabeth that he loved me. I sensed that she saw humor in his innocent, yet determined, affirmation of love for me, simply because she never doubted that and I knew that she would never interfere in any manner with his immutable worship and commitment to me.

Chapter 27- Enlightening Discoveries

I was energetic and positive when I woke up and could not wait to get on with my many and varied projects. I attacked the WD file first, skimming through earlier video and audio tapes between the Group of 5 and WD that were available on the computer system in the inner circle, before laboring over the more recent ones that revealed daily visits by members of the Group of 5. There was very little conversation in the beginning between WD and the androids. And, WD, laying lazily on his outstretched body, holding his upper body erect with his front flippers, exhibited no suspicious body language.

It appeared though that WD was more fascinated by them, than they were in him, because his eyes followed them closely when they spoke or moved, whereas the Group of 5 avoided eye contact with him and did inquire about his past or present life. They seemed to treat these visits as a routine task assigned to them to keep them busy.

There was something so surrealistic about their encounters that I wondered how prudent it was to let WD meet regularly with the Group of 5. Was he more diabolical than them? His inquisitive intelligence led him to take his time studying the members of the Group of 5, individually and together, before disclosing his concerns, like complaining to them about how loneliness might end up killing him, or that his vegetarian diet did not provide him with the vitamins and minerals he needed to survive.

One definitely had to be leery of his craftiness. I was not certain that the Group of 5 would intentionally align themselves with him. They were too conscious of Reinhart's power over them. And yet, they had remnants of their former emotional configurations that made them susceptible to flattery, something that WD was adept at using.

When I met with the Group of 5, in their large office, their reactions to his lamentations were predictable. I saw Crawford shake his head and throw his hands up in the air in total disinterest while Miller and the former Governor stood at attention, with a nod here and there, to hide their boredom.

Only Gordon and Flanders seemed curious, showing a genuine desire to learn more about him. Gordon suggested that his behavior was often times so emotive that she had the impression that he had either developed human-like emotions or knew how to convincingly simulate them; the reason why she wanted to study his behavior in more detail. She even argued that his reactions might give her more insight into issues of human instability.

Flanders suggested that perhaps by inadvertence-contact with a human before he devoured his victim or from the fairytales about humans that were passed on from one dolphin generation to another-he might be capable of emulating humans. Flanders also told me that he mentioned to WD that he would suggest that Reinhart move him to another part of Center.

"Yes, my suggestion definitely pleased him, because he clapped his flippers hard with enthusiasm and let out some boisterous dolphin cries of happiness." Flanders added in his monotone, android voice.

"I think that you all have to be cautious when you meet with WD. He is looking for allies and you seem to fit the bill for the moment."

"Ridiculous. We would never ally ourselves with anyone but Elisabeth." Crawford replied and the others nodded.

"Well, let's hope so." I said in a commanding tone and they lowered their heads in due respect.

"I wonder what he is going to offer today." I said in a whisper before thanking them for their candor and preparing to leave. I decided to meet WD on my own.

He was laying dotingly on his side, with his back to the outside world. He did not sense my presence, or if he did, he pretended not to. I cleared my throat loudly enough to startle him out of either innocent daydreaming. He turned slowly, with painful groaning, in my direction.

"Oh, which one are you?" He asked, hoping to hedge his bet, by engendering concern or sympathy from one of us.

I ignored his play for compassionate understanding and went straight to the point. "When I left last evening, I gave you an ultimatum." He pulled himself up into a sitting position, revealing his walrus tusks in all their splendor.

He let out a long, tedious sigh and began speaking. "Yes, I do have something to offer you besides just my body for scientific research." He moved to the glass enclosure and lifted his heavy body up, leaning on the glass protection to help him support his weight. I instinctively backed up in face of his imposing size, more out of surprise than fear, but he interpreted my reaction as an opportunity to gain control.

I stood my ground! When he was satisfied that his dramatic move had an impact on me, he let himself fall back away from the glass barrier into a comfortable sitting position.

"Now, where was I....Oh, yes, I was about to tell you, Pamela, why you might want to keep me in my present intellectual state."

"You better get on with your story, because I don't like to waste time." He stiffened when he heard Reinhart's voice, her accent ringing through loud and clear. He was no longer in command.

"Yes, Dr. Reinhart, I have an offer, one that I already made. But this time, I am ready to share information." He said as he slithered on his belly to approach for a second time the glass barrier. "I know what is in the high seas." He said softly, as if someone might be listening to our conversation. "I visited the region when I was very young. That is probably why I was so disgusted with the ludicrous stories of those foolish dolphins." He stared into my eyes, trying to read Reinhart's thoughts before going on. "There are large sea creatures, but not dinosaurs, dragons or sea monsters. They a kind of mutated whale."

"I don't see how this makes any difference to me." She said as she turned to leave.

"No, listen, I can scout for you and I will scout for you!" He screamed. Reinhart turned back to him. "I know that you dislike me

448

and consider me to be a despicable creature. Maybe you are right, but we were trained, educated and manipulated by our ancestors and...quite frankly, we had no choice but to mimic what they did." He stopped to make large circles on the sandy surface with his flippers, as if he was in deep concentration. "Today, I am the last of those creatures-the others are programmed to exist in that rosy colored world, thanks to you."

He got no reaction so continued. "Being the last of a species is already disconcerting. But, being the last and alone, is disarming. I am ready to surrender-to even bow in humiliation for the chance to live."

Reinhart laughed boisterously and he smiled insipidly at her mocking tone. "For all I know, you have followers out there in the high seas and it is in your interest to join them." She insinuated.

"I don't know." He said, lifting his heavy shoulders in doubt. "But, if you let me join your team, you won't be disappointed. I have nothing to lose, certainly...everything to gain by working with you. And," he looked up at the ceiling pretending to read the future, "I know that they have no chance against you and the others. Let's just say that I want to be with the winning side." He replied, with an unwavering glance.

"I don't trust you." He nodded. "But then, I am prepared for your disloyalty. But, are you prepared for mine?" He flinched. "One-and, I mean, one-mistake on your part and you're terminated. Do you understand?"

"It is a stressful situation you are offering me, even as I am offering you my life, as a scout. I am intelligent and capable of contributing to yours, and now, my cause, if I can be so audacious as to consider myself a member of your team. And, I shall be out there all alone confronting unknown dangers. But that is not enough. I'll be taking big risks, uncertain that you will even try to save me, if need be. To make it even worse, you are now telling me that no matter where, how or when I make a mistake, it is over for me." He rubbed his flippers slowly over his long whiskers, keeping an immutable eye contact with her. "But, I like confronting danger, so you have a deal, Dr. Reinhart. And, you will never regret it."

"I hope that there is some degree of sincerity in what you just said." She sighed. "In any event, for today, I don't know where to move you and this enclosure offers you space, water, and good food. I can never authorize the removal of the tracking devices and they will always be part of your dress attire." He nodded. "So, until you have proven your worth and your loyalty, which could take years, you will remain a prisoner, but a prisoner who gets to participate and contribute to the exploration of this planet."

"And, company, can I have any?" He asked pleadingly. "Maybe my female partner. Even programmed, she will be company for me."

"I'll have to see that with the others." She looked at the adjacent enclosures filled with stuffed animals and grimaced. "You will just have to ignore your neighbors for the moment, if they bother you that much. In the meantime, I want you to give all the details of the various creatures that you encountered on your early expeditions to Diana. There are specimens in our labs, and I want to know if any of them still exist, or have mutated cousins. She will meet with you every day to gather information."

"Diana!" He opened his eyes wide and shook his head. "She is dangerous." He swallowed hard, as if his collapsing ego was trapped in his throat and then mustered the strength to reply in an enthusiastic tone. "Oh, what the h___! She will be someone to talk to." He snickered.

"I'll be back again very soon." I said.

"Have a nice day, Pamela." He retorted. It was now clear that he could decipher the two personalities, not just with the voice tone but with the mannerisms. He was definitely a clever creature.

I went to see Diana and explained everything to her. "You are not afraid to spend time with him?" I asked.

"Yes, he is potentially dangerous and if ever he breaks through the barriers, he could devour me. But, I have a feeling-and I don't know why-that he likes the idea of being one of Reinhart's team players." She said firmly. "Nonetheless, I am taking a laser gun with me, just in case."

I returned to the lab in the inner circle to take another look at last evening's research. I decided that it was safer for me to use the more innovative, accurate equipment in the inner circle that was outside the watchful eyes of the Group of 5, even if it meant that

I might have friends popping in on me—the reason why Reinhart chose the other lab. Her research started to make sense to me and I no longer had to hide deep inside myself, but could watch and learn.

Jason would be the first, the guinea pig, simply because his physical side was deteriorating so rapidly that we had no other choice. If I were in any way worried, it was overshadowed by her strong satisfaction with her research and sincere conviction that everything would go well. Her earlier worries had long since disappeared and she was definitely more optimistic.

I sat back pondering the situation for a few minutes while she relaxed somewhere inside of me. My trepidations, inspired certainly by my more emotional self, jolted me back into the real world. What if it doesn't work, will she be as disappointed as I will be? Is she ready to sacrifice Jason and Ralph, if need be, to assure success with Ferdinand? Could I or would I blame her, or would I just be sad if her first two experiments failed? Only time would tell, was my last thought, before her warmth suffused me and I willingly let her regain control, while I watched and learned.

Immersed in the project Ralph, she worked diligently and rapidly, finding solutions and preparing the right code for his rejuvenation without any sign of bewilderment. It was as if she felt no challenge anymore; everything had become very simple and evident. Before I assimilated all the intricacies of that program, she was already studying Ferdinand's genetic profile. She was particularly at ease at this point and she needed very little time to complete the programming for his rejuvenation. When she finished, I was drowning in genetic codes and desperately needed to come up for air, so I was glad that she finally vanished inside of me.

I organized all the information and put the sealed envelope into a safe that could not be accessed by anyone else. I walked back into the lounge area and gave Ferdinand a quick kiss on the top of his head. "You will soon be young and dynamic again."

I then rushed off to join Peter and Frederic in the dining room. "Has everyone eaten already?

"No. The others will be joining us soon. They went to get Francis, so that we could bring him up-to-date on the trip to the botanical garden." Peter quickly changed the subject. "And has she completed the rejuvenation programs for the three candidates?"

"Yes, Peter, she finished it and will start with Jason when he returns." We exchanged looks of admiration for her. "She is incredible, huh?"

"Yes, she definitely is. But, she is so enigmatic, a bit like the members of the Group of 5. The closer I get to knowing her the farther away she appears to be." He let out a heavy sigh. "Her intellectual capacity is infinite."

Our discussion ended abruptly as the others arrived, escorting Francis to our table. Up until now he and the other members of his group were still confined to their cubicles for meals. He appeared stiff and ill-at-ease when he sat down to eat, apparently no one had explained to him why he was summoned. I sat back in my chair to study him for a brief moment, just to confirm my first impressions. He looked straight into my eyes, showing determination, instead of resistance or even fear. I liked that and smiled radiantly back at him. He responded without moving his lips. That interested me because he showed me character.

"Well, Francis-that is the name that I chose for you, I hope that you are pleased with it?" He shrugged his shoulders. "I shall explain to you why you were invited to join us today for lunch." He nodded, maintaining control over his emotions and body language. I explained the mission to him. He listened in silence, registering every word, before replying.

"I feel honored with your request, but am afraid that I shall have to decline the offer." He sat back in his chair and folded his arms.

"Why?" Stuart asked.

"Because the other members of my team-those of us you accused of violent behavior and have been punishing for months-might consider me to be a kind of...traitor." He sighed. "They are my friends and I don't want to offend them. You can certainly understand that." None of us reacted. "You should be making the same offer to all of us."

He pushed his chair back and moved to stand up to leave.

"Wait." John's thundering voice stopped Francis in his tracks. "What you just said is true. You demonstrate the kinds of human qualities like justice, concern, compassion, and so on that we are all happy to see." We nodded. "Nonetheless, we cannot take all of you in the transport vehicle, but we can involve them in another way in our mission."

I wondered what John was insinuating. "We shall be examining different plants and animal species." He looked at all of us, one after the other. "If all of us agree, Francis's friends could follow us on the visual screen, recording our discoveries and sending us vital information about the species and their potential toxicity. Even though they would not be with us on the outside, they would be contributing to the discovery in constructive ways."

"Yes, involving them in this project in vital and constructive ways is appealing." Francis broke the long silence.

"I agree." Ralph spoke up energetically. "They were all educated in agronomy and work very well for me. Of course, Francis is an agricultural engineer, which distinguishes him, in a way from the others, and justifies our choosing him to accompany us on the visit. And, well, John's proposal gives the others a chance to get involved." He stopped and rubbed the tiny bristles on his chin, before adding that he was definitely in favor of John's suggestion.

Mathilda cautioned us against creating any kind of animosity between members of the group, by liberating Francis from the restrictions and isolation that was to have been a group punishment and recommended following John's suggestion.

Stuart suggested that now was perhaps the right moment to reintegrate all of them into the human community, by suspending the punishment for good conduct over the last few months.

In the end, we all voted in favor of suspending the punishment and decided that Francis and Ralph would meet with the other members of the group and get their impressions. Ralph felt that the team members would be more relaxed and would not hesitate to show their feelings if they were only confronted by the two of them. It seemed logical.

"When do you expect to leave?" I finally asked.

"We are ready to leave the day after tomorrow." John, who was organizing everything, replied. "We must get on with this as quickly as possible." He pulled slowly, methodically, on his long beard.

"I thought that it might be a good idea to order Andrew to return momentarily to this center. We decided that it was too soon for him to join us on our explorations, but that doesn't mean that we should not pick his brain, so to speak, about the architectural aspects of that garden. We don't trust him, but we can still use him."

Diana was so opposed to having him prowl around the center that she vehemently registered her objection. We decided to take her feelings into account and have him meet the others at the floral garden and then return to the confines of his cavern after disclosing the architectural technics to Adam and Eunice. Our meeting broke up and we went off in our own directions to accomplish our various tasks.

Less than 48 hours later, we waved goodbye to a new group of explorers who would investigate the plant and animal life in place. The other members of the agronomy department were ready to participate in the assessment and analyses of the various specimens. And, Andrew, was on his way to join Adam and Eunice to explain how he conceived the floral garden.

"What an honor this is for me, Dr. Reinhart." He replied, bowing his head in deference, when I contacted him asking him to join the group at the floral garden. He might be as slimy as Diana said he was, but for the moment, his knowledge was useful and it was important for us to exploit him.

In addition to confirming that the English yew berry was responsible for Thomas's death, the group made other enlightening discoveries. Firstly, their cursory inspection of the animal life—relatively limited in species to foxes, wolves, rabbits, squirrels, chipmunks and hedgehogs, a few turtles and frogs living around the waterfall, and blue jays, robins, colorful parrots, several large cockatoos, small finches, red cardinals, eagles, hawks and parakeets flying complacently alongside each other. One of the startling points was that all the species were males and our research revealed that there were no sexual modifications underway.

From the agricultural perspective, large oak trees lived next to Palm trees, while roses and orchid lived in a symbiotic relationship. There were many types of berries and wild flowers in other sections of the garden.

A meeting was scheduled the day after the group returned from the floral garden and the former governor was invited to that meeting to comment. He informed us that he wanted to keep the number of occupants low and was worried that if the species reproduced that they would outsize the floral garden quickly. "This is, of course, why I chose to have only male animal life in the garden." He commented in a low tone. "And, I was also worried that recessive genes arising from reproduction could modify the olfactory systems that I had contrived and wanted to maintain in place, causing the animals to revert to predatory, carnivorous behavior."

The curious fact that the birds did not venture outside the confines of the garden did not seem of real interest to the former Governor. He could give no clear reason for this peculiarity and conjectured that it was because they had sufficient food sources and proper climate year around which meant simply that they did not have to seek new hunting grounds or migrate for better living conditions.

The research team drew our attention to the lack of insect life. They contended that insects were a source of food—their value undermined by the fact that they constituted a source of viable, living protein which would only be ignored by modified carnivorous animals---but that their existence was necessary to maintain a balanced eco-structure. "I, personally, would like to have insects available for our agricultural production." Ralph ventured. "And, do not understand the absence of these tiny creatures in the floral garden."

The former governor reminded us again and again that the garden was his distraction, both intellectually and visually, and that if the animals or plants did not survive, he would have replaced them. "Dr. Reinhart found the entire insect world repulsive and, even if she registered no fear of insects, she mentioned to me on many occasions that if she could exterminate all insect life she would." He forced a deep android crackle. "Dr. Reinhart must be grateful to us that we did not seek to recreate insects."

I registered her satisfaction with the former Governor's decision from the slight bubbling sensation in my stomach, but did not comment on this to the rest of the group whose mouths gaped in silence over the former Governor's revelation.

Ferdinand quickly changed the subject mentioning that Andrew shared his architectural knowledge with Eunice and Adam and even offered to help them build habitats out of the clay soil and open up other caverns for communal living. He informed us that the underground river was the source of water in this garden and in the center. "Apparently Andrew believes that he can easily provide water directly to the caverns if the rest of us want that." He announced in a throaty, vibrant voice. Building new outside communities appealed to all of us. And so it was agreed that Adam and Eunice would work with Andrew, using some of the androids assigned to the Agricultural unit to start construction in the near future.

Just talking about this in-depth study of the floral garden---which fascinated Reinhart on both an intellectual and sensory level---and imagining new housing popping up outside the various centers, reminded us that we had to leave soon to explore other parts of the earth's surface and ocean environment. We agreed on the need for a few weeks more to organize ourselves and celebrate the birth of a new generation of humans, after which our original group would leave for the northern hemisphere.

The meeting became very animated when Peter brought up the subject of space travel. "It would appear that space craft have been entering our atmosphere for the last 75 to 100 years, depending upon whether our calculations in earth years are based on the time warp in this center or the real, earth years on the outside." He stopped to observe our reaction, which brought a big smile to his face, before continuing. "The only real data regarding alien visits was in the computer at the Air and Space Center. Drager gave me that information months ago now. It took me some time to analyze it and..." he sighed, "much to my regret there were no survivors."

"We knew that already." Randolph interrupted sarcastically.

"Of course, we thought that. Now I can confirm it." He answered curtly. "Maybe I naively wanted to discover something different, something that would give us more hope." He let his remarks sink in before continuing. "The two astronauts, Anderson and Hadley, were the ones who communicated directly with this center. There is sufficient evidence that a vast number of space craft disintegrated upon entry and that the androids discarded the scrap metal and salvaged the instruments that were intact."

He sat back comfortably in his chair and stared into my eyes. "As she must suspect, the androids did recover ten space craft and those ten are in the Air and Space Center in a special room that was closed off to us during our last visit. I suggest that a small group of us go and examine the vessels and see if we can make contact with the Mother ship."

"You think that all these space craft were launched from the same Mother ship?" I ventured.

"Impossible to know." He replied brusquely. "I suspect that the later space craft was modified for better entry into our atmosphere. There must have been a problem with the gravitational force of the earth or the speed in which they entered our atmosphere or even the construction of the vessel itself that caused the other vessels to crash on entry."

Stuart finally broke his long silence. "So, if I understand, you think that only astronauts, Anderson and Hadley, or the ones that you actually heard contact this center, were killed by the androids."

"I don't know. It is all conjecture." Peter fidgeted in his seat as if he was trying to escape an awkward confrontation, before continuing. "The other vessels that were retrieved are intact, even though I have not yet inspected them. I believe that those astronauts did not survive the force of entry and the space craft landed on automatic pilot because there is no record of any communication between the astronauts and the androids. The only registered communications are from Anderson and Hadley. And, those registrations and commands came directly from this center."

"They might have erased the other communications." Randolph suggested.

"Maybe, but then they didn't have any reason to do that. They never thought that we would be back in control and that they would have to defend their position. The moment when they realized that we were interested in the incoming space craft, the crew at the Air and Space center surrendered all the information to us." He paused, taking the time to imagine the scenario.

"Yes," he continued, "they were programmed to kill the astronauts and retrieve the space craft. I think that they intercepted the space craft, followed it and when the vessel landed simply disposed of the dead bodies. I don't believe that they ever communicated with any other astronauts. This would also explain why there was a long time period between Anderson's entry and the other wave of astronauts. Hadley appeared close behind Anderson."

"Well, that just means that we must return to the Air and Space center to examine the different space craft, like you suggested." I commented. The others nodded. "I shall go with Peter and anyone else who is interested can accompany us. I think that we should leave tomorrow."

The meeting ended and we left with a new wave of enthusiasm, visibly evident the following morning when the entire exploration team, including the reptilian humans, were ready to leave. James and Reinhart piloted the aircraft and we were at the Air and Space Center in a short 30 minutes. Quite inadvertently, we formed our human group of five –Randolph, Stuart, Peter, Diana and I- while the others wandered off in different directions, looking over the large vessels that would be able to carry a large sized crew for space exploration.

Reinhart led us directly to the secret chamber. For an instance I could feel my throat tighten, as she entered the code that opened the door to the secret chamber. "Did she regret having forgotten to visit this chamber the first time, or was she annoyed that she could no longer keep it a secret?" I must be a skeptic, I thought, as I moved aside letting her lead the way, while I watched and learned.

There were 10 space craft, five of which showed severe erosion to their outer shells, caused certainly by the force and speed of entry. There were 3 others that seemed to have suffered less caustic damage, but sat in striking contrast to the smooth, unfettered exteriors of the remaining 2—the space craft of Anderson and Hadley. I suggested that we start with the 5 visibly damaged space craft to better compare the changes. After examining the space craft in evolutionary order, it was evident that the equipment, cockpit, sanitary facilities and survival units with medical, food and water supplies, were all the same. Each was also equipped with a cryogenic sack that was laid out, ready for use.

"How does this work?" Peter asked, looking straight at me, knowing that I would have to let Reinhart be the active player.

"I want to examine it in more detail." Reinhart was on top of the problem. "Yes, it is a cryogenic sack, or cocoon, that has biological readers in it. It is a like a sleeping bag." She pointed to the cryogenic cocoon that was laid out on a hard metal bed. "The biological readers are designed to react to the genetic code of a given astronaut. Very interesting, indeed." She gently placed my hand inside the cocoon to demonstrate that it did not respond to my genetic code. "Of course, the cocoon gently and slowly wraps itself around the astronaut, putting him or her in a cryogenic state. The biological readers monitor the vital signs of the astronaut, making adjustments in organ functioning when necessary."

She examined closely the interior of the cocoon. "The cocoon takes the appearance of the outer skin of the astronaut, but complex life support systems are hidden in the interior. These systems provide optimum comfort for the journey and will respond, if necessary, to maintain the life of a given astronaut, whose DNA profile is incorporated into the technical design of each cocoon." She said, as she pointed out the life support systems—breathing tubes, cardiac regulators, thermal detectors and more- so finely imbedded into the smooth interior of the cocoon that these integrated support systems were barely visible to the naked eye. "It is extraordinary—an incredible discovery, that I should have considered. Why didn't I?" She criticized herself.

"Of course, those bulky cryogenic tubes that took up so much space in the ships that I sent off have been replaced by a simple cryogenic covering. These are the product of technological geniuses or..." She didn't finish the sentence, just picked up the cocoon, which weighed no more than a couple pounds. "I shall take this with me to study it. I just want to compare it to the one in Hadley's ship, which, of course, is the most recent. I shall also be able to verify Anderson's and Hadley's contentions that they are the descendants of those who left on my exploratory mission because the cocoon's programming will give me their genetic code, or DNA."

We followed her to Hadley's vessel. She recovered the cocoon that he had disposed of and then picked up the one that was awaiting his return. "The Mother ship is not as close to us as I was hoping, otherwise these astronauts would not have had to enter into a cryogenic state." She went to the cockpit and looked over the controls. "They made only minor adjustments to what I had put in the control panels. We must test the material used in the construction of these vessels and compare that to what we used here on Earth. It appears to look the same."

"We should be able to retrieve the messages sent by the astronauts to the Mother ship and any sent on to the planet Earth. John would be good at this, but do you think that you can also work on this, Randolph?" He nodded vigorously.

We then spent the day testing and examining the substances used to construct the space craft, the telecommunications systems, and liquid and food substances that were stored inside.

The astronaut, Hadley, told Peter that they found a planet suitable for life, which meant that basic food substances existed and there was a liquid that was drinkable in its natural state or, at least, had a hydrogen and oxygen base that could be retrieved and converted to water. The energy drinks in the refrigeration unit of the space craft were comprised of the vitamins and minerals that normally come from the soil, plants, fruits, and other natural, nutritional substances growing in a given environment.

The telecommunications confirmed Peter's conjectures. The astronauts did contact the Mother ship just before entry into the earth's atmosphere to confirm their awakening and ask permission to proceed to a landing. The last communications with the Mother ship from the first eight vessels were distress signals indicating that the ships were gaining too much speed and that the ships were not responding to their commands. Whether they switched to autopilot and hid in another part of the spaceship hoping to survive a violent impact was impossible to confirm. The androids had cleaned the vessels so thoroughly that there was no trace of human remains.

Both Anderson and Hadley arrived when the Group of 5 was in Command. Anderson was apparently killed by the androids during the chase scene that Peter overheard when he was a deprogram-med human, living in the Center. He was hiding in a closet in the control room and heard the conversation between Anderson and the androids. He heard the androids order their pilots to intercept and destroy Anderson. The evidence of laser impact on Anderson's vessel confirmed that unfortunate incident.

Peter, who was at the command station for just a few minutes, gave Hadley permission to land. And he did properly land the space craft, which was in excellent condition. He was certainly one of their best. Nonetheless, the androids received the order to kill Hadley.

"So, Peter, what you witnessed or rather heard was real." I said in a low voice.

"We can contact the Mother ship." Randolph came running towards me with the news. "I have the coordinates. Do you want me to try?"

I felt Reinhart's warm energy moving rapidly inside of me. "I shall take the call." Reinhart said, exaggerating her special accent.

Randolph opened the communications for Reinhart to make contact. "Dr. Elisabeth Reinhart contacting Colonel Shannon." The five of us waited for what seemed like hours. No one replied.

Finally Reinhart repeated her request adding, "I know you've been reluctant to reply, but let me assure you that humans have regained control of the planet Earth. We are saddened by the horrors that have befallen the generations of humans prece-ding us and with the deaths of your brave and honorable astro-nauts." Reinhart hesitated before adding. "Although I do not re-cognize your name, Colonel Shannon, as a descendant of one of the original members of my team, I remember the progenitors of Anderson and Hadley. Let me assure you that we are contacting you in friendship."

Another long pause ensued before a voice came through. "Colonel Shannon to Dr. Reinhart. We have verified your voice, which indicates that we are in contact with you, Dr. Reinhart, or someone who is so cleverly using her voice." She cleared her throat. "My name did not appear on the list of the original scientists sent to explore other planets. I am the descendant of one of the few as-sistants that accompanied the group." Sarcasm was resonating in her voice. "How could anyone, even you, have survived all those thousands of years?"

"Colonel Shannon, your breach of protocol has been noted. I do not have to convince you or anyone of my existence. As you are so persuaded that I could not have achieved immortality, our conversation has come to an end." Reinhart switched off the communication.

"What did you do?" Peter grabbed me firmly by my shoulders.

"I did nothing." I replied. "You know how she is. She is not going to kneel down to anyone.-Shannon irritated her. We shall have to take another approach."

"A light is flashing on the panel, indicating an incoming message. I think that she is trying to contact us!" Stuart screamed. "Do you want me to reply?"

"Let Peter answer. Tell her that you were the one that was in contact with Hadley just before he was intercepted by the androids. Tell her your story."

"And if she asks about Reinhart?" He asked with trepidation.

"Just tell her that Reinhart is looking into the less distinguished members of the scientific team aboard the space craft that she constructed and launched thousands of years ago."

Peter answered and explained briefly his role with Hadley and why he was unable to protect him. When she asked to speak to Reinhart again, he repeated what Reinhart instructed him to say. There was tension in her voice when she replied. "I regret my doubts regarding the existence of you, Dr. Reinhart. I must consult my superiors and I shall be back to you with their decision as rapidly as possible. Thank you for your explanation, Dr. Feragan."

Reinhart's emphatic remark put all of us ill at ease, effacing our previous excitement. We worked in silence, collecting as much information as possible and transmitting it to John. I felt uncomfortable and avoided contact with the others' cold, dark, unwavering eyes.

Finally, I felt Reinhart surfacing and I quickly moved aside so that she could defend herself. "I said what was necessary. If I had tried to cajole her into believing that I was still alive, that would have been diametrically opposed to my legendary personality. You must trust me. They will get back to us and we will be working together again very soon." She disappeared inside of me, leaving me to dodge their sneers.

We were just getting ready to pack things up for the day and go for dinner when the display panel opened up. In front of us sat a middle-aged woman, wearing an officer's uniform. Large deep, blue eyes drew attention away from her thin, drawn face. "I want to extend my sincere apologies to you, Dr. Reinhart." There was tension in her voice.

Reinhart said nothing and they sat staring at each other. Finally, Colonel Shannon spoke. "I sit in awe of your genius and your beauty, Dr. Reinhart, both of which have survived time."

"I accept your apologies." Reinhart replied in a dry, administrative tone. "Now, if we can talk business. I am very interested in working closely with you and your superiors in continuing space exploration. But, before that, I want to be brought up to date on everything relating to the original voyage—the problems the androids confronted, the choice and the location of the planet selected---and how human life survived and developed. I also want to see all the scientific research conducted by my original team and those who followed."

"I shall do my best to get all this information to you rapidly." She cleared her throat. "The voyage was long, so our history is rather short. We are presumably living on Gliese 667Cc, in the Scorpion constellation. Although, I have heard mentioned that we are on a planet in the Libra Constellation." Colonel Shannon ignored Reinhart's visible choking response to that news and continued. "So, as I said, our story is not as voluminous as you might think."

"I don't understand." Reinhart interrupted. "You should have inhabited the exoplanet that I selected or, Wolf 1061c in the Wolf Constellation. Even though I considered either Gliese 667Cc in the Scorpion Constellation or Gliese 581g in the Libra Constellation as interesting options, I finally decided in favor of the exoplanet Wolf 1061c in the Wolf Constellation."

"Yes. But, as I said, we are not certain what planet or exoplanet we are living on. Nonetheless, the names and points of reference that Earthlings assigned to these exoplanets were ...lost." She said, the word riding on a breath.

"Is that all that you can tell me?" Reinhart asked sharply.

"The androids did wake up a number of the scientists on board who apparently agreed that the voyage should continue." She sighed deeply before continuing. "A lot of information was either lost or intentionally destroyed by the androids on board the ship, so much of what happened is pure conjecture on the part of the original scientists. The androids also claimed that they encountered many difficulties and that the ship was often times forced off course in order to avoid collision with celestial objects, black holes and space debris. That naturally prolonged the voyage."

"That still does not explain why the ship did not land on its original point of destination." Reinhart insisted. "The ship was equipped with sophisticated warp drive capable of stretching space time in a wave causing the fabric of space ahead of the spacecraft to contract and the space behind to expand. The ship was programmed to ride the waves, accelerating to high speeds."

Reinhart stopped to collect her thoughts. "I also programmed the route and laid out the various wormholes, or areas of warped space with great energy that create tunnels through space time, that the ship would engage during the course of its voyage to the chosen exoplanet. The spaceship was equipped with an effective thrust force which would activate before entering the mouth of the wormhole giving it the speed necessary to pass rapidly through the wormhole in a kind of free fall and exit at other end of the tunnel."

Reinhart sighed in disgust. "The only logical explanations are that the wormhole configurations were incorrect, which is extremely doubtful; or that someone manipulated the android programming and sent your ancestors on a more dangerous route."

"Your questions are valid, Dr. Reinhart. Maybe there was even an attempt to sabotage the mission. Unfortunately, I am not capable of answering them. Nonetheless, our planet is perfect for humans and the original scientists made extraordinary discoveries, continued asteroid mining which you developed, and ameliorated space travel."

She looked down at her hands, perhaps looking for the right words before continuing. "After Captain Hadley was killed, we withdrew far away from your solar system, under orders to protect ourselves from inhuman reprisals. I am surprised that we have such good visual and voice contact considering the distance between us."

"We shall launch two of our officers off in a small craft to meet with you." She continued. "I shall keep you informed and give you their coordinates so that you can follow their vessels. Even though it is a short trip with warped speed, they will be in their cryogenic cocoons until they arrive outside the Earth's atmosphere. Our vessel will be on alert should they incur problems. The voyage will take more than nine months."

"We look forward to their visit. In the meantime, please send me all the information I have requested so that we can study your progress and thereby facilitate our mutual cooperation in the future." The conversation was over and Reinhart disappeared inside of me, leaving me in an awkward position vis-à-vis my colleagues, who wanted reassurance.

Fortunately, Peter came to my rescue, articulating what we all were all thinking in harbored secrecy. "We must stop doubting her. She knows how to interface with others and get them motivated." Nervous laughter accompanied us as we dashed off to the dining room to eat.

The ambiance had changed for the better under the direction of Fleming and Jarod, who stopped by to see me and send their message of gratitude to Reinhart for assigning them to the Air and Space center.

The following day was more pleasure than work, exploring the enormous ships that were capable of carrying hundreds of humans to colonize new worlds. Reinhart was more interested in the vessels that would carry mining crews and return laden with natural resources that were necessary to rebuild the Earth. The androids at the center knew how they functioned and gave cursory instruction to Peter, Stuart, Randolph, Diana, James, Isabel and Mathieu on how to operate these vehicles.

"Well, any of you who are interested in piloting and working aboard these vessels can return at another time for further instruction." I said as I started to move in the direction of my aircraft and ready it for departure. "We need to get back to the Center and study the information that we will be receiving from Colonel Shannon."

I felt sad, just as sad as my friends, leaving these magnificent vessels behind, wishing that it were the right moment to jump aboard and leave for new horizons. And yet, I felt the Reinhart inside of me holding me back. Her warmth suffused me with more vigor and energy when we talked about scientific expeditions on the Planet Earth than when we spoke of space travel. Clearly, she was more interested in exploring the planet Earth, than rushing off to visit other celestial paradises. I knew that she would eventually determine my fate and that of the others.

Chapter 28-The Art of Manipulation

The next few weeks just flew by. The six new babies, 5 human and 1 reptilian human, were born and happy parents were rushing about showing off their descendants. Flanders was particularly pleased with the new born babies who were in his care. "Those artificial uteruses function extraordinarily well. It is amazing that the machine received Mathilda's daughter at three months and nurtured her until her birth. That was a new accomplishment for us. We already knew of their efficacy from the moment of conception, but we had never transferred a three-month old fetus into the uterus before. You have to admit, Pamela, that these machines have real value."

"Yes, these babies are as healthy as those carried to term in a human uterus." I replied in a whisper, as my thoughts moved closer to accepting this as the right solution for Peter and me. Mathieu's and Isabel's son spent his entire period of gestation in an artificial uterus and was as happy and healthy at his birth as my Frederic was. Of course, both sets of parents did spend time with their babies, interacting with them through tender words, as they lightly stroked the exterior of the machine, penetrating its surface with their parental love that vibrantly traveled through the embryonic fluid and reassured their children.

I was worried about Reinhart's ability to interfere with my body's normal hormonal level, or, even worse, impede my production of ova capable of being fertilized, simply because she was not at all interested in experiencing a pregnancy. And, under the spell of these thoughts, I was suddenly struck by despair. "Edward," I grabbed his arm and pulled him away from the others, "maybe you were right. Maybe I should just talk to Peter."

He looked at me, a glimmer of light visible in his android eyes, coaxing me to move closer to him. He gently wrapped his android arms around me and I laid my head on his broad shoulder, for an instance imagining myself being comforted in the arms of my father. He slowly stroked the side of my face, as he whispered in my ear. "Pamela, you have time. There is no rush." He drew my face up to meet his. "For the moment, it is important that you continue to explore this planet. Neither you nor I nor anyone else can be certain about her objectives concerning procreation, but the fact that you have viable alternatives should be enough for you, at least for the moment." My eyes met his in solemn agreement, before we returned to join the others.

"He is right", I said over and over again to myself during the next few weeks that would became months and would turn into years.

So in spite of my exasperations, life moved forward. The rejuvenation of Jason, Ralph and Ferdinand went without incident. Jason was the first to emerge young and dynamic- in first class physical condition. He was no more than 12 years old when he stepped into that cryogenic tube and, even though Reinhart could not bring him back that far, she did what she promised--- she released a muscular, 5 foot 8 inch man, in a 20 year old body.

The difference between that aged explorer and this young man was stupefying. Our mouths flapped open with delight when we cast our eyes on this stunning young man, with his rugged masculine face and square, determined jaw. His thick, short black hair and light brown skin made his twinkling hazel brown eyes more vibrant than ever. "Incredible how age changes us, remolds our facial features and wears heavily on our bodies." I remarked, as I tried to imagine Peter or Randolph 30 years older.

Ralph, the frail, crippled over old man, with a time-ravaged face and lifeless limbs, now flaunted a robust and sturdy 20 year old body, and a round, ruddy face, with bristling, reddish- brown hair and large, sparkling blue eyes.

Ferdinand was just a 20 year old version of himself. He was short, about 5 feet 6 inches, with a thin body. Surprising, this youthful version of Ferdinand, with long, thick, disheveled, coal black hair and bushy eyebrows, framing steel grey eyes protected under heavy eyelids, prominently displayed on a thin face, with a narrowing nose and a pointed chin, accentuated his seductively, intellectual side. I felt a strong burst of warm energy suffusing me as Reinhart's enthusiasm mounted inside of me. She had finally given youth to others—not just herself.

"How many times can one be rejuvenated?" Mathieu asked the question that everyone wanted an answer to.

Reinhart was cautious when she answered. "We are human and therefore we are by our very nature mortal. The rejuvenation machine gives us an illusion of immortality. We are vulnerable and our lives could end because of an accident or a disease or even because we decide not to continue to live. It is important to keep that in mind. I shall give you your youth until your own body and mind decide otherwise." She turned to Jason. "But, as I told you, Jason, this is your second and last chance to live, so live it to its fullest." And with that, she asked Gordon and Crawford to escort Jason to the learning center to start educating him in planetary sciences.

Exploration of the planet Earth was on the front burner. The reptilian humans were given permission to accompany Diana during her meetings with WD. Diana told me that the first meeting was very awkward and that WD used words and gestures to intimidate the reptilian humans and, in particular, to denigrate them because of their cross-breed appearance, which, he mentioned, lacked the harmony and beauty of his.

Their total indifference to his derogatory remarks and their refusal to enter into his game by casting similar insults in his direction eventually dissuaded WD, who abandoned this childish, unproductive approach to gain an upper hand. He started to exchange his ideas and information willingly with the Reptilian Humans. Diana contended that WD worked well with the Reptilian Humans, often times soliciting their company.

The Reptilian Humans shared their conclusions about ocean life with us at the next meeting. They relied upon the visual impressions of these creatures embedded in WD's mind and the marine samples in the inner circle, when they stated that the marine life that occupied the oceans today were mutants of the same and sometimes mixed breed species.

Diana suggested that the large creatures that the other dolphins took for dinosaurs, were a mixture of shark and blue whale. She further explained that the mutated species--- originating from sea worms, squids, sponges, jellyfish, crab, lobster and other shell fish---were definitely oversized creatures today. Even though some of them scavenged the seabed for food, from what WD remembered and reported to her, the ocean creatures were nonetheless very aggressive and fed off their own and other large species.

According to WD, these creatures considered him to be a very small food source for them, the reason why he was never chased or attacked. But then he took no risks and always distanced himself from these large creatures. All of this needed confirmation and Diana wanted permission to accompany WD and the Reptilian Humans into deep ocean waters, which she insisted should take place very soon.

Stuart immediately objected. "I don't think that Diana should go alone. She needs a larger team." He paused, covering his face with his hands in an attempt to hide his emotions, before continuing in a deep, strong voice. "Remember what happened to our Reptilian Humans when those crazy androids took over the ship. I know that you don't believe that this could happen again," he said as his eyes pierced mine, addressing Reinhart, "but, our entire team should make the trip. I know that it will postpone the exploration of the northern region for a certain time, but as the oceans are so vast, it is in our interest to determine what food and mineral sources they can offer." Heads nodded.

"Yes. Let's regroup the original team and take a longer trip out to the high seas, with WD leading the way." Randolph choked on his own words, realizing too late the absurdity of his comment, inferring that we could trust WD. "Will the tracking device that we inserted in him along with the tracking collar be enough for us to control him?" He asked, hoping to reduce the impact of his previously impulsive remark.

"Nothing is for certain." I suppressed a smile at his naivety. "He falls into the same category as the Group of 5. And, even with a tracking device and a collar, WD could always try to escape, or even turn against us when we are in a vulnerable position, like being attacked by other marine species." My eyes quickly scanned the group. "We must always be careful what we tell or share with them." I warned. "We must use them-meaning the Group of 5 and WD-manipulate them, but never trust them."

"So we postpone the space program for a few weeks?" Peter asked in a high croak, sounding like he was being strangled.

"Well, it is difficult to set priorities, but it is better to put the space program on hold for a few months." I hesitated before adding. "Reinhart took the initiative of asking Colonel Shannon to send us the design for the cocoons and the kind of material used to manufacture them. Of course, we can process them and determine the substances, but that takes time that can be better used for other projects. It will be easier for us to duplicate the process after we get the information."

I cleared my throat. "Reinhart is not certain that we have the same basic substance they used to fabricate those cocoons on this Planet. So, we must explore for minerals and fibrous plants everywhere, even on the ocean floor, to be certain that we have the right substance or a close substitute. If not we shall have to rely upon Colonel Shannon to provide us with the substance."

I tapped my fingers rhythmically on the table top to calm my nerves and keep their attention. "The technical side is no problem for Reinhart. She knows how to add the bio-readers." I was tired of trying to explain Reinhart's personality to my friends and colleagues. I sensed their confusion from the ensuing silence, but appreciated their steady gaze of studious effort to understand, so I added. "She knows that she should have consulted with all of you, but..." I didn't know what else to say.

After a long pause, Peter spoke up in my defense. "Ok, we all know that she is not a real team player." And then, suddenly ringing laughter filled the air. "Exploring this planet is pretty challenging as well and I like the idea of discovering the high seas!" He blurted out with gust and vigor. "I guess that it is time to start to pack for the Marine center. See you at dinner tonight."

Peter and I lingered behind the others, taking our time to leave the conference room. The corridor was filled with a lingering laughter, inciting us to walk rapidly to catch up with the others, who were moving in the direction of the inner circle, rather than the dining room.

Our first glimpse was of Randolph, with his arms around Isabel and Mathilda, their legs gripping his and their tongues running slowly over each other's throat. Stanislas and Benjamin, with Sarah closely entwined between them, were closely behind.

We watched as others skipped by us, following behind Randolph, as they slid through the wall into the inner circle. My thoughts turned back to another time, a time when I was the object of Gordon's study of human emotions. Probably to give me a very negative impression of human sexual practices, Miller encouraged me to read about libertine cultures throughout human history. The articles I read described dimly lit, cozy, warm parlors, with comfortable arm chairs, where men and women passed, in plain view, from one sexual partner to another.

Even though we are not bound by prudish morality, was the lounge in the inner circle being converted into a parlor, where players, conscious of the recompense of their lascivious desires, willingly surrendering to displays of dominance, as others assumed roles of dominance, or were they blindly following their partner or partners leading them into lascivious acts? No, I thought, as I shook off the images of those films, highlighting sexual orgies. "We are certainly more discrete in our quest for carnal pleasure than former generations of humans." I finally chuckled to myself for letting my imagination run wild.

I turned and looked at Peter, who hiding his laugher, behind his straight face, studied mine. "I would rather get something to eat." I said as I turned in the direction of the dining room, only to find Crawford standing near the wall, watching, like a peeping Tom.

"What are you doing here?"

"Observing, just observing." He replied. "And, I learned a great deal, just observing the promiscuous behavior of humans. I believe that I finally understand the human need for physical contact." His eyes popping from their sockets. "But, I still don't understand Gordon's fascination with sex."

"No matter." I actually wanted to reprimand him for watching the scene, but, he was not the only one "observing" the humans' behavior. "Just tell us why you were in this area." I said in a firm tone.

"Oh, yes, of course. I have a very good reason. Actually, I was looking for you, Pamela,--although I was hoping for Elisabeth." He caught my squinting eyes and went straight to the point. "I know that you are planning to explore the high seas and will probably be taking one of the large, marine transporters." I nodded. "I have a suggestion."

"And?"

"There are several aircraft that are designed to land on the marine vessels and I thought that it might be in your interest to have alternative means of escape, if you run into difficulty."

"Yes, that is an excellent idea, which we considered during our last meeting." Observant, he noticed that Elisabeth was back when I ran my fingers slowly along my lower lip.

The discussion interested Reinhart as her warmth rapidly suffused me, so I moved aside. "The ones that we need are at the Air and Space Center." He nodded. "Can you ask Jarrod to have a couple android pilots bring them to us?" Reinhart queried.

"Of course. There is no problem. I would suggest, however, that you ask for a few android pilots to accompany you on this exploration." He paused for a minute to read her reaction. "Androids can be quite useful and you are not exploiting them enough." He waited patiently, obviously realizing that he had perhaps overstepped his position.

"You are right, again, Dr. Crawford." Reinhart answered. "Ok, I want you to arrange all of that. They should meet us here and I shall take one of those planes and let the android crew take the other one. They are not that easy to fly and I am not certain my young pilots are ready for that." She paused. "We need you to move WD into that large aquarium he occupied previously to make the trip to the marine center. And, even if he could support a long voyage out of water, I don't trust him and will feel better knowing that he is in a confined place."

"Agreed." He shook his head as if he needed to revive his systems. "I have been observing the relationship between WD and the Reptilian Humans for quite some time now. I know that you trust the Reptilian Humans, but, I believe that WD is very manipulative and has been able to create a profound bonding with these hybrids."

"And...what are you suggesting?"

"I don't want to create adversity, but I believe that you and some of the other members of your team should meet with the Reptilian humans and draw your own conclusions regarding loyalties, and/or, misplaced loyalties." There was a long silence before he concluded. "I shall keep you informed." He looked at Peter and then at me and politely said goodbye.

"What unmitigated gall?" Peter burst out in anger, as his fist hit down hard on the side of the wall. "The Group of 5 is more unpredictable and dangerous than the Reptilian Humans."

"It is strange that he should want to create dissension between us by insinuating that our Reptilian Friends are changing camp?" Reinhart said pensively. "Divide and conquer was an effective tool in colonizing other human communities in the past. And now that he has put that idea in our heads, we have no choice but to summon all members involved in planetary exploration to a meeting so that we can evaluate the loyalty of everyone in our group to our cause."

Peter huffed and puffed before replying. "There is no natural allegiance between sea mammals and aquatic reptiles, is there?"

"Not to my knowledge." Reinhart let out a long stream of air. "We did take a risk letting anyone, other than Diana, get too close to WD. And yet, I cannot imagine Joseph, with Tirence at his side, or Adam being led into complacent comradery with WD."

"You are right. Unfortunately, because of that detestable Crawford, we have to investigate." He looked at me with a stern face. "It is a good idea anyway to meet as a group and exchange ideas and objectives."

Reinhart's energy slowly disappeared. Over dinner we all agreed to meet the following morning to organize the trip and define the objectives.

In the beginning of the meeting, I observed the reaction of the Reptilian Humans when I mentioned that WD, for security reasons, would be confined to the aquarium for transport and whenever he was out of the water. They all nodded. "Is there anyone who thinks that WD should be treated with more dignity?" I asked as I looked straight into Joseph's eyes.

He gave me one of his special iguana smiles, as his slim, more human, lips spread in a thin line reaching the far corners of his bulky human-reptilian face. "I know what is bothering you, Pamela." He snickered. "WD can be very charming but he is not a team player. We assure you that we are not naïve. Our objective was to get the maximum amount of information from him so we pretended that he was in command."

I turned away from him for a second to avoid being drawn into his large eyes, intensely focused on me. "He does not know that much. He ventured off into the high seas when he was young, and adventuresome. His memory of the creatures appears authentic." He stopped to stroke his chin. "Interestingly, he never paid much attention to the smaller aquatic species. One could say that it was a question of taste, as he had a preference for humans and dolphins, so he didn't care much about other sources of food."

"You think that you can keep up with him in the water?"

"Not at all. We cannot move that fast. Our advantage is that we can dive deeper and forage for plants, and our overall endurance is better than his." His eyes turned dark and severe. "I think that he needs to stay within a reasonably safe distance of the ship. Even though he can move far out for an undeterminable period of time, he will eventually have to return to the ship to recuperate. His mixed breed status could be a handicap."

"Ok, things are a bit clearer, although not completely convincing. He did swim a long distance when he was younger and there were no land masses in the deep sea where he could seek shelter or refuge. So, he must have relied upon his walrus side, using his air sacks to stay afloat to recover or resorting to unihemispheric sleep when he was travelling long distances." I said, repeating the information that Reinhart was uploading to me.

"Of course, he was smaller and maybe, when he was younger, his dolphin features were more dominant." I closed my eyes to try to visualize what might have happened, when Reinhart rapidly uploaded physiological information that convinced me that WD's walrus side was and is still dominant when it comes to long distant swims. I mentioned this to the others.

"We only have WD's side of the story." Adam protested. "He told us that he swam a long distance, but maybe the submarine that he and the others occupied when we found them, moved more inland over the years. He may have been closer to the deep sea limits when he was young."

"Excellent, Adam." Reinhart again replaced me in the discussion. "Admittedly, I hadn't thought about that. Let's hope that your analysis is right and that WD is not hiding his true capacities."

"We can always catch him." Stuart interjected. "And, he is not a loner...let's say, he likes being surrounded by others. He doesn't need to be liked. He just needs company."

"Despicable creature!" Diana exclaimed and then changed the subject. "Once we have located zones rich in flora and fauna, already identified by satellite images, shouldn't we just move the vessels into those areas and then dive?" Diana

"I don't think so---that could be risky?" Randolph spoke up and the rest of us agreed. "If there are giant mutated species, we have to move cautiously." He turned to face me. "We can't just take out small boats either?"

"No, that is why Crawford's suggestion is so relevant. We shall fly over the areas before moving the vessel. Even taking that precaution does not mean that there are no risks, because we shall have to dive to identify all life forms in the deep ocean waters. We might send down unmanned subs first and then use our small subs to investigate on our own." She stopped abruptly. "Regardless, I am going to skim the satellite images to get a better perspective of the area."

"Yes, good idea, Dr. Reinhart." John remarked. "And, while we are on that subject, I have found some images that may be very pertinent, at least in terms of ocean depth. You might recognize more in those images because I am only starting to understand how to read them."

The last point raised during the meeting reminded us that humans do have predatory instincts. "I want to know if we are going to become carnivorous again." Mathilda said in a very provocative tone.

Reinhart withdrew from this discussion and I sat back and liste-ned. We were apparently divided on this issue. Mathilda was de-finitely opposed to eating any life form other than plants and the fruits of the plants including grains. As Elisabeth shared her dis-gust for eating flesh, she had my support from the outset. The male members of the group, including the Reptilian Human males, were in favor of eating fish, mammals, or other living creatures. Diana was the only woman in our group who did not consider eating meat to be a barbaric practice. She nonetheless argued that she mi-ght consider eating another living creature, if there was no other source of nutrition available and she was close to death.

"Our objective should be to identify and study other life forms. Eating them should not be our priority." I said emphatically, when I finally moved into the discussion.

"Why is Reinhart so opposed to eating other life forms?" Benjamin asked derogatorily.

"Because she sees this as the primitive side of humans and does not want to be associated with instinctive, survival practice, I guess."

"We now know where we all stand on food so I don't think that we need to say more. You better get things together if you are leaving in a few days." John said in his deep, authoritative tone. "Sarah, Ruth, Mathilda, Linda, Eunice, Jill, Karen, Ferdinand, Ralph, and Ludovic will maintain the base here with me. Naturally, Jonathan and Imogen will continue in the music department." Jonathan nodded. He was involved in music and art, when he was not cuddling his son. "And Jason?"

"He will continue his educational program. We shall need him for land exploration." I said.

"I think that I might stay here as well." Clarence said. "I am not able to swim and I think that it is better for me to work with John and the others in preparation for the land trip." No one objected because he was right, his presence would be more valuable later on. Benjamin and Stanislas wanted to stay at the Center and assist John and the others with the analysis of the information we would be sending back.

Adam requested permission to stay at the Center and continue to work with Eunice and Andrew on the architectural projects. "I am sorry to hear that, Adam, as you trained in diving and we also need you to forage for marine samples." I said.

"I know." His eyes skirted the room to see if anyone was on his side. The others sat expressionless.

I finally broke the uncomfortable silence. "In the future, we will need to construct platforms for excavating minerals. That is if we find any. Your architectural knowledge will be very important." I tapped my fingers as if I were playing the piano.

There was no reason to force him to come with us, so I changed my strategy. "If you stay here, I expect you to take a look at the information that we send back and start to envisage the kinds of structures that are conceivable with the material we already have here in the Center, like metals and vegetable fibers and that which we have found on the outside, like clay soil and stones, as well as whatever we might find on this expedition" He started to thank me and I quickly interrupted saying that this was a voluntary trip. "In the future, we all have to be ready to sacrifice our time and energy for the benefit of the community."

Reinhart's warmth permeated me. I knew that when she spoke, her voice tone and words had the right impact on everyone. She quickly picked up where I left off. "Isabelle, Mathieu, and James, I would like you to work on the simulators for the larger aircraft that we will be using in a few days. And, Diana, you should familiarize yourself with the technical side of piloting the maritime transporter that we will be using. And, as we still have two days before our departure some of you might want to use the dive tank as last minute training. I shall mention all this to Crawford and he will get the programs for you. I shall arrange for Flanders to monitor the dive tank. The equipment and food will be ready for us when we leave, like the last time. The androids are already preparing all of that."

"Dr. Reinhart," Stanislas asked in a rough, low voice, "you continue to remind us that we cannot trust the Group of 5 and yet, you," he poked his finger in her direction, "never worry that they might poison our food?"

"Perhaps they might one day," she said as she leaned into the conference table, "if they get what they want from me." She smiled broadly, bearing her teeth, as if in amusement. "For the moment, though, we are all safe." She emitted an ear-splitting laugh that made everyone jump slightly.

Reinhart then looked at Diana and asked if she could send her research to John. "I don't want the Group of 5 to know too much about that, but if ever we need details, John and his team should have access to it. So please arrange for that. And, remember, John, you must not leave anything on the computers outside the inner circle."

The meeting was beneficial in many ways---clarifying the loyalty of friends and colleagues, soliciting help, revealing our human side---getting motivated for the trip. Randolph, Peter and Stuart followed John back to his lab. Diana sprinted off in another direction, with James following close behind her. Mathieu and Isabel walked hand in hand, while Tirence back-slapped Joseph, who led the way for the other Reptilian Humans.

I was the last to leave and headed directly to the inner circle to review the satellite images, something that I was now capable of doing, thanks to the knowledge Reinhart had uploaded to me. John was waiting for me. He sat patiently watching me compare in rapid sequence, the evolution of the earth from the moment the explosion took place until today as it appeared on old satellite images that were updated by the hidden satellite system Reinhart developed.

"I had difficulty retrieving data, even though you gave me the access codes to your invisible satellite system." He shrugged his shoulders in disgust. "I asked the Group of 5 if they had information. They pretended that they were unaware of satellite images and that, even if they had been aware of these photo images, they would have had absolutely no reason to study them."

"Do they know why you wanted to retrieve such a vast number of images and that you were using my satellite system?"

"No. I never discuss my projects with them." He hesitated. "But, because I requested their assistance, in the beginning, they...rather Crawford inquired about my work, until I told him that I abandoned the project because it was hopeless."

"Excellent strategy!" I exclaimed. "I want to show you something,

John." I pointed to the most recent images of the coastline near the marine center that I had found and were now visible on the large, wall panel. "The continental shelf where we encountered the dolphins, protrudes almost 300 nautical miles before sloping gradually into the deep ocean zone."

"Are you worried?"

"No. But it is unusual to have such a large continental shelf, with a sloping and not a sharp drop off into the deep sea, but then this planet was destroyed." I pointed to the coastline in the northern hemisphere. "You see the continental shelf is even larger—maybe 400 nautical miles." John looked confused, so she continued along another line. "I wonder if the continents are starting to expand outward, or the ocean is moving inland. And, I am unable to determine that from the satellite images that we have."

"Do you think that the Group of 5 has something to do with this? Maybe they altered the old satellite images that I requested, which made it difficult for me to compare them to the images we have today." His anger resonating in his voice.

"I doubt that they altered the ones that they had in their possession." I said, my hand slapping the table. "But they must have been aware of the continental coast line and the major changes that the explosion produced." I looked at John. "Crawford's suggestion about taking aircraft seems more than just an innocent inspiration." We laughed loudly, mocking the ludicrousness of his feigned innocence.

"Are you absolutely certain that the Group of 5 has not been able to access your research based upon my satellite system?" I said, changing the mood.

He stood up and paced back and forth, throwing his arms dramatically up in the air. "How can anyone be certain that the Group of 5 has not found a way to spy on us, Pamela, or to access all of our research?"

He was right. Only Reinhart, who they feared, was capable of getting them to confess to foul play and, for the moment, I could feel her energy focused on studying the images and identifying the marine zones that she thought we should explore.

"You are right it is futile to have this kind of discussion and, unproductive, to hallucinate over the worst-case scenarios that could be orchestrated by the Group of 5. They are certainly curious about what we are doing, but we should focus on practical matters like the course that the ship will follow and the intermediate areas we should stop to explore."

"Is she ready to take the ship out to the deep sea zone?" He asked when I finished logging in the coordinates we should follow along the continental shelf.

"There is every chance that she will move the ship out into the deep water zone—but then that depends upon how long it takes to accomplish the other tasks that are part of this mission. And it might be more prudent to have the small planes fly over the deep water zones, scout for danger—just in case the story about large mutated sea monsters has any validity." I found myself laughing, just thinking about those mythical monsters that WD rushed away from. "Oh," I changed the subject, "I have to contact Drager. I want him to select the android crew and verify the stability of the Captain, the one that Reinhart reprogrammed, whose presence would be desirable, but only if he has not gone astray again."

"I can contact Drager for you. He told me that he likes working with Reinhart."

"Thanks, John." I observed him closely. He had changed now that we were a team. Apparently what I took in the past for pretentious behavior was his reaction to stress. Today, I looked at him like a true friend. "I count on you to keep this center safe in our absence and to oversee the research of the others. Remember not to leave the Group of 5 alone." I caught a glimpse of his smile as I moved to leave. I stopped in my tracks because I felt the energy of my mentor, a term that I liked when I was alone with Reinhart, rising inside of me. I let her guide me in the next phase of the conversation.

"John," he looked up from his table, seemingly confused that I was still there.

"Something worrying you, Pamela?"

"Not worrying me. That is too strong a word. I would say, something is becoming a priority."

"Oh, I think that I know what you are going to say." He avoided my eyes, fixing his on the table top. "My age?"

"Yes, John, your age. I am so glad that you have been thinking about this, as well."

"I want to interrupt you before you go further." His eyes now met mine. "I don't know if I am ready to...rejuvenate."

"Why?"

"Because I have a comfortable life with Sarah and Ruth. I would end up being younger than them and who knows how they would feel about me, and worse...how I would look at them."

"That is a selfish position!" Reinhart's reaction startled me as well. Angry or annoyed, she left me to continue the discussion.

"We need you, John. You are now in your forty's---much older than Sarah and Ruth. And, even though 40 is still young, multiple rejuvenations are easier to envisage when the first one is performed at a young age. We need young, dynamic team members." He gritted his teeth, but I continued. "You will always have an emotional attachment to both Ruth and Sarah—your life with them goes back far. But, even if youth drives you to other relationships, it is a small price to pay for the right to continue to participate in building a new world---a world that we shall leave to our descendants and their descendants. You must think about those who will follow us."

I stopped to collect my thoughts. "And, John, relationships are not forever. Fortunately, we are not victims of an inhibiting morality that plagued the generations of humans that reigned over a world built upon irrational convictions. That world crumbled, as well it should have, and with it, crumbled those outrageous moral restraints."

"But, we have conformed, Pamela."

"Yes, we have evolved into people who believe in respecting life and liberty. We work for the benefit of everyone and we don't think about material gain. We believe in equality and no one is starving. Our clothing and living conditions are very comfortable—the list is long." Even though I could have explored this problem in more and more detail, I opted for ending this discussion and returning to the original problem. "And, we shall continue to pose questions and find solutions to other moral conundrums as we build our world upon a better basis."

I waited patiently for his response, as he stroked his long beard in contemplation. "But, this rejuvenation is forever?"

"Not really, because rejuvenation is not immortality. It is a way to return to a young, vigorous body so that you can continue to live longer, assuming that you don't have some unfortunate accident." I pondered the dilemma. Choosing to live in a physically rejuvenated body or to live in an aging body seemed an easy choice for me. Could the act of rejuvenating regularly be compared to reaching a state of immortality? Is immortality something that humans seek? I would be sad if Peter and Frederic did not follow me in my choice. And yet, if they chose to end their existence, would that be enough for me to decide to end mine? I turned my attention back to John who sat with his arms folded in front of him.

"Can I think about it?" He finally spoke up.

"Yes. It is not urgent, but I recommend that you recover your youth soon. It was difficult for Reinhart to give youth back to Jason, Ferdinand and Ralph. And she knows that she can never rejuvenate Jason again, because of his very long stay in a cryogenic state. Can she give youth to Ferdinand and Ralph through rejuvenation a second, third, fourth, or...more times? They were, after all, in their late 50's, when she brought them back in young bodies." I wanted my words to sink in and inspire John to make a decision soon. He was the right age to secure a very long future. "We need you, John, both here in the Center and out there discovering and exploring this planet."

"Ok, I promise to give you an answer when you get back from this trip." He was now slumping lazily back in his chair. Seeing that his eyes twinkled and his scalp raised in enthusiasm made it easier for me to leave.

I was not hungry so I stopped by to see what the Group of 5 was up to. They were huddled together in their common office, when I entered.

"Is there something that we can do for you, Pamela?" The former Governor asked, his eyes glowing with a kind of...guilt?

"Yes, we would like you to pick the android crew to accompany us in the transmutable aircraft –you know, vertical and horizontal rotation, with landing capabilities on large marine vessels. The ones you suggested to me earlier in the day. They should bring them to this center. I shall pilot one of them. I shall need an android capable of piloting, even under emergency situations. I want the androids to accompany us out to sea." Heads nodded. "And Edward, some of the group might need a couple practice sessions in diving. I would appreciate your supervising that." He nodded enthusiastically.

"I was wondering if you might need someone to evaluate the behavior of WD." Victoria forced her way into the discussion. "I think that you all will be very busy studying samples, diving, exploring and," she sighed, "whatever else you humans do." My furrowed brows pointed at her convinced Victoria to move on rapidly with her suggestion. "WD needs constant surveillance, and I don't have that much on my agenda for the moment. I would very much like to accompany you."

Her request was unsettling for various reasons. Firstly, I never imagined that a member of the Group of 5 would be interested in joining us; secondly, I thought that they would never consider leaving their group and their comfort zone; and thirdly, because her suggestion was not altogether disconcerting, but, to the contrary, very interesting. It would be a good idea to have someone assigned on a permanent basis to WD but...could I trust her. So I said that I would discuss her offer with the rest of the group and get back to her rapidly and then left.

I brought up her request over dinner. A brief discussion ensued. In the end, everyone, including Diana, agreed that her surveillance of WD would take pressure off of them. They were so positive and motivated over the idea of her joining us that when I said, "I am going to check her systems out before she boards the aircraft," I got no verbal response, instead they got up to leave, like my statement of concern didn't interest them or it just slipped by...unnoticed.

Chapter 29: Virtual Memories

The time warp in the center, caused by the doomsday exploration, did not affect our biological clock, something very evident every time we were with our children. Frederic wanted to accompany us to the transport unit and watch us board the very large aircraft, with vertical and horizontal rotor capacities, the same style plane that we used for our earlier planetary mission. The one that I would fly had a small plane positioned on top of it, so that I could take short discovery flights with a limited number of team members.

Even though I knew that James, with his previous training, was capable of flying the second aircraft, I preferred that we humans boarded the same aircraft together and thus invited James to be my copilot. I left the second one for the android pilots and their crew of 8, under the supervision of Drager.

"Mom, Dad, can I just see the inside of the plane?" Frederic's voice bubbling with enthusiasm.

Time stood still for me as I turned to admire my son for a brief instance, his 6 foot tall, muscular, athletic body, and erect posture made him appear physically older than his 12 years. I caught his glimpse of me from the corner of my eye, and was pleased when I saw his eyes, under slightly raised eyebrows-a classic expression of self-confidence. "Yes, Frederic resembles his father physically and also has his sober, rational approach to problem solving." I concluded, opening up the way for other thoughts to follow.

His interest in music had waned, becoming only a pastime, replaced by an insatiable scientific inquisitiveness. Even though I had mixed feelings, because I would have liked him to be more than a musical dilettante, I could not help but be impressed and proud of his scientific acumen. And, in spite of the fact that artistic fields are no less intellectual than those of science, meriting the same respect and consideration, at least Frederic, unlike me, was free to make his own career choice.

Mathilda mentioned to me on many occasions that even though she considered Frederic to be mature and dynamic, with very good interactive skills, she considered his thirst for knowledge both astonishing and worrisome. But then, she wanted this generation of humans to be free spirits and not those intellectually programmed human machines that we were. But, did that mean as well that they should be less productive in their contributions to our community?

I always doubted her assessment of Frederic's personality. And, I was right to doubt her, because today I saw another side of Frederic that pleased me, for he demonstrated my spontaneous curiosity, rather than his father's self-control or even Reinhart's hardened, logical approach to life.

I grabbed his hand. "Yes, come with me and I shall introduce you to the control panel. One day, you and your father might co-pilot one of these aircrafts," I caught Peter's eyes, "or even a spacecraft."

He marveled over the control panel, asking probing questions, and then opened up the various compartments and lockers, to examine their contents. And finally, he rushed towards me with that innocence of a child, and threw his arms around me giving me those indescribable hugs with kisses that totally bind you to your child. "See you soon." I called out to him as he dashed off the aircraft.

Our departure was imminent. Gordon came on board with us. I did not trust her enough to let her alone with WD, who was being transported by the android team. Unlike Gordon, those androids were not programmed to be inquisitive, but rather to carry out my orders and nothing else. I watched WD enter into his large tank and then wave to me as he was moved on board the aircraft with the androids. "What unexpected situation could we encounter this time?" I wondered, as I lifted up my aircraft with my team on board and led the way to the marine center.

Drager was waiting for me when I disembarked. He told me for a second time that the Captain's behavior had not changed over the last few months. Nonetheless, he was ready to assist me if I still wanted to assess the situation on my own. So I left the others to look over the large seafaring vessel and aircraft carrier with runways for aircraft larger than the ones we were flying. The androids were in the process of moving it out of the hangar which was not an easy task. In the past these large ships were docked in the outer coastal waters. "Look over the control panel, Diana and Isabel." I yelled over my shoulder, as Drager and I dashed off to the Captain's quarters.

"It is nice to see you again, Captain." I commented.

"It is an honor for me to serve under you, Dr. Reinhart."

"You are speaking to Pamela today." I corrected him.

The fact that he had been working very closely with Drager for a long time and showed no signs of programming reversal, was very encouraging. Nonetheless, I ran the tests we used before to be certain that Dr. Murdoc's programming was definitely deactivated. After being questioned, the Captain replied that, when we gave Murdoc's command to Attack, Kill and Dispose of humans, he was not programmed to carry out that kind of order. I knew then that the Captain was no longer prey to Murdoc's orders. So I told the Captain that it would be a pleasure to have him on board.

"What can you tell me about the high seas?" I queried

"We patrolled the continental shelf region, going about 200 nautical miles out close to the high seas during the revolution. After my reactivation, I never ventured off into the high seas. The stories of prehistorical monsters dissuaded me, in the beginning, from exploring the outer continental shelf." He stopped to retrieve more information before continuing. "Yes, after a long period of reflection, I did follow the dolphins out into deeper waters." He stopped abruptly, trying to convince me he had told me everything.

I was annoyed with his impertinence in ignoring the broad nature of my question, so I persisted. "I want you to share any information you have because, no matter how slight, it may be useful for us."

"My memory bank is feeding me highly improbable information. Do you want me to continue?" I signaled him with my hand to go on.

"There were large—gigantic—fish, maybe aquatic mammals,

about 200 nautical miles away from the slope of the continental shelf. I was unable to identify them with accuracy—but, that could be because they were some kind of hybrid." His piercing eyes were studying me so I kept a blank face. "They rushed at our ship, rocking it with their weight. I don't know if they could have sunk the ship, but I didn't wait to find out. I turned the ship sharply and moved at high speeds in the direction of the Marine center. Their pursuit stopped abruptly when we were out of the high seas and back in the waters of the continental shelf."

"Did you return?"

"No. Exploring the planet, and especially the high seas, was of no interest to anyone, including the Group of 5."

"I see." I replied in a low voice. 'Why didn't the Group of 5 care about other creatures inhabiting the planet? Something is missing here!

"Did you bring this up with the Group of 5?"

"No, but I was not myself at that time. If I had been in my present state of mind-if I can use that expression to describe my present robotic programming-I would certainly have raised the issue." His eyes had turned very dark and penetrating and I compared that to anger or frustration, none of which were part of his programming. "The Group of 5 did not take me seriously. It was Murdoc's programming that offset them and I understand that now. At the time, I was very cautious about what I said to them. The information that I am able to retrieve from that period is anything but rational or logical."

"And the dolphins? Did they ever tell you about the high seas?"

"I have no record of any discussion on that subject." He was now standing with his head bowed down. I waited patiently for him to continue. "We never expected to have to justify our choices and our decisions to you, Dr. Reinhart rather Pamela. What we did was not impulsive; of course, in my case, it was illogical and irrational. The dolphins were a problem and would have been a problem even if I had been in better control of my systems. The only thing that mattered to them was eating. They claimed that there were no more plants or fauna available. Giving them the humans was my way of getting rid of a nuisance in our coastal waters. When they were given food they left us alone."

"They could not eat you or otherwise harm you," I retorted, "so why were you so annoyed by them? You could have simply ignored them."

"It was not possible to ignore them. They were interfering with our routine maritime activities. But there was something else alarming about them. Their curiosity, yes, their curiosity, which was annoying as they were constantly interrupting us and asking questions. And, they were not subtle in the way that they pried for answers. They wanted to know about our technology, our center's living conditions and capacity, things like that.

Naturally, my programming at the time rendered me uncooperative. I believe that I also acted paranoid in their presence, although it is a strictly human state of mind that I naturally detest and thus I would rather not associate myself with it. I saw them and their contriving attitude as a menace to both my safety and that of the center." He stopped to observe my reaction. I had difficulty holding back my laughter. "We were not programmed to kill them. We were programmed to kill humans. So we got rid of them and their potential danger by giving them food."

"A repulsive, but logical decision." What he said made me very pleased that I had eliminated a number of those dolphins and programmed the remaining ones. "And, WD, how did you see him then and how do you see him today?"

"He was a cruel, brutal leader who wanted absolute obedience." I smiled in agreement. "Today, without his admirers surrounding him, he is harmless. You are right to exploit him."

"Thank you for your insight. I'll see you on board tomorrow morning. I have to meet with the other members of my team."

I found the others grouped in the dining area. "We have everything ready and the androids are working well." Peter said as he stood up to greet me.

"It looks like the kitchen staff is also working very well." I said as they appeared with heavily laden platters of vegetables and fruits that were sent from the agricultural unit at our center. The Group of 5 was on top of everything. A good dinner followed by a short walk along the sandy coastline, breathing in the saltwater air, was what we all needed to have a good night's sleep.

On our return, I noticed that Gordon followed Drager to his office, where she would spend the night, hoping to probe him for information. I laughed to myself as I imagined Gordon trying to seduce Drager, who, unlike Gordon, was incapable of emotional responses. Her efforts would certainly be futile, if not frustrating.

Peter was lying with his head resting on his arms, staring up at the ceiling when I slipped into the bed. "Are you worried, Pamela, about the horrors we might encounter?" I shrugged my shoulders.

He took a deep breath. "The marine center gave us a lot of difficulty the last time."

"No. I am not worried." I said in a soft voice. "I have confidence in all of us." He turned to look at me. I studied his beautifully sculptured face. His alluring, deep, brown eyes drew me towards him, effacing constraint by offering freedom.

His warmth melding with mine should have pacified me and invited sleep. But it didn't. Unaffected by my relentless tossing and turning, he fell asleep long before I did. And, when I did finally succumb to sleep, my dreams were but nightmarish visions of an ocean regurgitating horrific creatures whose monumental size so dwarfed our vessel that they ignored us in their search for food. Fish, with bulging eyes and large jaws with razor-sharp teeth passed rapidly in front of us, while large dinosaurian reptiles skimmed the surface in search of food. The sky above was clouded with predator birds, flaunting long, sharp beaks and impressive wing spans, as they dove in groups, violently ripping and pecking their prey into tiny pieces. And, the ocean, agitated from the hunts, retorted with crashing waves that swallowed up both the hunters and the hunted.

Before I woke, the nightmare vanished, replaced by a sublime, yet intense inner calm, as I sat on a large rock, in the middle of a floral garden, waiting, patiently waiting, for something to happen.

Chapter 30- Exploring the Briny Deep

One by one we entered the dining room, moving in bouncy steps, our eyes wide with excitement, like adrenaline fueled warriors ready for a challenging adventure. We ate rapidly, gathered up our gear and jumped into the small land vehicles that took us to the ship. WD was the last member of our group to board the vessel. We watched him as he exited the tank and labored up the Walkway.

Even though WD's walrus physiology gave him the possibility of spending long periods of time outside of water, he did need to spend quality time in water as well. So his tank was lifted onto the outer deck of the ship and placed alongside a small ramp, so that could easily enter the tank without assistance.

"Pamela, or Dr. Reinhart, I don't really care which one you are today. I want to thank you for giving me the opportunity to prove my value. I am ready to risk my life, if need be, to contribute positively to this mission." His voice was resonating a practiced enthusiasm.

"Welcome abroad WD." I replied, hiding any doubts about him.

We moved rapidly out of the coastal waters and onto the continental shelf. We dropped anchor in the area that was home to WD and his admirers in the past. He pretended to be emotionally affected by our choice of scouting grounds and asked for permission to remain on board the ship. Naturally, I refused and told him that I wanted him to show our team the exact route that he took when he was young and wandered off into the high seas.

"My memory is not like those machines." He said pointing to the android crew. He turned to study us. His eyes were warm and seemed to be offering friendship to the reptilian humans, who nodded politely at him, but those same eyes turned a sorrowful black color when he focused on us humans. "I never apologized to any of you for feeding off of your species. Now-and you can believe me or not-I consider what we did- rather repulsive. I regret our behavior and feel uncomfortable returning to former hunting grounds that will force me to face horrible images of my past."

I squinted at him in disbelief, which had no noticeable effect on him. Instead, he moved closer to the back of the vessel, rapidly pulled his heavy body onto the rail, and called out. "I shall just jump in and lead the way." And that is exactly what he did. He jumped in before we had time to get our diving gear on. I yelled to Joseph, Leonard and Daniel to follow him. Gordon made a crackling sound, before saying that she never trusted the slimy creature.

We hustled to put on our wetsuits and gather up our diving tanks. The ship was far too high above the ocean level for us to dive in, so the androids readied a few motor boats to lower us down. I was alone with Tirence for the moment, because Joseph and Leonard were following WD. Peter, Stuart, Randolph and Diana were together and Mathieu, Isabel and James were in the third boat, Daniel would join them later. We were able to catch up to our reptilian friends who were far behind the impetuous WD. Joseph had already warned me that WD would be able to move faster than them, so this was not a surprise. What turned out to be a surprise, was the dramatic return of WD.

When I saw him approaching my motor boat I wondered why he voluntarily returned. Even though we would have eventually located him because of the tracking device implanted in his shoulder area and his tracking collar, I wondered if his return was a sign of good faith, or a malicious strategy on his part to give us the impression that he wanted to remain with us, so we would trust him and relax our guard.

"Dr. Reinhart," his voice shook me from my thoughts.

I hesitated.

"Ok. Pamela, I located my earlier living quarters." He pulled his heavy body up onto the side of the small boat, which Tirence and I struggled to keep from capsizing under his weight.

"Yes. So what did you see?" I asked between clenched teeth,

refusing to hide my irritation over what looked to be an attempt to escape.

"Nothing, I found nothing. Even the remains of that submarine, were gone. It makes no sense." He replied in a very low voice.

"But, we destroyed the sub and, well, perhaps water currents moved any small debris?" I said looking for a rational reason why he found nothing of his former living quarters. He didn't answer. "Look," I pointed to the left, "Joseph, Leonard and Daniel are catching up with us. Ask them to dive with you." I suggested to WD. "We have to move these boats closer together and drop anchors."

"I'll take charge of grouping and holding the boats." Isabel called out. "Just bring them closer to me so that I can tie the ropes together to keep them in place, before I drop a single anchor."

We put on our half-masks that covered our eyes and nose and adjusted the mouthpiece that would supply us with breathing gas. We were all carrying two gas tanks to give us more dive time.

"Ok, let's dive." I called out to others.

We could either enter the water by stepping off the flat plank at the rear of the boat, or roll over the side of the motor boat, back first. I preferred the second method and particularly loved the ensuing sensation of a lifeless, vertical descend into deep ocean waters. Diving was very relaxing, effortless, for me, whether I was moving vertically or horizontally.

We had agreed beforehand that the group would stay together and collect any flora or fauna in the area and that I would search for any submarine debris and then venture out on my own.

I concentrated on my first assignment. We were surrounded with very thick vegetation, which could be concealing the debris. I skimmed the surface of the seabed, pushing aside the sand, hoping to dislodge even tiny pieces of the submarine, before sitting on the ocean floor and trying to imagine what could have happened.

My thoughts turned back to that day. The androids dragged the cages back to the center, where their human remains were incinerated. The surviving dolphins and the female WD, or the wife of WD who bore those two offspring that Reinhart killed, were in the marine center. An android demolition team received orders to plant a large number of explosives. "Of course, the android demolition team carried out their orders to the letter, completely destroying WD's very old and dilapidated living quarters."

I was ready to explore this oasis of plant life on my own and left the other members of my team to work together in the former submarine zone. Reinhart had already uploaded a vast amount of information regarding fauna and flora on the continental shelf, so I looked for anything that might correspond to her descriptions.

I was not that far away from the others before I made my first discovery. On first glance, I associated one of the plants with seagrass, a plant that grew in shallow waters where sunlight filtered into the water in abundance. I observed that it had long green, grass-like leaves, and that its roots were buried deep in the sandy soil in order to support its slim stems. Seagrass formed dense meadows or beds and could grow vertically and horizontally in the water, like the plant I was examining. Nonetheless, this new breed seagrass was much taller than its predecessor, reaching heights of 5 to 6 feet, or almost twice the height of seagrass at Reinhart's time, and its long, grass-like leaves were not fine, delicate strands like its predecessor, but rather wide, thick, almost, leathery leaves. I took some samples of the young seagrass and collected samples of a green algae that floated at low levels in this seagrass bed.

I swam another 500 feet to examine what resembled giant Kelp, a brown algae with holdfasts buried in the ocean bed that extended into a trunk with large, broad flat leaves that looked like blades. Dense canopies of giant kelp, which could reach very high heights, were referred to as forests. It was impossible for me to determine the actual height of these plants, although in the past they could grow as high as 173 feet. On close examination, I observed that the leaves were much larger and had sharp pointed edges, like the teeth of a saw. I carefully removed several leaves from the larger plants and uprooted several of the young plants, their jagged leaf edges were but tiny pricks. My bag of samples was nearly full.

I turned to leave this area of low meadows and high forests when I noticed a tubular plant growing in a small barren area about 50 feet up ahead. I felt Reinhart's energy spread through me when she recognized the plant. She very rapidly uploaded information to me and I understood that this plant, with its smooth, rubbery exterior and thick, flat, large translucent leaves might be a close cousin to the swamp plant she collected long before the doomsday explosion. It was very possible that this plant had the same qualities as that swamp plant and that its leaves could also be heated, melted and molded to form the covering, or thick skin, on the android bodies and on our bionic parts. I spent a lot of time cutting through the very tough plant fiber to have pieces of its tubular stem and removing a number of the leaves.

When I finished, I realized that my sample bag was heavy and my dive time was almost over. My two gas tanks were nearly empty. I had already registered the geographic coordinates of my finds into my wristband computer, so I sped off in the direction of the motor boats. The others were waiting for me when I arrived.

WD drifted lifelessly to the surface, still depressed over the disappearance of the sub. When we started our trip back to the Mother ship, with our small boats and suspension nets filled with various flora and fauna like turtles, sponges, crabs and small spiny fish, it was clear that we had not wasted any time.

Once on board the ship, I took my group aside, mentioning that I had something important to tell them, but we had to be alone. Gathered together in a small room, removing our dive gear, I told my friends that one of the samples I brought back looked to be a salt water version of the swamp plant that Reinhart used to create the android skin. "I have to run some tests but this may also be the right substance to construct the cryogenic cocoons." My voice mounted with each word. "Don't mention this to any of the androids." I warned. "We must collect as much as possible on this trip because it is also a source of food for aquatic animals and fish, and we shall need a lot of it if we are going to create cocoons for all of us."

"Hah" Peter screamed triumphantly. "This is wonderful news!" He tried to pick me up but I turned to face him with my finger over my mouth. He turned away with his lips turned downward.

"We will have time to talk about this again." I said and we split up. I looked for WD and finally caught a glimpse of him forlornly crawling inside his open cage. I found it both amusing and satisfying to watch this gigantic creature relegated to such a level of indignation. He sensed my satisfaction and broke the silence. "One of those furious creatures must have dragged the debris into the high seas."

A smile cracked my face, because what he said made absolutely no sense. "What do you mean by furious creatures?" I asked rhetorically adding that his story of prehistoric monsters was hypothetical. "There were no renegade dolphins living in the area who might have decided to move it somewhere else, assuming that there was anything left of the sub?" I queried.

"Ridiculous. It was too heavy for those kinds of animals to move. I was referring to the gigantic creatures that patrol the edge of the continental shelf." He stuck his walrus tusks out to remind me of his formidable size as opposed to those measly dolphins. "Maybe there was a kind of quake." He ventured. "Thinking about that makes me want to laugh at the irony of the whole situation because that would mean that you saved some of our lives by capturing us. We would have died in a natural underwater quake."

I sat down on one of the lounge chairs, listening to his theories on the disappearance of the submarine debris and observing his body. When he rolled lazily onto his belly and pouted, I had an excellent view of his massive size and his bulky, mutated walrus-dolphin face. "It happened once before- not in my lifetime, though." His voice sounded weak or strained. "The elders told us about it. It happened a long time after the earth was destroyed by those irresponsible androids."

I waited patiently while he changed his position. He was now sitting with his back held very straight up against the bars of the cage. "Maybe, though, the quake was your fault." His eyes beamed in on me, like sunlight, half blinding me, forcing me to blink. "When your drones fired on us and then the sub, they might have dislodged its foundation. I refuse to believe that they destroyed it-it was too massive. It was indestructible." He screamed in a grating tone that sent chills through me. "That being the case, the sub later succumbed to ocean currents and moved. That could be what happened. But where is it now?"

"Well, normally the sub should have been blown into tiny pieces." I clacked my tongue. "Perhaps we should have verified that when the explosion died down," I paused, "but, the android demolition team was ordered to annihilate the submarine, and the lack of debris in the area today proves that they carried out their orders." WD violently slapped the floor of the bridge with his front fins, before rolling on his side, his large eyes studying me.

"Why is there so much vegetation down there?" I changed the subject and the mood. "Was the vegetation as abundant in the past?"

"We had to eat something and after all the animal life disappeared in our area, we devoured the vegetation." He stopped for a moment to gather his thoughts. "Actually, I don't remember its being so abundant, but then we all had insatiable appetites. The only thing that really filled us up was meat."

"Well, WD, we both need time to think so I am going to leave you with your thoughts and join the others for dinner. See you in the morning."

Instead I looked for the android pilots who were standing next to the aircraft waiting for their next assignment. Rapid analysis of the specimens was crucial so I ordered the android pilots to take the various plant life we had collected back to our center so that John and the agricultural team could begin studying them. The Captain accompanied them on this mission.

I called John and asked him to sequester the specimens, especially the large, rubbery, tubular shaped plants with large, translucent flat leaves, which should be stored in the inner circle. Even though it was highly unlikely that the Group of 5 would draw the link between these plants and their outside skin, cautious exclusion of these plants from the Group of 5 was nonetheless imperative.

After unloading the specimens we had collected, these android pilots were to bring back equipment that could be used to harvest different varieties of plants, including algae that could be good sources of food. We also needed traps for shellfish, turtles, crabs, and other fauna, living in the area we explored. The android pilots arrived the following morning with the necessary agricultural tools, like shovels, picks, cutters, as well as traps designed to catch fauna.

Drager selected a number of androids skilled in diving to carry out the mission of collecting fauna and flora. These androids certainly had an advantage over us humans in that they did not need to carry gas tanks or wear wet suits to protect themselves from the cold water, making their movement in the ocean less cumbersome.

The Captain, under Drager's orders, moved a large freighter out of the Marine Center. The hull of the ship could hold tons of cargo, and even had a short runway for aircraft, to facilitate rapid transport of certain cargo. An android work crew and the divers were on the Captain's ship. I gave the Captain the coordinates of the meadow and forest region I explored and asked that the androids harvest all the large, mature tubular plants with wide, thick, translucent leaves, but leave the younger plants in tact to assure the continued survival of this species.

I also asked that they collect large quantities of seagrass and the smaller green algae floating in the seagrass meadows. Even though I knew that in the past smaller species of kelp and other algae were safe for human consumption, the giant kelp needed to be tested for its nutritive value. So, I stipulated that the androids harvest this giant kelp ecologically, by uprooting a limited number of those kelp trees for our research, leaving the greater part of the kelp forest in tact to ensure sufficient breeding grounds and safety zones for the various species of fauna. Regarding fauna, they were to bring back anything that they trapped.

I was pleased with the efficiency of both Drager and the Captain, who took command of the freighter, leaving Isabel and Diana at the controls on our ship. I would learn later that they carried out my orders to the letter.

I left a number of androids trained in navigation at the controls on our large vessel that was anchored in the area that WD and his community occupied in the past. WD asked permission to dive and scavenger with us and swam alongside the motor boat.

"Okay," I yelled making my voice heard over the sound of the motors, "we are just over WD's former habitation zone, so we shall continue ahead another few nautical miles." Joseph opened the throttle on our boat and the others followed our example, moving three nautical miles ahead, before grouping our boats. Daniel offered to stay with the motors boats while we dived, so that Isabel could join us this time.

We were not diving more than 200 feet so we did not need

pressurized diving suits. We were using ordinary diving gear with full masks, covering our eyes, nose and mouth that allowed us to breathe through the nose. The advantage of this system was that we could communicate with each other as audio systems were integrated into the masks. Our insulated wet suits were made from light weight fibers. Each of us carried two gas tanks.

We continued our dives over the next few days, with Isabel and Daniel taking turns holding the boats in place, as we covered large circumferences with each dive. The main ship followed us and anchored a safe distance from us, just in case we needed help. We were getting closer and closer to the edge of the continental shelf, which was approximately 200 nautical miles from the beach. We were all rather discouraged with the dives, some of us complaining about wasting our time in this seemingly empty ocean. Even though we humans were hoping to find life, I detected a certain reticence on the part of WD, as we got closer to the edge of the continental shelf, because he started to leave very little distance between himself and our group.

Our short dives of 50 to 100 feet at the very edge of the sloping continental shelf finally revealed some animal life. In the beginning, we discovered many varieties of brachiopods and small bi-valves animals resting inactive on pillars of sand, probably caused by submarine landslides, or tall, fascinating clusters of algae. We collected a few samples.

Today we were wearing our pressurized diving gear, prepared for a very deep dive of 300 feet or more; we stayed in a tightknit group, advancing at a depth of a little more than 200 feet, as we slowly moved another 500 yards ahead. I felt Reinhart's energy moving inside of me, encouraging me to lead the others in the direction of the metal and concrete remains of the foundation of an offshore drilling platform.

Oil, a fossil fuel, was a major source of energy until the end of the 21st century. Using our lamps to guide us, we moved slowly around the outside of this structure, taking photos and scrapings of the metal and concrete used in its construction, as well as samples of the fiber ropes, normally made of kevlar, which were used as tension legs to anchor the platform to the foundation. Algae was growing everywhere, forming a green carpet on the surface of this foundation and creeping up the short remnants of former tension cables.

We had almost finished our tour of this structure when we discovered a wide entrance, like that of cavern, that led us to a large, spacious, sandy area, cluttered with embossed, spiral shells, where metal, concrete, tension legs and algae should have been. We were fascinated, almost mesmerized with this sudden change of scenery and drifted lazily past these curious shells whose sizes ranged from a few centimeters in diameter to an imposing 6 feet or more.

Reinhart rapidly uploaded information about these creatures, which she referred to as ammonites. They lived during prehistoric times disappearing at the end of the Jurassic period. She said that they were believed to have had divine powers by the Romans who added embossed and spiral decorations to their helmets in deference to the ammonite. They worshipped them like idols in certain Asian cultures for their presumed intelligence and pacifistic behavior.

Archeological digs during different periods of history uncovered vast numbers of these fossilized shells that, eventually, became so common place that they were bought by tourists. Nonetheless, the mere fact that the ammonite's shells survived all those thousands of years certainly added to the mythical power attributed to these creatures and to the large numbers of ardent devotees.

"Are these shells empty?" Mathieu asked.

"I don't know if these shells are empty. If they're not, these shells are home to a reddish brown creature, the predecessor of the octopus or squid. The large shell inhabitants must weigh close to 75 pounds and measure at least 9 feet in length. Big or small ammonites all have 4 pairs of 2 arms, or 8 tentacles, a soft body and a beak, like a parakeet."

"Are they dangerous?" Isabel's voice trembled.

"From what Reinhart just told me, paleontologists considered them to be non-aggressive, pacifistic life forms." But, as we were to discover, those paleontologists were either wrong or these new breed ammonites had radically different behavior than their predecessors, because they turned out to be real predators.

We swam closer to the large ammonite shells to study the exterior, take photos and examine, what we thought were empty interiors. The ammonites waited in hiding for the right moment before they expelled a black, thick ink that so clouded our vision that we barely saw the rapid arrival of their long bodies, and eight-outstretched tentacles. Diana and Isabel screamed, under the seething grip of the two ammonites that captured them. Their terrified voices resonated in our audio systems and we scattered, trying to avoid the onslaught of tentacles coming at us from all different directions. A few of the large ammonites moved rapidly out of their shells, revealing bodies similar to that of an octopus.

Then I spied WD, who had been floating, his air sacks inflated, on the surface of the ocean, presumably recuperating from his long swim. He arrived behind the ammonites. At first he distracted them by hitting their shells with all his weight, toppling them, half burying them in the deep sand, at the same time that he used his dolphin voice to produce loud, piercing, sonic sounds that moved in waves drawing their attention in his direction.

He lunged at them, moving in a straight line, like a torpedo, avoiding their tentacles and slapping their bodies with his wide, hind limb, or tail, hard enough to send them spinning. He pounced on some of them, using his walrus tusks to shred their soft, spongy bodies. When the remaining ammonites backed away from him, I heard a high, piercing, crackling noise seep from behind WD's grinning mouth. 'He is laughing,' I thought. 'He is having fun.' I swallowed hard and watched.

He turned his attention to the two ammonites that held our comrades captive and charged at full speed, sinking his walrus tusks into their soft bodies and ripping them in half, allowing Diana and Isabel to escape.

Other ammonites finally left the protective confines of their shells, joining the others, grouping together like an army, as they stretched their bodies and long tentacles in WD's direction. He played hide and seek with them, disappearing rapidly from their view, using the element of surprise as he abruptly appeared out of nowhere, striking violently at those in the front line with his wide walrus hind limb. WD never gave them the chance to regain a position of force, for he continued his pursuit, ramming his dolphin bottlenose snout hard into their soft middle region, killing them instantly.

Before they had time to regroup for a second offensive, we were ready to launch our attack. We fired our needle guns with rocket propelled darts that exploded on contact, reducing their numbers. The remaining ammonites retreated rapidly far inside their shells.

WD helped the Reptilian Humans move a few of the dead ones into the netting on the sides of the motor boats so that we could transport them to the mother ship. A cursory examination of them later in the day, just before they were flown back to the Main Center for autopsies, confirmed both the crushing force of their tentacles and the lethal character of their long tongues, covered with rows of sharp teeth that could have ripped and shredded us as they devoured us.

The following day our large ship passed through rough, agitated waters for more than a 100 nautical miles before settling upon a calm region. The androids lowered us down in our boats. WD jumped in after us, his dramatic plunge violently rocking our motorboats. I wondered if he did that intentionally.

We moved a short distance away from the ship, WD leading the way, before attaching the boats to keep them in place and dropping anchors, so that we could all participate in the exploration of this, seemingly uninhabited zone. WD swam very rapidly in these bitter cold waters, leaving the reptilian humans to their relentless struggle to minimize the growing distance between them. With their legs hanging inactive, or useless, at their sides, they relied upon the force of their flattened tail and quick bursts of anaerobic energy to give them speed, keeping them within close distance of WD.

The rest of us dove around 300 feet hoping that at this distance and with the help of large dive lights we might be able to identify mineral and fossil nodules, or even cobalt rich hydrothermal deposits clumped together and rising in a chimney shape from the ocean floor. Deep sea bed mining was used in the past to recover magnesium, lead, zinc, gold, and other nodules of precious metals. Unfortunately, we were not equipped to dive deep enough to reach the seabed and our dive lamps were not powerful enough to reveal any of its contents, so we abandoned our search and returned to the surface.

We were swimming in the direction of our motor boats when we found ourselves surrounded by enormous, aggressive bull and tiger sharks and sting rays, their flat bodies an impressive 20 feet in width. It was strange to see these carnivorous flat, sting rays, native to warm waters, swimming alongside sharks, their natural enemies in the past. The stingray's razor-sharp stinger situated at the tip of its long, agile tail could easily pierce through our wet suits, releasing it deadly poison, killing us instantly.

Stuart and Randolph rapidly drew their needle guns and fired a round of darts, exploding several sharks and sting rays that were in close range. Even though our guns scared the sting rays, who retreated, they had the opposite effect on the sharks, who became more aggressive, launching an assault.

WD, our secret weapon, was now alongside of us. Relying upon his bottlenose dolphin side, he swam at full speed targeting the shark's soft abdomen and smacking his bottlenose hard into this tender area, causing the shark's delicate intestines to hemorrhage, as they fell helplessly into the jaws of the retreating sting rays.

He changed his approach in mid-stream, bumping his bottlenose into the sharks' gills, destroying their ability to breathe. I knew that Dolphins were natural enemies, in the past, for sharks, but I marveled over how ruthless the walrus side of WD could be. His hybrid characteristics worked so effectively together, as he sunk his walrus tusks into the flesh of these animals, after his dolphin butting left them disoriented and confused.

WD bought us the time we needed to board our small boats. He followed after us, pursued by a small group of these gigantic sharks as he led the way back to the ship. The androids were in charge, pulling up our boats and WD along with us. Isabel, who had remained on board, fired systemically and steadily at the predators, who finally abandoned their organized hunt.

I was busy taking off my diving gear, when I saw WD outstretched on the deck of the ship, moaning. I rushed towards him to examine him for injuries. He turned his lifeless, hollow eyes upwards for a moment. "Thank you for saving us." My normally soft voice now hoarse with thick emotion.

He nodded slowly, before his eyes rolled back in his head and his walrus tusks drooped from the sides of his mouth as he lost consciousness. Reinhart took over, quickly sealing the tiny, superficial wounds, with an aquatic veterinary laser, which she kept in her dive sack before verifying that he had no organ damage. She later explained to him that he lost consciousness simply because of the physical effort he exerted to save us.

I wanted to rally behind him, give him a friendly tap on his large walrus shoulder, or vigorously applaud him for his gladiatorial defeats of the aggressive creatures we encountered over the last few days, or even follow Isabel's and Diana's example and place a warm, affectionate kiss on his large walrus-dolphin forehead, but I couldn't. I was unable to show him trust and friendship yet, like the other members of our group.

Granted, he did what he said he was ready to do. He risked his life to save us. "But, did he really risk his life?" I was not so sure. He was a leader, a royal leader, for a long time and he enjoyed being honored and admired by others. That meant that he would resort to any form of manipulation to reach that same status. And, after all, I heard his laughter and saw his broad grin when he was killing the ammonites. Yes, I knew how much he enjoyed a "good fight" whether it was with ammonites or sharks. "Did he risk his life for us or did he do it for his own pleasure?" Repeated in my thoughts, reminding myself that I was right not to trust him.

We left the area inhabited by the sharks to explore a larger circumference. Reinhart uploaded information about sharks and stingrays to me throughout the day. Tiger and Bull sharks lived in very cold, icy water, so Reinhart was not surprised that we ran into them. But their behavior confused her because sharks were normally solitary animals, they did not hunt in pods. The only known shark that hunted in pods, at Reinhart's time, was the seven gill shark and only when hunting seals. Moreover, different species of sharks did not mate with each other so it was not natural for them to be socializing with each other.

The sting rays, carnivorous predators, believed to be related to sharks, troubled her as well. They were warm water creatures in the past, so either their internal thermic system evolved to support cold water, or these sting rays were a new, mutated species. She regretted that we were unable to capture any of these creatures for further study.

Weeks of diving, turned into months, as we added new varieties of fish, like salmon and tuna, to our growing list. Although Reinhart cautioned all of us many times about resorting to eating flesh, animal or fish, some of the members of our group were curious about the taste and did bite into freshly caught salmon and tuna. In the end, I was the only one who refused to taste the flesh of another living creature, not because of Reinhart's convictions, but because just watching my colleagues sink their teeth into animal flesh... nauseated me.

WD continued to guide us along the original route that he had taken when he was a young walrus-dolphin. "We have arrived." He announced to me one evening when we were alone together on the bridge of the ship. "It is dangerous here, Pamela." His voice was as sweet and humid as the ocean air when he pronounced my name, something he did quite often, trying to create some sort of bonding between us...instead, arousing my suspicions.

"I have to admit that I am afraid." He said, as he used his fore flippers, positioned at right angles, to support himself, pushing his body forward in a slow, sluggish, dismal manner, reminiscent of a funeral march, as he moved solemnly along the bridge of the ship in contemplation. "Listen to me." He rushed at me and grabbed my hands with his flippers. "It is better to let time efface the danger through evolution. They might become more manageable."

"Evolution would take a very, long time!" I doubled up with laughter. He covered his ears with his flippers and I heard him grumbling for a long moment.

I finally approached him, took his flippers in my hands and caressed them lightly. "We have to find out what those sea monsters are. That is if they still exist." I backed away from him. "Are you with us?"

"Of course, I am with you. I am not such a coward that I would hide here on this ship and let you risk your lives without my being close by to defend you." He sighed. "It is just that I don't want to lose any of you."

He was a great actor. I could almost feel the depth of his concern. "You are concerned about losing human meals?" I snickered. "Don't worry, WD, we are all going to survive." I commented.

"You don't trust me, Pamela." He turned his back to me, pretending to be offended.

"Trust must be earned." I said softly, hoping that what I was going to say next would have an impact on him. "You have shown me that you can kill and...that you like to kill!"

He turned slowly in my direction and fixed his ice-encrusted eyes on mine. "We are very much the same, Pamela. Yes, we have a lot in common. And, you are right, it is better not to trust anyone!" He laughed downwards, his walrus tusks showing through the rent in his dolphin lip. I quickly turned and walked away.

Our objective the following day was to venture further out. I wanted to start the very deep sea exploration with a small sub; the androids had the sub mounted on the bridge so that we could enter through the top hatch. There was enough room for six people. I invited Diana, Randolph, Stuart, Peter and Joseph to come with me. Everyone else, including WD, stayed on board the ship.

The androids lowered the sub slowly into the deep ocean before releasing the tether, and leaving us to maneuver through thick vegetation, similar to that which we encountered weeks ago on the continental shelf. We had an unobstructed view of the ocean by the top hatch and from the panoramic windows encircling the sub, projecting a calming visual image of the world around us, from every direction. We sat back and relaxed, observing the different algae, their long greenish brown, bushy stems swaying hypnotically in front of us before starting to work.

The sub was equipped with everything we needed to take samples of fauna and flora. There were six sets of extension tubes, like arms, which terminated with a covering for the hand that had separate parts for fingers and thumbs. They were encased in the wall just below the panoramic windows. Bio-readers were inserted into the flexible matter used to construct these tubes and hands so that they would adapt automatically to a given arm and hand size, making it easy to operate this equipment to capture and collect specimens.

There were traps just below the windows on the outside of the sub and self-sealing netting available in other outside compartments, accessible with our extension arms and hands, so that we could open them and store the specimens we collected. After working for hours we decided to move on and prospect.

We only went a few hundred meters before we encountered a remarkable variety of shellfish, some resembling lobsters and crabs. We stopped to catch a few live specimens and place them in the outside traps. "Should we surface?" Heads nodded.

In retrospect this was a mistake. Our first encounter was with a basking swordfish that was at least 15 feet long and probably weighed around 1, 500 pounds, if earlier species that Reinhart studied could be used as a basis for this visual calculation.

"Is that long projectile a sword?" Joseph asked, wrinkling up his thick forehead.

I repeated what Reinhart quickly uploaded to me. "The long projectile does resemble a sword, but is not used to stab prey rather to slash at prey or dig them out of hiding."

At this point Reinhart's energy vibrated through me and I sat back to listen and learn while she took charge. She expressed her surprise in finding another species of warm water fish living in these very cold waters. "Normally these fish live in temperate or warm waters. They are ectothermic and their internal physiology is not capable of regulating their temperature. Perhaps they are now capable of absorbing heat by basking in this hot sun or that special organ located next to their eyes is doing more than just heating their brain and eyes like in the past. We must capture this swordfish and study it."

She opened up one of the cupboards on board the sub and handed Randolph a needle gun loaded with five tranquillizer darts. "The sub is bobbing in the water so it is safe for you to exit by the upper hatch. One tranquillizer will be enough to keep this fish under control until we get it back to the main vessel."

There is a heavy, wire line inside a bobbin in the front of the sub. It will be easy for you to release the wire by pressing on the button on top of the bobbin. You can pull the wire the distance that you need to attach it to the fish. Signal me—wave—so that I can reel the fish back to the ship." She explained. "Randolph will need help attaching the line, is there anyone ready to accompany him?" She asked and Stuart volunteered. They put on their diving gear, just in case, then passed through the hatch. Randolph hit his target with the tranquiller dart before they entered the water. Within less than 15 minutes the sword fish was in our possession, enveloped in large, thick netting, tightly secured up against the outside of the sub.

They had just gotten back on board when the sub was seized by a strong, engulfing force rising from the ocean bed that sent our sub spinning rapidly in a tight circle, like a raft caught in a deadly whirlpool. Reinhart was at the controls, trying to move the sub out of the hollow that was forming in the center of this rapidly moving water, like the mouth of an underwater crater ready to swallow us.

She shoved the throttle forward, rapidly accelerating the sub and causing it to literally jump more than 30 feet out of the water, coming down in a violent splash, as it rolled from side to side until it finally settled in an upright position just outside the limits of that deadly, spinning funnel.

"Is everyone alright?" Her voice rising in tone with each word.

"For the moment, but look at what is up ahead!" Diana screamed, pointing out the side window. Our earlier predators, those from days before, were moving rapidly in our direction producing low, but powerful surface waves that were beginning to pound against the sides of our sub, slowly moving us back in the direction of that turbulent waters.

Diana let out a loud, shrill cry, while the rest of the crew sat straight and rigid clenching the sides of their chairs, watching the sharks gain speed, as if they were preparing to bear down on us. And, then at the last instance, they split up, lightly side swiping our sub as they sped onwards.

We imagined that the sharks were afraid of our sub and that we were no longer under pursuit, when Joseph sounded another alarm. "What is that coming at us now, just up ahead?"

"Oh no. Orcas, Killer Whales." Reinhart replied, her voice calm, as if she were in a trance. "We have got to get out of here as fast as possible." She quickly plunged the sub hoping to avoid them, but instead these gigantic creatures pursued us. They were moving at incredible speed. The gap closed, and much to our chagrin, it became evident that we could never outrun them.

They were practically upon us when Reinhart steered the sub into the thick vegetation. They followed us for a short distance, but, as Orcas need open space to move rapidly and catch their prey, the vegetation impeded their pursuit, saving our lives. We laid low in the water, for a long moment, hiding in the foliage of the various algae, to be certain that our predators abandoned their search.

All this time our hearts throbbed in our chests, sounding like faint, distant drums sending us the message that we were still alive. Reinhart disappeared inside of me, leaving me to pull myself together and check out the directional guide. I turned and looked at white faces and large, frozen eyes. We were not far from the Mother ship so I advanced cautiously, moving the sub delicately through the plants, which were our only protection from those wretched creatures. Once we crept out from under the thick underbrush, I put the sub in high gear and we sped back to the Mother ship. I called ahead to ask that they have the tether ready to lift us on board.

"We are safe now. We are on board the ship and we can climb out of the hatch."

"What did you call them, Pamela?" Stuart asked as he struggled to his feet.

"Orcas, large mammals that are a species of dolphin."

We were on the bridge of the ship and color was returning to our drained faces.

"What do you mean by killer whales?" Joseph asked.

"Orcas got their name, killer whale, because they were the only marine mammal that was capable of killing whales. They were also referred to as the "wolves of the sea" because they hunt in pods. Even though all species of dolphins hunt in pods, the Orcas that pursued us are much bigger than their predecessors, making them more dangerous for us and all other marine mammals, unless the whales have also doubled in size."

"They scared me!" Randolph slapped his hands hard together, getting everyone's attention. "Is that all that Reinhart communicated to you?"

"Reinhart did upload quite a lot of information to me when we were being attacked by the Orcas." I said. "Well, first they are apex predators, meaning that they have no natural enemies. They have ravenous appetites and hunt in pods, normally large family units. That is why there were so many of them rushing their typical food sources before getting interested in us. They were known to feed off of sharks, rays, swordfish and squid, as well as other forms of aquatic mammals, like seals, most of which we have already encountered. In fact, they might even eat those ammonites, because they are similar to the octopus or squid. They did chase and kill young whales, for fun, playing with their bodies afterwards, and did attack, kill, and eat adult whales."

"To kill those whales, which were the largest mammals on earth, they actually engaged in a well-orchestrated attack. Members of the group surrounded the animal, picking and biting at it, while others actually mounted the whale, using their body weight to force the animal to submerge and/or blocking its blowhole with their bodies to prevent it from breathing. They consumed the animal while it was still alive."

"Killing for food is understandable, even if it causes suffering, but devouring your prey while it is still alive or killing for fun is revolting." Joseph interrupted me, the muscles in his face and large reptilian neck were contorted and his eyes blurred with rage.

I tried to conceal the sick, anxious feeling worming its way inside of me by loudly clearing my throat and picking up my discourse in a monotone. "Actually, they were very protective of each other. They did not attack other pods and often times migrated alongside other family units." I sighed.

"Nonetheless, they did attack and eat other species of dolphin and walruses. I guess that we better keep WD away from them!" I emphasized.

"And humans?" Peter queried.

"In the past, they did not eat humans, but, well, based upon what WD and his followers were doing we are a possible food source for them. After all, they are in the dolphin family." I sat back and waited for Reinhart to upload more information.

"It seems unbelievable based upon what we just experienced, but according to Reinhart humans captured and trained Orcas to perform different tricks for the public in large marine arenas. The Orcas would jump 20 feet in the area and do sweet back-flips into the water. Some trainers actually swam alongside of them or rode on their backs like on a surfboard."

"Did they ever turn on their trainers?" Peter asked bluntly.

"Yes, they did. A number of trainers were killed. It was believed that the Orca's sudden change of behavior, from docile to aggressive, was caused by boredom and need for raw flesh. They are dangerous predators who need to hunt and roam, so, without warning, their basic instinct surfaced and they turned on their trainers and killed them."

"You are absolutely certain that those marine animals were really orcas?" Stuart asked as he plowed his fingers through his hair.

"No doubt. I don't know if you had a chance to get a glimpse of their appearance, but they have the physical characteristics: a black back with white chest and sides, as well as the long dorsal fins, with a white patch behind them. They were very large mammals before the explosion. Even though they measured between 23 and 30 feet in length in the past, the ones we saw today were almost twice that size. That means that they might even weigh close to 12 tons. Extraordinary! But, so dangerous."

"At a smaller size, they were capable of reaching speeds of 50 miles per hour, which was still less than a bullnose dolphin. Remember when the dolphins first attacked us, they were certainly at more than 64 miles an hour and their high jumps helped to accelerate their approach. These killer whales might have difficulty moving much faster than their predecessors, only because of their weight and size. But, as they attack in pods, they are capable of rapidly surrounding their prey."

Randolph burst out laughing. We looked at him with blank faces, too stunned by his sudden laughter to react. "Don't you remember WD saying that he saw horrible sea monsters, like dinosaurian reptiles, that frightened him so much that he hightailed it back home?" We nodded. "And, Pamela, you just told us that these orcas are members of the dolphin family. Do you get it?" He stopped to let his remarks sink in before blurting out. "He was terrified by his own kind."

In view of the fact that WD would be a rare delicacy for these animals who already ate other dolphins, Randolph's joke wasn't funny. And yet, his silly remark incited laughter simply because we needed to vent steam and regain control over ourselves. So, we all joined in his crazy baseless laughter until we felt calm. Exhausted, we slowly left the bridge and looked for the rest of our team. I asked the androids to give the fauna and flora samples to the android pilots and to tell them to fly high on their way back to the center.

I also asked them to tell the Captain, who was supervising the harvesting of plants and fishing, to return to our vessel, because his navigational skills were becoming necessary. He was with us before the end of the day.

I passed by to see whether WD had recovered from his exhausting battles with the ammonites and sharks. He told me that he felt much better and would be able to dive the following day, if we needed him, which did not turn out to be the case.

"We encountered the Sea Monsters today." I said in a calm, matter-of-fact manner.

"What? No one was hurt?" He asked, his voice quivering as if he were reliving that terrifying experience of his youth that continued to haunt him."

"They are not mutated, or hybrid animals." His walrus tusks dropped in surprise. "They are members of the dolphin species." He shook in head in disbelief. "They are what we refer to as Orcas, Killer Whales."

"Killer Whales." He repeated it several times before saying that it was an appropriate name for them. "But, I should have recognized them as oversized dolphins when I was young, if that is what I really witnessed." He protested. "There may be other horrific predators that you have not yet encountered that correspond better to the images that haunt me." He closed his eyes in thought.

"Perhaps." I ventured.

"You were right, though, to get out of the area when you passed by those killer whales." His eyes grew bright. "Were they fighting for control when you encountered them?" He asked, searching for answers."

"Doubtful. Orcas don't fight each other for dominance and they hunt in family units, pods is the name that was used to describe them." I didn't want to hurt him, but I knew that what I would say next would make him sad. "Even though Dolphins eat dolphins when there is nothing else to eat, the killer whale does not resort to that behavior. These mammals never eat each other. They defend each other. Perhaps you witnessed a battle between a killer whale and blue whale." I sighed. "But then, today, when their size and appetite is exorbitant, probably eating each other when there is no other food source available, is not outside the realm of possibilities."

"Of course." He shook his large head in disgust. "We are a wretched species."

"No, WD, you are a mammal species and react like other mammal species. You know humans will eat humans when there is nothing else to eat. And, in the distant past, cannibalism was practiced for rather heinous reasons. For example, victorious tribes sometimes ate their defeated enemies to acquire their strength, or, in some cases, for the simple pleasure of eating human flesh."

"Thank you, Pamela. That does make me feel less despicable. It is just that I want to be more civilized than I was before." I still had strong doubts about his honesty but played the game. I bent over and gave him a kiss on the top of his Walrus-Dolphin head. His naturally slim, upturned dolphin lips parted so slightly revealing his upper front teeth in what was undoubtedly an effort on his part to send me a friendly smile. I left him to his thoughts.

I joined the others over dinner, where the discussion turned around the Killer Whales. The ultimate question was whether or not we should continue to explore the area or return home and prepare for the northern hemisphere.

"I would like to take the small plane and fly over the area if anyone wants to come with me?" I said in a low, pensive voice. I believed that it was important to establish the breadth of the killer whales' hunting grounds and identify their actual prey. Were there still whales in the oceans? If so, that would be good news, because they fed off of plankton, copepods, salpa fish or tunicates, sea worms, larva and small marine animals. This would mean that the oceans were rich in food sources, offering large varieties of marine life. I was also curious about what kind of species of whales we might discover and their behavior. I sat patiently waiting for volunteers.

"Are they capable of jumping?" Leonard ventured.

"No doubt about that. The question is just how high can they jump?" I replied. "Earlier Killer Whales, were capable of jumping 10 to 15 feet out of the water. But they were smaller models of the Killer Whales we saw." I closed my eyes in thought. "Perhaps their heavy bodies and size today would make it more difficult for them to reach menacing heights. Nonetheless, taking into account their size, even if they lift only their upper body, they will be at least 15 feet above water level.

"Well, if we want to know if they live in a confined area and can jump, we shall have to take a look at them from the sky above." Randolph commented. "Ok," he stretched his arms out in front of him and cracked his knuckles, "I am ready to go with you, Pamela. I am not scared!"

With that remark, I had a crew ready. Joseph was the only reptilian human to join us and Isabel wanted to stay on board the ship with Leonard, Daniel, Gordon, Tirence and WD.

A good night's sleep and a hearty breakfast gave us the courage, inspiration, and maybe confidence to fly over the area. The Captain promised to be ready to move rapidly in our direction, to salvage the plane or to rescue our crew. He warned me not to go too far because the ocean could be very turbulent and there were often violent storms. He gave me the impression that he was concerned about our safety even though I knew that that was impossible, he was a machine and could not show emotions of any kind.

Gordon took me aside as well to caution me about this kind of risk. "You must keep everything in perspective, Pamela, and better evaluate the options and risks." I pretended not to understand, but thanked her for her concern.

I felt good in the pilot's seat because I shared Reinhart's love of flying. I looked at my co-pilot, James, sitting with his arms resting comfortably on the arms of his seat with his face alight with a big grin. "Yes, we are ready to carry our crew for a new adventure. And, we have enough weapons and ammunition to face any obstacle that might come in our way." I told myself. I sat back and let Reinhart's enthusiasm ignite me as she moved the aircraft high up in the sky, before passing the controls over to me.

"Diana," I called out. "I am counting on you to film the creatures. It is important to get as much audio and visual information during our flight."

"No problem, I am ready." She replied.

My objective was to maintain sufficient height in the event the marine mammals were capable of more valiant jumping feats than I anticipated. We were above our former destination within minutes. I circled out and around looking for predators. "I think that we have to move further ahead." I informed the crew. Finally, our slow and meticulous forward progression paid off.

"Look up ahead. I think that we are coming upon a Blue Whale." I ejaculated with excitement as the crew moved to get a glimpse, while Diana started filming. The closer we got the more certain I was that we had come upon one of those magnificent marine mammals.

"Look you can see the steam coming up from its blowhole. It is expelling stale air and will breathe in fresh air." I passed the information that Reinhart was uploading to me. Her energy, more dynamic than usual, moving rapidly inside of me suggested that she too was fascinated with this animal that was non-existent at the end of her lifetime. "It is that blowhole that those miserable killer whales try to block to suffocate the animal."

The Blue Whale was very large, but not much larger than its ancestors. Diana got a length reading of 100 feet and estimated its weight at about 2000 tons. We hovered over this beautiful creature as its undulating moves propelled it forward. And then, the worst scenario was upon us. From nowhere a pod of killer whales surfaced and surrounded the animal proceeding in the very manner that I had described earlier to my crew. We fired on these orcas, scattering them, giving the whale the opportunity to escape.

"Should we have interfered, Pamela?" Joseph asked with trepidation.

"Probably not, that is if we believe that that whale was destined to die today." I sighed a deep sigh of relief because the killer whales regrouped and headed in another direction. For the moment, the blue whale was safe. But, for how long?

"Should I continue out a bit further?" I heard only yes.

The farther out we went the more agitated the water appeared to be and, even more vexing, there was no visible marine life on the surface. "Perhaps they are hiding in the ocean depths," passed rapidly through my mind, as I prepared to turn around.

"What is going on over there?" Joseph screamed in a raucous voice, his long reptilian finger pointing in the northeastern direction.

"Let's get a bit closer." I suggested as I advanced cautiously in the direction that Joseph was indicating.

My eyes fixed on the ghastly drama, leaving me speechless for a few seconds, long enough for Reinhart to send information to me. "You are witnessing a fierce battle between a colossal squid and a gigantic sperm whale, or cachalot," I said pointing out the different marine animals engaged in a life and death struggle. "Both of them are terrifying predators---noticeably much larger than their ancestors. They normally hunt in the ocean depths which makes this an exceptional performance. I guess that we are, in a certain sense, lucky that they pursued their battle up to the ocean surface."

I stopped to take in the gruesomeness of the fight. "But...if history repeats itself, the sperm whale should be the winner, as the colossal squid was its preferred meal in the past." We sat back to watch what turned out to be a long and arduous battle between these two appalling creatures. The colossal squid fighting hard to save its life.

Diana was taking pictures and gathering readings of the sizes of these animals. She passed the following information onto us: "The squid weighs around 800 pounds, is 60 feet in length, and has 8 arms and 2 tentacles, which it is extending more than 20 feet outward in its attempt to capture the sperm whale." She turned to the sperm whale. "This whale weighs close to 60 tons, by my estimates, and is close to 80 feet in length, its head representing one-third of its body."

I picked up from there, adding more detailed information that Reinhart had uploaded to me. "As you can witness, the squid is reaching out with its long arms and tentacles in an attempt to attach itself to and perforate the cachalot's outer skin with its large suction cups that cover practically its entire body and are surrounded with serration rings, like teeth. Unfortunately, for the moment the squid is unable to attach itself to its predator, who is moving rapidly out of its reach."

"The cachalot has large, powerful jaws, with between 18 and 26 cone-shaped teeth, each tooth weighing around 2 and one-half pounds, positioned on each side of its lower jaw. These teeth can easily rip the squid into pieces."

Suddenly, in a desperate effort to save its life, the squid leaped out of the water and lunged, catching the cachalot off guard, as it wrapped its arms and tentacles around it, searing the animal with its suction cups and lacerating its outside skin. Red streaks of blood appeared on the surface of the ocean.

The cachalot responded rapidly to this attack. It jumped more than 20 feet in the air with the squid wrapped tightly around its body, and landed with a violent splash on its back, using its body weight to weaken its opponent and force it to release its grip.

The squid, stunned, by the impact, was rolling on the surface of the water, its arms and tentacles swirling in different directions, as it tried desperately to regain control of its body. We sat forward in our seats, our hands gripping the armrests so hard that our knuckles were white, and watched the battle come to a violent end, as the cachalot charged at full speed, sinking its teeth deep into the mantle, or body, of the squid, and began to devour its prey.

I quickly turned my eyes away, disgusted by the brutality of it, and found myself focused on the murky horizon shrouded with heavy grey clouds. I blinked hard, forcing my eyes to pierce through the hypnotic effect of this menacing imagery, finally deciphering the high waves that were now forming a dangerous barrier. The clear skies were turning dark and eerie as, at this moment, cumulous storm clouds were rising like towers in the distance. I could even hear the sound of distant thunder.

It was time to leave marine life behind. Before the crew had an opportunity to recover from the ferocious marine animals, they were jolted back to reality as I brusquely banked the airplane to the right to make a quick turn. "Brace yourselves. We are heading back to the ship at maximum speed!" I howled as I struggled to keep the plane on course and keep a distance away from the threatening, gusting winds that were creeping up behind us.

My flying experience was limited to clear skies so I surrendered to Reinhart who took over the controls and flew the aircraft while I hid frightened, but alert, inside myself.

"The storm is moving fast. You can already see the large storm clouds that formed on the horizon and are approaching us rapidly. The loud clashing noise that sounds like metallic parts exploding into pieces, is thunder. If you watch closely, you will even see lightning- large, sparks and streaks of white light- in the distance." She said, in a calm, didactic voice, which completely masked any anxiety she might be feeling.

"Our plane is too small to fly above the storm. We are at the plane's maximum flight level, or 10,000 feet, far below the 40,000 feet necessary to overfly a storm." She cleared her throat.

"But, don't worry. Hopefully we will have time to land before it overtakes us." She sighed. "But, we might experience some turbulence, if we get hit by the heavy rains and the winds, rushing at least 119 miles an hour. If this happens, the plane will react like a roller coaster, with rapid up and down movements. We might even spin around." She said, understating the real danger. "Just keep your seats and I promise to bring us down safely!" Even though her words were reassuring, the crew members were too aware of the approaching danger to be so easily bluffed.

She called the ship and asked the androids to move WD down below for safety. She ordered the Captain to send androids out onto the deck to prepare a safety net to receive our aircraft as we were going to need help maintaining it in place; that was if we could outrun what looked to be a hurricane.

What seemed like hours, was only minutes before the ship was in view. She had difficulty landing the plane. We spun around and moved up and down as she struggled to align the wobbling plane with the runway. The plane swayed and vibrated in the thrashing wind and torrential rain. It took several attempts before we finally landed. The androids virtually captured our plane in the netting, forcing the plane to land. They quickly opened the doors, shielding us in a makeshift corridor that protected us against the wind and rain. They grounded the aircraft with straps, retrieved all the equipment and put it in storage. The Captain was calling out orders to his crew, initiating the right manoeuvers to turn the vessel round and start our trip back to the coast.

"The storm . . ." No one could hear Reinhart's shouts as she entered the noisy bridge.

"It is ok. I know this vessel and it will withstand the storm. Just tell the others to sit in the lounge and protect themselves in case there is any violent jolt." She looked at the Captain and then did something that I did not understand, she moved her right hand to the right side of her forehead and he mimicked her gest. She later informed me that her gesture was a salute, a sign of respect or good will.

She rounded up the others and led them to the lounge. This was the first time any of us, apart from Reinhart, encountered thunder, lightning, heavy winds, and pouring rain. Grouped together in the lounge area with WD reclining next to me, we gradually started to unwind.

"So this is a storm, or did you say, a hurricane?" Peter asked, his voice feigning a reserved calm.

"Yes, the winds are very high, at hurricane level. Hopefully the wind and rain will die out, or at least calm down, before we reach the coastline or," I said with a half-smile, "we might have high coastal waves that make it difficult for the Captain to dock the ship."

"OH, not that." WD spoke up. "Not tidal waves." He wailed, comparing it with a tsunamis. "We don't need that!!"

"No, I didn't mean a tsunami or a giant, devastating wave caused by an earthquake or volcanic eruption in the ocean." He wrinkled his thick brow. "Did you ever experience a tsunami?" I asked out of curiosity.

Everyone's eyes were on WD when he next spoke. "Actually, I never encountered bad weather, but there were stories about high destructive waves." He shook his head in an effort to clarify his thoughts. "There were periods of violent storms and I think the tsunamis, our elders talked about, were caused by human destructive activity."

"What destructive activity?" Isabel's voice sounded like she was looking for a fight.

"Oh, Sorry, if I offended you." WD replied quickly. "I meant all the climate warming problems that were caused by the emission of carbon dioxide gas into the air by humans who used too much fossil fuel, especially in their transport vehicles. And, apparently, humans disposed of toxic material in the ocean." He shrugged his shoulders. "You are a scientist, so you should be able to determine the truth of that."

Reinhart disappeared inside of me, leaving me on my own to answer questions. "By the way, WD," he turned his eyes in my direction, "I owe you an apology for what I told you the other evening. Apparently, the Orcas are not the most violent or dangerous species in the ocean. Today we witnessed a battle between a colossal squid and a sperm whale, or a cachalot." I sighed and then described them to him. "They are imposing and frightening looking creatures." I blinked my eyes and continued. "Now I understand why you did not want to go too far out into the high seas."

His body collapsed up against the couch and I stroked his large head. "So my memories are real, Pamela." he said in a low voice.

"Yes, WD, those memories are real."

All this time, the Captain piloted the ship rapidly and meticulously. He kept the ship moving forward, giving it enough power that he could steer the ship to avoid getting pushed around by the waves. He was experienced and knew that he had to keep the bow, or the front of the ship, pointing into the waves so that the ship would plow safely through the waves, to avoid a massive wave striking the side of the ship and causing it to roll over or sink. And so, he steered the ship with dexterity through the middle of the storm.

After what seemed like hours, sunlight started to filter in through the lounge windows. An android messenger appeared to tell us that calm waters were just up ahead. "The storm broke, Dr. Reinhart, and we are now safe." Spontaneous sighs of relief filled the room.

"I think that I am looking forward to walking on "terra firma."" Randolph said in a convincing tone, as he stood up and stretched.

"I know what you mean." Stuart replied, his voice a bit raspy.

"So, we shall head back to the marine center and then leave for our center to pack for the exploration of the northern hemisphere!" I said in a voice animated with emotion, hoping to inspire enthusiasm.

"Well, I think that we," Joseph looked at his reptilian friends, "will need a couple days to recover before heading north."

That broke the tension and brought on that wave of laughter that our group resorted to, now instinctively, to release our stress and regain inner calm.

We disembarked tired but in good humor after the Captain docked the ship. We separated, walking laboriously, immersed in thought, our discoveries weighing heavily on our minds. I lingered in the corridor and waited until the Captain passed through the lounge area. I followed him to his office in front of which Drager was waiting patiently. We knocked. The Captain opened the door and we entered.

I thanked them both for assuring the success of this mission before opening up a discussion. "I was wondering if you could continue the exploration for us—in our absence." My eyes focused on both of them, and then moved to Gordon who had just joined us.

"In what respect...Pamela?" The Captain asked.

I would like to have more information about the ammonites, the colossal squid, the sperm whale, the killer whales, and the blue whale—perhaps other whale species. What do you think?" I wanted to know how they would evaluate their competences in this area, so resisted giving orders, because, if I gave orders, they would assume that they were coming from Reinhart and would just obey, hesitate discussing this with me.

"We can catch a few of the smaller killer whales." The Captain replied in his lifeless android style. I nodded. "Actually, as you might remember, there is a large basin." He moved in the direction of the door. "I shall show it to you. It has no water in it but that is not a problem. Follow me."

I was tired but curious. Reinhart seemed uninterested because

I got no feedback. I followed the Captain, Drager and Gordon into the transport unit. I thought that I had explored the entire area and then a thought hit me. "Was this all a trap?"

The Captain pretended to be oblivious to my lagging behind and kept his rapid pace. Eventually, he pressed a button on the right side of the far back wall, opening upon a large arena. This was when Reinhart surfaced again and took over.

"Of course, this arena was for aquatic shows." She started off. "I was opposed to all of this---humiliating for the animals and well, most of them were in very bad condition- suffering from bacterial infections, being underweight and lethargic- because of the air and water pollution. Their lifespan was reduced by 50% when they entered these pools."

"Interesting." The Captain replied. "Did you know that these animals were killed and eaten by the nonintellectuals who gained access to the center, just before the explosion?"

"Yes." She replied.

"Their visit was unexpected---they actually wanted to take refuge here. But, when Murdoc showed up, well...you know the rest." The Captain stood at attention. "We sealed off this room."

"I see. And how do you envisage using this space today?"

"We could fill the large basin with saltwater. The water, as your tests will indicate, is pure. There are no more polluting elements in the Earth's environment, so the air and water are clean." He stopped for an instance. "We could capture a few of those killer whales and put them in this large basin. You could study their behavior and their physiology." He suggested.

"I like the idea very much." She looked at him and Drager who stood in stiff android style. "I don't know if their attitude towards humans will be the same as in the past. We shall have to be careful. How can you catch them?"

"We can use the fishing vessels that were, in the past, very resistant and well-equipped to catch or kill aquatic animals." He replied.

"The weather conditions will not be a problem?"

"What happened today is rather unusual, but, of course, we must be prepared for that." He turned and moved past the very large wading pool for the killer whales and pointed to the large aquariums opening up into runways integrated into the ceilings. "We could collect a couple samples of those wretched sharks, if you want." He paused. "They are ravenous creatures like those killer whales, so we will have to find a suitable food source."

"Let me see this with the Group of 5 on my return. We can always use another protein-based substance as a food source."

"There are salmon and tuna and ray and others." The Captain commented. "Perhaps your humans would like to add them to their diet. We could always fish ecologically, or catch only mature fish and throw the small ones back, and, of course, not catch more fish or other marine life than is necessary. Your center could also simply order the quantity and species on a weekly basis. We could have the orders flown to your center."

"Treacherous—how I detest that carnivorous side of humans!" Reinhart said with strong emotion, registering her disgust. "But, yes, we may have to consider fish as a food source." She looked at the Captain. "We shall not offer much of that to our captives here. They will have to survive on substitutes."

"Intelligent fishing methods will not destroy the aquatic animals or wipe them out." Drager finally entered the conversation. "It was human irresponsibility -pollution, disregard of life forms, the waste of food, and, must I continue, that destroyed this planet's environment. Hopefully, this new generation of humans will be different."

"And the whales?" Reinhart's interest overflowed.

"The best that we could do is move them into a screened off area in a safe part of the continental shelf." The Captain ventured. "Even if we catch a small one, it will grow and for the moment we have no basin large enough for one of them. Your group could swim alongside of them and study them in an enclosed ocean environment. When they have finished with one study group, we could release them and collect other species.

"All that sounds very interesting. I would like to give that more thought. I do believe that for the moment the both of you could supervise the killer whale and shark project." They nodded.

"The ammonites?"

"They are very strange -creatures. Even though they have

octopus and squid characteristics, they have differences, like their razor sharp tongues. I think that it is better to study the dead animals that you collected before considering catching live ones." Drager suggested.

"Agreed." Reinhart looked at them pleased with their ideas and their interest. "Drager, I would like you to continue here for the moment?" Reinhart said.

"I like the Air and Space unit," he mentioned but knew that he would have to follow her orders and quickly added, "but I believe that I will be involved in interesting projects here."

"And, you, Victoria, would you be interested in studying the behavioral side of these animals?" Reinhart asked softening her order, while pursuing my divide and conquer policy

"Yes. But, perhaps I could work with someone like Mathilda, for example on this project." She suggested.

"I was thinking more about Dr. Crawford."

"She pulled her shoulders back and then flung her hands up in the air before saying. "Why not? It sounds interesting. I like the idea."

"Thank you all for your cooperation. I am going to go get some rest." Reinhart smiled at their unemotional android faces and disappeared inside of me.

I too wanted to be alone so I walked aimlessly. I noticed that the lounge area was empty and collapsed on one of the comfortable couches. I leaned my head back and could see the stars shining down on me through the domed ceiling.

"Hello, Pamela." Gordon said, as she handed me a glass of water, and then took the seat in front of me. "Is everything ok for you?" She asked, her arms folded loosely in front of her.

"Yes, but..."I stopped abruptly, taking a huge gulp of water.

"I believe that you and your team have made many interesting discoveries over the last few years." Worried about where she was heading, I bit down on my thumb, like a child, bracing myself for criticism. "Pamela, I know that you do not feel that you have moved forward as rapidly as you would have liked to." My body turned rigid and I sat up straight. "I am not flattering you, Pamela, I am simply stating facts." She forced an android smile that was as lifeless as if it were painted on a rubber doll.

"I am not as convinced as you that we have made a lot of progress. The only thing we have done is explore the areas within a reasonable distance of the main center." I said, hanging my head.

"True." She replied, adapting her voice to a pleasant mellow tone. "You must remember that it takes time to understand the past and to build a new world." She played with her long fingers. "Does Dr. Reinhart foresee a future for us?"

I heard her ask, as my mind drifted off to a distant past, when I was the subject of her study in human emotions. I could see myself, sitting in that uncomfortable, metal chair, trying hard to explain human emotions. . .some I had not yet experienced. . .to a machine. And yet, in spite of the stressfulness of these meetings, I saw her as an ally, a friend, a mentor, and, finally, an unselfish lover.

Memories, indelibly imprinted in my mind, of excessive sentimental yearning, swept through me. I could almost feel her hands, moving slowly up and over my body, fondling and caressing my breasts, dropping lower...and lingering, exciting me, as my legs parted, revealing my warm, wet desire, as I mentally relived that final moment of ecstasy.

"Pamela, does Dr. Reinhart foresee a future for us?" She repeated her question, jarring back to the present.

I quickly crossed my legs and put my glass of water on the table next to me. "She put something in it." Passed through my mind. "Something that would excite me. But why? To embarrass me with Reinhart or to send a message of defiance to Reinhart?" Neither response seemed credible. So, I breathed deeply, calming my mind and body, as a smile slowly worked its way across my troubled face.

"I believe so." I finally replied in a clear, steady voice. "Why? Are you worried?"

"We can't worry, Pamela." She protested, pretending that she was unaware of the wave of nostalgia that passed through me. "Humans worry. We just want you and Dr. Reinhart to know that we are committed to you and your group and appreciate being involved. I am pleased that you asked me to spend time here in this Center. I will be working on challenging projects."

"I am glad." I replied. "But you know that you will have to return with us to the Center. You and Dr. Crawford will be dropped off at this center later in the week by the android pilots, before they return to the Air and Space center."

She nodded, moved to get up and then stopped. "Of course, you and your group wasted time specifying your objectives. You spent too much time talking and not enough time acting, at least in the beginning." She moved her eyes rapidly in their sockets. "But then that is human-and you all needed to mature—if I can say that—and get focused on real life problems and serious scientific projects."

I looked at her askance and she continued. "Not everything you want to accomplish, nor everything you promised to do for others, are going to bring you satisfaction." Her lifeless android stare was unyielding. "Not everyone is your friend. You have rivals within your group." She warned. "Just remember, we, the Group of 5, are there for you whenever you need us." This time she got up and left me to my thoughts.

"Certainly she was right that we wasted a lot of time deciding upon the best way to deprogram the reptilian humans, how to reconstruct certain mutated humans and how to rebuild the android, Miller. But this was research oriented and a learning experience for everyone, because Reinhart was revealing very complex scientific information and procedures. The knowledge that we acquired will be useful today and in the future." I mulled this over in my mind.

"Yes, we may have lost a lot of time learning how to live together in a community—a larger one than we had on the outside. Nonetheless, we learned how to go beyond physical appearances, something that our predecessors had difficulty achieving. We also matured, learning how to assume responsibility and interact effectively. Our project "procreation" did become a priority and perhaps we did lose valuable time focusing on this. Nonetheless, it gave everyone the opportunity to learn more about in vitro fertilization and the utility of the artificial uteruses, thus acquiring valuable scientific knowledge."

"We also explored our environment." I said in a low voice as if I were speaking to someone close to me and not just to myself. "We have come to understand better how the planet Earth evolved after the explosion, the reason why different centers survived that dramatic explosion the Group of 5 instigated, and why the Group of 5 was in control for all those years. We also discovered new life forms, found former friends, and are starting to define our next objectives. We will build outside communities, continue to explore the large continent, search for new sources of food and natural resources. And, some of us will begin our next adventure on board a space craft."

It all sounded quite impressive to me. "So, why do I feel so melancholic when I think about our Group, when I should only have feelings of joy?" I thought to myself.

I sighed. "Did Gordon throw me off track, or did she put me back on track? What does she mean about rivals? If there were rivals, Reinhart would surface and protect us." I reasoned.

The beautiful rosy-colored aurora began to filter through the domed ceiling, arousing me from my thoughts. I realized that I spent the entire night in the lounge, ruminating over the implication of Gordon's final words.

I jumped up and rushed off to my bedroom to take a shower, waking Peter up as I ran into the room.

"Hurry," I yelled, "we have to get ready to leave!"

Chapter 31: Unity in Defiance

All of us were proud of what we had accomplished over the last few months, so friendly back-slapping, declarations of praise and laughter were the order of the day. We boasted about our oceanic discoveries, while the others boasted over their research. Sarah, Ruth, Benjamin and Stanislas had identified organic substitutes that could be used to reproduce vital pharmaceutical products and John had made considerable progress in his studies of the images he had captured from satellites, and Mathilda wanted to be complimented on the progress that the children were making. And, Ralph and his agricultural team wanted to share their research on the different species of plants recovered from the floral garden.

Still haunted by the final remarks of Gordon, I was unable to participate in their merriment and stood as an observer looking on, wishing that their waves of happiness would eventually sweep me up. But, it didn't happen.

Continually plagued by her warning, even as the days turned to weeks, I developed a foreboding perspective of our future. I felt uneasy interacting with the others. My suspicions grew stronger as I sensed something ominous invading our group which I was unable to clearly define. "Is it competition, or is it adversity, with rivalry and tension brewing within the team, that will eventually divide and tear us apart? Finally, is it that I'm worried the androids are secretly conspiring to take over the world again? "

John met with me in private soon after our return. "I decided to rejuvenate, Pamela—or, Dr. Reinhart." His voice took on a lofty, deep tone.

"You know, John, that I am not yet capable of doing that." I corrected him. "Reinhart already promised to do it for you. In fact she anticipated your favorable response and has already defined your parametric equation." "I replied. "We could schedule that for tomorrow, if you are in a hurry."

"Tomorrow is fine with me."

"You can meet me in the hospital unit. I shall program the machine today." Reinhart replied controlling my vocal chords so that her accent was recognizable.

The rejuvenation of John aroused and eventually unleashed that negative force, making Gordon's prediction of my future more dismal. John's physical appearance was remarkable. A tall, muscular athletic body flaunting brawny arms and legs replaced the slightly overweight and bulky body that we were used to seeing. A young, chiseled face and prominent chin, with dark, somber eyes stood in marked contrast with his former puffy eyes and aging face.

Unfortunately, the wisdom of age that should have accompanied him in his rejuvenation was gone. He was impatient and critical, downright aggressive and insulting, on many occasions. His quest for power, to be designated the acclaimed leader of our group like he was when we were a small community living on the outside, was something that I tried very hard to ignore.

Ferdinand set up a meeting several months later. I had already gotten the approval of everyone, except John, to send Gordon and Crawford to the Marine center, so their research was well underway.

I quickly brought the group up to date on their progress at the beginning of the meeting. "Gordon and Crawford contact me every day." I wanted to underline their loyalty. "The arena houses five young killer whales and a large variety of sharks are swimming in the overhead tanks with tubular runways. They are unable to explain why the different species of shark live in harmony with each other. Neither Gordon nor Crawford were able to identify any genetic mutations in these animals apart from their impressive sizes. They are presently studying the sperm whale and colossal squid in their natural environment and are dissecting the remains of the ammonite."

"I think that it is time that we name a leader." John said in a deep, harsh voice changing the subject radically.

"I thought that we agreed that we would make group decisions." Ferdinand interjected.

"That was a mistake." John turned his cold, menacing eyes in my direction. "Reinhart has taken control. She is making all the decisions. We just march behind her. She limits our research and defines our priorities."

"That is not true, John. You have lost your sense of rationality since your rejuvenation. I..."

"Stop it, Pamela!" He interrupted me in. "I am fed up with your patronizing language. You think that we don't know that you like, even enjoy, your symbiotic relationship. How can we be certain that you are not capable now of replacing all of us?" He asked in a thundering voice. "You should have shared everything with us, given us all the last level of research so that we could be going forward— improving on things. Instead you are pretending that she uploads information in you and that you cannot force her to reveal everything." He laughed scornfully.

"It is true. We could be so much farther ahead if Pamela had not switched loyalties by aligning herself completely with Reinhart. We are wasting precious time." Ruth affirmed, before continuing. "She could have given us all the information that she received from Reinhart."

"Ruth, I don't understand what you are talking about. We have made lots of advancements in our research because of the projects Reinhart has given us." Mathieu protested. "But, it is true, Pamela, that you have not made us privy to all of her knowledge."

"For example, I was previously involved in genetic research. Pamela explained the differences in the various reptilian humans, but never let me see the actual research. So, even if I want to create a new hybrid species, I don't know all the techniques that Reinhart used. It is very frustrating!" Ruth squealed, her face flushed red and finger pointing in my direction. The other members repeated in their own ways the same lies and accusations. Only Randolph and Stuart proclaimed their fidelity to me.

"I told you the truth." I protested. "In order to give you all her knowledge, I would have to force her to upload everything to me, which I am incapable of doing. What she reveals to me, I make available to you."

"Ask her, Pamela, to make a program for all of us." Peter pleaded.

"She could just upload everything onto a computer program that we could all download and access. Or, cajole her then, into making everything accessible to you."

I looked at him. My eyes were blazing and my teeth were showing, much like an animal ready to defend itself in a life and death battle. I felt betrayed by him and angry with the group. "Why was he taking their side? And why were they chastising me, like they did in the past, when I was the new arrival, sent by Gordon, to live with them in their outside community?"

My inhibitions and my self-control were disappearing. I knocked over my chair as I stood up rapidly, getting everyone's attention. I wanted to emit a piercing scream, like a battle cry to shock and intimidate my adversaries, but instead I stood with my mouth wide-open, unable to expel anything other than an inaudible stream of breath. I felt dizzy and my eyes were sending blurring images of all those in front of me. My head started to pound from the emotional build-up inside of me. And in the background, I could hear John's voice ringing in the air.

"Another melodramatic moment brought to us by Pamela." He spit out under raucous laughter as he applauded my performance.

His insult seemed insignificant in view of my cognizance of what just happened inside of me. Reinhart was gone. I no longer felt her energy, her warmth, not even a tiny flicker of her existence. ""Where is she? Why has she disappeared?" preoccupied my thoughts. My eyes stared hatred at those responsible.

"I am leaving this meeting now." I finally replied in a soft, unanimated voice, like the losing party in a war whose acquiescence is a mixture of shame and disgrace. "You can choose your leader." I looked at John. "Reinhart is gone. I don't know if she is gone forever, but she is gone for now. You got what you wanted so I hope that you are happy." I then turned to the others. "You can now start your own research from the point where you left off." I moved to leave, when Peter grabbed my arm.

"You are not serious, Pamela?" He sneered.

"Unfortunately, I am serious. And, I understand why she left." I paused, to build up the momentum and impact of what I would say next. "You didn't appreciate her." My eyes, red and inflamed, scanned the group. "You were jealous of her and jealous of me, because she decided to merge with me and not with one of you. Now, let your jealousy be your incentive to produce and show her that you can meet her expectations. Prove to yourselves that her belief in this generation of humans was correct." I sighed.

"I have had enough of your accusations." Feeling the repulsive contamination of his touch, I shook Peter's hands off of me, as I abruptly headed for the door and exited.

The three remaining members of the Group of 5, the former Governor, Miller and Flanders, were waiting for me just outside the door.

"Is everything ok, Pamela?" Flanders asked.

I knew that they were not privy to the conversation, nonetheless, I was suspicious of their curiosity. "No, nothing is the same." I said, dropping my head. "She is gone."

Chapter 32: Patience and Perseverance

"**C**ome with us, Pamela." Flanders said as he took me by my hand and led me back to their office.

"It is not possible." The former Governor insisted when we were all seated at the large desk. "She can't leave you, but she might have gone into a deep phase of meditation for the moment." The others nodded. "Give her time-that is what she wants."

"Time to do what?" I asked, my voice loud and clear.

"Who is responsible?" Miller asked, ignoring my question.

"John. Yes John is responsible." I replied because it felt good to put the responsibility on the one who deserved it. They all broke out into crackling android laughter that sounded like fingernails scratching a chalk board.

"It makes no sense to me." I pressed for answers. "You are not insinuating that Reinhart would disappear because she was intimidated by a rejuvenated, immature John, spouting off his young hormones?"

"Of course not!" Flanders said emphatically. "Her reason for tuning out alludes me, but I know that she is still inside of you and will eventually re-emerge." He insisted. "It is true, though, that she didn't get on well with his ancestor in the distant past, before the doomsday explosion, and he tried on many occasions to unseat her." Flanders replied. "The others will discover how incompetent he is during her absence. Now, you must stay positive."

"Is that why John is different now-ambitious and pretentious?" I asked.

"Yes, he is like his ancestor." Flanders said rubbing his chin in thought. "Strange that his rejuvenation should have brought back that ancestral trait." He looked at me. "Humans need outside stimuli to develop their personalities; you just don't inherit a personality. It is not genetically transmitted." He let out a long gust of wind and looked around the room. "Of course, it is possible that because of his self-proclaimed leadership of the outside community, his knowledge and competitive personality were incapable of being disentangled, much like an inextricable knot, so that after his rejuvenation, he came back an ambitious, power hungry young man." He stopped abruptly and asked. "Tell me, how does this rejuvenation work?"

"I can't even if I were capable of explaining it." His probing question made me feel anxious, and I pushed my chair away from the table to put more space between us.

"So, it is not just a physical restructuring then." Flanders commented as he tapped his fingers rhythmically on the desk top like he did in the past to distract me. "Then, she made a mistake." My eyes caught his in virtual combat and he quickly tried to qualify his statement. "I believe that my reasoning is right, but that the outcome was unexpected, perhaps even incompatible with normal physical rejuvenation, however rejuvenation is accomplished."

"Hum—so physical rejuvenation can have emotional side effects." He stood up and paced back and forth. "Well, there is nothing that we can do for the moment, except hope that Dr. Reinhart returns soon." He stopped pacing and looked at me. I sensed that we shared a common grievance. "You must not worry. She will be back."

I wanted to believe that she would return so what they said made me feel better. "Thank you all for reassuring me." I stood up slowly, wiping my moist hands on the sides of my robe. "I have to leave now."

"Where are you going, Pamela?" The former Governor asked.

"To play my piano." I yelled, as I rushed out of their office full of a new kind of enthusiasm.

Jonathan, who no longer participated in the meetings, was in the orchestra pit when I arrived. He was deep in thought and jumped when I sneaked up behind him and said hello.

"What a nice surprise, Pamela." He said in the mellow, warm tone of a cello. "It has been a long time since you passed by this part of the world." All my sadness disappeared when I looked into his glistening eyes and felt his hands gently caressing mine.

I sat down next to him and told him what had happened.

He sat calmly listening. When I mentioned the three android's comments, his eyes closed in thought.

"What they said seems very logical." He finally replied, his eyes open and moving rapidly in their sockets, as if he were analyzing a complex musical score. "Yes, she is a lot like them---incredibly logical. But would it have been a non-emotional thing to do?" He took my head tenderly between his hands and looked deep into my eyes. "Pamela, I have a feeling that her disappearance had nothing to do with the nature of the meeting, including John's overt quest for power, but rather with a project or a commitment that she had to complete and could no longer disregard." My eyes opened wide in awe of his perspicacious remark, as I marveled over his genius. "She will be back." He gave me a quick kiss on my forehead and then said. "Now let's have some fun with music."

I spent a long moment with Jonathan---a long, invigorating moment. When I left him, I went back to my former cubicle and curled up on the bed. I was angry with Peter, and needed to be alone. And, John was in charge for the moment. "Peter and John have known each other for a long time, they negotiated their small group's right to live on the outside. And, it is better for Frederic to be under his father's protection." My thoughts justified my decision to be alone.

I would spend a long week avoiding everyone except Jonathan. Playing the piano, eating when the others had finished their meals, and spending my alone time in my former cubicle.

No one came looking for me, not even Peter or Frederic, and I felt relieved that I was alone. Jonathan and I never talked about the others, something that made it so easy for me to spend curative time with him.

When I finally felt ready to reintegrate into the Group, I went to see Randolph. He and Stuart were there when I entered the lab. "I want to thank you for your silent support of me weeks ago." I said in a reserved tone.

"Are you feeling better now?" Randolph asked, a smile broke out, flashing his gleaming teeth. I didn't have time to reply. He wrapped, his strong arms around me, and I hid my head in his chest, until he finally relaxed his grip, releasing me from this comfort zone.

"Stuart and I have missed you." Randolph said. "We were shocked with John's attitude, which got completely out of control after you left." He broke off, shaking his head, while his hands came together forming tight fists. "John suggested that you were schizophrenic. He even went so far as to suggest that you might be a relatively brilliant scientist, but as you started as a musician, an accomplished pianist, your brain invented two different personalities-Pamela the pianist and Dr. Reinhart the scientist. He mentioned that you could be dangerous and should probably be confined, but he would let you live freely, if all of us to stayed away from you. He then put Mathilda in charge of Frederic and she follows Frederic's every move, reporting back to John." He kicked over his lab chair and knocked over some empty bottles on the lab table, watching them shatter into tiny pieces, as they hit the floor.

"And, no one defended me?" I hung my head in disdain, the pain of rejection weighing heavily on me.

"Stuart and I told him that the three of us worked together as a team in the past, for the success of our revolution and that we would do whatever the "h---" we wanted, meaning that we would work with you again."

"But, do Peter and Frederic miss me?" I struggled to blink back tears that were rapidly mounting in my deep, green eyes.

"Stuart and I told Peter to let us get in touch with you. He argued with us, but we convinced him that it was important for him to protect Frederic, by befriending John."

"But, neither one of you tried to contact me."

"We simply waited patiently for your return." Stuart entered the conversation. "We watched you from a distance and kept Peter informed about what you were doing."

"And Diana-she believes what John says."

"Not at all!" Randolph bellowed. "She pretends to be his ally so that she can attend the meetings and report back to us." He paused. "She is definitely our ally!"

"Reinhart is not back yet." I said, just in case their interest in me was really an interest in her.

"So-that is ok with us." Stuart replied adamantly. "The three of us can work together on our own." He then playfully tapped my cheeks with his hands, before picking me up and spinning me round, making me laugh.

"Ok. But, I only want to work with the two of you." They nodded. "I have some ideas. Do you want to hear them?" They nodded energetically.

"I think that we should contact Colonel Shannon. I don't know whether the two astronauts she promised to send have left yet. If so, we must be prepared for their arrival." I started off.

"I can contact her now." Randolph replied. "I am going to be honest with you, Pamela. I discretely studied John's research. I broke into the locked cupboard in the inner circle where he hides the research and took copies of the correspondence and imagery that he is studying." He hesitated before continuing. "Brace yourself—Colonel Shannon refused to let the astronauts leave." His brows corrugated. "Anyway, that is what she told him. Apparently, John tried to convince her that he was the right person to be in command of the Center and that she would have to trust him, like the rest of his team. She told him that she was following orders from her superiors who would only work with Reinhart. She even insinuated that the androids might now be in command and that John was one of them."

"That means that we cannot work with her either?"

"Yes and No—she has asked to speak to you, Pamela."

"Then let's contact her now." I felt stronger, more sure of myself, as if Reinhart had left me a bit of courage that I only now recuperated.

Randolph, Stuart and I sat together in front of the screen, as I repeated over and over again my request to speak to Colonel Shannon to the communications officer. It seemed like an eternity before she answered.

"Colonel Shannon, I am Pamela."

"I am listening."

"It would appear that you have been contacted by other members of our group." I did not give her chance to answer. "I took some time off to relax after all our months, years, of exploration, which is why you were unable to speak to me earlier."

"And, where is Dr. Reinhart?" She queried in that official military tone.

"You understand that we have a symbiotic relationship."

"Yes, she explained that to me on many occasions."

"Well, she is presently involved in analyzing the anatomical and physiological differences between a number of marine mammals existing today and their predecessors. She does not want to be disturbed and is not yet ready to assume ordinary administrative tasks, which is why I am the only one you can speak to you for the moment."

"What can I do for you?"

"I would like close range imagery of the supercontinent. Its topography, any visual evidence of movement of the continental plates, as well as, temperature readings in the northern and southern hemispheres and the earth's incline position while orbiting. I do not have much confidence in the imagery that we have captured from the satellites, even those that Reinhart manufactured, still in orbit around the Earth."

"We can send out several probes that will make this information available to you over the next month."

"Excellent, but I would like that information to be communicated to me at the computer terminal that we are using now." She agreed.

"In addition, I would like to know when the two astronauts will be arriving."

"They are orbiting the planet earth a considerable distance outside of its atmosphere but will not be given permission to continue their trajectory until Dr. Reinhart returns."

"Please explain." I requested.

"The High Commission does not want to take any more risks with the lives of our astronauts and only has confidence in Dr. Reinhart." She replied in a dry, administrative tone.

"Understood, even though I believe that they are being overly cautious." I added. "Nonetheless, if I forward you the genetic profiles of different members of our group who want to participate in space exploration, would you be able to fabricate cryogenic cocoons for them and have them available on another vessel that will land shortly after the two astronauts join our group."

"That can be done. I shall inform our engineers that the DNA profiles of certain members of your group will be forthcoming, for the fabrication and coding of five cryogenic cocoons per individual. And, I shall request that a certain number of non-coded cryogenic cocoons be sent, along with instructions on how to fabricate and program them so that you can personalize them by adding the DNA of the same or other members of your community who might want to participate in space exploration."

I sighed in relief over her last remark, which came as a surprise. I didn't want to give her my DNA, Stuart's, Frederic's because we are descendants of Reinhart and I believed that it would be dangerous for them to have access to Reinhart's DNA profile.

"This is excellent news. Reinhart will study the material used in the fabrication of these cocoons when she returns. It is possible that we have the same substance available here on Earth. And, she will have no difficulty following the instructions, thereby personalizing the cocoons with the DNA of members of our community." I replied officiously. "I have one other question. Have your astronauts encountered any of the inflatable Space Stations?" I continued to press for information. "I know that the major space stations were destroyed a long time ago."

"The astronauts have explored a number of the inflatable stations that went off course and are at a greater distance from the Earth. They are still functional. Would you like me to send you the reports?"

"Yes, please send them."

"Ok. Is there anything else?"

"No, not for the moment. Thank you, Colonel Shannon."

"I shall be in touch with the information over the next 24 hours."

"Excellent, Pamela!" Randolph screamed. "You were so convincing about why Reinhart was absent. Extraordinary! We are back to doing important things together."

I realized that time was passing by rapidly. Prioritizing projects that only Randolph, Stuart and I worked on was an insurmountable administrative task, as every project had its own primordial importance.

I continued to live in my cubicle and eat at off hours, avoiding everyone, except Stuart, Randolph and Jonathan. Colonel Shannon worked well with us. The cocoons were in production and the sharp imagery of the supercontinent arrived, with up-dates from time to time. I requested photos of the oceans as well, hoping that their probes would capture imagery of mineral deposits in the deep ocean beds.

In the beginning, even though I was a recipient of Reinhart's knowledge that was downloaded into me, the knowledge that she uploaded to me on so many occasions along with the scientific techniques and procedures that our group needed to continue their research, were now part of my knowledge bank.

I had uploaded and assimilated more of Reinhart's knowledge than I realized, something that became very evident as I worked with Randolph. He was an incredibly brilliant scientist, following closely in the prestigious footsteps of his ancestor, Dr. Murdoc. No matter what subject I consulted him about he was capable of finding solutions and moving the research forward. Reinhart's absence was also positive for me, as I gained more confidence in my own scientific acumen. And yet, we both knew that we were at a very elementary level in comparison to Reinhart.

Even though Randolph's sense of humor and playful style surfaced from time to time, helping both of us to unwind, our unfaltering regard for each other took on a new dimension. Randolph and I developed a strong scientific partnership, moving our relationship from its former physical level to a highly stimulating intellectual level. Incredible as it might seem, each achievement provided us with a healthy, explosive discharge of neuromuscular tension, like an orgasmic climax that moved through us, binding and fulfilling us, in a sublime intellectual intimacy.

Randolph or Stuart brought me news about the others. The only ones who really interested me were Peter and Frederic, both of whom were working together, preparing for space travel. "Peter understands how to operate the most recent space craft in the Air and Space center. He and Frederic spent a month together studying the equipment." Stuart mentioned to me.

Weeks later, Stuart brought up space travel from another angle. "Isabel and Mathieu are also involved in that program." He shuffled his feet around in front of him before proceeding. "I hope that you don't mind, Pamela, but I agreed to follow Diana to the Air and Space center for several weeks. James wants to join us there as well."

"I think that it is an excellent idea, after all, I have arranged for cryogenic cocoons for all of you. I anticipated well." I turned to Randolph. "You can join in if you want to."

"No, I am happy working with you, Pamela." He replied in a calm, reassuring tone. "I shall visit space later. I just don't think that it is the right moment for me. I want to explore this planet first." I was happy to hear that. I would not be all alone in this Center—rather I would have someone I trusted with me, if I decided to stay on Earth.

"By the way, Stuart, all of you will need to wait until Colonel Shannon provides the cryogenic cocoons, which will not happen before she gives permission to the astronauts to land."

"That is right, but I can't say that to John. So I pretend that we will be ready soon." He scratched his forehead. "You know that Gordon and Crawford are back?" Stuart intervened.

"Yes, actually I have met with them and reviewed the information that they collected." I stopped to consider our last meeting. It was, unfortunately, less informative than I expected, only because their research produced no extraordinary conclusions. The different species evolved into new social orders, where, for example, different species of sharks are now living together. It appeared that apart from this they were just physically bigger models. The only strange creature remained the ammonite, which, for the moment, was no more dangerous for humans or other marine species than the larger versions of early predators. I turned to them and noticed that they were staring intensely at me, waiting for me to continue.

"Yes, I asked the Group of 5 to introduce training programs that would be helpful for planetary exploration. None of us ever trained in Alpine sports like ski mountaineering. And, none of us have experience with mountain climbing. The most recent images of the northern hemisphere have revealed a number of high, mountain ranges in the northeastern and northwestern regions and cold, but not frigid, arctic weather near the northern polar region. The southern polar region is rather temperate. Nonetheless, the Southern hemisphere has a large mountain range dividing its continental surface practically in half. So it is important for the new group of planetary explorers to be able to use proper equipment, which is available at this center. Some of the training, like skiing, will have to be conducted by simulation."

"And, you, Pamela, what are planning on doing?" Stuart asked.

"I don't know."

"Don't you think that it is time for you to join the others?" Randolph asked.

"I am thinking about it." I turned my head away from them to hide my emotions, which were now visible in my watery eyes. "Give me a bit more time."

A week later, I again stopped by to see the Group of 5. "Hello Pamela." Gordon said, raising her head so slightly in my direction.

"Are there humans enrolled in the mountain climbing and alpine sports program?" I asked curious about the success of this project.

"Yes." Flanders replied. "I put up a schedule like I did for the deep sea diving program and even those who never wanted to explore in the past, like John, Sarah, Ruth, Benjamin and Stanislas have enrolled."

"And, the Marine center," I began, "is there anything knew happening?

"Well, yes..." Flanders replied. "WD asked to be assigned permanently to the center and requested permission to reproduce with his former programmed female walrus dolphin." I gasped and he continued. "John gave him permission. Apparently he convinced the others that it would be pitiful to prevent this rare mutated species from reproducing." I was speechless. "She is pregnant now." He ended the discussion.

I fell back with a thump into one of the chairs, like I had been slapped so hard in the face. I heard Flanders mention that Reinhart was certainly gone and there was little that they, the Group of 5, could do to prevent such irrational decisions. I finally forced myself to regain a semblance of control. I could not let them think that they were right and that the dreams of a new world governed by a new breed of humans were fading away.

"What are you doing?" I asked, as I stood up and moved closer to the lab table.

"We are creating the DNA profile of Pamela Series 15, as we

terminated series 14 far before her time." Gordon replied nonchalantly, flickering her long fingers at me. "You were not the right...
recipient for her so we are looking for a better model." She provoked me.

"But how, you don't have any more of our DNA here?" I replied
in a raspy voice.

"Of course we do. Remember we followed the various reproduction projects of your group." Flanders interjected.

"You stole the information." Suddenly, I saw him and the others
in a different light. The muscles in my throat tightened and those in
my shoulders and arms joined in. I wanted to slap Flanders hard in
his gloating android face.

"Stole." Miller said in a soft, therapeutic voice, momentarily calming my anger. "That is a harsh term." She continued her retalia-
tion. "I would say that we kept a reserve copy just in case things got
lost and our intervention was imperative."

"Despicable!" I screamed, my anger returning. "You are back to
genetic engineering--looking for new series of humans." I pushed
Gordon away from the lab table.

She swatted my hands aside and took her place behind the
lab table ready to resume her work. "And what can you, Pamela,
do about it? She abandoned you and we are now looking for your
replacement. We need to provide her with a human that will en-
gender her genius and who will not compromise her greatness like
you did. You let the others take control. You failed her---you stupid,
incompetent, musician!" Her android voice sending off crackling
sparks, like abrupt electrical discharges.

I backed away from her. I now had a clear view of all of them.
They were no longer worried. They believed that Reinhart would
never reappear and that they could easily take back the Center.
"Maybe they are all right, Reinhart is gone, but I am not going to let
them continue this research." I contemplated, quickly speculating
on my fate and that of the other humans. "I shall not let you decide
my destiny or hers!" I howled as I grabbed one vile of specimens
after another and threw them up against the wall, putting an end to
their present research. "I shall be back! And, when I come back, you
will be lucky if I let you continue to exist!" They were now standing

with their heads bowed down in deference. "Yes, in deference, but to who?"

I ran back to the sanctity of my cubicle and collapsed on that large bed. I closed them, imagining that effacing my vision of the outside world would be enough to rid me of the deplorable situation. Instead, my mind was invaded with a seemingly interminable display of truths.

I left my loved ones behind without regret or concern. I selfishly indulged myself in what was a very sterile existence. Even working diligently alongside Randolph, making scientific advancements, I knew that we were still so far behind the discoveries that Reinhart had made. And my nights were exhausting, often times terrorizing, as I passed from one nightmarish scene to another.

Yes, every night, I was plagued with dreams in which I wandered alone down dangerous paths as I struggled to find an answer, written on a piece of paper, taunting me, drifting in front of me, tormenting me as it came so close to my grip and then slid out of view, out of reach, at the very last moment. I followed this fluttering answer along winding streams, rugged paths, high mountains, and elaborate labyrinths. But, I was never able to capture even one word on that piece of paper that floated in front of me. I woke up every day covered with sweat. I told no one, not even Randolph, about these nightmares.

I let out a long painful sigh, just thinking about another restless night and decided to get up and take a long shower. The warm water flowed delicately over my body and the soothing odor of vanilla bursting through the soapy bubbles popped my melancholic mood, and I retrieved a glimmer of enthusiasm. I put on my long, white gown and stepped back into the bedroom and stretched out on the bed.

"Perhaps tonight my dreams will be different," I told myself, as I drifted off rapidly into a profound sleep, where I started down a dark, winding path. I stumbled many times and those painful tears of frustration and defeat flowed down my cheeks, leaving a burning sensation behind them. And, then as if by some strange miracle, my tears disappeared and I saw someone beckoning to me as she sat upon a large rock in the middle of a floral garden. I advanced slowly and cautiously, afraid and enchanted by her presence.

"I am back, my child." I heard her say in a soft, maternal tone. "I am sorry that I could not help you and that I left you to fend for yourself. But, I had no choice. My moment to evolve, to undergo an intellectual, or cerebral, metamorphosis came upon and compelled me to accept my destiny."

"It is you, Dr. Reinhart?" I asked in a dreamy voice.

"My beloved child please believe me when I say that I was always there inside of you and was aware of everything that happened to you and to those whom you love and admire. And, when you awaken, you will know that I never left you, you will feel my presence, and my warmth and energy will again suffuse you."

I rushed towards her and she took me in her arms, pulling me gently up onto her lap. I saw tiny sparkles pass magically between our eyes, as I reached up to touch the soft contours of her lips, smiling down on me. I laid my head against her chest and breathed in the comforting odor of maternal love, an intoxicating scent, like the ambrosial perfume. She ran her fingers delicately through my long hair, and placed warm, tender kisses on my face. I cuddled up closer to her, imagining her humming a Brahman's lullaby, as she rocked me, like a child, in her arms. Before I drifted off into a deep and relaxing sleep, I heard her say, "You did well, my child. I am proud of your courage and proud of your achievement. I love you, Pamela, and will always be there to protect you."

When I awoke, I could feel her alive inside of me, her energy and her warmth moving vigorously, as it suffused me. "It was not just a dream." I cried out. "You are back!"

Not only was she back, but I finally understood why I woke up so many times in the past, comforted and fulfilled, by the vision of someone sitting on a large rock in the middle of a floral garden. She tried to reach me in my sleep to prepare me for her absence and eventual return, but I never understood the underlying meaning of that visually beautiful scene of a woman sitting on a rock in the middle of a floral garden, waiting, yes, waiting for something to happen. I jumped up out bed, bursting with energy, and quickly prepared for the day.

The first thing I did was to drop by to see the Group of 5. I let Reinhart control my gestures and my walk because it felt good for me to feel her presence and I wanted to catch them off guard. But, they were one step ahead of me.

"Good Morning, Dr. Reinhart," The Group of 5 screamed in high, crackling android delight. "It worked." They said in unison.

"What worked?"

"You were gone too long, Dr. Reinhart." Crawford spoke for all of them. "We needed to provoke you by scaring Pamela. That is why we pretended to be creating a Pamela Series 15."

Reinhart slowly rubbed my hands together and then let out one of her exceptional, earthshaking laughs that made the Group of 5 move involuntarily out of position. "Well, your timing was right, as I was ready to return."

"One of my problems was under control." Occupied my thoughts, when I left the room.

My mind made up, I would not tell Randolph or Stuart about Reinhart's return before the meeting. I wanted the news to be a real surprise. Randolph was alone in the lab when I entered. "I thought about what you and Stuart mentioned. Yes, I am ready to reintegrate in the team. Do you think that you could set up a meeting with the group for tomorrow so that I can announce my return?"

"Great news, Pamela." Randolph said in a lively voice, giving me a friendly slap quite low on the bottom of my back. "I shall organize that straight away." He called out over his shoulder, as he rushed out of the lab.

I contacted Colonel Shannon. "Good morning." She said in her restrained military voice.

"You asked me to let you know when Dr. Reinhart was back." She nodded. "She has returned."

Before Colonel Shannon could request more information, I let Reinhart control my vocal chords, using her voice tone and accent, to continue the conversation. Colonel Shannon finally let her own voice expel enthusiasm as she spoke rapidly and energetically. "I have a verification of your voice in front of me. Yes, the High Commission has confirmed that your voice matches that which is registered in our computer system. And, I am personally so pleased to know that you have returned, Dr. Reinhart. We were very uncomfortable dealing with John, but did carry out Pamela's requests, to the extent possible."

Reinhart complimented her on the imagery that they had captured of the planet and for the reports on the inflatable space stations before asking her to give the various space ships permission to land. "They will land over the next month." Colonel Shannon replied.

Randolph was back rather rapidly with Stuart. I did not bring them up-to-date on my conversation with Colonel Shannon, just asked them if they could continue to work without me for the day, because I needed time to organize myself for the meeting.

I discretely passed into the inner circle, avoiding contact with anyone, entering the bedroom that I shared with Peter. I ran my hands nostalgically along the corners of the bed before I laid my head on his pillow and breathed in his odor of sandalwood and patchouli, marked with a hint of myrrh. My eyes closed, imagining him sleeping next to me, his warm, moist mouth slightly open inhaling the pure night air. Emerged in these sensual memories, I didn't hear Peter enter the room and jumped when he grabbed my shoulders and turned me in his direction.

"What are you doing here?" The muscles in his face were tight and his eyes...aflame.

"I missed you."

"You missed me!" He shrieked in a loud, brawly tone. "You missed me." A shrill laughter seeped through his seared teeth, making me shiver.

I moved to get up and he pushed me back down.

"You betrayed me, Peter." I replied in a whisper, as I turned away from him, frightened by his anger.

"I didn't mean too." He lifted my eyes to meet his. "I didn't say it well. I didn't mean to betray you. I wanted you to defend yourself!" He shouted in a loud, deep voice. "You didn't give me a chance to explain. You just left." He continued in that bellowing tone. "And you didn't just leave me, you also left Frederic!" He let my face drop back onto the pillow and hit the wall behind the bed so hard with his fist that I wondered why it didn't shatter.

"She abandoned me and I felt lost." I replied. "But, you never came looking for me either."

"But, she abandoned all of us. And, leaving like you did, pushing me away from you, sealed my fate." He took a deep breath, releasing the air in a rough, heavy puff. He again grabbed my shoulders tightly and spoke to me through clenched teeth. "Did you listen to what I just said? You not only abandoned me but you abandoned your son, you abandoned Frederic, for all these months and all you have to say is that I am responsible for your behavior." He stood up and paced back and forth, in front of me.

I never saw him angry with me before and did not know what to say or do to calm him down. He was right, I abandoned them, but I thought that he understood why. Randolph and Stuart assured me that they explained to Peter that I stayed away from them because I was worried about his and Frederic's safety. "Why was that not enough?" I asked myself.

I moved into a sitting positon, letting my legs hang over the side of the bed, and focused on the wall in front of me, looking for a message to magically appear, sending me the right words to turn his anger to forgiveness. He followed my example sitting down next to me and staring at the wall, like two lost souls unable to understand each other, until Peter broke the silence.

"I missed you, Pamela. I missed you in ways and for reasons that surpass me." He spoke calmly, repeating it many times in a soft voice.

"Randolph and Stuart told me about what John said after I left." We were now facing each other. "He insinuated that I was mentally deranged and threated to punish anyone who had contact with me." He nodded. "I was worried about you and Frederic. " I paused.

"All of you were a tightknit group of deprogrammed scientists when I arrived in the outside community, so it did not surprise me that John would get the support and approval from the majority of the board members to assume a leadership role." I stopped to let that sink in. "I felt certain that John would be particularly offended if you disagreed with him, after all you and John negotiated the conditions for your group's departure to the outside. There was a strong bond between you."

I noticed that the muscles in his face were taunt and that his eyes were still dark and cold. I gently took his hands in mine.

"Randolph and Stuart kept you informed about me and kept me informed about you. I thought that my strong desire to protect you and Frederic by avoiding contact with you would be a sign of my love for both of you." I could feel my eyes filling with tears and my lips trembling. "Perhaps my reasoning was wrong?"

"I should have tried to find you and reassure you of my devotion, but Randolph and Stuart were in a better position to protect you than I was, and I had to protect and care for Frederic." He replied. "I suppose that neither one of us had much choice but to avoid each other." He sighed. "You are back and that is all that really matters." His hands moved tenderly over my face, giving me the impression that everything was ok.

"And Reinhart, is she back?" He asked brusquely, opening up another point of contention.

"Yes. Yes she returned today."

"That is why you felt comfortable enough to wander out of hiding." He replied in a direct and unfriendly way. "So, you only feel protected by her? Or Randolph?" He asked raising his eyebrows.

"That is not fair." I moved to stand up and leave. "If you are not satisfied with what I said and you want to imagine that I left you and Frederic because I am a mean, cold, inconsiderate person or because I prefer Reinhart and Randolph to you, then do it!" I screamed at the top of my lungs. "No matter what, I shall always love you!"

"Wait, Pamela." He jumped up and pulled me back into the bed close to him as he gently enveloped me in his arms. I was swept up into the innocence of my past, feeling the strength and protection of my suitor, like I was about to discover for the very first time the intensity of our feelings for each other. When his warm, moist mouth met mine, my anger had already turned to passion something that I couldn't hide from him and didn't want to.

But, I didn't need to be caressed or fondled. I was ready and eager for him. I could feel the heat of my body, the hardness of my nipples, and droplets of moisture sliding along the inside of my legs, my body aching to be joined with his. So I tore off my long robe and let my naked body slither up under his robe as I breathed in his natural earthy odor mixed with that erotic, virile scent of masculine sweat. I ran my tongue slowly up and over him tasting his flesh and finally sipping his essence.

He broke free of his long robe and I moved rapidly on top of him, placing the palms of my hands firmly on his chest, releasing myself from those horrible months of celibacy by submitting to an unrelenting lustfulness. My inner muscles tightened on contact with him, holding him and dragging him deeper and deeper inside of me, as I moved in penetrating and vigorous cadences, until I felt that extraordinary wave of energy begin to build, trembling inside of both of us, drawing us closer together, culminating in an intense, explosive burst of physical and emotional euphoria, releasing excruciating, heightened screams of pleasure, as our bodies collapsed and rolled together in the frenzied, pulsating aftershocks of sexual fulfillment.

We finally unraveled and laid with our arms and legs spread out on the top of the bed.

I started to get up. "No, don't leave yet." He pleaded. "I want to ask you a silly question, Pamela, so please don't be offended." I nodded.

"I was making love... to you?"

Chapter 33: Indomitable Reinhart

I found Frederic in his Father's lab. He had his back towards me. I stood frozen, unable to move or speak. Only my eyes responded, trying in vain to blink back the tears, streaming down my cheeks from my swollen eyes. He turned round to pick up a vile and looked in my direction. His face lit up and he rushed towards me, throwing his arms around me. "I missed, My Mother. I missed you so much!" He exclaimed as he wiped the tears from my face. "It is ok. I am just so happy to have you back." He said as he kissed me tenderly on my cheek.

"I regret, Frederic, that I did not contact you before today." I said in a high voice trembling with emotion.

"Please, don't apologize." He said, moving a short distance from me. "Randolph and Stuart told me everything. I didn't want to believe them at first. I followed you often." He snickered. "I watched you eat alone in the dining room and I followed you stealthily when you returned to your bedroom. I could see that you were sad because you walked slowly, taking heavy steps, as if you were forcing yourself to go on living. I noticed that you ate very little, and the only time you smiled or laughed was when you were playing your piano in the company of Jonathan."

"I never even sensed your presence, I was so absorbed in my own sorrow." I said apologetically.

"I know. But, I realized that I would make a good spy!" He giggled at his own joke and I joined in. "Anyway, Stuart and Randolph told me how you were working with them on the space program and the exploration of the planet. I understood that you left to protect me and my Father. They asked me not to tell my Father because it would be dangerous for him to know what you were doing. They were worried about John's reaction." His eyes grew wide. "John is rather unpredictable. I avoid him." He grimaced and then picked up the conversation in a lively tone. "So I kept the secret." He hugged me again. "And, now you are back and that is all that matters."

"You have grown so mature and perceptive, Frederic." My warm voice echoing my maternal love. I reached out and took him in my arms, hugging and kissing him, until he was giddy with laugher. "So, you can keep a secret." He nodded. "Then I shall tell you mine, which I also shared today with your Father. But, you must not tell anyone else, not even Randolph or Stuart. "

"I promise."

"Reinhart is back inside of me."

He stepped away from me. "I guess that that is good news, but I would like to be sure." Before I could answer, he added. "Mathilda told me that you are schizophrenic and that Reinhart was just a personality you invented."

"She was mean to tell you that, when she understands my relationship with Reinhart is symbiotic." I sat down on one of the lab chairs.

"Please explain it to me then." He pleaded.

"Although I am not a psychologist, my recollection of the definition of schizophrenia is an individual's sub-consciousness divides into two or more personalities to compensate for weaknesses in the principle personality, or to evolve in more violent, or sometimes more rational directions." I sighed.

"The point is that when an individual's subconscious level evolves into different personalities, the primary personality may or may not be completely aware of the existence of all the others." He nodded in thought.

"My relationship with Reinhart is symbiotic. In the past, symbiotic relationships were envisaged in science fiction. A larva or another living entity would enter a human's body through an orifice like a mouth, ear, nostril, and so forth and the two different life forms would live in harmony, sharing the same body. My story is different."

"The Group of 5 downloaded Reinhart's knowledge bank, which she had registered on empty DNA strands, so that the androids could not access her knowledge. She left the vials containing the DNA with the Group of 5. She told them that if anything happened to her, they should download her knowledge bank into one of her biological daughters. They spent years, maybe centuries, reproducing gifted, biological daughters for Reinhart. She verified their DNA and studied their intellectual capacity and emotional structure, just like she did with me, but refused to share a body with them."

"The Group of 5 believes that she chose me because I was not a scientist." I coughed, to clear my throat. "In any event, her knowledge is also comprised of her very essence, her personality, emotional structure, likes and dislikes—because all that she was in her life time was part of her extraordinary intellectual capacity." His expressionless face bothered me, but I continued.

"She spoke to me after her knowledge bank was downloaded into me. And, she told me that I could choose to what extent her personality would manifest itself." I paused. "I am not afraid of her. So when her personality, her voice, her manner of walking, thinking, reacting and more were necessary, I simply moved aside and watched, listened and learned how she became such a power leader. Do you understand, Frederic?"

He shrugged his shoulders.

Let me digress for a minute to clarify things." I paused to collect my thoughts. "There were people throughout human history who were capable of great, extraordinary discoveries. Their genius spanned time. There were others who had different talents. Some, for example, had photographic memories. Their minds functioned like a computer registering everything that happened, regardless of its significance, around the world on a daily basis. Some of them were capable of analyzing the data, others simply stored it. Our human brain is a very complex organ and very few humans have ever tried to test its limits. In all honesty, humans have never used all the cognitive capacity of their brain, which is why there is a large place to store knowledge, for those with photographic memories. Reinhart is occupying vacant space in my brain."

He didn't laugh at that, instead sat pensively looking at me, trying to pierce my mind to find a greater truth. My eyes stayed focused on him, until he relented. "Please go on." He pleaded.

"Perhaps if I had been a scientist I would have absorbed and assimilated certain information she downloaded into me instantly. And, again, if I had been a scientist I would have assimilated the information when she uploaded it to me in rapid sequence. That was not the case. I was a musician and had no experience in the sciences. When she uploaded data to me because it was necessary for me to use and share this information with the others, she had to start from the very basic level so that I would understand. She used visual displays to help me to understand the data that she was transferring to me." I stared into his thoughtful eyes.

"You want more information of her power over me?" He nodded. "She is capable of controlling my vocal chords. Her voice, and native human accent, was registered into the android systems and they are programmed to carry out her orders. She can control my physical body, so that I walk very erect and march in her former military style so that the androids recognize their creator. She has controlled my hands to help me learn rapidly how to steer a land vehicle or an airplane. But, in emergencies, she simply takes over my motor skills and makes the decisions."

"She protects me and all of us. She chose to return as a symbiont, in a human body rather than as an android opposite."

"I know the story of her android opposite." He interrupted.

"I am glad that I don't have to repeat that story." I said sullenly.

"But why did she disappear and then return?"

"She disappeared because she needed to evolve intellectually."

"Then she is not human." He said firmly.

"She is different from us on an intellectual level, but nonetheless human. You and I are her biological descendants, meaning that I would not be here, and you wouldn't be here either, if she did not have human DNA." He nodded.

"So, if I understand, she is even more intelligent than before."

"There is that aspect, but I also have a feeling, because of the very high energy level that is now moving inside of me, that she has acquired new capacities and is capable of changing, transforming, moving, or destroying objects with her mind, by resorting to a highly developed form of psychokinesis." I told him, even though the reality of what she was capable of achieving was even more profound.

"So, is she going to challenge John and bring our community back together?" He asked, slapping his hands together like he was already applauding the final outcome.

"Let's hope so!" I chimed in. "The meeting is tomorrow, so between now and then, do not mention any of this to anyone." He nodded. "I love you Frederic and am so proud of you!" I said in a strong voice. I enveloped him again in my arms and kissed him tenderly before leaving.

I spent the night alone in my cubicle. I wanted my appearance to be a surprise and if the group found me in the inner circle, the impact of my, rather Reinhart's, arrival would not have been as traumatic.

I slept well and woke up ready for the tasks ahead. I did not want to arrive at the same time as the others and purposely lingered about, passing slowly through the long corridors. The group was seated when I opened the door and I noticed that an empty chair was waiting for me between Peter and Randolph. The chair was directly in front of John, who was at the head of the large oval table, with Ferdinand seated at his right and Ruth at his left.

"Well," John chuckled, "what brings you out of hiding, Pamela?"

"I decided that it was time for me to observe your meetings and learn more about what you were doing." I said in a low, calm voice.

"We don't need you, Pamela." He looked at the others. Only Ruth nodded in agreement.

"That is ok for me, because you are no longer addressing Pamela." I felt Reinhart's warmth alive inside of me and enjoyed feeling her adapt my vocal chords to her voice tone.

John's eyes drew narrow and he clenched his teeth. "You are not happy to have me back, John?" Reinhart asked him.

He leaned back in his chair, and forced a smile, trying to hide his earlier anger and pretending that he was in no way bothered by Reinhart's presumed presence. "Where have you been, if I might ask?"

"I have been undergoing a transformation, or a metamorphosis, whichever term you prefer---which has helped me to evolve on an even greater intellectual and scientific level." Reinhart replied calmly.

"Oh, Pamela, this is outrageous. You have gone mad and I think that perhaps I should order your internment." He looked at the others. "It is sad, but this woman is dangerous. She could kill us!" He wailed, each word getting louder than the one before.

"As you can see, John, you stand alone. I notice that even Ruth, your most faithful companion, has lowered her eyes and leaned away from you." Reinhart stood up. "I suggest, John, that you let Ferdinand take his place at the head of the table."

"I shall take NO ORDERS FROM YOU!" He replied in a thundering voice, hitting the table with his tight fists.

"I am afraid, John, that you will have to bow to my will, whether you want to or not."

She suppressed a smile at his overt, pretentious behavior, while he burst out in raucous laughter, drawing everyone but Peter, Randolph, Stuart and Diana into the folly of his behavior. "You are a great actress, like you are a great pianist, but this farce has gone on long enough." He spit out through erratic waves of laughter. "Pamela, just sit down and listen.

"If I understand, John, you want proof of my power." Reinhart replied, accentuating her original accent.

He tilted his head in her direction. "Yes, give some proof!" He ordered.

I could feel the muscles in my face and neck grow tight, under Reinhart's anger. My hand made a rapid upward movement and John's chair backed up 5 feet from the table. He stopped laughing. "I have a perfect scan of your body in front of me, John. Let me show you how fast I can make your heart beat." Within a split second, she accelerated his heart beat and he began pressing down on his chest. But, he was not yet ready to concede, stumbling as he moved out of his chair to rush her. With a quick, intense, almost burning, movement of my eyes, she tapped into his neurological system and paralyzed him from the waist down. He fell flat on his face.

"You are a charlatan!" He screamed, lifting his torso, as the other members of our team shouted and pointed to his face that had taken on its previous aged appearance.

"So, it really is you, Dr. Reinhart." He said in a low voice, as he touched the contours of his face that were now sagging with age.

"Yes, I have returned, John." She took her time before continuing. "And, I am angry, saddened and disappointed with the way in which you exiled by ostracism, my daughter, Pamela."

"I was wrong. But, I seriously don't know why I acted like I did and why I feel so persecuted today." His voice trembled as he spoke.

"I want everyone to know that I made a mistake in the rejuvenation of John. I could have made minor adjustments to his personality, or blocked any changes in his personality, maintaining that emotionally mature man who acted in the interests of all of us, or that man who we trusted and relied upon. Instead, I brought back a young, aggressive, intolerant, power hungry, young man, who took advantage of my sudden absence to persecute my daughter, and subjugate all of you, except Randolph and Stuart, by exerting his power and will." She breathed deeply.

"You all know that I no longer need to rely upon complicated technology to make someone old... or make someone young." She said. I felt that burning sensation behind my eyes return as she scanned John's body, giving him back his youth and restoring his neurological and cardio-vascular systems."

We watched John regain the use of his legs and move his chair back to the table, quickly changing places with Jason, who was now sitting in center stage, with John at his right hand side.

Reinhart did not give John the chance to say anything, instead she gave him an ultimatum. "I can either change you back to your former self or let you stay young. If you choose the latter, I shall give you time to think about how you were before and why we all appreciated you, and show me that you are capable of making the necessary changes in your personality so your youthfulness will be an asset for all of us." She stopped to let her words sink in. "If neither offer appeals to you, John, I can make you disappear forever with a click of my fingers."

He gradually revealed his downturned eyes and frowning, droopy mouth. "I have been rather dictatorial and intolerant." He admitted in a low, practically inaudible voice. "So, today, I shall follow former procedure. I suggest that we take a vote, if you agree to that, Dr. Reinhart?" She nodded. And so we voted on one of the three options. Whether real or feigned, his face lit up with energy, when the vote was unanimously in favor of a young, rational John who could be a real team player.

That drama behind us, Reinhart gave way to me and I brought the group up-to-date on all the progress that Randolph, Stuart and I had made in secret.

"We have a lot to do now. The astronauts and supply ship will be landing over the next two weeks. The cryogenic cocoons, five per person, for those members who expressed interest in space travel are ready. The inflatable space stations," there were loud gasps, "are now operational so that we can conduct different experiments closer to our planet. Those who want to join Colonel Shannon will be happy with the training program she has in place. You will learn how to pilot different space craft in outer space and will participate in mining activities on asteroids and work on research projects dealing with her native planet and other potentially habitable exoplanets."

I stopped to collect my thoughts. "I am glad that so many of you have been training in alpine sports, like skiing, and mountain climbing. I have very clear imagery of our planet and would be happy to discuss it with those interested in exploring our planet."

"The imagery confirms that the Earth offers us a large variety of minerals on its continents and in its deep sea beds, which we shall eventually be able to extract. Those of you involved in agronomy, architecture, and natural sciences will be very active. Building habitable zones on this planet and discovering and interacting with new life forms will keep us busy for years to come."

"I believe that we should all take time to study the information that I have received from Colonel Shannon and prepare to engage in the exploration of our planet or outer space over the next month."

"There is one more topic I would like to introduce. I learned yesterday that WD was given permission to live in the marine center and to procreate. Apparently, his programmed female opposite is now pregnant."

"I made that decision." John replied. "I have the feeling that you do not agree."

"And the rest of you---where do you stand on this?" I asked, scanning the faces of my colleagues.

"If I can speak for the others, "Benjamin started off, "letting him reproduce was not a real issue for any of us. I think that we all agreed on that." I noticed that the group nodded. "But, giving him the autonomy that we did was perhaps reckless. I think that you, John, authorized the removal of his tracker."

"Yes, I did authorize it, but the Captain and that Drager refused to carry out my order." I breathed a sigh of relief with that news.

"I would like WD to return to our Center. He can accompany us on planetary explorations." I suggested. "Should we vote on that?""

Everyone, even John, agreed that WD should return. It was decided that Reinhart should contact the Marine center and arrange things.

There was a long silence. Finally Ferdinand spoke up. "I am very happy to have you back with us, Pamela. I suggest that we all meet next week to keep closely informed."

He ended the meeting with an applause and the others joined in. My eyes met John's eyes in what I hoped was a new-found comradery. I stood up and hugged my friends one after the other. Diana was moving slowly, a round belly protruding from her normally tall, thin, muscular frame.

Peter and I were the last to leave. "I have not seen our team so inspired and enthusiastic about our future and excited about working together since the day you left, Pamela."

"Thank you, Peter. But, as you witnessed, I am not the inspiration, Reinhart is."

John was waiting for me just outside the door. "I should apologize to you, Pamela, for the way I treated you. It is going to be difficult for me to resist my power hungry side." He tugged nervously on the sleeve of his gown. "I am going to try, but hope that you will be patient with me."

"I might be patient, John, but she won't!" I said keeping the pressure on him. "Let Ruth help you."

Reinhart contacted the Marine Center, just after the meeting.

She spoke to the Captain and Drager who were quick to tell her that they were pleased that she was back. They informed her that WD was not giving them any trouble and often times told them how much he missed Pamela and Reinhart.

"I would like to speak to WD." Reinhart requested in a dry tone, as if she was annoyed with the conversation.

"He is waiting outside the control room. We shall call him in." Drager replied.

She watched WD approach the visual display screen and bow his large walrus-dolphin head when he saw me. "I know that it is you Dr. Reinhart, because I recognize your style, your proud straight posture and your penetrating eyes." She nodded. "I am relieved that you have finally returned to us. If I can be so pretentious, I would like to be reassigned to the main center. I am bored. I am not interested in being with these programmed dolphins or my former programmed walrus-dolphin partner. I begged John to let me leave for the Marine center because I was so uncomfortable living in that place with him in command and was concerned about my future." He spoke slowly, his voice had a sweet air of serenity and respect.

"I see no problem with your returning." That was exactly what all of us wanted, but she hid her pleasure and spoke formally. "I suggest that you return to our center with your child who will be raised under proper supervision."

He nodded vigorously in agreement, flapping his flippers on the floor, as he uttered a dolphin cry of pleasure. "Wonderful news! I have been so worried about my child living among these programmed marine mammals. My partner had no idea that she was inseminated." His voice croaked, as if he were feeling strong emotions. "She doesn't know that she is pregnant, and in her programmed state, she won't even be aware of the baby's birth."

"I understand what you are implying, but I am not ready to remove the visual receptor from her brain."

"The baby will arrive very soon." He continued, pretending that my remark had no relevance. "I shall do my best to support the boredom of this center until he or she arrives." He bowed his head in deference. "I remain your most devoted ally!" I was back now and I thanked him for his fidelity to all of us, which, in my mind, still needed to be tested.

I had chance to see all my other friends over dinner. When the reptilian humans, in the company of Jonathan, Imogen, Eunice and Tirence saw me at the table, they rushed towards me. Joseph picked me up. "Where have you been?" I heard them pronounce at the same time.

They listened while I quickly brought them up-to-date. I knew, by their inquisitiveness, that Jonathan had not revealed my association with him or with Randolph and Stuart to anyone. He was definitely a true friend. "Can we join you for dinner?" Adam asked. I stood speechless, looking for an explanation from the others who moved nervously in their seats.

"It is my fault." John eventually spoke up. "They were constantly criticizing my ideas, so I told them to stay far away from us, especially during meals."

"Another bad decision on your part, John." Just slipped out, as I invited the others to join us. I noticed that everyone, except me and the Reptilian Humans, had fish or shellfish on their plate.

Ruth told me after dinner that she was going to take John back to the cavern on the outside of the Center. She believed that this might help him to recuperate his previous personality.

And, she patiently helped and guided him to recover his former personality. A week in that isolated environment turned out to be long enough for him to relive and understand the frustrations of those early years of exile, when he was the leader of a group of brilliant, deprogrammed scientists living a sterile existence, dependent upon the Group of 5 for their food, clothing and water. Ruth told me that she comforted him when he told her how worried he was in the beginning that they would all perish in a barren wilderness. And she praised him, when he spoke of his persistent search for a solution that finally materialized when they found access to the tunnel that was linked to the Center.

She even shared one of John's confessions: "Those were difficult times, Ruth, and I was at the point of abandoning everything when Pamela arrived. Her naivety, curiosity, emotional highs and lows amused me. I forgot what it was like to discover emotions. I enjoyed watching her trying to find an emotional equilibrium and even empathized, at times, with her frustrations."

"And then one day I realized that Pamela was our hope and could be our savior. She was like the missing link in the chain. So I pressured her into spying for us whenever she was summoned back to the main center for Gordon's study in human emotions. She did well. She sent us vital information and gave us access to the tools we needed to open the end of the tunnel so that we could enter the transport unit. She gave me the courage I lacked to launch an attack. Alone, she was a formidable ally, but with Reinhart inside of her, we were assured a victory."

Ruth said he cried, wiping his eyes and nose on the cuff of his sleeve. "How could I have turned against the person who helped us to realize our dream of a new world ruled by humans?"

He came to see me in the lounge in the inner circle soon after my meeting with Ruth. He took a seat next to me. I already knew that the old John was back. "I understand that I acted rashly and am embarrassed with my behavior. I am ready to work with everyone, as a member of the team, in the interest of humanity, if Reinhart will accept me as a team player."

"I am counting on you." Reinhart answered with her beautiful accent. "So, be ready to start work tomorrow." He thanked her profusely and rushed off to tell Ruth.

The remaining three weeks went by so rapidly in spite of the longer days exacerbated by the time warp of our center. I met with those who wanted to spend time on Colonel Shannon's ship, or in one of the inflatable space stations. "Why do we need those cocoons to reach the Mother ship or go to the inflatable space center?" Stuart asked, his voice sharp with irritation.

"You don't need the cryogenic cocoon for a short trip to the expandable activity module that can revolve independently and can connect to create a larger, more complex space center." I could see the expandable module design that existed in the 20th century that Reinhart found fascinating and usable over the ages.

"The fabric layers are fortified and can resist radiation and shield the module from impact." I said in a low, pensive tone. "Colonel Shannon sent an android team to regroup certain modules that were rotating independently, to form a larger unit. Even though the rotation of these inflatable centers produce a gravitational force, it is not sufficient to offer a comfortable living environment for humans. Today they are all equipped with microgravity units, making them habitable."

"If you want to join Colonel Shannon's ship, to reach the travel distance, measured in light years - a light year being the unit of distance that light can travel in one year away from us-you will need to use the cocoons. The travel speed and the zero gravity environment throughout the voyage also necessitate the use of cocoons."

"These small spaceships are, nonetheless, equipped with a microgravity system that activates whenever the astronauts are awake or need to be awakened from their cryogenic state to pilot the spacecraft for takeoffs, landings or emergency situations. Colonel Shannon did, however, inform me that androids will pilot the small spaceships carrying members of our team and that you will be awakened from your cryogenic state when you reach the Mother ship, which is, naturally, equipped with a gravity system."

I looked at Peter who had mentioned to me on many occasions that he was more interested in traveling to the inflatable space modules, which thankfully meant that he could rapidly return to Earth. I sat in deep thought. Reinhart recognized that the descendants of the former astronauts had made extraordinary progress in space travel.

"Why are they called inflatable? Were they like a balloon that you blow up?" Peter asked the question that bothered him and the others.

"Yes, to a certain extent. Actually, they were transported on larger space craft as flat cargo. They inflated when they were released into space. It was an ingenious idea that was used from the beginning of the space program." I was speaking rapidly. "They were even conceived to provide housing, like a tent, for astronauts who would be spending time on the Moon or another planet, examining the surface."

"The more elaborate Space Centers that were built with metallic frames were destroyed, as I mentioned before, during one of the numerous wars that took place before Reinhart's period.

And, after these destructive wars, the space program, along with its complex technology, also disappeared. Even the comfortable living conditions, transport facilities, food sources, and more, were destroyed." I sighed, reflecting on the misery that humans inflicted upon themselves.

"You can read more about that in the Library." I continued. "The Group of 5 saved the worst of human experiences, so you will be getting accurate factual information from the library. Nonetheless, Reinhart rebuilt a technologically advanced planet by ameliorating, creating or adapting older scientific research, which she managed to retrieve from different abandoned scientific facilities." I stopped, for an instance, imagining the efforts she made and the frustrations she encountered trying to bring back a technologically advanced world, before I picked up the discussion. "Actually, there was very little land surface during Reinhart's time and she had difficulty finding comparable material to build the ships and to create new technology."

"How did the inflatable space stations survive?" Randolph queried.

"I don't know, but assume they survived because they moved far enough away from the Earth that they were not easy targets." I replied curtly and changed the subject. "Whether you spend time on board the Mother ship or in one of the expandable module centers, it will be an incredible learning experience." I rambled on a bit. "The basic design of the Mother ship, which was constructed using comparable material found on their planet or through asteroid mining, is the same as the design that Reinhart created." I stopped for a minute, not quite certain where the truth was. "Actually, it may be the spaceship designed and launched by Reinhart."

"Pamela," Dr. Crawford rushed into the conference room, interrupting the meeting. "The astronauts are requesting permission to land from Dr. Reinhart."

Reinhart's thoughts invaded me. By her calculation, the slow rise in the temperature inside the cryogenic cocoons was activated more than 24 hours ago, giving the astronauts the time to peel away the exterior of the cocoon and recover their physiological independence. They were in command of the vessels when they entered the Earth's atmosphere.

We were all in the control room within a few minutes and Reinhart took over.

"Hello, Captain Robert Cray .... Captain Jennifer Marshall, at the commands. We are requesting permission to land, Dr. Elisabeth Reinhart."

"Permission granted." Reinhart answered.

"Your voice verification has been approved. We are sending you our landing coordinates. We shall be landing in the next 30 minutes your time. Over and Out."

We rushed to the transport unit, and drove rapidly to the landing site which was very close to the Center. This time, incoming astronauts were not going to be disintegrated by android fighter pilots, but were welcomed and received by all the members of our human and reptilian human community when they stepped out of their spacecraft. They saluted us, in the tradition of another time and Reinhart gave them the same sign of goodwill and respect. The others offered friendly handshakes and warm hugs.

Reinhart drove the two astronauts back to our center in her vehicle. They both hesitated when Reinhart invited them to follow her through the wall to the inner circle, but later mentioned that it was an incredible experience, marveling about the sophistication of a wall imbedded with bio-readers. They were not hungry but very tired so we gave the astronauts a few days to recover in their bedrooms, serving them meals made in the inner circle, until their energy level returned and their bodies adapted to the gravity and atmosphere of the planet Earth.

The following day, we received an incoming call from an android piloted aircraft requesting the right to land. I left in a large land rover with Peter and Stuart to pick up the cryogenic cocoons. There were five containers, containing a dozen cryogenic cocoons, bearing the name of Mathieu, Isabel, James, Peter, and Diana, who was not ready yet to participate in space travel. There were five other containers with a dozen cryogenic cocoons that had no name labels.

"I don't see mine among these containers." Stuart threw his hands up in the air. "What happened?"

"You mustn't worry, Stuart. I acted cautiously. Your DNA, like mine and Frederic's reveals Reinhart's DNA."

"Of course!" He said, as if reality slapped him in the face.

"Reinhart is going to program the cocoons for the three of us." I added.

"Wow! Good thinking on your part, Pamela." He slapped me lightly on my shoulder.

The android pilots took off to join the Mother ship and we returned to the Center.

The astronauts met with us two days after their arrival and gave us a very brief account of their history. Curiously enough, all generations of humans were born on board the large Mother ship and never stepped foot on the planet presumably inhabited by their ancestors, members of the original crew. Some humans left to explore new worlds. Apparently none of them every returned. "All of us astronauts dreamed of the day that we would meet Dr. Reinhart and her prestigious group of scientists." Jennifer's voice bubbled with enthusiasm.

From what they were told by others, who never visited their home planet, the androids landed the original spaceship, waking the humans upon arrival. The humans continued to live in the spaceship while the androids explored the planet and built communities.

Reinhart did not pursue that discussion, probably because she found it slightly absurd, and focused on two other major points. "I am very interested in the technological changes and improvements that my former scientific team made in space travel and in planetary and asteroid mining.

"But, Dr. Reinhart, aren't you coming back with us?" Robert asked, hoping to distract us from the glimmer of astonishment that reflected in his eyes.

"That is rather irrelevant for the moment." Reinhart replied. "I would like to see this information before I leave, if it is available. And I would like to have more information regarding your home planet, which is not the one I selected, and appears to be located in the zodiacal constellation, Libra." She paused. "It is very strange that none of you have ever visited or lived on this presumably magnificent planet."

"Understood." Robert replied, sitting stiffly in his chair. "I am not in a position to speak for Colonel Shannon, but believe that she will be willing to send you the information you want. I think that you should make the request directly to her."

Reinhart contacted Colonel Shannon who forwarded her request to the High Commission. Days later she informed Reinhart that the Commissioners believed that the information was highly sensitive, Top Secret. They would reveal this information to her in person when she arrived on the Mother Ship. Reinhart ignored the decision of the High Commission.

Over the next few weeks, the space explorers, James, Stuart, Peter, Frederic, Mathieu, Isabel, and myself actively trained with Captains Cray and Marshall, concentrating on how to support zero gravity conditions which they would encounter if they maneuvered outside the ships or modules.

I was informed that those team members who wanted to explore the planet Earth had split up into two mains groups, those who would explore the interior of the northern continent and those who would explore the coastal area, inland rivers and lakes. The choices of location were logical and evident. All the male and female Reptilian humans, along with Tirence and Eunice, were interested in the coastal and river zones. I put Joseph in charge of the Reptilian humans. Jason was fit to lead a group and I would select someone, like Randolph, to lead another group to explore different inland areas, like mountainous and thick vegetation zones. We would discuss this further over the months to come.

Originally Diana wanted to go into space with Stuart, but, after giving birth her strong maternal instinct manifested and she changed her mind about taking a long absence in outer space. She recuperated her former slim, muscular body rapidly and requested permission to be part of an exploration team on Earth. Having her as part of the Earth exploration team was excellent news because good combat skills might be necessary.

John had become a real team player and could be trusted on the inside or on the outside of the Center to act in the interests of everyone. Although he wanted to eventually explore the planet, he wanted to stay in the Center in the beginning, like in the past, to help Sarah, Ruth, Jonathan, Imogen, and Mathilda. Even the Group of 5 were working well with John.

I spent as much time as I could in the company of Peter and Frederic, hoping to make up for my months of absence and reassure them of my love and devotion. I grew more and more dependent on Peter and sought his comfort and encouragement on a daily basis. His very presence gave me courage and inspired my enthusiasm to confront the never-ending challenges. I spent long days and nights watching and learning how Reinhart programmed the cryogenic cocoons to accept the genetic identification of myself, Frederic and Stuart.

She discovered that the substance used to create cocoons was practically identical to that tubular plant that we harvested almost two year ago from the seabed. In fact, she believed that our plant would be more resilient and durable than the substance they were using. In addition, she marveled at the simplicity of the technologically and coding system used in the fabrication of these cocoons.

"Sometimes humans tend to over complicate technology and miss the easy, simple, direct route to achieving a technological masterpiece," I heard her say to me when she was explaining to me with the use of visuals how to fabricate these cocoon.

The night before the beginning of our last week in the Center, I sat watching Peter sleep. He asked me often if I had made a decision about going with him and Frederic into outer space. "I will wait until the last moment to give him my answer." I promised myself, as I cuddled up close to him and fell into a deep sleep.

I woke up in the morning feeling ill and left in a fury, looking for Dr. Flanders, as I rushed from one lab to another until I finally found him alone in the in vitro unit.

"Pamela, so nice to see you. Is everything going well?" He didn't give me chance to answer. "There is so much happening since Reinhart's return that even the 5 of us are drowning in work. Here, let me..."

I interrupted him. "I am not feeling well, Edward. I wonder if I ate something contaminated. Is someone overseeing the preparation of food?"

"Please sit down and try to calm down." He pointed to one of the low comfortable chairs with arm rests. "No one is trying to poison you. Dr. Miller and Dr. Crawford are supervising the kitchen staff." He scratched his android chin. "Are you pregnant?"

"Of course not!" I screamed. "You know that I tried all those years to get pregnant and it just didn't work. After I left Peter and the others, I started taking birth control pills." I sat up very straight in my chair, my hands gripping the arm rests. "I do not want to be pregnant now. I have other plans."

"Oh, Pamela, all this emotional reaction for nothing." He tapped me lightly on my shoulder. "Well, I shall run some tests. Perhaps you are just tired."

"You will have to stand up for a moment." He said, before he took a small device, a body scanner, and slowly ran it over the length of my body. He then turned away from me pretending that he was studying the results, which I knew were already on the scanner's small screen.

"Peter and Frederic want to explore outer space...spend some time on the Mother ship?" He asked perfunctorily.

"I think that they will probably be on the inflatable modules."

"No matter. They won't be on Earth, if I understand." He said as he turned in my direction.

"You have the results---so what did I catch?" I replied brusquely.

"You are pregnant." He said almost shyly.

"What are you talking about?" Give me that scanner." I ordered, as I grabbed it out of his hand. Perplexed and emotive, my body began to tremble and my legs grew so weak that I fell back down into the chair.

"But, how did this happen? It doesn't make any sense." Repeated over and over again in my mind, as I felt a dreadful sinking feeling engulf me. That euphoria that made me sing and dance in heightened pleasure, when I learned that I was pregnant with Frederic, was absent today, replaced by a strong apprehension or uneasiness about my future, an alarm sounding in my head. "My whole world is crumbling around me."

Flanders rushed towards me and bent down next to me. He hugged me with as much paternal kindness that he could muster from the fragments of his primitive emotional programming. "Now then, Pamela, this is wonderful news. And, of course, there are solutions.

You could use the artificial uterus---we would take special care of your child, which, by the way, is female. And, of course, if you would rather let time pass, we could interrupt the pregnancy." He rambled on. But, I barely heard his words of comfort, distracted by the tone of his voice, sounding like the background music of Carl Orff's, "O Fortuna," in a film about my life, signaling my impending doom.

I shoved him away from me. "So, it is girl." I exclaimed as I stood up, pacing up and down the small room, swinging my hands out in front of me like I wanted to hit something or someone. "Reinhart is responsible."

"Of course Reinhart is responsible." He watched the color drain out of my face. "You know that she can control your motor skills, vocal chords...so I don't see why you are surprised that she can control the functioning of your organs." He paused. "She simply neutralized the birth control treatment so that you would get pregnant." He turned away from me.

"But why?" I said softly.

"She wants you to give her the time to finish exploring this planet and building a new civilization before moving onward." My head dropped. "She also wants, and I know that, to explore outer space, which certainly will happen. For the moment, you can explore this planet and your wisdom—something that even I have come to respect---and hers will be vital to the many and varied projects and problems that you will encounter."

He was right, but hearing that did not make me happy. I wanted to be the only person that could determine my fate.

Reinhart sensed my anger, her warmth suffusing me, as she uploaded the answer. I saw things in a new light.

"Of course." I said to myself and Edward took that for a confirmation of his theory. I looked at him, standing patiently waiting for me to explain my change of heart. I could not tell him the truth. It was better to continue the discussion along his lines. "Yes, I do agree with you, Edward." I sat back down in that comfortable arm chair and he waited for me to continue. "In exchange for staying here and letting her participate in the rebuilding of this planet, she is giving me a baby girl."

"Yes, exactly! And, Pamela..."

I interrupted him. "She has a deal!" I said in a lively scream. "I must go now."

I looked for Peter and Stuart and told them that I absolutely had to speak to them together.

⊕⊢3⊹⊹⊱⊱3⊹⊹⊰⊛

I was looking up at him, staring intensely into his serious, yet compassionate and loving eyes, when I heard Peter's voice breaking into my thoughts and forcing me to return to the present.

"So what is your decision, Pamela?" He asked in that lively spirited tone one uses when the answer seems so evident. "Frederic and I decided to spend time on the Mother ship---we don't want to ease into space exploration, we want to dive into the middle of it. So what do you think—there is room for you on board the ship? It is time to give me your answer."

I stood speechless, my thoughts distracted by the burning enthusiasm in his voice and the sparkles illuminating his eyes. I didn't know exactly what to say but knew that I had to be decisive. So I finally confessed. "I want to go with you but I can't."

"I don't understand. Is it because Reinhart won't let you go. If that is the case, Pamela, I shall convince Reinhart." He said in a terse voice.

"No, she would also like to visit outer space."

"Here I am." Stuart screamed as he rushed into the lab. "So what is the matter, Pamela?" He said with lots of energy, before he turned to Peter. "And what is wrong with you, Peter?" He asked, his voice trailing off.

I didn't give Peter a chance to answer and jumped right into the reason for this meeting. "I am going to explain everything to the two of you who will in turn explain all of this to Frederic." I said in a calm voice. "Stuart, you will be going to the Mother Ship with Peter. James will take your place and go to the modulated space center."

"I am ok with that, Pamela, but why?"

"I don't know if you paid a lot of attention to the strange behavior of our two astronauts." They both shrugged their shoulders.

571

"Ok, I see that you were just swept up into the glamor of space travel. I understand this because, at least for you, Peter, this is your lifelong dream." He nodded.

"Reinhart is worried. She requested information from the High Commission regarding the reason why the androids did not land the spaceship on the exoplanet she chose, or Wolf 1061c in the Wolf Constellation, because it would appear from her calculations that they are on a planet, uninhabitable for human life, in the Libra Constellation. She also requested the designs for the improved technology that they were using for space travel. They refused to send her any information, indicating that the exoplanet they inhabited and the technology were top secret." A dead silence resulted....

"The original scientific team was comprised of twenty members who were accompanied by their android foils, or opposites, as I prefer. These androids were privy to all the scientific projects of their human opposites and worked alongside of them."

I folded my hands together and cracked my knuckles to release my inner tension. "In the beginning, scientists were so fascinated with android potential and downloaded their memory banks, their personalities, their voices, and emotional configurations into their android opposites. For certain scientists, it was their route to immortality. I explained that to you a long time ago."

"Reinhart realized that it was dangerous for humans to make their android opposites an identical version of themselves after her android opposite challenged her for authority. But that was years after this space mission was launched. We all know that she contaminated the Group of 5 with that debilitating virus that has made them dependent upon humans for creative scientific progress. If she hadn't done that, we would be their non-intellectual slaves just like the crew on board that Mother ship."

"You mean that the android opposites of the original scientific team are ruling their world?" Stuart choked out. "And that we are dealing with programmed humans?"

"I am not certain that the humans are programmed. But, there is reason to believe that the High Commission is comprised in whole or in part of the android opposites of the original scientific team. And, I don't know how many of those twenty android opposites survived." I stopped to consider his second question. "And, even though the humans may not be programmed, the Colonel and her commanding officers do not appear to have any decision making power."

I recounted Reinhart's impressions of what happened. "Actually, Reinhart believes that there could be at least two different possibilities for a change of command. The first is that these androids may have replaced their human opposites once they landed on the planet, by enslaving or killing them. But, perhaps there were other reasons why the humans did not survive. For example the air may have been too toxic for humans, but the androids were not affected by the environment. Whatever the answer, they are most likely in control, just like our Group of 5 was in control of the Planet Earth for hundreds of years. And it is possible that the Group of 5 knows this!"

"There is also the possibility that the android opposites were activated during space travel by members of the android crew who were programmed to do that and that they disposed of their human opposites and changed the course of the spaceship, directing it to another exoplanet in another constellation."

"Our Group of 5 and the High Commissioners do not have the same interest in Reinhart." I paused. "Our Group of 5 brought back Reinhart, their Creator, in the hopes that she would help them to achieve their ultimate objective and free themselves from human dependency, which, of course, she has not done. The androids living on that exoplanet want Reinhart, their Creator, simply because she is the only one-human or android-capable of putting an end to their reign and destroying them."

"So they are waiting for her to blindly walk into a trap when she boards the spaceship so that they can kill her?" Stuart asked, a glimmer of hostility in his deep voice.

"I don't think that they want to kill her. They may even imagine that she might work with them and even abandon me for an android opposite." I hesitated, my expression pensive. "But, that reasoning assumes that they actually believe that Reinhart exists in a symbiotic relationship with Pamela and that Pamela is not in reality, Reinhart's android opposite." I raised my eyebrows. "And, again, they might doubt Pamela's existence in any form, supposing that Reinhart is using Pamela as a preposterous, ludicrous, subterfuge to hide her immortality."

I breathed deeply and picked up the conversation. "They are probably not easy to reason with, because unlike the Group of 5, they have the emotional structures of some of Reinhart's very competitive colleagues, who vied for power, resorted to trickery and deception, and looked for allies to help them overthrow Reinhart, who was held in high esteem by a large majority of the intellectuals, until the outbreak of the revolution."

"Maybe, but why didn't they just get in touch with the Group of 5 and work to destroy Reinhart?" Peter asked.

"Oh, they are uncomfortable with them because they were the android opposites of the most brilliant, the best of the best, la crème de la crème, of the scientists working with Reinhart. And, the group of 5, like their human opposites, were loyal to Reinhart. They coveted and protected her."

I felt Reinhart's energy moving vigorously inside of me as she jumped into the conversation, using her voice. "They don't know that the Group of 5 has that debilitating virus that makes them dependent upon humans for creativity." She sighed. "And, regardless, I did treat the Group of 5 differently, with more respect, and worked very closely with them, like I did with their defunct human opposites. I did not treat the human opposites of the High Commissioners in the same manner. For example, I gave them interesting projects but I never gave them autonomy or even the right to initiate their own projects."

Stuart and Peter stood tall and straight. "We should never have revealed so much information to Colonel Shannon who gave detailed reports to the members of the High Commission, the Android opposites of my former colleagues. We even told Colonel Shannon that humans waged a revolution, acquired control, and subjugated the Group of 5. And, worse, we told them that I was in a symbiotic relationship with Pamela." She paced back and forth.

"Nonetheless, I doubt that they believe much of what we told me. In their android logic, all these "stories" are being used to confuse them. And, a strong point for us is that we did not mention Murdoc's absence. Dr. Murdoc was my closest friend and strongest ally. I foolishly ignored Murdoc's warnings that these humanoid machines were potentially dangerous."

"No matter how much you want to believe that you can control them," Elisabeth, "he repeated often, "they will turn against us one day—try to destroy us then control, or use us humans to carry out meaningless tasks. Your creations are the beginning of the end of the human race." She smacked her lips impulsively. "He did not cherish my creations like I did and admittedly, he was right to be suspicious of them."

"So when the subject of Murdoc comes up, and it will, tell them that Dr. Murdoc is a vital member of my team but never mention in what form he exists. They will probably imagine that Reinhart created an android opposite for him. If they believe that he is still around, they will act cautiously."

Reinhart disappeared inside of me. "And, even if Robert or Jennifer mention the submissive nature of the Group of 5, the High Commissioners will certainly draw the conclusion that their submissiveness is because Reinhart is more powerful than before." I sighed.

"Regardless, they must be worried about the power the Group of 5 has acquired since they left the planet Earth." I felt like I was caught in a conundrum and wanted to escape, so I ended the conversation by saying that no matter what the High Commissioners believed or didn't believe in the reports sent to them by Colonel Shannon, the fact that Reinhart is present now can only mean that the Group of 5 has grown stronger.

"But, the astronauts---Anderson and Hadley---, especially Hadley, described the devastated condition of our planet." Peter mentioned.

"Yes, of course, but that doesn't matter, because they never lived on a planet and had a glorified image of what the planet Earth should look like." I sighed. "The High Commissioners knew that there were barren areas on Earth and probably paid little attention to their remarks. Regardless, they were sending them for another reason. They wanted to know who was in control. Their lives were not that important for the Commissioners."

"So what do you want from us?" Peter asked, looking straight into my eyes.

"I want you to do what I did for all of us all those years before our revolution. I want you to spy on the humans and the androids, and find as much information as possible about the planet they pretend that their ancestors inhabited, their objectives and their technology." They both nodded. "After you are satisfied with your findings, you must request permission from Reinhart to return and you must not stay longer than is necessary."

I shuddered thinking about what I was asking them to do. "They won't harm you because they want Reinhart. And, you must constantly assure them that Reinhart intends to visit the spaceship and meet all the members of the crew!" I stopped to gather my thoughts. "Reinhart will regularly confirm that." I turned away from them. "Please never reveal to them the handicaps that Reinhart downloaded into the Group of 5. Pretend that they are dangerous, vicious and contriving, whatever, to keep the High Commissioners worrying."

Stuart left saying that he was up for another round of spying and fighting. "My life is too sedentary for me at the moment! I am ready for a bit of fun!" Peter and I both burst out laughing.

"What kind of an excuse are we going to give to explain Reinhart's absence?" Peter moved closer to me, taking my face tenderly in his hands.

"Reinhart has created a very good excuse for her absence. I am pregnant." I whispered in his ear.

"What?" He pulled away from me and I saw that he had the same morose reaction to this news as I did. "She should have talked to us about that." His eyes turned grey and sullen. "This sounds like a rather ridiculous excuse that will make the High Commissioners even more suspicious of her ultimate objectives." The muscles in his face were so rigid, that I thought that they might just crack. "Can't the baby survive with you in the cocoon?"

"It has never been tested. And I can't leave now because of my safety and that of Reinhart, so I think that your question is of no consequence." My voice sounded high and screechy, like someone playing the wrong chord of a violin." I don't think that I am ready to take that risk with my life and that of our daughter."

"So, we are going to be separated again"

"But, for less than a year and, during that year, you shall be living your dream. You will be learning how to operate spacecraft, visit asteroids and observe mining operations. You will be learning new techniques in space travel...the list is long."

"You are right, Pamela, but I am going to miss you." He said, unable to suppress the broad smile spreading across his face, just thinking about spending time in outer space. "And the baby?"

"A little girl."

He approached me and wrapped his arms around me, rubbing his right hand slowly over my stomach, caressing his child. "Promise me that you will take care yourself and our daughter." I nodded. "I still wish that you were coming with me."

"I do too, but we shall travel together in outer space when the time is right for me to leave. You have a very important mission to carry out so concentrate on that. The sooner you accomplish it the sooner you can return." I saw Frederic coming in the door with Randolph just behind him and let Peter announce the good news.

"See you all later," I yelled as I dashed out the door. I contacted Colonel Shannon who answered straight away. "Dr. Reinhart, we are looking forward to your arrival."

"There is a change of plans." Reinhart said slowly. "I cannot leave at this moment. Pamela is pregnant, and the fetus will never survive if Pamela enters into a cryogenic state."

"OH!" The word vibrated in the air. "The High Commissioners will be very disappointed. I don't know how I am going to announce this news." Her face flushed red.

"You will simply tell them the truth. They will understand." Reinhart paused. "You will tell them that you will be receiving a very prestigious team. Dr. Peter Feragan, Pamela's husband, Dr. Stuart Rever Reinhart, my son, and Dr. Frederic Feragan Reinhart, Pamela's son and my grandson. And, you will use these words when you speak to them: 'Should anything happen to any member of my family or that of my daughter, Pamela, I shall stop at nothing to destroy the High Commissioners and everything that they have created." Reinhart didn't wait for her response.

The launch date arrived. I wished James, Isabel and Mathieu, who left on Robert's ship for the modulated space station, good luck and reminded them to activate the communication system before doing anything else so that we could keep in touch. I also asked them to avoid questions regarding our lives on the planet Earth, the role of the Group of 5, and our objectives.

I said goodbye to my brother, Stuart, who I had come to love and cherish, giving him a big kiss on his cheek. "I am counting on you, Stuart, to protect Peter and Frederic, like you protected me and Randolph in the past. And, please be careful. I want the three of you to come back to me."

Saying goodbye to Peter and Frederic was the most difficult moment in my life. Vivid memories returned of those farewell marches from the Cavern to the Center with Peter and Frederic by my side appeared.

"I love you both so much... and am going to miss you." I turned my head to hide the tears welling in my eyes.

"Frederic and I are an invincible team and with Stuart there with us, well...you don't have to worry about anything." Peter's voice cracking with emotion.

"You must take care of each other." I smiled feebly and then grabbed Frederic and hugged and kissed him until he begged me to stop.

I heard Jennifer's voice. "It is time to board."

Peter took me in his strong arms and gave me a tender kiss that would make me long even more for his return. "Knowing that you are there waiting for me will be my motivation to accomplish this mission as fast as possible." He said as he started to run towards the ship. "We shall be back, Pamela." He yelled over his shoulder, his voice echoing in the air.

Reality set in and my heart stopped for an instance when I watched them board the vessel. "They will soon be asleep in the confines of their cocoons and will wake up in a space ship light years away from me." I drove rapidly back to the Center and rushed off to the control room.

I heard my breath coming in loud short spasms, during the launch, and I felt my body tremble when the ship disappeared from the screen, dwindling into a tiny, flickering speck of light, emitting a low beeping sound. "Was I right to let them go?" Passed through my mind, while tears flowed down my face. And, at the very moment that a profound emptiness began to invade me, I was jarred back into reality by the red light of an in-coming call flashing on the control panel. I quickly pressed down on the button.

"Colonel Shannon for Dr. Reinhart." I opened up the visual and saw Colonel Shannon's weathered, wrinkled ridden face, in front of me.

"Pamela." She asked hesitantly.

"Yes, you are speaking to Pamela." I replied in an officious tone.

"I want you to know that we are tracking the vessel with your crew on board. The ship will be going into Alcubierre drive soon, and will pass through a number of worm holes that will reduce travel time considerably. They should be arriving in five months, your time. I shall keep you informed on a regular basis."

"Thank you." I took advantage of what she said to ask her to send me the exact route they would be taking and indicate the various worm holes the spaceship would engage."

She nodded before clearing her throat and saying. "I have a message for Dr. Reinhart from the High Commission."

"I'm sorry but Dr. Reinhart is not available, do you want to give me the message?"

She hesitated, taking a long, deep breath, before answering. "The High Commission wants Dr. Reinhart to know that they were sorry to learn that they will not have the honor of meeting her this time, but promise to treat her distinguished team of scientists with the highest respect." She paused, waiting for me to comment, before coaxing me for a response. "Is there anything else that you have to say, Pamela, before I sign off?"

"Yes, actually, I have a message for the High Commissioners from their Creator."

"Their Creator? I don't understand." She said in a high tone.

"Don't worry. They know who their Creator is." I sat for a moment looking at the expression of bewilderment, her eyes motionless and her lips slightly parted, on the face of Colonel Shannon.

"Their Creator wants them to know... that their time is running out!" I bowed my head slightly to Colonel Shannon and switched off the audio-visual system.

A Generation Returns

Reinhart's energy was now permeating me, moving rapidly and vigorously inside of me, prompting me to smile at the future, accept with open arms the daughter she was offering me, to laugh heartily at the adventures and challenges that awaited us and to seek the sweet taste of victories.

Chapter 34- The Scales Tip

I n the bowels of a cavern, shielded from the high surface temperature and greyish green toxic gas of the exoplanet that offered them shelter for hundreds of years, six figures, enshrouded in the florescent light reflected off the cavern walls, sat patiently around a large, round stone artifact, awaiting Reinhart's message.

With bowed heads, they listened in silence to the words Colonel Shannon transmitted to them. They gradually raised their heads and stared into each other's steady fixed eyes, knowing that the decision that they would make today would decide the fate of the human race.

The silence was broken by the impetuous, Dr. Charles Deringer. "Did you register Reinhart's threat?" He asked, slowly pronouncing each word.

The others stared at this tall, willowy man with that oblong face that drew attention away from his stubby nose and heart-shaped lips. His deep set brown eyes gave him an air of authority. He slowly moved his long fingers from his folded hands into a steeple position, as he patiently awaited response from his five colleagues.

Dr. Graham Christenger finally replied, with a loud, crackling android sound that immediately degenerated into uncontrollable laughter that ended only after his short heavy upper body and round, pudgy face plummeted from the weight of this laughter onto the hard table top.

"How can you laugh?" Dr. Dorothy Lansley asked, her hollow, android voice crackling, exaggerating her stress. "Have you forgotten who Reinhart is- her power, her cruelty, her love for vengeance?" Have you- have we- grown too sure of ourselves?" Her trembling mounted when Graham turned his small grey eyes shrouded in heavy black eyebrows in her direction.

"Calm Down! Control those emotions that have never served us well." Dr. Elena Yung admonished.

"There is no reason to worry." Dr. Jeremy Milhouse replied. His eyes scanned the group, stopping when they fell upon Elena. She was even more beautiful than her human opposite. Her oval face, her large, ocean blue eyes, her slim nose, her inviting, pulpous lips, and her long black, silky hair enticed him. He was easily distracted by her tall hour glass body, long legs and graceful arms, whenever she passed in front of him. He imagined that with his tall, robust body and immaculate oval face with dark, brown eyes and full lips, they would make a perfect child, if only androids could reproduce.

"Why? How can you be so sure?" Dorothy broke into his thoughts.

"Think about it." He replied, as he leaned back into his chair. "The information we have received thus far," he cleared his throat, "that is if we can believe what Colonel Shannon has told us, is... ludicrous." He pretended to swallow. "Even Reinhart could not have survived all these hundreds, or thousands of Earth years." He flicked his fingers as if he were swatting a fly. "Even though time alludes me, I am certain that her human life must have ended."

"So you believe that her android opposite has been in touch with Colonel Shannon?" Charles suggested.

"But, then why did she mention an explosion on the Earth, a revolution waged by humans against androids, and...the most incredulous of all...Reinhart's symbiotic relationship with a human, who looks exactly like her in every detail." Graham said as he got up and walked around in circles.

"Reinhart knows that we exist. But, she does not know how many of us android opposites survived. And, she is uncertain about our objectives." His eyes grew wide. "So, she is hiding her true identity. It is a brilliant subterfuge." Charles replied.

"And, the pregnancy—her reason for staying on the planet Earth?" Dr. Meredith Webber asked in that screechy, android voice that was as unattractive as her small, frail body and sharp featured face.

"Perhaps she realized too late that the humans on board the spaceship are our slaves—obedient and loyal slaves, but slaves nonetheless." Graham snickered. "She made a mistake. Yes," he said slowly, "she made a mistake. She trusted Colonel Shannon. That is why she is pretending that she is in a symbiotic relationship and her symbiont is pregnant. She needs time to devise a scheme before she leaves the planet Earth."

"Reinhart does not make mistakes." Dorothy replied, in an icy cold tone. "She has been playing games with us which is why she sent us so much incredulous information." She sighed. "I am warning you. If she has survived all this time, she is more powerful than ever."

"Your paranoia bores me!" Elena's human-like cries of anger resonated in the air.

"Dorothy might be right. We have to be cautious." Graham reminded the Group.

"We can test her." Jeremy suggested.

"Do you have a plan?" Elena's lips curved slowly upwards.

"Of course, I have a plan." Jeremy stood up and stretched, while the others waited with bated breath. "There is a risk. As, Dorothy mentioned, we are confronting Reinhart, but she seems to have a sentimental weakness for the three astronauts she is sending us."

"Not at all." Charles interrupted. "Reinhart is incapable of profound sentimental feelings. She is playing with us. She is dangerous."

"Let me remind you that we have also evolved. She does not know that. And, we have an effective military force at our disposition." Jeremy pleaded, but Dorothy and Charles shook their heads in doubt. "And the rest of you, do you want to know my plan?" He continued. They nodded.

"We have to force her to come to us before she has time to mastermind a strategy."

"And, how are we going to do that?" Charles asked, under a shallow smile.

"We are going to arrest her three astronauts on arrival." Jeremy stopped to let his idea sink in before explaining more. "We already sent a nice message back to Reinhart today promising to treat her three emissaries with distinction, but instead we shall order their arrest and hold them in custody. We shall pick their minds for all the information we need to confront Reinhart before we reveal the truth." His eyes grew bright. "The effect of our unanticipated defiance will plunge her into a state of turmoil where she will make rapid, impulsive, irrational decisions to save them. And, when she arrives we shall capture her."

"It all makes me uneasy." Charles spoke up. "I can laugh at her silly messages, but I know that my human opposite worked in fear of her and that emotion is very much alive inside of me."

"I agree with Charles." Dorothy protested.

"Her astronauts are her spies!" Elena screamed. "I agree with Jeremy. We must take her off guard."

"We could pick their minds without arresting them." Dorothy suggested. "We could befriend them and get information that way."

"Your fear is interfering with your reasoning." Graham commented.

"What are we going to do about Colonel Shannon?" Charles asked.

"What are you talking about? She is faithful to us. We shall just tell her that we discovered that the Earthlings are not friendly and that they want to gain control of her ship and destroy the androids and humans on board." Jeremy replied.

"I believe that we should follow Dorothy's suggestion." Meredith said in a whisper.

"Do we all agree then?" Charles asked, ignoring Meredith's comment.

Everyone, except Dorothy, nodded. "If you are not with us, you are against us, Dorothy. Need I remind you of the fate of our other colleagues who spoke of morality." Jeremy warned.

"You leave me no choice." She said as she joined in the unanimity of the vote.

⊕⊢⊟⇥⊩⇦Ɛ⊢⊷

Five months later Colonel Shannon received a written order from the High Commissioners. She shuddered when she read it, knowing that she had no choice but to carry out the order even though she had committed herself—given her word to Reinhart through Pamela that the members of her family would be treated as high dignitaries. She would be a traitor if she carried out the order and a traitor if she didn't. But…perhaps, yes perhaps, there was a way, she thought as she opened the interstellar communication system.

"Colonel Shannon," her heart fluttered "the shuttle craft has arrived and the human members of the crew are ready to enter our vessel." The highest ranking android officer, Lieutenant X, announced.

"I shall leave now to meet them in the arrival area, with several high-ranking human military officers." She breathed deeply. "The High Commissioners have sent the following order which I want you to carry out to the letter. You should send several members of your android forces to the arrival area now. And," she hesitated, "this order should be read over the loudspeaker." She handed him the order.

Stuart, followed by Peter and Frederic entered the arrival area, just as Colonel Shannon and her officers arrived. Their excitement, like the smiles on their faces, rapidly disappeared when a strong, crackling android voice came over the loudspeaker.

"In the name of the High Commissioners of the planet Gliese 581g, I hereby arrest Dr. Stuart Rever Reinhart, Dr. Peter Feragan and Dr. Frederic Feragan Reinhart for Crimes committed against our friends and allies, the Group of 5, which include, but are not limited to, their capture and enslavement, and for their Intended Acts of Espionage with the purpose of conquering and holding captive the High Commissioners and the Androids and Human Members of the Spaceship Benevolence."

After a short pause Lieutenant X added the following.

"Your trial will take place over the next few months. If found guilty, you will be executed in a manner that the High Commissioners decide proper."

Colonel Shannon moved discretely across the room and whispered into Peter's ear that they should do whatever necessary to stay alive until Reinhart arrives, just seconds before the android guards entered the room and escorted them to the prison.

THE END

Patricia Lee Strunk

M s. Strunk, author of Pamela Series 13, grew up in a poor, working class neighbourhood, in a small town in Pennsylvania, where she dreamed about becoming an astronaut. Instead, Ms. Strunk became a lawyer. She holds an LL.M. Degree in "International Business Law" from the "London School of Economics," a Master Degree in "Comparative Law" from the "Institut de Droit Comparé, Paris" and a Juris Doctor Degree from "Duquesne University School of Law." She is also a member of the California and Pennsylvania Bars. Patricia spent the greater part of her legal career in academia and had the privilege of being a Lecturer in Law with many distinguished French Law Faculties, like "L'Université de Paris Ouest-La Défense, Nanterre" and "L'Université de Paris 1, Sorbonne," as well as many Institutes of higher learning, like "L'Institut de Droit Comparé" and "L'Institut d'Etudes Politiques" (Science Po, Paris). Ms. Strunk never completely forgot her childhood ambitions and fascination with science. Pamela Series 13, Volume 2, "A Generation Returns," like volume 1 of the Pamela Series, reflects her academic interest in Bio-Ethical and Environmental Law, as well as her overwhelming support and advocacy of responsible Scientific Research at all levels.